BLADE IN SHADOW

FALLEN BLADE VOLUME 1

BLADE IN SHADOW

THE FALLEN BLADE SERIES

Broken Blade
Bared Blade
Crossed Blades

Kelly McCullough

SCIENCE
FICTION

BROKEN BLADE   Copyright © 2011 by Kelly McCullough
  Publication History: Ace mass market, December 2011
BARED BLADE   Copyright © 2012 by Kelly McCullough
  Publication History: Ace mass market, July 2012
CROSSED BLADES   Copyright © 2012 by Kelly McCullough
  Publication History: Ace mass market, December 2012

First SFBC Printing: August 2013

Selected by Michael Phillips, SFBC Senior Editor

Published by arrangement with
The Penguin Group (USA), Inc./ The Berkley Publishing Group, Ace
375 Hudson Street
New York, NY 10014

Visit The SFBC online at *http://www.sfbc.com*

ISBN # 978-1-62490-649-7

Printed in the United States of America.

Contents

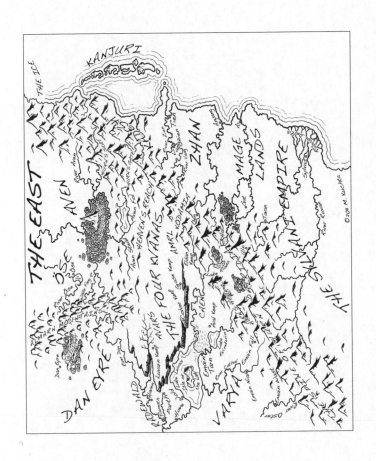

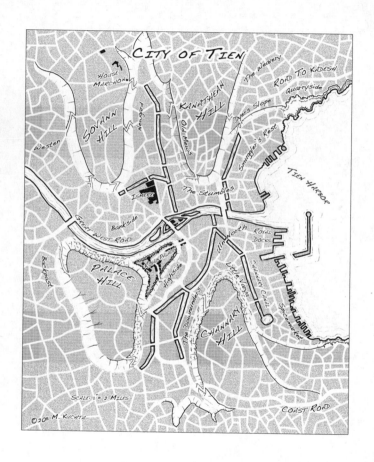

BROKEN BLADE

For Laura,
forever and always

Acknowledgments

Extra-special thanks are owed to Laura McCullough; Jack Byrne; Anne Sowards; my mapmaker, Matt Kuchta; Neil Gaiman for the loan of the dogs; and artist John Jude Palencar and cover designer Judith Lagerman for a truly amazing cover.

Many thanks also to the active Wyrdsmiths: Lyda, Doug, Naomi, Bill, Eleanor, and Sean. My Web guru, Ben. Beta readers: Steph, Dave, Sari, Karl, Angie, Sean, Laura R., Matt, Mandy, April, Becky, Mike, and Benjamin. My family: Carol, Paul and Jane, Lockwood and Darlene, Judy, Lee C., Kat, Jean, Lee P., and all the rest. My extended support structure: Bill and Nancy, Sara, James, Tom, Ann, Mike, Sandy, and so many more. Lorraine, because she's fabulous. Also, a hearty woof for Cabal and Lola.

1

Trouble wore a red dress. That was my first thought when the girl walked into the Gryphon's Head. My second was that the dress didn't fit as well as it should for a lady's maid. It was cut for someone both bustier and broader across the hip than the current occupant. Not that she looked bad. The wrapping didn't fit right, but the contents of the package more than made up for any lack in presentation.

The poor fit of the dress was a definite puzzler. Red was the coming fashion for servants in the great houses of Tien, and while your average duchess might not give a cracked cup whether her servants' clothes fit comfortably, she cared enormously whether their looks reflected poorly on her. The fashion was too new for hand-me-downs, which meant the dress had to belong to someone other than the girl wearing it.

She turned my way and marched across the room without so much as a glance at the filthy straw covering the floor of the Gryphon's common room. Jerik, the tavern's owner, changed it out once a year whether it needed it or not, much to the annoyance of the rats and their more exotic magical playmates, the slinks and nipperkins. When I added her indifference to the awful things in the straw to the length of her stride and the set of her features, I had to revise that "girl" to woman though she was quite young.

"Are you the jack?" she asked when she reached my table. She leaned down toward me as she spoke, silhouetting herself against the only light in the room—a dim and badly scarred magelight chandelier.

"I'm *a* jack, and open to hire if you're looking for one." A jack of shadows, the underworld's all-purpose freelancer—how very far I'd fallen from the old days.

"I was told to look for Aral . . ."

She drew the word out almost into a question, as if hoping I might supply something more than my first name. It was a tactic I recognized from long, personal use and one I didn't much like having turned back on me. But if I wanted to keep paying my bar tab, I needed to work, so I nodded.

"Aral's a name I'll answer to, among others. Why do you need a jack?"

"First, let's find out whether you're the right sort for the job I have in mind."

Out of the corner of my eye I saw my shadow shifting slowly leftward as if seeking a better view of the young woman. I leaned that way as well, to cover the shadow's movements, and accidentally elbowed my whiskey bottle off the table. It thudded into the straw but didn't break. Not that it mattered. I'd finished the last of the contents twenty minutes ago. Which, in all honesty, might have had something to do with my knocking it over.

"Hang on a tick," I said, and bent to pick the bottle out of the moldering straw.

I took the opportunity offered by the cover of the table to make a sharp "no" signal to Triss with my left hand. I couldn't afford to let anyone notice my shadow moving of its own accord, not with the price on our heads—prices, really, as there was more than one interested party. And even this darkest corner of a seedy tavern had light enough for a trained eye to make a potentially fatal connection.

I swore silently at my shadow familiar while I returned the bottle to the table. *Cut it the hell out, Triss!* That was just frustration. If I didn't say it out loud, Triss couldn't hear me, and if I did, I might as well just cut my own throat and get it over with. The Shade did stop moving, but whether that was because of my hand signal or simply because he'd gotten an adequate eyeful, I didn't know.

I did give the woman a more thorough looking over myself at that point. Triss never pulled anything *that* obvious without a damned good reason. He owned the cautious half of our partnership. Besides, as noted earlier, the lady merited plenty of eye time on her own account.

Tall for a woman, perhaps matching my own five feet and eleven, and built and muscled more like a Zhani warrior-noble than the lady's maid her dress proclaimed as her station. Hair a few shades darker than my own middling brown and nearly twice as long, with a luxurious braid that reached just shy of her waist. Her eyes were dark though I couldn't tell the exact shade in the dimness that had originally drawn me to the Gryphon. More telling still, she had sword calluses on the inside of her left thumb.

That made the dress a lie for sure. It more likely belonged to her girl than to her. Which left me with an interesting question: Why, if she really was a minor noble of some sort herself, hadn't she simply had her seamstress do her up one that fit properly? But that was more a matter for idle curiosity than any real concern. I didn't much care where my jobs came from. Not anymore. Not if they paid enough to cover my bills. Besides, in the jack business, the client *always* lies.

The whole point of coming to a jack is that we don't belong to anyone and so don't answer to anyone. A sunside jack might find your stolen necklace for you without asking any of the inconvenient questions that the watch would be obliged to because of their allegiance to the law and the Duke of Tien. Questions like: *Where* did you get the necklace in the first place? Or *why* does it look so much like a necklace that was reported stolen by someone else last year?

On the shadowside, the questions we don't ask have even sketchier answers. Why do you want me to steal that? What's in this box that needs to be delivered to a dockside location at four in the morning? How come Taurik Longknife isn't getting his cut of this little deal of yours? What did they do that you need them roughed up? Or, for a black jack, *why* do you want him dead? Sometimes the client supplied an answer anyway, but it was rarely an honest one. Not that it mattered. Mostly, I just don't want to know. That's part of why I became a jack in the first place. A jack doesn't have to care.

I *did* wonder about a couple of interesting little scars showing where my potential new client's neck met her right shoulder—but it was an idle sort of wondering. While I was studying her, she was doing the same with me. Judging by the slight crease between her eyebrows, she didn't think much of what she saw. She wasn't the first to make that judgment. She wouldn't be the last.

"Well," she said, after a moment, "what sort of jack *are* you?"

"Me? I'm a shadow jack, of course, but never a black one. I'll take risks if the money looks right and I'm not fussed about the law, but I won't ghost anyone for you. Not for anyone else either, for that matter."

I was done with the blood trade. Triss and I had long since sent our share of souls to the lords of judgment and their great wheel of rebirth. More than our share.

It was her turn to nod though the frown stayed. "I'm not looking for contract murder, just a bit of sensitive delivery service."

That was good and, if true, probably why she'd chosen me from among Tien's many shadow jacks. Courier work and its close cousin, smuggling, provided the bulk of my income these days. Shadowside, but not the deep dark. Few jacks anywhere could boast a better reputation for quiet deliveries, but then, I had Triss. And that was the sort of advantage that not more than a score of people in the whole wide world could boast.

"How much are you offering?" I asked.

"Don't you want to know the where and the what?" For the first time since she'd come through the door, my lady of the red dress looked knocked off her stride.

"Not really, or at least not until I find out whether it's worth hearing any secrets. Those always come with their own risks."

She pulled a small but full silk pouch from the depths of her bodice and dropped it on the table with a clank, tipping its mouth toward me. I picked it up and flicked it open. It was full of silver Zhani riels still warm from her skin and smelling faintly of lavender perfume. A thefty bit of cash, but not ridiculously so for the right job.

I set the bag back on the table. "Is this the whole payoff in advance, or the first bit of a half-now, half-later sort of arrangement? Or is it simply by way of showing me what's to be paid on proof of delivery?"

"This is a third down, with the rest on proof of delivery."

"It's dangerous, then?" I asked.

It had to be if she was willing to go so high before the haggling had even opened. Danger worked just fine for me. The longer the odds, the better you got paid and the less you had to work. And if someone ghosted you along the way, well, then you got out of working entirely. Nobody expects anything of the dead.

She shrugged at my question, then flipped her braid back over her shoulder when it fell forward. "It's only dangerous if things go wrong." Her eyes narrowed. "Do you object to *all* killing or just when it's the point of a job?"

"I try to avoid ghosting anyone when I can avoid it, but I'm no renunciate." My shadow moved again, and so, perforce, did I, leaning back this time, though mercifully without knocking anything over.

Dammit Triss, stop dancing around! It wasn't a big move, but even half an inch was half an inch too much. Too many people wanted to see my head nailed up over the traitor's gate or sent off to the Son of Heaven in a jar of rice wine. To distract from my little shadow two-step, I gestured for the woman to take the other seat.

"I'd offer you a drink, but . . ." I sadly flicked the empty bottle—Kyle's fifteen-year, the rather expensive Aveni whiskey I favored when I could afford it. It rang emptily and rocked, giving off a tantalizing little whiff of peat and honey. "So unless you're buying the round you'll just have to settle for going dry while you tell me what you want done, Lady . . . ?"

I gave her the courtesy title that might belong to a duchess's first maid in hopes of getting her to give up more information. She ignored the bait and shook her head impatiently.

"Call me Maylien." But she did not yet sit. "You *will* take my commission then?" She smiled a smug little smile.

That made me want to turn her down flat. Unfortunately, sending her away would leave my purse even flatter. If I wanted to keep drinking the good stuff, I had to work. And I wanted to keep drinking the good stuff. It was one of the few things left in my life that gave me any pleasure.

"Let's just say that I'm open to the idea," I said. "The fee looks adequate for some things, less so for others."

"I can't tell you more without some surety . . . of silence at the very least."

I raised an eyebrow at her. "If you've learned enough of my reputation to find me here, you've learned enough to know I don't discuss my clients. Not even my offers."

"May I presume that constitutes your word?"

"If you want to; though why you'd accept the oath of a jack of the shadow trades, I don't know."

She smiled like a woman holding a secret. "Most jacks I would not, but I've reason to believe I can trust yours. Have you ever heard of the Baroness Marchon?"

It took an effort not to start at that name, though perhaps a wasted one, since my shadow jerked a good inch on his own. I had, of course, heard of the Marchon, but I rather doubted that the person I'd chosen to become would have. Thinking daggers at Triss and his sudden tendency to jerk and start, I pasted a confused look on my face and shook my head. The gesture made the world bob and twist—a not wholly unpleasant side effect of the empty bottle.

"Is this Marchon a city noble? Or country?" I asked.

"More the latter than the former, but she does maintain a city house—a big estate right on the north edge of town, just off the royal preserve. That's where I need the delivery made."

I knew it well. The Marchon place had once housed the old king's last mistress, the younger sister of the then Baron Marchon. I had slipped into the house on no less than three occasions while trying to catch a quiet moment alone with the king.

"That's a neighborhood with an ugly reputation for the shadow trades, heavy security on all the estates plus the occasional royal patrol in the streets," I said.

Not to mention the fact that the Elite had a clandestine chapter house near there and watchers in the park most nights, but I certainly wasn't supposed to know that, nor how to slip past them.

I pushed the purse back toward her. "I think you'll have to find another jack."

She bit her lip in a quite convincing and quite fetching imitation of worry. I wondered how often she practiced.

"How about a bigger fee?" she asked. "I think I could come up with half again more if I had to."

I had just opened my mouth to tell her no, when I felt a tugging all along my back, sort of like peeling away a sweat-soaked shirt. Triss again, letting me know he wanted me to take the job for some reason. I didn't like the smell of the thing, or Triss's pressuring me on it, but I really did need money. I decided to push Maylien a bit and see how she responded.

"Half again *might* do," I told her. "But indulge me for a moment by biding here, won't you? I have an urgent matter that I need to attend to." I flicked my eyes in the direction of the back door and the sign marking the privies beyond and gave her a what-can-you-do sort of look.

It was a rude request under the circumstance, and she had every right to take offense, but I actually did have something that needed my private attention. Also, if she chose to see it as an insult and walk away, I would have solved my dilemma over whether to take the job.

Before she could answer, or do much more than blush angrily, I pulled myself to my feet and tipped her a ragged tradesman's bow—it wouldn't do at all to deliver the proper Zhani high-court version. Besides, I'd put enough whiskey away over the past two or three hours that I might not have been able to manage the more formal one if I'd tried.

"Back as soon as ever I am able, my lady."

A couple of lanterns filled with the cheapest oil money could buy guttered and sputtered in the yard. There was no risk of fire out on the cobbles, so no need for a magelight, which meant it was as dark out there as old King Ashvik's heart had been. Some of the noble neighborhoods could afford to use magelight to illuminate the main streets, but the Stumbles was about as far away from being a noble neighborhood as it got. On nights like this, with the moon near her nadir, even night-trained eyes like mine had trouble, and Jerik's lamps provided just enough illumination to find the privies.

I slipped inside, trading the stink of one sort of shit for the stink of another. Given a choice, I preferred the yard and the horse; but I needed the privacy. I closed the door behind me and wedged it shut with a thin knife pulled from the sheath on my left wrist. The light inside was better than the yard's, provided by a fading magelight nailed firmly to the ceiling—night-market certainly, but still costly. I presume the more expensive choice had been made because Jerik didn't like what happened when the drunks couldn't find the holes, and so he wanted to give them as much help as possible.

I turned a stern eye on my now much-clearer shadow, and demanded, "What are you trying to pull?"

Though my arms remained tight to my sides, the shadow's arms lifted and broadened into wings at the same time its legs fused themselves together into something much longer and narrower. Combine that with the way the head and neck respectively flattened and lengthened, and you no longer had a shape that looked even remotely human. In fact, were you to go by the form and movement of my shadow alone, you could be forgiven for making the assumption that I had become a rather small and agitated dragon.

My shadow, or rather the Shade that inhabited it, tilted his head to one side and shot out a long slender shadow of a forked tongue to touch my cheek. And that was Triss.

"I want you to take the job," he said.

I say "his" and "he," because Triss lives in *my* shadow, and I'm a man, though "its" and "it" would probably be more accurate, for what is sex to a shadow? His smoke-and-syrup voice reinforces the ambiguity, lying as it does midway between tenor and contralto.

"Why?" I asked him.

"Because you're broke and you're bored, and when you're working, you drink less."

I shook my head. "I'm not buying it, Triss. That's been true of the last dozen job offers, none of which made you break cover like you did with this one. That's dangerous. What if someone had seen you?"

Triss reared up. "Since when did you care if something was dangerous? I can't even count the number of times your frankly reckless attitude about the kinds of work we take has nearly gotten us killed in the last five years!"

"That's different. Killed in action on a job is a risk I've *always* been willing to take. Getting tumbled in a tavern and nailed to the traitor's gate or sent off to provide amusement for the Son of Heaven is a fucking amateur's death! Do you want that to be our legacy?"

"As opposed to what?" demanded Triss, his wings vibrating with agitation. "Killed while delivering a stolen painting to its buyer? You're not seriously comparing the risks of the last five years to dying on a mission from the goddess. At least if someone sells us to the King of Zhan or the so-called Son of Heaven, we'll be dying for what we used to be. Back before the fall of the temple, what we did mattered. We worked for a cause bigger than just getting paid."

"In case you hadn't noticed, Triss, the goddess is dead, murdered by her heavenly peers, and most of her servants followed her into the grave. The Son of Heaven pronounced the ban on our entire order. *Nothing* we do matters anymore and it never will again. The fucking gods themselves have decreed it through their official human mouthpiece."

"May he rot from within," snapped Triss.

I threw up my hands. "There is no *cause* anymore, just you and me and the work and getting paid. So we might as well hold on to our professionalism because we sure as hell don't have anything else left. Which is why I'd really rather not get taken down for the kind of mistake a rank amateur would make."

Triss's wings sagged. "Dead is dead, Aral. *How* doesn't really matter." Before I could answer, Triss contracted briefly—his version of an embarrassed shrug. "But I am sorry about moving around like that. I hadn't intended to be so obvious. It's just that this Maylien is more than she seems, possibly much more. It made me curious."

I sighed and accepted the peace offering. "I'm sorry, too, Triss. I know it's harder for you, always hiding in my shadow, having to pretend you don't even exist." I hated fighting with Triss. Far more than the work, he was what I had left. His friendship and love were what made me keep getting up and going on even when I no longer saw much point. "If you want me to take this job, I'll do it."

"Thank you."

"I'll go tell Maylien now." I reached for the dagger I'd used to wedge the door.

"It's wrong," said Triss, his voice barely above a whisper, "what the gods did to us, to the whole order. Their ban is wrong, and so is the Son of Heaven, even if he is the head of the high church of the eleven kingdoms. We should be free to return to the duties laid upon us by the goddess. I will never concede otherwise. Why have you?"

I looked away from a certainty I could no longer bear. "Because the unblinking eye of justice has closed, Triss. The goddess has gone into the grave, and the rest of heaven and all its priests are against us."

"If the gods truly approve of the actions of the Son of Heaven, they're wrong, too. You've done nothing to earn such a ban. I've done nothing to earn such a ban. None of the Blades or the Shades who companioned them did anything beyond what was needful and just."

"That doesn't change the fact that every last one of us is under religious sentence of death and meat for any man's hand. Nor that the Emperor of Heaven himself struck down our goddess."

Triss closed his wings sadly. "If you cared so very much about living, I do not think you would have started to drink as you do."

I wanted to argue with him, but nothing I could say would make him any less right. Just then, something banged into the door from the outside.

A moment later, the handle began to rattle. "What the hell's wrong with the door?" asked a slurred voice.

"Nothing," I replied, "just finishing up."

Triss sank back into a reasonable semblance of my shape, and, a moment later, I stepped out into the night, pretending to fumble with the buttons of my pants as I went. I was actually glad of the interruption and glad of an excuse to return to the common room as well. If Maylien hadn't walked out yet, she'd certainly be getting suspicious about what was taking so very long.

"Well?" she asked when I got back to the table. Her lips were tightly compressed, and her tone was freezing. "Did your business go as it ought?"

"Near as needs be," I replied. "I am sorry about that, but it was a most urgent transaction."

She snorted, then, much to my surprise, smiled. "I suppose that we've all had to face such a need for haste on occasion. Now that it's passed, though, what do you say to the job?"

"Is the package small?" I intended to take the job but not before I'd gotten all the information I needed.

"Two sheets of folded parchment."

"Where does it have to be delivered?"

"There's a large balcony on the third floor of the Marchon great house, around the back of the main building. You'll need to wait beside one of the windows—I'll tell you which. You'll meet the person the message is intended for there. And that's all you need to know until you accept the commission."

I still wanted to turn her down, but I had promised Triss. Besides, the money was very good, and Triss had it right—I was bored and I was broke.

"Two conditions." I tapped the pouch, which lay right where I'd left it. "Double the fee, and tell me where you got that dress."

"For the first, done." She reached into her bodice and pulled forth a second identical pouch along with two sheets of tightly folded and sealed parchment. It made me wonder what other treasures she might have tucked away in there. "The delivery has to happen tomorrow night, five minutes past the tenth hour bell. Wait by the fifth window from the right on the back balcony. The recipient will be there."

"At the Marchon city house?" I wanted us clear on terms.

She nodded and rose from her chair with a smile.

"And the dress?"

"Why, I stole it, of course." Then she turned and walked away.

2

Maylien had barely made it through the front door when Jerik slid out from behind the bar and came my way. He was a big man with a thick patch of scar tissue where his left eye and about half his scalp used be. When asked about it, he always pointed to the gryphon's skull hanging behind the bar, and said, "The other guy got it worse. I nailed his sorry ass to the wall."

"Work?" he asked me.

"Looks like."

"Pay up."

I tossed him one of the pouches. "Put half on my room tab and the other half toward the bar bill. That ought to pay both forward a bit."

Jerik glanced into the small bag and smiled. "That it will. Shall I get you a fresh bottle of the Kyle's?" He snagged the empty as he asked.

I really, really wanted to say yes, and I might have if not for the gentle pressure I felt rippling all along my back, where my shadow lay against my flesh, like dozens of disapproving centipedes march-ing angrily from my hips to my shoulders and back again. I shook my head regretfully.

"Not tonight, I'm afraid. The job."

Jerik shrugged casually and turned away. I might be done drink-ing for tonight, but he knew I'd come back whenever the work ran out. For the second time in an hour, I ducked out the back door into the dark of the yard. This time I went into the stables and up the ladder that led to the loft and the tiny room I'd been renting for the last two years.

There was no light above, just the musty-dusty scent of last summer's hay and near-perfect darkness. The hay made an unattended lantern too risky, and Jerik wasn't going to waste the cost of a magelight on the likes of me. Not that it mattered. I'd been trained by the temple priests to operate in the dark from the age of four, when they first took me for the order.

I made a show of fumbling with my key when I got to the door though I was alone and there was no light to see me by even if I weren't. The priests had taught me to *live the role*, a lesson quite as useful for my jack work as in my old trade.

While I scraped at the door with my key, Triss did the real work. Effectively invisible in the darkness, he climbed and enfolded my body, sheathing me in a nearly transparent layer of shadow, like a smoky second skin. It felt a bit like being wrapped in icy silk. Then he extended the portion of himself that covered my right hand, sliding a tendril of hardened shadow into the keyhole. Through our temporarily shared senses I could feel/taste the tumblers and the spell binding them as he twisted the extension of himself to release both.

The door opened with a barely audible click, and I slipped into the even darker room beyond, closing and locking the door behind me. It was a far better lock than the room demanded, Durkoth work and damned expensive. But I valued my privacy.

Reaching up, I touched a shadow-gloved hand to the small stone globe I'd mounted above the door—its magic visible in magesight as a dim green spark. That released the spell of darkness binding a tiny but very bright magelight and illuminated my room. It was more the habit of a lifetime's training that had made sure of the door before I exercised my power than any real worry about being discovered there and then.

Stretched thin as he was now, Triss did little more than darken my skin by the same degree a few hours in the noon sun might achieve. Of course, those who had been trained to observe might also have noticed that when I went clothed in shadow, I cast none, not even in the brightest of light. Fortunately for me, individuals with such training were exceedingly rare.

The small magelight revealed a narrow room tucked under the slope of the eaves, with my pallet wedged into the corner where steeply slanted ceiling met rough plank flooring. The only other furniture was a low table and, beside that, a small trunk that doubled as a bench. A tattered and much-stained rug prevented any glimmers of my magelight from leaking through the cracks between the planks to the stalls below.

Except for its shape, the room wasn't all that different from the cubicle the priests had given me at the temple complex all those years ago. Well, that and the fact that my old cubicle now lay under several hundred tons of rubble surrounded by acres of barren fields sown with salt by the forces of the Son of Heaven. I pushed the thought aside, but not without a sharp pang of regret at turning down Jerik's offer to bring me another bottle.

Triss squeezed me in a sort of whole-body hug, then relaxed onto the floor, taking his otherworldly senses with him and returning me the semblance of a shadow. If said shadow belonged to a small dragon, of course.

"Thank you for taking the job," said Triss.

I shrugged and knelt to rub a finger along his jawline—as always fascinated by feeling scales and warm, living flesh where my eyes showed nothing but shadow lying on a threadbare rug. Even in that shape, he had some substance to him. "You're all I have left, and you wanted me to. How could I deny you?"

The shadow of a dragon ducked his head abashedly. "I worried that the way she lied to you and concealed her magery might drive you to turn her away."

"Magery?" I closed my eyes and rubbed the lids for a long moment. "You didn't mention *that* part earlier, only that Maylien was more than she seemed. Perhaps you'd better elaborate now."

"I know she wasn't showing any visible spells, and I couldn't spot her familiar. But when she first leaned over you, her shadow fell across me and it tasted of mage gift—very recently used, or I wouldn't have been able to detect it." He cocked his head to the side thoughtfully. "She probably had her familiar wait for her outside, though it's possible she's allied with a lesser spirit of some sort, and it was simply invisible."

I suppressed a desire to growl at Triss. But we'd done more than enough fighting for one night. "Well, if she is a mage and a noble, it's no wonder she's hiding her familiar, whatever it is." Perhaps something that left scars on your shoulder when it perched there? A hawk maybe, or an eagle? But it really wasn't important. "The Zhani take a dim view of their peers using magic. They claim it distorts the whole challenge system of succession." Which it did, and that might explain why she had to come to me in disguise.

I sat down on my trunk and wished I had a drink handy. The

last thing in the world I wanted was to get mixed up in Zhani high-
court politics . . . again. I still had the scars on my leg and the price
on my head from the last time, a decade ago. I massaged my temples.
    "Triss . . ."
    "I know. I should have told you. You're not going to back out of
the job, are you?"
    "No, I took her money, and it's not like I really expect clients to
tell me the truth. You, on the other hand . . ." I sighed. "Next time
you taste magic on someone's shadow, signal me secretly, and we'll
go talk about it." We both knew he ought to have done so this time,
but I let it slide—he's a willful sort of creature when he wants to
be and quite possibly smarter than I am. "No more of this jerking
around like someone poured a cupful of shadow ants into your
shadow pants, all right? It makes you look like a twitchy tyro."
    "I . . . You . . . I never . . . Hmmph."
    Triss relaxed back into my shape, raised shadow hands to
shadow ears like a set of antlers, then rudely wiggled his fingers at
me, effectively terminating the conversation. *Gotcha.* I grinned and
went to reshade the light. I'd need a solid ten or twelve hours of
sleep if I was going to refill the wells of magic and be at my best for
tomorrow's delivery.

I got up late in the afternoon and killed time while I waited for the
sun to go down by alternating shadow-fencing with Triss and pretending to read a book I had "borrowed" from the Ismere, a wealthy
merchant's lending library. It was a ridiculous adventure story set
in the long-destroyed realm of the Necromancer, which used to lie
on the northern edge of the mage wastes. I was so distracted by
thoughts of Maylien as mage and wondering what her real game
was that the words just flowed through my head without leaving
any real imprint. I vaguely gathered there was something in this
most recent chapter about methods for strengthening various breeds
of the restless dead, but that was about all I got out of it.
    When the sun finally fell within a handsbreadth of the horizon,
I snapped the book closed with real relief and hurried back up to
my little room. There Triss wrapped himself around me, and we
opened the spelled lock I kept on my trunk—another bit of Durkoth
work. The Other smiths were the best in the world though I couldn't
afford any but their cheapest pieces.
    From the inside I pulled a matched pair of battered short swords,
straight-bladed and double-edged, with simple cross hilts and the

blades darkened for night work. Decent smithwork, but not fancy and nothing like as good as the pair of curved temple blades they'd replaced. I checked their fit in the hip-draw double back sheath I'd had made to replace my old temple-supplied shoulder-draw rig. Then I set the whole on the pallet.

Working clothes came out next, and I put them on as I went. Shirt first, then loose trousers cut very full in the leg and tucked into soft knee boots, all in nondescript shades of gray—the sorts of things any Zhani peasant might wear. Crushing the oris plant made for an easy dye and a cheap one as long as you didn't want to concentrate it enough to make a true black.

A heavy belt with a short, plain knife went on next, followed by my broad, flat trick bag. Then my sword rig, with its straps and darkened steel rings for attaching other gear—left empty for the moment. Finally, I pulled on a dark green and much-stained poncho. It smelled of old wool and fleabane and came down far enough to cover the hilts of my swords. Over that I added a traveler's hood to complete the picture.

Triss watched quietly from the wall opposite the open window, content to sit where the westering sun put him though he did retain his dragon shape. After I finished dressing, I had only one task left before we could leave—reading the letter. I didn't trust Maylien, and even if I did, I wasn't about to walk into a job any more blind than I absolutely had to be. I set the folded parchment on my little table and pulled a six-inch strip of flexible copper from my trick bag.

"Triss, could you give me a hand?"

The little dragon flowed down off the wall and back along the fall of my shadow to puddle around my feet before slithering up my body and pressing himself tight to my skin. For work of this sort I needed very fine control, so Triss subordinated his will to my own, putting his mind into a sort of waking dream that tracked but could not direct our joint actions. His physical self—inasmuch as a shadow can be said to have such a thing—now moved to my commands, a necessary condition for most higher-order magic, which needed to be guided by a single will.

The mage and his familiar are like the swordsman and his sword. The swordsman makes the swing, but the sword delivers the killing blow. The raw stuff of magic, the nima, comes from the mage, power drawn from the well of his soul, but without a familiar to provide a way to focus and deliver that power, nothing happens.

I directed that part of me that was temporarily a thing of animate darkness outward, enclosing the thin metal tool in shadow and charging it with magic. In my magesight, the strip of copper took on a bright blue glow. Then I slipped it under the edge of the seal on the letter. Through Triss's senses, I could taste dye and bees and turpentine in the wax of the seal but no concealed magic, which made things simpler. With a tiny flash of power, I separated it from the parchment without hurting either.

Unfortunately, Maylien, or whoever had prepared the letter, had anticipated the possibility of seal lifting—one of the easiest of the gray magics. The exposed pages appeared as blank as if they'd come fresh from the stationer. That made exposing any message significantly harder. There were easily a dozen magical means of blanking the pages, ranging from a fairly simple charm of concealment up to a destruction-primed soul key, though most of those would leave some visible light of magic on the page. The wrong sort of spell could as easily wipe away what I wanted as reveal it, and I couldn't tell enough about this one to decide on the right approach. Time for a second opinion.

I released my hold on my familiar's will and tapped the parchment sheets. "Triss, what do you make of it?"

He slid off my shoulders and onto the table, shrinking into the shadow of a dragon perhaps ten inches from nose to tail. As I passed my hand back and forth between the sheet and the light, he spread his wings and flew across the surface in tandem with my motions. Then he settled beside the paper and extended a shadow tongue again and again until he'd tasted every inch. Finally, he shook his head.

"Not only can I not tell you *how* any words might be bound away from prying eyes, I'm not at all certain there's a real letter here to be read. The spell is either too clever, too strong, or too absent to unravel."

"That's what I thought, and I don't like it. Not even a little bit. It's magic out of proportion to the scope of the job, and more expensive by far than my courier fee. Though, if our Maylien's a mage, it's possible she managed it herself."

Triss shrugged. "Possible but unlikely. This is specialist's work, and I don't see a noble devoting herself to the necessary study. I wish I could show this to Serass or Malthiss or one of the other old Shades. They might have done better, and Serass in particular would have enjoyed the challenge. But they all faded into the great black when the temple fell." His wings slumped.

I ran a fingertip along the shadow of a spinal ridge from Triss's neck to his tail, but I had no soothing words for my familiar. Only shared pain at the loss of so many of our friends and fellows. Names slipped through my mind. Master Kelos, Devin, Sharl . . . beloved teachers, close friends, lovers, all gone, and with them their Shades, Malthiss, Zass, Liess. Triss and I were virtually the last of our kind. A four-hundred-year tradition would end with us.

I pushed anger and grief aside for perhaps the ten-thousandth time and resealed the letter, tucking it into my trick bag along with the copper strip. We had a job to do, and the prospect of action offered distraction if not comfort.

"Triss," I said.

"Yes." He didn't look up.

"We ought to go."

"You're right."

He relaxed into my shadow, his dragon shape fading into a dark mirror of mine. But only briefly. A moment later, he was flowing silkily up my body, covering me from toes to top in a soft skin of darkness. No sooner had he finished that transformation than he began another. This time he extended himself outward in every direction. As he grew in size, he became ever more diffuse, like cream stirred into a fine froth. By the time he reached maximum size, I could no longer feel him as a physical presence at all.

The blackness that enclosed me was absolute. I could see nothing and no one, and no one and nothing could see me. Not even with magesight, because the effect wasn't a spell. It was a part of Triss's nature.

From the outside we would appear as a sort of dark moving hole in the vision, a lacuna, like the blind spot some headaches bring. As long as I stayed away from bright lights and places where no shadow had any right to go, we could move about virtually unnoticed by normal eyes. And as long as I kept from using magic, magesight couldn't see us either. That was why we Blades so rarely made use of actual preset spells. The glow negated our biggest advantage.

It wasn't quite invisibility, but it was the nearest thing available and vastly superior to what any other order of mages could achieve. The powers of the familiar defined and shaped the powers of the master. A barely gifted hedge witch with a snake for a companion might be able to do a lot with poisons and potions, things that even a master sorcerer would find nearly impossible if he happened to be bound to a fire elemental.

I stood in the dark until Triss again subsumed his will to my own, giving me control over our joint actions and allowing me to take in the world through his senses. Though I had given up my eyes to the darkness, Triss now provided me with a sort of unvision tuned far more to textures and the interplay between light and darkness than the shapes and colors so central to human sight.

Through Triss's senses, I could feel the level of light in the room as almost a physical presence, a painful sort of pressure against the skin that faded away as the sun slid below the horizon and left Tien to the night and to those whose work required darkness. The housebreakers, the smugglers, the night watch, and me.

I opened the shutters over my window and slipped through onto the narrow ledge. Once I'd closed and set the spell-lock on the shutters, I leaped and caught the edge of the stable's tiled roof, pulling myself up on top. A spring breeze coming in off the sea made me shiver and briefly long for a warming drink in the tavern below, but I pushed the thought aside. Exercise would heat my blood faster than any whiskey and leave me feeling better the next morning to boot.

Standing astraddle the roof's peak, I ran through a series of quick stretches while I reset my expectations of the world around me to accommodate my enshrouded state. With the very different range of Triss's unvision distorting my visual picture of the city, I had to rely more on my other senses, and I wanted them operating at their peak.

The sounds of the streets below gave me clues about the immediate vicinity. A boot scuff could speak about cobblestones or packed dirt. The way it echoed and traveled said things about alleys versus wider streets or even open squares. The sudden flutter of a bird's wing might warn me of the arrival of another traveler in the chimney forest—a thatch cutter or burglar perhaps. Or, more dangerous, a hunting ghoul or some other strain of the restless dead. Though they mostly stayed out of the open, this moon-dark night would allow them more freedom to haunt the streets.

Smell provided a broader sort of map of the city. Here in the heart of the Stumbles, the odor of badly maintained sewers blocked out most other scents. Farther along, I would find spicy sauces designed to cover the flavor of elderly meat, which would in turn give way to the perfumes favored by the better-off merchants. And that would shift to the floral aromas of the ornamental gardens only the truly wealthy could afford.

Touch didn't matter as much up on the rooftops, but it might become critical if I had to move inside later, so I made sure to attune myself to the messages sent by skin and bones. I let myself really pay attention to the way the rounded ceramic tiles of the roof felt through my soft-soled boots, the roughness of my woolen poncho as it rubbed against the backs of my hands, the sharp cold touch of the sea breeze on my cheeks and neck.

Only after I felt fully settled within Triss's enshrouding darkness did I begin my run through the city's chimney forest. Tien was ancient and had accreted rather than growing to any real plan. In most places, the roofs stood so close together that I could actually pass more easily from place to place on the chimney road than in the twisting and often crowded mess of the streets below. Even when I hit the broad canyon of Market Street, which separated the decrepit maze of the Stumbles from the saner Dyers Slope neighborhood, it didn't slow me much.

I simply spread my arms and had Triss spin himself into great wings of shadow like sails. Then I took a run and launched myself into space to glide across the open area. Sail-jumping was more than a jump, if less than true flight, and could be extended by magic if necessary or if you weren't worried about being spotted. The one real drawback of the technique was that there wasn't enough of Triss to both enshroud me and make wings. For the brief seconds of flight, I was exposed to watching eyes.

But that seemed a small price to pay for the joy of the experience. It always made me feel fifteen again, when Triss and I used to sneak out onto the temple roof at night just so we could leap off the edge and make the long, giddy glide down into the lake. When I landed on the far side of Market Street, I felt a brief stab of jealousy for the birds. They got to feel that way every day of their lives.

Racing across the rooftops with Triss made for a weird dichotomy of experience, at once dual and singular, familiar and alien, Shade and human. In moments like this, with my familiar surrounding and overlapping me, we were more one being than two, living within each other's skin if not actually mixing our minds in the way some familiars did with their companions.

The powers Triss wielded became an extension of my will, his senses mine to use, and yet there was still a fundamental separation. It wasn't just that Triss floated in dream while I controlled our conjoined bodies. The Shades interacted with reality in a manner wholly alien to human experience. Even if Triss could have approached the melding of our beings fully awake and aware, we had no common frame of understanding. If we wanted to share thoughts or even the sort of simple abstract ideas that a human familiar-bound to a cat might have easily managed, we would always have to resort to speech.

Twice more as we moved across the city, we had to cross a too-broad gap, and I got to be a bird for a few shining seconds—both times for canals coming off the Zien River. The nearly three-mile run took us from the ugliness of the Stumbles to the skirts of the Sovann Hill and up along the western edge of the carefully crafted faux wilderness of the royal preserves. There we had to descend to ground level for the first time.

It was the long way round. If I'd wanted to make my way along the east side of the park, I could have gotten much nearer my target before I left the shelter of the rooftops, but that would have brought me very close to the secret chapter house maintained by the Crown Elite. Not the sort of risk I wanted to court under any circumstances. Alternatively, I could have stayed concealed by taking to the sewers then, but I preferred to avoid shit's highway if I possibly could, and I didn't see the need here.

Making my quiet way across the parkland to the Marchon estate seemed almost childishly simple, needing little more than the occasional freeze in place when routine patrols passed by. In this one thing, the death of my goddess eased my way, for most believed that the fall of her temple had destroyed or driven into deep exile all of my kind. That meant that certain measures the patrols might once have taken had been much relaxed in recent years.

And why not? Though it hurt me to think it. In the five years since the fall of the temple, I had seen only one other of the Blades of the goddess alive, and Kaman had been nailed to a cross, with his shadow staked to the ground at his feet. When I offered to try to free him, he spat at me and cursed the goddess's name before begging me to make an end of him. I'd used an arrow from a distance and spent the next month playing a game of death tag with the Elite who'd hung him up there.

A ten-foot stone wall surrounded the Marchon estate. The wall was far too long to ward or guard effectively, but the owners had done what they could. It had shards of broken pottery set edge up along the top to deter human intruders, along with sprigs of dried mistletoe to keep out the restless dead. Silver nails would have answered better for that second purpose, but those tended to be stolen faster than they could be replaced, even in this sort of neighborhood. They hadn't bothered with slivers of iron, though I expect I'd have found those at the Marchon country house, where the creatures of wild magic posed a greater threat.

Getting over the top unharmed drained a bit more of my nima away as I had to use a minor sort of spell to protect me from the sharp edges. The baroness had dogs roaming the grounds, big vicious brutes who hunted as much by scent as sight. Triss's enshrouding presence was no help there, but I only met four, and in each case a snoutful of hollowed robin's egg loaded with powdered opium and efik worked the trick nicely. I made a mental note after the last to use some of the funds from this job to buy more of the finely ground and very expensive powders needed for their making. The slender brass case I kept them in was nearly empty.

Like most freestanding great houses, the Marchon place was built more than half as a personal fortress. It had no outward-facing windows on the ground floor, showing the world a blank limestone face. A dense hedge of imperial bush roses grew tight against the building as a further defense, with climbers growing up the wall as far as the second story. That cost me in blood lost to thorns, and I wished I dared use magic to push them aside, but the heavenly smell of fresh blossoms paid for at least some of the pain.

The third-floor balcony was broad and deep, supported by four thick columns faced with slick marble. Had I climbed one of those, I could have avoided the roses but only at the cost of facing an overhang deeper than I was tall—far more trouble than it was worth. Especially since the decorative stonework at the corner of the building was more than half a ladder for my purposes. So I went up the corner and across the top of the second-floor windows to the edge of the balcony, where I froze for several minutes while I checked the current state of things against my memories from earlier visits.

There I found more roses, some on a central trellis that would serve to provide a shaded area for dining outside in the brutal Tien summer, others scattered about in planters of various sizes. These were of more gentle varieties than the vicious imperials of the guardian hedge below. When you combined the roses with a small grove of decorative oranges that topped out just below the level of the balcony, the overall effect was of a floating garden sailing on a sea of blossoms. Quite lovely, even in the dark, and much as I'd remembered it. But I wasn't there for the view, so I soon slipped over the railing and crossed to the small window where I was supposed to meet the recipient of the letter.

I'd just lifted a hand to check the latch when the balcony doors opened behind me spilling light across the marble floor from the chandelier within. Quickly and quietly, I took three long steps and dropped into a crouch within the deeper shadow offered by a large stone planter. I was almost relieved at the interruption. Until then, the job had been far too easy to justify the fee I'd been offered though a jack without Triss's help might have found it a much more difficult task. Combine that ease with the too-expensive magic used on the letter, and it made for a very suspicious package.

As I settled in to wait and find out what might come next, I relaxed my control over Triss so that he could observe as well. Though I maintained a low-level contact with his mind that allowed me to use his senses along with my own, I wanted a more complete picture. So I drew one hand across my face, signaling Triss to thin the shadow veil enough for me to see with my own eyes.

A couple of red-clothed footmen came out through the open door with seat cushions and a cloth for the table and chairs sitting under the shelter of the trellis. Though they maintained the impassive expressions expected of servants to the high nobility, the hesitance of their bearing expressed a certain amount of bewilderment. Who could blame them? It was late and oppressively dark and growing steadily chillier, a strange time indeed for such a one as the baroness to be taking the air.

I didn't recognize her beyond the insignia on her chain of office and the cut and fabric of her clothing. As a noble, she wore the divided skirts and loose shirt that would allow her to instantly defend her seat if duel-challenged by a rival. She had a heavy gold chain around her neck supporting a medallion of office with the Marchon insignia of a jade fox on a gold background. She was not atypical of the breed, tall and broad-shouldered, with the muscles of one who visited the salle daily.

True black hair and an unusually plain face were the only factors that distinguished her from seven-and-seventy other ladies of her standing, though not recognizing her face came as something of a shock to me. There had been a time not all that long ago when I could have identified every major noble in Tien and nine other kingdoms at a glance. But then, she was obviously quite young and probably only recently risen to the peerage.

"Bring the drinks and a small light, then go away," she called in a voice deeper than I'd expected.

The servants did as they were told, adding a tray with two steaming pots and cups to match as well as a dim red magelantern that was only just a hair brighter than a thieves-light. Then they closed the doors, cutting off the brighter light from the room beyond once again. That left only the lantern to fight the darkness and made me much more comfortable. The thin layer of shadowstuff over my eyes would prevent them from reflecting much light, but not all of it. If I wanted to see, I had to risk being seen.

With her back to the house, the baroness settled in to wait, occasionally sipping at her tea. I could probably have tried for the window again then, but curiosity held me. Who was she waiting for? And how did she expect them to arrive? Even without the second pot, there was no question she was waiting for someone, and very impatiently at that—every line of her body told the same tale.

I wasn't terribly surprised when I heard an almost imperceptibly faint rustling in the roses below a few moments later. I shifted my position slightly to give me a better view of the far corner of the balcony—the same place I had come up and the most logical entrance for a climber.

I don't really know who or what I was expecting, but it was not what I got. For what seemed an awfully long time after the rustling stopped, nothing happened. I was just beginning to think I'd dreamed the whole thing up, when a man appeared in the seat across from the baroness, looking for all the world like he'd been there all along. He nodded casually at the baroness as he picked up a cup and reached toward the second pot.

"Devin, you're very nearly on time," said the baroness, her voice harsh. "However did that happen?"

She probably saved me from betraying myself then, because I'm sure I gasped aloud in the same moment she spoke her piece. That noise was all that prevented Devin from hearing me. Never in my life had I regretted more the way that Triss's assumption of shroud form made it virtually impossible for him to communicate with me. In that shape, he couldn't even give me the sorts of squeezes and prods he indulged in as my shadow, though I could tell by the way he focused his attention on Devin that Triss was every bit as shocked as I was to find him here.

Devin!

I wanted to shout that name aloud, to leap up and hug the man it belonged to, a man the temple had raised me to think of as my brother. Even in the dim light, I couldn't possibly mistake the familiar features, the Blade-trained hearing, the well-worn sword hilts jutting out above his shoulders.

But Devin was dead. Along with so many others, he had died when the temple fell. At least, his name was carved with all the others into a great granite obelisk in front of the ruined temple. The Son of Heaven had ordered the stone erected to commemorate the triumph of the forces of heaven over the "self-declared goddess of justice, rogue of heaven, and her twisted cult of regicides and priest-murderers."

There had been over five hundred names carved in that stone, priest and Blade, novice and master. Of all the servants of the goddess, fewer than two score had escaped the list of the dead, and every one of those names had appeared on the posters that declared the ban and offered a reward for our heads.

That as much as anything was what had convinced me that heaven really had turned against my goddess, that every last name was there. The complete roll of the Blades was a secret known only to full members of the order and to a few of the highest priests, and we were all bound by mighty oaths and deadly magic never to reveal it. But there we all were, our identities exposed to the world by divine fiat.

Devin Urslan was dead, his name set forever in black granite on the tombstone of an entire religion. Yet here he sat, with a high noble of Tien calmly pouring a cup of tea—no. Efik. The rich smoky scent rolled over me as he poured, and I felt a moment of intense longing that I reflexively suppressed. That life was gone forever, murdered by the Son of Heaven and his gods. But then, so was Devin.

I couldn't seem to make my mind deal with the contradiction of Devin both dead and buried and alive and drinking efik. But where thought failed me, temple-taught discipline took over. Aral the jack vanished, and I reverted to Aral the Blade.

The priests and teachers who had molded me into a living weapon for the hand of the goddess had set out to create a tool that could do its job in the most confusing circumstances and under the worst conditions. Routines set as deep as my bones took over.

Stop. Assess the situation. Act decisively.

And so, rather than rushing to embrace the brother I'd believed lost, I listened and I waited. The time to act would identify itself.

3

<hr>

"**B**aroness Marchon, you're as lovely as ever. And," Devin paused and took a sip of his efik before continuing, "if anything, your manners are more charmingly direct than I remembered."

The baroness looked as though she'd been slapped and, well, she had been. "How dare you! You're nothing more than a filthy peasant with an overdeveloped sense of his own—"

"Do shut up, Baroness, and remember what I am." Devin's voice came out smooth but firm, cutting across her diatribe. "Our contract doesn't cover bowing and scraping, and I don't have the time or the patience to pretend that it does. Your noble blood doesn't impress me a whit. Zass and I have spilled bluer on a number of occasions, and, frankly, it all looks the same when it's leaking into the dirt."

He took another drink, wafting the scent of the efik my way. I drew in a slow, deep breath through my nose—good beans steeped just long enough. How I missed that.

The baroness was snarling, "I . . . You . . . How could—" But she stopped abruptly and straightened her spine before nodding ever so faintly and regally. Her voice when it came again was icy cold and perfectly contained. "I see. Thank you for the reminder of why and for what I hired you, Assassin. In return, you ought to remember that casting no shadow puts you under one. The temple of Namara is a smoking ruin, and your goddess is as dead as you are purported to be. The proscription of Namara's Blades is quite clear about—"

"Ssst," said Devin, raising a hand and cutting her off for a second time. As he spoke, he stood, pulling a short, curved sword from behind his shoulder with his other hand. "We're not alone, Baroness."

I wasn't sure what had betrayed me, probably a sharp breath drawn when the baroness had spoken the name of the goddess. It had been years since I'd heard or said her name aloud. For me it hurt less that way. For others . . . well, what was the point of calling on a dead goddess?

"I know you're here." Devin carefully scanned the area, and I ducked my head to hide my eyes. "Whether you're a simple burglar, an eavesman, or follow some other flavor of the shadow trade, you can't hope to hide from me. You heard what the baroness just said about my shadow, and you know what it means, or you wouldn't have given yourself away then. Will you come out so we can discuss this in an amicable way, or will you declare yourself my enemy by remaining in hiding?"

What to do? It was the hardest question I'd faced in years and one where my training couldn't help me. Part of me still desperately wanted to talk to Devin, to embrace him as a brother returned past all hope and from beyond the grave. But the time that ingrained discipline had given me to think had raised too many questions.

How *had* Devin escaped the fall of the temple when so many others had not? Why, if he had, was his name on the list of the dead and not beside mine with the proscribed? I didn't want to believe that someone I'd trusted might have betrayed the goddess, but what other explanation was there? For that, or for his presence here and in such company for that matter?

The young baroness, with her contempt and her talk of filthy peasants and the hiring of assassins, was exactly the sort of unjust authority Namara had created the order of Blades to address. To find Devin, who'd once killed corrupt generals and deranged duchesses in the name of the goddess, working for such a creature . . .

But was I really so much better? I might not kill for money, but I'd taken my own goddess-trained talents and gone into business as a shadow jack, smuggling goods and letters, playing bodyguard to thugs and jackals, even the occasional bit of contracted theft when I got broke enough. I didn't know what to think or do.

While I crouched there, paralyzed with indecision, Devin drew his second blade. As it came free of the sheath, I looked up and caught a flash of the lapis-inlaid oval of its guard shining like a blue eye forever open—the unblinking eye of justice. It was the message I needed. For me, Devin must remain as dead as if I'd buried him myself, one more part of a past I'd left behind forever.

I might have made a wreck of my life that mirrored the wreck of the temple, but I'd done it without turning the blades of justice into murderer's tools. My swords rested now on the bottom of the sacred lake whence they had come. A weighted bundle that held my every image of the unblinking eye had gone with them. I might ply the shadow trades to keep body and soul together, but I refused to carry any token of the goddess while I did so. I refused to pretend that I was anything other than the petty shadow tradesman I had become or pretend that the goddess would have approved.

Training took over again. Once you have decided to act, act decisively.

I signaled to Triss that we needed to move, and he ceded control back to me. Slipping a black coil of silk line free of my bag, I dropped a loop over the stone planter I'd chosen as my hiding place. Then, as Devin dashed toward us, I took two long steps and leaped over the front of the balcony—putting me clear of the roses. Were it not for a thickened patch of the stuff of shadow acting as a glove, I'd have badly burned my hand on the rope when I used it as a friction brake on the way down.

In the instant my feet touched the ground, I let go the line and started into a gentle lope. I knew that Devin was right behind me. If I wanted to give him the slip, I needed to get as far away as possible as quickly as possible, and I needed to do it without breaking into the kind of hard, noisy run that would allow him to follow me by ear.

Focusing on the task helped me ignore the mad tumble of emotions that kept trying to suck me under. Though I couldn't read specifics from Triss, I could feel weird and wild echoes spilling over from his dreams that suggested an even-more-turbulent state of disorder than my own.

As I hurried along, I made several sharp changes of direction in the hopes of further confusing things, but I always kept moving toward the nearest corner of the estate. At another time, I might have chosen to hide within the grounds and wait for the pursuit to move out and away from the center of things, leaving behind a void I could exploit. But the combination of having a major contingent of the Elite so close and the unknowns represented by Devin's presence decided me against the idea in this case.

The outer wall was in sight, and I'd just started to breathe a little easier when I crashed headlong into another of the baroness's dogs. An opium-and-efik egg smashed across his nose put him out of the game a few seconds later, but not before he'd made noise enough to betray me to someone with Devin's training.

That left me a major dilemma. To get out, I had to get over the wall. Since the estate was properly maintained for security, there were no trees close enough to the wall to jump from unaided by shadow wings, which meant dropping my shroud. If I wanted to maintain my lacuna of shadow I either had to climb out at the corner, where I could brace myself in the angle of the stonework and vault over the pottery shards on top—my original intent—or I had to use the same sort of magic I'd used to get in. If Devin was close by—and I had to assume that he was—I couldn't do either undetected, and we both knew it.

Climbing the corner would make more than enough noise to allow Devin a free shot with dart or blade, and the active use of magic was visible to any practitioner who cared to use his magesight. That was a large part of what made the enveloping darkness Triss and his fellow Shades could offer so valuable. It was passive and innate to the breed, a near invisibility that would baffle even the eyes of a mage.

Moving a few yards away from the place where I'd left the unconscious dog, I put my hands on the hilts of my swords and settled in to listen and wait on Devin's next action. I couldn't afford to give him very long—no more than a couple of minutes—but I didn't want to attack him without giving him the chance to choose another way.

Several seconds slid past. If he hadn't been close before, he certainly was now. More time. Perhaps a minute. I silently slipped the loops that held my swords tight in their sheaths. I needed only to move my hands down a few inches more, and they would drop free.

Devin spoke then, his voice coming from a point some yards off to my left. "I don't know who you are, but I know what you are, Blade of Namara."

No one had called me that in years, and until that instant I'd had no idea how much that hurt me, nor how much more it would hurt to hear it now. I had never in my life felt a stronger desire to kill than I did then. If I'd had the slightest idea who it was I really wanted to kill, I don't think I could have stopped myself from making the attempt. As it was, my knuckles burned from squeezing the hilts of my swords so tight.

"Actually, that's not quite true," said Devin. "I may not *know* who you are, but I bet I can make a very good guess. Let's see, you're no apprentice assassin."

I had to suppress a hiss at that. "Assassin" wasn't normally a word a Blade used when referring to his fellows—however true it might be.

"An apprentice I'd have caught before they made it off the balcony. I don't think you're one of the escaped journeymen either, not having gotten this far running free, though that stumble with the dog was very sloppy tradecraft. There are only four masters that are yet unaccounted for. Jax and Loris both refused the bargain the Son of Heaven offered to those that survived the fall of the temple. They called those of us who took the deal *traitors*."

Deal? What deal? I knew nothing of any deal.

I wanted to shake Devin and make him answer that question, but I knew that moving against him physically would only stop the flow of information. I wondered, too, how the pair could both have been captured and yet remain unaccounted for, and played out what I knew of them in my head. Loris was of the previous generation, and I didn't know him well, but I'd always liked Jax, who was a year or two younger than I. She had a good head on her shoulders.

Devin continued, "Though they later escaped, they both spent a certain amount of . . . time with the Hand of Heaven first. I think either of them would have moved to kill me rather than running."

In that moment, I regretted that I hadn't. The Hand provided the Son of Heaven with his enforcement arm, which included a lot of torture and burning of heretics. I didn't move. Devin knew things that I wanted to, and he was still talking.

If your enemy is doing what you want, don't interfere.

"That leaves Siri and Aral," he said, "the shining stars of my generation. Both in the field at the time of the fall. Which are you, I wonder, my former sister or my lost brother? Mythkiller or Kingslayer? In either case, a potential adornment to the new order of the Assassin-Mage."

This time I did hiss. A mistake.

Devin chuckled in response. "Oh, I didn't like the name much the first time I heard it either, but it's a hell of a lot more honest name for what we are than 'Blade' ever was, and it grows on you if you live long enough. I'm going to make you an offer. If it will make you feel better, you can choose to believe that's because I don't think I can take whichever of you I'm talking to in a fight. And you might be right, or then again, you might be surprised. It makes no difference to me what you believe. What matters to me is what you decide.

"Those of us who took the Son of Heaven's deal have moved on from the ruin of the temple. We had no choice. The goddess really is dead, and there's no bringing her back. The Blades of Namara are gone forever. But that doesn't make us a spent force. We still have the Shades and the skills we learned from the temple. We can take on new apprentices, teach the assassin's arts, summon more Shades from the everdark. We have the potential to be one of the most powerful mage orders this world has ever seen. To rule from behind every throne."

And to betray everything we ever were. I slid my swords free of their sheaths and rolled my shoulders. I didn't want to kill an old friend, but I couldn't see any other way out.

"I know I speak for the order when I say we'd love to have you with us," said Devin. "I won't demand an answer this instant, but we can't afford to leave you running loose for long if you won't side with us. You have forty-eight hours from this moment to decide. If you want to join the future, send a note for me here care of the baroness. If you insist on remaining a part of the past, we'll have no choice but to make sure your name is added to the list of the fallen. Goodbye for now."

The time for words was over.

I started toward the place where I thought Devin's voice was coming from but had only taken a couple of steps when the world came apart with a blinding flash and a tremendous boom. For a good ten seconds, I couldn't see anything but a lavender pattern of branching lines left on my retinas by one of the most violent bursts of magelightning I'd ever encountered. It was well beyond what Devin should have been able to manage without a more formal spell. If he'd wanted to kill me then, there's a good chance he'd have managed it. Instead, he vanished, leaving me alone beside the giant hole he'd blasted in the baroness's wall.

I briefly contemplated looking for him, but I had no doubts that the display was going to draw a lot of the wrong kind of attention, including the Elite. Promising myself that this thing with Devin wasn't over, I slipped out through the hole in the wall and headed back toward the city proper.

I picked up a bottle of Kyle's as I passed through the Gryphon on my way back to my room over the stables. It had been an excruciatingly long and nasty night, and I really needed the drink. I set the bottle carefully beside a borrowed glass on my little table before I started to strip off my gear.

Triss flowed up the wall and into dragon form. "I don't think that's such a good idea."

I yanked off my hood and dropped it on the pallet. "I do. In case you weren't paying attention back there, my old friend Devin's become some kind of fucking assassin for hire along with who knows how many of the others. Not to mention that he wants us to join him in his abomination. If that's not the best reason for getting drunk this side of Namara's murder, I don't know what is."

Triss let out a loud, hissing sound and reared back, but didn't say anything. The purpose of a Blade of Namara was to bring a just death to those who deserved it. Killing was part of our job, and both Triss and I had once been damned good at it; but even the idea of doing it for money seemed the most horrible sort of perversion of what we had once been. I shrugged out of my poncho, throwing it down beside my hood. As I unbuckled my swords, I nodded toward the trunk.

"Open that for me, would you?"

Triss slid down from the wall and briefly covered the trunk in shadow. With a sharp clicking noise, the lid popped open. I flipped the poncho from bed to trunk with the toe of my boot. It landed in a lump guaranteed to leave creases. The hood followed, then my shirt.

"You normally put your swords on the bottom." Triss's voice came out quiet and worried.

"Fuck normal." I grabbed my sword rig off the bed and rebuckled it over my bare shoulders. "In fact, fuck everything."

"What are you doing?" Triss sounded more than a little alarmed as I crossed to the door.

I didn't answer, just grabbed the handle and wrenched the door open. Triss dove back into my shadow as the mage-light threw it across the floor of the hayloft. As I strode over to the hay pile, my shadow slid across the trapdoor that led down to the stables. When it did, one dark arm stopped mirroring my own movement long enough to flip the door shut—a sensible precaution on Triss's part though I barely registered it.

I pulled a half dozen of the rough bundles of hay free of the pile, and started leaning them against various of the roof posts. Two fell apart at once when the dried loops of braided grass that held them together for transport to the city gave way under my rude handling. The others held, more or less. I added more, putting a couple along the walls and two against the hay pile itself.

Stepping out into the middle of the big open room, I rolled my shoulders and fixed the positions of the bundles in my mind. A deep breath in, and . . . I let the rage free with my breath. Seemingly of their own accord, my swords dropped into my hands and flicked out, the left taking off the top of a hay bundle in a beheading stroke, the right going home in a heart thrust that sank the tip deep into the post behind it. Pivot and wrench my right blade free while back-cutting with my left to split the beheaded bundle. Stomp and cross swords in a blade-breaking parry. Turn, lunge.

I sliced and chopped and parried and thrust until every bundle was destroyed. Until the sweat rolled down my sides, and the air grew thick with chaff. Until I could barely breathe for coughing. Until my eyes streamed tears from the dust, and I could no longer see Devin's face even in my imagination. It wasn't enough.

With a snap of my wrist, I sent one sword flying down the length of the loft to embed itself in the door of my cubby. Then the other. An utterly useless little trick and suicide in combat, but it felt good, and it freed my hands to collect more bundles. When I was done, there were no more bundles, just a big loose pile of hay and a thick cloud of dust, like smoke. And it still wasn't enough. So I cleaned and resheathed my swords and closed myself up in my little room and reached for the bottle again.

And again, Triss said, "I don't think that's a good idea."

And he was right. So when I twisted the cork stopper free, I only poured two fingers into my glass and sealed the bottle again. Then I knocked back the whiskey and set the glass aside. My poncho came back out of the trunk and got folded properly on the bed. My hood and shirt, too.

I put my swords neatly away beside my knives and laid the trick bag down on top. That's when I remembered the letter and my failed courier's commission. Another in a long string of failures. You'd think I'd be used to them by now, but they never got any easier to face. I reached for the poncho.

"Aren't you going to take another look at the letter?" asked Triss. "There are stronger measures we might try, more destructive per-haps, but—"

"No." I laid the poncho down over the bag.

"You know there might be some clue in there about Devin, don't you?"

"Of course." I didn't for a second believe that the near-simultaneous arrival of Devin and me on that balcony was a coinci-dence. "Maybe after eight or ten hours of sleep, I'll even care enough to look Maylien up and rake her over the coals about the whole thing, but not tonight."

Or then again, maybe I wouldn't. Maybe I'd just have a drink or six and forget about the whole thing. I added the hood to the pile in the trunk, then my boots. As I changed pants, I could feel Triss glaring at me, so I took extra time and care in putting the grays away—I'd had all I could take of pushing for one night. He made a little hmmphing noise when I closed the lid, but he didn't grouse. I reached for the lock . . . and stopped. I just couldn't do it.

As a Blade, you learn that it's all right to choose not to act. Choosing not to think is another thing entirely. Though I was no longer a Blade, the lesson remained.

With a sigh I opened the trunk again and retrieved the letter. As Triss had noted, there were things we could do now in regard to exposing its secrets that we couldn't have when I'd cared about keeping it intact. I was running through some of those in my head when I took a closer look and discovered it was going to be a simpler task than I'd expected. Since I'd last examined the letter, words had appeared on the previously blank space above the seal.

"For Aral Kingslayer, last Blade of fallen Namara."

Un-fucking-believable. I laughed then, and it was a bitter and black sound like efik left too long a-steeping. I cracked the seal and began to read, with Triss following along over my shoulder. "I seek the redress of Justice," it began.

After the first few lines, I reached for the whiskey bottle. This time Triss didn't try to stop me.

4

My day started with pain. Throbbing pain and cruel light and a truly foul taste in my mouth. Nothing I hadn't experienced before. In fact, I'd been there often enough that I knew better than to open my eyes right away. I groped upward with my left hand, feeling along the top edge of my pallet until I found a plump wineskin.

Keeping my eyes firmly closed, I brought it down and pressed the cool leather against my forehead while I fiddled with the seal. Finally, I very carefully placed the neck in my mouth and took a long pull of small beer. It was bitter and harsh and warm, and it tasted like ambrosia. Good country water would have been better yet, but in a city like Tien, only the crazy and the desperate drank from the wells. Some might have preferred tea, but since I gave up efik, I no longer drink hot drinks. Not if there's any polite way to avoid it.

I didn't try to move or open my eyes till I'd downed half the skin. At that point I still felt like week-old shit, but I knew that just lying there wouldn't help anymore, so I reluctantly cracked an eyelid.

The first thing I saw was the shadow of a dragon. Triss peered down into my face from a position on the angled ceiling a few feet above my head and gently shook his own. That put my shadow ninety degrees away from where the light would have and announced Triss's unhappiness with me. It wasn't the first time *that* had happened either.

"Morning, Triss," I said. Husked really, since my throat felt like I'd been pouring paint thinner down it. "How are you?"

"It is *not* morning, and I am very angry." His voice came out flat and hard, but quiet enough that it didn't hurt my head. Much. "But you knew the latter and ought to have known the former."

He was right, my one window faced west. Sunlight slipped between the slats of its battered shutters. From the angle it had to be five or six hours past midday. Bad sign. I took another long pull of small beer, then discovered a worse one. When I recapped the skin and tossed it aside it landed with a clink of bottles. Plural.

"What day is it?" I asked.

"Atherasday, the tenth of Seedsdown."

"Oh, thank you." I paused for a moment, hoping for memory to allow me to sidestep the next question. But it failed me, and I had to ask, "What day was it when we saw Devin?"

Triss growled low in his throat and shook his head again. "It was in the last hour of the eighth day of Seedsdown."

"That could be a problem." I sat up and forced myself to stay that way.

I didn't much enjoy it, but it didn't kill me. I had about five hours to make a decision on Devin's offer. No, that's not true. I already knew my answer. There was no way in hell I was going to make common cause with my former brothers and sisters if it wasn't in service to the goddess. Not when any alliance would be made atop her divine corpse. No, what I had to decide was what to do about Devin.

"I need a drink," I said, then felt ashamed of myself. I knew what I had become, but that didn't make me proud of it.

"No," said Triss, "you may want a drink, but it's the last thing in the world that you need."

"Point. What would you suggest instead?"

"That you pack up and we leave this city and never return."

That surprised me. "You don't think we should seek Devin out? Devin and . . . Zass with him?"

"No. I do not want to join anyone who would betray the goddess's memory as they have. I do not want to have to kill them or, more likely considering the way you've let yourself go the last few years, be killed by them." There was a lot of anger in his voice, and I really couldn't blame him.

"So why run?" I asked. "Why not just stay here and ignore them? Them, and that damn girl both." More of my night-before was coming back to me. I found myself glancing into the corner where I'd thrown Maylien's crumpled letter when burning it proved beyond me.

"The girl found you. Do you really think Devin won't if he tries? Or the Elite, should Devin choose to keep his own hands clean? The only reason we have remained safe here for so long is because no one who wanted to find us would have believed we were foolish enough to come back to Tien after we killed its king."

I didn't have an answer for that. Instead, I made a show of dragging myself across the room to retrieve the letter. There were smoke stains along the edges from where I'd held it in the flames of one of Jerik's filthy oil lamps, but no other evidence of my attempts at burning. As I sat down at the table, I glanced at the front again.

For Aral Kingslayer, last Blade of fallen Namara.

I should have torn the letter into shreds. It wasn't for me anyway. The Kingslayer had died with his goddess. All he'd left behind was a broken-down wreck who wore his face. A shadow jack who drank himself unconscious most nights because that was the only way he could get to sleep. I opened the letter again. It beat facing Triss's reproach. Besides, I couldn't remember what was in it.

I seek the redress of Justice. My name is Maylien Tal Marchon and I am the true heir to the Barony of Marchon. If you are alive to read this, then I know that you are the Kingslayer and the one person who can help me regain my baronial seat.

If I'm your only hope, Lady, you might as well walk away from that chair right now.

I thought it was you from the moment I first saw you across the common room of the Gryphon's Head several months ago, but I had to make certain. I knew that the baroness's pet assassin—I won't sully the title of Blade by applying it to that Devin-creature— could never hope to stand against you in open combat.

Against the Kingslayer, maybe not. Against me . . . now those were much shorter odds. I shook my head. Devin. What was I going to do about Devin? That was still the only question that mattered. Triss was almost certainly right. We *should* run. But when I thought about walking away, something deep down in my soul said "no." It wasn't a loud voice, barely a whisper even, but it was very firm. My eyes flicked to the page again.

I'll have to lie low for a while after this, but I will look for you in the Gryphon's Head as soon as I am able.

The rest of the letter babbled on and on about her bona fides and the horrors the current Baroness Marchon was visiting on the heads of her people. Doors broken down in the middle of the night, people disappearing, burned-out crofts, all the usual mayhem and murder and exactly the sort of thing that would once have drawn the attention of the goddess. What Maylien completely failed to mention was anything that I actually cared about at the moment. Like how she knew who Devin was and what he'd been up to these last five years. I crumpled the letter and threw it into the corner again.

"You don't seem to like the contents any more today than you did the first time you read them," said Triss, his voice acid. "I hope that doesn't mean you're about to replay the drunken binge the last reading brought on."

"I don't really have time for that, now do I?"

The shadow of a dragon flicked his wings in a shrug, then flitted down to the table in front of me. "That hasn't stopped you in the past."

"In the past, I didn't know about Devin or any deal my former brethren might have made with the Son of Heaven."

Triss raised his head to stare at me. "That almost sounds like the old Aral, the stubborn one. I take it that we won't be leaving town?"

"Not till we find out a bit more about what happened at the fall of the temple."

"What of Maylien and unseating her wicked baroness?"

"Getting rid of the baroness isn't my problem. My interest in Maylien goes only as far as finding out what she knows about Devin. Oh, and collecting the rest of my fee, of course."

Triss cocked his head to one side skeptically.

"Don't look at me like that," I said. "I delivered her damned letter, didn't I? That's *all* I contracted for—none of this baronial seat bullshit. Come on, let's go have a look around."

I slid from my seat on the trunk to my knees, moving gently to avoid jarring my head. Then, drawing Triss around me, I reached for the lock.

The Spinnerfish was a good tavern in a bad neighborhood. It lay a few streets in from the docks on the Smuggler's Rest end of the harbor. That wasn't what anyone official called the area. Not where they could be heard at any rate. But everyone knew what happened down there.

The shadow port was one-third of what made the Spinnerfish such a successful venue. The second third was Manny Three Fingers, the best seafood cook in the city. Last was Manny's boss, Erk Endfast: a onetime shadow captain and black jack from Oen in the Magelands—he'd left rather quickly as an alternative to making a command performance on the Magearch's gallows. Now he ran the Spinnerfish as neutral territory, a safe place to meet or simply relax for all the players in Tien's shadow trades.

It was also a good place to dig for information. Devin's current company put him well beyond the ken of the sort of dregs and drifters that frequented the Gryphon. Though I didn't normally run in the richer circles of the shadow world, I knew most of the faces, and I knew how the game was played at that level. Perhaps more importantly, I had enough of a rep as a straight-back jack to spring a few locked doors.

I arrived at the Spinnerfish as the sun was setting, which put me ahead of the crowd. So I was able to snag a small table in a corner of the front room. When the waitress came around, I tossed her a silver riel and told her to bring me a tucker of Kyle's with a clean glass and the catch of the day, whatever it happened to be.

The place filled with people at about the same rate as my belly filled with peppered snapper. Things were really hopping by the time I put aside my plate and poured myself a second glass of whiskey from the small bottle. About halfway through sipping it down I noticed Erk himself making his way among the tables, waving at this one, leaning down to have a word with that, asking all and sundry about the fish.

He was tall and very fit and all-over brown, from his hair to his skin to his conservatively expensive outfit. He openly wore a pair of cane knives on his belt, forward curved and heavy—brutally effective weapons and better by far than a sword in a crowded and enclosed space like the Spinnerfish. I was rather surprised when his progress brought him to a halt across from me.

"Aral, how have you been?" he asked, his voice pitched to carry to the nearby tables. "It's been an age. I don't see you down this close to the docks very often. Mind if I join you? I've maybe got some jack work for you."

I pasted a smile on my face and waved at the other seat though I was feeling mighty uneasy. "I always have time for a man in need of a jack." I knew that Erk knew my jack face, but we'd never been on a casual basis.

As he sat down, he pulled a small bronze bell from some inner pocket and set it in the center of the table. "Drum-ringer."

"Sensitive business then?" I could feel Triss clinging tightly to my back as he paid extra attention.

The bell was an expensive little piece of permanent magic. Anyone more than a few feet away who tried to casually listen in would hear nothing but the distant ringing of bells. If someone employed magic to stick an ear in, the ringing would get a whole lot louder. Possibly even deafeningly so if the drum-ringer was a sufficiently powerful one as the spell-glow of this one suggested.

"Sensitive enough," answered Erk. "I've a favor to ask."

I cocked an eyebrow at that. Favors were not a common item of trade in the shadow world, and I doubted very much that he meant that word in the traditional way.

"It's like this; see those three gentlemen at the second table past the door, the one right by the corner of the bar? They're planning on causing you some harm, and they're planning on making their move soon. I really don't like that sort of thing happening inside the Spinnerfish. So if you'd do me the favor of stepping outside before you ghost them, I'd really appreciate it."

I flicked a glance around the room, making sure not to spend too much eye time on the table in question. I didn't for a moment doubt what Erk was telling me though I did idly wonder how he knew. The trio in question looked more like Kadeshi mercenaries than the bravos I'd have expected. They sported two swords, an axe, a mail shirt, and couple of breastplates between them. I'd noticed them when they came in but hadn't really paid any attention at the time.

Apparently, Devin had decided not to give me the full two days though why he hadn't come for me himself I didn't know. But that was a puzzle for later. In the meantime, I had a more pressing concern, two really. Erk's request had set a small worm of icy cold to stirring itself in the pit of my stomach.

"Why is it," I asked, keeping my voice as casual as I could, "that you're so certain about *me* ghosting *them*? I'm just a jack, and not exactly dressed for a fight." I tapped one of the long daggers that were my only visible weapons, then adjusted the collar of my light leather jerkin. "And those are hard men armed and armored for war."

One man with knives against a trio of veteran mercenaries doesn't a fight make, more like a massacre. If you bought my jack face, those were fool's odds.

Erk leaned back in his seat. "I was running a skip in the court of the Magearch when Lord Baskin met his much deserved and ever so timely end."

"Oh." Triss squeezed my shoulders hard but didn't make any more obvious moves.

Not that it mattered. Baskin was one of the very few jobs I'd ever been forced to perform in front of witnesses. The first thrust had glanced off a magical chest piece I hadn't known about. He'd managed to get out the door of his rooms and halfway to the great hall before I caught up and finished him.

"Hell of a sprinter, Baskin," said Erk.

"He was that, though I thought all the eyes in that hallway belonged to servants."

"That was certainly how I was faced at the time."

"You do know what my head's worth?"

"Of course," replied Erk. "But that's not my problem. When I left Oen behind, I left all the skips and plays with it. My world is this bar, and as long as nothing bad happens in here, my clients' business is entirely their own."

And that was as nice a threat as anyone had ever made me. Even if Erk didn't choose to sell me directly, he possessed something that a number of people would pay very highly for; a postgoddess view of my face. In the days when Namara still lived she had prevented the making of any likenesses of her Blades, jostling the elbows of artists who tried to capture images of our features and twisting the tongues and memories of those who might otherwise have described us. Now that she was gone, and Erk had refreshed his memory of me, he could make himself a tidy sum simply by having a good sketch done.

"I'd better see that I take care of my little problem outside then, hadn't I?" I said.

"I *would* appreciate it."

I downed the last of my second glass and looked regretfully at the tucker holding what would have been my third and fourth, then rolled my shoulders to loosen them.

Erk recorked the small bottle. "I'll have this kept aside for the next time you stop in if it comes soon enough."

"Thank you."

"You're welcome." He picked up the bottle, then reached for the drum-ringer, pausing in the instant before he lifted the bell as though just remembering something. "One last thing; going forward I'd also appreciate it if you didn't trail that sort of stupid trash in here in your wake ever again. I don't appreciate having to step in like this."

"I'll see what I can do," I said.

I stood and headed toward the counter, holding my empty glass in front of me as though I wanted a refill. That took me straight toward the trio of Kadeshis, who looked quite pleased and started oh-so-subtly loosening weapons and sliding their chairs back. It also put me on a line to pass within ten feet of the door. As I hit the closest point to the exit, I set my glass on the nearest table and bolted out into the night and a light drizzle.

When I hit the street, they were less than three yards behind me and had already drawn steel though they had to pause briefly to open the small magelantern the leader carried. I could still have lost them if I'd wanted to. Between the dark and the rain, I wouldn't have even needed Triss's help, but I wanted to send Devin a message, written in blood. Besides, I desperately needed a break from running and hiding, even if only for one night. I sprinted just far enough down the street to put a polite distance between me and the Spinnerfish before pivoting to face my attackers and drawing my daggers.

As I did so, Triss gave a questioning squeeze, offering to enshroud me or take a more direct hand in eliminating my attackers. I shook my head. I preferred not to reveal my nature to any third-party watchers if I could avoid it, and vanishing into shadow or having one kill for me would have made for a pretty unmistakable calling card.

Then they were on top of me. They were actually very good, attacking all together in a coordinated rush. The axe-man, who also held the lantern, charged me head-on, while the other two slid forward to his left and right so they could come in on my sides. It was smart tactics and a sign of good training and plenty of combat experience.

Someone was going to miss these boys.

I waited for the axeman to make the overhand swing that was his best bet, then slipped forward, moving inside his guard and blocking his descending arm with my own. At the same time, I jammed my right-hand dagger up under his chin and through the roof of his mouth, driving it deep into his brain. I felt something like the sudden electrical shock of magelightning as the coppery smell of blood feathered the air.

That was one.

He dropped the light as he died, but it stayed open, which was too bad since I didn't have time to do anything more direct about it. Using the embedded dagger as a push-off point, I shoved myself downward. Letting go of the hilt as I dropped, I balanced on the ball of my right foot and the knuckles of my left fist and pivoted backward in a sweeping kick. The dead man's left-side swordsman was exactly where I had planned for him to be, and my spinning calf caught him across the shins. He went down in a heap, while the falling corpse of the leader protected me from the right-side swordsman.

Which put me in the clear again.

As I came back upright, I flicked my right wrist, dropping the much shorter knife I kept in a sheath there into my hand. The right-side swordsman was turning around, but his companion had only gotten back up onto hands and knees, hampered perhaps by the water lightly slicking the cobbles. I sank both my blades deep into his spine, one above his breastplate, one below. Again, I felt a sort of electric charge at the kill.

That was two.

I used the hilts sticking out of his back like the handles of a pommel horse, pivoting and launching myself through the air feet-first. I hit the last man in the side of the knee, shattering the joint. It was a calculated risk but necessary given our relative positions. He was damned good and had come around faster than I'd hoped.

Two and a half.

He managed one solid swing at me as he went down. I blocked his blade with the inside of my left forearm, where I had a second wrist sheath. His sword broke the knife and tore the sheath loose. The straps burned across my skin, drawing blood. Then I was rolling away, and the second swing of his sword struck the wet cobblestones behind me.

That marked the effective end of the game.

Flipping myself to my feet, I drew my second-to-last blade from the top of my right boot and walked back toward the fallen man. He rolled onto his back, bringing the sword up between the two of us and pointing it at my chest.

"This doesn't have to end this way," he said desperately. "Just tell me what you want. Anything. I'll do it."

I kicked the lantern shut, plunging the street into deep darkness. Then I reversed my grip so that I was holding the dagger by the blade.

"I don't think so," I said.

I snapped my arm down and forward, throwing the knife. Master Kelos would *not* have approved, and he'd probably have been right—throwing a weapon was always a risky bet and usually a dumb move against a better-armed opponent, no matter what the barroom toughs claimed. Of course, that risk was small here. My enemy could move neither far nor fast, and I had another knife. Besides, as the blade's sinking deep into the Kadeshi's throat proved, sometimes a risk paid off nicely.

And sometimes it didn't.

As he died, the dagger flashed blindingly bright—a burst of magelightning arcing from its pommel to my right hand. More lines of lightning shot from there to the other two corpses, centering me in a web of burning light and pain. My view of the world exploded into a wild rainbow cascade of nonsense shapes, and for just a second, I could both taste and hear the colors.

I'd been deathsparked, and I was an idiot.

I slumped to my knees in a filthy puddle. I'd never seen it coming. Because, you see, Blades are immune to death-sparking. The goddess protects us. But the goddess was dead. If I'd ever needed more proof of that, I had it now.

That hurt more than the deathspark, and the pain carried me into darkness.

5

The world tasted of blue, which in turn tasted rather a lot like badly burned bacon, and it smelled like mage-lightning. The world also hurt, especially my head. Oh, and I had a powerful urge to vomit. Sadly, waking up feeling like I did just then was no more than a strange new variation on an old, familiar theme. I automatically reached for the skin of small beer that sat at the top of my pallet. Or, tried to, actually.

That was when I discovered I couldn't move my arms or much of anything else. I was bound. Then I remembered the deathspark, and that explained the pain and my situation and tasting colors. *Thank you, Devin, you shit-eating bastard.* Rather than fight my bonds, I stopped moving completely as routines that had been carved into my bones came to the fore. I could almost hear old Master Kelos drilling me on what to do when captured.

Hide your strength.

I cracked an eye the tiniest margin and found . . . myself severely disorientated and once more fighting hard against the impulse to throw up. In part because of the eye-jabbingly bright magelight hanging a few feet in front of my face. But also because of my sudden mental change of orientation. Rather than lying on my back as I'd initially believed, I was upright and facing a basement room that just screamed dungeon.

Count the opposition, locate the exits, catalog your assets.

I forced down the nausea. In addition to me and whatever I was hanging from, the dungeon contained various implements of torture—many of which I could use as weapons if I could get my hands on them. A quartet of rough-looking men played at dice in a corner. One of them had a few faint glimmers of magic about him— poorly crafted spells probably. Above them was a barred window laced over with some sort of minor spell that blurred what lay beyond. That and a door off to my left provided the only exits I could see without moving.

The place stank of mold and piss and old blood. Especially that last. A lot of blood had been spilled in this room, and not just as a side effect of torture. Not with a bleeding-table standing just a few feet off to my left. The angled marble slab had deep gutters cut into it to direct the blood into the basin at its foot. Though not magical in itself, an exsanguination table was a tool used for some of the darker magics and one more reason to get the hell out of there as quickly as possible.

Test your bindings.

None of the men was currently looking my way, which suggested one of two things. Either they were stupid, or they were very confident about the efficacy of my . . . what *was* I hanging from? It didn't feel like any of the sorts of manacles I'd learned to slip as a child. There were too many fastening points for one thing . . . ankles, knees, chest, throat, elbows, wrists. All snug.

Very carefully and very slowly, I turned my head to the right. The taste of blue came back, but I ignored it. Looking along my bare arm I could see that there was a heavy leather strap buckled just above my elbow and another at my wrist. The buckles were brass. It was hard to tell given my angle of view and scrambled senses, but they all seemed to be mounted to some sort of magically active wooden framework. I strained weakly at my bonds, but they didn't move, and the effort brought back the nausea, so I stopped and went back to trying to make sense of the framework that held me. Its shape seemed far too complex for its purpose.

"It's a sheuth glyph, Blade," said a rough voice.

I glanced up to find that one of the dice players had turned to look my way. The one with minor bits of magic hanging about him.

"I don't think I know that one," I replied.

"No surprise there." He got up to come closer, approaching me from one side. "It's not anything your kind is supposed to know about. Came straight from Tangara, God of Glyphs, it did." He chuckled then, and it was an evil sound. "He made it special like for the destruction of that bitch Namara's temple."

How could Devin bear to employ such a man? I took a moment

then to really fix him in my memory. I wanted to be absolutely sure I would know him anywhere. If I didn't kill him on my way out of here, I was going to make a point of looking him up later.

Middling tall and middling dark, with narrow shoulders and a bit of a paunch, he would have blended into any Tienese crowd without raising an eyebrow. He *was* better dressed than his fellows, wearing bloused pants of rough silk and an embroidered leather vest, where the others wore cotton and badly tanned hide. He also had a slender spit-adder wrapped two or three times around his neck.

It raised its head and hissed at me when they got within a few feet. Its attitude mirrored that of its mage, for that was clearly what the man was, though of a minor enough sort that I didn't recognize the school. Seeing the familiar made me realize that Triss hadn't tried to signal me in any way yet. Though I could feel him lying against my back, he didn't seem to be as present as normal, and that worried me. A lot.

"Sheuth, huh? What's it do?" I asked.

The man smiled, showing uneven teeth. "Can't you guess?" Before I could answer, he went on, "It's got another name; the pillory of light. Working along with the stone there"—the snake's head rose to point at the brilliant mage-light hanging in front of my face—"the sheuths's a binder of shadows. The light makes your pet monster act like a *real* shadow, substanceless and inanimate, and that rack you're on trusses it up even tighter than it does you."

I didn't panic though I felt the first edges of real fear. Quickly I moved my hands through a half dozen of the signals I used with Triss when we couldn't speak aloud. But the device was custom-designed by a god to hold Blades and Shades, and Triss made no response, not even the slightest change of pressure across my back.

Fuck. Fuck, fuck, fuck.

I wanted to bust loose, to kill the bastards who'd messed with my familiar. I couldn't even move my arms though I strained against the straps until the muscles in my chest and shoulders felt raw and shredded. The mage just watched me, smiling all the while, and there was nothing I could do to him. Nothing at all. That was what finally made me stop fighting like an animal and start thinking like a Blade again. And that began with making an honest assessment of my situation, both in terms of my options and how I got there.

If they didn't kill me outright, there might come a moment when I had a chance to act. If I was exhausted, I'd fuck up, and that would

be it. I would die, and Triss would die with me, and there'd be
nobody to blame but the miserable drunk that had inherited the
Kingslayer's skin. But I wasn't going to let that happen.

I didn't much care about me. If I'd had the choice, I would have
followed my goddess into the grave when the temple fell. But I
didn't have the choice because Triss's life was tied to mine, and I
loved him far more than I hated myself. Now, if Triss was going to
live, I had to live. That meant I had to get smart, maybe even become the Kingslayer again, if only for a little while—I didn't think
I could bear the weight for much longer than that. I took a deep
breath and looked my captor in the eye.

"Does it hurt him? Your glyph, I mean."

"Does it hurt the Shade?" He laughed. He. Laughed.

Dead man.

"I sure hope so," he said.

Again I wondered how Devin could have let himself get involved with this sort of human filth. Or with the baroness for that
matter. What had happened to him in the years since the fall of the
temple? I couldn't imagine the Devin I'd grown up with doing any
of this.

As I was calculating what I ought to say or do next, the dice
game finished up, and two of the other men came over to join the
conference. A big rawboned fellow with a deep scar on his forehead
and a shorter one who reminded me of a weasel. The fourth man
remained by the door.

"Be damned careful you don't block that light," said the mage.

"Don't worry, Lok," said "Scar."

"There's really no need to be careful on my account," I said.
"The regular light's more than adequate for anything but reading,
and I left my book back at my inn."

Never let them see you sweat. The lessons were still all there.
Now, if I could only get back to the place where I lived them without
having to think them, I might be able to really call myself a Blade
again.

The snake hissed again, and the mage said, "I'm going to enjoy
hurting you. Lads, whenever you're ready."

The pair moved to stand close to the wall on either side of me.
By tilting my head, I could see one or the other but not both at the
same time. I was looking at the one on my left, Scar, when Weasel
hit me from the right, striking me just under the front edge of my
rib cage on bare skin—they'd stripped me naked. He used a freshly

peeled willow branch about as thick around as a dagger's hilt, simultaneously heavy and whippy. Damn! It hurt as bad as any punch or kick would have but wasn't nearly so likely to do lasting damage.

I turned and tried to spit at him, only to catch a shot across my cheekbone from the other side—Scar using a much thinner branch to do the fine work. *Fuck!* It didn't split my cheek, quite. Weasel hit me again, about midway down my thigh. Things got ugly after that as the pair worked me over for a bit. They were very good. They never hit hard enough to break anything, and they kept their blows far enough apart so that I felt each one sharply without any merciful blurring. But the sticks didn't hurt me half as much as my fears for Triss.

Control the pain, don't let it control you.

I forced myself to step outside the pain as I had been taught, to assess what they were doing to me on a tactical level instead of experiencing it viscerally. On the personal level, it was a very professional beating. But what was the point? I couldn't make the bigger picture make any sense at all.

They couldn't be after information. They hadn't asked any questions before they started in with the sticks, and beating was a shitty way to get real information anyway. Most people would tell you whatever they thought you wanted to hear just to make it stop. More importantly, I didn't *know* anything. I hadn't done one thing that really mattered since the temple fell. Devin knew all the same secrets that I did from the days before the goddess died, and even if he didn't, Namara was gone into the grave. None of it mattered anymore.

It didn't make sense as a recruiting tactic, either. If I'd had the least inclination to sign on with Devin and the other traitors to Namara's memory, this would have put a knife in the heart of that plan. Devin knew me well enough to understand that. It was just as bad an idea for sending a message to the other remaining rogue Blades. Jax, Siri, Loris, none of them liked being pushed any more than I did.

The only thing I could think of was that Lok and his boys were freelancing, beating me in a way that wouldn't leave a lot of marks for the sheer joy of kicking the shit out of a Blade. In which case, Devin was an incompetent bastard. Once again I found myself wishing I hadn't hesitated back at the Marchon estate. If I'd killed Devin as soon as I saw him dishonoring his Namara-given swords, none of this would have happened. But that would have killed Zass as well, and even in the middle of a beating, I knew I didn't want any Shade's death on my conscience if I could possibly avoid it.

Which brought me back to my fears for Triss. I lost control then, maybe went a little mad even, screaming and swearing and wrenching at my bonds again and again for some unknown length of time. An open-handed slap brought me back from that edge, though it was more the different sound of the impact than the sting of the blow driving my lips against my teeth that registered.

"What?" I shook my head in an effort to return the world to proper focus. The part of me that had heard the slap also vaguely remembered there being a question asked or an order given in there somewhere. "Could you pass that one by me again?"

Lok caught me by the chin and turned my head to the right so that I was looking directly at him. With the intense white shock of the magelight only a few feet away, he looked like nothing human. Half of his face lay in such deep shadow that for all purposes it didn't exist, and the other half was washed out, pale as any night-walking undead.

He leaned in so close we were practically kissing, and his breath was foul. "I said, *Blade*, that I want you to tell me everything you know about the man who calls himself Devin Nightblade."

"Wait, what now?" I squeezed my eyes tight shut, then blinked several times while I tried to make sense of the words.

What he'd just said was so far off the page of my read on things that I almost couldn't make sense of the words. Weren't these Devin's trained rats? What possible reason could they have for beating me to get information about Devin?

Lok let go of me and stepped back, speaking very slowly and clearly. "Devin Nightblade, your onetime comrade in arms, tell us about him, or what you've suffered so far will seem like so many love-caresses from your dead goddess."

I put another mark on Lok's dead-man tally sheet, then opened my mouth to answer. But nothing came out. Night-blade. Nightblade? Really? When had Devin bartered Urslan away for a use-name that all but spat on the grave of the goddess? More importantly, if these boys didn't belong to Devin, my emerging view of the bigger picture had just gone from blurry to spilled paint in a dark studio.

"Hit him again," said Lok.

Scar laid one on the side of my neck, just above the leather collar. It stung like the gods' own bumblebee. It also helped bring me out of my stupor. More because of the threat than the pain. An inch forward, and he would have crushed my larynx. I couldn't afford to die right now, mostly for Triss's sake. But I also very much wanted to have a few steel-edged words with these fellows and with my dear old friend *Nightblade* before I followed my goddess.

"Wait," I said. "Assuming your Devin is the same as mine, I'll happily tell you everything I know." Hell, if it weren't for Zass, I'd have been more than half-tempted to help them string him up in my place here.

Lok looked incredulous. "If they're the same man? You're not seriously suggesting that there's more than one ex-Blade named Devin running around this city, are you?"

"Point." I nodded as firmly as the straps would allow. "What do you want to know?"

"Let's start with his long-term plans for the baroness."

I didn't say, "How the fuck would I know that?" Though it's what I was thinking. "That could be a problem. I haven't seen Devin in five years. I have no idea what he's planning right now."

Lok shook his head sadly. "Are you going to try to tell me you weren't the man that Nightblade talked to on the Marchon estate two nights ago? Because I don't believe you. Think carefully before you answer because I'm starting to think I ought to just let the boys give you another working over before I ask any more questions, this time without playing so gentle."

I wanted to tell Lok I was going to ghost him. I wanted to make him understand what a *really* bad idea all this was, particularly messing with my familiar. But in the short term, that would only put Triss in more danger. And in the long term, Lok was a dead man.

"No," I said. "That was me, but it was my first and only contact with Devin since about a month before the fall of the temple. I didn't even know he was alive until I saw him on the baroness's balcony. Honestly, at the moment I'm wishing he'd stayed as dead as I thought he was."

I don't know whether Lok believed me, but he didn't immediately have his men start in with the sticks again, so I continued, "I can't tell you what Devin's doing right now, or where to find him, or anything like that. I can tell you what his favorite foods were as a kid, and who his first lover was, and a thousand other little details, but you don't want all that. If you could just tell me why you want the information, I could probably narrow it down to the stuff that's actually usefu—ungh!"

Weasel this time, a jab to my floating ribs with the point of the rod.

"I'm not sure you understand the situation here." Lok leaned in close again. "I ask questions. You give answers. Anything else leads to pain. Got it?"

I nodded. I wouldn't do Triss any good if I were a broken bloody mess when the time came to move.

If you control yourself, you control the situation, and your chance to act will come.

As the words slid through my mind, I found myself incredibly sad to realize that I could never thank Master Kelos for his lessons. Without them, I might well have already died here.

"Good," said Lok, "then we can continue. Oh"—and he smiled—"and I think it might help us to get to the point if I explain what I want from you. Yes?"

I painted a smile across my swollen lips and nodded again. At the same time, I made my three-thousandth attempt at breaking loose. It was just as effective as all the ones that had come before.

Lok grinned at my struggles. "My boss wants to know everything you know about the baroness's little assassin, right down to the color of his underwear. Understand?"

"That's crazy."

Who was Lok working for? A rival to the baroness other than Maylien? Why would anyone care about that level of detail? Everything I learned just made me more confused. These people were the weirdest damn mix of professional and amateur I'd ever met.

"Was that the answer to my question?" asked Lok. "It didn't sound like an answer. It sounded like a comment, and I was pretty sure you weren't supposed to do anything but answer questions."

Before he could do or say anything more, I heard a low thrumming twang and saw a flare of magic at the window. It burned a line across the room from there to the magelight, where it ripped the stone free of its string, then continued to a spot an inch or so to the right of my bleeding ear. At that point, there came a sharp crack, and I felt a spray of pinpricks across my neck and that side of my face.

I didn't know what had just happened, but neither did I care. My chance had arrived, and I wasn't going to fuck up this time.

The tumbling magelight hit me on the chest as it fell, bouncing and rolling away across the room, sending the shadows wild. Against my back, I felt Triss come to life. I snapped the fingers of my right hand to draw his attention to the bindings there. I needed a free hand soonest. An instant later, I felt the first of the straps part: wrist, followed by elbow.

As my arm dropped free of the restraints, the pain of full circulation returning hit. It felt like someone had set fire to the blood in my veins. I blocked out my awareness of the pain while I glanced around, checking to see if I had time to finish cutting myself loose.

I didn't.

Lok was already moving, one hand going for a knife while the other rose to point at my face. I brought my free arm up and across in a blocking motion, signaling my needs to Triss with the positioning of my half-clenched fist.

A stream of magefire burst from Lok's fingers only to vanish into the oval of shadow that suddenly enveloped my arm from elbow to first knuckle, like a buckler carved from the stuff of night. One for me. But only barely, and at the cost of remaining a trussed goose all hung up and ready for the slaughter.

If I couldn't get loose of the rack fast, I was a dead man. Triss had a very limited ability to cope with fire magics—a stronger mage or a true spell would have done him real harm—and even a petty mage like Lok could get through given time.

Scar's stick came in hard then, catching me just above the eye so that bursts of sparkling purple flashed across my vision. At the same time, the spit-adder on Lok's shoulder reared back, ready to send a stream of venom at my eyes. I tilted my shadowy shield to try to catch both that and the inevitable next round of magefire, but I didn't have much hope.

Lok opened his mouth like a man about to laugh. But just then there came a low "thwock" sort of noise. A thin trickle of blood dribbled out of his mouth, and Lok crashed to his knees on the hard flags. I heard bone break with the impact but he just slumped quietly forward, beyond caring. Lok was dead, killed by the crossbow quarrel sticking out of the back of his skull. As his face hit the floor, the snake went into convulsions, dying with its master.

That left Weasel, Scar, and the fourth man.

Scar struck again, but I anticipated the blow this time, blocking it with my Triss-covered forearm. The stick shattered in a burst of white fire as my familiar used the contact to turn the wood into a conduit for a flare of magelightning. Scar screamed and fell to the floor, clutching at his ruined hand. I turned to kill Weasel. But he had already dropped his stick and bolted, heading toward the place where the fourth man was wrenching at the door.

That moved both men from threat to target.

Magefire poured in through the window as the fourth man opened the door, turning him into a human bonfire. The room filled with the scent of charring flesh, and Weasel dropped to his belly, begging for mercy.

He wasn't going to get any from me.

Triss cut me the rest of the way free, and I dropped to the floor. It was all I could do not to go face down like Weasel after the beating and the hours pinned to the glyph. I managed to stay upright, just, but I couldn't walk for shit. I staggered into a big butcher-block table covered with all sorts of sharp and pointy nastiness, much of which cascaded off the back in a little torture-implement avalanche. Iron and steel smacked into stone with a sharp series of clangs and bangs and a couple of deep booongs when bits bounced against a giant copper cauldron.

"Are you all right?" a half-familiar woman's voice called from the window. Even with the spell that had covered it broken, I could see only darkness beyond the bars.

"I will be, thanks to you. What do I owe you for the rescue?"

Triss was going to live because of this woman, whoever she was. She could name her price.

There was a merry laugh and then a smiling face leaned in close to the bars. "Why, a shot at my baronial seat, just as I asked for in my letter . . . Kingslayer."

It was Maylien, my lady of the red dress. The one I'd hoped I'd seen the last of. And now I owed her a barony. At least my life is interesting.

"Damn," Maylien said, suddenly thrusting herself away from the window. "There's someone else out here with me. I—"

There came a faint thud, like a sap catching someone behind the ear, followed by the sound of a body falling, then silence.

6

I dashed to the window, where Maylien had just disappeared from view. Or, I tried to anyway, but my much-abused muscles didn't want to cooperate and I tripped on Weasel instead of stepping over him. As I began to fall, I felt Weasel twist sharply beneath me and heard the scrape of his knife against the floor as he drew it.

Dammit, I don't have time for this.

I did what I could to avoid his thrust, bending awkwardly to my right as the blade came in. Instead of going deep, the knife cut a shallow furrow along the back of my ribs. I rolled farther to my right, trying to get some distance between us as Weasel slithered to his knees and pivoted toward me. Before I'd gotten very far, I slammed into the legs of the bleeding-table, hitting the fresh cut on my ribs and sending little spikes of light across my vision.

Weasel lurched toward me, raising his dagger to sink it into my chest. Under normal circumstances I could have dealt with him easily, even naked and unarmed. But I was still so stiff and sore, I could barely shape a fist, much less hit someone with it. That left magic, but my nima was at least as drained as the rest of me. Not that I had any choice. I signaled Triss for magelightning, but he had his own plans.

The shadow of a dragon rose between Weasel and me, hanging in the air for a moment like a falcon ready to stoop on its prey. Weasel screamed and threw himself back and away, dropping the knife. Triss fell on him anyway, enfolding him with wings of darkness and hiding him from view. Then Triss squeezed, closing into a tight ball of shadow with Weasel hidden at its center. Slowly, the ball contracted, shrinking to the size of a pinhead while I dragged myself upright. I didn't understand what Triss was doing, not initially, but I could feel the tremendous strain of it echoing along the connection between us.

When Triss sprang back to his normal size and shape, Weasel had simply vanished. While I tried to make sense of that, Triss beat his wings sharply and climbed toward the roof. The connection between us attenuated to little more than a slender thread of shadow. His head whipped angrily this way and that as he ranted and raved in the language of the Shades, a sharp, sibilant sound like the swearing of angry snakes. I could make out only a few words, "kill" and "make suffer" and "all"—it's not a tongue they use much with humans.

His attention fell on the injured Scar then, and he stretched across the room, looming above the fallen man like a figure in some mummer's shadow play. Scar screamed when the shadow fell on him, just as Weasel had screamed. Triss squeezed and strained, pushing himself almost to the edge of endurance . . . and then Scar, too, had vanished. That's when I realized what Triss must have done. He had made a gate of himself and sent them to the everdark. I wondered how long they would survive there in the cold and infinite blackness—always falling but never hitting bottom—and I shivered.

I actually shivered.

I'd been trained to kill almost from the day I'd learned to walk, and I *had* killed. Many times. I'd intended to finish both Weasel and Scar myself. I would have done it with a smile on my face and no hesitation. But it would have been quick and clean, an opened vein, a dagger to the heart, a crushed throat. Nothing like what Triss had just done.

The plunge into the everdark was a terrible death, and a rare one. I'd heard whispers of berserk Shades opening the gates of shadow, but I'd never seen it happen nor expected to. It was not something we asked of them. Not ever. Until that moment, it hadn't occurred to me to wonder why. Now I knew the answer. Fear. What Triss had just done to my enemies, he could also do to me if he chose.

Every time I hid myself within his darkness, every time I exercised my magic through him, every time I drew my familiar around me for any reason, I placed myself on the threshold of the everdark with nothing more than a shadow between me and doom. If I didn't trust Triss more than I trusted myself . . .

I shivered again, this time from the subterranean cold of the

damp dungeon. Between that and the abuse I'd taken, I was court-
ing shock just by standing there. I needed to get moving. More importantly, I needed to find out what had happened to Maylien. I
owed her that and more for helping me to save Triss.

"Triss!" I called as I staggered to the window. "Triss, come
here!"

I had to hold on to the bars to stay upright while I looked out into
the night. But all I could see was a narrow stretch of empty cobblestones with a blank brick wall beyond and no sign of Maylien.

Shit.

I turned away from the empty night. Triss was still flitting this
way and that through the room, looking for something more to kill
and still muttering in his own tongue. He'd taken Lok into the
shadows, too, though the mage was already dead, and he kept stoop-
ing to examine the charred corpse of the fourth man.

I almost wished he'd go ahead and take the bastard. The stink
of burned meat had me on the edge of gagging. For a couple of seconds after I called him, I thought Triss wasn't going to come to me.
But, after a few more dives at the dead man, he slid back to the place
at my feet where the dungeon's lights would have put him.

"Are you all right?" he asked. "They hurt you, and I couldn't
stop them." His voice was high and fast, laced with anguish. "I
couldn't do anything at all. It felt like one of the nightmares that
sometimes take you humans while you sleep, like it had me in its
teeth shaking me and shaking me and shaking me, like it would
never stop."

"It was pretty nightmarish for me, too," I said.

"I know." My dragon shadow suddenly lifted off the floor and
wrapped his wings around me. "I know. I wanted to kill them all,
to make them pay for hurting you, and I couldn't. I couldn't! I'm so
sorry."

For just an instant, I felt the threat of the everdark in his touch
though Triss had not put it there. Then I pushed the feeling aside,
relaxing into the embrace of my dearest friend. He was a trained
killer and plenty frightening, but then, so was I. We were both of us
products of a system designed to create living weapons.

"It's all right, Triss. I'm all right. We need to get out of here and
find out what happened to the girl."

Of course, by this point, whatever had happened to Maylien
was almost certainly over. There had been neither sound nor sign
from outside since her first outcry, which suggested she was dead
or taken. I couldn't do much about either of those things naked and

unarmed, so I figured I'd better take a few seconds more to do something about both conditions.

All the gear I'd had on me when I got deathsparked was lying in a rough pile, but that didn't help much. They'd cut my clothes and boots off me, probably after they hung me on the rack of the glyph, and most of my knives had stayed behind with the dead Kadeshis. I didn't have a lot of other options either. Three of my four captors had gone from the world entirely, taking all their belongings with them. The fourth had burned.

Grabbing the wreckage of my pants, I started to tie myself a breechclout. I'd gotten it just about to the point of addressing Tien's decency laws, when a nervous voice called from somewhere beyond the partially opened door to the dungeon.

"Lok!" it said. "Are you all right? What the hell happened?"

"Shit." I picked up my remaining knife and something that looked like a vicious cross between a fireplace poker and a bone saw and quickly crossed to the doorway.

A hallway lay beyond, with another prison door at the far end. A torch in the passage reflected off a pair of eyes peering through its little barred window at me.

"Lok?"

Triss hissed something in his own language and stretched down the hall, reaching for the far door. Before he could get there, the eyes vanished with a muffled curse and the sound of the viewing panel slamming shut. A moment later, an alarm bell started to clang.

That accelerated the schedule.

I closed and locked the door at my end, then broke the key off in the hole and wedged it before heading for the window. It was narrow, but if we could cut a few of the bars loose, I'd fit through all right, and it was a better bet than fighting our way out through an unknown building. I called to Triss and made my hand into a knife shape to let him know what I wanted, but he kept sliding back and forth along the surface of the door, either not listening or ignoring me again. He wanted more blood.

I did, too, but this wasn't the time.

"Triss!" I snapped. "Do you think you can drop that for a minute and help me with these bars? We'll come back later and we can kill them then. For now, we need to get clear and see what happened to Maylien."

He turned his head my way and hissed something angry and unintelligible.

"Triss, please. Let it go for tonight."

With a sigh, he came back toward me. I made the knife-hand gesture again, but rather than settle around my hands and shoulders, he threw his wings wide, hiding the window and a good bit of the wall around it. For nearly a minute he hung there like a leaf pressed in a book. With a brutal effort I could feel through our bond, he flexed his shoulders and snapped his wings forward, contracting into a pinpoint in an instant. The section of wall vanished into the everdark along with the window it contained. It left behind a hole in the shape of a man-sized dragon. Then Triss collapsed back into my shadow for a moment in exhaustion. This newly revealed talent took a lot out of him.

"That'll work." I climbed up into the hole, using the outline of a hind leg as a step.

About half the hole lay below the surface of the ground. Between that and my still-rocky condition, I ended up slithering my way up and out, smearing myself with dirt and nearly losing my breechclout in the process. I came up in a narrow stone-flagged alley, quiet, dark, completely empty.

No girl. But then, I hadn't expected her to be there. No girl's corpse either, which was a relief.

Though I didn't recognize the alley, I could tell by the paucity of trash in the corners and the lack of sewer smells that I was in one of the city's better neighborhoods. Maybe professional, maybe residential, but still not rich enough for street lighting. Tailor's Wynd or the Underhills or someplace like that. By the stars, it was still a couple of hours short of dawn, which explained the quiet.

Glancing back at the hole I'd just climbed out of, I wondered briefly why anyone would put a dungeon someplace like this. But the very affluence of the neighborhood would provide good cover. And someone who could keep even a petty mage like Lok in their pocket could also afford the spells that would keep the screaming and stink from passing through the window. That reminded me again of the girl, who must have broken the spell to find me. The fact that I needed a reminder said very bad things about my general state.

I took a quick look around for signs of what had happened to her though I didn't hold out much hope on that front. I'm no tracker, and even if I were, deep city is no place to go hunting without a hound. When I didn't find anything in the brief time I figured I had before my new enemies started to be a problem again, I turned to leave. That's when Triss, who had recovered enough to look around the alley behind me, made a noise like a kettle boiling over onto the coals.

"What is it?"

Triss circled an apparently unmarked spot on the cobbles. "Zass was here. He came from above. I can taste him in the stones where he and Devin landed."

I could feel my eyebrows heading for my hairline in surprise. Zass meant Devin, but that wasn't what had startled me. I'd more than half expected his involvement if for no other reason than my current run of luck—all bad. No, what startled me was the fact that Triss could tell Zass had been there. I'd never so much as heard a rumor of any such ability among the Shades.

Before I could ask him about it, a noise from the nearer end of the alley suggested we'd overstayed our safety margin. I glanced briefly up toward the rooftops whence Devin had come and whence he had probably returned. But even with Triss's help I knew I couldn't make it up the smoothly stuccoed wall in my current condition, much less run the rooftops. My nima was overtapped already. If I pushed my magic any further, I'd die and take Triss with me. Even if I'd been up to it, Triss wouldn't have been—I could feel the pain and exhaustion leaking down the link between us though he tried to shield me from it.

Part of being a professional is knowing that sometimes you have to let go, no matter how much you might want to keep trying.

So, instead of going after Devin, I asked Triss to hide me within himself and started walking. We left the alley by its farther mouth and turned left, plodding downslope in what I hoped was the direction of the sea and the docks. After a block or two, I figured out where I was—the Old Mews, which meant I needed to reverse my course and go over the top of the Kanathean Hill to get back home.

I paused a moment to set my position in memory so I could find the alley and dungeon later, after I'd had both rest and food. Then I turned toward the Stumbles and the Gryphon and began my slow walk again, letting Triss relax back into my shadow after a little while to preserve his strength against emergencies. It was a slog, and I desperately needed about fifteen hours of sleep and a triple portion of breakfast.

The few people I encountered along the way gave me a wide berth. Who could blame them? I must have looked like a holy beggar, clad only in a breechclout and covered in scrapes and bruises. When the first of the street vendors started setting up, I was half-tempted to actually try to beg a few coins here and there so I could buy a bit of breakfast. The boiling congee and frying sausages smelled like a little slice of heaven. But I couldn't afford the trouble freelance begging would buy me with the real guttersiders, so I let it go. Gutterside had a most ungentle way of settling quarrels.

I'd just reached the edge of the Stumbles when it finally occurred to me to wonder about how *exactly* I'd ended up in that dungeon. That's when I realized that going back to the Gryphon might not be the best idea I'd ever had since I had no answers for some very important questions. Most notably: How had the parties who put me there known right where to find me and exactly how to take me down? Parties as yet unnamed who might well try to pick me up again. It probably should have struck me earlier, and it might have if I'd been more than half-alive, or less focused on Devin and what he might be doing to Maylien.

Maylien. Dammit!

If Devin killed her, I'd have no choice but to kill him, and probably the baroness as well. Debts owed to the living can be negotiated. The dead can only be paid with absolutes. Justice. Revenge. Redemption.

I shook my head. Worry about it tomorrow. For now, I needed to worry about making sure I had a "tomorrow." So when I passed a certain alley, I turned into it. This one didn't smell nearly as nice as the one up in Old Mews had, and I tried very hard not to think about the stuff squelching over the tops of my bare feet. Triss had sheathed the soles in a toughened layer of shadow stuff to keep me from injuring myself when we got close to the Stumbles, but the muck was ankle-deep here.

About fifty feet in, I found the crumbling stone wall I remembered and used it as a ladder to take me up onto the rooftops. From there I made my slow way to an old brick-faced tenement that had burned two years ago. Most of the place was a dangerous ruin, but one old turret on the southern corner had survived mostly intact, and I'd set it up as a fallback.

You always have to have a fallback in case the plan goes bad, even when the plan is as simple as drinking yourself to death.

It was nearly eight stories up, and the stairs were gone. The only way in involved a thirty-foot vertical climb followed by a short diagonal traverse to get to a slightly canted window. Even so, it would have attracted summer squatters had I not spent considerable time and magic making the climb look worse than it was and the floor appear as if it had gone in the fire. In winter, of course, it would have been deathly cold and a complete nightmare to heat, and even I would have been hesitant about making that climb with the bricks iced up.

It took everything I had left to make it up a wall I could normally have managed in my sleep. At the end, I literally fell in through the window of my hidey-hole and crawled to my little straw tick. I barely had the energy to wrap myself in one of the worn woolen horse blankets I'd stashed there before I tumbled into the ocean of sleep and sank into the depths.

I had evil dreams and woke from them both too early and gladly. My everything hurt, and I was as stiff as boiled leather though I'd escaped with no serious injury. Lok's beaters had been very good at their job, and I was glad they were dead though the satisfaction that gave me did nothing for the pain.

Wind woke me, a chilly blow coming in off the sea and whistling through the myriad cracks in the ruined old building. Fortunately, the warm afternoon sun pouring in through the shutters I'd forgotten to close offset the worst of the wind. I'd slept a good ten hours. I could have used ten more, and I really didn't want to move, but I needed a piss.

As I rolled off the straw mattress, most of my fresh scabs stayed behind with the blanket they'd stuck to, and I had to bite back a scream. A couple started bleeding again, though none badly. Not even the long gash Weasel had left on my ribs, which looked shallower than I'd expected—though I'd have to get Triss to double-check it for me.

Getting to my feet made me feel about nine hundred years old, but I managed it. I staggered my way over to the open hole where the stairs had once been. I undid my filthy breechclout and dropped it into the opening, then followed it with the contents of my bladder. It was only when I was done that I realized Triss hadn't said a word yet. Turning back toward my bed, I saw a thin line of shadow stretching from me to an irregular patch of darkness where I had lain.

If you sketched our connection as a tail, the patch looked rather like a dragon with its nose tucked under one wing. I stepped closer, and called Triss's name. The shadow didn't even twitch. Triss was dead asleep, and that told me just how awful yesterday had been for him. In the twenty years since we'd bonded when I was seven, he'd outslept me less than a dozen times, and only twice had he slept through my getting out of bed.

I left him lying there and crossed the little room to my supply cache, a big, lidded earthenware amphora sealed with spelled wax. I'd lifted it special for the purpose from among an upscale tavern's empties. There wasn't anything better for keeping the rats and other vermin out of your goods, not that could be scavenged on the cheap anyway. Inside, I'd left a worn but still wearable change of clothes, a couple of battered daggers, a smaller jar full of rice, and a bottle of Kyle's. I set one of the daggers where I could reach it, ignored the clothes and the rice, opened the whiskey, and took a long pull— purely medicinal.

At least, that's what I told myself, that the Kyle's was the best way to file the sharpest edges off my collection of aches and pains. I'd just had my third hit off the bottle when Triss made a sort of unhappy clucking noise.

"Don't you think it's a little early for that?" he asked.

"It's medicinal," I said. "And it's midafternoon."

"But the meal you're drinking is breakfast. I think that trumps the actual hour, don't you?" He cocked his head to one side, and I got the distinct impression of a disapproving stare. "Especially considering the day we have ahead of us. Or have you already forgotten about Maylien?"

I hadn't, not quite, but he was still right. With a sigh, I took a last drink, then recorked the bottle and set it aside. Sometimes it's a pain having an external conscience, especially one that won't shut up.

"Better," said Triss. "You're going to need your wits unscrambled if we want to find Devin and stay out of the hands of Lok's crowd." He sounded angry when he mentioned Lok, but the homicidal rage of the previous night seemed to have lightened enough to shift his focus to Devin.

"Lok's crowd." I shook my head. Their behavior didn't make any more sense looking back than it had at the time. "Who do you suppose they are? And what do they want?"

Triss shrugged his wings. "Whoever they are, they know far too much about our kind for my comfort. Once we've recovered the girl, we'll need to find and kill them and their master. The sheuth glyph would be enough to condemn them even without that trick they pulled with the deathspark and those Kadeshi mercenaries. That's all information we don't dare allow to spread."

I shrugged. "With only four Blades left beyond Devin's lot, I don't know that the information matters all that much." Triss froze and gave me a hard look, and I held up a hand. "I'm not saying we shouldn't kill them, just that Blade secrets don't seem to matter that much anymore."

"Do you truly believe that?" asked Triss, and I heard real sadness in his voice.

"I don't know, Triss. If Devin's assassins are the future of the order, maybe it'd be better if more people had ways to take us down. Maybe it would be better if we died out completely."

Triss shook his head wordlessly, then laid his chin on my thigh. I scratched him behind his ears, and we sat like that for a while.

"I'm sorry, Triss," I said finally. "I just get depressed sometimes."

"I know. I'm sorry, too. But that doesn't mean we should give up."

I wanted to say that I gave up a long time ago, but I couldn't do that to Triss. Especially since it wasn't really true. I might have given up on many things, but I'd never give up on him. And now after last night, I was maybe even starting to see some hope for me again. Which meant we probably did need to make some plans for the future.

"You're right about that glyph's being all kinds of bad news for the few of us that remain," I said. "But I'm a lot less worried about the deathspark."

"Why so?"

"A deathspark's a mighty chancy bit of magic under the best of circumstances, even more so when tied to more than one man like that. If your target doesn't take the bait within a day and a night, you've done nothing more than kill the ones you set it on to no good purpose. Beyond that, I doubt it'd even bother any of the other remaining Blades. I didn't see any other swords on the bottom of the sacred lake when I put mine there."

Triss shook his head. "That assumes it was the magic in the goddess's steel that protected you instead of the touch of the goddess herself."

I thought about it for a moment. Some of the powers that resided in the swords of Namara were intrinsic to the weapons themselves, but not all. And a deathspark was damned powerful magic to have to counter. Sacrifice magic always is—not to mention dark as night-spilled blood. It's a sort of necromancy, burning up the life of a person so that their death will rebound on whoever killed them.

"Could be you're right, Triss." Then I shrugged. "Either way, I'm screwed. I've neither sacred steel nor goddess left to protect me."

"Which means," said Triss, sternly, "that we need to start thinking about how to prepare you for another deathspark."

He had a point. "I assume there are things a person can do to ward against them. I just don't know what since it never mattered to me before. I guess that's one more item to put on the giant list of things we need to know yesterday. Along with who Lok was working for, how they found me, why they wanted to know about Devin, where Devin is, what his plan is, where did he take Maylien, who is Maylien really, and so on."

"None of which can be solved from here," said Triss.

"None of which can be solved from here. Which, I suppose, means that I need to get dressed." I reached for the whiskey again, and Triss stiffened grumpily.

"For external use this time," I said, "much as it pains me to say it. These cuts need cleaning." Triss furled his wings and settled back down. "I need a bath, too, but that's going to have to wait till we're in a better neighborhood."

Half an hour later, I was back on the street dressed as a much poorer and more travel-worn version of myself. Down in the street, the wind wasn't half so cold though it still kicked up a lot of dust and grit. Many of the people I passed had wrapped scarves around their faces or turned up the collars of their vests and jackets. I made a quick stop at a public bath and another at an armorer—the one necessary before I could bear to put my boots on, the other to pick up a hard-used short sword. And that reduced to the brink of starvation the already thin emergency purse that had been tucked into the bottom of my cache.

Half an hour after that, I was making my way through the crowded streets and over the top of the Kanathean Hill toward the Old Mews, hoping desperately that the giant banner of smoke trailing away in front of me wasn't coming from my erstwhile dungeon. Then I got close enough to see the fire.

It wasn't the dungeon.

It was the whole damn neighborhood.

7

The wind off the sea had whipped the flames into an all-devouring madness. The entire neighborhood was lost. I had a damned good idea where and how it had started, and I swore bitterly at the sight. Accidental fires didn't spread this way, not in good neighborhoods, where they could afford to keep the antifire wards in top shape. Not even with these winds.

That made this emberman's work. Lok's mystery boss was covering his tracks and Devin's, too, though I figured that last was an accident. Devin might have fallen a long way, but I simply couldn't imagine him playing emberman. Fire killed wholesale. Using it like this marked you out as someone who couldn't hit the target clean. Incompetent. A temple-trained Blade would sooner cut his own throat.

Though I didn't think it would do me much good, I moved upwind and slipped through the cordon of stingers that were keeping people away from the fire. The line of watchmen, in the black and gold uniforms that gave them their nickname, were fending off a mixed crowd. Gawkers and opportunists mostly, leavened with the occasional concerned resident. I didn't get very deep into the burning neighborhood. Even with the smoke mostly blowing away from me, the heat forced me to turn around before I'd traveled much more than a block.

"Dammit, dammit, dammit!" I turned away from the flames, toward the nearest wall and my shadow. "Triss, what are the chances of us circling around and picking up Devin and Zass's trail somewhere beyond the edge of the fire?"

My shadow leaped and danced in the wild interplay of fire and light-cutting smoke just as you might expect of a normal shadow.

The movement cleverly concealed what I recognized as a careful scan for other observers. But we were alone, though whether that was because of the effectiveness of the guards or because no one else was crazy enough to go so deep into the fires, I couldn't say. And my shadow soon slid into the familiar shape of the dragon. He looked nervous and kept a close watch on the closest flames—even normal fire can hurt a Shade if there's enough of it.

"I'm sorry, but it's just not going to happen today," said Triss. "It probably wouldn't have worked even if we were able to start from that trailhead we found last night. Too many hours of spring sunshine have already passed since Zass last touched the stones there." He spread his wings to take in the fires around us. "And now . . ." He shook his head. "Heat and light will have burned the trail completely away."

"I wish you'd told me last night that we'd lose the trail if we waited. We could have—"

"Could have what?" interrupted Triss. "Chased a renegade Blade across the rooftops in the darkness when we were both injured and exhausted? Done so virtually unarmed? Facing who knows what traps Devin might have left on his back trail? With your nima drained to the dregs? And if we *had* caught him, then what? There are simpler and less embarrassing ways to commit suicide than facing Devin under such circumstances."

I wanted to argue, but the heat of the flames was tearing at my back like a fiery scourge. Besides, Triss was right again. There are ways to wield power beyond the ends of your nima, but they require physical reserves I simply hadn't owned the night before.

I sighed and nodded. "I suppose that trying for magelightning and bursting your heart instead is probably not the smartest way to end your life."

"Neither is burning alive." Triss looked around worriedly, and I nodded again.

"Point. We'll have to find another angle on Devin and Maylien." A coughing fit prevented my saying anything more. So I threw my arm across my face and started breathing through the fabric of my sleeve as I took us away from the fire.

Once I got out in the clear again, I turned toward the Spinnerfish. I figured I had just enough cash left to cover a meal and a few tongue-loosening drinks. With the shadow trail broken, I needed to find Devin some other way, and the Spinnerfish provided good food, rich information, and a pleasant place out of the wind where I could play bait.

If you want to catch a shark, you spill blood in the water—another thing I'd learned from Master Kelos. And since mine was the blood Devin wanted most . . .

I'd barely put my ass in the chair at the same table I'd had last time when Erk appeared from the back. He was holding my half-finished tucker bottle of Kyle's, two glasses, and the drum-ringer. It saved me the trouble of asking after the bottle but also made me mighty nervous to be singled out like this again.

"Don't you look sour," he said after he poured the two glasses full. "I hope it's not on account of your buying me a drink. I didn't have to save the bottle for you in the first place."

"Nothing on you and the Kyle's," I replied as I picked up my glass, then coughed to cover my jerk when Triss kicked me in the ass. "I'm thinking I should maybe be drinking a bit lighter anyway. Though I do find myself wondering about being graced with your presence at my table two nights in a row."

Erk frowned. "If you're that badly out of count on the days, maybe you have been tipping the bottle too much. But that's not why I came by and not my business by any means."

"Wait," I said, "what do you mean 'out of count'? What day *is* it?"

Erk raised his eyebrows and took a drink, then said flatly, "Sylvasday."

"Oh." That was four days after Atherasday, which was when I'd been deathsparked. I hadn't realized I'd been out nearly so long. It was my turn to take a drink though, out of deference to Triss, I sipped the whiskey instead of knocking it straight back. Which is what I wanted to do after that news.

"Lose a couple days?" asked Erk.

I nodded. "Though not to drink." I paused then, remembering Erk's reputation as a former black jack. "Actually, you might be able to help me there. Do you know any way to avoid a deathspark?"

"Ouch." He whistled. "That's bad magic, and I can't say I've heard of any way to avoid it except not hitting the target."

"I'd never have thought of that." I couldn't keep the sarcasm out of my voice.

"No, seriously. There's no point in killing a man walking under that mark. He'll burn away from the inside soon enough on his own. Why bloody your dagger? You just need to learn to spot the signs and walk away. Looks a lot like caras-dust addiction actually, bright eyes, lank hair, sweaty, talking too much. The main difference is that your caras snuffler doesn't have an ash-drawn glyph on the back of his neck."

"And if it's him or you?" I asked.

Erk's eyes went far away for a second, then widened. "The Kadeshis, you mean. From the other night. That explains several things." Then he shook his head and seemed to be looking inward. "I'm surprised I didn't notice that. Must have been a very freshly set spark. Well, that, and I'm not really in the business of watching out for that sort of thing anymore." Finally, he shrugged. "Him or you is always a tougher question, but I'd think someone like yourself could have just faded into the shadows and walked away if you'd chosen."

He had me there, but if we started talking about all the mistakes I'd made recently, we'd be there all night, so I moved on. "While I'm asking you questions, I've another. I met a girl recently, and I was wondering if you might know anything about her. That's why I stopped in actually."

"To ask me questions?" He crossed his arms and gave me a very hard look. "If she's a customer, I don't know anything more about her than I know about you when someone asks."

"No, not to ask you questions, but to ask some of your other customers," I said. "You just happened to sit down first. Besides, it's not like that. She's a client of mine, a noble one and she . . . let's just say I owe her one. I'm not looking for anything confidential, just common city gossip. Besides, I doubt she's spent much time in the Spinnerfish. Her name is Maylien and she's related to the Baroness Marchon."

"Sorry," said Erk, his expression closing further. "I'm afraid I can't help you."

Which told me that she *had* eaten at the Spinnerfish often enough for Erk to recognize the name. And that meant someone else there could probably give me something useful. I smiled and took another sip of my whiskey.

"Fair enough. That runs my line out," I said. "What are *you* fishing for tonight? You said the Kadeshis' being tied to a deathspark explained a lot. Is that it?"

"I'm not fishing, and yes, it's the Kadeshis. I wanted to warn you about . . ." He turned in his seat and looked toward the door. A moment later it opened and a tall woman came in. She wore a gold and black uniform with a watch captain's insignia on the shoulders. "Well, that," Erk said as he slipped the drum-ringer into his jacket and headed toward the newcomer.

"Captain Fei," said Erk, "as always, I'm delighted to see you come in. Would you like your usual table?"

Fei nodded absently as she scanned the room. She was broad

across the shoulders and hips, with the heavy muscles of a jindu master. A thick brown braid hung almost to her waist, plaited flat for ease under a helm. She was too pale to be highborn and had freckles on her cheeks and arms as well as light green eyes that marked her as having a foreigner in her ancestral line, and that all too recently. Her face was round, her features plain but pretty, almost soft, an impression belied by the knife scar that ran down and back from her left cheekbone to the point of her jaw.

I hunched my shoulders a bit and looked down at the table when she glanced my way. In other circumstances, I might have made a point of smiling and meeting her eyes to show my innocence, but not in the Spinnerfish. Here and now, not looking like I had something to hide would have marked me out as different from my fellows, suspicious. I didn't play it too big because that would have drawn unwanted attention, too. Especially since Fei knew me. She knew everybody in the shadow trades, having worked with all of the heavy players at one time or another and most of the independents, including me.

Captain Kaelin Fei was something of a Tienese institution, the perfect model of a corrupt cop. She had hooks in every major shadow operation in town, and everyone who mattered knew it, including Fei's boss, the watch commandant, and his boss, the Duchess of Tien. Maybe even King Thauvik himself.

Unlike a regular district captain, Fei had no set area under her watch and no investigatory responsibility. Fei's only job was maintaining stability in the capital city. It was almost surprising that more places hadn't invented a Captain Fei since the role she filled went a long way toward making the locals feel safe and secure. The ones who mattered to government anyway. It was Fei's job to see that shadow wars didn't spill out of places like the Stumbles and Smuggler's Rest to trouble the more upright citizens, and to make sure that what crime there was in the better neighborhoods didn't cause civil unrest. Fei was very good at that job. She was also coming my way.

Fuck.

I ignored her right up until she sat down across from me, at which point I put on a sick smile. "Buy you a drink, Captain?"

"Thank you, Aral, that would be lovely." She raised a hand to signal the waitress and ordered a glass of rice wine. "Been a long time since I last saw you in here."

It was a request for information.

"I like the food well enough, but I'm rarely so much in pocket I can indulge myself."

"And you are now?"

"I'd say that's self-evident."

The captain's sake arrived, and she took a sip before continuing, "S'funny, you don't *look* in pocket." She reached across and touched a stain on my cuff. "Not at all."

Shit. I'd forgotten the clothes. I wanted to blame the dungeon and the deathspark, but too many years of booze and easy jobs made a more likely answer. My heart tried to beat faster, but I forced it to stay slow and steady. The captain might not be able to hear the beat, but she'd see the secondary signs if I let myself get too nervous. For a brief moment I regretted having given up efik—a dose of calm would have gone down very nicely just then.

I darted a look around, then lowered my voice, "Don't tell anyone, but I got rolled last night. In my best clothes no less. Finished up a nice little job and went on a binge. Passed out in the wrong place just like a green fool."

When a tough question comes too close to the truth, the easiest way to throw off the scent is to give an embarrassing confession to something completely different.

"That was a damned stupid move, especially for a jack of your experience and reputation. Even a drunk. Might be time to cut back on the booze."

"It is that," I agreed, and a pressure along my back let me know that Triss thought so, too. When I spoke again, it was as much to him as Fei. "I learned an important lesson last night, and a dangerous one. From here on out I'll be mastering my drinking instead of letting the drink master me. I really am getting my act back together"—I leaned forward—"and I'd take it as a personal favor if you wouldn't pass that story along to anyone, Captain."

She took another sip of her rice wine and gave me a long, considering look. "Your eyes have seen what the bottom looks like. I can see it there, and that didn't used to be the case." She nodded. "You're a smart man, Aral, and a good jack. Every time I've given you a job, it's gotten done without any mess or fuss, which is why you've gotten more than one and will likely see my coin again in the future. Don't let the bottom suck you down again."

"I don't intend to." Triss rubbed my back companionably, and I started to relax.

Mistake.

"Now tell me why you reek of smoke and not from a brazier. The Old Mews is on fire, and you've been up that way today, or I'm a fresh-hatched chick. That's well outside your normal territory. What brought you there?"

"A delivery." How had she smelled that? I hadn't washed my clothes, but I wasn't sitting all that close to her, and there were plenty of stronger scents in the packed tavern. "I can't say more."

"Not even for me?" She batted her long eyelashes at me. On her it looked predatory.

"Not even for the Son of Heaven," I replied. "Where it comes to my hires, I'm a mute, Fei. That's *to* you and . . ." I drew out the pause, "about you."

Fei laughed. "You drive a sharp point there, jack. Fair enough. But if I find out you had anything to do with starting that fire, I'll nail your flayed hide up for display behind the gallows. Nobody does that in my city and lives."

"Then we're fine. Emberman's so far out of my line, you can't even see the shadow from where I stand. That's black-work of the worst sort. I don't kill for money and I'd sooner slit my wrists than take a job that involved fire."

"Glad to hear you so emphatic," said Fei, but her eyes narrowed slightly—curious but not suspicious, though I don't think anyone who hadn't been trained to read faces would have caught it.

I'd slipped somehow, exposed something I oughtn't.

I took a sip of my whiskey and leaned back in my chair and tried to decide how to cover whatever it was I'd given away. But I just didn't know enough. Fei took another drink as well and I could see her weighing things up in her head like a warboard player trying to decide what piece to move next.

"S'funny," she said eventually.

"What?" I asked after a few seconds of silence told me she wanted me to.

"You speak the language so well that I sometimes forget you're not a native, and that despite your looks. Where are you from originally? Your bones are Varyan, but the accent's too faint for me to be sure, and there's enough outbreeding between Varya and Dalridia or the Kvanas to blur things."

"You're very good, Captain. I'm from Emain West, right on the edges of the mageburned lands."

Which was half a lie. I was Varyan right enough, but I'd been born in Emain Tarn on the shores of the sacred lake and less than a day's walk from the temple of Namara. Anyone who knew Namara would know that didn't really matter, that her Blades came from every one of the eleven kingdoms that had survived the great burning. But I didn't want Fei putting Namara and me in the same thought even in passing, and Emain West lay as far away from the

temple as you could get in Varya and still be in a city. I didn't think
the captain would buy me as a country boy.

"What were you there, I wonder?"

Fei didn't sound like she was really talking to me, but I answered
anyway, "Shadow jack, same as here. Or maybe just a bit shadier." I
grinned and flicked my eyebrows up, inviting the captain to share
in the joke. "Left the place a half step ahead of one of your counterparts in the law."

"Price on your head?" asked Fei.

I nodded. "Though not big enough to be worth the shipping fee,
if you're thinking about trying to collect on it."

"But it *is* big enough that you can't go home."

"Nor anyplace else in Varya or the Kvanas. It taught me a lesson
that's stuck, too—that there's good work and bad in the shadows
and that I won't touch the latter ever again."

"Once burned . . ." she said.

"I don't think I'll complete the old saw if you don't mind. No
burning for me. Not then and not now. Let's just say that I'm cautious about the jobs I'll take and leave it there. But that's more than
enough talking about me. What brings you down to this end of
town? If the question's not treading on any dangerous ground, that
is. If it is, forget I asked."

Fei rolled her glass between her fingers, warming the sake,
which had cooled while we talked. "It's not dangerous ground at all.
Not for you at any rate, unless you're hiding a mage under those old
rags you're wearing. Actually, there might be some coin for you in
this job if you're interested and not otherwise engaged."

"Hang on a second." I pulled my shirt out and looked down the
collar. "Nope. Nobody in here but one slightly sooty jack." I forced a
grin. "Figured I'd best check for mages since the odd spot of night-
side delivery *does* fall into my line though not usually so big a package as all that, and I'd rather play honest with you where I can."

Fei snorted, then drank a bit more of her sake. "No. Whoever
set this play up runs a couple of cards up from the jack. I'm looking
for a king or an ace if it's really a shadowside job and an earl or a
baroness if the sunside royalty is playing."

My ears pricked at the word "baroness." "Sounds messy."

"And political. Someone ghosted a couple of Kadeshi mercenaries about a hundred and fifty yards thataway." The captain waved
vaguely toward the door. "Which circumstance would normally be
grounds for celebration in my office. There's no one like a Kadeshi
for making trouble."

"But . . ." I had to fight to keep the interest out of my voice.

"But these bastards all had deathmarks on the backs of their necks of the magelightning variety. A deathspark's a tricky and expensive bit of magery even without tying it to three deaths instead of just the one. And that's saying nothing about how illegal it is. But again, not something I'd normally worry about. My job's making sure things run smooth and quiet, not enforcing the law."

"What happened to the killers? Charcoal? That's how a deathspark works, right?"

"It is and I wish, but no. Whatever party or parties sliced these boys up—a *very* fancy piece of knifework, I might add—has vanished away completely."

"So where *do* you come in? And, more importantly, where do I? I'm always up for a bit more coin, but . . . Bad boys get marked. Bad boys get killed. Killers go completely bye-bye. That sounds about as smooth and quiet as you could ask for things to run. I'd think you'd want to leave it there."

"Nothing would make me happier," said Fei, "but this one's got its very own set of noises and bumps in the person of a baroness of the royal house and her own pet colonel of the Elite, both of whom want to know what happened and why justice has not yet been served on all involved."

Fuck, Elite.

"Okay, I'm still not seeing where I come in," I said.

Meanwhile, Triss started doing the routine where he marches invisible centipedes up and down my back.

"I thought you might want to play ear for me. Outside your normal line, I know, but it's clean, and you're a smart player. The noble pressure means I need to get this one done quick, and that calls for a wide net. If you hear anything I might want to know on this one, I'll make it worth your while."

"Now that sounds like . . . Oh, shit."

The door of the Spinnerfish had just opened.

"What is it?" asked Fei.

"Your Elite colonel, skinny little quink with a bit of a limp?"

"That's him." She wrinkled her nose.

"Well, he's about to join us."

In the moment before Fei turned in her seat and waved to the colonel, I saw the faintest trace of fear ripple through her eyes. It was erased an instant later by the adamantine nerves that had made her such a power in Tien's shadow trades, but it was there.

Blade training or not, I started to sweat.

8

Physically, the colonel did not impress, but he practically burned with magic. Seething light danced around him in wild patterns of oranges and browns for eyes that could see it, a network of active and preset spells that must cost him hours every day to maintain. One thick rope of fiery orange looped around his left wrist and plunged from there into the floor like a fall of molten iron from a blacksmith's crucible or a leash for hell's own hound.

I forced my eyes not to follow its trail down into the earth, not to look for the colonel's buried familiar at the other end of that spell, his stone dog. Because Aral the jack was no mage, and Aral the Blade rated a prominent place on the Elite's death roster. Though the colonel didn't seem to be aware of me in any way, I knew that he had seen who sat with Fei and that he would be watching me too-too close. On my back, Triss's utter lack of movement made a presence of absence as he played at being nothing more than a shadow.

I kept my gaze fixed on the man's feet, expressing deference in expression and posture, and I sweated. The Elite had accounted for more Blades than any other organization in our history. They were nearly as good with the weapons of the body as we were, and much better where it came to magic. But more than that, they had the stone dogs.

Like the statues that guarded Zhan's temples come to life, they stood five feet at the shoulder with thick, strong bodies, and heads like lions. The stone dogs could cut the earth like sharks slicing through clear water. Softer than granite but harder than sandstone, they were fanatically loyal to their Elite companions and to Zhan's rightful ruler. They had killed at least two of the three Blades who died trying for Ashvik VI before my knife spilled royal blood and forever tied me to the name of Kingslayer.

As the colonel made his slow and careful way toward our table, I used the edges of my vision to study his face. Thin and pinched, marked by long pain and the fanaticism endemic to the Elite. An ugly and familiar expression on a stranger's face . . . No, I suddenly realized as he got closer, a familiar face, if you can call a moment's frantic meeting ten years in the past grounds for familiarity.

Fuck, fuck, fuck!

I recognized the colonel though I prayed to lost Namara's memory that he wouldn't recognize me. I had last seen his face on the night I killed a king. Of all the trouble I ran into that night, the worst was a young lieutenant of the Elite.

Dressed and masked in grays and wearing my shadow as a cloak, I had seen him before he saw me. I'd been so proud then, filled with youth's ignorance—for I was younger even than the lieutenant—convinced of the approval of my goddess and flushed with thoughts of success. Certain that I was the best there'd ever been, I'd wanted no dead guards staining my record of a clean kill on the king. I'd tried to slip past him unseen, but the hall was too brightly lit, and the darkness that concealed me also betrayed my presence.

He lunged at me, missing his thrust and leaving himself open to a low return as Triss shifted one way and I the other to confuse his aim. That and his position in the Elite made him a fair target. None of Namara's servants would have faulted me for killing him, but I wanted no other arrows showing on the butt to distract from a perfect bull's-eye on Ashvik. Instead of aiming for an artery, I'd thrust for the big nerve cluster where thigh met groin.

Fool.

The lieutenant went down screaming as my goddess-blessed sword punched through his wards and went deep. I spun away, then used the wall as a backstop and launched myself high over the body in a bit of overfancy and frankly showoffish footwork. That jump was an arrogance that saved my life when his stone dog came up through the floor clawing and biting. The dog shredded my boot and carved bloody furrows in my left calf. I bore the scars to this day and counted it light payment for the lesson driven home.

You can never let your pride trump your professionalism. Not if you want to live.

In combat, you have to sort people into two categories. There are targets, and there's everybody else, and you kill the targets. No exceptions. I'd forgotten that then and it had nearly gotten me killed. Now, as the colonel came closer, moving with a limp I'd given him, I wondered if that "nearly" was about to be removed from the record. If so, it would make for a bitter coincidence though perhaps a not wholly surprising one.

There were never more than a few score of the Elite to start with, the familiar-paired sorcerers who made up the officer and operative class of the Crown Guard. Most of those stayed close to the king's person and the capital, though a few were assigned permanently to Vangzien and the summer palace or Anyang, where special winter courts were sometimes held.

But then the colonel had arrived at our table, and I was out of time for thinking. I moved my gaze from his boots to the tabletop and kept it there. The effort of keeping my shoulders hunched and submissive instead of rolling them into a loosened state of readiness felt like a stone weight pressing down on my mind and back.

"Captain Fei," said the colonel, his tone clipped and contemptuous, more indictment than greeting.

"Colonel Deem." Fei lowered her head in something halfway between the nod of an equal and the bow of an inferior.

"Any news?"

"Not yet." Fei sniffed and tilted her head my way. "I've just been making inquiries while I waited for you to arrive."

"Is this a person of interest, then?" Deem seemed to really look at me for the first time.

Fei barked a laugh that sounded more than a little false to me. "No, Aral's just a broken-down jack I occasionally employ for odd jobs. I thought he might have heard something that wouldn't have risen to the top of the shadows yet."

"Aral?" Deem stepped even closer, and I could see the network of active spells that enclosed him shift and brighten, ready for action. "That's a very unlucky name."

Breathe, Aral. To keep itchy hands from reaching for a knife or a sword, I rolled my whiskey glass between my palms, breathing deep of the rich smoky aroma released by the heat and motion.

"Tell me about it." I let my very real nerves color my voice. "I was born under an unlucky star, which is why my little brother ended up with the shop in Emain Wast, and I ended up doing shit work a thousand miles from home." I knocked back the last half of my drink in a single swallow, barely tasting it.

"Fell in with the wrong crowd," I continued, babbling intentionally, though I still didn't look up. "Started taking the kind of jobs that don't make a man proud. Got in a fight over a woman. Knives. Won it, too, nearly killed the guy. Turned out he was a noble's son. When the bailiffs came after me, I started running. Didn't stop till I hit the fucking ocean." I waved vaguely toward the docks.

Before I could say more, Deem turned very deliberately back to Fei. "And this is the sort of person you deal with on a regular basis?"

"My job doesn't leave a lot of time for sipping chilled wine with the highborn in the palace," replied Fei, her voice acid. Then she got up and gestured toward the back of the Spinnerfish. "Come on, I've got a private booth where we can talk."

As Deem started to walk away, Fei turned that curious look on me again, and I knew I'd slipped a second time. Maybe by making my sob story a little too smooth and a little too easy to reconcile with what I'd told her earlier. I'd been so focused on Deem, I'd forgotten the quality of my secondary audience. Master Olen would have had very hard words for a cover story that didn't layer properly for *all* my listeners, and the fact that I'd had to cook it up on the spot wouldn't have excused me. I should have remembered that Fei was sharp enough to notice things like how well you lied.

In my line of work, it's much harder to appear bad at things you do well and often more important.

But worrying about it now was like stopping to sharpen your knife *after* you'd already made the sloppy cut. I waited just long enough for the curtain that hid the passage to the private booths to stop moving. Then I made a show of finding my bottle empty and getting up and heading for the door. I'd wanted to learn more about Maylien, but this was no longer the time or the place for it, and I didn't think Erk would miss my business all that much. I had no doubt I was high on his list of least favorite customers at the moment, between the Kadeshis and Fei coming in wearing her city-watch hat instead of the shadow-captain one.

Actually, that made for an interesting study in Erk's ethics. I had no doubt that Erk would have left me hanging without a warning if Fei'd had shadowside reasons for asking after whoever ghosted those Kadeshis. It was only the fact that the captain's attention was official watch business that made Erk give me a shout. Shadowside was us. Sunside was them.

When I hit the street, the sun was already yawning, so I went up a nearby wall and looked around for a place to lie up out of the wind while I waited for full dark. The process made various cuts and bruises sing out for my attention. I found a temporary snug in a steeply slanted niche between two battered dormers on the lee side of a roof. A onetime temple to Calren the Taleteller, first and former Emperor of Heaven, now deceased. It was better built than most of the buildings in the area.

I wedged myself into the gap and settled down to think through my next move. Fish was clearly off my menu for the next couple of days, and I really didn't want to spend any time at the Gryphon, on the off chance that my enemies hadn't marked it yet. There were a couple of other taverns I could try if I wanted to trail a bit more of my blood in the water. But after my chat with Fei and the subsequent dance with Deem, I felt there were way too many sharks swimming around at the moment to make that a good idea.

I needed solid information about Maylien and House Marchon. Especially if the royal baroness who had Deem chewing on Fei's ass turned out to be Marchon. I didn't remember Marchon having any ties to the royal house. Nothing beyond the way the old baron's sister had catered to Ashvik's need to bed girls half his age, that is. But perhaps things had changed. I had to find out what had happened there.

If I could get the information someplace quiet and far enough from my regular haunts, I could use the whole thing as an opportunity for a fadeout and make the trip serve double duty. I knew just the spot, but I couldn't go there without making a brief stop at my main snug in the Gryphon's stable. That was a problem, both because I didn't want to mark the Gryphon and because I didn't want to lead them on to my next destination if they had.

If I really wanted to make a fade, I had to find some way to break my trail to the Gryphon both coming and going, and that was a skip that would run a whole lot smoother if I had any idea how they were trailing me in the first . . . Wait. Could it really be that simple?

I turned to where my shadow lay along the roof slates, almost invisible now in the twilight. "Triss, you can . . . I don't know, is 'smell' the right word for what you did with Zass up in the Old Mews?"

Triss shifted into dragon form and spoke softly, "No. We would say . . ." And here he dropped into his native tongue, making a sort of guttural hiss with liquid undertones. "'Taste' would be closer to the right meaning, but there's really no good word for it in human speech. You just don't have the right senses. It has to do with the interplay between light and shadow and the nature of the everdark." He shrugged his wings. "It's very hard to explain the sensation."

"All right . . . I guess we'll go with taste then. If you can taste where Zass has been, can he do the same for you?"

"Of course."

"Why have I never heard about this before?"

Triss's wings sagged, and he looked ashamed. "The Shade elders and the senior masters instructed us not to speak of it to our companions, said it was a secret of Namara. I never liked that, but I could not disobey the elders, not while . . ." He trailed off and didn't speak of the goddess's death though I knew that was what he meant. "Then, after the fall of the temple, it didn't come up since we never saw any other Shades."

"How does it work?"

"When a shadow falls on something, it leaves a sort of . . ." More hissing. "Call it an *afterflavor* of itself that gets slicked on the surface, at least for a little while. The darker the shadow, the stronger the *flavor*." He spread his wings, then flicked the tips back and forth in a gesture I'd come to recognize as searching after a thought. "Every shadow, no matter how faint or briefly cast, partakes of the everdark. We who are born from the substance of the everdark can sense where shadows have touched—taste the flavor of home in the darkness. If the impressions are strong enough, we can follow them like a trail."

"Could you teach me to do that?" I was grasping after something here, but I still hadn't gotten hold of enough of it to know what its final shape would be. "Or someone else?"

Triss shook his head. "No. You don't have the . . ." He hissed again, sharper this time. "Your mind isn't shaped right."

"What about a spell? Could you help me cook up something that would have the same effect? Magically? Or at least that would let me follow a . . . a taste trail?"

"Maybe." Triss flitted back and forth across the slates like a pacing cat. "If the spells were set on a spyglass or a dark lantern, it could probably be made to"—long, involved hissing—"the trail so you could follow it, but only for the very"—more hissing—"*Everdarkest*-tasting shadows, like yours where it has been reinforced by my presence."

"Or Devin's because of Zass?"

"Yes, or any Blade's, really. A shadow that holds a Shade is much"—hissing—"realer than a regular shadow, yes, realer. And the more the Shade is present in the shadow at the time, the realer the impression it will leave."

"I'm not sure I followed that one," I said.

"When I am hiding in your shadow, as I did with the colonel a few minutes ago, the shadow would taste stronger than a regular shadow but only to a"—hissing—"truly refined palate. Whereas when I am in my chosen shape"—he flapped his wings for emphasis—"I will leave a much stronger and longer-lasting flavor, easier to track—more real. And the same would happen when I enshroud you."

Now he cocked his head to one side. "Yes, the more I think about it, the more I think it would be possible to set a spell in some item that would allow such a trail to be followed. This is how we are being found, yes?"

"I think so, but it still leaves me confused. Lok's people seemed genuinely to want to know everything I could tell them about Devin. If they're working with or for Devin, why would they need that information? And if they're not, how did they get ahold of such a tracking spell? I seriously doubt there's a third Blade involved. There were never that many of us to start with, and I can't imagine *any* Blade going along with building that rack-thing they had us strapped to."

"Perhaps Devin's allies do not intend to stay his allies."

A little electric thrill danced across my shoulders, like the after-effects of a big burst of magelightning. Yes. That felt right, a double cross. I nodded.

Don't fight your instincts. A trained mind works on multiple levels, and you have to learn to listen to yourself even when there are no words.

"I think you've got it, Triss. The baroness and Devin struck me as very uneasy partners. It wouldn't surprise me at all if there's a betrayal on someone's schedule. Or, considering what we know of the new Devin, more than one someone's. We'll use that as our working assumption going forward. Next question, what breaks a shadow trail?"

"Summer sunlight is best, but fire will work, too."

"Like the Old Mews."

"Like the Old Mews," agreed Triss.

"Do you think Devin started . . ." But I couldn't finish the question, still couldn't even imagine the answer being yes. It would be too big a betrayal of what the goddess had expected of us.

"No!" Triss sounded utterly emphatic. "A fire that big in that kind of neighborhood had to involve magic, and Zass would never help in such a thing."

I really hoped Triss was right about that, but I couldn't help imagining the arguments I might make if I were Devin, and I wanted it bad enough. I remembered how angry Triss had gotten at the people who had held us prisoner, how willing, even eager he had been to kill and destroy. Zass hadn't been bound to the rack as we had, but if Devin had wanted to start the burning with that glyph, how much of a push would it have taken?

Evil thoughts. I shook my head and tried to push them aside. We had things that needed doing and . . . hey, maybe I'd just figured out how to manage them.

"Why don't we use our enemies' own tools against them?" I asked.

"What do you mean?"

"The fire in the Old Mews."

"I don't understand," said Triss. "I know you're not suggesting we start a fire to cover our trail."

"Heat and light you said, right?"

"Yes . . ."

Even with the torn-away sleeve of my old shirt tied across my mouth and nose to fend off the worst of the smoke, I couldn't stop coughing as we jumped from one field of coals to another through what had once been a thriving neighborhood. Triss had wrapped himself around me from the knees up to keep away from the fire. I could feel his comforting presence against my skin like cool silk, and I needed all the comfort I could get. The stench from the burning of the Old Mews was horrific.

Wood, of course, a hundred kinds, horsehair that had been used to reinforce plaster and stucco or stuff furniture, straw, cotton, wool, silk. Those were the good smells. The paint and lacquer, lead, copper, the shit from the chamber pots, those were worse. But worst of all was the horrible smell of burned meat. Horse. Dog. Human. Whoever had done this had to die.

"I'm going to find out who started this fire, and I'm going to kill him," I said between coughs. "I owe it to the dead."

And as I said that, I stopped right there. In the middle of a ruined house with smoke rising from the soles of my slowly burning boots and the sweat pouring off me in sheets, I listened to the words coming out of my own mouth, and I really heard them. It froze me where I stood because I had realized a great and terrible truth.

Someone had done real evil here and they needed to die for it. I owed it to the dead. Not just those killed in the fire. I owed it to my goddess and to all my fallen comrades, who would never again have the chance to bring justice to the guilty.

For five years, I had forgotten or chosen to ignore what I was and why I had been given the gifts I had been given. I might not be a Blade of the goddess anymore, or the King-slayer, or even the kind of man who could consistently tell good from evil—there was too much gray in my world now to ever be sure of the black and white again. But I had no right to ignore wrong when it slapped me in the face. I would stop whoever did this and I would stop them forever. I had to.

I owed it to the dead.

9

The Ismere, a club for gentlemen-merchants, stood only one narrow alley away from the private library of the same name. The former also provided the opportunity for a necessary stop along the way to the latter. My second round of coal-walking through the burned-over Old Mews neighborhood had left me even more committed to tracking down those responsible than the first round had. People were going to die for that. It also left me hot, sweaty, and covered in filth. So when I finally slid into the shadows beneath the club's rooftop water tank, I did so with a rather intense feeling of relief.

After carefully unfastening my heavy pack from the steel rings that attached it to my sword rig, I tucked it into a niche in the tank's supports. Then I stripped off my smoke-stained clothes and briefly contemplated tossing them into the river behind the building. Having recovered the rest of Maylien's silver, I was flush enough to replace my whole wardrobe and use my current best and cleanest to replenish the cache in my fallback. But you never know when a set of old rags might come in handy, so I stowed them beside the pack instead.

Then, naked except for a pair of daggers in wrist sheaths, I climbed the short ladder to the top of the tank, opened the trapdoor, fastened a length of rope to the edge, and lowered myself into darkness. The reservoir was on the low side, less than a quarter full, and a long day in the sun had turned the chest-deep water in the dark-roofed and -sided tank blood-warm. I sank into it with a happy sigh. In the dark, I couldn't see Triss, but I could feel him sliding about on the bottom of the tank, enjoying the water in his own alien way.

Washing the smoke stink out of my hair and skin felt wonderful, despite the extra attention I felt the need to give to my myriad of small cuts and bruises. Unfortunately, I lost my little bar of rough soap when I was still half a leg short of clean. As I made do with even harder scrubbing, I idly wondered if it would survive long enough to slip through the big clay pipes and slide down into one of the large private soaking pools that made club membership so popular with the traveling merchants and wealthier caravaneers. Honestly, I would have liked nothing better than to stay and have an hourslong soak myself, but I had urgent debts to both the living and the dead and couldn't afford to tarry.

Besides, there was always the chance that one of the club's servants might decide to have a quick bath. The exposed rope would make them very suspicious—they always went to such care to hide it from the owners. I could almost certainly fade my way out of any such encounter without having to hurt anyone, but it would be much smarter to avoid the need.

With a regretful sigh I hand-over-handed my way out of the tank. After I'd restowed the rope and changed into clean grays, I sorted my pack into two smaller bundles and carefully hid the larger, smellier one in the top of one of the club's chimneys—cold and dark at this time of year but with enough of a smoke smell of its own to mask the stink of my gear.

Next, six running steps and a Triss-assisted leap carried me across the narrow alley to the Ismere Library. I touched down on the steeply sloping lead roof of the library, then let myself slide down and over the edge to land on a third-floor balcony. The slatted doors were latched but not barred, and the thin strip of copper from my trick bag opened them neatly. The ward of alarm on the door was more tricky, but I'd had plenty of practice at bypassing it over the years.

Inside was a marble-floored reading room with a central table, and several smaller study carrels lined up along the rough mulberry-paper panels that served it for walls. The panels were often used in places where flexibility of floor plan might come in handy or where it was advantageous to let light bleed from room to room. Stopping only long enough to pull out a small leather-wrapped package, I left my swords and pack in one of the carrels. I didn't think I'd missed anything with smoke smell, but caution is always the best strategy when dealing with a librarian, and anything that might harm one of his books. Especially if he's a sorcerer of some repute.

Dealing with a dead king's bodyguard is much less fraught than facing a librarian who thinks you've just taken one of his precious charges through a fire, even a fire as burned-out as the Old Mews. Before slipping out into the main part of the library, I sniffed at the leather I'd wrapped around the book one last time. Clean, or at least, clean enough. Partially hooded magelights mounted on the ends of the shelves cast a dim yellow glow that could easily be brightened by raising the shutters.

I'd once asked Harad, the master librarian, about that and about why there were no actual windows in the stacks. He'd told me that prolonged exposure to direct sunlight was bad for books and that intense magelight was worse. Whatever the reason, I liked the way the shadows lay thick in the library, and Triss liked it even more—it gave him greater freedom. That and the peace and the smell of the books reminded me of the more contemplative parts of Namara's great temple. It wasn't quite like coming home, but it was as close as I was ever likely to get again.

More out of habit than concern, I checked each of the other three reading rooms that occupied the corners of the big square floor plan. It was well past the library's official closing time, but the collection was owned by a private fellowship whose members included the club next door, and merchants sometimes kept weird hours. Catering to that trade was half the reason the Ismere had a built-in apartment for the master librarian.

The other half was so that he could provide security for a lot of valuable property. Thanks to magical techniques borrowed from the inhuman denizens of the Sylvani Empire, the actual production of books was relatively inexpensive; but the materials' costs were high, especially the high-quality paper needed. The Ismere had been started by an extremely successful Kadeshi-born merchant who had paid for the building and provided the bulk of the initial collection. It had been added to steadily over the years by its members— donation of new titles could be used to offset the hefty fees the library charged.

As soon as I'd cleared the third floor, I catwalked down the back stairs to the second floor and gave it a once-over as well. That's where I found Harad, wandering quietly among the rows of books and checking to see that everything had gotten back to its proper place after the departure of the day's visitors. Even in the dim light, the many complex spells that wrapped him round made him easy to spot with magesight. Once I'd made sure we were alone, I got ahead of him and stood quietly in plain view, waiting for him to look up and see me. After a few moments, his eyes lifted and met mine, and he waved.

"You're up late," I said.

"I'm an old man and don't sleep as well as I used to. I like to take the opportunity to check on my charges and see that they are resting better than I am."

"You don't look that old to me." And, in truth, he didn't, no more than fifty, a well-preserved sixty at most, and that in a society where magical healing saw many of the better off into their eighties and nineties.

"But I am old, older by far than anyone most people will ever meet." He waved a hand. "I exclude you, of course, young Aral. You walk strange roads and see much that is hidden from the ordinary run of folk."

I smiled, and, for perhaps the twentieth time, asked, "How old are you, Harad?"

He smiled back and winked, and I waited for the usual coy dodge, but it didn't come. Instead, his smile faded into a thoughtful look.

"Do you really want to know? Truly?"

"Curiosity is one of my besetting sins." Even though I had more pressing questions and duties, Harad hadn't visibly aged in the ten years since I'd first met him, and I really did want to know more about that. This might be my only chance to find out. "That curiosity's what brought me here the first time."

"A decade ago, in the year that butcher Ashvik—may he burn eternally in the deepest of hells—was slain. I remember it like it was yesterday." He smiled again. "And in the long book that is my life, that is not so far from the truth. All right, curious boy, I will answer you . . . in a few minutes. Come back to my kitchen, and I will make us tea."

I wanted to refuse the tea, since it always reminded me of efik, but that might have shut off the potential flow of information, so instead I snorted and grumbled, "Now you're teasing me." Triss's brief squeeze of my shoulders told me that he agreed.

"No, I just prefer to tell things in their right time, and the right time for this tale is still a short way off."

"Have it your way, *old* man."

"For far more years than you've been alive I have done precisely that. I see no reason to change my ways now."

I grinned. After Triss, Harad was the nearest thing I had to a friend these days. Unlike Fei or Jerik or any of my other Tienese associations, there was no flow of debts between us, neither of blood nor of money. Just a mutual interest in books and all that lay between their covers. We'd first met because of that. I had snuck into the library one night because I felt the need to get away from my assignment to kill Ashvik—things hadn't been going well, and I was frustrated. I wanted nothing more than to read some slight volume and let the story lift me out of myself for a while.

Harad had found me at it, sitting in the very reading room where my gear now sat, my nose buried in a particularly lurid sort of adventure novel translated from the original Kanjurese. It was an odd moment really, him knocking very politely on the door frame—the door itself having soundlessly vanished when he approached—and lightly clearing his throat to let me know he was there.

I was mortified, of course, a Blade caught out by a librarian. But as I later learned, he was an exceptionally powerful sort of mage, and that certainly had something to do with it. To this day, I'm not sure why he chose to knock rather than throwing me out or calling in the stingers. Whatever the reason, it put me at my ease in a way I'd never have expected before it happened. Rather than drawing a weapon or some other hostile action, I'd simply set the book aside, and said, "Hello?"

He'd come in then and gently questioned me about my presence in his library and my intent. And, also, by the way, how did I like the book? I'd explained that I liked the story well enough, but that I thought the prose of the translation was pretty awful. That had led to a rather spirited discussion of translation in general, both on the page and in person. Ever since then, I'd had a sort of unofficial library membership and one person in Tien whom I could talk to without the weight of anything beyond mutual interest.

Once the water for the tea had cooled down a bit from its boil, Harad poured it over the powdered tea and carefully stirred with a whisk. An unusual method for Zhan, it spoke of foreign origins in a way much more forceful than Harad's Kadeshi name. It also reminded me of the efik ritual, a thought I pushed aside forcefully.

He'd just finished preparing the second cup—his own—when the timesman at the temple of Shan Starshoulders struck the great bell to signal midnight. Normally, I was too far away to hear it, but here in the wealthiest of the merchant districts, it rang quite clear. It reminded me time was pressing, but somehow I still couldn't bring myself to push Harad.

"There." Harad touched his ear. "That is what I have been waiting for. It signals the right time for this story."

"Which is?" I asked into the silence he left for that purpose.

"My birthday. With the tolling of the midnight bell I enter into my six hundred and eleventh year."

"Your what?"

"Don't give me that look, Aral. You don't feign shock well. The teacher who trained you to it emphasized the open mouth too much, and you have a touch of the ham in you, which pushes the whole thing just a *shade* too far."

The inflection on the word "shade" was so subtle as to be barely there, but it *was* there, and I had to suppress the impulse to twitch when I heard it. Triss, on the other hand, didn't feel any such constraints. He gave me a sharp jab in the ribs.

Harad went on. "Shock's not really a good look on you anyway. It undermines the whole tragic but dangerous image. I'd suggest you stick with the eye twitch and then a quick slide back to the blank stare of the gambler, like now. It plays to your strengths."

I'd recovered by then and also decided he might have a point—Master Kelos had once told me something similar. So I hung on to my closed face. Holding a hot cup in my hands helped there, reminding me as it did of old times and old disciplines at the same time it spiked my desire for a cup of efik.

"But I am shocked," I said, in a tone that belied the words. "Six hundred years old. That's awfully hard to believe."

"No. It's not. We both know that I'm a sorcerer and a powerful one. It's a requirement of the job here. The Ismere holds the largest and most valuable collection of books in all of Zhan—mostly because it is private and thus free of the censoring impulses of generations of Zhani royals." Harad's smile looked more than a trifle smug. "Like any sorcerer, my life is tied to my familiar's. As my companion's is the longer span, we have both measured our threads to his."

Unlike my dead buddy Lok and the spit-adder, where the lengthening of life went the other way—well, right up until Maylien killed him. I wondered what the nature of Harad's familiar was but knew better than to ask. If he'd wanted to tell me, he would have.

He continued, "Don't pretend that you don't know how that bonding works. If nothing else, you've read up on the topic. I know. I lent you the books."

I looked Harad flat in the eyes. "You know what I am, don't you?"

I set my untouched tea aside as Triss pressed himself hard against my back. But Harad simply shrugged and smiled.

"Since you ask, yes, though I would not have raised the issue had you chosen to leave it lie. I have known it from the first moment you snuck into my library a week before you rid the world of King Ashvik, the sixth and hopefully last of that name. It's in the way you walk and the way you hold your head when you lie, techniques passed down through dozens of generations."

"Like this." He shifted subtly in his chair and for just an instant I faced one of the masters of my order. Then he relaxed, and it was gone.

"Oh"—Triss slid out from behind me so that he could see better— "that was Kelos to the life. Very good." Shadow hands applauded.

Harad gave a half bow from his seat, as elegant as any actor's, but said nothing.

"I don't understand," I said after several seconds of silence while I reviewed my options.

They were much constrained by Triss's choosing to expose his presence. Funnily enough, attempting to kill Harad never ranked as a serious choice. Whether that was prudence or curiosity or simply friendship is still an open question.

"Three hundred years ago, servants of your Namara asked me to help out with the training of her Blades. At the time I was running a theater company in Varya and had been for perhaps fifty years before that. The masters wanted to add some refinements to their techniques, and who better to ask than an acting master. I had become bored with the theater at that point and I thought that teaching assassins might make for an entertaining change of scene. I was right, and I stayed a decade or three."

"What happened?" I was fascinated but also a tiny bit horrified at learning about Harad's involvement with my order. It was also funny how the word "assassins" bothered me not at all coming from his lips.

Triss assumed his dragon shape and settled on the floor by my feet. I suppressed an urge to whap him on the nose for exposing our secrets. That pot was already a decade spilled if Harad was being honest with us.

"I got bored and left the temple," said Harad. "It was a bit too much like working with the acting company, really. Then I moved on to another career and another after that. So far, I think that I like librarian the best. I've been here for a hundred and twenty years and might well stay a hundred more. Now that we've dealt with that, what brings you to see me tonight? You can't be done with that necromancer book already." His eyes flicked to my still-full teacup. "You don't read that fast or that steadily—it cuts into your drinking time."

I opened my hands to acknowledge the truth of his dig. "No, I haven't finished it. It's both a little too gruesome and a little too silly for me at the moment though I'd like to try it again someday. I was going to pretend that I had read it and ask you to find me something on what's been happening with the royal family and the succession since the death of Ashvik."

I continued, "I've been going out of my way to avoid as much news of the royal court as I could, but I didn't want to admit that to you as it might give something away. So I was going to make up a cover story about a new client, but somehow that all seems a little ridiculous now. Instead, I'm just going to tell you what I really want to know, why I want to know it, and everything that's happened so far. Then I'll see if you can point me at the right information."

So I did, with helpful pointers from Triss wherever I failed to mention a mistake I'd made—drat him. And when I was done, Harad found me what I needed.

"This is banned in Tien as propaganda." Harad handed over a thick pamphlet written in Kodamian: *Thauvik, the Rise of the Bastard King.* "Which it is, of course, but with a core of truth. The banning means that it's in high demand here at the library. Please don't keep it too long or, if it should come up, let anyone know where you got it. Everything you want to know about the Marchon girls you will find in there."

I nodded and flipped the pamphlet open. The city-state of Kodamia was tucked into the great gap of the Hurnic Mountains just to the west of Zhan. It had fought several bitter wars with its larger neighbor over access to that passage and the kingdoms of the west. Kodamia's strategic position made it the fattest of prizes, and only an astonishingly competent army officered by the dyads—warrior-sorcerer familiar pairings who also served as spies and assassins—and constant vigilance had kept them from succumbing to one of the many invasions they had faced from both sides of the gap. If anyone paid closer attention to the ruling dynasty of Zhan than the Zhani, it was Kodamia.

"Thank you," I said, "but there's no need to worry about my returning it late. I don't have the time to waste. If it's all right with you, I'll just park myself in the third-floor reading room I use as a foyer, and it'll never leave the building."

Harad nodded. "If that's what you want."

"What I want is to go to my fallback and sleep the night and day around, then get so drunk I forget that this whole stupid job ever happened." Triss expressed his disapproval of that suggestion with a grumpy snort. "But what I need to do is make a serious fadeout while I figure out my next move. That means staying away from anyplace that might already have been compromised and minimizing the chance that anyone will pick up my trail again. So, assuming I got here clean, my best bet is to hold still until it's time for the next move, and then to move quickly and decisively."

Harad gestured toward the stairs. "Then, after you."

When we reached the reading room, Harad went straight to the outer doors and opened them. Then he knelt on the threshold and placed one palm on the limestone of the balcony floor.

Looking up, he beckoned to me. "Come here."

I could have asked why, but I figured I'd find out quicker if I just did as I was told. Life is like that sometimes.

"Give me your hand."

I did, and he took it in his free hand. Harad closed his eyes and muttered something under his breath, causing one of the network of spells that wrapped him round to twist and kink slightly. The words sounded like some sort of archaic Kadeshi, but I couldn't make it out well enough to be certain. When he stopped speaking, I felt a shock like a tiny burst of magelightning run from my hand into Harad's.

Triss slid around for a better look then, as the floor of the balcony flared briefly green over most of its surface. The exception being a large black symbol like a circle bounded by crescent wings that ran spiderweb-thin through the stone—some kind of extremely sophisticated ward.

"I've just rekeyed it to you personally," said Harad. "As the most likely entrance for one of your kind, I have long left this door open to anyone companioned by a Shade, but if what you tell me about this Devin and his society of assassins or whatever he wants to call it is true, that's no longer a smart choice."

"Has this ward always been here?" I hadn't ever seen it before, and that was a very neat trick.

"Only for a hundred and twenty years or so. My predecessor used a different system."

I opened my inner eyes as wide as they would go. "How do you hide . . . oh!"

I realized then that the whole of the building was impregnated with just a touch of active magic, barely more than the background noise of the world, and just enough so that the faint lines of the ward were concealed within the greater light. I was impressed: that took a lot of power to set up and maintain. It was far beyond anything I could have managed, both in terms of technique and raw power. But the ward itself looked so weak . . . what could you do with it? Only by looking closely and knowing just where the ward lay could I even make it out now.

"The obvious ward on the door is just another layer of distraction, to keep people from looking for this, isn't it?"

Harad smiled. "Very good. What else can you see?"

"Let me look a little more closely." Again and again, I mentally traced the lines of the spell worked into the balcony, trying to figure out what it did.

"The ward on the balcony floor is just a triggering spell, isn't it? For something much nastier? What does the nasty look like? Is it hidden beneath the surface of the stone?"

Harad shrugged. "Trade secret. Suffice to say that if your friend Devin comes knocking on my door, he will cease to be a problem for you."

"If that happens, let me know. I'll come take care of the body. It's the least I can do."

Harad laughed. "If that happens, there won't be a body." Then he left.

I settled down to read, and Triss took a little nap. He's generally bored by books, and in this case I couldn't blame him. Most of the pamphlet was blah, blah, Thauvic's a vicious bastard, blah. But there were a few things worth knowing. I took a sheet of paper and a quill from a small box by the door—the carrel had its own inkwell—and made notes as I went, just as I had been taught.

—Succession of the Royal House of Tien and the Barony of Marchon.

—When Aral Kingslayer (I really, really hate that name) ended the reign of Ashvik (by sticking a sword through his throat) in 3207, Ashvik's bastard half brother, Thauvic, then Chief Marshal of the army, took the throne with the support of the leading generals and the order of the Elite.

—That he was able to succeed his brother despite his bastardy was due to three factors.

—First and most important, he was very popular with the Elite and the military, where he had risen through the officer ranks based on merit rather than the favor of his brother, who publicly ignored him for most of his career.

—Secondly, though Ashvik had three legitimate children by his queen, he had executed all of them for "treason" to the realm and "attempts against the throne." (All three were innocent, part of why Namara had marked him for death, the rest being the brutal murder of more than ten thousand innocent Kadeshi villagers.)

—Third, though Ashvik's bastard daughters by the Marchon woman (oh, shit) might have had a slightly more legitimate claim on the throne, they were both underage and had been missing and presumed dead for some weeks at the time. The official story was that they'd been sent to the court of the Thane of Aven for finishing, but it was assumed they had been murdered by the late king—their bastard status precluding the need for a trial. (names?)

I hadn't written this much in ages. I stretched my fingers to relieve the cramping and wished whoever had written this book had more sensible priorities, namely the same as mine. I wanted to know what the supposedly murdered girls' names were though I feared one was Maylien. Anything else would have made my life easier, and that didn't seem to be the way the dice were falling. With a sigh, I plunged back in. More blah, consolidation of Thauvik's rule with a little judicious bloodletting including Baron Marchon, blah, enlargement of army and increase of power for the ministry of war, blah. And then something I could use.

—Six years after the disappearance of Ashvik's illegitimate daughters by his last mistress, Juli Dan Marchon (younger sister of the baron), two young women were presented to the court by that same Juli Dan Marchon (now Baroness Marchon) as the long-missing heiresses. At that time, she asked that Maylien, the elder, be confirmed as her successor in the Barony of Marchon. There was no mention of any relationship to the late Ashvik. (I just bet there wasn't).

—Thauvik disinherited Maylien because she had taken mage orders in her exile and settled the succession on Sumey (apparently he was comfortable enough on the throne by then to want to avoid the odium of executing his nieces). A short time later, Juli killed herself, and Sumey became Baroness Marchon. At that point Maylien vanished again, and rumors began to float around that she had murdered her mother, rumors that were hotly (too hotly) denied by her bereaved sister.

There was more about Thauvik and what the author perceived as his ambitions, but nothing that interested me. And that was it. I read my notes aloud both for Triss's benefit and because that made them easier to memorize. Then I asked him to destroy them for me while I tried to think of what to do next. I had neither time nor good options.

I was pledged to help a girl who might have murdered her mother reclaim a baronial seat that the current king had already refused her. Assuming she was still alive, of course. Throw in the fact that I'd assassinated the king's predecessor, who was also Maylien's father and that I was going up against a man who'd once been one of my closest friends and . . . my head was spinning.

"How the hell did I get here?"

"By killing a king," said Triss.

10

I killed a king once upon a time. I was seventeen and armored in the certainty of my faith, completely confident in my purpose in life. I was Aral Kingslayer, Blade of Namara and proud of it. That man was gone now, lost somewhere in the depths of a soul shattered by the murder of his goddess.

I could sense him sometimes, down there in the darkness, showing through in the skills I brought to some shadow-trade task he never would have consented to touch. Or in the momentary outrage I felt at some injustice, a flash of the morals I'd had etched into my bones by the priests and masters. Or, occasionally, in a black sense of humor that had grown somewhat rusty from lack of use over the last five years. I needed him now, to help Aral the jack pay his debts—to Maylien, to Devin, to the dead—but I didn't know how to find him anymore.

I got up from the little desk, leaving the pamphlet for Harad to collect later, and I began to pace and to think. From the very first day I was brought to the temple, I'd been taught how to hunt men and women, how to sneak up and catch them unawares, how to kill them in any of a hundred ways. I was a manhunter to the marrow, trained in the arts of stalking and death by the very best in the world. But that didn't do a damn bit of good when the man you were hunting was yourself.

Or did it? Could I apply the manhunter's skills to myself? If so, where to start?

Then, like it was yesterday, I seemed to hear Master Kelos, "If you don't know how to get at your target, or worse, can't find him, look to his history. If you truly understand a man, if you know his background and habits, you can predict his actions, his location, even the exact moment to strike. Understanding starts from the beginning. What made him the man he is today?"

Where did Aral Kingslayer begin? That gave me my starting point. Because the Kingslayer had not been born with the death of Ashvik; that was merely the moment that made the name. No, the Aral who became the Kingslayer had taken shape at the temple school, where he trained with Siri and Jax and a dozen others, including his good friend Devin.

Some of my earliest memories were of me and Devin together. Our cubicles had sat side by side in one of the hallways of the boys' wing, and since we were of an age, we were often together.

Dalridia, the kingdom in the clouds. I was eleven, Devin twelve. Master Loris had taken us there so that we could train our bodies and our minds to operating in the thin air of the heights. For the first couple of weeks, we did nothing but run and spar and practice combat forms, ending each day with a collapse into the long sleep of exhaustion.

This was the first night where we'd both been able to keep our eyes open past dinner. Loris had gone into the local village for reasons that I no longer remembered, leaving Devin and me alone in the big tent, which gave us extra incentive to stay awake. Truly unsupervised time was rare in the early years at the temple.

Triss and Zass wrestled and chased each other on the canvas walls in a shadow play just for us—the dragon and the tayra. I laughed when my familiar pinned his ferret-wolf opponent. Zass was faster than Triss and more slippery, but not as strong or large— they were well matched.

"That makes it your turn," I said. "Tell me about the mountains of Aven."

"They're much of a height with the mountains of Dalridia, but there's a lot more snow and ice." Devin took a sip of efik.

"Is that why you drink that stuff?" I pointed at his steaming mug and the various implements used to make it. "Because it's so cold where you come from?"

He snorted. "It's a Varyan drink, Aral. I don't think anyone back home even knows the stuff exists. I drink it because I like it and because it calms me down."

"But it's so bitter." I shuddered in mock horror.

Most of the older Blades swore by the calming effects of efik, but among the younger trainees only Devin and Siri had yet acquired a taste for the stuff.

"You're such a puppy," said Devin. "Hey, Zass just won a fall, it's your turn. Tell me about being born in sight of the temple."

Varya, the great temple of Namara, just after the service of mourning. I was seventeen and heartbroken. Alinthide Poisonhand had just been killed in action, the third Blade to die making an attempt on Ashvik VI, the butcher of Kadesh. Mistress Alinthide had been one of my favorite teachers and one of the oldest Blades still in active service at a hundred and fifty-four.

Beautiful and warm, always ready to answer a question about the poisons that were her specialty and looking not a day over twenty-five. I'd had a burning crush on her for almost two years and a completely unrealistic hope that I might be able to do something about it once I'd finished my classes and earned myself a working name.

Once the priestess had returned Alinthide's spirit knife to the goddess—casting the black steel kila into the shaded depths of Namara's pool—we had taken a barge back across the lake from the holy island. When we docked, I had turned away from the temple and into the setting sun, walking blindly along the shores of the great lake, weeping. Triss hung at my back, gently rubbing my shoulders and whispering wordless comfort in my ears.

After perhaps a half mile, I took conscious notice of Devin trailing along at a polite distance—close enough that no one Blade-trained could have missed him but far enough back not to intrude. I waved him forward, and we walked a while in silence, the four of us, Blades-to-be ahead, Shades trailing behind.

When the tears finally stopped, I pulled a couple of roasted efik beans from the little pouch I always kept about me and began to chew. I nearly gagged at the bitterness, but I had neither the time nor the tools to steep and prepare a proper pot. I needed something to calm me down and take the edge off the pounding in my skull right now, and since the priests despised alcohol . . .

"Three!" The word burst out of me, almost against my will, and I felt Triss jerk in startlement as I turned to face Devin. "Three Blades dead in as many seasons. How can the goddess let Ashvik get away with it?"

"Namara is not the only goddess," said Devin, his voice barely above a whisper. "Perhaps in this, she is too strongly opposed."

Zass, who'd been slipping back and forth across our trail, jerked and vanished completely into Devin's shadow at his words.

"Impossible!" I said, and in that moment I believed it utterly. "Namara is unstoppable."

"Then why are there so very many Blades who return to her only as a black steel dagger cast into deep waters?" Devin asked. "So many whose bodies are burned on foreign pyres?"

At first I had no answer. But then, almost as if the goddess herself were putting it into my mind, I heard a phrase from the book of Namara. The words were spoken in the voice of that high priestess who had died in my first year at the temple, and whether they came from memory or from the goddess, I cannot say.

"The sheath must find the right Blade," I said, and Triss nodded his agreement.

"Sure, and 'those whom Namara would slay are like sheaths for her Blades.'" Devin didn't quite roll his eyes, but I could see that he wanted to. "I'm familiar with that one."

Zass slid back into view, peering up at me from the ground. "Alinthide was one of the very best. If she couldn't do it, then who can?"

"I can." The words came out of my mouth, but it didn't feel like I'd said them, more like they had said me—as if everything I'd done up to this point, all my training, all of what I had become was a prelude to that simple statement. That I could kill a king.

Triss froze, and Devin started to argue with me, to tell me I was crazy and a fool and that I'd never even make it as far as Tien. I could barely hear him. Instead, I looked out over the deep blue waters of the sacred lake and listened to . . . what?

I don't know. At the time, I thought I was listening to the goddess, and things that happened soon thereafter seemed to reinforce that idea. But I'm older now, and not so sure. Not of that, nor really, of anything. The world has become a gray place for me, filled with shadows where once it was all black and white. That inner voice might have been my pride, or folly, or simply a heart filled with anger by the death of someone I loved. Whatever the reason, in that moment I resolved that I would be the Blade who brought down Ashvik.

"I will kill the king," I said, cutting across Devin's argument, while Triss slumped unhappily against my back.

"You can't mean that," said Devin. "You're not even a full Blade yet. You haven't taken your kila. The Elite will tear you to pieces and feed the bits to the stone dogs."

I should probably have felt fear then, but I didn't. All I felt was certainty.

"The goddess has spoken to me."

Perhaps it was the look on my face. Perhaps it was the tone in my voice. Perhaps Zass gave him a nudge. Whatever the reason, Devin stopped arguing.

"You're serious, aren't you?" he finally asked.

I nodded, and his expression changed. The look on his face held something of awe and something of pity, and maybe just the tiniest bit of envy. Yes, envy. I think that it started in that very instant when he finally believed me though I didn't recognize it then, nor for a long time afterward.

"How will you do it?" asked Devin.

"I don't know. I just know that I must." For a brief instant, I felt the enormity of what I had to do pressing down on me like a great weight, could see the barriers ahead—the travel, the expense, the Elite and their stone dogs—but only for an instant.

"We'll have to go to the goddess," said Triss after a moment, "directly. Ask her to give you your kila early and make you a Blade. You have to sheathe the spirit knife in the altar before you leave, and you can't go after Ashvik without an eye and your swords."

He was right, of course. I needed to seek the formal blessing of the goddess. Without it, I would be nothing more than a common assassin.

"I'll go now." I turned on my heel and started back along the shore.

Devin caught my arm. "Don't be a fool, Aral. Even if the goddess approves, the masters won't want to let you go. The easiest way to prevent you is to keep you from ever crossing to the island. If you're seen taking one of the boats, they'll figure it out, and they'll stop you. You'll have to go after dark, and you'll have to swim."

"Point. But how will I get my blades back across?"

I had no worries about swimming out to the island. It was nearly half a mile, and there were things in the lake that devoured the unwary, but I'd swum farther in training, and the creatures would leave me alone because the goddess had called me. But the weight of all that steel would be a problem.

Then I had it. "I can borrow a rush basket from the temple fishermen." They used the floating baskets to keep the fish fresh when they went spearing in the shallows.

Devin nodded. "Good plan."

And Zass asked, "When?"

"I'll wait till an hour past the sun's setting to grab the basket—better not to ask for one, I think—then I'll go. I wish I could leave it till later, but I'm going to want to be well on the road by dawn. It'll take at least another hour just to swim out to the island and back with the basket slowing me down. As to the rest . . ." I shrugged.

I had to petition the goddess. How long it would take for her to decide what to answer, if anything, I wasn't even going to try to guess. I knew that I had been called, but I also knew that the goddess worked when and how she wanted. If I approached her with arrogance in my heart . . .

For perhaps the dozenth time I pressed my forehead against the age-smoothed granite of the flagstones that lay in a ring around the sacred pool, praying silently for permission to deliver the unblinking eye of justice to Ashvik. I was facing outward, toward the heart of the lake where the goddess made her home. A natural stone arch separated the pool from the greater waters while allowing for its continual refreshment.

Triss was with me, but nearly undetectable in the darkness since he chose not to insert himself in the process. Addressing the goddess was my challenge alone.

I tried to push earlier images of this place out of my head, to think only of the mission I wished the goddess to grant me. I tried to banish my memories of Alinthide's kila held high in the hands of the priestess before she cast it into the pool, but I just couldn't do it. Once again, the eyes of my heart followed the ghost of the spirit-dagger as it sailed through the air and landed in the water, watched as it sank with an unnatural slowness into the shaded deeps, stayed focused on the last place it had been visible, a sort of watery window into the darkness of death.

But this time, I found a sort of answer there in the peace of the grave and the stillness of deep water, a place I could lose all thought, even my sense of self. This time the thinking part of me plunged into the deeps, too, following a dead love into darkness and oblivion.

Time passed like a stream flowing through my mind. It could have been hours or minutes or days. Eventually, I raised my head. Now I faced Namara. An idol of polished granite, she seemed, risen from the deeps, cold and unmoving and yet somehow more alive than I could ever hope to be. No words passed her gray lips, nor expression touched the stone of her beautiful face, but I felt myself summoned. Without thinking or wondering, I stepped out onto the surface of the water, walking across it to meet my goddess.

From the waist down she was submerged, her lower half hidden in the darkness. Above, she was naked, her bared stone breasts hanging a few feet above my head, her six arms extended in front of her. Namara had come, risen from the deeps to accept me into her service.

I . . . how can I express it? Find a place on the side of a hill on a perfect summer evening. Lie back on the heather and look up. As the blue turns to red and then fades to black velvet, the stars spring out one by one. Imagine what it feels like to be the sky filling up with starlight and moonlight and liquid midnight and to know this is why you exist—to hold the beauty of the night. That's how I felt when I bowed before my goddess and accepted her blessing.

Namara's uppermost pair of hands held two daggers. The black kila that signified my service to the goddess was extended on the open palm of her right. Normally such magical blades would have glowed in magesight, but because this magic was divine, their light was hidden. The eye of my mission was gripped firmly in her left. Her middle pair of hands cradled twin swords, short and curved, unbreakable, unrusting, and forever sharp. With her lowest pair of hands she extended a tray that held the harness and sheaths of the three greater blades as well as many lesser knives and tokens, the hunting gear of the Blade.

First I took up the harness, sliding it over my shoulders and fastening the straps as I had been taught. It should have been wet, slippery, smelling of lake. It was dry and smooth and utterly devoid of any scent, even the faintest hint of fresh-cut leather. Then I took my swords, seating them firmly in their shoulder-draw rig and fastening the catches that would hold them in place.

Next I reached for the black steel of the kila. For the first time since the goddess had risen, I became aware of Triss as he flowed outward silkily along my arms so that we touched the spirit knife together. Clad now in shadow, I picked up the heavy black dagger with its tripled blade, clutching it in both hands.

"Wind and wave." I raised its point to the sky, then lowered it to touch the water. "Stone and heart's blood." I pressed the tip between the breasts of the goddess, then reversed it to prick the left side of my chest. "I bind myself to the will of Namara, her Blade forevermore." It flared brightly in mage-sight, then faded back to a normal dull black.

I lowered the kila to my side then, for there were only two possible sheaths for the spirit knife, and neither of them was a part of
the Blade's gear. Going to one knee before the goddess, I lowered my
head and closed my eyes.

"Command me."

*Ashvik must die for the horror he wrought in Kadesh and for his
crimes against his own blood and people in Zhan. Will you show the
tyrant that Justice never sleeps?* The voice seemed to come from everywhere and nowhere.

"I will," I said, though I did not yet lift my head.

Then take him the unblinking eye.

Now I looked up. The stone hand that held the short straight
dagger we called an eye was now open, though no sound had betrayed its movement.

I stood and took the eye. Pressing it to my lips, I whispered,
"For Ashvik," then slipped it into a downward-facing sheath fastened to one of the chest straps of my harness.

I looked one last time into the cool gray face of my goddess—
beautiful and utterly still, a form carved in stone and yet so very,
very alive. Then I turned and walked back across the waters to
shore.

I see her like that sometimes, in my nightmares, just for an instant. Then she becomes nothing more than a statue on the bottom
of the lake, dead granite bereft of all presence, the way she was the
last time I saw her. I start drinking early on the days that follow
such dreams.

Devin and Zass were waiting for us when we swam back from
the island. "That was fast," Devin said, when I stood up in the shallows. "I'm surprised you were even able to swim out and back. Did
Namara refuse you?"

I was too surprised by his words to speak, so I reached into the
basket and lifted out my kila by way of an answer. A sharply indrawn breath was his only response. Once I'd waded ashore, I set
the spirit knife aside while I pulled out the harness. This time the
collection of leather straps and sheaths dripped vigorously, and I
caught the faint scent of lake water as I started to buckle it into
place.

"How long was I gone?"

"A bit more than an hour," replied Devin. "You're a faster swim-
mer with that basket than I would be. And that must have been the
shortest investiture vigil in the history of the order. Did you sprint
from shore to pool?"

"No. It felt like I was there for ages and ages, much longer than I was gone, even without the swimming." I snapped my last buckle into place and rolled my shoulders to make sure everything was hanging properly. "Are you certain it's only been an hour?"

Devin nodded, and I thought I saw Zass do so as well though he was nearly invisible in that light. "Perhaps the goddess bent time for you," said the Shade. "Triss?"

My familiar poked his head over my shoulder, and I felt his shadowy scales rub my cheek. "I don't know. Whatever happened, I was inside it and felt nothing. But time is running now, and we have to be quick if we want to avoid days wasted in arguing with the masters."

As usual, Triss was right. I scooped up the kila again and turned to Devin. "Will you come with me to witness the ceremony?"

His teeth shone white in the dark, marking a brief smile. "Of course."

It was easy enough for two Shade-cloaked boys to slip past the priest attendants at the door to the inner temple and move on from there to the Sanctuary of the Blades undetected. We paused there at the entrance to draw aside the shadows over our eyes and look for any senior Blades within. I couldn't see anyone, but that meant less than it might in any other place. Blades often paid Namara their respects or made prayers while hidden in shadow.

Still, as a new-forged Blade, I had both the right and the duty. Signaling my intent to Triss with a gesture, I stepped across the threshold and out of his shadow. The sanctuary was a large, domed oval with tapered ends, perhaps thirty feet across at its narrowest and entered by doors at either end.

Over the very center of the room was a circular skylight open to the weather. Underneath the opening lay a wide circle of lapis lazuli with a great sphere of obsidian sunk in its center. From above and in concert with the white oval of the dome, it presented the aspect of a great unblinking eye with the globe as its pupil.

Walking quickly but silently as I had been taught, I crossed from the door to the edge of the lapis band, where I knelt briefly and bowed my head to the orb. I couldn't tell whether Devin had accompanied me in shadow or if he hung back a bit, somewhere behind me, and I realized that it didn't really matter. Not that or the presence of any other Blade. This was between me and my goddess.

Rising, I approached the chest-high sphere. The obsidian was smooth and polished. I could see my own face in a reflection clearer than the lake on the calmest day. The only thing marring the perfection of the stone was the hilts of the kila standing out from the surface here and there. Unlike pitons hammered into rock, they looked as though they'd been simply slid into the orb as cleanly as the sharpest stiletto going into an unprotected back.

I looked for the place where the high priestess had withdrawn Alinthide's spirit knife, but there was no hole to mark its passing and I could only make a rough guess. Bending forward, I kissed the stone where I thought it had been and whispered a prayer for her soul. Then I lifted my own kila high over my head and drove it down toward that same spot with all the strength in my body.

I had seen the investiture of other Blades several times in the past. But some part of me still expected the black steel to glance away from the black stone with a ringing sound and a shower of sparks, braced for the shock of that impact to transmit itself up my hand and arm to my shoulder, anticipated numbness and pain and the shame of failure.

None of that happened. The kila went into the sphere as neatly and smoothly as a practice thrust going into the throat of a hog or goat—when the cooks needed an animal slaughtered, it was always done by a trainee. It slid in until the guard touched stone, then stopped smoothly. But when I tugged at the hilt briefly before releasing my grip, the blade felt as firmly planted as if it had been welded in place. There it would remain until I died, and some future priest or priestess came to return it to Namara. Or so I believed at the time.

I was wrong.

11

It's funny how two disparate moments in time can become forever tied together by memory and pain. I can't look back on the transcendent joy of the night of my investiture as a Blade without also seeing what came later. It's part of why I try never to think about something that was once one of my most important memories.

When I do let the memories loose, it's impossible for me to revisit the moment when my kila joined me to the goddess through her great orb without also returning to the day five years later, when I came home from a mission and found the temple in ruins and my goddess murdered. In one memory, the orb sits in the heart of the temple, whole and symbolically wedding the goddess to her Blades through the marriage of stone and steel. In the other, the orb is cracked and ruined, a broken stone promise lying just outside the temple gate. The kila were pried loose and carried off to lie at the feet of the Son of Heaven.

I've been told that the knives of the last few living Blades are sunk in the back wall of the Son of Heaven's privy, where the man can piss on them each morning. I don't know if that's true, but I do know that several of the surviving masters died trying to recover the lost kila over the last five years. I wonder if the Son pulled their blades out when they died and let them splash into the depths below. It would have a certain sort of obscene symmetry, wouldn't it?

Pain from the cramping of clenched muscles drew my attention back to the now. I pushed even the thought of memory aside for a moment, forced myself to see only the library and the present. It was that or go and find a bottle of Kyle's, knowing I wouldn't stop drinking till I hit the bottom. I wanted that drink, I wanted it so very badly, and I might have gone looking for it if not for my debts to the living and dead. That, and my unspoken promise to Triss, not to give up drinking—I hadn't the strength for that—just to stop being a drunk.

I went to the balcony and looked out over the city. It was dark and still, almost quiet here at the nadir of the day in a wealthy part of town. It was a few hours yet before the delivery people and the house servants responsible for feeding the well-to-do would start to make their scurrying pre-breakfast rounds. A sharp contrast with the Stumbles or Smuggler's Rest, neighborhoods where things never quieted down completely.

Places like the Gryphon and the Spinnerfish never closed. The night traders needed havens where they could meet and eat. The whores and their clients wanted dark corners and beds by the hour. And always, always, always in those neighborhoods there were damned souls in need of a drink. That last was half of why I'd taken a room there once upon a time.

Turning away from the balcony and its doorway on the night, I pried my hands loose from the death grip they'd taken on my shoulders and prepared to dive back into the deeps of my own past once again. I didn't want to go there, but I still hadn't gotten what I needed, and I didn't know where else I could find it.

Turn back the years and find . . .

After I'd placed my kila in the great orb, a voice came out of the darkness, and it hadn't belonged to Devin.

"Ashvik?" Master Kelos had asked.

"Ashvik," I'd answered, ready to argue with him. "For the goddess and for Alinthide."

"Good hunting," was all he'd said.

I'd nodded and turned back toward the door. I saw neither Kelos, nor Devin, though as I went out into the hall, a hand had briefly squeezed my shoulder. Another had placed a small fat purse in my hand. Devin and Kelos? That's what I'd believed at the time, but things that came later make me wonder if both weren't Kelos.

But that wasn't the memory I needed right now. Perhaps I could find it in my first visit to Tien, in the months leading up to the night I killed a king. During the first few weeks, I'd tried to catch him away from the palace, twice at the Marchon place when he went to bed his mistress, once on a progress through the Duchy of Jenua, and another time when he met with his brother Thauvik at military headquarters. Each time I'd been thwarted by the Elite and their stone dogs, unable to get within even a long bowshot of the king.

Ashvik was guarded too well. I began to understand why Alin-

thide and the others had died. It should have been frightening, or, at
the very least, sobering. Instead, I found it the reverse. The challenge
intoxicated me. *I* was going to succeed where the great had failed. I
was going to deliver justice to the tyrant. I was going to prove the
power of Namara to the world. All that because only I could, and
because she had chosen *me*, and most of all because I was the best
there was.

I was an arrogant fool. I was lucky. I was also right.

At that time and for that situation, I really was the best in the
world, and that was why the goddess had chosen me for the mission. I won't lie to myself and deny it, but neither will I lie to myself
about my sins of arrogance and ignorance. Being one of the world's
best at anything is a funny sort of situation. It's a bit like walking
along a fence top between two very deep pits. On the one side is
overconfidence, on the other self-doubt. A misstep in either direction can set you up for a fall into ruin. And lying to yourself is one
of the easiest missteps to make.

That's part of why I say that I was the best, because it's the
truth. I was, for a year or two. I'm not anymore, not with what I've
become. For that matter, I wouldn't be even if I were the Kingslayer
still, not if Siri the Mythkiller is alive at any rate. She took the honors from me when I was at my best and held the title for a little less
than half a decade before the temple fell, which isn't a quarter so
long as Kelos held it fifty years ago when he was in his prime.

But back then, I was so very, very good. I watched and I waited
and I worked my way ever closer to the king. First, I learned the
guard routines in the grounds, penetrating a little closer to the castle every night, slipping past dogs and guards, groundskeepers, and
courtiers out for clandestine fucks in the gardens.

When I could come and go as easily as any shadow in the night,
I moved in closer, entering the castle proper, moving through the
halls, burrowing my way steadily deeper. It took a month and a half
from when I started to sniff out the palace's secrets to finding my
doorway into the Grand Tower where the royal apartments lay.

The details don't really matter except in the broadest sense. I
could enter the grounds any of a dozen ways, up through a culvert,
over the walls in five places, through the main gates with the non-
resident courtiers, in by the postern with the deliveries . . .

From there my path narrowed. Only three routes into the castle
proper left me in a good position to approach the Grand Tower. Via
the kitchens and up the shaft of the dumbwaiter to the monarch's
informal dining chamber, hanging in wait in the rafters of the

audience hall after the court had retired, or trailing behind the shift change of the Crown Guard as they made their way from the barracks to their positions around the outer perimeter of the Tower.

All had their problems. The route from the audience hall was long and heavily guarded. The dumbwaiter was a rat trap, hard to climb undetected and easy to seal if they spotted us. Trailing the guards meant treading very close behind the soldiers and the pair of Elite who officered them for close to ten minutes, plenty of time for the stone dogs to hear an extra pair of feet.

Unfortunately, that last was also the best route because of timing. The Crown Guard's officers checked in with the Elite providing internal security for the Grand Tower while their own men took up position. Likewise, the exiting troop's Elite checked in then. It gave everyone an important chance to compare notes. It also gave Triss and me a brief window when there was no exterior Elite presence covering the wall where the gate from the pleasure gardens entered the Tower.

The gate itself was hopeless, but a fast climber with the right equipment could make it up the outside of the wall to a small overhung niche between the supports of a fifth-floor balcony, and he could do it before the Elite lieutenant who supervised the gate finished his conference with his fellows.

The first time we'd made the climb, I'd bored two small holes in the mortar where the stone corbels met the wall—completely invisible from the ground level—so that I could set a pair of anchors whenever I wanted. Of course, by the time I was done, the lieutenant had arrived, so Triss and I had to wait for the next shift change to descend. But that was the whole point of the anchors, they allowed me to hang a narrow rope sling between the corbels like a sailor's hammock. There we could lie safe while I observed the security arrangements.

An awful lot of a Blade's job involves sitting and waiting.

Killing someone is relatively easy if you don't care about who sees it happen or about getting away. No security is so good that it can keep out a determined professional assassin willing to die to reach his target. Fortunately for the people who guard kings, there are very few professionals interested in dying for the job. Even among the Blades.

I know that the stories paint us as fanatical assassins totally devoted to the goddess and ready to martyr ourselves at Namara's whim. That's true enough, but it's also beside the point. If Namara had ever asked one of her Blades to go on a suicide mission, I don't think any of us would have refused the goddess, or even resented the order. But the goddess never asked. If you'd questioned me about that back in the day, I'd have told you it was because she loved her Blades and would never allow unnecessary harm to come to us.

Again, that would be true but largely beside the point, because it's only one truth. Another is that children with the right sort of mind-set to become a Blade are few and far between. Those with the mind-set and both the familiar and the mage gifts are even rarer. The Shades are quite picky about who they will bond with— probably two-thirds of the children presented to them are turned away. Finally, it takes more than a decade of training to make even a novice Blade. The goddess can't afford to throw a single one away.

Which is why Triss and I spent four hours hanging in a scrap of silk over a multistory drop, chewing carefully measured-out efik beans while I watched and listened. If we were going to get away clean after I killed the king, we needed to get in clean. That meant watching and waiting and thinking and planning. It also meant dealing with the permanent ward built into the tile mosaic of the balcony.

Permanent wards come in two types, keyed and unkeyed. Keyed wards react only to people who haven't been spelled into their memories. Unkeyed wards react to everybody. In both cases, it's basically impossible for a person to cross the ward without triggering it. That's why people generally don't bother to hide them; they're as much a warning as a barrier. When people do try to cross them, what happens when the ward is triggered is limited only by the power and imagination of the wardcaster.

Permanent wards are very dangerous. They're also stupid. They can't be adapted to changing conditions without a lot of work on the part of the wardcaster. Even just adding a new person to the key takes time and a good deal of power. Beyond that, if they're someplace like the balcony, where they're exposed to wind and weather, they can't be too sensitive.

You don't want a fifty-foot column of magical fire shooting into the air every time a passing pigeon lands for a minute or a couple of leaves blow across the balcony. That's hard on the nerves and trains guards not to pay attention to the wards when they trigger. If you do it enough, it drains the ward. At the same time, you don't want some clever mage with a pigeon for a familiar landing his companion safely on the ward to spy on you. So you make compromises. You set the ward to have a nasty but not flashy reaction if something living and smaller than a cat lands on it. You also set it to ignore leaves and other wholly dead stuff.

Say, for example, a piece of silk with weights sewn in all around the edges so it can be cast like a net. If you're really cautious, you'll build some sort of magic detection into the ward so that something with an active spell on it like an eyespy or hearsay will get the pillar-of-fire treatment. But say your piece of silk doesn't have an active spell on it, say it's just been prepared to be magically sensitive itself, and say that it works slowly. Now, that is *very* hard to detect.

So, for the last hour we were hanging under the balcony, a silken net lay atop it soaking up a perfect mirror image of the ward. When we got back to our snug, I took that sheet of silk, attached it to a prespelled mat of felt with Triss's help, and created a custom wardblack that would render the ward effectively blind.

That's how you penetrate really good security without getting caught: slowly, carefully, one custom-built piece at a time.

The second time we climbed the tower, I spent a good half hour lying flat on the wardblack with a tiny ear trumpet pressed to the iron-bound oak door before pulling a corner-bright out of my trick bag and slipping the end under the door so that I could peer inside. Like every aspect of this job, it was a risk, but a calculated one.

Take a strip of silver an inch wide and a bit thicker than a sheet of parchment. Tarnish it dead black, then polish the two ends up into tiny mirrors. Enchant it so that what one mirror sees the other shows. Now you have a way to see around corners and under doors. The magic involved is small, passive, and inherent to the device, which means it barely glows to the sorcerer's eye. The bigger problem comes from the mirrors. You can't do it without them, and mirrors shine, but a cornerbright's less risky than the alternatives.

Once the cornerbright revealed a dark and empty room, we slipped inside, where I pulled a tiny magelantern from my trick bag. I opened the directional shutters just enough to illuminate a narrow band in front of me. The stone was a dim one and dark red, so the light wouldn't be visible from any distance—a thieveslamp.

The beam revealed a small council room with a heavy wooden table, a half dozen chairs—including one meant to evoke the throne—and a small side desk where a secretary could stand. A floor below the king's apartments, the room provided a private venue to meet with a few trusted advisors. There were no windows, only the two heavy doors. The one leading into the tower was flanked by a pair of shallow alcoves for guards.

Not a good place for an ambush. I might, barely, have contrived to sling myself under the table and wait there for the king to arrive. But even on the incredibly tiny chance that I succeeded in hiding out till he arrived and killing him with a dagger to the groin, I'd never make it out alive.

It would have been tempting to try something fancy with the royal chair and poison if I didn't know that Alinthide had been killed after trying a similar trick. There was no way the council room wasn't being checked for poison on a daily basis.

I might, if I were very lucky and very stupid, be able to get Ashvik with a poisoned dart from the edge of the balcony, if the door happened to open at the right time, and I wasn't spotted from below, and there was no one sitting in the nearer chair to block the shot. I couldn't make my move here. So I spent another long span with my ear to the inner door.

This time I had something to listen to. Every few minutes someone, or rather two someones, passed the door. First one way, then the other. One of the few real disadvantages the Elite had was that the stone dogs made a lot of noise once they came up out of the earth. No matter how graceful and gentle-footed you are, when you weigh a thousand-plus pounds, and your feet are made of stone, sneaking is not your forte.

The noises from the guard rounds suggested a short hall lay beyond the door, one with stairs at either end and a few doors the Elite had to check. The latter probably magically, or they'd have rattled the handles. After an hour or so of the routine, I decided I'd have to risk the cornerbright if I wanted to learn anything more. I waited until the stone dog had just passed, then slipped the tiniest edge of the device under the door.

I could see a narrow band of hallway and another door as well as the retreating backs of a young Elite lieutenant and his familiar. By tilting the strip as much as the narrow crack under the door would allow, I was able to follow their progress as far as the base of a set of stairs, where they waved upward—probably at a second Elite on the landing above. Then I pulled back the cornerbright before they could turn around and spy it.

I rolled onto my back beside the door and waited for the pair to pass again. The heavy, grating footsteps of the stone dog got closer and closer. Even though I knew it couldn't have sniffed me out, I had to work to keep my heart from speeding up.

Everything had gone fine so far. Everything was going fine. Everything would be fine. I repeated that to myself again and again. I even believed it.

Right up until the moment the stone dog's head came through the wall two feet above my face. My skin burned with cold as shock rolled over me like a powder-snow avalanche in Dalridia's mountains. Every muscle in my body went rigid—bone-deep reflexes that wanted me to jump and shriek warring with a lifetime's training in stealth.

The training saved me. Mine and Triss's. Rather than jerk away from those great stone jaws or reach for a knife to defend myself, I held my breath and froze. In that very same instant Triss burst outward from my skin, covering us both in his enshrouding darkness. The next few moments seemed to take as long as my entire life up to that point. I could hear the stone dog snuffling around a foot or two above my face, feel his cold, dank breath through the shadows that shrouded me every time he breathed out. I turned my head to the side so that he could not feel mine in return.

Moving as quietly as I possibly could, I slid a hand to the hilt of the eye of the goddess and slowly slipped it from the sheath on my chest, holding it ready. If I moved before it sensed me, I could probably drive the knife into the stone dog's neck. The eye was a magical blade like my swords, and the only weapon I could reach that had any hope of killing a stone dog.

In my mind's eye I pictured the positioning of the beast's head, lower now than when I had first seen it sliding through the rough stone surface of the wall like a seal surfacing in Tien's bay. My best chance for living out the night involved striking now, before it spotted me. But if I did that, my chance of completing the mission and killing Ashvik dropped to nothing, both because the Elite would be forewarned and because I would have profaned the eye of the goddess.

The snuffling grew louder as the dog's head dropped lower. I squeezed the hilt of the eye tight. Tighter. Stopped. Relaxed my grip. Both on the knife and my fear. The goddess had sent me on a mission. If I killed the stone dog now, I might live, but I would also fail in my charge. If I held still and left things in Namara's hands, she might see fit to allow me life and success both. More time slid by in heart-tearing slowness. The dog did not find me. Neither did it leave. Years seemed to pass. Then, with a noise like splashing mud, it was gone.

I slid the eye back into its sheath, drew my swords, and placed them at my sides. Then I reached a hand up and ran it across the stones of the wall where the dog's head had come through. They were unmarked. The shakes took me, and Triss returned to dragon form.

"Are you all right?" he asked, his voice anxious.

I nodded though I couldn't stop shaking.

"You'd better chew another bean," he said. "Efik'll help."

"It's too soon after my last one."

You had to be careful with straight efik. Too much, and it'd level you instead of leveling your nerves. Do that too often, and you might get to like it. Maybe you'd end up sitting in a back alley with the rest of the sleepwalkers, cutting stripes in your arms and rubbing powdered efik into the gashes. Maybe it'd kill you. But even after I stopped shaking I couldn't get my heartbeat to stop rabbiting. Finally, Triss opened my pouch and pulled out a bean. Holding it between claws of shadow, he offered it to me.

"Really, I think you need it."

I nodded and took the bean. Dropped it into my mouth, chewed slowly. In moments I could feel my calm returning, my heart's pace slowing. The stone dog and its master passed by on their rounds several more times, each without looking in. On the fourth round I rolled over again and slipped my cornerbright under the door though I did not resheathe my swords.

This time they were going the other way, down the stairs. They were gone for perhaps five minutes. Leaving the corner-bright exposed as I waited for the top of the returning Elite's head to appear coming up the stairs almost had me shaking again, but I needed to know exactly how long the hall would remain open. On his next trek downstairs I examined the ward of alarm that hung in front of the door across the hall—a simple temporary spell.

There are a lot of reasons to avoid the hassle of using a permanent ward. There's duration—you have a space you want warded only at night or only for a few hours each day. Creating a moving target—you want to keep changing things around so no one can make a wardblack. Adaptability—you want different results at different times, silent alert instead of immolation, or whatever. Timing out—you're using it as part of a system that involves guards, and you want it to make all kinds of noise if they don't check in with the spell every so often.

Whatever the reason, they're much harder to deceive than permanent wards. Take the one on the door. It would probably trigger if the Elite took ten minutes instead of five downstairs. It would certainly trigger if I opened the door, and it was inaccessible if I didn't. There were ways I could deal with that, but not without leaving signs of tampering.

That meant I couldn't go beyond this point until I was ready to go all the way. So I turned away and went looking for a better route in. But three more rounds of spying over the following week proved what I'd already guessed—it was the balcony and the council room or nothing, and I wasn't going to walk away without taking a shot. So, on a quiet afternoon in Harvestide I made my decision. It would be tomorrow.

I would kill the king or die trying.

12

Even though I'd managed to successfully slip into the Grand Tower previously, this trip felt different. Every noise was louder, every check and pause longer, every surprise more startling. Various techniques I'd learned to slow my heart and quiet my breathing helped. So did a carefully gauged series of efik beans chewed on the run. But I still felt as tight as an overdrawn bowstring by the time I reached the little council chamber.

After I'd shut the outer door, I laid my length on the floor and pressed my tiny ear trumpet against the crack of the inner door. I stayed there for nearly half an hour listening to the patrolling Elite, making sure the routine remained unchanged and working myself up to the next step. Once I felt sure of both the guard and the steadiness of my hands, I slipped the cornerbright under the door and did a final check on the hall and the door wards.

Everything looked the same, so I quickly fixed a pair of long leather straps across the width of the door and slid two thin wedges underneath it. The straps had been prepared using a simple spell of binding and stiffening that would keep them in place and rigid for some hours. One went just above the floor, and the other about a foot above that and an inch or so below the bottommost of the heavy iron bands that bound the thick oak planks together.

Next I drew a slim dagger and gestured Triss to action—unless something went wrong, there would be no speech between us until the end of the mission. At my sign, Triss slid down my arm and enveloped my hand and the dagger in a dense layer of shadow. Concentrating his presence most heavily along the blade's leading edge,

he exerted himself and created a knife-thin gate into the everdark—
not that I realized it at the time.

Placing the shadowed edge against the wood of the door a hairsbreadth below that bottommost iron band, I began to saw silently
away at the planks. I had to stop and wait out the passing of the guard
twice in that time. The seam, lying in the shadow of the iron band,
was nearly invisible, but the knife's tip was another story. When I
was done, I had converted the bottom foot of the door into a free-
floating horizontal plank held tightly in place by the wedges. Next,
I reattached it to the main body of the door with a second pair of
leather straps mounted vertically. These were shorter and more flexible, serving as hinges.

When the guard next went down the stairs, I quickly pulled out
the wedges, flipped my impromptu trapdoor open, and slid most of
my body out into the narrow hallway. Above me, the door ward
glowed peacefully away, untriggered because the door itself remained shut. I was really working against time now; the pass-through
I'd just cut simply couldn't be repaired without leaving traces any
mage could see.

Cracking the door across the way took much longer because I
had to duck back into the council room every time the guard came
back, and I couldn't rig it with straps until I was inside the second
room, out of sight of the guard. But eventually I had a second pass-
through rigged. This one opened into the sitting room of a large and
apparently vacant suite, probably belonging to the recently executed
crown prince.

Using my dim red thieveslamp, I quietly explored the apartment.
Beyond the sitting room lay a withdrawing room and a sleeping
chamber, all beginning to develop the empty smell that even the
best-kept vacant rooms start to acquire after a while. Most importantly, I found the garderobe. It was hidden behind a small door off
the withdrawing room.

In a less secure castle, such a privy would have been situated on
an outside wall and simply voided its contents into empty space.
Not in Tien Palace. Here, the broad ceramic pipe that angled back
from the hole in the marble bench disgorged itself into a central
shaft that led down through the building into the sewers below the
castle. For ease of cleaning—it wouldn't do to stink up the royal
quarters—the central shaft was big enough to easily accommodate
a man.

Were that shaft less carefully secured, it would have provided a

perfect route into the royal apartments. But it was simply too heavily guarded down in the deeps at the sewer level. Master Urayal had
demonstrated that by his death, and I had further verified it with my
own extensive explorations of Tien's undercity. But it wasn't the
shaft or the sewers I was interested in.

Working quickly, I levered up the marble bench with its central
hole and set it aside. Then, more tricky and more messy, I pulled out
the pipe. The former I left leaning against the garderobe wall. The
latter I tucked into the late prince's wardrobe. That opened a path
to the central shaft that a fleeing assassin could quickly and easily
take.

Next, I opened my trick bag and pulled out a good-sized smudge
candle, attaching it to the wall of the shaft as far down as I could
reach. Looking at it from above, I could just see the faint glow of the
spells that had been cooked into the wax and its half dozen wicks. I
was just pulling back when the glow was partially occluded as a
ragged and rotting hand reached up from below to catch at my wrist.

That momentary silhouette gave me a critical instant to set the
grip of my other hand on the lip of the privy above. Without that,
the sharp yank the reaching hand delivered would have tipped me
over the edge and sent me plunging headfirst down the long stone
shaft. Even so, it was a close-run thing. Pain hammered up my arm
as the bones of my wrist ground together in the inhumanly strong
grip of the thing lurking below. Then it started pulling.

I had to clench my jaw to keep from screaming as my right
shoulder tried to come out of its socket. It hurt even more when I
twisted my hand, grabbed its wrist in turn, and started to pull back.

"Triss!" I hissed. "Help me with this thing!"

Shadow surged down along my right arm to enclose both my
wrist and the hand gripping it in liquid night. Immediately, there
was an easing of the pressure. At the same time, tendrils of darkness wrapped themselves around my upper back and shoulders,
adding Triss's strength to my own as I fought to bring the thing up
into the garderobe. It fought back hard though it made no sound
other than a sort of dreadful scrabbling and scratching on the stones
of the shaft as I dragged it slowly up into the light.

"Ware!" said Triss, his voice soft but urgent. "It's going to—"

The thing suddenly stopped resisting, somehow managing to
launch itself up out of the throat of the garderobe, lunging for my
neck with its free hand. It met a shield of night and slid off without
finding its target and together we fell back against the door of the
garderobe and on out into the room beyond, knocking over my

thieveslight in the process. That caused the shutter to snap shut—it was designed to do so at the slightest impact—and plunged the room into complete darkness.

We landed hard with my attacker on top, its bony knees pressing into my ribs as it started to squeeze with its legs, but I was ready. Even as we'd gone through the door I had flicked my left arm, sending the knife in my wrist sheath sliding into my hand. Now I drove the slender blade up into the soft flesh in the hollow of the monster's right armpit.

It didn't even flinch as the steel went in to the hilt. Instead, it brought that hand back around for another grab at my throat. This time Triss couldn't keep it off, though he did manage to form a thick layer of himself into a sort of shadow gorget that kept the thing from crushing my throat outright. Between that and the band that was protecting my right wrist, there wasn't much Triss left to do anything else.

If the thing had been one-tenth as smart as it was strong, Ashvik's defenses would have accounted for their fourth Blade that night. But once it had a grip on my throat, it seemed to forget entirely that that left me a free arm. Reaching back over my shoulder, I drew one of my swords—the guard dragged along the floor as I did so, making a grating noise that seemed horribly loud by comparison to the near silence of our fight so far.

With purple starting to flash around the edges of my vision as its scissoring legs slowly squeezed my lungs empty, I brought the sword around and lopped its head off. For three long beats of my heart, I thought it was going to keep right on squeezing, but then the pressure eased, and it slumped forward onto my chest. Whether it was the beheading or the virtue of the goddess's sword that did for it, I couldn't say.

What I really wanted to do just then, more than anything, was collapse in a heap for a few minutes and then go home to the temple. Instead, I put an arm on a dead shoulder and shoved. The thing came apart like a child's straw doll gone rotten.

"Triss, light," I husked.

A moment later, I had the thieveslight in my hand. I flicked it briefly over the corpse of my attacker—some variety of restless dead by the look of it. The people of the Kvanas dispose of their fallen by exposing them on tall platforms. What the crows don't take quickly stiffens and dries into the consistency of jerky.

This thing looked liked six months on the drying rack. The general state of decay marked it as one of the risen—mistakenly called zombies by some—and a devilishly clever move on Ashvik's part. Not only dangerous on its own, but also for the curse it carried. Without the protections the goddess wove around her Blades, I might already be on my way to becoming this thing's replacement. I shuddered and said a quick prayer of thanks to Namara.

I still see it in my nightmares occasionally, but at the time I put the horror aside in a little box, as I had been taught. *It is acceptable to feel fear, it is folly to hold on to it.* Then I went to listen at the door to the withdrawing room to see whether the fight had attracted the attention of the patrolling Elite. But it had been fast and it had been quiet and I got lucky. No one came.

I looked back over at the corpse and noticed that it now looked like ten months a-drying. I put a heel on the exposed end of a thigh-bone and started to shift my weight. It gave off a distinct sewer smell as it powdered, and I decided that maybe I'd leave the shit-soaked risen out of the story if I ever got to tell it to anyone. Class it with magical defenses and call it an animate ward maybe.

But that was getting ahead of myself. I had a job to do, so five minutes later I was back in the damn garderobe. After making sure the smudge candle remained in place—thank Namara for small favors, it did—I made quick use of the hole. The encounter had rather forcefully reminded me of my bladder—fear will do that. Then I stepped up onto the lip of the privy. That put me high enough to rub a potion into the plaster of the ceiling over an area a couple of feet across.

It made more noise than I'd have liked as it liquefied and slowly dropped onto the rug, but there was no avoiding it, and at least it was quieter than the damned risen had been. When enough plaster had dissolved away, I attached another set of trapdoor straps to the planks of the floor above, this time making sure to set a latch.

Time pressed ever more heavily on my shoulders. Like the pass-throughs I'd cut into the outer doors, the dissolved plaster left a trail that couldn't be erased. Still, I listened carefully for several minutes before I started cutting into the planks above. This time I used one of my swords so I could cut faster. As soon as I had a big enough opening, I blacked out my thieveslamp and unspelled the latch, easing the trapdoor open. There was a gentle fluttering noise and a light thud as the rug dropped through from above. I was in.

Thankfully, it was as dark above as below. I reopened my lamp then and affixed a sheet of paper with a ward of fire to the hanging edge of the trapdoor. Then I leaped and caught the lip, pulling myself up into the king's garderobe. Even with the hole in the floor, the space felt stuffy because of the tightness of the door's seal. That was one of the many reasons I'd taken the risk with the pass-throughs rather than just cutting through the ceiling of the council room.

Garderobes had thick, well-set doors intended to spare noble noses. Those same features meant they also spared noble ears from the noises of my entry. They also stacked. There was no way of knowing what lay above the council room, but because of the placement of that central sewer shaft, the garderobes had to be built one above the other, and the suite above my original entry point belonged to King Ashvik.

With my feet straddling the hole in the floor, I pressed my ear trumpet against the door. I wanted nothing more than to act fast, but I had to know if there was an Elite bodyguard stationed in the withdrawing room. I thought the sitting room a much more likely choice, and a niche in the hall just outside the royal suite most likely of all, but I wasn't going to let incaution ruin me at this point. Only after I felt sure of the room beyond did I ease the door open.

The withdrawing room was dark save for a thin line of light coming under the door that corresponded to the bedchamber in the room below. I was at the most dangerous stage of my mission, with the king likely sleeping behind one door and Elite bodyguards and stone dogs possibly behind the other. The temptation to go for the king as quickly and quietly as possible was almost overwhelming. Instead, I drew my left-hand sword and forced myself to listen at the door to the sitting room. There I heard . . .

Nothing.

It was empty. I checked the eye the goddess had given me for the king. It was loose in its sheath, ready to find a home in a royal heart. I crossed to check the door to the bedchamber. Faint noises of habitation came from within, little creaks of the sort furniture made when you shifted position, the occasional deep breath . . . the king was in, and likely awake. The door opened away from me and was hinged on the left side, so I switched to my right-hand sword.

Now!

I turned the handle and quickly pushed the door open. Ashvik was sitting on the edge of a chaise, facing a window that looked out over the palace, his back to me.

"I told you I was *not* to be bothered," he growled without even turning my way. "If you're here for anything less than an invasion from Kodamia, I'll have you boiled alive. Maybe in the bath right here." He pointed at a big red marble tub in the corner.

I slipped my second sword free of its sheath.

"Well," he demanded, "spit it out. Why have you come?"

"To bring you justice."

"What!" Ashvik spun in his seat. "I—"

His words ended in a rasping gurgle as I plunged one sword into his chest and the other into his throat. For a couple of heartbeats his eyes blazed hate at me, but then, as easily as a sheep slaughtered for the table, he died. I don't know what I had expected to happen at that point, a suddenly hammering alarm, a great cloud of evil smoke rising from the corpse, wild cries of celebration? Whatever the answer, I didn't get it.

Ashvik VI, King of Zhan, Butcher of Kadesh, and murderer of his own royal sons simply slumped gently backward and slid off my blades, and I felt nothing.

As I had been taught, I flicked the swords to clear the blood, then resheathed them at my back. Next I arranged the dead king on the chaise as though he were sleeping. I took the Eye of Namara from its sheath and sank it deep into Ashvik's chest, making sure that the blue lapis eye on its pommel stared straight at the door. And still, I felt nothing, not even satisfaction at a task well done.

With a lesser villain, the goddess might have given me a scroll detailing the man's wrongdoing to leave at the scene of the execution. But Ashvik's crimes were great and known to all. His next life would not be a good one.

Turning away from the body, I left the room and closed the door behind me, never looking back. In the withdrawing room, I used magic to lock the king's bedroom door. Then I took a second paper ward from my bag and put it in place across the outer door. This one would howl like the wolf of the underworld when the paper tore. Then into the garde-robe, shut the door, drop down, seal the trap with the fire ward, and on through the dead prince's apartments. Five minutes after the death of the king, I was back in the small council chamber, sealing the door to the hall with the last of my spelled straps. They wouldn't stop the Elite and their stone dogs, but they'd buy me a few precious seconds each.

Taking a small risk, I slipped out onto the balcony and tucked myself up against the railing in a shadowy corner. Now I just needed the body to go undiscovered for the hour or so until the next shift change gave me a chance to slip out without being spotted by the Elite in the courtyard below. It was hard to fight the impulse to just go now, but my chances of getting away clean would go up dramatically if I was patient.

Haste kills.

After about ten minutes, the enormity of what I'd just done started to sink in. Not the part about killing my first man, that particular horror wouldn't hit me until months later, when I first had to kill a guard. No, for me on the balcony that night, Ashvik wasn't yet human. He was simply evil.

What I started feeling then was another thing entirely, religious ecstasy riding atop a golden wave of triumph. My goddess had set me a task, and I had succeeded where three older and more experienced Blades had failed. Namara had put her faith in me, just as I put my faith in her, and for her I had removed a monster from the world. More, I had done it clean without being spotted or harming a living soul other than my target. The risen, being neither alive nor possessing a soul, I felt I could discount.

Though it took months for the name to attach itself to me, I was in that moment more Kingslayer than I would ever be again. I really and truly believed in myself as some kind of invincible weapon of justice in the hand of Namara. I *knew* I was going to rid the world of evil. The feeling lasted about thirty seconds.

That's how long it took before my alarm ward got triggered. A single hellish howl from above alerted me that someone had just entered the royal withdrawing room. Which meant I needed to go, middle of the guard shift or not. I rose into a crouch and peered down through the rails of the balcony, waiting for the general alarm to go up and counting seconds in my head. The call would bring chaos in its wake, brief but exploitable, and I wanted to wait until that happened if I had the time, hence the count.

One. Two. At three, the Elite who had set off the ward would have crossed the room and tried the king's door. He wouldn't bother knocking, not with my ward howling away. *Four.* At five he would break the door in. *Eight. Nine.* By ten he would have checked the body and found it still warm though not warm enough. After that, things got fuzzier. *Eleven.*

If I was lucky, the Elite would make a quick search and find the trapdoor I'd cut in the garderobe floor before sounding the alarm. *Seventeen.* Opening it would trigger my fire ward and light the smudge candle I'd left in the waste shaft. *Nineteen.* The logical conclusion then would—My thoughts were interrupted at *twenty* by the sound of a door crashing open a floor above me and halfway round the tower.

A magically augmented voice cried out, "Assassins in the sewers!"

A half second later, alarm trumpets started blaring out all over the palace—more magic. The Crown Guards below me had begun looking around anxiously in the first seconds after the howl of my ward. But their Elite commander, a young lieutenant, had held his ground with complete professionalism, keeping his area under tight watch. Now he started barking orders though he didn't move otherwise.

There was no way he'd miss me blotting out the stars as I sail-jumped across the courtyard above him nor fail to see me when he looked up, but I couldn't wait for a better opportunity. I stood, took two running steps, jumped, and launched myself from the rail of the balcony, spreading my arms wide and commanding Triss to spin us wings of shadow.

I traded a two-story drop for about seventy feet of horizontal glide to land on the curtain wall that separated the Grand Tower from the main palace. At that point, I had to make a sudden change of plans when what looked like half the Zhani army stampeded out of their barracks and into the middle of my exit strategy. I'd intended to make another sail-jump down to the grounds and leg it for the outer wall, but I didn't think gliding into a seething mass of armed soldiers would do much for my long-term survival prospects.

Instead, I turned and ran along the top of the wall to the farther of the two towers it connected, the one that housed the royal kitchens. From there, I started working my way toward the formal ballroom. That's when I ran into an Elite lieutenant named Deem and his stone dog—name unknown. I won the pass but almost lost a leg in the process.

The rest of my trip out of the palace went by in a sort of nightmare blur. At Triss's insistence, I took a couple of extra efik beans to help ward off shock while he clamped a bandage of shadows over the gashes on my calf and heel. Of course, he had to thin himself out everywhere else to do so, and that made me a whole lot less invisible. Combine that with the attention summoned by the wild grating howls of the fallen lieutenant's stone dog and the deep tearing pain in my leg at every step, and I honestly can't tell you how I managed to come out the other end in one piece.

I don't even remember how I got from there to the snug I'd set up as my fallback in case I couldn't get out of Tien immediately after the execution. I'd like to say that Namara guided and guarded me, and I know I thought so at the time. But these days I've come to doubt that the gods intervene so directly. If Namara were that powerful, why did she need us to act as her hands? No, the answer is probably Triss, whispering in my ear and guiding my steps in the right direction, just as he so often has.

My snug was an attic storeroom in a great house not too far from the palace. It belonged to an out-of-favor viscount who had removed himself to his country estates for "health reasons." In other words, he thought it healthier to stay far away from the king, whose displeasure he'd incurred. The place had only a skeleton staff for the duration, and the room I'd adopted as my own chiefly held storm shutters and other winter necessities.

I spent the next several days wandering the edges of delirium, waking only now and then to chew a few efik beans handed me by Triss and wash them down with tepid water out of a skin I'd cached the week before—I didn't have the energy to brew up a proper pot. I would have recovered a lot faster if I could have put my teeth to the dried fruit and jerky I'd left with the skin instead of all that efik, but for the first time in my life, I simply had no appetite.

I felt terribly weak and shaky when I finally decided to venture out on the fourth day, but I'd run out of beans the night before, and I needed efik then more than I've ever needed alcohol since. Wrapping bandages around my torn calf made the flesh feel like I'd poured boiling water over it. Up to that point, Triss had kept my wounds bound in his own shadow-stuff, providing another of the many benefits to partnering a Shade. For reasons we didn't understand, that proximity to the everdark cooled and soothed as well as any snowpack while simultaneously warding against wound rot.

When I felt up to moving, I slipped downstairs to the master's quarters. There I borrowed a beautifully made but long-out-of-fashion suit of court clothes from the depths of a wardrobe that looked like it might not have been opened in the last century. Green and gold silk patterned with water tigers and twining vines, cut loose for ease of dueling. It was part of a set with a beautiful, if antiquated, matching court dress that had no doubt belonged to the lady of the house. I also found a pair of overlarge riding boots that accommodated my bandages though I had to pack the other boot with rags to make it fit.

Sandals or light court shoes would have been more appropriate considering the weather and my attire, but I didn't want to advertise the fact that I had a badly ripped-up leg right at the moment. Not after leaving so much blood and a boot behind in the palace. Besides, if I stole a shabby enough horse, the boots and the unfashionable clothes would blend right into a cover identity as some noble's down-at-the-heels rural cousin. Though I'd also need to do some careful work with cosmetics if I wanted anyone to believe I was a Zhani noble from anything closer than a few yards away.

Getting one of the cart horses saddled and out of the stables was easy enough once I'd set the mulch pile on the far side of the house afire. Everything but my swords packed down into the saddlebags with room to spare. After I removed the guards, the swords slid easily into a pair of thick bamboo tool handles I'd prepared for the purpose.

As I rode out onto the road in front of the estate and turned left toward the palace, Triss hissed quietly in my ear.

"Where are we going?" he asked.

"Little Varya," I whispered back.

"That's on the wrong side of Tien!" His voice rose, and I made a quelling gesture.

"That's what they'll be thinking, too, if the search hasn't already moved out of the city. If the lieutenant lived, he'll have told them it was a Blade. They'll be watching the roads to Kodamia, so I'm going to go south along the coast into the Magelands. Then I can cross the mountains through the high passes at Dalridia. It'll take longer, but it's less risky."

"Except for the part where we have to ride so close to the palace."

"I need efik for the trip home, Triss, and Little Varya's the only place in Tien I can get it. My leg's still pretty bad."

Triss hissed. "True, though I wish it wasn't. All right. But we'll have to be quick about it."

I nodded. "Really, Triss, it'll be fine. I'll be fine." But if I didn't get another bag of beans soon, I was going to shake myself to pieces. "I know what I'm doing."

13

Maybe the past did hold the keys to the present. I hadn't found my lost self in my memories—though the quivering efik addict who'd just killed a king had all too much in common with the drunk wearing that same skin today. But I did know exactly where to look for Devin now, and for that I could thank the efik. It was funny, really, that when I'd been a Blade, it had never occurred to me to think of efik as anything other than a tool of my trade. A dangerous one, to be certain, but just another tool I used.

Even when I'd given up efik after I came back to Tien, I hadn't seen it as more than that. I'd quit because the old Aral, Aral the Kingslayer, drank efik when he could get it and chewed the beans when he couldn't, just like all the other Blades. And every damned bean provided another reminder of the life the Son of Heaven had stolen from me. At the same time, Aral the Kingslayer had never touched alcohol.

So, when it came time to let the Kingslayer go, to really become Aral the jack, I drank myself unconscious every day for a week. It was the best method I could see for making a break between the two lives. It had honestly never occurred to me that I was just swapping one drug for another. Looking back now with the eyes of a drunk, I could see that back then I wasn't all that different from the sleepwalkers with their razors and efik-crusted scabs. Still wasn't in some ways, no matter that Triss had approved of my efik habit and hated my drinking.

I hadn't touched efik since then, but I remembered exactly how it tasted and how it made me feel, and I knew exactly where to find it. I knew how much it sold for by the mug and the ounce, and when the shipments came in from Varya, and which smugglers made the deliveries. Because efik was moderately illegal in Tien, there were only three alley-knockers where you could find a proper cup or pick up a bag of roasted beans.

All three of the illegal taverns were in Little Varya. If Devin wanted efik, that's where he'd have to go to find it, and that's where I'd find him. It's a good thing that most of the world had known so little about the habits and workings of the Blades back in the day, or people like the Elite would have known right where to look to find us. But the Blades had always been rare—a few hundred in a continental population that ran into many tens of millions—and more a matter of legend and speculation than anything real for most people. Beyond that, the power of Namara had blurred the memories of those few who did encounter one of us.

Figuring I'd have better luck traveling light and fast, I left my larger pack behind in the chimney of the Ismere Club. It'd be safe enough there, and none of the stuff in it would matter to me this side of setting up a new snug. As I stepped out onto the library's little balcony, I turned and looked over the river flowing by on my left. A thought occurred to me.

"Triss, could you follow a shadow across running water?"

"I don't think so. Not for long, anyway. Water will hold the—" He hissed something in his own language. "When we used to play tag on the lake's surface on a very still night, Zass and I and the other Shades could follow each other easily enough across the surface. But in a wind or on a river, the movement of the water would break up the"—hissing—"too quickly."

"I was hoping you'd say that."

The Zien River bisected Tien, entering between two of the hills that held the wealthier neighborhoods and exiting by way of the harbor. In the lower parts of the city, several long canals extended the reach of boat traffic outward from the hub where river met bay. By stealing a dinghy, I was able to slip from the river into the Channary Canal, which took me right to Little Varya's doorstep. A slower route than the chimney road, but not by much, and the advantages of leaving no trail more than made up for the lost time.

"It feels strange to be looking for efik again after all these years," Triss said in a very quiet voice. "It's almost like the old days."

"We're not looking for efik. We're looking for Devin. Now hush.

We don't want anyone noticing me talking to myself and answering back in another voice."

I stretched then and rolled my shoulders before reluctantly reaching for the oars again. It was unusual exercise for me, and every pull reminded me forcefully of the cut Weasel had made across the back of my ribs. None of my other injuries liked it much either, but it was the ribs that made me sweat.

Even at this hour, the river and canals carried a lot of traffic. Farmers bringing in early vegetables and greens from the southwest— bok choy, pea pods, baby daikon . . . Fishermen hauling the late catch upriver to restaurants and great houses. Shippers moving loads they didn't trust to the crush of the day traffic. And, of course, the smugglers pretending to be one or another of the other sorts of traffic. The rain had stopped, but it was still cloudy and dark as the inside of a miser's wallet—perfect smuggling weather.

Twice as I made my way toward Little Varya, customs cutters slid in close and played their big magelanterns over my boat. But there was nothing to see except for me, my shadow, and a tiny pack tucked under the thwart. That last might possibly have gotten me stopped and briefly searched on a slow night, but not now. Not with so much bigger game on the prowl. Still, it was a relief to slip into the quiet waters at the foot of the Channary Canal.

The canal ended at the base of the Channary Hill, in an artificial bay where the nobles living at the top of the slope kept a small but fancy marina. A narrow brick lane ran along the western shore, marking the edge of Little Varya, and it was there that the first alley-knocker lay. From the water's surface, the whole area looked almost empty in the small hours of the morning, almost bleak, much quieter than the open waters behind me.

I rowed us in to shore on the west side of the canal a few yards short of the marina gates, where things looked considerably less fancy. I didn't bother to tie up because the last thing I did before hopping onto the dock was to rake a shadow-edged sword blade along the bottom of my little boat, scuttling it. I didn't want to leave any ideas for Devin to pick up on if he hadn't already figured out the running-water trick.

Behind me, sewage-laced canal water fountained up through the great rent I'd made in the planks, raising a truly delightful smell. You could get a pretty serious fine for dumping shit in the water, but that didn't stop some people, and unlike the main river, the canals didn't have a steady flow to keep it all moving out to sea.

Before I'd made it the length of the dock, my little rowboat had already sunk to the gunnels. I'd have felt worse about that if I hadn't made sure to steal my dinghy from an ostentatiously rich yacht anchored in the river between the Ismere and the Palace Hill. The owners could afford the loss.

I paused at the foot of the dock and took a second look around, borrowing Triss's senses for a moment so that I could see beyond the end of my nose. I didn't spot anyone other than the dozing guard at the marina gate and a couple of day-working drunks staggering their way home from the taverns to catch a too-short sleep. It was just past four bells now, and the casual drinkers had gone home hours ago, while the night workers, both shadowsiders and sunsiders, had only just settled in to drink. That left the streets mostly empty. It was a marked change from the tens of thousands of people who would pour into the streets with the rising of the sun.

Normally, the relative emptiness would have made keeping an eye open for threats easier, but if Devin was around and enshrouded, I'd never know it until I stumbled into him or he struck. If he got it right, I'd never know another thing at all. With that in mind, I flipped my sword to an underhand grip and tucked it back against my shoulder rather than resheathing it. The darkened steel of the blade would blend well enough with the gray of my overshirt in this light. Both derived their shading from the juice of the oris.

As long as no one got very close or produced a too-bright magelight to shine on me, I could keep the sword in hand without alarming any potential passersby. Somehow that didn't make it any easier for me to climb up to the lane. I'd never had to worry about being stalked by a Blade before, and I didn't much like the idea. I did have the grace to wonder whether my own targets had felt that same little lead ball sitting in the bottom of their stomachs at the thought of an invisible assassin stalking them that I did now.

Probably. With a roll of my shoulders, I started forward, soft-footing my way up the half dozen stone steps that led from dock to lane. At the top, I turned right and headed for a narrow unmarked door wedged into an improbably short wall between a tailor's and a cobbler's. The door headed a steep stair that led down to the Cat's Gratitude. The illicit tavern occupied a low cellar filled with dim light, tiny tables, and people who'd rather not be recognized.

I didn't bother going inside, just walked past about six inches from the door while Triss had a bit of a sniff around. When he didn't signal me, I knew that we'd missed the mark, so I continued along my way till I hit a slim gap between two of the buildings fronting the lane.

When I turned in, the scuttling flight of a startled rat allowed me a moment's relaxation, signaling as it did an otherwise empty darkness. Not even a Shade could hide you from a rat's nose. A pass down the clogged and stinking snicket behind the alley-knocker yielded another miss. As I headed for the next alley-knocker—two blocks in from the canal and a couple farther north—the tension slowly returned to my back and shoulders. The only other soul I saw was the driver of a cart making the run from the Coast Road to the canal end with a dim oil lantern bobbing along just above his head to light the way.

The Manticore's Smile topped an old tannery. The bar and tables were hidden from curious eyes on the hill above by a bunch of tattered old sails dipped in oris and strung up awning fashion over the whole area. Because it was open to the air on all sides, I actually had to climb up and circle around the whole perimeter to let Triss check for Zass's spoor.

When I ordered a tucker bottle of Kyle's and a clean glass to give me an excuse to mingle with the other patrons, Triss gave me sharp pinch on the heel. I stumbled at that and had to bite back a snarl. What did he want me to do? Wander around empty-handed? Because that'd go down great with the management of an illegal club. Ask for a pot of tea?

The Manticore didn't sell anything but alcohol and things that made alcohol seem as tame as candy. I didn't really have a lot of options if I wanted something with an intact seal from a reputable distiller. So I silently promised Triss that I'd just have the one glass, and myself that I'd tell him about that promise as soon as I got to someplace we could speak again. Then I walked to the edge of the roof and pretended to look out over the city as I drifted along.

Twenty minutes later, I'd made the full circuit and drunk a glass and a half—I had a brief talk with Ashelia, an old smuggling acquaintance who thought she might have some business for me. Again, I didn't have much choice but to play friendly. Getting loose of her cost another half glass and a promise to look her up as soon as I finished my present job.

"Well?" I asked Triss as soon as I'd gotten clear of the rickety stairs that led back to the ground.

"Nothing," Triss said, his tone falling somewhere between

depressed and angry. "No Zass. No Devin. Nothing to make it worth the . . . effort involved."

I winced at the obvious message. "Look, Triss, I'm sorry about the Kyle's. I needed to be drinking something for cover purposes."

"So you bought a whole bottle?"

"In a place like the Manticore, you want to see the seal. Besides, it's a small bottle. And I was only going to have one drink."

"I counted two."

"That was because of Ashelia. If I hadn't kept drinking, she might have gotten suspicious."

"That *would* be out of character, now wouldn't it?"

I yanked the bottle out of the pocket I'd tucked it into and threw it over my shoulder to shatter on the cobbles.

"Happy?" I growled.

"Delighted," he snapped back.

"Good."

Without another word, I turned up the street and headed for the western edge of Little Varya where it butted up against the Down-unders as the Coast Road entered Tien. The Downunders had started out as a shantytown catering to the drovers and traders who dealt in goods and animals that were too cheap or otherwise un-suited for ship travel, and it had never really recovered from its squalid beginnings. The streets got narrower and dirtier as I got closer and closer to the Dead Man's Pouch, offering a thousand hid-ing places for a Blade waiting to strike. Once again, I slipped my left-hand sword free of its sheath to carry against my shoulder.

The Dead Man stood between a more reputable sort of tavern on its right and a flophouse on its left. A signpost without a sign hung over the front door in a subtle nod to the alley-knocker's name. In Tien, a dead man's pouch was usually gone before the body hit the ground.

The building leaned to the left, as though it wanted to have a lie down at the flophouse, or perhaps feared catching an incurable case of legitimacy from its other neighbor. The windows were boarded over, and several big planks appeared to have been nailed across the door as well, though the latter were just for show. You *couldn't* open the door from this side, but that was because of a huge iron latch that opened easily enough from the inside. Quite a few patrons left by the "front" door, though most entered by knocking on the alley-side door. Which was the origin of the term alley-knockers, also occasionally called three-knocks.

I'd just turned toward the pitch-black gap on the flophouse side when Triss slapped me sharply in the soles of both feet to let me know he'd tasted Devin's trail. I kept walking as if nothing had happened, though it took a huge effort of will not to look around or reach for my second sword. The narrow gap ahead suddenly seemed twice as dark, a perfect place for an ambush. As I walked, I edged to my left, steadily shifting my practically invisible shadow so that it reached out toward the gap ahead of me.

As soon as my shadow's head touched the near-absolute darkness of the space between the buildings I felt Triss flowing out and away from me, extending himself to invisibly check the whole of the narrow passage. A moment later, I got a reassuring squeeze on my left foot. The way was empty, both of Devin and his traces, but I didn't relax. He could still have set up with a crossbow in the courtyard that backed the Dead Man. The open area outside the main entrance provided a secluded place to park extra tables in the stifling heat of Midsummer and Sunshammer.

"We're clear," Triss whispered, when I stepped into the deeper shadows.

"The trace in the street out front, coming or going?" I asked.

"Going, and quite recently. It got stronger as it moved away from the Dead Man's Pouch, but I couldn't sense any hint of his arrival here."

"Let's circle round the main door then and see if Devin came in that way before we decide whether to follow him or see where his back trail leads."

A quick slide around the courtyard revealed that Devin had arrived by coming north across the roofs from the direction of the nastiest part of the Downunders. Looping back to the front of the alley-knocker, we checked Devin's departure trail, which headed north and west toward the Palace Hill and the bulk of the city.

So, follow Devin? Or see if we could find out what brought him to the Downunders? I didn't have time to do both, not with dawn less than two hours away. It was the hint of a double cross that decided me. If Maylien had told me the truth about being the true heir, then she represented a major threat to Baroness Marchon. That was a card that might come in damned handy for Devin in the event of a falling-out. The Downunders were very nearly as far away from the Marchon estate as it was possible to get without leaving Tien, well outside the baroness's easy reach. It was a perfect place to stash a backup plan.

Over the next hour, Triss and I painstakingly backtracked Devin two-thirds of the way across the rooftops of the Downunders looking for where he'd come from. It was slow, frustrating work. Between the many breaks in the trail made as Devin jumped across lanes, the various aches and twinges coming from my cuts and bruises, and the dilapidated nature of the buildings, I spent a lot of time swearing.

I must have put my foot through a half dozen roofs, and only just avoided doing so at least twice that many times more. Maybe the most annoying part of the whole thing came from knowing that Devin had probably made the trip in about ten minutes. At this point he could easily have finished his errand to the north and gotten back around in front of us again.

We'd come to a temporary halt atop a tiny temple tucked in tight against the base of the western bluff of the Channary Hill. Dedicated to Govana, goddess of the herds, the temple was built of sandstone blocks and much sturdier than the buildings around it. Devin's trail had come to an unexpected dead end on top of its small tower. We'd checked every roof within sail-jumping distance and found nothing but the trail we'd followed to get there.

"It's like he came up through the roof of the tower." Triss was flitting back and forth across the close-set stones, sniffing and tasting with his tongue. He'd shifted back to dragon form when we returned to the tower after our fruitless search of the surrounding buildings, and I didn't have the energy to argue with him about the wisdom of that. "That, or he simply dropped out of the sky."

"Now there's an unhappy thought." I glanced up at the bluff. "And one that should have occurred to me before you said something."

Seven or eight aging and out-of-fashion great houses hugged the cliff edge a hundred and fifty feet overhead, and that only counted the visible ones in easy sailing distance given the height. There were probably a dozen more out of sight that would have allowed Devin to make the jump to the temple. Unlike the houses around the palace or the Marchon estate, where the nobles and merchant princes kept the neighborhood exclusive, the Channary Hill great houses could belong to practically anybody.

All four of the hills of Tien had been colonized by the nobility over the thousand-plus years of the city's existence. The Palace Hill held the bulk of those still in use, with the Sovann Hill, where House Marchon stood, coming in a distant second. The abandoned great houses on the equally abandoned Kanathean Hill had long since been torn down, and their stones incorporated into the streets and homes of the Old Mews, Dyers Slope, and a half dozen other neighborhoods.

The Channary Hill was much more of a mixed bag. On the eastern slopes overlooking the ocean and the harbor, you could find quite a number of country nobles who didn't want to venture too deep into the evil city, intermixed with bankrupt city nobles clinging to these cheapest of Tien's great houses by their fingernails. While on the western bluff the remaining houses had a dusty popularity among social climbers who wanted to claim a palace view or shadow captains who needed a whiff of legitimacy for portions of their business.

In short, the place provided a perfect environment for a renegade Blade looking for a snug, as long as he had the funds. Knowing the money I could have made as a black jack, I had no doubt that the freelance-assassin business kept Devin solidly in funds. Time to start looking for the fastest way up the bluff.

"Come on, Triss, we'd better climb up and have a look."

"We don't have enough time to check even half of the houses before the morning sun burns off Zass's trail." Triss sounded gloomy.

"So we'll do what we can and hope we get lucky."

We didn't get lucky, at least not in terms of tracing Devin's trail back to its source. There were just too many jumping-off spots on too many great houses for us to have any reasonable chance of checking them all. Every third-story window on the bluff side provided a potential point of departure. It would have taken hours to search any single house and days to search them all, possibly longer. No, finding Devin's snug that way would have been virtually impossible. Finding the Crown Guard watching Devin's snug on the other hand . . .

Them, I practically tripped over. The first pair lay hidden in a hollow carefully excavated under the thickest part of a huge patch of imperial roses gone feral. I'd never have seen them if first light hadn't started me nosing around for someplace I could lie up for the coming day. I'd wanted to stay close and keep an eye on several of the better candidates for Devin's base of operations.

The dense rose thicket provided a good vantage on three of the five best choices, and I'd actually started to crawl into its depths when a small noise ahead warned me to freeze. The Crown Guards wore mottled green from head to toe, and green and brown paint on their faces. The only way I could even tell they were Crown Guard was by the dragon-crown insignia engraved on the deliberately verdigrised guard of the sword strapped across the nearer of the pair's back. It was clearly visible even in the predawn light, so close had I come before I saw them.

If not for Triss's enshrouding presence and the fact that I'd approached them from behind and with a good deal of stealth, they would certainly have seen me well before I spotted them. Even just crossing in front of them might have given me away if they were there waiting for Devin—and I had to assume they were. Trained soldiers actively lying in wait for a Blade would certainly have picked out light-colored sight points, and would be watching for any telltale obscuring darkness to pass between them and their marks.

They'd be just as happy to nail up my skin as Devin's—might not even know they'd gotten the wrong man. That made for a very cautious exit on my part. It took me fully three times as long to back my way oh-so-carefully and even more stealthily out of the rose thicket than it had to sneak in. Which, I suppose, gave me plenty of time to admire the fragrance.

As soon as I'd retreated to a safe distance, I set out just as cautiously to look for other likely hiding places around the area. I wanted to see how many of them held similar surprises. Their placement and numbers could tell me a lot about what the target was.

I found a round dozen, including a command post a fair distance back from the main perimeter on the upslope side. It held a captain of the Elite and his stone dog along with three more Crown Guards. Cold sweat started all over my body when I spotted them. I found it all too easy to imagine the consequences if I'd tripped over the stone dog and his master instead of the pair of guards in the rose thicket.

The smart thing to do at that point would have been to go home. Better yet, I could follow Triss's original advice and leave town entirely and permanently. Trying to slip past a cordon of watchers set up for the express purpose of spotting a shadow-shrouded Blade was a lousy recipe for even short-term survival. On the other hand, if this *was* Devin's snug—and the presence of a surrounding troop of Crown Guards commanded by an Elite captain sure as hell suggested it was—then Maylien might be in there somewhere. I really hated decisions like this.

14

Devin had co-opted a decaying great house of ducal size and state, a massive pile of badly pitted sandstone leaking rotted mortar from a thousand joints in need of repointing. It still looked sturdier than most of its neighbors, perhaps because it had further to fall before it finally hit bottom.

The tallest tower stood a bit over five stories, which gave it between one and two floors on the other four. A virtual maze of steeply angled roofways connected the five towers into a figure with several more sides than it had any right to.

I couldn't see any lights or other evidence of anyone's moving around the house or grounds. That was one benefit of a house run on assassin's hours. In a normal great house, the kitchen and pantry staff would certainly be preparing breakfast at this time of day. They might be doing the same here—impossible to tell since great houses never had windows below the second floor—but the odds were much lower.

I could only see two doors, both clearly in view of several of the watching posts, which observation pointed up my primary dilemma. Go in or walk away? The problem was that I didn't *know* Maylien was inside. If she wasn't, breaking into an unknown great house under these conditions was profoundly stupid. Maybe even borderline suicidal. If she *was* in there, I could at least cross off the stupid part. I didn't see any way around suicidal.

The funny thing was that if this were a mission for the goddess, I'd have walked away right then. That might sound counterintuitive, but really it's just part of the job.

Mind before heart.

Namara taught her Blades to treat assignments professionally, not emotionally. That meant balancing risks and rewards honestly and walking away more often than you might think.

On the walking away side of the table there lay the Elite and his stone dog, a heavy argument even without the Crown Guard. Add to that the admittedly slim possibility that they were here after someone other than Devin. Alternatively, if they *were* hunting for him—as I believed—there was a decent chance they'd solve my Devin problem for me. Conceivably my Maylien problem, too, if they chose to release any prisoners their target might be holding.

Balance that against the argument for going in. Maylien might be there. She might be alive. And it was barely possible that if both those things were true, I could sneak her out in one piece past the Crown Guard and the Elite.

That's the point where you walk away if you're looking at things professionally. Emotionally, on the other hand . . . Maylien had saved my life. More importantly, she'd saved Triss's life. I owed her whatever I had the power to give. I also kept coming back to the fact that Colonel Deem had been under pressure from a royal baroness. A baroness whose name seemed all too likely to be Sumey Marchon, who would certainly prefer that Maylien died in the coming crossfire.

But who did I think I was kidding? Of course I was going in. The real question was how. The Elite captain had placed his teams very well. The only thing that made it even remotely possible was the combination of knowing they were there and the fact that they'd had to choose their positions more in terms of concealing themselves than for perfect surveillance. They couldn't afford to scare off the target. With a target who could make himself invisible, that meant playing things very conservatively.

Half an hour after I'd admitted to myself that I had to try, I was sliding down the leaded roof into an oddly shaped little valley made by the nearby intersections of several roof segments. As long as I stayed low, the various bits of steeply slanting lead would hide me from the watchers on the ground.

The sun was up by then, but not yet so high I could see it over the rooftops. The thought of making noise still made me nervous, but I really needed to let my familiar know where we stood. I also needed to give him the option of talking me out of my insane little plan since I hadn't been able to drop my shroud and consult with him before. Now I released my hold on Triss, and, an instant later, a small dragon's shadow lay beside me on the leads. I spilled the story to date in the ghost of a whisper.

"What do you think?" I asked finally. "This is our last chance to give this up and slip away clean."

"I owe Maylien as much as you do. She saved you for me as much as she saved me for you."

I suppressed an urge to tell him that balance didn't come out even, not with the current Aral on one side of the scales anyway. I didn't think he'd appreciate the sentiment, not even in jest.

Instead, I drew a knife and placed its edge against the lead of the roof, and said, "Then we go in."

Triss nodded, and the familiar cold-silk feeling of his presence slid up my body and down my arm to the knife's edge. It took less than a minute to slice open three sides of a square, allowing me to pry up a flap of lead and expose the underlying planks. I didn't want them tumbling noisily to the floor of the attic below, so I was more careful now, working between two joists and lifting the boards out as I cut them free. Another few minutes, and I was able to poke my head through the narrow gap and take a quick look around.

The attic ranged in height from next to nothing at the edges to over twelve feet at the nearest visible peak. It was also a maze, mirroring the tangled structure of the roofs above. The detritus of generations of owners lay strewn around, all of it covered in dust and the various leavings of the house's less official residents. Without moving, I could see clear evidence of slinks, pigeons, rats, and nipperkins.

The roof hung within a few feet of the attic floor here, which allowed me to collect the planks and, with Triss's aid, lever the flap shut behind me. The whole process was quiet and fast but not silent. There was nothing I could do about that except tuck the fresh-cut planks as far back under the eaves as possible and move fast. That, plus the size and cluttered nature of the attic and the closing of the flap, would conceal my point of entrance even from a dedicated searcher. Hopefully for long enough.

"Triss, can you scout around and see what options we have for getting downstairs?"

"Of course." The near-total darkness of the attic allowed Triss the freedom to thin himself out and expand to many times his normal area, sliding along the floor's surface and encompassing the space within himself.

"There are two small trapdoors," he said, when he returned a few seconds later. "There's also a main stair down to what's probably the servants' wing, and a second, narrower stair going who knows where. More importantly, I found a good-sized gap that opens into the top of one of the interior walls. It's covered by a trunk that's nailed to the floor."

"False bottom in the trunk."

"Almost certainly."

"Nice! I haven't seen that trick in ages."

A lot of great houses had secret passages or rooms. Some provided hidey-holes for goods or people. Many opened into escape routes or provided access to nearby chambers for clandestine affairs. Others had been put in for purposes of spying on the guests, or murdering them in their beds. All of them were an assassin's friend.

"Guide me to the trunk."

Triss shifted so that I could feel his presence as a pair of invisible hands on my shoulders. He steered me swiftly through the darkness to the trunk. It was a huge thing of oak and rusted iron, with a couple of giant splits at the corners. The no-doubt carefully-thought-out combination made it look too heavy to bother moving and too ruined to sell. Opening the lid revealed a mess of moth-eaten old wool that seemed to cry out for mice and rats to come and make a nest of it.

"Triss?"

Shadow gloved my hands as I reached into the tangle, groping for . . . there! A few inches under the surface, I found an iron loop. Pulling on it pivoted the shallow tray full of wool up and out of the way, revealing a dark opening.

Sliding a leg over the lip of the trunk, I felt around with my foot until I found the top of a wooden ladder leading down into the wall. Another iron loop pulled the tray back into place above me, while a long rod connected to the trunk's hinges quietly closed the lid. The ladder descended perhaps twelve feet to a wide plank set loosely across the deep floor joists. Pulling my tiny thieveslight from the trick bag, I shined the dull red beam around. I was in a narrow space between the walls, with a dead end a few feet to my left and a narrow passage heading away on my right.

Every couple of yards a gap between planks opened down into the joists, where more boards had been mounted just above the ceilings of the rooms below, allowing a person to crawl down and into those ceilings. At a guess, some of those would cross-connect to other passages in the walls. It made for a pretty typical network of the spying and murdering sort.

"Triss, can you slip around through the walls and see if there's any light or sound coming from anywhere close at hand?"

The shadow of a dragon appeared on the wall, and Triss nodded once before extending himself like a snake, slithering down
into the depths of one of the floor gaps. Almost as soon as Triss had
gone, he returned. Shaking his head, he tried another. On the fourth
attempt I felt a sudden tug along the thread of shadow linking us.
He'd found something. Closing up my lamp, I bent and slipped into
the gap, scraping my still-healing back against the bottom of the
wall as I did so.

Fuck, but that hurt! Clenching my jaw to keep from swearing
aloud, I started crawling. It was hard on my much-abused body,
harder than all the climbing and roof jumping had been earlier.
Maybe because climbing and roof jumping were a part of my regular
routine even as a jack.

I passed under a second overhead passage and into another ceiling before I saw daylight shining up through a gap just beyond the
next wall. It was coming around the edges of a tiny wooden slide
affixed to the floor. When I moved it, I could see about three-quarters
of a large room that might once have been an audience chamber of
some sort. Judging by the angle and the restrictions on my view, the
peephole was hidden in the crown molding, an observation the professional side of my brain made and filed away independently of the
emotional side, which had an entirely different and more intense
focus.

Maylien! She sported a number of minor cuts and a really spec-
tacular black eye, but she was alive. She sat sullenly against the far
wall, not far from the filthy eastern windows that provided the light.
She wore a loose shirt and something midway between a split skirt
and pair of bloused pants, similar to a noble's dueling clothes, but in
coarse peasant fabrics. It was not all that different from what I was
wearing, actually.

She had chains on her wrists and ankles. And she wore the most
murderous expression I'd seen on any woman's face since Siri had
missed her shot at the High Khan of Avars after we'd gone through
a week of maneuvering to set up the kill. The khan had died old and
in his sleep—bastard.

Maybe ten feet to Maylien's left a man sat with his feet up on a
scarred oak table. He had one hand hooked through the loop on the
end of a rope pull. The rope, in turn, ran across the table, connecting to the release on a very heavy steel blade suspended between
two wooden tracks. I recognized the design as having been stolen
from the Sylvani Empire's latest device for making beheading more
efficient.

Underneath the blade sat a small wicker cage holding something gray and fluffy. I couldn't tell what it was from that angle, but judging by the way it kept pacing and growling, it was very, very angry.

"They're threatening her familiar to keep her under control!" Triss hissed in my ear, his voice aseethe with rage. "We've got to do something!"

"Sst!" I made an angry chopping motion, signaling him to shut up.

He did because it was the smart thing to do. But the way he kept sliding back and forth across my back like an agitated snake told me everything I needed to know about his continued fury. I felt the exact same way. Threatening a familiar was the usual way you controlled a mage. We'd both seen it dozens of times in the past, but after our own recent imprisonment, it struck a lot closer to home. The man with the rope didn't know it yet, but he was about to meet the lords of judgment.

The cleanest way to come at the problem would have been to back up about two rooms and find a quiet way down to the lower floor. Then sneak around to nail him with a shadow-sharp thrust through the wall he was leaning against. Done properly, it would kill him so quickly he'd never have a chance to even think about tugging on that rope. But clean took time we really didn't have.

Not when Devin might come back at any moment. Not with a small army waiting to attack the house, likewise at any moment. And especially not with that bastard holding a rope he could pull at any moment. No, I needed to do this quick and dirty and I needed to find some way to pin that rope down for a bit.

A spell-guided throwing knife might have served, but there was no way to get that to work through the peephole. Likewise an arrow if I'd had a bow and room to draw it. I had a few blowdarts in my pouch, but the broken-down blowgun was stowed with the bulk of my gear in a chimney on top of the Ismere Club.

Come on, Aral. Think! There must be something. But my mind kept going around in the same circle: knife, arrow, dart, knife, arrow . . . Wait a moment. Could I . . . ?

"Triss," I breathed in a voice lighter than any whisper. "Do you think you could make yourself into a tube for a blowdart? I need to pin that rope."

Triss froze on my back, digging his claws in lightly.

After a moment he replied just as quietly, "Maybe." Then, more confidently, "Yes. Yes, I could."

The rest of the plan fell together in my head. Quick and dirty to be sure, but also reasonably likely to succeed. I slid the peephole closed and neatly laid my tools out on the planks around me. First, my swords, about a handspan behind the peephole with the hilts toward the hole. Next, a long steel blowdart, one of six in my trick bag. After that, I very carefully reversed my position so that the bulk of my body lay above the audience chamber. Finally, I told Triss what I wanted him to do. As soon as he nodded in agreement, we began.

Opening the peephole once again, I took a quick look to make sure nothing had changed. Then I rose as high as the constricted space would allow and set the blowdart between my teeth. It was instantly surrounded by a hollow tube of night that ran from my lips down and through the peephole. Without looking—it was Triss's job to make sure it hit the target—I blew as hard as I could. As soon as the dart left the gun, I reached for my swords.

In that same instant, Triss shifted back to dragon form and pressed himself flat along the boards beneath me, pushing hard. Just as he had when he freed me from Lok's dungeon, he slowly forced his wings forward while contracting down to a pinpoint. Then I was falling through a dragon-shaped hole in the ceiling, my swords in my hands. I landed on my feet and let myself tumble backward into a roll. Spinning as I came upright again, I leaped forward to chop the guard's hand off at the wrist before he could free the rope from the dart temporarily pinning it to the table.

The guard clutched at his hand and started screaming, but not for long. I silenced him with a thrust of my second sword. As I started to tug the chopping blade free of the table, Maylien shrieked an unfamiliar word in a voice both louder and more frightened than the guard's.

I turned to find her pointing back over my shoulder toward the hanging blade, and I knew without looking there must have been a second guard concealed in the peephole's blind spot. I left one sword stuck in the table as I pivoted on the ball of my foot and dove, sliding on my belly across the floor toward the falling blade. The distance was short, but so was time.

All I could do was punch the little wicker cage hard with my empty hand and hope I'd gotten there fast enough. The cage bounced away in the instant before the falling blade dropped into the space it had just occupied. I should have lost a hand then. Would have, too, if Triss hadn't managed to catch the blade in the inches before it could hit the floor.

That took all his strength and focus, at least for a few seconds. But even with Triss intervening, the blade pinned my wrist, leaving me dreadfully exposed. Trying hard not to imagine the feeling of the guard's weapon driving deep into my back, I slid my sword under the edge of the bigger blade and used it as a lever.

As soon as I freed my hand, I started rolling, aiming toward the place I'd last seen the guard who had, very obligingly, not yet stabbed me in the back. That probably had something to do with his shrieks and the squalling and hissing of Maylien's familiar, all of which came from the same direction. But I really hadn't had time to look.

Reflex or chance guided me into the guard's shins, and he went down in a heap. I didn't bother to get up, just flipped my sword from overhand to under and sank it deep in his side, twisting and levering in search of something vital. Somewhere in there the man stopped moving, Maylien stopped yelling, and her familiar stopped snarling. For a few brief seconds, all was bliss and silence, and I had leisure to figure out that the cage must have come apart when I hit it, freeing the familiar to save my life.

Then came the applause.

"Very nicely done, Aral. Oh, very nice. If you'd managed it even a few minutes earlier, you'd be out the door and gone by now."

It was Devin's voice.

Fuck.

I rolled over onto my back, bringing my sword up defensively. It wasn't much of a shield, but it was all I had.

"There's no need to be so dramatic," he said. "If I'd wanted to kill you, I wouldn't have spoken. I'd just have pulled the trigger."

Devin stood in the doorway holding a small crossbow, its quarrel aimed directly at my left eye. I had no doubt that a moment before it had been pointing at the spot where my spine connected to my skull. I also had no doubt that the dark smear of stuff on the head would kill me in a matter of minutes, whether it hit a vital spot or not. I couldn't tell what the poison was from here, but none of the options made me want to try my luck.

"Maylien," said Devin. "Tell your pet to land next to Aral, or I will be forced to kill it and, tragically, you."

Maylien didn't say a word, but the gray and black cloud of fury that had been hovering a few feet from Devin and hissing angrily, turned in the air and came to land beside me. It wasn't until then that I finally got a good look at it.

Miniature gryphon, or gryphinx. Which meant that Maylien had spent those missing years with the Rovers, a semi-nomadic order of mages that spent much of their time clearing the roads and hunting bandits and highwaymen. Maylien's partnering of a gryphinx meant she'd taken mage orders with them, or at least started along that path, and that spoke well of her. The Rovers had always had good relations with Namara's priesthood and shared many of the same values.

"There's a nice pet," said Devin. "That wasn't so hard, was it?"

The little gryphinx hissed and mantled at that, which pretty much mirrored my feelings.

"Gently, Bontrang," said Maylien, and I recognized in his name the word she'd cried out earlier.

Bontrang let out another angry squall, then dropped back onto his haunches and flicked his tail around to cover his front feet. He *looked* calm that way, but I could hear the very faint scraping as he repeatedly flexed and released his talons under the tail. The gryphinx was about the size of a large house cat, with the head, wings, and front legs of a hawk and the body and coloring of a gray tabby.

"Very good," said Devin. "Aral, I'm going to ask you to stay right where you are. Flat on your back in the middle of the room is about as safe as I can make you this side of dead. Triss, please don't try anything clever. I don't want to have to kill Aral, but I will if you force me to it. So I'd like you in plain sight."

Triss slid out from under me, assuming his dragon form as he did so. "How's this?" His voice burned with anger.

"Perfect. That puts everyone where I want them. Now we're going to have a little talk."

"Don't you want to move me over with the others?" asked Maylien. "It's going to be hard to keep an eye on me way over here."

"Not at all. I like you in chains. If anything, I'd prefer to lock Aral up next to you. *That* would simplify things, but I can't think of a safe way to arrange it at the moment, so we'll just leave him there. Besides, with your pet sitting next to Aral like that, I've got all the leverage over you that I need."

"Bontrang's not a pet," snapped Maylien. "He's my familiar, and a damned good one."

"Call him whatever you wish, child. He's still a glorified house cat. Now, do shut up, or I'll have to shoot him. The adults have things we need to discus."

Maylien shut up though I could read rage in the angle of her chin and the tension in her neck and shoulders. I felt the same way but made a conscious effort not to show it.

"Aren't you going to ask me to throw my sword aside?" I asked, keeping my voice casual.

"No, I think you'll feel safer with a weapon in hand, and that'll make you easier to deal with, more rational. It also keeps you from getting any ridiculous ideas like throwing it at me. That's a reasonable trade-off for the risk. I take it from your arrival here that you've chosen not to accept the deal I offered you at Marchon House?"

I nodded and tried not to look over Devin's shoulder into the hallway. I wanted the Crown Guard to have one clean shot at his back when they finally got here.

"Pity that. You'd be a real asset for the new Order of the Assassin Mage. It would make our path much easier if I could just get you to come in with the rest of us." Possibly in response to some unintentional cue from me, Devin stepped deeper into the room then, moving to the side so that he had a wall at his back. "Hell, you wouldn't even have to participate in any of our funding activities if you didn't want to."

"Contract murder, you mean?" I asked. "Not interested."

Triss hissed his agreement.

"I prefer 'paid assassination' if it's all the same to you." Devin moved again, stepping to the side and resting a hip on the table where his henchman's hand still lay beside the sword I'd used to chop it off—the crossbow never wavered from its aim at my left eye. "But that's not all we do. We hire out for a lot of freelance work these days. Some not so different from your jack work here in Tien. But you wouldn't have to play that game.

"After our last encounter, I checked in with the ruling council, and we've agreed you're an important enough catch to offer you a new deal. You and Triss can join us in an advisory capacity, teaching the next generation the skills that you know so well. You wouldn't be allowed a vote on the council, of course, but your hands would be completely free of blood."

"This council you keep mentioning. Who are we talking about?" And where the hell were the Crown Guard? Had they missed Devin's arrival?

"Sorry, but until you're on the inside, you don't need to know any of the involved names but mine. For that matter, if you didn't already know about me, we wouldn't give you that much." Then he shook his head sadly. "You're not going to see reason, are you?"

"Reason? Really? It's not like you're asking me to train a new generation of Blades. Namara's dead. No, you want me to help you create an army of assassins unbound by any ethical restriction. An order of murderers that would answer to no one but itself in the shape of this council of yours. Then you tell me that if I do this, I won't have blood on my hands? Secondhand blood is still blood."

"You're sure you won't reconsider? No, I can see that you won't. I guess—"

Devin's voice cut off abruptly as he spun in place and fired the crossbow at an angle back through the door. There was a choked gurgling noise in response—the distinctive sound of someone taking a quarrel in the throat.

The Crown Guard had arrived. Now I just had to survive long enough to get Maylien free and make a break for it.

15

Devin vanished into a pool of shadow. As the first Crown Guards burst through the doorway, the shadow licked out, and the guard lost his head. I was already moving by then, rolling back up onto my shoulders, then flipping myself forward onto my feet.

"Catch!" The shadow shifted again, and the sword I'd left embedded in the table came spinning my way. The enemy of my enemy, and all that.

I put out my right hand and the hilt slapped into it, a perfect toss on Devin's part. I lunged toward Maylien as two more Crown Guards died in the doorway. Before I could do anything about the chains that held her, the back wall of the room exploded inward, propelled by magic. A dozen more Crown Guards charged in through the choking cloud of wood and plaster dust.

The nearest tried to skewer me with her woldo, a pole-mounted short sword, and I had to turn away from Maylien to parry the blow. Dust began to fill my nose and throat, and I coughed violently but kept moving. Before the guard could recover from her thrust, I stepped in and opened her throat with a backhanded cut.

As I fended off another attack, I croaked back over my shoulder to Maylien, "Hang on, I'll get you loose in a second."

"Screw that," said Maylien, between her own coughs. "I'll get myself loose. You deal with the Crown Guards. Bontrang!"

The little gryphinx shot past my head as I slid between two of the guards, killing one with a thrust up and under the ribs and breaking the knee of the other with a spinning back kick. Triss tore out that one's throat when my shadow fell across him. As I moved past the dead guard, an arrow passed just behind my head. I turned to look for the archer, but Devin's shadow abruptly hid him from sight, and I stopped worrying about him.

I killed three more guards in quick succession and had moved to go after a fourth when Triss's voice suddenly yelled "Down!" and I dropped to the floor. All the hair along the back of my body stood on end as a sheet of magelightning sizzled through the place I had just been. I rolled sharply to my left, just dodging a thrown axe, then spun myself back up onto my feet in time to bat another axe away with my sword.

Then the captain of the Elite was on me, a short axe in each hand, and I found myself backing up fast as he pressed me. The next few seconds passed in a blur as we exchanged a dozen blows and counters at a pace I hadn't had to sustain in years. He was better than I, at least as I was now, and I couldn't touch him. I kept him from scoring on me, but only barely and with the constant worry that his stone dog might take me from behind at any moment.

Then Triss came to my rescue, enfolding me in shadow all in an instant and surrendering me his senses. The captain very nearly had me in the moment of transition before I'd fully submerged Triss's consciousness in my own. The tip of his left axe tore away a huge strip of my shirt between armpit and waist, while the back of its head slid bruisingly along my ribs.

I countered with a thrust straight toward the captain's groin. He leaped backward just in time, wisely moving away from the sword he couldn't see within the moving shadow he could. I followed, pressing him back and back again. Triss's presence gave me other advantages beyond the invisible attack, including the ability to "see" all around me in three dimensions through his unvision.

It revealed why the stone dog hadn't taken my life earlier. The dog and a half dozen Crown Guards were engaged with the shadow that hid Devin—they had not been prepared to meet two Blades. The unvision also showed me Maylien and Bontrang working together to free her by repeatedly directing some sort of low-magic force burst against the locks of her shackles. Slow work that. Much slower than a pick if you didn't want to accidentally rip your hand off. Most importantly, my unvision spied subtle movement in the hall beyond the door where the first guards had entered. More archers probably.

"Devin! Ware the door, we've company coming!" For a moment it almost felt like old times, and I had to remind myself we were at best temporary allies.

"Busy here! Deal with it!"

But four more guards had also arrived from the other direction, backing up their captain and putting me once more on the defensive. This group all had woldos, and they were using the sword-spears to blindly thrust again and again into my lacuna of shadow. Easy enough to avoid on an individual basis, but much harder coming from multiple directions and with the captain and his axes and possible spells to keep an eye on as well. That was the situation when the first arrow sank into the floor at my heels.

The archers couldn't go for a straight shot with the captain and his spear-wielders in the line of fire but they *could* plink away in the general vicinity of my feet and hope they got lucky. I was just trying to decide if I could afford to turn and rush the archers when Maylien let loose on them with a truly hellacious burst of magefire.

At which point, the world came apart. The magefire ignited the cloud of dust still hanging in the air in a massive explosion. The blast took out what was left of the wall between the audience chamber and the hallway, at which point the ceiling fell in.

At least, that's the way I thought it happened, looking backward at the results. In the moment, I heard a huge noise like thunder experienced from the inside and found myself thrown toward the captain and his companions. Somehow I managed to avoid a skewering as we all tumbled together into the large dining room that had backed the audience chamber.

I'd balled up by then, dropping my swords and rolling with the force of the blast as I'd been taught. It took me halfway across the room, throwing me into and through the legs of the nearer rows of chairs with bone-jarring force. As I bounced to a halt under the table, I thought sure my luck had run out. I was badly tangled up with the remains of two or three shattered chairs, disarmed, and easy meat for anyone still standing. That's when the ceiling came down, bringing with it various bits of junk from the attic and a goodly piece of the roof above that, reversing the direction of my fortunes.

Instead of a trap, the huge oak table had suddenly become a refuge. Oh, I still had to free myself from the wreckage of the chairs, but I did that quickly enough. I had a new collection of cuts and bruises layered over the old, of course, but none too severe, and nothing like what I'd have had if the ceiling had landed on me. As soon as I could manage it, I slithered stiffly out from under the table and surveyed the damage.

Various cries and faint stirrings in the rubble marked other survivors of the battle and collapse, by implication if not immediately by position or persuasion, though nobody else seemed to have mastered the trick of digging themselves out yet. It seemed a perfect time to make a quick exit, so I started toward where I'd last seen Maylien in hopes of finding her alive and ready to travel.

That's when Devin called out, "Aral, help! The dog's got me!" His voice was gasping, laced with pain and panic.

With his cry to orient me, I spotted the stone dog, a massive presence near what had once been an outside wall, its paw pressing down into a low-lying pool of shadow. The huge beast was covered in dust and debris, which is why I hadn't seen it earlier, but it seemed otherwise unharmed. I started to turn back toward Maylien, but I couldn't help picturing Devin—my onetime friend—lying there under the great weight of that stone paw, his ribs creaking as it slowly pressed down.

I couldn't leave him to die like that. Damn me, but I couldn't do it. Even knowing that he'd betrayed the memory of our goddess, I couldn't leave a fellow Blade in the hands of the Elite.

The funny thing is that the old Aral would have done it in a heartbeat. Aral Kingslayer would have looked at what Devin had done and seen only the black and white, and he'd have condemned Devin to death without a qualm. But the new Aral had lost that clarity of purpose. He understood too much about bending to circumstance.

I didn't know what pressures had been brought to bear on Devin. I didn't know what I might have done in the same situation. Oh, I wanted to believe that I'd have chosen to die by torture rather than betray my goddess, and I really think that I would have. But I didn't *know* I'd have done it, especially if they'd threatened Triss. Because of that and because of Zass, I couldn't just let an old enemy kill the new one who had once been my friend. With a snarl of frustration, I released my hold on Triss.

"Find the Elite," I said, "quickly!" Triss dove into the wreckage near where I'd come out.

"Here!" he called a moment later, raising a shadowy tail above a heap of broken lath and shattered plaster. Then he started digging.

Within moments, Triss had exposed the Elite captain's head and right arm. I flicked a wrist, releasing the dagger there into my hand, then knelt to press it against the captain's chin. There was a time when I'd simply have cut his throat, but I wanted to give him a chance.

"Call off your dog," I said.

"Fuck you." He had dark blood on his lips, and he spat some of it into my face.

"Aral!" Devin's voice was weaker now. More desperate.

"Do it now, or die," I said.

"I'm already dead," said the captain. "We both know you're going to kill me."

"Only if I have to."

He spat at me a second time, and I drove the dagger up, through the soft place behind his chin and the roof of his mouth, into his brain. Behind me the stone dog gave one great howl, then fell over with a crash that shook the floor.

"Devin?" I called. "Are you dead?"

"I don't think so."

"Then you owe me. Get the fuck out of my city."

I'd taken a life to save a life. And somehow the fact that the life I'd ended belonged to someone who'd cheerfully have killed me if our circumstances were reversed didn't make me feel any better about the whole thing. But sometimes that's just how it is. So I wiped the blood off my face and went to see if I could find Maylien.

We still needed to get out of there, and I didn't think we had a whole lot of time to manage it. A big and more or less intact chunk of the roof had fallen atop the place where I thought she ought to be, so I sent Triss into the wreckage.

He emerged a few moments later and gave me a shadowy grin. "She's fine, trapped in a little pocket between the wall and a big piece of ceiling, but essentially unharmed. I didn't want her to attempt anything drastic with magic from where she is, for fear she'd make it worse, so I told her we'd get her out soon."

"Great, any idea how do we do that?"

"You don't," said Devin from somewhere behind me. "At least not right away. We weren't done talking. You know I can't let you leave until we come to an arrangement."

"You're not serious." I turned around to find Devin aiming an arrow at me from somewhere near the place the door used to be. He'd apparently salvaged one of the fallen guard's bows. "For fuck's sake, man, I just saved your life."

"That's why I didn't shoot you in the back. I wanted to give you one last chance to change your mind. We need your expertise, Aral. You could do so much for us. Don't make me throw a treasure like you away."

"Zass," said Triss. "My master just saved your master's life. You will *not* let him do this."

Zass said nothing, but the string of the bow suddenly broke with a sharp twanging noise, momentarily disarming Devin. Somehow, it felt like a loss.

"I won't say it again, Devin. Get out of my city and don't come back. Don't force me to kill you." There was a time where I might have been able to make that threat stick. Now . . . I just had to hope he wouldn't make me try.

I turned my back on Devin. "Triss, what if we went out what's left of this window and you cut a hole through the wall behind Maylien. Can you make that work?"

"Yes, I think I can. I'm tired but not impossibly so."

"Then, let's do it." I put one foot up on the twisted frame.

Behind me, I heard Devin's swords slide out of their sheaths, a deliberate threat on his part, since we both knew he could have drawn them silently. I kept going, climbing out through the window. Either he would kill me or he wouldn't. At this point, there was very little I could do to stop him except run away, and I wasn't leaving Maylien behind. I'd lost my own swords in the blast and cave-in, and there was no possible way for me to defeat another ex-Blade knives against swords. Not on this ground at any rate.

As I slid around to hang on the wall just outside where Maylien lay trapped, I heard Devin swearing behind me. Then he put his swords away just as noisily as he'd drawn them.

"This isn't over, Aral. If it wouldn't have upset Zass, I'd have killed you just now."

"Fuck you, Devin. I—oh, shit." Out of the corner of my eye I'd seen movement on the road in front of the great house. More Crown Guards on the way, along with at least a half dozen Elite judging by the stone dogs. "We need to speed things up, Triss, the next wave's going to be here in a couple of minutes."

He spread himself out on the old masonry of the wall for a time, focusing his strength, then flapped his wings and sent the stones to the everdark. It was still as creepy as all hell to watch him do that, but I was beginning to believe that I might someday get used to it. Bontrang exploded outward through the hole, with Maylien sticking her head out a moment later.

"Thank you," she said. "I knew you wouldn't let me down, Kingslayer." I looked away from the admiration in her eyes.

"Look, we don't have a lot of time here, and I don't have a rope. Can you climb onto my back?"

"Of course."

Maylien slid farther out of the hole, putting her arms around my neck and shoulder, then pivoting to hang free for a moment before she wrapped her legs around my waist. As I took the strain of her full weight, I had to suppress a groan. She was a tall woman and sword-trained, and I was a bruised and battered wreck. Without Triss's help, we'd have fallen off the wall.

"Ready?" I asked through gritted teeth.

"Ready."

I started down, moving as fast as I could. When I got about eight feet from the bottom, Maylien let go and dropped, touching down only lightly with her feet before dropping into a backward roll to soak up the force of her fall. Apparently, she'd taken me at my word about needing to get out of there fast. A moment after she dropped, I kicked off and followed her. By the time I'd rolled to my feet, she was beside me. That was good because the deep baying of one of the stone dogs started then—we'd been spotted.

"Take my hand," I said, "and run."

She did, and Triss widened himself out into a broad curtain of shadow between us and our pursuers while I aimed us straight toward the edge of the bluff. In this light, Triss's intervention wouldn't allow us to slip away, but it would make it much harder for any archers to hit us, especially since they'd have to shoot on the run. If any of them tried, they shot wide enough of the mark that I didn't know about it.

We had to slow a bit when we crossed from the ruined gardens into the wall of overgrown shrubs that had colonized the broken ground along the top of the bluff. Branches slapped at my face and chest, and weeds clutched at my boots, while Bontrang flitted in and out above us.

Maylien went up several points in my estimation over the next minute or two. Both because she kept her mouth shut to save her breath for running and because she would have soon pulled ahead of me if she'd let go of my hand. When it came to running, she was in decidedly better shape than I was. Not having to worry about Maylien gave me more leisure to worry whether Triss would be able to manage the task ahead.

If not, we were all going to die. As fast as we ran, the stone dogs were faster still. The three following us had started out less than a quarter mile behind and they'd gained ground fast as we sprinted toward the edge of the bluff. The brush and trees that so hampered us barely registered for the dogs, who left a swath of crushed and shattered greenery in their wake. The only good thing about the dogs' speed was that they'd left their masters behind, temporarily saving us the necessity of dodging magefire and -lightning and other nastier sorts of magic. They'd closed to within twenty feet when we abruptly ran out of running room.

"Trust me," I said to Maylien, as we broke through the last of the brush before the cliff's edge.

Then I scooped her into my arms and leaped into space. As I did so, Triss caught hold of my shoulders and spread himself out above us like a great black wing. I frantically fed Triss nima as we moved lurchingly out and away from the bluff, filling that wing from the well of my soul. Somehow, we stayed aloft.

It was more of a slow and loosely guided fall with a lot of wild swings and random turns in one direction or another than a true sail-jump, but we didn't just fall. That felt like a miracle, really, since we normally used my arms as supports for Triss's shadow wings and they carried half the weight. Even the massive quantities of magic I was pouring into the effort were barely enough to keep us aloft under the circumstances. I desperately hoped we could hold it together long enough for something roughly resembling a success-ful landing, and wished I still had a goddess to pray to on the subject.

Behind us the stone dogs bayed wildly and briefly, then dove down through the ground into the rocky bones of the Channary Hill, heading for the base of the bluff. We hadn't gotten away yet, not by anyone's count.

"I love this," Maylien said suddenly, reminding me that she was more than just deadweight.

"You what?" With all the nima it was taking to fight the twist-ing and bobbing, I didn't really have the spare energy or breath for conversation, but I was simply too shocked not to ask.

"I've always wanted to fly," she said. "Bontrang makes it seem like such fun. Look at all the people down below." She pointed to-ward the Downunders, where the morning crowd had filled the streets. "Don't they look surprised?" Quite a few had noticed us, and they started pointing and calling out to their fellows. "Oh, this is glorious!"

Crazy woman.

We lurched abruptly left at that moment, nearly flipping over. I was still trying to think of some way to respond to Maylien that didn't involve a lot of swearing when a bright whip of magic like a giant chain forged from links of green fire slashed past a few feet to my right.

Triss screamed, and we jolted sharply to the right, dropping a dozen feet as he jerked in his wing on that side. The spell, whatever it was, had grazed him, and magic was one of the few things that could really harm a Shade. Below us, the people in the streets started running and shouting.

I ignored them in favor of feeding Triss even more of my rapidly failing magic. I took a risk by taking my eyes off our landing zone to glance back over my shoulder. I wanted to get a mark on the bastard who'd hurt my familiar. I couldn't do much about the attack right now, but I promised myself a reckoning later. I'd just spotted a mounted figure on the slope now far above and behind us, when a second glowing chain of power lashed down toward us from his raised hands like some giant magical whip.

The spell missed by a much wider margin than the previous burst—Triss's injury had transformed an already frighteningly erratic descent into something completely unpredictable and terrifying. The burst of light that accompanied the spell also gave me one instant's bright and perfect view of the caster, burning his image into my mind. Colonel Deem, mounted atop his massive stone dog as if it were a horse. I had a brief moment to hope he hadn't gotten an equally clear look at me. Then Maylien screamed, Triss screeched a warning, and I turned back frontward in time to see a thatch roof coming up to meet us.

The perfect, soft landing place. There was only one little problem. Deem's spell had landed first. The roof was on fire.

16

We missed the worst of the flames, crashing through the roof in a cascade of smoldering thatch and shattered bamboo poles. There was a sharp jerk up and back on my shoulders as Triss caught at the edges of the rotten bamboo roof supports in an attempt to slow us even further. Then they gave way like the rest, and we fell the last couple of feet with burning thatch raining down all around us. I'm not sure who was more surprised, the occupants of the little leather shop at the sudden fire and the manner of our entrance, or me at our having survived it.

But there was no time to worry about that or do more than marvel briefly at the fortune that had kept us from hitting a more solid roof. It was a good thing for us that the Downunders was one of the few parts of Tien where the odds of hitting a rotten roof were better than even. My feet had barely touched the floor when Maylien slipped from my arms and started for the door. Much as I needed to follow her, I paused a moment longer.

"Triss, are you all right?" I asked.

"Yesss," he said, but I knew from the hiss in his speech that he was in pain. "Go! I will recover sssoon enough if I resst. Fire and sun, but that hurts." Then he let go of his dragon form and collapsed into my shadow.

I wanted to do more for him, but the smoke was getting thicker by the second, and somewhere nearby the stone dogs were swimming through the earth in pursuit. I did take a moment to open my trick bag and pull out one of the half dozen heavy gold riels I kept there for direst emergency.

"Sorry," I said, tossing it to the old man standing in open-mouthed shock behind the counter. "Now, run."

Then I took off after Maylien. As I crashed through the door and out onto the street, I was glad to see that a bucket brigade had already started to form. I couldn't bear the thought of a second neighborhood burning in my wake. Better to let the Elite kill me than that—curse them! If I'd known they were going to do this, I'd have . . . what?

I honestly didn't know the answer. I'd never succumbed to the particular cynicism endemic among the Blades that painted abusive rule as a thing of uttermost routine. No matter how many times I'd seen corrupt officials abuse their powers, it always shocked me when someone like an officer of the Elite casually harmed the people under his protection.

Even as that thought crossed my mind, another lash of the great magical chain fell from above. It struck across the street, about a half dozen buildings up, and ignited another fire. Two really, one in the just-blasted building and another within my heart. There was no way Colonel Deem could possibly have picked us out from the rest of the milling crowd at this distance. No, he was just blasting away and hoping to eliminate us in the general destruction. As I looked around at the flaming ruin authored by one of Zhan's "authorities," I swore that this would not go unanswered. I half turned back toward the bluff, though what I intended to do I couldn't say.

Then Maylien caught my arm. "Do you have any of the money I paid you? Devin's people stole what coin I had on me."

"Sure," I reached for my pouch, "how much do you need?"

"Five silver riels should do it."

I handed them over, and Maylien darted away. "Wait, what do you need it for?"

"Come on," she called back over her shoulder. "Hurry! There's a man over here who'll lend us his cart horses for a fee, and we need to ride."

I shook myself free of the anger that had taken me, forcing it back down into the depths for later use, and followed Maylien across the street to where she was cutting a couple of horses loose from their traces. She was right, we needed to be gone, and I shouldn't have lost sight of that. Nor let the weight of arranging our escape fall on her. I was the one who was supposed to be rescuing Maylien, wasn't I?

Just who was rescuing whom became even more debatable when Maylien practically had to push me onto the back of one of the horses a few moments later. I'd stopped moving after catching up to her, lost track of everything for a moment, really. And not for the first time. Odd batches of seconds seemed to be slipping away from me and leaving no memory of their passing. It wasn't until Maylien gave me a shove toward the horse and ordered me to mount up that I did so.

It was a damned good thing the two horses had been harness mates, because it meant that mine followed Maylien's without any prompting on my part. Bits of the world kept vanishing into white nothingness around the edges of my vision as we rode, and it took most of my attention just to stay ahorse. The white blots rang old alarm bells in the back of my head, but I couldn't make my mind work well enough to think of why.

Then, without any sense of transition at all, I found myself sitting in a thick bed of ferns beside a fire, with a tin cup in my hand, and that seemed very strange. Especially since the sun had gone away somewhere along the line, replaced by the moon and a slice of starry sky bounded by overhanging branches.

What the hell . . . ?

"I said that you should try to take another drink." It was Maylien's voice, coming from somewhere off on the other side of the fire though I couldn't see her. She sounded concerned.

That didn't make any more sense than the darkness or the bed of ferns, but she seemed pretty sure about drinking. Almost absently, I raised the cup to my lips and took a big mouthful of some incredibly raw alcohol. It burned gloriously as it went down.

"What the hell is this stuff?" I asked, in something halfway between a cough and a croak.

"You'd have to ask the very sketchy-looking fellow I bought it from back at the crossroads for the details, but it probably started out as rice, and it's certainly not legal." Maylien laughed then, a wry, earthy sort of sound. "But I've told you that twice already. What are the chances it's going to stick this time?"

"I don't know. I don't remember asking before. Actually, I don't remember anything much after we got on the horses. Where are we? What happened?"

One of the shadows on the left side of the fire moved, resolving itself into Maylien's face as she pushed back the hood that had covered her until then. Beside her, Bontrang stirred, fixing me with one bright eye and making a small, inquisitive, trilling noise.

"You sounded almost coherent there," she said to me. "And Bontrang's paying attention to you for the first time in hours. Are you really back?" She got up and came to kneel beside me, looking into my eyes for several long beats. "I think you are." She produced a rough clay bottle from somewhere and poured a clear liquid into my cup. "You'd better have some more of that."

"I don't think Triss would approve of . . . Wait, Triss!"

"Shh." Maylien put a finger to my lips. "He's sleeping, and he needs it even more than you do if I am any judge. Now have another drink. It's the nastiest rotgut I've ever tasted, but it'll do you a world of good to get more inside you."

She eyed me sternly, and I sniffed at my cup—hellfire but it smelled raw—then took another drink. It tasted awful but somehow wonderful at the same time. And again I could feel it burning as it headed down my throat. At least at first. When it hit my stomach, the feeling simply went away.

"That's really strange," I said.

"What?" asked Maylien.

"Normally with liquor this strong I'd expect it to light a fire in my belly, but it's just going away."

Maylien laughed again, still earthy, but lighter this time. "Then it's working. 'Spirits for the drained spirit.' That's what the Rovers used to say, though *you've* probably never heard the phrase, what with the way Namara's priests were down on booze."

She cocked her head to one side. "Someday you'll have to tell me how you ended up pretending to be a drunk. That was inspired, you know. The way you put away your whiskey at the Gryphon is why it took me six months to decide you really were Aral King-slayer."

My head started to spin, and I took another drink. Surprisingly, that seemed to bring things back into focus again, so I drained off the rest of the cup. Maylien topped me up again before I could argue.

"You need all you can get right now," she said.

"Can we back up to the part where I asked you what happened and where we are? Only this time with you answering?"

Again the laugh. "All right. Where should I start?"

"How about what happened after we got on the horses? The world started to flash white around the edges about then, and I don't really remember much between then and waking up here a couple of minutes ago." I felt a sudden twinge. "You're sure Triss is all right?"

"Yes, and stop saying his name. You'll wake him." Maylien settled back beside the little gryphinx. "Those white flashes are what happens when you overtap your nima. Which is why I've been feeding you the strongest moonshine I could find every chance I could get since we left the city shortly after sunrise."

"'Spirits for the spirit' . . ." I said.

"Exactly. There's nothing like strong drink to carry you over until you can get some sleep if you're an overextended mage. It's useless or even counterproductive under normal circumstances, but when you've pushed yourself beyond your limits, it can save your life. Of course, you didn't know that, what with Namara's followers being so notoriously down on alcohol. The thing that really surprised me was how very much of it you kept putting away without ever coming back to full consciousness.

"Well, that and the fact that you managed to stay on that horse even when you were nine-tenths unconscious. The first was your Shade's fault, of course, though *I* didn't know it till he explained it to me an hour or two ago, but I still don't know how you can hang on to something as tight as you did that horse when no one's at home in your skull."

I took another drink from my cup, hoping to calm the headspinning effect Maylien's conversational style seemed to induce. "Well, if you spend much time climbing buildings while under fire or exhausted, you tend to develop a serious reflex for hanging on to things. But even so, you've lost me again. Twice. What did Triss tell you that explained my continued problems?"

"Nima, of course. Shades need to eat, the same as anyone. That's what your Shade said, anyway. Now, during the night they can draw strength from the darkness itself, but in daytime, if they overextend themselves, they have nothing to feed on but the nima of their human companions. Your Shade got pretty badly clipped by that firechain spell. So, the only way he could keep it together was by tapping your nima. But you were *already* pretty much overtapped before that happened. Without that moonshine I've been feeding you, I think you'd probably both be dead. With it, I was able to get you through till nightfall, when your Shade could rest and soak up the dark."

I took another drink while I let all of that settle in. It was frighteningly bad stuff, and yet I found myself wanting more, which meant it was probably time to put it down even if it had saved my life. I set my cup aside.

"All right, I think that answers the 'what happened' part of my question, but I'd still like to know where we are."

Maylien smiled, her teeth shining bright in the firelight. "We're a bit less than a half day's slow ride south and west of Tien by the shortest road. We took a much longer and more roundabout way, so it took us from dawn to dusk to get here."

"And *here* is?"

"Nowhere really, a little dell on crown lands about a quarter mile back from the smuggler's track we took to get here. Between the trees and the hills, the campsite's invisible to anyone not right on top of it. It's frequented mostly by poachers. They're going to be a little bit grumpy about my using up a bunch of their woodpile without replacing it, but I'll square it with them later."

"You sound like you know the area well, and the poachers."

"Well enough," said Maylien. "I've spent a good part of the past four years traveling in this part of the country. The smuggler's way"—she gestured off behind her—"is one of the three best routes from the Barony of Marchon to Tien proper if you don't want to meet up with either the Crown or Baronial Guards. The Rovers taught me how to survive in the wilderness while the crown and my dear sister taught me to avoid the various guards."

Maylien leaned back against a log and stretched her feet toward the fire. "As for the poachers, and the smugglers, too. Well . . ." She shrugged. "We all get along well enough. We live much the same lifestyle, and the same people would see us all hanged if they could."

"But you were raised by the Rovers." I nodded at Bontrang. "Don't they frown on your shadowside acquaintances? They hunt bandits and other wilderness criminals as a part of their holy mission, don't they?"

Maylien laughed. "Bandits, yes. Bandits prey on travelers and pilgrims, and the Rovers kill them wherever they find them. But as long as the poachers and smugglers leave the people on the roads alone, the Rovers leave them alone. The order was established to protect travelers, they don't give a damn about protecting taxes and tariffs."

"I didn't realize that."

"They don't advertise the fact. Otherwise, people like the various Barons of Marchon might decide that they didn't want to dedicate house lands to Rover chapter houses."

Something struck me then. "You talk about the Rovers like you're not really one of them, but the nature of your familiar says otherwise. I know that you and your sister spent six years off the edge of the map of official history, but I don't know what happened beyond that or how you came to join the Rovers' order."

"I didn't. Not really, though I desperately wanted to once upon a time. My mother gave Sumey and me to the Rovers at the Marchon chapter house when we were thirteen and fourteen to protect us from our father. They handed us over to one of their traveling bands, which happened to be spending a few weeks at the chapter house, and the band whisked us right out of the kingdom.

"Between fourteen and twenty I spent more nights under the stars than under a roof. I've walked or ridden over most of the kingdoms of the east, from the northern marches of the Sylvani Empire in the south to Kadesh in the north and from the eastern ocean to the western mage wastes. I think those were the happiest years of my life . . . and the worst of Sumey's."

"How so?"

"Sumey hated every minute of the road. She complained constantly. After a couple of months of that, the Rovers parked her in a chapter house in Aven. But I'd fallen in love with the road, so I stayed with my traveling band. I learned to hunt and ride and fight as well as any Zhani warrior-noble. I even fell in love with a Rover, Serak, and I took Bontrang as my familiar when it turned out I had both gifts. I even went so far as to ask to take the Rover's oath."

"And then what happened?" I asked.

"What makes you think something happened?"

"The fact that you're here with me and fighting for a baronial seat instead of off on the road with the Rovers maybe?"

Maylien looked into the fire. "We were in the Kvanas. A lesser khan took a fancy to me, knocked me on the head, and carried me off. It was a really stupid move on his part. I'm a decent mage and a better swordswoman. When I woke up, I killed him and slipped away, but not before the other Rovers of our band came after me. There was a big fight, and Serak was killed along with about half our band."

She got up and walked away from the fire, turning her back to me. "We went to the High Khan for redress, but the khan I'd killed was a nephew of his. He threatened to sell the lot of us into slavery in the Sylvani Empire if we didn't get the hell out of his lands. So we went. We didn't have any choice. I had been supposed to take my Rover's oath a few weeks after that, but I was devastated and angry and terribly bitter. The senior members of our band told me that I needed to wait, that vows should never be said in anger.

"While I was waiting, I got to thinking about what makes a good ruler and what makes a bad one, and the fact that I had fallen heir to Marchon when my uncle died without issue. I hadn't been back to the barony proper in years, but the chapter house there made sure that the news made it to me. And then I started thinking about how I would feel if someone else took the seat when my mother died and did something horrible like what had happened to me and Serak. It would be my responsibility, you see. So I left the Rovers, and collected my sister, and we came back to Tien so that I could take up my seat . . .”

“And then it all went to hell,” I said. Having read some of it, I could make guesses as to how, but I wanted to hear it from Maylien.

Maylien nodded. “And then it all went to hell. Thauvik advanced my sister’s claim over mine. Which was all right. It meant that I could go back to the Rovers once things settled down. Except they didn’t settle down. My mother died within a few months, almost certainly by poison. At first I believed Sumey when she said that Mother had committed suicide. But then, bit by bit, I came to believe that she’d been murdered and that it had to be my sister who’d done it. I’d already started to hate Sumey more than a little by then.”

“Why?” If I was going to put Maylien in her sister’s place—and my debts bound me to do just that—I wanted to know as much as I could about both of them.

“As soon as Sumey took the seat, she started to do . . . things to our people, treat them like animals and worse than animals. I don’t know if she was always that way, and I’d just never seen it before, or if something happened to her during her years in Aven, and that changed her, or what. Whatever the reason, my nightmares about someone else doing horrible things from the baronial seat that I ought to have inherited started to come true. And it was made a thousand times worse by the fact that the person doing horrible things was my sister. How could someone so close to me turn into something so awful?”

I looked away from Maylien, into the fire. I didn’t have an answer for her question. If I had, Devin’s betrayals of the goddess and her ideals might have hurt less. Or then again, they might not. It would all depend on the nature of that answer.

If Devin and Sumey were simply bad people waiting for the right moment to go rotten, then we could bask in the armor of righteousness. But if they were just people like Maylien and I were just people, and the only reason that it was the two of us here and the two of them there was a matter of circumstance . . .

One of the things I’d learned over the years since the temple fell was that nothing was ever simple. Maylien hadn’t moved since she stopped talking. She just kept staring out into the darkness. I was still pretty weak, so I rolled onto my hands and knees before I tried to get up.

When that didn't kill me, I slowly and carefully pushed myself to my feet. It wouldn't do to fall into the fire and make her rescue me again. I walked over to stand behind Maylien, making plenty of noise so she'd know I was there. She didn't turn around, so I put a hand on her shoulder. I could feel her crying, though the tears made no sound.

"Maylien, what your sister has done belongs on her conscience, not yours."

She shrugged my hand off. "I *am* Marchon, or should be. Sumey has tortured and murdered people . . . my people, and done it under the banner of the Marchon. What Marchon does is my responsibility. Those deaths are on my head."

"Did you make your sister Baroness Marchon?"

"No, of course not! That was Thauvik's doing. And my sister's . . . when she murdered my mother to take the seat."

"And you've been trying to fix it ever since?"

"Yes, but that's not enough." Maylien turned to face me. "Don't you see? It can never be enough. My sister is a monster. She's already done things at least as bad as what happened to me and Serak. I should have seen it coming, done something about it earlier, prevented it somehow."

"You want to make it never have happened, right?" I asked, and my voice sounded to me like it was bubbling up through bitter waters—an aftereffect of my nima loss, maybe.

"Yes!"

I shook my head. "That's not how it works. You can't change the past . . . No matter how much you might want to, no matter how awful it was. Not even gods can change the past. You can't let the weight of might-have-been fall on your shoulders, or it will crush you."

"You're not just talking about me and Sumey anymore, are you?"

I looked through Maylien, into the past, and saw deep water with the sun shining dimly down from above. Beneath me a broken stone goddess lay sprawled on the floor of the lake, weeds starting to grow in her hair. Though my lungs burned already, I swam deeper so that I could place my swords in one cracked stone hand.

"No," I said, "I'm not. But that doesn't make what I'm saying any less true for you and Sumey. When the temple fell, I took the weight of a dead goddess onto my shoulders, and the guilt destroyed me."

"I don't understand." Maylien canted her head to the side. "You're here now, talking to me. How can you say the guilt destroyed you?"

"Because I'm not the man I was then, not the man you were looking for to help you with your sister, really. Aral Kingslayer, the Blade of Namara, didn't get the opportunity to die in defense of his goddess, and the guilt of that drove him so deep into the bottle that he never came back out again. I might wear the same face, and I might have shared the same bottle, but I'm not really him."

I laughed, and it sounded harsh in my ears but also strangely hopeful. "Maybe that's why I've actually managed to poke my head out into the light again, because I'm finally beginning to understand that."

Maylien stepped in close and kissed me gently on the lips.

"What was that for?" I asked after a long moment.

"For understanding."

She kissed me again, longer this time.

"And that?"

"For caring." She smiled then, in the dark. "And this next is simply because I want to."

I kissed her back this time and didn't have to bend down to do it. For a little while we simply held each other there in the night. It was the first time in more than five years that I'd held a woman like that, and it felt good. Maylien felt good. She was strong and athletic, like Jax or Siri or one of the other female Blades I'd shared a bed with, but softer somehow. She smelled of the road and hard riding, but also of woman, and she brought back memories long lost. Of camaraderie and shared purpose and nights spent together out of simple companionship. I found that I wanted her badly.

But it had been a very long day on top of a very long night, and I soon felt the world slowly tilting to my left. When I lurched rightward to compensate, Maylien slipped from my arms and half dragged—half led me back to my bed of ferns.

"Finish your drink," she said, handing me the cup, and I did.

Then she pushed me gently back into the ferns and tucked a rough blanket over me. "Now get some sleep."

I reached up and ran a hand along her side from ribs to hip. "And in the morning . . ."

"We'll see." She smiled at me, then got up to deal with the fire.

17

I jarred awake once in the night when I sensed someone leaning over me. Reflexes put a dagger in my left hand with a flick of the wrist, but vaulting to my feet proved beyond me. I was far too weak and dazed to do much more than sit up.

"It's just me, put that away and go back to sleep." Maylien put her hand gently on my chest and pushed me flat. Then she dropped a second blanket over me, and tucked herself in against my side. "It's going to be a cold night, and we'll be warmer if we share."

I was out before I had time to respond.

I woke when the dawnlight reached over the treetops and touched my eyelids, though I didn't look around right away. Sometime in the night, I'd turned and curled myself around Maylien, and I pressed my face gently against the back of her head, trying to put the day off a little bit longer. I wanted to prolong the pleasure of holding a woman while she slept. I hadn't done that in years, not since Jax and I had last traveled together.

As I woke further, I did a quick assessment of my general state of being. Where our bodies touched, I felt warm and wonderful. Every other part of me was sore and stiff and cold, especially the arm that pillowed Maylien's head. My right hand was three-quarters asleep as well as half-frozen where it stuck out from under the blankets in front of her face. All too soon, the aches and pains started to outweigh my resolve to hold still, and I was forced to shift around.

"Mmm." Maylien grumbled sleepily. "Stop moving around." But

then she sighed and stretched. "Too late. I'm awake." She turned her head to look at me over her shoulder and smiled. "Good morning."

"Good morning yourself," I said, speaking into her shoulder. I wanted to kiss her, but after all the raw rice alcohol I'd drunk the night before, I figured my mouth probably tasted like one of the more decayed varieties of restless dead. "Any thoughts on where we might find breakfast?"

"I can offer you yesterday's cold bacon and last week's stale black bread," said a disgustingly chipper male voice from somewhere on the far side of last night's campfire.

I jerked in surprise and looked up, but that was all I did. The voice didn't sound like it belonged to someone with dire intent. More importantly, by getting so close without waking us, its owner had proven that if he'd wanted to kill us, we would have already died.

The stranger was sitting cross-legged on a thick pad on the ground about fifteen feet away with the sunrise behind him. I couldn't make out a lot of detail against the sun, but I could tell that he had on a large, round, peasant hat and dark clothes, and no visibly exposed weapons. Instead, his hands were in his lap, where he was quietly scratching Bontrang's head.

The little gryphinx's presence reminded me to worry about Triss—who would normally have warned me about any stranger's approach. Reaching out through our bond, I could feel Triss's presence but only dimly. He was still very deeply asleep, and I decided to leave him that way for now.

"It's not much of a breakfast, I know," said the stranger, "but it's all I've got to hand."

Maylien had stiffened in my arms at the newcomer's first words and slid half out of the blanket. Now she relaxed and shivered before sliding back down to snuggle against me.

"That sounds pretty dreadful actually. Why don't you go find something better and wake us when you get back." When our unexpected guest showed no sign of moving, she sighed. "Yeah, I didn't think that was going to happen." Then she glanced over her shoulder at me. "But where are my manners? This is Heyin, one of my oldest friends, and—as you will no doubt soon agree—the world's worst cook."

"Don't be like that," said Heyin. "I'm offering you the same food I was planning on having for *my* breakfast."

"Doesn't matter," said Maylien. "Your digestive system is made of old leather and leftover bits of yak intestine. Whether or not you

can eat something has no bearing on its relationship to actual food."
Maylien shrugged then. "On the other hand, I doubt we'll get a better offer. So, what do you think, Aral? Should we take him up on
his revolting breakfast?"

"Aral." Heyin whistled low and soft before I could answer. "Then
you *have* found your famous Blade."

"Actually, this time, he found me." Maylien squeezed my arm
under the blanket. "He saved my life yesterday. Aral, Heyin. Heyin,
Aral."

Heyin clambered to his feet—startling Bontrang, who squawked
loudly and flapped over to complain at Maylien. Then Heyin gave
me a deep bow.

"For saving my baroness, I owe you whatever is in my power to
give. Sadly, for the moment, that mostly consists of a rather inadequate breakfast. However, if the baroness will consent to get herself
out of bed and on the road, I will be happy to promise a better meal
later, when we get back to Marchon's house-in-exile."

"All right," Maylien mock-grumbled, "all right. I'm getting up.
See, this is me getting up."

Maylien rolled out from under the blankets. When I started to
follow, she put a hand on my chest and gently pushed me back down
again. "You stay. You're nowhere near recovered, no matter what
you think."

I wanted to argue, but the fact that she'd hardly had to exert
herself to keep me from rising lent weight to her case, so I let myself
be convinced. She started poking at the coals, then added wood from
the pile.

"Might as well toast the bread and make sandwiches." She looked
up at Heyin. "I don't suppose you thought to bring along a teapot?"

"No, though I've got a tin pan and a couple of moderately fresh
cakes of Kadesh Jade I can shave into the pot."

"Ooh, that changes things. For good tea I can forgive the food."
She pointed over the hill. "There's a little stream just over that way.
Why don't you go fill your pan while I get the fire built back up."

"As my baroness knows, I live only to serve."

Heyin nodded at me and sketched a little bow to Maylien, then
started off in the indicated direction. As he moved out of the direct
sunlight, I saw that he was much older than I'd have guessed from
his voice, with streaks of white in his long ponytail and mustache
and several old scars visible on his hands and arms.

I waited a few more minutes, until Maylien had the fire built
up, then slowly pushed myself into a sitting position. It was a lot

more work than it should have been. I felt like a heap of ground-up mystery meat ready for the sausage maker. Admittedly, I felt like a significantly better cut of mystery meat than I had last night, but that wasn't saying much. I gently poked at the fresh bruise on my ribs, sliding my fingers though the giant hole in my shirt where the axe had nearly opened me up.

"I think I'm going to need some new clothes."

"You and me both." Maylien tugged ruefully at the tornout left knee of her divided skirts. "We'll have to fix that when we get to Exile House. These have moved from the category of convenient disguise to polishing cloths, and yours are worse."

She was right. Between the dust, the dirt, and the travel stains, it was hard to even tell what color my clothes had once been. Add in the rips and tears and the stink, and the only practical use I could imagine for anything I was wearing was lining the nest of a not-very-picky rat.

I decided it was time to wake Triss then and gently poked my shadow. "Triss, are you all right?"

My shadow stirred sluggishly and slowly reshaped itself into a small dragon. "Whazzat?"

"I asked if you were all right."

"Oh, sure. I've never felt better in my life." He reached back and licked his right wing at the shoulder joint, then growled before going off into an extended string of Shadetalk. It sounded like someone shaking a sackful of angry snakes, and I was pretty sure a translation would have come out all kinds of obscene.

Finally, he shifted back to Zhani, "Still, I think I'll live." Then his voice dropped lower, filling with concern. "How are you?"

"Likewise, thanks to Maylien." I decided to omit any reference to the rummer's overproofed rice-whiskey—or whatever you wanted to call it—on the grounds that if Triss didn't remember it, he'd be happier not knowing. "She got us out of Tien and clear of the Elite without much help from me. And now . . ." I looked at Maylien as I realized I didn't know what happened next. "Well, better ask her that, I guess."

Maylien frowned. "Back to Exile House to clean up and resupply, though I suspect we won't be able to stay long. I sent Bontrang there yesterday afternoon with a message for Heyin, to let him know where we were then and that we were coming. I'd expected him to wait there, not come out and meet us on the road. The fact that he's here suggests all is not well in Marchon."

"Who is Heyin?" I asked.

"A foolish old man who refused to die when he was supposed to," Heyin replied as he came back over the hill.

Beside me, Triss started to shift his shape, but I patted him and shook my head. "He knows what we are, Triss. There's no need to hide."

Triss nodded at that, then curled up on my shady side, tucking his nose under his tail and going straight back to sleep. That worried me rather a lot, but there was nothing I could do about it. I rested my hand lightly between his wings, trying to reassure myself with the contact of fingers against invisible scales that felt strangely insubstantial.

Maylien gave Heyin a stern look. "That's not true. Heyin was the captain of my mother's guard before my sister had him stripped of his position and thrown into the street for failing to prevent the old baroness's death."

"Which may be the only thing in the whole world that your sister and I ever agreed on." Heyin set the pan down on a rock Maylien had laid among the coals for that purpose. "Though she really ought to have had me flogged and beheaded as well." Heyin's voice was casual, but his eyes seethed with rage and shame. "I would not have resisted."

"She couldn't very well do that," said Maylien. "Not when your failure was to stop a *suicide*."

"Not without admitting it was murder, no." Heyin opened a small paper package, pulling out a slab of smoked bacon, which he proceeded to slice up. "And if she'd done that, then someone might have thought to investigate just who it was that had murdered the old baroness. Which is why I would not have resisted. I did fail to protect your mother in life; if my death could bring your sister to justice for that murder, I would quite happily commit formal suicide in the market square of Marchon tomorrow."

"That wouldn't do anything but provide my sister with a great deal of satisfaction." Maylien admonished him.

"Which argument is how you talked me out of it the first time." Heyin finished with the bacon and started cutting a loaf of black bread into thick slices, handing them off to Maylien to arrange on another rock for rough toasting. "What I still don't understand is how you convinced me to become the captain of your guard-in-exile. Or why you chose to do so, when you would have been fully justified in spitting on me and sending me into the wilderness to die." He leaned his head to one side as he started in on making the tea. "You still could, you know. You have but to say the word."

Maylien rolled her eyes theatrically. "How many times do I have to tell you that I need you, old man? Without you I could never have set up Exile House or even begun to oppose my sister properly. I was a stranger to my people and far more Rover than baronial heir; you were one of them and respected. Without you to vouch for me, I would have had to choose between fleeing Zhan and remaining to die by my sister's hand. Now, finally, because you paved the way for me among my people, we may have a chance to see my sister pay for her crimes." She turned then, and they both looked at me.

I shrugged. "I'll have to get some fresh clothes and rest up for a few days, but if you want me to kill your sister for you, I can certainly manage that. Even with Devin protecting her, it shouldn't be impossible. She just doesn't have the resources to keep a"—but I couldn't bring myself to say "Blade"—"to keep me and Triss out." I ran a finger along the spinal ridge of my dragon's shadow, but he was too deeply asleep to respond—very worrying.

"I wish that were all I had to ask of you," said Maylien. "But it wouldn't do the trick. If I am to take the baronial seat and not have Thauvik simply assign it to some unknown cousin, I have to kill Sumey myself in a proper duel and seize the coronet. I need you to get me to Sumey in a setting where she will have no choice but to accept my challenge."

"You need me to do what?" I blinked. "I think I missed a step there. You're a mage." I nodded at Bontrang, who had settled down where he could keep a sharp eye on the bacon. "You don't even have standing to issue a challenge. Do you? I thought Zhani law forbade the mageborn from dueling for peerages."

"Not quite. The crown despises the practice because it is believed that a mage has an unfair advantage in combat. But the Right of Challenge is much older than Crown Law. It's a survivor of the Code Martial of the ancient kingdom. If I can get to Sumey in front of proper witnesses and forswear the use of magic for the duration of our duel, she cannot deny my challenge—we are too close in blood."

Bontrang made a little growling noise though whether he was responding more to Maylien's words or to her angry tone was impossible to tell.

Maylien continued, "The trick will be getting there. Crown Law can't deny Right of Challenge, even from a mage such as myself. What it can do is make it *very* hard for any mage to live to issue such a challenge."

I was still flailing. "Could you elaborate on that? Obscure dueling codes weren't really a major topic of study at the temple. Namara issued sentences of death, not challenges."

Maylien nodded. "If I weren't a mage and I wanted to challenge my sister, all I would have to do is walk up to the entrance of wherever she was and demand that I be taken to her to issue my challenge. Whoever met me at the door would then have to take me to her at once. She wouldn't be allowed to use guards or other direct measures to prevent me from entering her presence, and we would duel on the spot. But Crown Law has put all sorts of barriers up around the conditions of challenge in the case of the mageborn."

"Such as?"

"To start with, I have to send a formal announcement of my intention to challenge. Both to my sister and to the crown. In it, I have to name a day and a place, and that place must be on Marchon lands. The crown then sends a pair of witnesses to the event, and if I don't show up, the challenge is considered forfeit. At which point, they declare me an outlaw and under sentence of death throughout Zhan." Bontrang growled again.

"I think I'm starting to see how this works now," I said. "I take it all those rules about not using guards or other direct measures to stop you from reaching your sister go out the window, too."

"Exactly. She may use any means that were available to her at the time of the announcement of intent to challenge, though she may not increase the size of her guard or beg help of the crown."

"Do you have to tie both your arms behind your back, too?" I asked.

"No. The Code Martial describes the conditions of the duel itself and those they have not been able to alter though I have little doubt they would like to do just as you suggest. That or simply have anyone with both the mage gifts and noble blood killed outright."

"As much as I hate to interrupt," said Heyin, "the toast will all too soon go from done to burnt if I don't, and the tea is almost ready as well."

Heyin handed out rough sandwiches then. As soon as I took a bite I realized just how hungry I was after two nights and a day of putting nothing in my stomach but alcohol. I took the tea when it was ready, too, since there was no graceful way to refuse, and drank a token sip before quietly setting it aside. As always, it reminded me too much of efik and what I had lost. Heyin finished eating quickly, then immediately started to clean up the campsite and pack away our small stock of gear.

"So, how bad is it?" Maylien asked Heyin as he reached for our blankets.

He shrugged. "Honestly, I don't know."

"How bad is what?" I asked.

"Whatever it is that's making my captain very politely but very firmly push us to get moving."

"I'm not pushing. I'm easing the way." Maylien gave him a hard look, and Heyin held up a hand before she could say anything. "No, really. What I know doesn't justify pushing. Reports of the place were both vague and unreliable, and we haven't been able to get inside. But something about it nags at me."

"The place?" prompted Maylien.

"A little keep not far from the Marchon seat," said Heyin. "There's been talk of your sister going there in secret, but no one knows why, and we haven't been able to get inside. And we won't without magic or a major assault."

"Which needs either me or my orders."

"More or less," said Heyin. "But really, it would be better to show you. Tomorrow. After both of you have rested and eaten and bathed." Heyin sniffed. "Especially that last."

"Heyin!" Maylien glared at him, but he was impervious.

"It's more than a day's ride from here, and Exile House is almost on the way. We won't lose much time by stopping, and I think it would be better if you arrived looking more like a baroness and less like a rag-seller. Your people expect you to look the part."

Maylien tossed the last bits of bacon from her sandwich to Bontrang, then started helping Heyin with the packing. I got up to help, but Triss continued sleeping and wouldn't be moved. As soon as I got more than a few feet away from Triss, though, I became aware of just how much of my nima was steadily draining away down the link between us—much as pulling a bandage off a seeping wound will make you aware of all the blood you're losing. The feeling made me go all dizzy and staggery. That's when Maylien ordered me to sit down again and poured me out the last of the rummer's moonshine. That took the edge off my growing worry and made me feel a false sort of cheer, but only for a little while.

When it was time to go, I managed to wake Triss long enough to get him in the saddle with me, where he hid himself in my shadow, but then he went right back to sleep. Within an hour, I'd started seeing white blots again and lost track of everything but staying on the horse. Somewhere close to lunchtime, we stopped at the house of a prosperous farmer who hailed Maylien as his baroness. He cheerfully supplied us with a meal and a large jar of something almost painfully alcoholic that he called rice-white. It was basically a more polished cousin of the rummer's stuff, and I spent the rest of the day teetering back and forth between keeling over from overtapped exhaustion and keeling over from the booze.

I got a bit of my strength back at sunset, shortly before we arrived at Exile House. So I was alert enough to register a sort of blurry impression of lots of ruined stone walls and collapsed structures wrapped around a tight core of carefully renovated and camouflaged buildings. There were a few dozen men and women around, most in rough martial attire with bands bearing an inverted emblem of House Marchon on their sword arms—upside down, the jade fox sitting in its gold field looked subtly wrong. Maylien and Heyin had put together a substantial counterforce. Unfortunately, getting down off my horse and into the bathhouse soaked up most of my reserves, so I didn't find out any more then.

I dozed off twice in the soaking tub and had to be prodded awake by Chul, the young soldier Heyin had assigned to make sure I didn't drown. He also found me a robe, and after I'd dragged myself to the privy and back, he led me to a tiny stone-walled room where a thick feather bed lay atop a low platform and some quite beautiful and obviously hastily-thrown-down rugs. It smelled strongly of last summer's apples.

"I'm very sorry about the state of your . . . bedroom," he said, sounding both deeply embarrassed and confused. "The baroness has told us to treat you as the most honored of guests, and we would normally have given you one of the tower rooms, but she also asked that we put you in a place where the sun doesn't shine. She specified no windows and as many feet of wood and stone between you and the sky as we could manage. That made things . . . difficult."

"It's perfect," I said. "Mayl—your baroness is a very wise young woman." I lowered myself gladly onto the bed. It felt wonderful.

"We had to take the latch off the door because it wasn't really designed to be opened from this side. So just give it a shove when you want to get out. There's no privy down here, but I can bring you a piss-pot if you'd like."

I tried to answer, but all I managed was a mumble before sleep reached up and pulled me under.

Something cool and wet touched my forehead, and I blinked my eyes open. A shadow crossed through the dim lanternlight that came in through the door of my little sleeping chamber. My eyes flicked upward. Triss hung on the wall above and to my left, his paw extended toward my face, where a wet cloth lay just above my eyes.

"How do you feel?" he asked quietly.

I stretched. Tentatively at first, then with more enthusiasm. I was stiff and a little weak but not really sore anywhere except my throat, which, for reasons unknown, felt awfully hashed. I was also *seriously* hungry.

"I feel pretty good, Triss. Apparently a solid night's sleep in a nice bed was just what I needed."

A wry chuckle drew my attention to the foot of the bed. Maylien stood just inside the doorway, with Bontrang perched on a leather pad on her shoulder.

"What's so funny?" I asked.

"Try a week's sleep interspersed with bits of delirium," said Maylien.

I looked at Triss. "Really?"

He shrugged his wings. "That's what they tell me, but I couldn't really say. I've only been up and around since sunset yesterday myself."

"What happened?"

Triss contracted briefly in embarrassment. "Apparently, I did. The magelightning hurt me much worse than I let on—"

"Triss . . ."

He looked off to the side. "At first I didn't want to worry you because you were in rough shape, too. You needed to stay focused on getting us clear of the Elite. After, I knew you'd be mad that I hadn't told you, and I was so busy just holding myself together that I could barely string two words together. It just seemed easier not to have to argue about it." He shrank again. "I'm feeling much better now . . ."

"You should have told me, you muttonhead." I reached up and ran a fingertip along the underside of his jaw, reveling in his scaly solidity.

"I know. I'm sorry. When we couldn't get you to wake up after I did yesterday night, I was really worried."

I glanced a question at Maylien.

She shrugged, but only with the shoulder opposite Bontrang. "I don't know. You'd need to talk to a healer who specializes in mage care to figure out what happened there. If I had to guess, I'd say that for most of the week, Triss was draining your magical reserves away faster than you could replenish them, and it took you some time to recover after he stopped. Call it soul-exhaustion maybe, since nima rises from the well of the soul."

"That sounds ugly," I said.

Maylien nodded. "We weren't entirely sure either of you was going to make it. If the healers hadn't been able to get you to drink some clear soup and rice-white in your brief rounds of waking delirium, I don't think you would have."

"That'd explain the throat then. That rice-white stuff tastes like it runs three parts paint thinner to one part water."

Triss gave me the hairy eyeball but didn't say anything. I pushed myself up and back to lean against the wall in a half-sitting position—the longer I was awake the better I felt . . . and the hungrier. Like a monster that had been wakened by hearing its name, my stomach let out a quite audible growl.

"So, if it suddenly occurred to me that I was ravenous, what would be the chances of my getting something to eat?"

"Well, if you're up to moving, I can take you to the kitchens and see what's available. Otherwise, I'll send someone to get you something."

"Let's go then!" I flicked the blankets off, then hurriedly recaptured them when I realized I was naked.

Maylien blushed prettily and looked away. "I forgot about that. Let me arrange some clothes for you." She backed into the hall.

"You weren't so shy on the road," I teased.

"Uh, about that . . . just a moment." She turned and said over her shoulder into the hall, "Chul, could you find a pair of pants and a shirt for our guest?"

"Of course, Baroness." From the tone of his voice, Chul didn't much like the idea of leaving his baroness alone with me, but he didn't argue either.

Once the sounds of Chul's moving away had grown faint enough to indicate some real distance, Maylien looked back at me, her expression carefully blank. "I have to apologize for my conduct on the road, Aral. As Heyin has been at pains to remind me, the duties and conduct demanded of a baroness are not at all the same as those of the Rover's apprentice I used to be. When we were alone together on the way here, I treated you as I might have treated a fellow Rover in my traveling days. I said and did things that were not in keeping with my present obligations. I'm very sorry if I gave you an impression I shouldn't have."

I felt like all the air had abruptly left the room, or like I'd caught a solid kick just under the ribs. In either case, I found it very hard to draw the breath I needed to reply as I should. It wasn't about sex, though it could have been nice if things had gone that way. It was about the sudden severing of a connection that had only begun to form, the first such connection I'd tried to make in years.

"I'm sorry, too," I said quietly. "I should have remembered why you sought me out and treated you like the baroness I intend to help you become and . . ." I trailed off lamely, unable to say "not like Jax or one of the other Blade women"—that wouldn't be appropriate either. Finally, after the silence had gone on too long, I forced out, "I should have treated you like a baroness and not an old friend."

Bontrang hissed sharply, and the look on Maylien's face shifted from blank to tightly closed. I felt even worse. But before I could do anything to repair the situation, Chul returned, and Maylien stepped aside to let him into the room.

"Thank you, Chul. Could you make sure that . . . my guest is dressed properly, then bring him up to the kitchens for food? Aral, I'll see you later. I've got things to attend to."

And then she left me.

18

"I guess the real question is whether you want to try to shut the place down cold now or just have someone nip in and take a quick look around," I said.

With sunset a half hour off, Maylien, Heyin, and I sat high up in a massive old oak tree on a heavily forested slope. Across the deep narrow valley below us, a small stonewalled keep stood on the edge of a fast-moving little river. Bontrang had chosen a perch above us, up where the branches wouldn't support a human's weight, while Triss opted to stay hidden within my shadow as he did most of the time I was in company.

The keep sat well down under the shoulder of the opposite ridge, centering the open scar of the cut where they'd quarried the limestone for the outer walls. The setting of the tiny stone-and-timber fort felt more than a little off to me, as though the builders had been more interested in keeping the place out of sight than making it truly defensible.

Oh, it had most of the usual defensive accoutrements, high outer walls of smooth-cut stone, a narrow moat fed by the stream that ran through the valley, corner towers with light catapults . . . But big ancient trees stood all around it within easy bowshot of the walls, and a ballista or other siege engine on the ridge would be able to hammer the central tower almost unimpeded. An attacker using burning pitch could set the place alight in minutes.

It might be strong enough to repel a casual assault by unskilled rabble, but it would never hold against a determined assault from even a moderately well-armed force. On the other hand, its tiny size made it a damned hard problem in terms of infiltration. That was why Maylien had asked me to have a look at it now that I was up and around again. She didn't want to pay the blood tithe of a frontal assault for an unknown return, especially since Sumey might be able to use such an attack against her at court. And Heyin had flat refused to let his baroness go in there herself when they "had a damned sneaking specialist sleeping off a bender in the basement!"

I'm pretty sure I wasn't supposed to have heard that particular debate, but then, I *am* a sneaking specialist.

"I think we should start with a quick look around, Aral. If you'd be willing to oblige me." Maylien's tone sounded just as stiff and formal as it had every time we'd talked since I shoved my foot down my throat two nights before. "We might need to make a major assault at some later point, but I'd like to know what my sister is using the keep for first. She's got a habit of tucking her dirty work away where it's hard to find, like that dungeon she had you locked up in back in Zhan."

I nodded. As I'd found out yesterday, Maylien had tracked me down by the simple expedient of having a spy in her sister's house who'd gotten her a list of Sumey's city properties. The Old Mews dungeon had been in the basement of the fourth building on the list. Knowing that told us that it had probably been Sumey who started the fire as well rather than Devin. I was frankly relieved by the thought—it felt better to believe that my onetime friend hadn't sunk so low.

"Whatever she's doing here, she's kept it awfully quiet," said Heyin. "And I don't like the feel of the place. We're only about an hour's hard ride from the Marchon seat at Shaisin, but the countryside's as empty as if we had a nest of petty dragons living in the forest, and that's just not right. The ground's lousy for farming and technically baronial land, but the timber's damn good. There ought to be illicit loggers and charcoal-men about, or poachers at the very least. It's not natural."

"Has Sumey declared the area off-limits in any formal way?" I asked.

"No," replied Heyin. "There aren't even the usual dire warnings posted at the bounds. Everyone knows it's baronial land and legally off-limits, of course. But most times and places that only makes sure the poachers stay extra quiet. It doesn't scare them away."

Maylien spoke. "When Heyin and I came out here last week, I asked a couple of the smallholders around the edges of the land what they knew about it. These are people who aren't afraid to defy

my sister's rule. If they were, they wouldn't be talking to me or I to
them. But not one of them is willing to trespass here, nor talk much
about why that is. I got a few bleats about the haunted castle and a
few more about the night-walking dead, but that was it."

"Seems like awfully fresh construction for a haunted castle," I
said.

Heyin nodded. "I checked into the rumors of night-walkers as
well—I'd heard from those same folk before ever I brought Maylien
to see them. But there don't seem to be any more disappearances or
unexplained corpses turning up around the edges of the wood than
you'd normally expect to see in this kind of country."

"The forest proper is completely empty of people?" I asked.

"It is," said Heyin. "But you can't confine ghouls and ghasts to
one area like that. Especially not when there's potential prey to be
had by crossing the boundaries."

Triss flickered into dragon shape, showing himself. "You and I
can't, maybe. But a powerful enough necromancer could."

"Is that what *you* think is in the keep, Triss?" I asked.

"No." Triss's tongue flicked out. "The deeper shadows in the
forest on the way here didn't taste as I would expect them to if there
were someone like that around, not enough rough magic. But it can
be done, and the shadows don't taste quite right either . . ." He
shook his head in frustration. "There's something almost familiar
there though I haven't been able to place it."

"Well, the sun's nearly down," I said. "So, why don't I just slide
over there, have a look around, and save us further speculation?"

"I agree that's our best course of action," said Maylien. "Shall
we go?"

"I don't think that 'we' should go anywhere," I said.

Heyin spoke at the same time, saying, "Baroness, we discussed
this already. Surely you're not planning on going with him?"

"Of course I'm going," replied Maylien. "The whole reason for
bringing Aral into our plans was so that he could get me through
my sister's defenses come the day of the challenge. If that's going to
happen, we need to practice working together against the nastiest
security my sister can put together. If either one of you can think of
a better way to do that than to have me go with Aral here and now,
you're welcome to tell me about it."

"I'm convinced," I said, though I didn't much like the imper-
sonal sound of "bringing Aral into our plans." It made me feel like
a piece on a game board instead of a human being. "Let's go."

Heyin said something unintelligible under his breath, but he
didn't elaborate or make any other argument, just sighed loudly
when Maylien and I started down the tree.

I pointed across the moat to the guard slowly walking back and
forth atop the nearest of the keep's little towers. All of the towers
had guards, but this one was farthest from the front gate and the
weakest link in the defense.

"That's our first hurdle, right there. We can't get over the outer
wall without doing something about him. You can't anyway. I could
probably get past him on my own, but if I'm going to carve a hole big
enough for you to follow me through, he's got to either die or take a
convenient nap. This is your domain and your mission, so it's your
choice as to which."

Maylien grimaced. "Which would you recommend under the
circumstances?"

"There are pluses and minuses to both choices. Dead is easier,
and it's permanent. There's no chance of the guard waking up and
sounding the alarm. It's also not something we'll be able to conceal
later. Leave a corpse, and they *know* someone ghosted a guard. Get
rid of the body, and they'll still be pretty sure that someone killed
the guy. Perhaps most importantly, if I do ghost him there's no bringing him back. Right now all that we know he's guilty of is working
for your sister. He could be every bit as bad as those torturers who
had me strung up in Tien, but he could just be a local kid who needs
to make a living."

"What about putting him to sleep?"

"That's significantly harder to manage without using magic,
which would light us up if your sister's got another petty mage like
Lok around. I have to get in close and dose him with opium and efik
or cut off his air for a bit. Either way is imprecise. He could die, or
he could wake up too early, or not all there. Best way to deal with
too early's to tie him up, but that's as good a calling card as ghosting
him would be if he's found or wakes up. There's no way to pretend
we weren't here if he's discovered gagged and bound. Even if he's
not, there'll be rope burns and other signs. Knocking him out and
tying him up's still my first choice, though. I'd rather not ghost anyone who might not deserve it."

Maylien frowned. "My sister's kept this place even quieter than
she did that nasty little dungeon in Tien. Considering the kinds of
things that was set up for, and the unholy . . . pursuits my sister has

taken a liking to in the last few years, I really doubt that anyone here is an innocent lamb. But you're right that we can't know that without investigating first."

She closed her eyes for a moment, then opened them and straightened her spine. "I'm the rightful Baroness of Marchon. That man over there is one of my people, even if he does work for my sister. He deserves the benefit of the doubt. If you can put him to sleep without too great a risk to yourself, do it. If you can't . . . if there's any real chance that he'll give us away or harm you, kill him."

"Wait here. I'll throw a rope down when I've taken care of him." I slipped down to the edge of the moat and eyed the water.

It looked cold and smelled wrong somehow, swampy and rank where it appeared clean and clear. I didn't really want to swim, but the heights of the walls relative to the surrounding trees made for an impossible sail-jump. Also, if I swam, I'd be much harder to see coming. So I edged my way out onto a root in order to ease myself into the moat quietly. Dim moonlight cast my shadow on the surface of the water, and Triss let out a hiss, then quickly changed shape and spread dragon wings wide between me and the water.

"Back up," he whispered urgently.

"Why?" I asked, but I was already moving.

"Faster."

Up on the tower the guard turned and looked our way, raising his lantern as he did so. I flattened myself in the leaf litter under the trees, and Triss flowed over me, covering me in shadow. Together, we waited for the guard to turn away.

"What's wrong?" I asked once Triss finally signaled that the guard had moved back to his normal pattern.

"Something in the water," said Triss. "I don't know what, but when I touched the surface, I could feel things moving around down in the deeps. It tasted like the shadows under the trees. I don't think swimming would be wise."

"And I don't think we can make the tower's deck with a sail-jump," I replied. "It's simply too far above the nearer trees."

"So we don't jump for the top. There's a little ridge in the bedrock just below the base of the wall, a few inches above the water. If you aim for that, I don't think we'll have any trouble."

"Except for the part where I smash face-first into the wall and fall into the water if we come in too fast. Oh, and the bit where you have to shift from wings to claws in the instant between hitting the wall and falling into the water."

"We've done harder jumps in the past," said Triss.

"We were a lot younger then, and in better training, and you hadn't been recently injured."

"Are you saying you're too old and out of shape to manage your end of things? Because I'll understand if you are. I know I can do my part, but I'm sure we can find some other way for an old man like you to get in if we need to."

"Listen here you lizard-brained excuse for a shadow-puppet . . ." I trailed off as I realized I was grinning.

For the first time in I couldn't remember how long, Triss had simply teased me for teasing's sake. For years now every one of his pokes or prods had a hidden nag underneath—worries about my drinking, or my choices in the jobs I took to keep us off the streets, or simply how dangerous it was for us to be living in Tien with a price on our heads.

Triss grinned back at me. "Does that sudden silence mean you've decided you're not quite too decrepit to pull off a trick you could have done in your sleep a few years ago? Or, to put a finer point on it, that I'm right? . . . as usual."

"Let's just say that we'll make the attempt. The worst that happens is we blow it and die horribly, and my last words will be 'I told you so.' "

"I can live with that."

"Why doesn't that surprise me? We'd better fill Maylien in on the new plan before we go."

After all the discussion, the jump itself was almost anticlimactic. I did hit the wall quite a bit harder than I'd have liked—hard enough to knock the wind out of me and make a noise that drew the guard's attention. But I managed not to slip off into the water, and Triss kept us hidden in shadow until the guard gave up and went back to his slow march again. Climbing up the tower wasn't much fun. The stonework was all fresh-cut and very clean and straight. And the mortar had been applied with care and an eye to eliminating fingerholds.

Without Triss's ability to cling to cracks finer than any sheet of paper, I'd have had to swim back across the moat or spend the night balanced on the three-inch ridge we'd used as our landing point. Add in the need to do things very quietly, and it took close to half an hour to make it up a tiny little forty-foot wall.

As I waited under the edge of the parapet for the guard to pass by on his rounds, I reached into my trick bag for the case holding the last of my opium-and-efik-packed eggs. What I got when I opened it was a handful of eggshell shards and drug-dusted fingers. Dammit!

It was all right before the sail-jump, so it must have shattered when we smacked into the base of the wall despite the special packaging. One of the hazards of working with eggs.

I'd lost the easiest way of dealing with the guard, which meant I had to revisit whether it wouldn't be better simply to ghost him. It was much easier to kill a man silently than it was to knock him out without making a lot of noise or seriously hurting him. But I found that making the right decision about when to kill had become the hardest task of all, and I froze.

A younger me wouldn't have hesitated for an instant if a man's life had lain between me and the most efficient execution of my charge. But that version of me had the certainty of the goddess as the bedrock underneath his feet. My definition of justice had been no more and no less than whatever my goddess desired. If she chose to order a person killed and another stood in the way, then killing that other was a necessary expedient. You couldn't let sentiment, or pride, or any other emotion get in the way of duty and professionalism.

But the goddess was dead, and I had only the shifting sands of my own conscience to stand on. Here and now, the choice was mine, no matter what I told Maylien. If I spilled this young guard's blood, the stain would be on my hands. Long seconds slid past as I hung there dithering.

"What's wrong?" Triss whispered in the faintest ghost of a voice.

I just shook my head because I needed to work it through on my own. I'd been avoiding this choice for five years though I hadn't realized it until now. This was really why I'd chosen to lose myself in minor sorts of shadow work instead of trying to hunt down the Son of Heaven or looking for some other real purpose for my life.

I was a trained killer, one of the half dozen best in the world. In the five years I had served the goddess as a full Blade, I had taken at least a hundred lives. I had been a human weapon, honed to the finest edge possible by the training of the temple. The Blade of Justice made flesh. I knew my purpose then: to bring death to those who deserved it. I was so very, very good at the job, and I loved my work and my goddess.

More than efik, or alcohol, I had been hooked on the feeling that came with being the living embodiment of Namara's will. Not the killing—that had brought me no pleasure—but the certainty. Knowing that I was born to destroy the enemies of justice was the sweetest feeling in the world. When the other gods killed Namara, I'd lost that along with everything else.

That was the problem with relying on gods instead of thinking for yourself. When you base your morality on what heaven tells you to do, heaven can always cut you off at the knees by changing its mind.

Oh, I'd killed since the temple fell. Mostly it had been in self-defense, though I would cheerfully have killed Lok and his men for what they did to Triss. But until this moment, I hadn't had to face the choice whether or not to kill someone in pursuit of some other goal. The temptation, really, as I now realized. That was the real reason I'd tried to put the decision off on Maylien, to make it her mission instead of mine. More than anything, I'd wanted to give my will over into another's hand again, to do what I did best without having to take the weight of decision on my own shoulders.

It would be so easy to do, to kill this faceless guard and believe that I'd done it because Maylien had ordered me to. That I owed her Triss's life and mine and that paying that debt meant doing whatever she asked of me. It would be so easy to let her become my new goddess, if only for a little while. And I wanted it. I wanted it so badly, the luxury of turning off my mind and simply being what my training and aptitude had shaped me into. A weapon for another's hand.

A scuffing sound from above told me that the guard had come close again. If he followed his pattern, he would look out over the woods behind me for a count of five, then turn around and walk to the other side of the tower. *One.* Through Triss's unvision I watched as he leaned out above me craning his neck and exposing the pale skin under his chin.

Two. All I had to do was flick a dagger into my hand, bring my arm up, straighten my legs . . . he'd die without a sound. *Three.* So easy to let my reflexes decide for me. *Four.* I pressed my face into the limestone, drawing its dusty smell deep into my lungs. *Five.* He started to turn away, but I could still just manage it . . . if I let myself. *Six.* And he was gone, stepping back from the edge in the same moment that I did.

Seven. A hand up onto the lip of the parapet. *Eight.* Another. *Nine.* Pull myself up and over. *Ten.* Drop down and grab. I hit him fast and from behind, wrapping my left arm tight around his neck, cutting off air and blood flow at the same time that I pinned his right arm to his side with my own. I lifted him back off his feet as Triss wrapped around his legs and his other arm, holding him immobile.

It would have been simpler to break his neck. Much simpler. Even then. I fought the temptation, keeping the pressure on until he went limp. Counted carefully. Cut off the blood too long, and something happened to the mind. Too short, and he'd wake up within minutes. Finally, I let off and eased him to the ground, hoping I'd gotten it right. A gag, bindings at wrists and ankles, a couple of loops of cord tying him tight against the base of the catapult, and done. He still might die—bound and unconscious people did sometimes—but I had made my own decision, taken the hard road and done what I could to preserve his life within the constraints of my assignment.

I signaled Maylien, and she sent Bontrang over to take the end of a rope back to her. We pulled it tight between the nearest tree and one of the crenellations and she hand-overhanded her way up the slightly inclined rope.

Maylien peered through a low, barred window in the back of the central keep. "That looks familiar."

"All too," I agreed. The dimly magelit room was a much-expanded version of the torture chamber where I'd been held.

"Except here she hasn't bothered hiring out an illusion to keep the neighbors from seeing what goes on down there. Maybe you *should* have killed that guard. He had to know what happens here. As soon as I can get a big enough force together, I'm going to destroy this place."

"Why wait?" I asked. The sight of the glyph rack and memories of what its twin had done to Triss had my blood burning.

"You can't be serious. A keep this size must hold at least thirty of my sister's guards. I know Blades are good, but there's just the two of us."

I opened my mouth to point out that two mages, one a former Blade, with the element of surprise to help ought to be more than adequate to the job. Before I could say a word, several drops of cold rank water fell on my face and Triss slapped my shoulder, hard. I caught Maylien around the waist, dragging her with me as I dove to the left.

"What are you doing!" she demanded as she landed atop me.

"Moving!" I started us rolling across the cobbles.

Something that smelled like it ought to have been buried a long time ago landed with a soggy thump in front of the window where we had been kneeling only a moment before. Chalk one up for those rumors of the night-walking dead and another for Triss's concern about things in the moat.

19

The undead moved fast. Rising from where it had just missed its pounce, the creature threw itself after us within seconds. Because we were already rolling onward, it missed again, this time ending up flat on its belly.

I threw Maylien a few yards beyond where the roll had carried us, then flipped back to my feet before it came at me again. I went right back down a moment later when I couldn't get my new swords clear of their sheaths in time to prevent the creature's clawing hands from striking me full in the chest. Maylien had given me a beautiful pair to replace the ones I'd lost at Devin's, but they were a tiny bit too wide for my old hip-draw rig—a problem I thought I'd fixed already.

Triss briefly shaped himself into a shadowy breastplate then, or the thing would have torn my heart out. As filthy fingernails skittered across hardened shadow, I had a moment to desperately hope Triss's efforts would also suffice to keep the creature from passing its horrible curse along to me. With the death of the goddess, I'd almost certainly lost my magical immunity to the restless dead.

Then I went ass over ears and had to let go of my still-sheathed swords as I turned the fall into a clumsy backward roll. I expected to have to fend off another attack as I came to my feet again, but Maylien had entered the fray by then, scything in with a crouching spin-kick that knocked the legs out from under the risen. Or whatever it was—it was hard to get enough of a fix on it in the moonlit courtyard to make more than a guess.

Maylien's maneuver finally gave me time to free my swords. As the monster started to push itself to its feet, I stepped in and swung simultaneous cuts from both sides. Aiming to take the damned thing's arms off just above the elbows, I struck with maximum force. Instead, of shearing neatly through rotted flesh and decaying bone, as I'd expected, I felt more like I'd chopped into wet oak. And, where the magical swords of my goddess might have done the trick anyway, I had only ordinary steel.

It wasn't enough, and my swords stuck fast as undead muscles bunched and twisted, pinching tight like a half-sawn branch nipping a saw blade. I had to leave them behind a moment later as I threw myself backward into another roll when the risen lunged toward my groin, its mouth gaping wide to tear and rend.

Bontrang tried to claw the monster's eyes out then, but it batted him aside. Even with my swords stuck deep in its biceps hampering its movements, the thing moved scary fast. Maylien snarled something incoherent as Bontrang fluttered weakly back to land on her shoulder, then she sent a wave of magefire washing over the creature.

The flames momentarily filled the narrow courtyard between the keep and the outer wall with light and heat, wiping out my night vision in the process. The risen screamed as the horrible smell of burning rotted flesh filled the air. Bits of cracked and blackened skin fall away, but the risen was far too soggy from its time in the moat to actually catch fire. Still screaming, it turned and lurched toward Maylien.

She'd drawn her own sword by then, a slender double-edged dueling blade of the sort favored by the Zhani nobility. She swung a backhanded cut as she dodged out of the way of the creature's charge. Several of its fingers fell to the ground with a noise like demented hail. I had a perfect opportunity then to sink a dagger in the back of its neck, but didn't bother. This was a chopping job if I'd ever seen one.

What it really wanted was an axe. Failing that, I needed to get at least one of my swords back. Short and broad, they'd do a much better job on the risen than Maylien's dueling blade. So I lunged forward, catching hold of the sword sunk in the creature's left arm. Putting one hand on the hilt and the other on the crosspiece, I applied my whole weight, twisting and torquing the blade out and down.

The blade bent alarmingly, then came free with a wrench and a ringing sound, as it sprang back straight. Somewhere in there, I caught a sharp knock on the side of the head. It sent me spinning away, with red sparks dancing across my vision and the taste of blood in my mouth from a cheek torn by my own teeth. If Triss hadn't taken the worst of the blow, I'd have lost my ear. I whispered a quick thanks, then the risen was coming at me again.

I wasn't in a good position for an effective shot with my sword, so I turned side on and kicked the thing full in the chest. A knee to the groin would have been easier and a more effective target on a living man, but I didn't think it'd help much here. What I really wanted was to shove it back and away long enough to let me think. I managed that, knocking it onto its ass, but only at the cost of filthy hands and undead fingers digging painfully at my shin and calf. Triss was there again, sheathing my leg in shadow, and again I hoped it would be enough to spare me the risen curse.

As the creature clambered back to its feet, Bontrang dove at its head from the side, slapping the creature with his wings, then shearing off before it could make any move to catch him. An instant later, Maylien hit it with more magefire. It snarled and turned toward her, and I finally saw my chance.

"Triss, I need an edge!" Then I stepped in, set my feet, and swung a double-handed blow right at the base of the thing's neck.

It was like hitting a tree trunk. The shock of the impact numbed my hands and nearly sprained my wrists as the sword tried to tear itself free of my grip, but Triss came through. With the essence of the everdark transforming my sword's edge into a sliver of deadly night, the blade slowed but never quite stopped, plowing through undead flesh and bone to behead the monster.

Not that that killed it. The head was still angrily snapping its jaws as it rolled away, while the body kept right on going in a straight line. It would take a long and hot fire or powerful and properly tailored magic to fully destroy the thing. We had time for neither, as a crossbow quarrel struck the cobbles near my feet and shattered just then. One of the other guards had gotten into firing position.

"We have to get under cover!" I yelled.

Maylien had ended up back by the low window into the dungeon, and she turned to it now. Calling Bontrang to her, she moved her hands through a quick and intricate pattern that left lines of magical light behind in a beautiful cat's cradle for those that had the eyes to see it. Then she touched the palms of her hands to the two closest bars and spoke a word of opening.

Blue light erupted from the point of contact with a tremendous shattering boom like someone had broken a bottle filled with thunder. Maylien flew back and away from the window at the same time that the bars ripped free of their moorings and fell inward. A second quarrel struck the place she'd just been crouching even as

Maylien—who had landed neatly on her feet—started back in my direction.

"Go!" she shouted, and I went, diving to slide headfirst through the gap she'd opened in the bars.

She followed a moment later, dropping down beside me out of the line of fire. She had a satisfied smile on her face and gave Bontrang an appreciative scritch on the top of the head.

"Pretty fancy spellwork for such short notice," I said as I started to check over the places the risen had touched me—if it had drawn blood, the wound would need to be cleansed with fire.

"Thanks." Maylien's breathing sounded ragged. "Bontrang and I practiced, though I wish it took less out me—I need to sit for a moment."

"Gotta check for risen contamination anyway," I responded.

Maylien spoke again as she checked herself over. "That spell's what I'd intended to use when I came to get you out of that dungeon in Tien. But then Devin dropped a net over Bontrang, bopped me on the head, and carried us both off as easily as a couple of sleeping children."

I looked away for a moment. "I'm sorry I didn't come after you right then. I wanted to, but I just didn't have anything left to do it with."

"I wouldn't have let you if you'd tried," interjected Triss before turning to Maylien. "Aral was overtapped, inches from dying."

"It's all right." Maylien put a hand on my shoulder and squeezed. "Best thing you could have done, truly. Devin had a bunch of traps laid for you. He really wanted to capture you for something though he wouldn't say what, and he was furious when you didn't come after him right away. It threw his plans off."

"Do you know that those plans were?" I asked, feeling a little sick—what else had my old friend intended to do to me?

"No. He ranted a little about how you and Sumey were both making things hard for him, but he wasn't dumb enough to spell anything out for me. Sorry."

By then we'd both finished checking for cursed wounds, and I noticed how very sad she looked though I didn't know why, so I reached up to cover her hand with my own. For a moment we sat silently like that, then she pulled gently away. Before I could do or say anything in response, we were interrupted.

"I don't know where they went." The voice was outside but close by. "That big flash blinded me, and they were gone when I could see again."

"Just get out of the courtyard, you idiot!" someone yelled back from somewhere above. "Another of the baroness's pets is on the way in from the moat, and you don't want to be there when it arrives."

"Oh shit! I—" The other voice rose into a scream, then cut off suddenly.

Fuck.

"I think it's time we got moving again." I climbed to my feet. "Too bad we can't put the bars back."

Maylien nodded and followed as I started quietly across the room. In addition to duplicating the equipment of the other torture chamber, this one had a large rack, an iron maiden, and a cauldron full of oil atop a fire grate. And just inside the door we found a huge, red marble tub and a large copper for heating water.

"What the hell is that for?" asked Maylien.

"I don't know." After glancing into the empty hallway beyond the door's narrow barred window, I bent to work on the lock with Triss's help. "Maybe your sister likes to lounge in a hot bath while she watches people have their fingernails pulled out."

"I wish I could put it past her. Or pretend she wasn't my full sister." Maylien shuddered and hugged herself. "But blood-madness runs in my family. First my father, then my sister, and lately my uncle. Sometimes I wonder when it will take me."

I felt the lock give and stood up. "You seem to be doing all right so far." It was an inadequate response, but I was too horrifyingly aware of the possibility that she was right to make a better one.

As I started to open the door, something smacked into it from the other side and slammed it back shut. Before I could force it open again a solid thunk announced someone's dropping a heavy bar into place. I glanced through the tiny window again, but couldn't see anything.

"Triss," I said, my mind racing ahead to try to anticipate the kind of resistance we'd face after he took the bar off for us— crossbows certainly, maybe woldos or other pole arms, possibly attack from two sides . . . "You're going to have to—"

Maylien tugged on my sleeve. "I hate to interrupt but another one of those things just came in through the window."

"Always wondered what it'd be like to see someone ripped to pieces by the pets." A man's face appeared in the window, leering evilly through the bars as he spoke. "Give us a good show, won't you, love?"

"Watch *this*." Maylien slapped her hand against the bars and sent a blast of magefire through the narrow opening.

The man on the other side shrieked horribly and fell away, which gave me an idea for the risen. I started back across the torture chamber toward the window.

"Follow my lead," I called over my shoulder as I raced to get into the right position.

The monster met me halfway, charging forward in the same eager and powerful but uncoordinated manner as its predecessor. That was just what I'd hoped for. As its bony hands reached for my chest, I caught it by the wrists, dropping onto my back and pulling. It lost its balance, falling toward me, and I planted both feet in its stomach, lifting and thrusting so that it passed over me and went sailing through the air. It landed headfirst in the big cauldron with a splash. For a moment, only its lower legs stuck out above the surface.

"Maylien!" I yelled but she had already anticipated my request, blasting the oil-filled cauldron with magefire.

The oil ignited with a whumpfing sound, and further trails of fire radiated out around the cauldron from the risen-spattered oil. Burning undead hands rose from beneath the oil's surface and clutched at the edge of the cauldron. Maylien grabbed a heavy cleaver from a nearby table and brought it down with a sharp whack that severed the thing's left hand. Unbalanced, the risen fell back into the flaming oil. When it tried to get out again a moment later, Maylien removed the right hand as well.

The burning hands started to crawl away. Since I wanted a closer look, I skewered them on the end of one of my swords instead of just flicking them back into the cauldron. This risen—and a close look showed it was definitely one of the risen—seemed further gone than its predecessor. What little flesh was left on its bones stretched out in narrow ribbons of muscle and tendon. The fingernails were gone completely though it looked like someone had filed the finger bones themselves to ragged points. It was harder to get a fix on the thing's head, as we didn't dare let it get out of the cauldron, but in the brief moments it was above the surface it, too, seemed more stripped down and skull-like.

After a couple of minutes of our shoving it repeatedly back into the fire, the body seemed to lose the coordination necessary to make a serious attempt at escaping the cauldron, though it continued to thrash and flail feebly. That was right about the time a badly aimed crossbow quarrel came sailing in through the window of the inner door and gonged off the cauldron. Maylien sent a burst of magefire at the door while I scraped the hands off my sword and back into the cauldron.

I would have liked to let the risen cook a little bit longer, but the guards had just become the bigger threat, so I slid my swords under the edge of the cauldron and levered it over. A cascade of burning oil washed across the floor, quickly lighting the door and every bit of wood near it on fire. Since that included a couple of major support posts, I figured it would make for a hell of a distraction. I hated to use fire under most circumstances, but I figured the people guarding this chamber of horrors had earned it.

Rather than attempt the rapidly growing inferno around the door, we reversed course and went back out the window. Between the smoke pouring out of all the lower windows and the distraction of the angry headless risen that was still staggering around the courtyard, nobody noticed us at first. We made it back to the rope we'd left on our way in and most of the way up the wall before the first crossbow was fired our way.

"Do you think there are any more of those risen in the moat?" Maylien asked as she dropped down on the roof of the little tower.

"Why?"

"Because if we stay here, someone's going to think to use one of the catapults on the other towers to lob something a lot more lethal than a few quarrels at us, and if we try to climb down that line I crawled up, we'll be easy targets." She shrugged. "I guess there's only one to find out." Then she vaulted over the parapet.

"Crazy woman!"

"But you're going after her, aren't you?" Triss sounded resigned.

"Of course I am. What if there *are* more risen? She'll need help." I followed Maylien over the parapet and into the water.

Before I'd taken three strokes, Triss made a little relieved sound. "I can't taste them in the water anymore. I think we're clear."

Maylien was already out of the water when I reached the shore, and she offered me a hand up.

"That was insane, you do know that, right?" I asked as she pulled me up.

"A little, maybe." She grinned and her teeth shone white in the darkness. "But then, so's this." She stepped in very close and put her arms around my neck. "Don't you think?" Then she gave me a kiss that just about melted my knees—enough so that Triss had to steady me.

"I dunno. Seems like a great idea to me. But I thought the future baroness wasn't supposed to do things like that." I'd intended it as a joke, but it came out sharper than I'd intended—I guess I was still stinging from her earlier rejection.

Maylien's cheeks flushed. "I'm sorry about that but . . . well, I'm *not* supposed to be doing things like this. Heyin would tear his hair out if he could see us here, but I'm not going to worry about that right now if you won't. Just for tonight, I'm going back to being the Rover I spent most of my life as and letting the future baroness take a well-earned break. We could easily have been killed back there, and confronting my sister's going to be even more dangerous. So the chances are pretty good I'm going to die rather than become a baroness anyway, aren't they?"

I nodded because she was right, though it hurt me to acknowledge it. I was quite certain I could kill Maylien's sister if I needed to. Getting Maylien into position to do it herself after sending a formal warning to Sumey that she was coming and when? Not so much. For that matter, even if I got her there safely, Sumey might simply turn out to be the better swordswoman.

"If I don't die," continued Maylien, "I'm going to have plenty of time to wear the shackles of baronial etiquette later on. So, right here, right now, I intend to do something just because I want to do it and not because I'm supposed to do it, maybe for the last time."

I glanced over my shoulder to the place where flames were starting to crawl up the side of the keep. "What about the keep?"

Maylien nipped my earlobe. "The way its going up? It'll just add to the afterglow."

"Crazy woman . . ."

"Uh-huh. Does that mean you're turning me down?"

"No, but let's get a little farther away first."

"Fair enough."

When we'd put some distance between us and the fire, I pulled her in under the shadow of a pine and gave her a kiss. She returned it in a way that left me breathless.

"It's been an awfully long time for me," I husked. More than five years.

"Me, too." And she sounded more than a little breathless herself. "Since I returned to Zhan, actually. All right for the future baroness perhaps, but not easy for the Rover I used to be." We kissed again.

"Oh, how I've missed this." She drew her fingers across the base of her belly then, setting the simple spell that prevented pregnancy.

A wasted effort that, since I had long since chosen to give up my ability to have children. Most of the Blades of Namara did so rather than run the risk of creating divided loyalties.

*   *   *

A worried-looking Heyin was waiting in the woods across the river when we turned up some time later.

"I thought you said you were only going to take a quiet look around." He pointed accusingly back the way we'd just come, to where a huge column of smoke stretched toward the moon, and flames were pouring out of what remained of the keep's upper stories.

"Things got complicated." Maylien sounded contrite but gave me a wicked wink when Heyin glanced back at the fire.

Heyin sighed. "Tell me about it."

So, we did, or most of it at least.

"You're damned lucky there weren't any more of those things in the moat, Maylien," he said when we came to the end of our tale. "What madness possesses you that you do such damn-fool things?"

"Aral keeps calling me a crazy woman," she replied. "Does that answer work for you? If not, call it a calculated risk. I figured if there were more, they'd have shown up by then."

Heyin shook his head and sighed, but didn't argue. "What were they, anyway? I thought the risen were supposed to be slow, shambling sorts of creatures. The thing you described sounds more like what you'd get if you could somehow hype a ghoul up on caras dust."

I nodded. "As far as the way they moved, yes. But they definitely weren't ghouls. No fangs and no real claws for starters, just ragged nails on the one that still had the flesh to hold them. They were stronger and tougher than ghouls, too. No, they were risen all right, but someone had done something special with them. I want to say I've heard or read something like it somewhere before, but I can't pin down when or where."

"Speaking of pinned down," said Heyin. "We should be going. That fire's likely to draw the attention of any patrols that Sumey has out in the area, and I'd rather not run into one of them."

"**Baroness** Marchon!" a young woman ran in and knelt before Maylien's chair.

Two weeks had passed since the destruction of the keep—the fire had burned it to the foundations, robbing us of any opportunity for learning anything further from the site. We still hadn't settled on the details for a plan to get Maylien through to her sister for a duel though we had the broad outlines down. It pretty much had to happen at Marchon House in Tien, for example. We were sitting in

Exile House's formal dining room going over a map of the Sovann Hill for about the forty-seventh time.

"What is it?" asked Maylien.

"A carrier pigeon just came in with a spell-sealed message for you," said the woman.

Maylien took the tiny scrap of paper and started reading. Within moments, her expression turned dark.

"What is it?" asked Heyin.

"It's from our *friend* in Sumey's household. My sister is going to move to have me impeached before the king. She's planning on using the loss of the keep we torched as cause to have me declared outlaw though how she can prove I had anything to do with that, I don't know. This says she will bring the charges when the king next holds formal court in five days' time. If she succeeds, I will no longer be eligible to issue challenge. We have to move now, before that can happen."

"I'll draft the letter for you," said Heyin. "When should I say you will be coming for her?"

20

---·•·---

Down! I tapped Maylien on the shoulder, giving her the prearranged signal. She dropped flat on the wet roof, and I dropped on top of her, while Triss settled over both of us. We stayed there in the dark and the cold spring rain, getting steadily damper and more frustrated for about a quarter of an hour before Triss finally whispered that we could move again. Then we crawled backward toward the narrow street that ran behind the large and expensive apartment house we'd only just ascended.

Above and ahead of us on the Temple of Athera, one of the Elite hunkered down on the lee side of the bell tower, resting his forehead against the shoulder of the stone dog staring off to the northwest. The dog stood atop a thick limestone buttress that made for one of the few rooftop positions that could both support its weight and provide a way for it to get up there. Between the night and the rain, they'd have been nearly invisible to normal eyes. But in magesight, the glow of the Elite's many active spells illuminated them from within.

When we'd first slipped up over the edge of the roof, the man had been hidden by the bell tower, and his unspelled stone dog had all but vanished against the stone and slate of the rooftop. But then the Elite came around the corner, all aglow with his spells, and started scanning the southern rooftops. Triss and I could still have gotten past him and his familiar unnoticed on our own, but there simply wasn't enough of Triss to cover both Maylien and me fully if we tried to move. So we'd had to wait until the Elite took his little break for an opportunity to move back off the roof.

Now we dropped over the roof's edge onto a third-floor balcony, putting the building between us and the watchers. From there it was easy enough to climb down a floor and drop the rest of the way to the street below unseen. We retraced our steps further, moving back into a dark and stinking alley that provided some shelter from the rain as well as from the eyes of our foes. Bontrang briefly stuck his head out of Maylien's bag then and made a piteous little squawking noise. It sounded to me like a complaint about the awful weather.

I couldn't help but agree with him. Both because I sympathized about the misery factor and because it would have been awfully nice to have his eyes in the sky to warn us about things like all the damned Elite on the rooftops. On the other hand, at least the storm was keeping everyone who didn't have to be there off the streets.

"That's the third roadblock we've run into in the hour since sundown," I said, "and that smells bad. One member of the Elite blocking a chimney road route up onto the Sovann Hill could easily be there on some business unrelated to ours. Maybe even two. But make it three, and add in the Crown Guards who are crawling all over the fucking place, and it means that the king or someone close to him is trying to cordon off the area. Now, there might be some reason for that other than your challenge tomorrow morning, but I'm having trouble believing in that much coincidence."

"It's no coincidence, I'm sure of it." Maylien's eyes were downcast, her voice discouraged. "My sister seems to have enlisted crown support."

"I thought the crown was specifically forbidden from interfering in this sort of challenge," Triss said from within my shadow, "that your sister could only use her own resources."

Maylien sighed and shook her head. "Against *me* yes. Against an unidentified renegade Blade? Or, depending on what she's told them, Aral the Kingslayer? I don't think she'd have any trouble enlisting crown support in that case. Hell, if she's really got Deem in her pocket, she might not even need to talk to Uncle Thauvik."

"When did you come up with all that?" I asked. I didn't like it one little bit, but it fit the circumstances.

"A few minutes ago, as we were climbing back down the third wall that we'd just climbed up."

"That's a major problem," said Triss. His voice seemed to be coming from somewhere near the entrance of the alley then—he'd spread himself out to keep an eye on things as soon as we ducked into the deeper dark. "We can't do a big sail-jump with Maylien riding along. That plus all the royal attention severely limits our number of possible routes up the hill."

"So you two can't get to Marchon House *with me*, and I can't get into Marchon House *without you*," said Maylien. "Basically, we're dead in the water."

"There's got to be some way around this," I said. "Maybe we can split up and meet on the hill somewhere. If we didn't have to cover you, Triss and I could get past the cordon easily enough. If the crown's really not allowed to interfere with your challenge, you *should* be able to pass through without any problems, right?"

"In theory," said Maylien. "But I've got a nasty feeling it's not going to work that way in practice. You're right about this whole thing stinking. I don't know whether that's because Thauvik has decided to support my sister's claim against me as actively as he dares, or if it's just antimage prejudice. Either way, I'm afraid there'll be trouble with the guards."

"I'd love to say something reassuring at this point," I replied, "but I suspect you're right. The question is do we try it anyway? If we do, then how do we do it without blowing the whole game if you turn out to be right?"

"Well," said Triss, "there are a couple of Crown Guards coming along the street at the far end of the alley—I can see their lantern. How about we have Maylien step out that way and see what they do when they spot her? We should be far enough from the Elite on the temple there to keep things quiet if we have to take them down."

I didn't like the idea much, but I couldn't think of anything better, so I just shrugged and said, "Maylien?"

"Let's do it."

As we hurried toward the farther street, we put together our basic plan. When we reached the end of the alley, Maylien set Bontrang on my shoulder and touched his forehead lightly, giving him mental orders. He squawked complainingly again but bobbed his head. Then Maylien stepped out into the street and turned away from the oncoming guards without ever looking their way, heading toward the hill. I pulled Triss around me and stayed in the shadows, waiting for the guards to go past.

The pair were tall and professional, the picture of crack troopers and much of a size, though the woman didn't have quite the same breadth of shoulder. After they went by, I launched Bontrang into the air and slipped in behind them. Maylien, who'd been walking slowly to start with, slowed even more as she approached the intersection ahead, as though unsure about where she was. It was really intended to keep down the number of potential witnesses. The guards obliged us by catching her up just short of the crossing street—a wider artery leading up onto the Sovann and important enough to have a scattering of streetlights.

"My lady? Could you answer a few questions for us?" asked the man, his voice extremely polite—as it ought to be when dealing with an obvious noble.

Maylien had put on an elaborate and expensive dueling blade that had belonged to her mother. It marked her as a member of the high nobility, as did the rich silk of the clothes she'd chosen to wear. Now she played the part as well, turning to give the soldier a sharp, annoyed look.

"Why?" she demanded. "What do you want to know?"

"We're looking for a serious criminal," he answered, keeping his voice polite. "One of those Namara cultists that the true gods proscribed a few years ago. The assassins."

There was a time those comments would have sent me into a rage that I'd have had a hard time restraining. But after five years on the run, I'd gotten very good at controlling my responses to nasty things said about me and mine. If I hadn't, I'd have died. Now I just tightened my jaw and moved in closer.

"I thought the Blades were all supposed to be dead," said Maylien.

"We're working on it," answered the guard. "But there are a few left around, and one of them's in the area right now . . ."

He had more to say, but I stopped listening as his partner's actions suddenly drew my full attention. She'd very quietly opened her pouch, using her partner and the wet darkness to hide her movement from Maylien. As she reached inside, I decided I had to take a risk, and so, hoping there were no mages about to see me, I summoned a charge of magelightning, focusing it in my right hand.

When she pulled out a small piece of paper with a line drawing of Maylien and a tiny dimly glowing rune on it, I extended the shadow that surrounded me to touch the back of her neck and released the lightning with a brilliant flare. I didn't know what the rune was for, but I knew I couldn't let her activate it.

She went down in a heap, dead or unconscious. Her partner whirled around in surprise at the flash, half-drawing his sword. I summoned a second charge and touched his chest, and he went down, too, dropping the lantern, which shattered, spilling its light-stone into the street. Then I released Triss and knelt to check the nearer guard's pulse.

Maylien kicked the light into a nearby sewer grate, where it vanished, plunging us back into near-total darkness. No one opened any shutters to see what was going on, so I had to assume that we'd been quiet and fast enough to avoid any attention. Not a huge surprise given the hours and the noise of the storm, even with the flash and the sizzle of the magelightning, but not something to take for granted, either.

"I take it they were about to cause us some trouble?" Maylien asked.

I nodded. The man was unconscious but not dead. I moved on to the woman, scooping up the soggy sheet of paper and handing it to Maylien to look at, while I checked the guard's pulse. She was out but not gone, too—a pleasant surprise. I'd expected to kill at least one of them. It probably had something to do with the rain and the wet street. I'd noticed that seemed to drain off some of the strength of lightning magic, dispersing it into the surrounding area somehow. Actually, now that I thought about it, that might well have been what kept the Kadeshi deathspark from killing me.

Maylien whistled. "This is a summoning rune. Touch it, and it'll alert whoever's at the other end and give them a trace to follow. What do you want to bet that if I tap this with my finger, a whole swarm of Elite will be along shortly."

"Do you want to call this off?" I asked.

She tore the sheet in half, breaking the rune, then dropped it after the magelight. "No. If I walk away now, I'll be outlawed. I'll have to leave Zhan forever and surrender Marchon to my sister. If I can get through to her and challenge successfully, Thauvik won't have any choice but to acknowledge my claim to the barony. He might try to have me declared outlaw anyway, but the other peers won't like that, and I'll have a damn good chance of fighting it off."

She glanced at the fallen guards. "Are they . . ."

"Down but not dead." I caught the man's arm and pulled him into a sitting position, then up onto my shoulder. "We'd better get them out of the street."

Maylien let out a little sigh of relief, then bent to lift the woman. "I'm glad of that, even if it is inconvenient for me. It's not their fault my sister's a monster, and the king is supporting her." She got the woman onto her shoulders, and we headed back toward the alley. "I just wish we could erase their memories of the past few minutes, but that's magic far beyond my skill. When they wake, and the last thing they remember is my face, it's going to make it that much harder to fight any charges the king might bring."

"I could . . ." I drew a thumb across my throat. I didn't particularly want to kill them, but I'd do it if I had to.

"No. I'll deal with it when and if I need to. There are way too many ifs between here and there to justify killing anyone we don't have to. We might not even make it up the hill. If we do, we might not get past Sumey's guards or Devin. If we manage that, I might be killed in the duel. If I win, Thauvik might choose not to try to have me removed. We'll leave them as they are."

"Good." I turned into the alley and dumped my load in the shadows. "I hate when I have to kill people for being in the wrong place at the wrong time."

Maylien dropped her guard beside mine, opening up a space on her shoulder that was quickly occupied by the return of a sopping-wet and very grumpy Bontrang. She soothed him a bit and quickly dried him off with a rag before coaxing him back into the bag. While she was doing that, I arranged the guards so that neither one of them was going to keel over and drown in a puddle before they woke up.

"So now what do we do?" Maylien edged back to look out the end of the alley. "It's not getting any earlier, we're still miles away from our goal, and I'm not seeing any way to make it up that hill. Not with the Elite blocking the high road and the Crown Guard blocking the low road."

"Actually," I said, "the guards are blocking the *middle* road."

Maylien whipped around to face me, her face a pale blur in the darkness. "You're not suggesting the sewers, are you? In the middle of a rainstorm? That's insane."

"It is. Which is exactly why I think we might able to make it work. Only three sewer lines coming down off the Sovann Hill are big enough to pass a person walking upright. In dry weather I'd bet money on all of them being covered by the Elite and the stone dogs, but with all this rain, no one sane is going into the sewers."

"How do you know that much about the system?"

"Back when I was working out a plan to kill Ashvik, I had to learn enough about the basic layout of Tien's main sewers to know whether they were a good option or not. There've been miles and miles of the things built over the last five hundred years."

"Did you go in through the sewers then? I've never heard any-one talk about the details."

"No. The sewers that lead to the palace are a nightmare for any-one trying to use them to get at the king. Full of dead ends and traps—many of Durkoth design—plus all kinds of patrols and checkpoints."

Triss nodded from my shadow. "Which is why Master Urayal and Patiss died down there. Nasty place."

"All right, but the palace is on the other side of the river. Why would you know the ones over here so well?"

"Because we've been living over here, and that's what I was taught to do. But I really only know the mains. I'm sure there are at least another dozen lines coming down off the hill that would pass someone willing to crawl through sewage on their belly in the dark. Depending on how they're connected to the storm drains, one of them might well provide us a better and safer route, but I couldn't tell you where those were if my life depended on it."

"Oh, how sad. Here I was thinking how much fun it would be to crawl through sewage on my belly, and now you've dashed my hopes. I guess we get to drown instead."

"If you've got a better idea, I'm all for it," I replied. I decided not to mention the possibility of restless dead in the tunnels.

Maylien just shook her head.

It took us two miserable hours underground to travel the five short blocks I felt we needed to get past the cordon. We nearly drowned half a dozen times, but with ropes and magic and Triss's help, we did finally make it. The only positive things I can say about the trip were: One, the rushing storm waters had cleared out the worst of the stench and all of the shit that wasn't permanently glued to the bricks. And two, we didn't run into any of the restless dead, risen or otherwise.

We came up out of the sewers in a narrow street lined with the walled homes of the lesser well-to-do. From there we dragged ourselves into an even narrower alley, where we collapsed against some wealthy merchant's or minor noble's back wall. Unspeakable muck coated the bricks beneath us, but it couldn't be significantly worse than the unspeakable muck we'd had to wallow through to get there, so it probably all equaled out.

Beside me, Maylien poked at her ruined clothes and sighed ruefully. "So much for going into the duel looking like the rightful baroness."

"Don't worry about it. We can always stop by your sister's rooms on the way in and steal you something more appropriate."

"I wish we could, but someone might recognize the outfit. As much as I hate it, the manner of my defeat of Sumey is going to have almost as much to do with whether I can hold the barony successfully as the fact of the defeat itself. Which means we *will* have to do something about my clothes, I'm just not sure what or when yet. Maybe I can find something of my mother's at Marchon House, though that doesn't solve the immediate problem."

Before I could respond, an utterly soggy Bontrang dropped out of the sky and into Maylien's lap. He didn't bother to complain about the weather this time. When she scooped him up, he just tucked his beak under her chin and started purring frantically. The little fellow had practically gone berserk when Maylien insisted he stay aboveground while we went into the sewers, but it was safer for both of them that way.

In the darkness of the alley, I couldn't see Triss, but he must have felt some of the same sympathy for Bontrang and Maylien that I did. He shifted into dragon shape and draped his head across my lap affectionately. I scratched him behind his invisible ears and wished we could just stay like that for the next four or five hundred years. Unfortunately, that wasn't an option. I could already feel the warmth of exertion losing the fight to the cold and wet.

"Maylien?" I dragged myself up out of the muck.

"Yes."

"Why don't you and Bontrang stay here while I hunt us up that change of clothes. I can do it quicker alone." I stripped off my sodden woolen hood and vest and draped them over Maylien and Bontrang. It wasn't much, but it was all I had to offer.

Maylien pulled them around her gratefully. "Thank you. Bontrang's freezing, and I'm starting to get cold, too."

I nodded. "I noticed the way he's shivering between the purrs. We all need to get dry and get moving, and that starts with clothes. You'll need something to carry Bontrang in, too. That bag's no good anymore."

I'm not, in general, a big fan of theft, though I'll do it when I absolutely have to. So, I promised myself to leave a couple of Maylien's silver riels in the bottom of whatever petty noble's wardrobe I ended up raiding for our clothes. I also prefer not to scare the life out anyone who hasn't earned it. Which is why I intended to pick a wardrobe in an empty bedroom.

Here on the lower slopes of the Sovann Hill, people couldn't afford the extensive magical protections and alarms that I'd have found up closer to Marchon House. It was relatively simple to pick a large house that felt mostly empty and use Triss and a bit of minor spellwork to open the delivery door that led into the dark kitchen.

From there it was a short jaunt up the servants' stairs to the upper floors, where Triss found me an empty guest room. Of course, it being an old house, there was a certain inevitable amount of creaking and squeaking as I moved around, no matter how careful I tried to be. But the wind and the storm seemed more than adequate to cover it, and since no one showed up right away to disabuse me of the notion, I went about my business.

As was often the case in the smaller noble houses during spring and the switchover from winter wardrobe to summer wardrobe, a guest room had been pressed into service for temporary storage. It held the winter clothes that had to be kept handy for a few more weeks yet in case of cold snaps as well as little sachets of fleabane and worrymoth.

As I dug around through the clothes spread across the bed, I found a moment to be thankful I was in Tien. Here loose silks and cottons provided the outfit of choice for the upper class, a marked contrast to someplace like Aven, where everyone favored tailored wool and fitted leather and lots of boning and laces. It meant that I could manage with stuff that was merely near my size, and also that if it worked for me, it'd probably work for Maylien. I did make sure to pick out women's clothes of the best fabrics for her given that she might have to use them for the duel. The divided skirts were fuller than the pants I nicked for myself, but only a little.

After changing my own clothes, I wrapped up a bundle for her, using the bed's top blanket as my sack. I was just finishing that up when Triss gave me a sharp poke in the ribs. I'd had him watching the hall, and that was the signal that someone was out there now. I doused my thieveslight.

"Window," hissed Triss, and I started moving. "Now! It's the steward, and he's got an axe. I think he must have heard something."

That was when the door to the guest room burst open. Damn all old houses with their creaky floors, and damn efficient servants, too, the bane of the housebreaker's existence. I'd intended to at least open the window first, but I didn't have the time, so I just put Maylien's bundle of clothes in front of my face and crashed right through the shutters. I suppose the fact that they were light summer shutters and not the heavy winter storm shutters counted as a point in the favor of efficient staff, but I didn't feel it really balanced out.

I hit the ground running. With Triss providing a shroud of darkness to hide me, I knew the man would never be able to spot or follow me. On the other hand, the way he started screaming for the watch was going to present a real problem in fairly short order. The window was on the front side of the house, and Maylien was out back and a few houses down. So I doubled back around the house as soon as I had shed the impetus provided by the drop.

When I vaulted over the back wall, I found Maylien already

waiting for me, with Bontrang hissing angrily on her shoulder. "What the hell went wrong?"

"I picked the only house in the neighborhood where they pay the servants well enough to care, apparently. Now, come on!" I turned and started running, and Maylien fell in behind me. "We have to get out of here."

Normally, I wouldn't have been that fussed about it. Put a couple of blocks between us and the break-in, and we'd be set. But normally the neighborhood wasn't crawling with Crown Guards and—a deep grating howl went up from somewhere behind us, punctuating my thought—stone dogs.

21

Maylien threw herself down on the muddy ground and rolled under the low canopy of a golden willow, following Bontrang into the natural tent. I entered more cautiously, duck-walking to preserve the knees of my stolen pants. They were already the worse for twenty minutes of climbing walls and running through backyards with the forces of the crown in howling pursuit.

We'd shaken them loose somewhere on the outskirts of the royal preserve by slipping in and out across the borders between crown land and various private estates. Our current hiding place lay on a tiny island centering the miniature man-made lake on the Earl of Anaryun's city estate—a spot I'd scouted for just such a temporary refuge years ago when I was nosing Marchon House as a venue for killing Ashvik. Luckily, nothing seemed to have changed since then. We'd been able to follow a narrow calf-deep track built for the use of the gardeners and concealed among the lily pads out to the island.

I had no doubt the Crown Guard was still out there looking for us, but they'd gotten much more circumspect about it now that they'd completely lost sight of us. That quiet might also have something to do with the fact that we were getting close to Marchon House and a much greater potential for charges of crown interference with a scheduled challenge.

I'd brought us to the island because we needed to hole up for an hour or two, and the shelter of the willow was perfect for the purpose. Not even crack troops like the Elite and Crown Guard can maintain maximum alertness for very long without dulling their edge. Our chances would look much better if we vanished for a bit before making our next move. It also gave Maylien a chance to finally change into clean dry clothes.

"Sorry about all the running and hiding," I said. "I really didn't expect I'd get pinched by an elderly steward for stealing clothes." I handed them over. "Do you want me to hold anything for you?"

Maylien grinned, her teeth shining briefly in the darkness. then shivered. "I bet you say that to all the girls when you're trying to get them out of their clothes. Here, take Bontrang. He's half-frozen. Oh, and you'd actually better hang on to the clothes, too. I can't strip and keep them off the ground at the same time."

I took the little shivering gryphinx and stuffed him into the front of my shirt against my skin. He was cold and wet and smelled of soggy cat, and was very, very happy to be out of the elements. He started purring at once, and I rubbed his neck affectionately. Triss, who had come to quite like the little fellow, wrapped himself protectively around the gryphinx as well.

Meanwhile, Maylien skinned out of her ruined shirt and pants, leaving me wishing for better light. She was a beautiful woman, and we hadn't gotten another chance to be alone together since the keep fire. Heyin had gone out of his way to prevent us. I couldn't fault him for that, however much it might have frustrated me. Protecting Maylien *was* his job.

"Hand me that shirt." Maylien took it and slipped it on. "Skirt next. Ahh, much better. Now, what's our next move?"

"We stay right here for at least an hour. We've still got four hours till daybreak and we need to let the heat die down a bit."

"Well, damn," said Maylien, and she gave a throaty chuckle.

"What?"

"If we've got an hour to kill in here, and we want to have any hope of staying warm and limber while we do it, I'm going to end up taking these clothes right off again."

Triss let out a derisive snort. "You'd better let me hold Bontrang since he's still half-frozen, and we can keep watch. Humans would be so much easier to deal with if they had mating seasons like everybody else does."

Even the richest neighborhoods have cheap taverns. Little hidden hole-in-the-wall-type places that cater to servants of the high-and-mighty. The Footman's Step was one such, marked out only by the coach step nailed to a narrow door in the middle of an otherwise blank wall. It was tucked into a little wedge of property between two wealthy estates and had matched its façade to the walls of its well-to-do neighbors in an effort not to offend anyone's delicate sensibilities.

Normally, it would have been closed here in the brief hours before dawn, but a well-paying private party had rented the front room. So, when I knocked lightly on the door, it was quickly opened. Inside, Heyin and a dozen of his best people waited for us. They wore heavy canvas work clothing of the sort favored by masons and carpenters and had appropriate tools and equipment neatly piled in one corner.

The only thing remotely suspicious about them was that they were carrying more in the way of ladders, rope, and bamboo poles for scaffolding than such a group might normally have. A fact explained by the very real-looking work order they had for cornice repair on the notoriously tall great house of the Duke of Jenua.

"You're late," said Heyin. "We were worried. Especially with all the noise and fuss. What happened?"

So we filled him in, minus any description of how exactly we'd killed time under the willow though I'm sure he had his suspicions. One unexpected plus from said time killing was it had warmed both of us up enough to take a quick bath in the lake, leaving us something approaching clean.

"What about you?" I asked Heyin after we'd finished bringing him up to date. "Were you stopped?"

"Twice. Both times they checked faces against a drawing of Maylien with a rune at the bottom."

"We saw one of those," I said. "Did they do anything else?"

Heyin nodded and lowered his voice. "It was subtle, and I doubt any of the others noticed since they wouldn't know to look for that kind of thing, but one of the guards made sure to step on every single one of our shadows. I thought I saw another rune scribed on the sole of his boot."

Triss squeezed my shoulders and hissed very quietly. I felt more than a little like hissing myself. Instead, I asked, "Is everything ready?"

"Whenever you are," said Heyin.

"Then let's go."

I led the way through the edge of the royal preserve, where we had to move in a series of short dashes and long pauses. Triss and I would scout ahead, then slide back to lead the others forward. This close to Marchon House, the royal patrols were actually significantly lighter than normal though I couldn't say if that was more to avoid the charge of interference or simply because the outer cordon had soaked up all the available troops.

When we got to the place where the Marchon estate met the royal preserve, we split up. Triss and I led the bulk of Maylien's guard one way while Maylien took Heyin and a couple of others in the opposite direction. The estate was a large one, and I left the men and women of the guard spaced out along the wall at fifty-pace intervals, each with a length of rope with a metal tool tied to one end. I kept going after I ran out of guards, speeded up even, though I had to climb into another estate to do so. I wanted to put as much distance between me and them as possible before the timesman at the temple of Shan struck the fourth hour.

When the bell rang, I started counting to a thousand. I needed to give our planned distraction time to work. With the ringing of the bell, each of the guards I'd left behind would be noisily throwing their tool-weighted ropes over the wall, then dragging them back to the top, which would make a sound like so many grappling hooks being pulled tight.

After that, they were supposed to scatter and meet back at the Footman. Some of them were bound to be picked up by the Crown Guard, but that was a price they'd all agreed to pay if necessary. Since none of them was carrying anything illegal, the worst they'd get was a light beating and a couple of weeks in jail for trespassing. And, if Maylien won her duel, she could bail them all out as soon as she was confirmed as Baroness Marchon.

At the end of my count, I silently placed a light ladder against the wall—a single bamboo pole with shorter lengths driven through it to form rungs. I went up and over the wall, carrying a second ladder, which I placed on the other side. I left them both in place since we wanted them to be found.

We also wanted to leave the thickest possible shadow trail for Devin, so instead of my taking control, Triss covered me as I dashed a couple of hundred feet into the grounds. That presence would strengthen the spoor he left behind. At the end of the dash, we dodged left and right as though we'd encountered a couple of patrols. Then we turned and ran back along a slightly different path to my ladders. The goal was to make Devin think Maylien and I hadn't been able to get past the guards and had backed off to come in from another angle.

Maylien was actually on the far side of the estate, coming in by a completely different route. If all had gone according to plan, she was already over the wall and in the company of her spy within the house—the chief cook. The cook was going slip her into the house with the morning deliveries. Easy enough to do since they'd already been thoroughly checked at the main gate of the estate. Then she would take Maylien to a hiding place in the kitchens to wait for the dawn.

Heyin would get rid of Maylien's ladder and take care of Bontrang for the duration. No familiar could be trusted to stay out of a fight if his companion's life was in imminent danger, so Bontrang had to be kept away from the duel.

After our run-ins with the Elite and Crown Guard, we'd argued about my part in the next bit of the plan. Maylien wanted me to get clear so that I wouldn't encounter whomever the king chose to send as his witnesses to the duel. She suspected Deem and possibly a second officer of the Elite—people who would happily try to kill me given any chance. She'd already made me swear not to interfere with the duel as long as it was conducted honorably, and now she figured I was better off out of it completely.

I'd insisted we stick to the original plan, with me providing a backup in case of treachery, and I'd refused to be budged. So, after using the neighbor's decorative trout stream to break my shadow trail, Triss and I doubled back to the estate and made a second climb onto the wall, this time using a rope and a leather-wrapped grappling hook.

Then we made our slow and painstaking way to the house by moving from tree to tree and touching the ground as little as possible. Since the whole estate was crawling with Sumey's guards, it took Triss and me the better part of two hours and three major backtracks to get within sail-jumping distance of the house, which had its compensations. The spring was starting to fade, but many of the trees were still in bloom. The smell of the myrtle and flowering pears was particularly lovely and made doubly sweet by the very real chance that this was the last time I'd ever smell them.

I ended up about thirty feet up a grand old katsura, perched on a branch a bit bigger around than my thigh. The leaves chattered quietly away in the predawn breeze, a lovely but dangerous sound, as it masked the noises made by the patrolling guards below. After half an hour of waiting for a good gap, I concluded that the timing was never going to come out right for a clean jump.

That left two choices. Jump anyway. With the rain still coming down, there were no stars to blot out, and I was all in gray and black—not easily visible against the backdrop of Triss and the darkness above. Or, remain fully enshrouded and drop to the ground to slip between patrols on foot, which would leave a trail for Devin. Either way, I needed to make my move. Dawn was coming on fast. If not for the clouds, the sky would already have begun to lighten. For about the millionth time, I wished that Triss and I had a good way of communicating under these sorts of circumstances. Then I jumped.

I landed on the narrow ledge of a second-floor window and stayed there for a few seconds while I checked to see whether anyone had noticed. If so, they were playing things mighty casual, so I headed for the most difficult of the possible routes up this side of the house. I felt pretty sure that at this late hour, Devin would already be in place for the duel, but I wanted to confuse my shadow trail just in case.

At the top I perched myself on the narrow strip of lead roofing that lay between one of the house's many chimneys and the wall I'd just climbed. I wanted to give Devin a little more time to get in place if he hadn't already. The duel was supposed to take place in the hour after dawn in the receiving garden out front, between the main house and the forward-thrusting wings. I knew it well from my attempts to catch a king there once upon a time.

Devin's problem now was quite similar to the one I'd had then. If he intended to provide a backstop for Sumey's sword-handling skills, he needed a place to hide. Somewhere from which he could both watch and act if the duel started to go wrong. He had four major constraints. First, he had to stay hidden from any Elite witnesses. I didn't think that any deal Sumey had cut with Deem would extend to ignoring the presence of a former Blade—the enmity between Blade and Elite just ran too deep.

Which led to Devin's second problem. He needed to not get caught. There are a very limited number of ways to affect a witnessed sword duel from a distance. The constraints get even tighter if you can't use magic because the witnesses are also mages. He couldn't just nail Maylien with an arrow in the back or push her onto Sumey's sword with a spell. The scandal would finish Sumey as thoroughly as losing the duel would. And that would be true even if she were able to convince people she hadn't ordered her sister's death herself.

That left Devin an extremely short list of options, all of them small and inaccurate over any distance. I was figuring a blowgun loaded with tiny pebbles from the carriageway. Delivered with the right timing and to the right target—an ear, say—the distraction could easily prove fatal, and the pebble would effectively vanish among its mates.

Third, deniability. If Deem—or whoever the witnesses turned out to be—did spot Devin, he needed to be someplace where the baroness could reasonably claim to have had nothing to do with his presence. It probably wouldn't save her if Devin was caught in the act; but if he was spotted beforehand or couldn't be linked to any obvious tampering afterward, it might keep her neck off the block. That put any position within the house off-limits to Devin, leaving him on the roof or somewhere on the ground.

Finally, he had to know he couldn't trust the baroness. Especially if he'd seen the glyph rack in the torture chamber Maylien had rescued me from. He'd want a quick way out in case the baroness decided to sell him to the Elite.

All of which meant Devin only had one really good option for his sniper's nest, a particularly deep niche between the end pair of dormers on the west-facing wing of the house. There *were* other choices but none as good: a similar perch atop the east-facing wing, but at that hour it would be in full sun, which would make him easier to spot as well as putting the sun in his eyes. There was also a second-floor balcony on the main house that would provide a cleaner shot and better concealment, but it would make escape virtually impossible if the Elite did spot him.

It would be the dormer. Of course, that all assumed the baroness really had set Devin up as a backstop, but I had no doubts. People who hired the sort of person Devin had become never played fair.

Over the next three-quarters of an hour, the rain tapered off, and the clouds started to break up, exposing the dawn sun as a half disk lying on the crest of the Kanathean Hill. If everything had gone right with Maylien—and I felt sure there'd have been a serious commotion if it hadn't—she would be issuing her challenge in short order. Time to move. I ducked around the chimney and crept along the back of the wing. I wanted to come down on Devin's position from above and behind.

When I finally poked my head over the peak of the roof I spotted a pool of too-deep shadow exactly where I'd expected to find Devin. He really didn't have another good choice. Ducking down, I moved back far enough to put the nearer of the two dormers between us. Then I slipped over the ridgeline and moved silently out onto the dormer, a process made much easier by the thick lead of the roof. One of the things I loved about working great houses was that they never went for the cheaper and noisier options like slate or terra-cotta tiles.

It took a while, but eventually I was lying along the roof of the dormer directly above and out of sight of the dark blot that concealed Devin. I wanted to wait until events below provided a distraction before making my move. Obligingly enough, I'd only just come to rest when a small coach pulled up beside the arched stone gate at the foot of the garden. It was pulled by a stone dog. As I lifted the curtain of shadow from in front of my eyes so that I could see better, the coach's door opened, and Colonel Deem climbed down from the cab.

He was followed a moment later by another familiar face, a stiff-backed Captain Fei of the watch. Though it was hard to tell from this distance, the combination of her posture and demeanor suggested Fei was mighty unhappy about something. As Deem passed the stone dog on his limping way to the house, he waved his hand and triggered a small spell that released the creature from the traces so it could join him. At no time did he or his familiar so much as glance back at Fei.

A noise from the main doors drew my attention away from Deem then. Sumey was descending the front stairs, followed by a virtual explosion of servants and guards. She wore both the baronial coronet and her chain of office. While she continued down the path toward Deem, most of her retinue peeled off at the base of the steps. Some started setting out chairs, tables, and all the other accoutrements of a formal audience while others took a length of rope and began staking out a large dueling ring.

"Colonel Deem," the baroness called as they closed. "So nice to see you." She offered him her hand to tuck into his elbow. "Come sit with me while I wait for this charade to be over."

She nodded vaguely at Fei as she turned back toward the house, but that was the only acknowledgment she made of the other woman. Clearly she was no more happy with the second crown witness than Deem was. Not happy, but also not surprised. I wondered what that meant but had no way of finding out, so I pushed it aside for later thought. Fei didn't look happy either, wrinkling her nose at the retreating back of the baroness.

Soon Sumey and the colonel were seated side by side at the center of the furniture arrangement, with the colonel's stone dog at their feet. Fei was shunted off to a slightly smaller but still comfortable seat on one side. Servants continued to dash back and forth from

the house, bringing tea and cakes and other dainties. As the minutes slid past I began to worry about Maylien.

Then, the baroness leaped to her feet and pointed at a young
maid in an ill-fitting red dress, demanding loudly, "You there, girl,
what's that you're carrying?" The girl had a long slender bundle of
fabric tucked under one arm, which she now raised in both hands.

"Your death, Sumey," she declared in ringing tones, and I recognized her voice as Maylien's.

"What!" yelled Sumey. "Wait, guards, stop her!"

But Maylien was already too close for anyone to interfere with
the challenge, and, with many a sidelong glance at Deem and Fei,
the guards did nothing.

When she saw that, the baroness turned a sneering gaze on her
sister. "You come to challenge me in the clothes of a maid? How
humiliating for you." As she had all along, she pitched her voice
high and clear, a noble used to playing for her court.

Maylien didn't say anything, just reached inside the bundle and
withdrew her sword. Then she slipped the tip of the blade into the
front of her bodice and, in a surprisingly graceful move, slit the dress
completely down the front. It fell away to reveal a loose divided
skirt and a shirt, all in a rich jade silk. For reasons not readily apparent, the baroness stiffened angrily.

Maylien shrugged off the remnants of the dress. "I come to challenge you in the clothes of the woman you murdered, our mother,
Juli Dan Marchon, last true ruler of Marchon. I am Maylien Dan
Marchon Tal Pridu and I claim my right under the Code Martial of
Zhan to offer blood challenge to Sumey Dan Marchon Tal Pridu. I
challenge for the rule of the Barony of Marchon and I call on the
representatives of the crown here present at my request to witness
the duel." She, too, spoke for the audience.

Deem rose from his chair, a tightly closed look on his face, and
addressed the baroness, "I am honor-bound to point out that I know
this woman to be a mage." He turned to Maylien. "As a duly sworn
representative of the crown, I may recognize your right to challenge
under the Code Martial if and only if you forswear the use of any
magic for the duration of the duel. Do you so forswear the use of
magic?"

"By my honor and my blood, I do so forswear it."

"Then I will witness your challenge for the crown."

Captain Fei now rose from her chair. "Likewise, I'm sure."
Deem turned a glare on the captain, and Fei shrugged, but then

nodded. "As a duly sworn representative of the crown, I will witness the challenge here issued. That make you happy, Colonel?"

Deem turned to the baroness. "Baroness Marchon, the challenger has forsworn magic and her blood claim is valid. Will you accept the challenge and duel to the death? Or will you refuse it and concede the baronial coronet, going into voluntary exile forthwith?"

"I accept. Captain," she called to the head of her guard, "bring me my sword." She turned to Maylien. "This is going to end with me bathing in your blood." Then she laughed. "Oh, I'm going to enjoy spilling your life away as I've enjoyed nothing else in years, sister mine."

"Then you've become a true child of our father the butcher, Sumey." Maylien shook her head sadly. "I loved you once. You know that, don't you? Somewhere down in the hell that has come to fill your head, you have to remember what it meant to be sisters."

Sumey didn't answer, just smiled and drew the sword her guard captain offered her. I used the noise to cover the drawing of a long dagger of my own. When Sumey gestured for her sister to proceed her into the ring, I noted that her sword was unusually broad and heavy for a dueling blade—an odd choice.

Maylien stepped over the rope, crossing to the far side of the ring and turning back to her sister. "Having recently seen evidence of the depravity you take pleasure in these days, I've no doubt spilled blood brings you joy. I only hope you can still smile when the blood on the ground is yours. Then at least one of us will be happy with what has to happen here today." She raised her sword. "Whenever you're ready."

Sumey took off her coronet and the formal chain of baronial office with its insignia of a jade fox on a golden background, handing them both over to Deem to be presented to the winner. Next she took off her formal jacket and other outer garments, stripping down to her own shirt and divided skirt for the duel. Then she entered the ring and likewise raised her sword.

The two sisters faced each other now across a distance of perhaps twenty-five feet. They were much of a size, though Sumey was slightly broader across the shoulders. Both wore loose silk, Sumey's a golden brown that complemented her sister's green. As the two began to slowly circle and move together, I edged closer to the lip of the roof and Devin below. Soon.

Sumey suddenly lunged at her sister, swinging a low cut at Maylien's right knee. Maylien parried while simultaneously hopping back. There was a bright clash of steel and Maylien's sword bent sharply, slowing Sumey's just enough to allow her jump to carry her clear, before springing back straight as she brought it up and around.

What the hell? I'd fenced with Maylien only a few days previously, helping her train for the fight, and not even my heaviest strokes had that kind of effect on her sword. Unless Sumey was a good bit stronger than I was, that shouldn't have happened.

If Maylien was surprised, she didn't show it, using the impetus of her sister's blow to flip her blade around into a neat backhanded slice at Sumey's throat. Without showing any sign of effort, Sumey brought her much heavier sword up in a hard parry that slapped Maylien's blade aside. Again, Maylien flowed with the movement, eeling her blade down and around in a corkscrew to slash at Sumey's thigh.

Rather than parry, Sumey moved forward so that Maylien's hilt caught her rather than the blade, though she didn't stop there. She bulled forward and crashed chest first into her sister. Maylien flew back and away, losing her footing. Though she managed to turn the fall into a backward roll, it almost took her clear of the ring, which would have been very bad form.

I lost track of the duel over the next few seconds because whatever happened to Maylien, I needed to settle with Devin, and Maylien's fall offered the perfect distraction. I rolled over the edge of the dormer, dropping about five feet to land on Devin. I'd intended to use my dagger and the weight of my body to nail him to the roof—you don't let a target live. Especially one as dangerous as Devin.

Deem's presence in the garden below should have been more than reminder enough for that. But when the moment actually came, I found that I just couldn't kill a man who'd once been a brother to me. Not like this. Not stabbing from behind in cold blood. As I fell, I shifted the dagger out from between us, smacking him behind the ear with the pommel as soon as contact allowed me to judge that target instead. Devin grunted noisily, and I hoped that the sounds of the duel below would cover it. I moved my dagger to lie against the right side of his neck, just above the big artery.

"Hello, Devin," I whispered into his ear. It was just him and me at the moment, since Zass and Triss were both in cloud shape and submerged by our respective wills. "We need to have a little talk."

"Why not just kill me and get it over with?" he asked after a moment, and I could hear strain and pain in his voice. "It's what I'd do to you."

I really didn't have an answer for that, not one I was willing to tell Devin anyway. Telling him that he still mattered to me would

BROKEN BLADE   *223*

be like handing him a dagger with my name on it. Instead, I looked back down at the duel. I couldn't say why, but I wanted to know the results there before I made any final decisions about Devin.

There had clearly been several more passes to the fight, though none conclusive. Maylien was orbiting her sister now, moving in fast for tiny cuts at wrist or foot and refusing to fully engage. From what I could see over the next minute or two, it was her best strategy. She was clearly a better swords-woman than her sister, and she should have been able to parlay that into a quick victory, but she had two major disadvantages.

Sumey's much heavier sword and seemingly unnatural strength and stamina. Normally, the weight of that sword would have worked against Sumey in anything longer than the briefest of matches. Whipping it around as wildly as Maylien was forcing her to should already have tired her out, but the weight didn't seem to bother Sumey at all. That strength allowed her to use the heavier blade as a hammer on her sister's more conventional dueling sword, smashing it repeatedly in a clear attempt at breaking Maylien's blade.

"What the hell is happening down there?" I asked, though I didn't expect any answers.

Devin let out a cruel little snort. "What's happening is that Sumey is going to carve her precious older sister into cutlets while you watch from the sidelines. Of course, it could never have ended any other way."

"If you're so sure of Sumey's victory, why are you here?" I felt around in the shadows with my free hand until I found the blow-gun I'd expected. "And what's this for?"

"You really don't know what's going on, do you?" Devin's tone fell somewhere between incredulous and bitter. "You've never in your whole fucking life known the real score, Aral. You've always just charged in and trusted to the old King-slayer magic to carry the day. And do you know what the funniest joke of all is? It always fucking works. No matter what the odds, Aral the gods-be-damned Kingslayer always comes out on top."

"I don't understand."

"How do you do it, Aral? How do you always manage to fail upward? No matter how half-assed your plan. No matter how much others who've worked harder and actually thought things through try. No matter what you actually deserve. The dice always come up crowns for you. Well, this time, buddy, the dice are loaded, and you're rolling nothing but skulls. This time you're going to lose, and I'm going to be here to watch."

Below, Sumey executed a particularly quick turn and counter, smashing Maylien's blade so hard that I fully expected it to snap on the spot. But somehow Maylien managed to flow with the blow, throwing herself sideways into a cartwheel and saving her sword.

"What in the world are you talking about, Devin? You're here with this and . . ." As I shook the blowgun, a long steel dart fell out of the end.

It hit the lead roof with a dull tinkle then started to roll away. Its end was heavily coated with something dark and sticky, manticore venom by the green undertones. What the hell . . . ?

"That's not for Maylien," I said. "You'd never be able to hide something that blatant from the witnesses. Who are you here to kill? And why?"

"Just watch the duel, Aral. If your Maylien is good enough, maybe you'll get to find out."

"Sumey? Deem? Fei?"

"Just watch."

Another minute went past, and I could see that Maylien was tiring. If she didn't pull a trick out of her bag, she was going to die soon. And there was nothing I could do about it without breaking my promise and throwing away everything she was fighting for. Another pass, and another. She had to—Oh, beautiful!

Rather than parrying her sister's blow, Maylien had thrown herself flat on the ground, feet toward Sumey. It wasn't the first time that she'd dodged rather than parry, but it was the first time since the earliest moments of the duel that she'd moved in tight with her sister instead of out and away. When Sumey shifted to follow the expected move back and away, she stepped right into a scissors kick that took her at knee and shin.

Sumey landed flat on her belly at right angles to her sister, with her sword momentarily trapped on the wrong side of her body. She was wide open to Maylien's slithering thrust. It was a beautiful blow, driving deep between Sumey's ribs, up and in, straight into the heart. Sumey died instantly. You could tell by the lack of blood flowing out of the wound that her heart had stopped pumping. I relaxed, though I didn't remove my blade from Devin's neck.

Below, Fei rose and started toward the fallen sisters. "I think that about does it."

"So much for your mind games, Devin," I said. "Now let's . . ."

Sumey moved. It was impossible. Maylien's blade transfixed her heart, but she was getting up anyway. And still the blood didn't flow.

"I told you to watch." Devin's voice sounded smug.

"What's the hell is going on here!" Captain Fei reared back and away from Sumey.

"I'm killing my sister." Sumey rose onto hands and knees. "And you're going to witness it for the crown like a good little pet if you know what's good for you."

And now I had a pretty good idea who the dart had been for.

Reaching back with her left hand, Sumey caught Maylien's sword between her fingers and casually snapped it off where it emerged from her rib cage.

22

I couldn't force what was happening below to make sense. Sumey Dan Marchon had taken a thrust to the heart and simply shrugged it off. Even now, she was calmly rising to her feet despite the length of Zhani steel sticking out of her side. I was totally unprepared for the current turn of events.

I didn't realize Devin had been counting on it and the distraction it would provide until I felt him smack my dagger away from his neck. Before I could do anything to regain my advantage, Devin gave a hard kick that sent us both spilling over the edge of the roof and tumbling into space some five stories above the ground. Through my connection to Triss, I tried desperately to form a shadow sail. He was less than halfway through the transition when we slammed into a narrow fourth-floor balcony.

I landed on my back, with Devin on top of me, both of us having shed our enshrouding shadows along the way. He took advantage of the shock and the impact to smash my wrist against the marble railing. Pain ripped through my arm, and my dagger tumbled away into the air beyond the balcony.

Devin popped up into a crouch, drawing a long knife as he pivoted to face me. "And now, I'm going to kill you."

If he'd acted immediately, he might well have managed it. I was still stunned, and though I had released Triss to his own recognizance, he hadn't yet manifested himself in any significant way. But whether Devin had the same problem killing an old friend that I'd had, or he wanted to gloat first, or was prevented by Zass, or whatever, I couldn't say. All I know is he hesitated and lost the moment.

"Assassins! Assassins on the balcony!" It was Sumey's voice as clear and strong as ever. "Deem, Blades, kill them!"

Her cry was answered by the deep grating howl of a stone dog and a great chain of green fire lashing along the marble posts of the railing. Heat licked through the gaps, chewing at the right side of my body. I felt pain shock through Triss as parts of my shirt started to smolder, but Devin caught it much worse. The top of his head was above the protection of the railing. He screamed wildly and dropped his knife to slap at his scalp when his hair burst into sudden flame.

I kicked him in the chest, sending him backward into the side railing. It saved his life as a second chain of fire lashed vertically through the place he'd just been, wrapping over the edge of the railing and burning across my shins. It hurt like nobody's business, but my boots took the worst of it, and I wasn't badly crisped. I scooted back into the corner of the balcony, where there was more cover, while Devin did the same opposite me.

Our swords came out in the same instant, his left, my right. Before either of us could make a move toward the other, his shadow shifted, twisting into the shape of a tayra and sliding onto the floor between us.

"Truce!" cried the ferret-wolf. "Truce until the Elite is dead. It's our only chance."

"Done," said the dragon that suddenly appeared to sniff noses with the tayra. "The stone dog will be here in seconds."

Then both shadows flowed to the railing side of the balcony, weaving a shining curtain of magic between them that deflected the next fall of Deem's lash. Devin clenched his jaw so tight I thought his teeth might shatter, and he glared at me as if daring me to argue.

Since I figured it would piss him off even more, I smiled, mustered my cheeriest voice, and said, "It's always good to know who's the boss. So, what's the plan?"

We weren't exactly in the best tactical position I'd ever occupied. The wooden doors and window that led from our balcony into the house were burning madly, as was the room beyond. That only left down or up. Both directions posed problems.

"I got the damned dog last time," said Devin. "It's your turn." Then, as the stone dog's head came up through the floor of the balcony, Devin did a neat backflip over the railing behind him.

I shouted, "You're the one with the magic swords, asshole!"

But he was already gone, and the stone dog seemed to agree with him as to who got to fight whom, turning a snarling glare on me as its front legs emerged from the stone. But terror is a wonderful driver of inspiration, and I jumped straight out of my crouch and up onto the railing.

That left me exposed to another blast from Deem, but I figured he wouldn't take the risk of hitting his familiar. It was only as I leaped from there to catch the edge of the roof above that it occurred to me that the damn dog might be proof against its master's magical fire. But Deem didn't fry me just then, and my plan moved to phase two.

The dog was fully up and through the balcony now. It leaped after me, which was actually what I'd counted on. As a great stone paw swiped at my legs, I pulled my feet up bare inches above the swing. Long claws sank deep into the stone wall below me, and I planted both boots on the back of its paw before it could move again, using that momentary footing to launch myself the rest of the way onto the roof.

The dog came after me, charging up the limestone wall as easily as a squirrel might run up a tree. I took three long steps. Then, just as the stone dog came up over the lip of the roof, I let myself fall forward as if I'd tripped. Landing on palms and toe tips, I could feel the roof already starting to warm from the magically generated fire below.

"Triss, joist!" I slid my right hand over a seam in the lead roof to guide him.

The dog pounced, and I pushed off with my right hand, rolling madly away. In that same moment, Triss released a blast of pure magical force focused on the thick joist running beneath the seam in the lead. It shattered one of the main supports for the patch of roof where I'd just been. Combine that with the fire beneath, and there was never a chance it would stand up to the incredible impact of a thousand-pound dog trying to crush a man.

The stone dog went straight through into the fire below while I reversed course, spreading my arms as I leaped off the roof. Time to join Devin in going after Deem. The colonel was by far the more fragile link in the Elite partnership. Triss made wings of my arms, though much narrower than usual, and we went down *fast*! After our last experience sail-jumping around the colonel, I couldn't blame him for the caution.

I used our abbreviated hang time to take quick stock of the situation below. The garden was in total pandemonium. The guards and servants had scattered, variously running for the house, the hills, or the koi pond—presumably to get buckets of water to throw on the rapidly spreading fire. Maylien, who only had about two-thirds of a sword left, was dodging in and out between the hedges and larger bits of sculpture to avoid closing with her sister again. She didn't look happy, but I was pretty sure she'd be all right on her own for a few more minutes.

Devin, on the other hand, was in real trouble. He was unshrouded and fighting against both Fei and Deem. The latter was using his free hand to hurl short bursts of mage-lightning at Devin every few seconds. That forced Zass to focus all his energy on magical defense and explained why Devin hadn't shadowed up.

I lost track of things for a few moments then as I hit bottom and had to go straight into a series of diving rolls to bleed off the extra speed from our precipitous descent. As soon as I was up, I drew my second sword and dashed toward the whirling knot of steel and magic that was the Deem-Fei-Devin fight.

"Aral!" Maylien yelled from somewhere off to my left. "I could use some help here! Call Bontrang, dammit!"

I mentally kicked myself. We'd prearranged a signal with Heyin to release the gryphinx in case of treachery, and I'd forgotten all about it until then.

I made a half turn to orient myself properly and pointed my swords skyward. "Triss, now!"

He flowed over the blades, momentarily masking them in shadow, and together we sent a great V of magelightning up into the clear morning air, brilliant green so there would be no mistaking the intent. Then I turned back toward the more urgent problem. I'd taken barely two steps before I heard a tremendous crash from above and behind me.

I glanced up in time to see a huge horizontal pillar of flame extend itself from a gaping hole in the Marchon House. The stone dog led the fire like the head of a comet, dropping out and down from the doors it had just shattered. It didn't look any the worse for wear and was already bunching its legs for landing. While the few remaining servants finally bolted, I mentally calculated angles and distances. The dog was going to land in front of me and much closer to Devin and Deem. There was no way I could get to them before it did.

I still had to try. But before I'd gone two steps, Zass let out a horrible hissing screech and Devin went down hard, falling flat on his back. The stone dog landed with a noise like a building coming down, plunging deep into the ground and vanishing under the surface. Fei and Deem both moved in on Devin.

They were going to kill him, and then me. Sumey would kill Maylien. It would all be over, and there was nothing I could do about it because I was too damn far away at the critical moment. But then a mad idea occurred to me.

With a rolling snap of elbows and shoulders I disarmed myself, throwing both of my swords at Deem's back as I continued to run forward. Magic never would have worked; the colonel was too wrapped around with spells of protection for me to unravel them all in the time I had, and I simply didn't have anything else to try. Master Kelos was probably rolling in his grave at the very idea— he'd given us enough lectures about the uncertainty involved in throwing even a knife in anything but a distraction tactic. A sword thrown to kill was the ultimate fool's bet. Doubly so in this case since I hadn't ever practiced the trick with these blades.

But sometimes even fools win. My left-hand sword hit Deem high in the side, but it had underrotated, coming in more like a slice than a stab and it bounced off without seriously hurting him. The right-hand blade, on the other hand, sank a foot and a half into the colonel's back, right at kidney height, and he fell forward, fouling Fei's thrust at Devin.

A moment later, Fei was leaping backward, with blood sheeting down over her sword hand from a nasty slash on her forearm. Deem was lying flat on his belly, unmoving. And Devin had rolled over and up onto his feet, though his left leg was also covered in blood, and he had to move by hopping. The stone dog hadn't yet re- surfaced, and now Devin made sure it never would by beheading its fallen master. I crossed the last of the distance to Deem's corpse in a mad dash and retrieved my swords. I was exhausted, but I still had Devin, Fei, and Sumey to manage and no idea what to do about any of them.

I pointed one sword each at Devin and Fei. "All right, we need to stop—"

I was interrupted by a piercing scream from the direction I'd last seen Maylien heading. But then she let out a wild string of pro- fanity, and I knew she was still in the fight. In fact, it sounded like she was coming back our way.

"I think your girlfriend's about to die, Aral," said Devin. "Don't you think you should go do something about that?"

"What *is* Sumey?" I demanded. "Tell me right now, or I'll kill you, right now."

The shadow of a dragon fell on the ground between us. "I'll help."

"Killing me won't save her. You know that, right?" Devin smiled, though I could see it cost him. "You can probably beat me right now, but it'll take time you don't have." In addition to the deep gash in his left thigh, he had numerous minor cuts and a truly ugly band of blisters running across his brow and up into the charred remnants of his hair. "But I might be willing to cut a deal. I want to walk away from this."

I glanced from Devin to Fei, wondering what she thought of all this. I really didn't want to kill her, but I wasn't sure I was going to have any other options. When my eyes met hers, her nostrils flared, and she gave a faint shake of her head, opening her wounded hand— she'd shifted her sword to her uninjured side.

"I've got nothing, Aral." Then, as if she couldn't help herself Fei asked, "You're the Kingslayer, aren't you?"

"He is that, honey," Devin said with a sneer. "Pride of fucking Namara."

I moved without thinking, lunging at Devin, one sword going for an eye, the other for his groin. His double parry was slow and wouldn't have saved him, if he hadn't leaped backward at the same time. But he'd forgotten his wounded leg, and he went down on his back when it folded under him.

"Here's the only fucking deal you're going to get, Devin. You tell me what Sumey is in the next ten seconds, and I don't kill you for the next ten seconds."

"Fuck you." He raised his swords, and I wanted to cry because he was right.

I *didn't* have time for this. I could kill Devin, but not easily and certainly not quickly. Even wounded and on his back, he could cost me minutes I didn't dare waste.

"I'll help," said Fei, raising her sword to point at Devin. "We can work out our own deal later."

Maylien suddenly came into view, emerging from behind a bit of hedge maybe a score of yards beyond Devin. She was limping badly, and covered in blood and mud from the ring and garden. She'd lost her sword somewhere along the line and she had an unconscious Bontrang clutched against her side. She saw us and started in our direction.

Sumey followed her out from behind the hedge. She was walking slow and steady, her sword held casually in front of her. If it weren't for the gleaming steel stub sticking out from between her ribs, I'd never have known she'd been stabbed. Where the hell was the blood? She should be covered in the stuff. And then I had it.

"She's one of the risen, isn't she?"

I didn't realize I'd spoken aloud until Devin answered me. "She is that. Give the man his prize. Not that knowing it is going to do you a damn bit of good. You can't kill her—"

But I was already ahead of him, and I interrupted. "Not with these swords maybe, but with one of Namara's . . ." I pointed one of mine at one of his. "Looks like you get to live, Devin. I'll trade you one of my swords and your life for one of yours if you hand it over right now. I'll even give it back to you once I'm done. Oath to Namara."

"Deal." He flipped his left-hand sword around to offer me the hilt.

I dropped one of mine at his side and took it. Sumey and Maylien were barely twenty feet away, and I started toward them. Devin laughed.

"What's so funny?" I asked.

"It won't work. I was about to tell you that when you cut me off. I've already stabbed her through the heart with that very same blade. I did it right after the bitch burned the Old Mews down to hide her plans to eventually betray me. She just smiled and asked if we still had a deal. What could I say? Namara's dead, Aral, and her magic with her."

"She may be as dead as your soul, Devin. But I'm not." I dashed forward, putting myself between Maylien and her sister. "Sumey!"

The risen looked up at me, a cold dead smile curling her lips. "Yes?"

"This ends here and now."

"Yes," she said. "It does. Take your best shot." She dropped her sword to her side and laughed. "Then I'll take mine."

I lunged forward and drove Devin's goddess-made sword straight between Sumey's breasts. It was a futile gesture, and I knew it was a futile gesture. But Sumey, with her torture chambers and her cruelty and her contempt, was everything the goddess had ever stood against, everything I had ever stood against. I couldn't not try.

The sword went home to the hilt and Sumey smiled at me. She opened her mouth to speak, but all that came out was a sort of sigh that might have contained the word "Namara." For an instant, I thought I felt something like fingers touching my forehead in the ghost of a benediction. Sumey's expression twisted from contempt to hatred as her body went limp, and she slumped slowly to the ground. For a few long seconds she glared hate at me. Then the animating will left her body, and she died.

"I don't understand," Devin said, as I withdrew the sword from Sumey's chest. "That's the same damn thrust I made."

I turned and walked over to where he lay. "Here's your sword." Only it wasn't his. It hadn't been his in years. It was ever and always Namara's. And maybe, just for a few seconds, it had been mine.

"How did you do that?" Devin demanded, without taking the offered hilt.

"*I* didn't."

"Namara's dead, Aral. Dead. Dead. Dead."

And suddenly I pitied him. "Somewhere along the line you lost sight of the one thing that really mattered, didn't you, Devin? The Emperor of Heaven may have killed Namara, but no one can ever kill Justice."

I dropped the sword at his feet. I didn't need it, and maybe, just maybe, it would help him find his way. It was all I could do for him, or to him, for that matter. Then I turned my attention to Maylien and Fei. The latter was binding a strip of clean red fabric around a deep burn in the former's arm. Triss put himself between me and Devin in dragon shape, guarding my back.

"What happened?" I asked Maylien.

"Sumey clawed my arm, and I burned the wound clean because I'd realized what she was by then. The backlash of the pain is what knocked Bontrang out."

I put an arm around Maylien's waist and gave her a squeeze. "You all right?" She squeezed me back and nodded.

"I will be once Bontrang comes around. It hit him pretty hard, but I can feel him starting to wake up now. What are we going to do about . . ." She indicated Captain Fei with her chin.

"The simplest answer would be for me to kill you, Captain. You know that, right?"

Fei shook her head and put away her sword. "I don't think so, Aral. If you really wanted me dead, we wouldn't be talking. No, the way I see it, you need at least one live official witness prepared to swear that Maylien here delivered the duel's killing blow in a completely legal and magic-free manner."

"That would certainly make things easier," I said. "Maybe we need to make an arrangement."

"Arrangement is practically my middle name," said Fei. "Tell me what you want, and we'll talk."

"Two things. Maylien takes Marchon."

"Of course."

"Aral Kingslayer was never here."

Fei smiled. "As far as I know, Aral Kingslayer hasn't been seen or heard from since the fall of Namara's temple."

"And in exchange?" I asked.

"Oh, all kinds of things. For starters, Marchon's a rich barony, and I'm a poor civil servant."

Maylien nodded. "I'm sure we can manage a big donation to Captain Fei's fund for the betterment of Captain Fei. What else?"

"Well," Fei said to me, "you know the kinds of things I get up to. I'm sure you'll be very helpful with all sorts of jobs in the future. Take for example the matter of . . . no." She glanced meaningfully at Devin, who'd just gotten to his feet and shook her head. "Let's talk about this later, in private. Suffice it to say that you owe me nine-and-ninety kinds of favors, and we've got a deal." She sniffed, then turned her head toward the burning wing of the house. "Smoky. Shouldn't you two be doing something about that fire?"

"Yes," said Maylien, "probably, though I have no idea what. I suspect we'll lose the whole wing though I can hope the fire wards will protect the main building."

That's when Heyin and his people came running up the carriageway. Maylien hurried to meet them while Devin began to limp away. I started after Maylien.

Out of the corner of my eye I caught the shadow of a tayra touching noses with the shadow of a dragon. Then the tayra sadly bowed its shoulders, and the dragon fell in behind me.

Epilogue

I paused at the edge of the orange grove and drew aside the curtain of shadow that covered my face. I wanted a better look at the third-floor balcony and my goal. The moon was high and near to full, providing a clear view. The climb was easy enough, but the dense thicket of imperial roses I had to pass through to get to the wall made for a painful obstacle. Sadly, in the first clutches of fall, they were long past their blooming season, which would have provided some small recompense for the blood I'd lose slipping through them.

I crossed the open ground to the roses fast and low, staying hidden within Triss's enshrouding presence. Then I worked my way quietly through the wall of thorns to the corner of the building. From there it was easy enough to climb to the level of the second-floor windows and use them to make my way across to the balcony. A short jump got me from there to the railing. Over and down into the shadow of a planter, and I was in position. Now it was just a matter of waiting.

And not long either. I couldn't have been there more than a quarter of an hour when the door from the house opened. Two footmen came out carrying a tray and some cushions, quickly moving to the small marble table that sat within the shadow of the arbor. They put two glasses and two plates on the table along with a lamp and a variety of decanters and small covered dishes. They arranged cushions on three of the four chairs. They wore red shirts and pants, as was the current fashion for servants, as well as slightly baffled expressions, which were always in fashion for anyone who had to deal with the whims of the nobility.

Once the table was set, they withdrew into the house, leaving

the door open behind them. The Baroness Marchon came out a moment later. She was tall and athletic, with long dark hair drawn
back in a braid and a wicked smile I knew well. She had a little gryphinx perched on her shoulder.

"Aral"—she sat down at the table—"come, sit down. Talk to me."

I let the shadow covering Triss had provided fall away, then
crossed the marble tiles to take the second seat. A dragon's shadow
curled up in the third and was soon joined by Bontrang. Maylien
poured me a small glass of Kyle's, an eighteen and cask-strength.
Triss made a tsking noise but didn't insert himself any further into
the conversation. He approved of Maylien if not the drink.

"It's good to see you," I said.

"You, too; I'm glad you agreed to come this time. You haven't
answered my last couple of invites."

"I've been out of town, trying to find out more about the risen
and when your sister might have succumbed to the curse. That sat-
isfies curiosity and necessity both since I'm trying to lie low at the
moment. I'm going to have trouble with Fei sooner or later, and I
figure if I keep myself out of her sight as much as possible, that will
help. Besides, Heyin was here, and I know it gives him hives when
you see me, so waiting for him to return to Marchon seemed pru-
dent."

"You might have a point there." Maylien nodded. "Speaking of
Fei and curiosity, there's something I've been wondering about the
good captain."

"What's that?"

"Why was she so willing to cut a deal? She works for the king,
and you're pretty much at the top of his most-wanted list."

"She doesn't actually," I said.

"What?"

"Work for Thauvik. Fei works for Fei first and Tien second.
The king and the law don't even enter into it. Besides, she owed me
one."

"You just lost me again."

"That poison dart Devin had prepped. It was for Fei, in case
Sumey was revealed and Sumey and Deem couldn't get Fei to play
ball. At least I'm pretty sure that's what it was for."

"But Fei didn't know about the dart, not when we first started
talking deal anyway."

"No, but she knew by then what Sumey was and that she had
owned both Deem and Devin. It's not a long jump from there to realizing that Fei's own survival odds went way up when things came

out as they did. Even if Fei'd agreed to a deal with Sumey, she'd have had a target on her back afterward, and she knew that. Also, you'll note, I made a point to mention the dart later."

"Well, maybe." She shrugged. "While you were away, did you find out anything more about Sumey's plans?"

"Her plans, no. But I've learned more about the risen than I ever wanted to, and I know how she managed to keep herself looking healthy and normal all this time. Remember that big marble tub in that torture chamber in Marchon?"

"That was really creepy."

"More than you know. She used it for bathing. In blood. Apparently, the blood of the living can keep the risen from decaying if it's good and fresh and they soak in it often enough. It's how she kept her looks and her mind."

"That's horrible."

I nodded. "What about you? Have you found anything here at the house?"

Maylien nodded and lifted the cover on one of the larger plates. There was a narrow scroll on it.

"This was in a stone casket inside a hidden vault in the wine cellar. It was behind a rack of my mother's favorite reds. There were some other things in there that made it pretty clear Sumey has been using it in the years since my mother died, so she knew about it."

"What is it?"

Maylien looked away from me. "It's a proclamation legitimizing Sumey and me. Ashvik made the two of us his legal heirs. Now that I've reclaimed my birthright by taking Marchon, that document means that the throne ought to have gone to me. It's dated a few days before you killed Ashvik, and I suspect that its existence is why my mother sent us into hiding. She didn't want us to follow our half brothers to the headsman's block. I think the real reason Sumey hired Devin was to help her kill Thauvik and make her Queen of Zhan."

I whistled. "That would certainly explain a few things."

Maylien didn't say anything, and I realized there were tears on her cheeks.

"What's wrong?" I put a hand on her shoulder.

"Do you remember that first night we spent together, sleeping by the campfire? When Heyin interrupted us in the morning."

"Of course. What about it?"

"Do you remember all those things I said about why I had to oust Sumey? About how every horrible thing Sumey did was my responsibility because the barony was mine by right?"

"I do."

She was crying openly now. "It's all still true with Thauvik. My uncle is a bad man and a bad king. Not as awful as my sister or my father, to be sure, but not good, and he's getting worse all the time. And every damned evil thing he does is being done from a throne that was supposed to go to me."

"What are you saying?"

"That I have to take the throne or accept all the evil my uncle does as my own." Now she looked up and met my eyes and there was steel in her gaze. "I don't want to have to do this, but I have no choice. Will you help me remove Thauvik from the throne?"

I have to admit that I thought about it. The temptation I'd experienced at Sumey's keep was still there. The temptation to let Maylien take the place of Namara as my personal goddess, to become an instrument for someone else's hand and let her make all the hard decisions. But I'd only just started to find out who Aral the jack could be. Who *I* could be if I let the Kingslayer go and became my own man once and for all.

I couldn't let myself be drawn into Maylien's sphere. Not yet. Maybe not ever. It'd be almost as bad for me as crawling into the bottle of Kyle's sitting there on the table and pulling the cork in behind me once again.

"No," I said. "I won't. I just . . . can't. Not as I am now." I was Aral the jack now; Aral Kingslayer was as dead as the goddess that made him, and I needed to finally bury my dead. "I'm sorry. Triss, come on. We're going."

Maylien didn't say another word. Not until I'd reached the edge of the balcony.

"Aral?" Her voice was low, quiet, hurting.

"Yes." I didn't turn back, but I did stop. I owed her that for helping me put my feet on the right path once again.

"I'm sorry, too. I thought that would be your answer, but I had to ask." Her voice dropped even lower. "You do understand, don't you?"

I nodded. "I know you did."

"I have one more thing I have to ask you."

"What is it?" I said through a throat gone suddenly tight. I didn't know what she wanted, but I knew from the sound of her voice that I wasn't going to like it.

"I know you won't kill my uncle for me, and I don't blame you. Truly, I don't. This isn't your fight. But I *will* be queen someday." She said that hard and fast, and I knew she meant it. "I have no other choice, but it terrifies me, too. What if it's the power that does this to my family? What if I'm going to become my sister all over again, or worse, my father? Not the risen part—there's been no evidence of the curse since I burned out the wound—but the slow slide into evil." She paused, and I could tell that she was crying again. "I think you love me, at least a little."

"I do." That's more than half of the reason I had to leave her now, because loving her would make it that much easier to give myself into her keeping. To surrender the chance to find out what I could be on my own.

"Good. Because I want you to do something for me." Her voice changed again, becoming firm, almost cold. The voice of the queen to come. "If I become a monster, I want you to kill me. I won't live like that, and you're the only one who can stop me. Will you promise to do that for me?"

"Yes." And now I was the one who was crying.

"Thank you."

I didn't say "you're welcome," and I didn't look back, just jumped over the railing and glided to the ground. Then I walked home to the Gryphon and asked Jerik to get me a glass of Kyle's. A glass. Not a bottle. I couldn't kill another king for Maylien. That was still beyond me. But maybe, just maybe, I could do a little good here and there, save a life, rescue a hostage, stop a robbery. Bring a little justice to the world. Find out who Aral the jack really was. And if I wanted to do any of that, I had to be sober.

It wasn't much, but it was a start.

Terms and Characters

Alinthide Poisonhand—A master Blade, the third to die making an attempt on Ashvik VI.
Alley-Knocker—An illegal bar or cafe.
Anaryan, Earl of—A Zhani noble.
Anyang—Zhani city on the southern coast. Home of the winter palace.
Aral Kingslayer—Ex-Blade turned jack of the shadow trades.
Ashelia—A smuggler.
Ashvik VI or *Ashvik Dan Pridu*—Late King of Zhan, executed by Aral. Also known as the Butcher of Kadesh.
Athera Trinity—The three-faced goddess of fate.
Balor Lifending—God of the dead and the next Emperor of Heaven.
Black Jack—A professional killer or assassin.
Blade—Temple assassin of the goddess Namara.
Bontrang—A miniature gryphon.
Calren the Taleteller—God of beginnings and first Emperor of Heaven.
Caras Dust—Powerful magically bred stimulant.
Caras Snuffler—A caras addict.
Cat's Gratitude—An alley-knocker in Little Varya.
Channary Canal—Canal running from the base of the Channary Hill to the Zien River in Tien.
Channary Hill—One of the four great hills of Tien.
Chimney Forest—The city above, rooftops, etc.
Chimney Road—A path across the rooftops of a city. "Running the chimney road."
Coals—Particularly hot stolen goods.
Code Martial—Ancient system of Zhani law predating the conquerors who make up the current noble class of Zhan.

Cornerbright—Magical device for seeing around corners.

Crown Law—Zhan's modern legal system.

Dalridia—Kingdom in the southern Hurnic Mountains.

Dead Man's Purse, the—An alley-knocker in Little Varya.

Deathspark—A piece of magic that turns a human being into a trap triggered by his own death.

Deem, Colonel—An officer of the Elite.

Devin Urslan—A former Blade.

Downunders—A bad neighborhood in Tien.

Dragon Crown—The royal crown of Zhan, often replicated in insignia of Zhani crown agents.

Drum-Ringer—A bell enchanted to prevent eavesdropping.

Dustmen—Dealers in caras dust.

Eavesman—A spy or eavesdropper.

Elite, the—Zhani mages. They fulfill the roles of secret police and spy corps among other functions.

Emberman—A professional arsonist.

Erk Endfast—Owner of the Spinnerfish, ex–black jack, ex–shadow captain.

Everdark, the—The home dimension of the Shades.

Eyespy—A type of eavesdropping spell.

Face, Facing—Identity. "I'd faced myself as an Aveni bravo."

Fallback—A safe house.

Familiar Gift—The ability to soul-bond with another being, providing the focus half of the power/focus dichotomy necessary to become a mage.

Fire and sun!—A Shade curse.

Ghost, Ghosting—To kill.

Govana—Goddess of the herds.

Gryphon's Head—A tavern in Tien, the capital city of Zhan. Informal office for Aral.

Guttersiders—Slang for the professional beggars and their allies.

Hand of Heaven—The Son of Heaven's office of the inquisition.

Harad—Head librarian at the Ismere Library.

Hearsay—A type of eavesdropping spell.

Heyin—Lieutenant of the exiled Baroness Marchon.

Howler—Slang name for the Elite.

Imperial Bush Roses—Living security fencing.

Ismere Club—A private club for merchants.

Ismere Library—A private lending library in Tien, founded by a wealthy merchant from Kadesh.

Jack—A slang term for an unofficial or extragovernmental problem solver, see also "shadow jack," "black jack," "sunside jack."

Jax—A former Blade and onetime lover of Aral's.

Jenua, Duchy of—A duchy in Zhan.

Jerik—The bartender/owner of the Gryphon's Head tavern.

Jindu—Tienese martial art heavily weighted toward punches and kicks.

Kaelin Fei, Captain—Watch officer in charge of Tien's Silent Branch. Also known as the Mufflers.

Kaman—A former Blade, crucified by the Elite, then killed by Aral at his own request.

Kanathean Hill—One of the four great hills of Tien.

Kelos Deathwalker—A master Blade who taught Aral.

Kila—The spirit-dagger of the Blade, symbolizing the bond to Namara.

Kodamia—City-state to the west of Tien, controlling the only good pass through the Hurnic Mountains.

Kvanas, the Four—Group of interrelated kingdoms just north of Varya. Sometimes referred to as the Khanates.

Kyle's—An expensive Aveni whiskey.

Liess—A Shade, familiar of Sharl.

Little Varya—An immigrant neighborhood in Tien.

Lok—A hedge wizard with a spit-adder familiar, works for the Countess Marchon.

Loris—A former Blade.

Magearch—Title for the mage governor of the cities in the Magelands.

Mage gift—The ability to perform magic, providing the power half of the power/focus dichotomy necessary to become a mage.

Magelands—A loose confederation of city-states governed by the faculty of the mage colleges that center them.

Magelights—Relatively expensive permanent light globes made with magic.

Magesight—The ability to see magic, part of the mage gift.

Mage Wastes—Huge area of magically created wasteland on the western edge of the civilized lands.

Malthiss—A Shade, familiar of Kelos Deathwalker.

Manny Three Fingers—The cook at the Spinnerfish.

Manticore's Smile, the—An alley-knocker in Little Varya.

Marchon—A barony in the kingdom of Zhan. The house emblem is a seated jade fox on a gold background.

Maylien Dan Marchon Tal Pridu—A client of Aral's.

Mufflers—Captain Fei's organization, so known because they keep things quiet.

Namara—The now-deceased goddess of justice and the downtrodden, patroness of the Blades. Her symbol is an unblinking eye.

Nightghast—One of the restless dead, known to eat humans.

Night Market—The black market.

Nima—Mana, the stuff of magic.

Nipperkins—Magical vermin.

Noble Dragons—Elemental beings that usually take the form of giant lizardlike creatures.

Old Mews—An upscale neighborhood in Tien.

Olen—A master Blade who taught Aral.

Oris Plant—A common weed that can be used to produce a cheap gray dye or an expensive black one.

Others—The various nonhuman races.

Palace Hill—One of the four great hills of Tien.

Patiss—A Shade, familiar of Master Urayal.

Petty Dragons—Giant acid-spitting lizards, not to be confused with noble dragons.

Quink—Slang word, roughly: freak.

Rabbit Run—An emergency escape route.

Restless Dead—Catchall term for the undead.

Riel—Currency of Zhan, issued in both silver and gold.

Right of Challenge—Part of Zhan's old Code Martial.

Risen, the—A type of restless dead, similar to a zombie.

Sellcinders—A fence or dealer in hot merchandise.

Serak—A Rover, deceased lover of the young Maylien.

Serass—A Shade, familiar of Alinthide.

Shade—Familiar of the Blades, a living shadow.

Shadow Captain—A mob boss.

Shadow Jack—A jack who earns his living as a problem solver in the shadow trades.

Shadowside—The underworld or demimonde.

Shadow Trades—The various flavors of illegal activity.

Shadow World—The demimonde or underworld.

Shaisin—Small town in Zhan, baronial seat of Marchon.

Shan Starshoulders—The god who holds up the sky, current Emperor of Heaven.

Sheuth Glyph—A glyph for the binding of shadows.

Shrouding—When a Shade encloses his blade in shadow.

Siri Mythkiller—A former Blade.

Skip—A con game or other illegal job, also a "play."

Sleepwalker—An efik addict.

Slink—Magical vermin.

Smuggler's Rest—The unofficial name of the docks near the Spinnerfish.

Snug—A resting place or residence.

Son or Daughter of Heaven—The title of the chief priest or priestess who leads the combined religions of the eleven kingdoms.

Sovann Hill—One of the four great hills of Tien.

Spinnerfish, the—A shadowside tavern by the docks.

Stingers—Slang term for Tienese City Watch.

Stone Dog—A living statue, roughly the size of a small horse. The familiar of the Elite.

Straight-Back Jack—A shadow jack who gets the job done and keeps his promises.

Stumbles, the—Neighborhood of Tien that houses the Gryphon's Head tavern.

Sumey Dan Marchon Tal Pridu—Baroness Marchon and sister of Maylien.

Sunside—The shadowside term for more legitimate operations.

Sunside Jack—A jack who works aboveboard, similar to a modern detective.

Sylvani Empire—Sometimes called the Sylvain, a huge empire covering much of the southern half of the continent. Ruled by a nonhuman race, it is ancient, and hostile to the human lands of the north.

Tailor's Wynd—An upscale neighborhood in Tien.

Tangara—God of glyphs and runes and other magical writing.

Thauvik IV or *Thauvik Tal Pridu, the Bastard King*—King of Zhan and bastard half brother of the late Ashvik.

Thieveslamp/Thieveslight—A dim red magelight in a tiny bull's-eye lantern.

Tien—A coastal city, the thousand-year-old capital of Zhan.

Timesman—The keeper of the hours at the temple of Shan, Emperor of Heaven.

Travelers—A seminomadic order of mages dedicated to making the roads safe for all.

Triss—Aral's familiar. A Shade that inhabits Aral's shadow.

Tuckaside—A place to stash goods, usually stolen.

Tucker—Tucker bottle, a quarter-sized liquor bottle, suitable for two or for one heavy drinker.

Underhills—An upscale neighborhood in Tien.

Urayal—A Master Blade.

Vangzien—Zhani city at the confluence where the Vang River flows into the Zien River in the foothills of the Hurnic Mountains. Home of the summer palace.

Warboard—Chesslike game.

Wardblack—A custom-built magical rug that blocks the function of a specific ward.

Westbridge—A bridge over the Zien upriver from the palace, and the neighborhood around it.

Worrymoth—An herb believed to drive away moths.

Zass—A Shade, familiar of Devin.

Zhan—One of the eleven human kingdoms of the east. Home to the city of Tien.

BARED
BLADE

For Laura,
the bright star at the center of my universe

Acknowledgments

First and foremost I want to thank Laura McCullough; Jack Byrne; Anne Sowards; my mapmaker, Matt Kuchta; Neil Gaiman for the loan of the dogs; cover artist John Jude Palencar; and cover designer Judith Lagerman.

I also owe many thanks to the active Wyrdsmiths: Lyda, Doug, Naomi, Eleanor, and Sean. My Web guru, Ben. Beta readers: Steph, Ben, Dave, Sari, Karl, Angie, Sean, Laura R., Matt, Mandy, Becky, April, Mike, Jason, Jonna, and Benjamin. My family: Carol, Paul and Jane, Lockwood and Darlene, Judy, Lee C., Kat, Jean, Lee P., and all the rest. Lorraine, because she's fabulous. My extended support structure: Bill and Nancy, Sara, James, Tom, Ann, Mike, Sandy, Mandy, and so many more. Also, a hearty woof for Cabal and Lola.

I'd also like to thank the many people at Penguin who do so much to make me look good: Kat Sherbo, Anne Sowards's fabulous assistant; production editor Michelle Kasper; assistant production editor Andromeda Macri; interior text designer Laura K. Corless; publicist Brady McReynolds, and my copy editor, Mary Pell.

1

Every story has to start someplace, though it's rarely at the beginning. I came into this one when it came into my office. I had two sips of good Aveni whiskey left in my glass when the woman walked into the taproom at the Gryphon's Head. Women, really . . . or, well, it's complicated. I believed there were two of them at the time, so we'll go with that for now—two women walk into a tavern. My tavern.

The place I work out of is named after the skull the owner nailed up behind the bar. Jerik used to hunt monsters for a living. Poach monsters, really, but it's not the kind of poaching that gets you arrested, because the royal game wardens don't want the damned things around either. He retired when the one behind the bar nearly bit off his head. What the Gryphon lacks in elegance it more than makes up in character, every one of them dangerous and most of them wanted by the Crown. My silent partner and I fit right in, though no one ever sees him.

They call me Aral these days, or shadow jack. The one is my name, though not quite as it appears on all the warrants and wanted posters. The other is my new job. I've become a jack of the shadow trades, a fixer of problems that you'd rather not bring to the attention of the law.

Anyone who knew me in the old days would call it a huge step down. But only if they missed the place in the middle where my world shattered. I may be nowhere near the man I used to be, but I'm infinitely more than the wreck I was a year ago. Someday I might even figure out how to bridge that gulf and get back in touch with the old me. There are some pieces that I'd like to collect for future use.

In the meantime, I work out of the Gryphon because it's the kind of tavern that attracts people with shadowside problems. Well, that, and because my partner, Triss, likes the ambiance—it's always dark in the Gryphon and he lives in the shadows. Quite literally.

He's a Shade, a creature of living darkness and a legacy of the days before my fall. Triss is my partner, my friend, my familiar. Yeah, I was a sorcerer once upon a time. A sorcerer and what some would call an assassin, though I don't much like that word. I never killed anyone for money.

But back to the women. I was trying hard to make sure my second drink didn't turn into a third—I'd followed that road all the way to the bottom. The eighth hour bells had just rung when the first of the pair stepped into the Gryphon, briefly occluding the red gold light of the westering sun. The doors and windows were all open to help with the heat of high summer, which put me in a chair next to the empty hearth. It was the only windowless wall and it offered me a perch where I could keep an eye on front and back doors while staying as much in shadow as possible.

The first one came in fast and immediately stepped to one side, getting out of the light and putting her back to the wall while she waited for her eyes to adjust to the tavern's gloom. Add in the way the woman moved—smooth and quiet, balanced on the balls of her feet amidst the dirty straw on the floor—and I marked her down as some sort of trained killer. Though whether that meant hunter, mercenary, black jack, or something more exotic, I couldn't say without the closer study I proceeded to give her.

She was tall and broad shouldered, built like a farm girl or a soldier. Wide hipped and busty, she had thick muscle showing on her bare arms along with a number of interesting, if minor, scars. She had black hair and dark eyes, which was common enough in Tien, and golden brown skin almost as pale as mine, which wasn't.

Her clothes were foreign, too, tight green breeches and knee-high brown walking boots below, with a short sleeveless cotton tunic the color of rust above. Over that she wore a heavy leather vest that hung to midthigh—too warm for this weather and closer to armor than clothing, though not as close to armor as she would have liked, if I was any judge. Her stance wanted chain mail or possibly plate. She had a pair of short iron-tipped rods hanging where another might have carried daggers, an interesting choice.

The woman who followed her in a few moments later was short and lean with almost no breasts or hips to speak of and the whipcord muscles of a dancer or acrobat. Her outfit matched the larger woman's in style, though she wore blues and grays instead of greens and browns. She headed straight across the bar to a little table right in the center of the room, moving fast and without any of the hesitancy you'd expect of someone suddenly crossing from light into darkness. She even managed to avoid stumbling over a stray chair that had been left between tables, deftly stepping around it without actually appearing to see it.

When she got to the table, she took a seat facing back toward the front door and started idly tapping her foot. Between the dancer's build and the nervous energy she reminded me of my fellow assassin and onetime fiancée, Jax. A lot. That would have been enough to focus my attention even without the sudden pressure Triss exerted on my back as he slid up to peer at the two of them over my right shoulder. A surprise, since he's normally not that interested in strangers. Once she was in her chair, the larger woman headed across the bar to join her.

Like her companion, the little dancer type wore her black hair short—cut just above the collar on the sides and back with bangs in front. Her skin was darker than the taller woman's, though still light for Tien, and her eyes were a shockingly pale blue. Really, she looked nothing like Jax, and yet there was something about her bearing that made me think back to soft lips and whispered words of . . . I shook my head. Those days were gone. Focus on the now and the woman in front of me. From the way she kept rolling her shoulders and neck I didn't think she liked the heavy leather vest any more than the bigger woman did, though for reasons I guessed to be pretty much the opposite of her friend.

Or, should I say bodyguard? Because that's what I made them initially—some foreign noble and her minder. Which meant I could safely ignore them. And I tried, really I did. But Triss kept peering over my shoulder, and somehow I found I couldn't take my eyes off them either. Oh, I didn't make it obvious—the priests who raised me had taught me better than that. But I did watch them as close as I'd have watched one of my goddess-assigned targets back in the old days.

A lot of that was Triss, of course. What he cares about, I care about. He's all I've got left of the old me and these days he has to spend the vast majority of his time hiding in my shadow and pretending he doesn't exist. When the Emperor of Heaven murders your goddess, orders his head priest to burn your temple to the ground, and then declares your entire order anathema, it kind of puts a cramp in your social life.

It didn't help that the goddess Namara had made herself and her followers deeply unpopular with the world's secular authorities. Seeing to it that justice applies to kings as well as to commoners is not a recipe for making those kings love you. Quite the contrary. But that was my life once upon a time: a Blade of Namara, bringing the Unblinking Eye of Justice to those too powerful to find it in the courts.

Torture the innocent? Foment wars of aggression? Murder your way to the throne? Namara would send me or one of my fellows to have a few words with you. Usually "rest in peace." Occasionally "burn in hell." In either case, we arranged an immediate interview with the lords of judgment and a chance to ride the wheel of rebirth. For that, some lumped us in with paid assassins, mostly the sort of people with guilty consciences and high titles attached to their names—king, general, Son of Heaven. . . .

But those days were gone, destroyed with the temple, or buried with the goddess, or simply hiding in the shadows like me and Triss. Hiding or lost. It's hard for me to tell the difference between those two things these days. Once I was a Blade of Namara and I knew my purpose, believed in it absolutely.

Now? I'm not sure. I think I can be more than just a jack, or I hope so at least. But is it even possible to be a Blade without the goddess? To serve Justice when its avatar has left the scene? Those were the questions I'd been asking of late. But with Namara gone there was no one to answer me but me. And who could trust the word of a shadow jack? I sighed and once again tried to focus on the moment.

The Gryphon is full of dim corners and mysterious smells and even on summer days when the sunlight spilled in at doors and windows, it seemed to hold onto more of the night. That affinity for shadow allowed Triss considerable extra freedom of movement. He used it now as he studied the two women from his resting place on the wall behind me.

After the big woman stopped at the bar to place their orders, she'd taken a seat at a right angle to her fidgety companion, which meant that neither of them could see both doors. Overconfident or foolish—it was hard to tell the difference. They split a bottle of wine, with the taller one doing the opening and pouring while they waited for our host Jerik to send someone over with the specialty of the house—fried bits of anonymous meat and lightly bruised vegetables served on a bed of brown rice.

They weren't doing anything but eating and drinking in the

most casual fashion but there was something about them that kept drawing my eye, and it wasn't just the way that the smaller one reminded me of Jax. There was something off about their body language and I couldn't figure out what. That was irritating enough, but I might have been able to drop it if Triss hadn't been equally fascinated.

The only obviously strange thing about them was how quiet they were. They spoke only rarely and then barely moved their lips, speaking so softly I hadn't been able to hear a word from where I sat despite the relative emptiness of the tavern when they arrived. They also moved with a sort of intermittent dance-like grace, though I hadn't yet figured out the pattern. For a while I'd thought they might be a couple, but they didn't have the right sort of interactions, so I went back to my original guess.

By the time they'd finished eating, the sun had well and truly gone to bed, which meant the Gryphon started to wake up as the night crowd rolled in. I ordered another Kyle's somewhere in there, just to give me a reason to stay in the bar and keep an eye on the women. I could feel Triss's disapproval, but I watered the whiskey heavily, so it hardly should have counted.

It wasn't long after sunset that the trouble started. Boquin, a young shadow lieutenant—about third in the hierarchy of the gang that claimed the Gryphon as part of its turf—swaggered in the door and almost immediately headed for the table with the two women.

"How much?" he demanded.

"For what?" replied the taller of the pair, speaking loudly enough for me to hear her for the first time.

Her voice was low and sweet, gentler than I'd have expected from her appearance, and carrying only the faintest trace of some foreign accent—Kvanas maybe, though I couldn't place it firmly. Her companion froze. It was the first time I'd seen the smaller woman hold still all evening.

"The two of you together in one of the rooms upstairs," replied Boquin. "I like the look of you. How much?"

I don't know whether he was serious or just messing with them, but it didn't really matter. Either way, things looked like they were escalating. The tall one dropped her hands down to rest on her fighting rods, while the short one slipped a hand inside her vest then went still again. Perilously so. That air of precisely focused danger *really* reminded me of Jax. What was going on with these women?

"Why don't you go away before you get hurt," said the tall one.

It was a challenge, and Boquin took it as such, flipping back his

light jacket to expose the hilt of a short heavy sword. He didn't yet
put his hand on the blade, but the implication was there.

Normally at that point, my impulse would have been to slip
back even deeper into the shadows while I waited to see what happened next. I didn't have a stake here. Somebody else's problem, and
all that. Not to mention that the action to come might well serve to
reveal whatever it was about the women that kept hitting my sense
of something off.

But I still hadn't so much as moved my chair back when Triss's
voice whispered in my ear, "Help them."

Since he was incredibly careful about not breaking cover under
anything but emergency circumstances, I'd already popped to my
feet and crossed half the distance to the women's table before I had
time for second thoughts or even first ones. By then, of course, it was
too late. Boquin had spotted my move-in—his eye likely attracted
by the suddenness of my actions.

He turned and gave me an appraising look. "These two with you,
Jack?"

I nodded, but made no other move, and it hung there for a moment. I could almost hear Boquin weighing up my reputation against
the possible loss of face from backing down. I didn't have a hard
name, not as Aral the jack anyway—no major notches on my sword
hilts, no history of playing the enforcer, but not a single lost fight or
turn-tail moment either. My reputation was all about getting things
done on the quiet and without costing large. It was close, I could see
that from his eyes, but in the end he made the right choice.

He shrugged and let the jacket cover his sword. "Well, keep 'em
on a shorter leash in the future."

I nodded again and snagged a nearby chair, sliding it over to the
women's table. It put my back to the bar and to the door into the
kitchens, which made my bones itch, but I didn't have a lot of choice.

"I don't recall inviting you to sit down," said the tall one, and
again I wondered about her accent.

Her companion remained still and quiet, though she had removed her hand from her vest. The change in the character of her
actions didn't fit with my original assessment of noble and bodyguard, but so far I hadn't come up with anything I liked better, and
she wasn't giving me any more clues.

"I'm only planning on staying long enough to convince Boquin
I wasn't just twisting his dick for the fun of it." I spoke as quietly as
they had earlier because I didn't want Boquin or any of his friends
to overhear me. "Name's Aral."

"Stel," the tall one said grudgingly after a long thoughtful pause, though she too spoke quietly. "And we didn't need your help with this little problem." Her companion ignored me, or pretended to.

"Actually, you did." There was something about the way she said that they didn't need help with *this* problem that made my business ears prick up, but I decided to come back to it in a bit. "Boquin's a lieutenant in the Cobble-runners, and several kinds of bad news."

"What's that, some Tienese gutter gang?" She shook her head. "We could have handled him."

"Physically, probably—you look like someone who knows how to use those Kanjurese fighting rods you're carrying. But you wouldn't have been able to do it without seriously injuring or killing him. That would have bought you a world of hurt when you tried to get out of the Gryphon. His Cobble-runner buddies would have been all over you before you got fifty feet."

"We can deal with gutter slime easily enough." There was a sneer in her voice now, like she'd taken my measure and found it wanting. "Even in numbers."

"Can you deal with a crossbow quarrel in the back of the neck? Because that's how they'd do it if they saw you take down Boquin too easily. They're mean bastards, not stupid. You wouldn't do your boss much good then."

"My boss?" She looked puzzled.

I glanced at the shorter woman for emphasis, wondering why she hadn't added anything to the conversation, but she continued to look past me as if barely aware of my presence.

"You think I'm working for Vala—" But whatever she was about to say, she never finished the sentence.

Instead she leaped to her feet, drawing the rods from her belt and spinning toward the door. In almost the same instant a big man in the uniform of a lieutenant of the Elite came striding in with his huge stone dog behind him. Preset spells wrapped them round in a network of multicolored light like dew-hung spider webs catching the reflections of a shattered rainbow—beautiful and deadly for those with the eyes to see it. Mage's eyes.

The shorter woman, Vala, kicked her chair over backward and somehow turned the motion into a back handspring. I twisted up and out of my chair with vague intentions of heading out through the kitchen, but even as I turned that way, a Crown Guardsman came in—one of perhaps a dozen entering through various doors and windows.

I had one of those brief moments of clarity then, the kind you sometimes get in the midst of incipient chaos. I realized that I could turn my lunge out of the chair into a drunken-seeming fall and hope that the Guard was there for someone else—Stel and Vala most likely, though Boquin or a score of other possible offenders of one degree or another offered other options. That seemed likely enough given the numbers, only a dozen guards and one Elite. If they'd come for me they'd have come much better armed.

If I played the drunk and they were here for someone else, there was an excellent chance I'd get lightly roughed up and then thrown back as a small fish. After all, the wanted posters with my name on them didn't yet come with a picture—a leftover gift from the goddess, if you will. Of course, if I was wrong, and they *were* here for me, they'd have my head nailed up over the traitor's gate by this time next week.

Though I have to admit Vala's resemblance to Jax weighed on my decision, it was Triss's "help them" that made the difference. I still didn't know why my best friend had taken such an interest in the women, but it was enough for me that he had. I reversed course then, moving away from the bar and back toward the lieutenant and his stone dog. I was lightly armed, daggers only, but there was no other possible choice. The Elite mage-officer, with his stone dog familiar and his network of powerful spells, was a greater threat than the rest of the soldiers combined.

He shrugged his right arm now, sending a golden loop of spell stuff sliding down off his shoulder into his hand—some sort of entrapment magic by the look of it and one of his presets. With a snap of his wrist he lashed the golden line at Stel. Good. Tying her up might keep him distracted long enough for me to get in close and— *blood of the goddess!*

Instead of being caught by the line, Stel dropped under the ensnaring spell while simultaneously lunging toward the Elite lieutenant in a fencer's extension with her righthand rod. Far more startling was the way she brought her left-hand rod up and back, using it to snag the spell-line. Looping it quickly around the tip a half dozen times, she brought it down and around behind her back, jerking the lieutenant off balance and into her other rod. The iron tip caught him in the floating ribs with an audible crack of breaking bone.

His stone dog lunged forward then, and would probably have bitten her arm in half if a blast of raw magical force hadn't caught him squarely in the chest, spinning him half around. A second blast hit him in the shoulder and threw his thousand-plus-pound bulk into the wall just to the left of the door frame, scattering stone chips in his wake. The wall came apart in a cloud of shattered boards and plaster and I turned a quick eye toward the source of the blast. Vala.

She held a pair of short wooden wands, hilted like fighting daggers and likewise positioned. Both glowed with an intense green light in my magesight and I wondered what had gone into their making. But I didn't let that distract me from my main goal—the lieutenant was still alive and that meant he was still a threat.

For about two more seconds. Stel let the spell-line she'd caught fall across her shoulders. Then she pivoted, using her own body as a sort of spool to take up the line and pull the lieutenant in closer before she crushed his throat with her right-hand rod. She was terrifyingly fast, completing the whole maneuver before the Elite had time to even begin the process of unweaving his spell. Somewhere outside the stone dog thrashed and gurgled as its own life boiled away in sympathy with its dying master's.

Suddenly, Stel dropped to the floor. I had an instant to wonder why before a beam of bright blue light passed through the space she'd just been occupying. About as thick around as my thigh, it came from the door behind her and punched a hole through the dust and debris from the broken wall. It likewise punched a hole through Boquin, the post he was leaning against, the guy across the table from him, an unknown drinker near the fireplace, and the fireplace itself.

A moment later, a second stone dog charged into the room through the wreckage left by the first, and a third came in through the front door. Panic ensued as everyone, including several of the Crown Guards tried to find someplace else to be. One particularly clever shadowsider took a moment to throw his shirt over the magelight chandelier, plunging the already dimly lit room into near blackness. I left the second Elite by the back door to Vala and her friend and headed toward the one coming in through the front.

I went by way of rolling under the nearest empty table, picking up the gods-alone-know what kind of vermin from the filthy straw in the process. An odd choice perhaps, but one that came out of a lifetime of hiding what I am. In the dark and the chaos, the table provided plenty of cover as I called on Triss to cover me with his darkness. In a world where spells shine bright in magesight, there's no such thing as true invisibility, at least not from your fellow mages. Triss and his Shade cousins can, however, provide a very effective substitute.

Triss is both a part of my personal shadow and apart from it, a creature of elemental darkness. With the table and the madness around it hiding us from most eyes, he flowed up from the floor to encase me in a thin layer of condensed darkness like a second skin made of icy silk. But the sensation only lasted for a moment before he expanded outward into a cloud of enshrouding night.

It was a bit like being wreathed in thick smoke. No one could see me and I couldn't see anyone else. But that's less of a handicap than it might seem. The priests that raised me as a weapon for the hand of a goddess now dead, had trained me from earliest childhood to operate comfortably in complete darkness. Moreover, while I can't see in the conventional manner when I'm shrouded, I *can* borrow the senses of my familiar.

Triss possesses a sort of 360-degree unsight, focused much more on texture and differences in light and dark than on the shapes and colors that dominate human vision. It's a very different way of seeing, and it took me years of practice to be able to make sense of it at all, much less use it effectively.

As I slipped out from under the table, the unsight provided a sort of confused view of turbulent motion as Crown Guards tried to hold the exits against the mass outpouring of panicked shadowsiders. I narrowed my attention to the slice of the taproom near the front door, where I'd last seen the third stone dog. It wasn't hard to spot, not with the giant circle of completely empty space around it. People stayed away from it even in the dark and half mad with fear. Who could blame them?

Stone dogs are flat terrifying. Imagine one of those guardian statues that sits out in front of the bigger temples. You know the ones; size of a small horse, deep chest, broad shoulders, a head more like a lion than a dog. Now imagine that one of them's come to life and is sizing you up as its next meal. Figure in that it can swim through earth and stone like a fish through water, and then add in whatever protective magic its sorcerer-companion has wrapped around it, and . . . brrr. Just brrr.

This one was moving fast, charging toward Vala and Stel. I let it go past and headed back the way it had come, looking for its master. I didn't have a lot of choice. None of the weapons I had on me would do much more than irritate the stone dog, and I'm only a middling good spell caster at my best. If I revealed myself, it'd tear me to pieces before I cracked its protections. No, the only chance I had of removing the dog from the equation was to take down its master.

A captain of the Elite, he was just coming through the front door then. Drawing a long knife from the sheath at my belt, I moved toward him as quickly as I could manage without making any significant noise. In the dark tavern, I was effectively invisible, and he didn't know to watch out for me or my kind, not if they were there for Stel and Vala at any rate. But the Elite were very, very good and I would only get one free shot. I had to make it count. I was coming in from the front, because that was faster, and just about on top of him when the captain raised his right hand and pointed at the darkened chandelier, calling out a spell of illumination.

The room practically exploded with light as the old and faded magelights Jerik had bought secondhand suddenly kindled into eye-tearing brightness. The captain's gaze flicked across the darkness surrounding me, flicked back, froze. He knew I was there.

Somewhere behind me, Stel screamed.

2

──◆──

Shade invisibility has its strengths and weaknesses. Biggest strength? In the dark you are essentially invisible. Biggest weakness? The blind spot. In a brightly lit space—like the Gryphon's taproom had just become—the Shade's dark shroud registers as a sort of large moving hole in your vision. A lacuna, or void.

Most people will barely register it if it goes away quickly enough or, if they do take notice, they will dismiss it as a symptom of too much drink or incipient headache. But for people who have been trained to look for Shades and their companion Blades, people like the Elite captain I was trying to kill, it's a clear sign that one of my kind is close at hand. In this case, too close.

The captain was good and he was fast, flicking a bundled coil of deep purple magic loose of his wrist and lashing out with it in the very instant he noticed me. But I was already inside his guard. I drove my knife up and in, under his ribs and into his heart, twisting as I pulled the blade free. Hot blood followed it, contrasting sharply with the cold ice that wrapped my spine when the captain's already dissipating spell lashed across my back.

Triss shrieked in pain and the lower half of my body effectively went away, as I lost all feeling below the waist and collapsed. I caught a boot in the ribs—someone tripping over me while bolting toward the momentarily unguarded door. I rolled away, hoping to get clear before they had time to think about what had just happened. That's when I noticed that I'd lost my shadow, or rather that it had returned to being no more than a dark outline on the floor.

I didn't know what the spell had done to Triss, only that he was still alive or I wouldn't be. As much as his absence scared me, I didn't have time to do anything about it if I wanted us both to survive the next few minutes. I was half-paralyzed, exposed and vulnerable and that was after taking only the dying aftereffects of the Elite's spell. What would the full treatment have done? I shuddered and pushed the thought aside. I needed to get under cover. I started dragging myself toward the closest refuge—the dark space under a nearby table—sweating ice water all the way.

Up close, the filthy straw on the floor was more noisome and foul than ever, lousy with centipedes and nipperkins. Not that this was the first time I'd ended up crawling around on the Gryphon's floor, just the first time I'd ever done it sober. I'd just about made it under the table, when the feeling started coming back in my lower body. I had to clench my jaws to keep from swearing aloud, because I didn't think I'd be able to quit if I got started. It felt like ten thousand tiny imps had decided to use me for target practice with their tiny bows, every one of them shooting fire-tipped arrows. If you've ever been jabbed with hot needles, you know the sensation. Yes, I have. No, I don't want to talk about it.

But with the pain came the ability to move, and as much as I just wanted to lie there until the hurting stopped, I had things to do, starting with checking on my familiar.

"Triss!" I hissed, forcing myself to hands and knees. "Are you all right?"

My shadow shifted beneath me until it looked as though it belonged to a small dragon—Triss's preferred form. The dragon nodded his head briefly, though he didn't speak, then collapsed back into my own outline a moment later. That really worried me—he's normally much more circumspect, and this was a case where words would have spoken more quietly—but he *had* nodded and I still couldn't afford to stop moving.

I had to find out what had happened to Vala and Stel, help them if they were among the living, and make my escape if they weren't. Grabbing the edge of a table, I pulled myself upright and scanned the room. Compared to the chaos of a few minutes before, the Gryphon seemed positively peaceful. Three dead Elite and two stone dogs lay on the filthy floor along with a dozen other mixed casualties. The Crown was going to be profoundly unhappy—it took years to make an Elite and their numbers were few.

Stel was down and out, though presumably not dead, judging by the light of healing magic Vala was applying to her fallen companion. Most everyone else on both sides of the conflict had fled. As I staggered toward the women I noticed an unspilled drink sitting at the edge of a table—a short glass filled with something clear and no doubt brutally alcoholic. Rice-white or one of its cousins.

I thought about it, I really did. I'm not sure if that makes it better or worse that I picked it up and lifted it to my lips, and at that moment I really didn't care. The effort of getting to my feet had left me shaking and sweating. I *needed* that drink.

It was harsh and warm, the cheapest stuff imaginable, and it went down like a shot of liquid silk—sleek and soft and oh-so-soothing. Not as effective as a hot cup of efik, or even a few of the fresh roasted beans that wonder brew came from, but I'd turned my back on the Blade's drug of choice long ago. Almost against my will, I thought about all the bottles sitting behind the bar, even half turned that way. But I knew what following the impulse would make me, and I forced myself to head for the women instead.

Vala was sitting cross-legged on the floor, facing away from me, with Stel's head cradled in her lap. She was doing some sort of intricate spellwork, healing magic well beyond my meager training in that direction. The details of the spell were far less interesting than the fact that she was doing it without a familiar anywhere in sight. I'd been watching her and her companion rather closely all night, and I'd never seen even the hint of a familiar. Nor did I now. The obvious answer to that puzzle was that she'd partnered an air spirit like a qamasiin, or some other invisible creature, but I was beginning to suspect a very different solution.

I took another silent step closer just as Stel's eyes flickered open, meeting mine. Though Stel didn't move her lips or even twitch, I saw Vala go suddenly still, and I froze. She couldn't know I was there, and yet, she did. Moving carefully and deliberately, I opened my hands and extended them out to the sides, palms toward the two women to show that they were empty. If I was right, I was on very dangerous ground. If I was wrong, the worst that would happen is that I'd make myself look the fool.

"I'm not your enemy," I said quietly. "There's no need to start up the bloodletting again."

Though she kept looking in the other direction, Vala half turned toward me, lifting her right arm away from her body. Revealed in the gap between elbow and ribs was the tip of one of her battle wands. She was pointing it squarely at my chest with her hidden hand. Stel's eyes never left mine.

"Can you give me a good reason not to use this?" asked Vala, still looking away. Her voice sounded tight and clipped.

"I killed that third Elite, the captain. If I hadn't, your pairmate would be dead now, and so would you . . . Dyad."

Vala nodded. "So you know what I am."

"I do." Though I hadn't been sure until that moment.

"All the more reason to kill you." This time the voice came from Stel's lips.

But it was the same entity speaking, the Dyad. Two bodies, two brains, one creature. A single being with three distinct minds and personalities. Stel, Vala, the motes, and their Meld, the master entity formed from their conjoined souls—together, a Dyad, and about as far away from the familiar partnership Triss and I had as you could get. On a personal level the thought of Dyads had always struck me as a little creepy, and I found myself wondering how I could have compared one of them to Jax. On the other hand, there were the fallen Elite to consider. I couldn't argue with their deadliness, and right at the moment, with Triss incommunicado, I almost envied their ability to read each other's thoughts.

"Aren't you going to bolt, or at least try to convince me not to kill you?" the Vala half of the Dyad asked after the silence had stretched out between us.

"No," I replied. "I don't need to. If you were going to make the attempt out of hand you'd already have attacked. Since you haven't . . ." I bowed my head lightly, indicating it was still her move.

The Dyad made a little growling noise in the back of both her throats, but nodded the Vala head. "Stel took a solid hit from one of the stone dogs. It broke a half dozen ribs and she's barely up to walking. Under the circumstances, I'd rather not start a fight with anyone who can kill an Elite. Not if I don't have to. You're still talking to me instead of running for the hills. That suggests that it was skill rather than luck that did in the Elite. Also, that you're interested in some sort of alliance. What's your proposal?"

"That is the question, isn't it?" I only wished I knew what the answer was—this was Triss's gambit, not mine, and he wasn't talking. "But it's one I think would better be discussed somewhere else, don't you? Somewhere safer."

It was mainly a play for time, but that didn't make it any less true. The Crown Guards had very sensibly scattered when their Elite officers fell, but they were good soldiers and would be back with reinforcements as soon as possible. I made a quick mental calculation of the round trip time from the Stumbles to the customs house at the docks, the nearest place likely to have an Elite or two on hand—over half an hour but not by much. If they wanted to come in force, we might get an hour and a half—the time it'd take those Elite to send a message to the palace and summon more troops—but no more than that.

"Did you have a place in mind?" asked Vala. "Is it close? I don't think Stel's up to a long trip." There was something different about the tone of the second question and its followup, something more normally human, and I suspected it came from Vala rather than her Meld.

"I'll do whatever I have to," Stel spoke firmly, but I could tell she was having trouble breathing.

"I've a fallback not far from here," I said. Several actually, which made the thought of exposing any one of them less worrisome. After the events of the previous spring had reignited my interest in life, I'd started to rebuild old habits of caution and contingency planning. "We should be safe there, for a while at least."

"Take me there," said Vala, speaking in the clipped tones of the Meld.

Before I could move to offer Stel a hand, the Dyad flowed to its feet. Using the two bodies in perfect cooperation, it made the difficult task of getting the injured woman upright look like a carefully choreographed bit of dance. I realized then what it was about the women's behavior earlier in the evening that had made it so hard to ignore them: the inhuman coordination.

Any time the two had interacted directly, handing a wine glass across the table say, they'd done so with none of the wasted movements or minor corrections that normal people made under similar circumstances. That told me that they'd never learned to pass for standard-issue human. And, that in turn, meant this pair was almost certainly operating beyond the range of their normal duties and training.

I hadn't had much direct interaction with the Dyads; none of the Blades had within my memory. Kodamia was a much better and more humanely run enterprise than any of the surrounding countries, which meant it mostly avoided the attention of my goddess. I *had* encountered a few of them over the years, mostly while working undercover in various of the courts of the east; Kadesh, the Kvanas, Zhan. . . .

The Dyads I'd seen under those circumstances—mostly spies, eavesmen in diplomatic drag—had appeared perfectly normal except when they deliberately chose to emphasize their alien nature. Vala and Stel had pretty clearly not gone to whatever spy school those others had. An interesting detail that. So was their comparative youth—not much more than twenty-five, either of them—which was a good decade younger than the other Dyads I'd met. I wondered what it meant, finding them so far from home.

"Come on," I said, nodding toward the back door. "We're less likely to be seen going out this way and I've a brief stop I need to make on the way."

"For what?" Vala asked suspiciously.

"My gear. I rent a room over the stable . . . or I did up till today." I started walking. Either they would trust me and follow along or not. Whichever happened, I needed to grab my stuff and get out of there before the guard returned in force. "The whole place is burned now. After this I'm not going to be able to come back here for quite a while, if ever. Not with three dead Elite and reports of a rogue Dyad heating the neighborhood up. Too many people saw me with you."

I'd been too busy staying alive and in one piece to think ahead, so that hadn't occurred to me until that very moment, but it was true and it actually hurt me a little to realize it now. The Gryphon's Head was the worst sort of dive and it lay in the heart of one of Tien's most miserable slums. None of which changed the fact that it had been my home for more than six years—longer than any place other than the temple of Namara itself. I was going to miss it.

I glanced around sadly as I ducked out the back door. In the earlier panicked stampede for the exits someone had knocked over one of the cheap oil lamps that normally lit the yard. It had landed in a filthy pile of used straw from the stable, and now the flames provided a bright if fitful light that made my shadow dance wildly on the wall behind me. I spared a surreptitious glance at the spectacle, hoping to see some visual evidence that Triss was back with me. I didn't get that, but I did get a brief reassuring squeeze on my shoulder, and it sure wasn't from Vala or Stel.

The Dyad was trailing along at a safe distance behind me. They had arranged themselves so that the Stel mote could lean heavily on her smaller counterpart. She'd put away her rods but now held one of Vala's battle wands in her right hand while Vala held the other in her left. Both had reversed the short wands so that they lay mostly concealed against their wrists, but as I turned toward the stables, Vala flipped hers around again, pointing it loosely in my direction.

"I don't think I like the idea of letting you out of our sight," she said.

"Well, it's that or use that thing," I said over my shoulder as I kept walking. "My gear is in the hay loft and I'm going to go get it now."

"I could come with you. . . ."

"But Stel couldn't, not up the ladder. Besides, I don't want you to. There are certain protections I have to disarm and I don't want you watching." More importantly, I wanted to talk to Triss, and for that I needed privacy.

"But I don't know what you are!" This time the voice came out of both throats and the second wand slid around to point at me. "You killed an Elite and that's no mere jack's work. You're a mage at the least and much more than you seem. It makes you a serious potential threat."

"Or a potential ally. It's your choice which you want to make me. But if you're not going to try to kill me, *stay here*. I'll be right back."

Since no blast of magic followed me through the door of the stable, I had to assume they'd opted to continue our protoalliance. I dashed to the ladder and hurried up the rungs—time was getting ever more precious, and I had things to do.

"Triss?" I said as I got to the door to my little room.

"Here." In the darkness I couldn't see my shadow-companion, but something about the tone of his voice told me he'd reassumed dragon shape.

"What's the plan with the Dyad?" I asked.

"There isn't one." Triss sounded a little abashed.

I groaned. "Why am I not surprised? Did you at least know what they were when you asked me to help them?"

"No, only that they didn't move like anything human and that they were in trouble. They were foreign and alone in Tien, as we were when we came here after the death of the goddess. They needed help. What more did I need to know?"

I gently smacked my forehead against the door.

Triss said, "You have said that Namara is dead and you are a man without a people or purpose, no longer a true Blade. But also that you hope you can still do some good in this world. Here was an opportunity to do just that."

"Well, yes, but—"

"But nothing. You told me that was the path you wanted to walk going forward, *and* that I should help you stay on it. Consider this helping."

Somehow I was losing an argument with my own shadow. Again. "Later, you and I are going to have a long talk about exactly what helping me means."

"But there is no time now," said Triss, and rather smugly in my opinion.

"No there isn't, so if you'll just . . ." But I could already feel him flowing up my legs to encase me in a second skin of cool shadow.

A moment later, he released his will to me. Using the part of my-self that was temporarily Triss, I touched the lock on the door and extended a tendril of shadow-stuff into the keyhole. From the out-side the lock looked simple enough, the sort of crude iron mecha-nism you might expect to find in the stable of a run-down inn, but it was more than it seemed. Much more.

The inner workings were of Durkoth make, though not their best, nor even the best they sold to humans. I couldn't begin to afford the finest the Other smiths had to offer. What I could and had done was add spells devised by the priests of Namara to reinforce and en-hance the Durkoth workings. It would have been far easier for an intruder to break down the thick oak door than to pick the lock.

Shaping and hardening the shadow-stuff into a key—the origi-nal, I had long since destroyed—I sent a pulse of magic through the lock and twisted. The door opened inward. The room beyond hardly seemed worth the effort, tiny and tucked into the wedge where the roof met the wall of the stable. It barely had space enough for the pallet and low table that were my only real furniture—a small trunk provided a rough bench as well as storage for my more precious possessions.

I closed and latched the door behind me before I reached for the shaded magelight fixed to its lintel. Closing up wasted time, but not much, and it was hard to push aside the cautious habits of a lifetime. With a touch I moved aside the shade, filling the room with an in-tense and expensive white light. A mosaic of threadbare rugs would prevent it shining through to the stable below and I'd chinked all the cracks in the walls long ago.

I released Triss then and he dropped to the floor, briefly provid-ing me with a normal sort of shadow before shifting to dragon form and extending himself across the room. While I applied the tip of a knife to the socket holding the magelight, Triss cracked the spelled lock on my trunk and popped the lid. I was going to miss the trunk, but it was too bulky to move quickly.

I tipped the trunk up on end, dumping its contents across the rug, then grabbed my sword rig off the top of the resulting pile. The arrangement of leather straps and steel rings held two short straight swords in a matched set of hip-draw back-sheaths as well as several smaller sheaths for knives and other tools of the Blade's trade.

Fixing a heavyweight canvas pack to several of the rings was the work of a few moments, as was filling it. I tossed in the best of my clothing, a few durable items of food, a tucker bottle of Aveni whiskey—Kyle's fifteen—and finally the magelight, plunging the room into darkness once more. Put that on my back, add my much worn trick bag, and the pouch that held what little money I currently possessed and I was ready to go. Figure five minutes total, and back out to the ladder.

I didn't bother to lock the door behind me. It wouldn't have slowed down the sort of searchers I expected to come once some witness connected me with the Dyad. There was also the slim possibility that if no one had to deal with the lock, no one would look at it closely enough to see that it was more than it ought to be. There were clues there as to what I was for those with magesight and the training to see them, so that would be for the best.

I was almost disappointed to find the Dyad waiting for me in the courtyard. Since they didn't look very happy to see me, I guess that made us even. Vala in particular looked as though she'd bitten into a rotting pastry, as she stood there angrily tapping one toe. That they hadn't bolted while I was out of sight told me that whatever else the pair might be, they were pretty desperate. They *needed* me. And that, more than anything else, was why I was going to help them, because Triss was right. My goddess might be gone, but I was ever and always her Blade, and even if I didn't entirely know what that meant in her absence, part of it had to be helping those who really needed me.

"Where to?" grunted Stel.

"Follow me." I headed for the little gate that led from the courtyard out onto the streets.

"Not till you tell us more about yourself," said Vala.

"How about this then?" I asked without slowing down. "I'm leaving. And I'm leaving right now, because the fucking Elite and their Crown Guard minions are going to be crawling all over this place in something between ten minutes and half an hour. If you want to stay and meet them, that's your lookout. But if you want my help, you'll be coming with me. It's your choice."

Vala said something in a gutter Kodamian that I didn't understand, but it sounded rude. Then they fell in behind me.

"We're not used to being treated so high-handedly," said Stel.

I didn't answer and I didn't stop moving. I've never held any sort of noble in all that high of esteem, and I wasn't about to make an exception for Dyads just because they did a better job than most of a bad lot.

In the ruling houses of Kodamia the mage gift and familiar gift

ran in different bloodlines, and a mage with no familiar was no
mage at all. The lack of proper mages to defend them could easily
have led to the ruination of the city-state.

Instead it had become one of Kodamia's greatest assets. As it
turned out, it wasn't having a familiar that was the important
thing, it was having a *familiar bond*, a pairmate of some sort who
could act as a lens to focus your magic. So the children of Kodamia's
mage-gift-bearing sorcerer caste became the bond-companions of
the children of the warrior caste who carried the familiar gift.

Because both halves of the pairing were human, the bonding
was the tightest of any mage/familiar coupling in the whole of our
world. Too tight by my standards. The two literally became one. But
that, along with intense training, allowed them to accomplish things
no other school of magery could even hope to manage.

The streets of the Stumbles were quiet and unnaturally empty
and dark. Normally at this time of night, you couldn't have gone ten
feet without fending off a couple of half-a-riel-a-lay whores, three
caras snufflers, and a slit-purse pretending to be a sleepwalker, most
of them carrying their own lights. But even the beggars and other
gutterside players had vanished. News like three dead Elite traveled
fast in a place like the Stumbles.

Windows were closed and doors barred on houses and taverns
alike, and everywhere lights were out. The only illumination came
from the stars and the half-full moon, but that didn't make me feel
one jot less exposed. I could feel eyes looking out from the cracks
between shutters and various other peepholes. Not to mention the
fact that the lack of light would make an ideal hunting environment
for the restless dead. They were rare in the city proper, but this sort
of deep darkness would draw them out of their lurking places if
there were any around.

Taking the Dyad back to one of my fallbacks instead of simply
vanishing into a cloud of shadow seemed ever more dumb. For
perhaps the dozenth time I glanced over at the laboring Stel and
considered how much simpler my life would be if I just walked
away right now. If it weren't for the part where I knew I'd have to
look at myself in the mirror to shave, I might even have tried it. I
sighed.

"What is it?" asked Vala, sounding suspicious. "Why do you
keep looking at us that way?"

"It's this—" I waved an arm to take in the whole neighborhood.
"There's no one around, which means we can't pull a decent fadeout. Not on the streets anyway."

"What would you do if you didn't have me to carry?" demanded Stel.

I couldn't tell her I'd vanish into shadow, not without admitting what I was, so I offered my second choice. "I'd head up onto the chimney road." I pointed toward the rooftops. "There's never much of a crowd up there to begin with, and we pretty much all agree not to see each other when we do meet. But there's no way you're going to make it up there, so we need to think of something—"

A sudden brief blast of light and sound cut me off. What the . . .

"Stel, you idiot!" It was Vala, who was glaring up toward the nearest low rooftop—a tannery. "That hurts, *and* you could have killed yourself, us . . ." She trailed off into a string of obscenity as she started up the wall after her pairmate.

It was only then that I realized what Stel must have done. She'd aimed the battle wand at the ground, triggered it, and ridden the resulting shockwave up onto the rooftops. I was just about to follow the Dyad roofward when I heard a shout from somewhere behind me.

"Look there's one of them now, by the tannery! Get him!"

3

Later, if we lived through the next couple of hours, I was going to strangle Triss for getting us involved in this.

"Go," I called up to the Dyad. "Head north until you run up against a big street with square stone cobbles and actual lights. Then find someplace to hole up for a bit. I'll draw them off and catch up to you there."

That was when the first crossbow quarrel stuck itself in the wall a few feet from my head. There was a slender gap between the tannery and its nearest neighbor, providing a narrow breezeway. I ducked into it and started to feel my way into the pitch-black depths.

Another quarrel followed me in, but the angle was too steep and it didn't come anywhere close to me by the sound of it. The lack of any hostile magic thrown after it suggested that I was going to be spared further Elite attention at least for a little while. That greatly increased my chances of pulling pursuit away from the others without getting myself killed in the process.

Every cautious step I took involved the sorts of crunching and squishing sounds that make you happy you can't see what you're stepping on and depressed that you can smell it. Mostly rotten food and dead rats, if I had to guess. I'd gone less than ten feet when I felt the familiar sensation of Triss wrapping me in a skin of shadow, like that moment of welcome transition when you step from the hot street into a cool tavern on a sunny summer day.

"Shroud up?" he asked.

"Not yet, we have to give the guard something to follow. I will need your eyes, though."

"Done."

With that Triss put himself into the dreamlike state that allowed me to use his senses as my own, expanding my "view" of the immediate surroundings to a full 360 degrees of Shade-style unvision.

That let me pick up the pace to a fast jog and reach the alley at the end of the breezeway just as the pursuing guards got the necessary angle to send more quarrels my way. They were still effectively shooting blind, and the majority of the quarrels stuck in the walls somewhere behind me, but even a blind shot can kill you if your opponent gets lucky. There was more light in the alley proper, so I had to close my eyes as I approached it. The overlay of the two different ways of seeing becomes especially confusing in situations where my own vision moves back and forth from useless to barely helpful.

I turned right as I moved out into the alley, away from the original direction of pursuit and started really laying down boot leather. The guards weren't stupid, so I had no doubt they would already have sent runners to try to close off both ends of the little alley. That wouldn't stop me. I could always head up to the rooftops or have Triss shroud us up and fade away into shadows. But neither of those options would draw attention away from our Dyad friend, so I preferred to avoid them as long as possible.

I could hear pursuit in the alley behind me by the time I reached the street. Triss's senses picked out the bright points of the guards' magelanterns as they chased after me, but I couldn't actually see the ones carrying them. Not without turning around and using my own eyes. Triss's unvision just doesn't work that way. The lanterns washed out his view of the area immediately behind the lights.

In some ways, Triss's analog to our vision is more like touch than sight, or maybe hearing. The Blade masters at the temple taught us that bats see with their ears. They scream and listen for the echoes to come back and tell them about the world around them. Texture is important and edges, soft and hard, rough and smooth, colors not at all.

I don't know how the masters knew about the bats—probably from quizzing mages with bat familiars—but it's not really important. What is important is how that relates to the unsight of the Shades. Triss and his fellows see by reading . . . well, call them dark-echoes that they feel rather than hear, and you'll be as close as anyone can get to describing it using the human vocabulary. All you really need to know is that the darker it is the better he can perceive things, and that it never ever looks like what you or I would see through our human eyes.

Whatever the mechanism, it makes for a surreal view of the city. Doubly so since the human mind just isn't properly equipped to see equally well in every direction. You have to sort of keep your main attention focused on where you're going, while at the same time setting aside a part of your mind to constantly flick through a rotating view of the entire circle.

I'd lost the last of my pursuers maybe a quarter mile ago and had just turned to head back to the Dyad, when the street rose up to meet me. And not in any wind-at-your-back, traditional-blessing kind of way. No, this street was decidedly hostile. The muck-covered cobblestones under my back foot dropped away as I was about to push off, robbing my running stride of all its power. At the same time, the street in front of me rose like a low stone wave. I was already off balance when it caught me in the thighs, and I flipped over it like I'd run full tilt into a stone fence.

I landed more or less on my head, and then slammed down onto my side, driving the breath from my body. On a cleaner street I'd probably have broken a couple of ribs and maybe my neck, but the accumulated filth of years cushioned my fall. Even so, I was stunned half unconscious by the impact and lost my grip on Triss's mind and senses. Then Triss did something he almost never chooses to do.

Normally, when Triss encloses me with a shadowy second skin, it feels as though I've got a thin layer of cold silk covering my entire body. Now that skin tightened and hardened, becoming something more like chitin. Then it started to move, first rolling me over and up onto hands and knees. Picture an empty suit of plate armor moving of its own accord. Now picture a person inside that armor, moving with it, but not out of any volition. That was my situation as Triss started us scrambling toward the nearest building—a dilapidated tenement.

I was still pretty dazed and didn't know what was going on, but I knew that it had to be urgent and dangerous. Otherwise Triss would never have seized control like that. I was just about to ask him why he didn't stand us up and run if it was that bad, when the ground dropped out from under my hands and we tumbled forward. My forehead hit the cobbles hard, but Triss's rigid presence saved me from the worst of the impact. This time I was looking directly at the ground when it started moving. I felt a feather of cold touch the back of my neck when I noticed that whatever was happening, it didn't show up in magesight.

Triss quickly got me back up onto hands and knees, but by then it was too late. The cobbles beneath my hands lifted and twisted at the same time the ones under my knees dropped and parted. The street set me neatly on my feet in a knee-deep hole in the ground, while simultaneously turning me to face toward my left. Then the cobbles closed back in, gently but firmly pincering my calves, all without any visible sign of magic. To make matters even more confusing the street was empty.

"What's going on?" I asked.

"Durkoth," said Triss, his voice a bare whisper in my ear. Then he relaxed his hold over my body.

"Interesting," said a cold, perfect voice, and it was only then that I saw my first Durkoth.

I knew that a score or more lived in Tien, but they mostly dealt with the outside world through emissaries. I'd never encountered one in the flesh before, and I really didn't know much about them. Subterranean, though I didn't know if that meant they lived in caves or castles or just swam through earth like the stone dogs. Like their Sylvani and Vesh'An cousins they were inhuman and beautiful, demi-immortal creatures of a much older breed than ours.

Or that's what the legends said at any rate. I only knew of one interaction between my order and any of the Others in the last hundred years—the assignment that had earned Siri her second name of Mythkiller. That was the big stuff. Beyond that? What I didn't know about the Others would have filled books.

The Durkoth was crouched in the middle of a shallow hole in the street, his bare hands and feet pressed against the roadbed. He was utterly still in a way that no human could ever achieve, and I would have mistaken him for a statue if the earth hadn't been bringing him swiftly and steadily closer. *He* wasn't moving, but the hole in which he crouched was, with the cobbles parting around it like water around the hull of a ship, complete to filling in behind him.

At first, he was the exact color of the cobbles, skin and cloak and all, but when he finally came to a stop a few feet away, it all began to shift and lighten. By the time he stood up to face me, he had returned to his natural coloration, looking like a statue fresh hewn from white marble. Only no statue in Tien had ever been so clean, not even as it stood in the sculptor's studio. No scintilla of dust or misplaced chip of stone marred his perfection.

Zhan had a long artistic history, including the previous century's heroic school, a movement dedicated to the artistic embodiment of the human ideal. Chang Un was considered the greatest of all of

Zhan's heroic sculptors. The Durkoth looked like what Un's wildest dreams might have looked like if he'd had the skill to chisel them out of stone. I couldn't help but stare.

The impression of perfection extended to every facet of the Durkoth's appearance. His face was human in layout, two eyes, two ears, one nose, one mouth, etc. But no human had ever possessed such symmetry of feature, or fineness of line. Each pale round ear perfectly mirrored the other in every detail, including an ideal flare and height that seemed intentionally designed to balance and highlight the shape and placement of his other features and his hair. He was slightly taller than the human norm and muscled and proportioned like the realized ideal of what an athlete *should* look like. A typical example of the breed if the legends spoke true.

While I studied him, he studied me. At least, I thought he did. It was hard to tell. In living under stone, the Durkoth have become like stone themselves—taking some of its stillness and hidden depths into themselves. His eyes were blank white spheres that did not appear to move. Neither did he seem to breathe, though I knew that was something of an illusion. The Durkoth do breathe, just far too slowly for the human eye to see. After a little while—a very little while by Durkoth standards—I broke the silence.

"What's interesting?"

"You are not what I expected to catch," said the Durkoth, and again I noted how cold his voice sounded. The only thing about him that moved when he spoke was his mouth, and even that looked wrong and unnatural, as though stone had decided to flow like water.

"Then perhaps, having mistaken my identity, you'll be so kind as to release me." I was in an incredibly bad position, with my legs held in a stone clamp. If I could avoid a fight I would.

"Perhaps, though not at once, I think. I can sense that you do not have the Kothmerk. And you are obviously not the Dyad. But you did run from the guards when they pursued that creature. Why?"

"Maybe because they were shooting at me?" Then, because I had no idea if Durkoth even understood sarcasm, I continued. "I feared for my life." I let my mouth run on by itself—I needed to keep the Durkoth occupied while I tried to think of some way to convince him to let me go. I was pretty sure that knowing what a Kothmerk was would help there, but it didn't ring any bells. "The guards were using crossbows. Running away from them looked like the best way to keep them from killing me."

The Durkoth didn't respond immediately. He might have been thinking about what I said, or he might have simply forgotten I existed. His expression didn't change at all, and I had no way to tell what was going on inside his head. It was maddening. Deception and misdirection are a significant part of the Blade's job. You have to be able to sneak in close to a target if you want to kill them. In many ways it's like running a successful skip or con, which involves learning to read physical and facial cues. Cues that the Durkoth simply didn't provide.

"Could we move this along a bit?" I asked, but the Durkoth held up a hand.

"Bide." It knelt and touched the ground with its fingertips again. "One comes."

The cobbles let go of my knees, but before I could do anything about it, the ground caught hold of my feet and pulled me under. For a brief moment I stood at the bottom of a hole just big enough for one. Then the cobbles closed above my head, cutting off the light and imprisoning me under a roof of stone. I reached up and started hammering on the underside of the street, and found that the stones were moving. Or rather, as I discovered a moment later, when the cobbles above gave way to the underside of a rough plank floor, that I was.

The Durkoth's voice spoke into the darkness then, saying again, "Hush. I will release you when our business is done, but the guards come now. Bide in silence if you want to remain free."

"Triss?" I whispered.

"Just a moment." I felt him flowing off my skin and up through the wide cracks in the floor above. "There, I can see now. We're just under the lip of the tenement's porch."

"Oh good." The words came out higher and tighter than I'd planned. The narrow space reeked of piss and rot.

"It's all right," whispered Triss. "These planks won't even slow us down once we decide to move."

I forced myself to breathe deeply and evenly despite the smells, as I had been taught: *Calm the body and the mind will follow.* It would have helped if I could have borrowed Triss's senses, but that trick only worked when he held me within himself.

"What's the Durkoth doing?" I asked.

"Looking at a spot on the stree—oh." His voice grew even quieter—a shadow of a whisper, audible only because he spoke directly into my ear. "A stone dog has just swum up through the cobbles . . . and here comes his master."

I froze. The stone dogs are elementals, creatures of the earth at a level even more fundamental than the Durkoth, and I didn't know what might draw its attention when I was in its element like this. I'd never felt more vulnerable.

I tried not to think about the smoky-sweet burn of a sip of the Kyle's in my pack hitting the back of my throat, or about how much better I would feel with a glass inside me. But that only turned my mind to efik, and how very nice a couple of roasted beans would go down, or better yet, an entire, properly brewed pot of the stuff. Faster than alcohol and more reliable, efik soothed the nerves at the same time it cleared the mind. I hadn't wanted it this bad in a very long time.

"Master Qethar," the Elite called—the first syllable of the Durkoth's name coming out something between "hch" and the sound of someone clearing their throat. "Have you found something?" I could hear him quite clearly through the many gaps in the battered old porch. "Graf heard you working your earth-magic and he led me here."

"It is not magic, Major Aigo," said Qethar, his voice as flat and cold as ever. "I do not compel, I persuade. I am Durkoth. The earth and I are children of the same house. I need no conjurer's tricks to convince my sister to help me."

"Of course," said Aigo, his voice soothing, though I could hear strain under the surface. He was clearly under orders to play nice with the Durkoth. "My apologies. Graf heard you *speaking* with your sister. What did you find?"

"Nothing," said Qethar. "I thought I had found the Dyad, but I was mistaken."

"That's odd," said Aigo. "Graf told me that your . . . conversation was quite extensive. It seems a lot of effort if there was nothing to find."

"I saw someone running from your men," said Qethar. "But it was not the Dyad, so I decided that I had no need to keep him for you."

"Did you then?" I could hear anger in the Elite's voice. "We've learned that they had help at the tavern, a man named Aral. A jack, and one who works the shadowy side of the business. We think he might have been fronting for someone who wanted to buy the Kothmerk." There was that word again. "He's wanted for questioning. You're telling me you just let him go?" The Elite's voice rose with the question.

"Perhaps," replied the Durkoth, and if he noticed the Elite's anger it didn't show in his voice. "You could draw me a sketch but I have trouble telling your kind apart by faces. This one was male and alone. He did not have the Kothmerk. I couldn't tell you more than that."

"But you won't mind if Graf and I look around a bit, right?" There was a hell of a lot of tension between the two of them, the kind that required some history, and I found myself wishing I knew what that history was.

Qethar didn't answer right away, though I couldn't tell if that was from uncertainty or deliberate provocation. Finally he said, ". . . no, of course not, search all you want, though you won't find anything."

"We'll see about that. Graf, seek."

The giant dog began to sniff around. Between its hard stone feet and enormous bulk, you'd have expected the thing to make at least as much noise as a shod horse. Instead, with nothing between it and the cobbles that were a part of its native element, its footfalls were nearly silent. I could only just make out the snuffling, but that was all.

What I *could* hear was my own breathing growing steadily thinner and more ragged, despite my best efforts to keep it under control. Triss gave me a reassuring squeeze on the shoulder, but that really didn't help. As the stone dog worked its way ever closer, I felt sure it would discover me. It took a huge effort of will to keep from simply blasting away the floor above me and leaping out to face my enemies.

Of course, the stone dog would rip my head off before I could get halfway out of my hole and I knew it—which is why I stayed put. *Your mind must always rule your heart.* I couldn't even draw my swords in the available space. My only hope lay in concealment. I kept still, but it was brutally hard.

The dog got closer, and closer still. It was snuffling along the base of the little porch. I held my breath. It took one deep sniff and froze like it knew I was there. Then, miraculously, it moved off, still snuffling loudly. A few more minutes passed like hours.

"I told you that you wouldn't find anything, Major," Qethar said after a while.

"You did," replied the Elite, his voice contemptuous and angry. "But sometimes you Durkoth have different ideas about the way the world works than we humans do. I don't suppose you want to tell me which way he went?"

"Does it really matter?" asked Qethar. "He's surely beyond your reach by now. Still, if it will make you happy, I can say with some degree of confidence that he was headed toward this very tenement when last I saw him."

"Did he go inside?"

"I didn't notice it if he did," replied Qethar, and I couldn't help but wonder why the Durkoth kept handing out obvious evasions instead of smooth lies. That was bound to put a twist in the Major's tail. No one held out on the Elite. Not in Tien. Not if they had any sense.

"Well, I'd best rely on my own devices then, hadn't I?" growled Aigo. "Be sure that I'll inform my superiors of the very telling degree of your cooperation, Master Qethar. I don't think King Thauvik will be at all pleased with your performance."

Mention of the king made my ears prick up. His name wasn't something you heard very often in my normal run of affairs, and not something you wanted to hear. In fact, I generally went way the hell out of my way to avoid situations that would bring his eye anywhere near me. If he was directly interested in this business with the Dyad . . . well I didn't like to think about it.

"How very sad for His Majesty. You'll have to tell him how deeply sorry I am that I couldn't be of more help." Qethar didn't sound sorry. If anything he sounded like he thought pissing off Thauvik was something of a perk.

Triss whispered in my ear again, "The Elite and his familiar are turning and walking away now, but the Durkoth remains. He's coming this way, so I'd better go quiet again."

The porch creaked alarmingly above me and a swath of my very limited light vanished.

"Now, where were we?" the Durkoth asked.

"I'm pretty sure you were about to let me go about my business," I said without much hope.

"No, I don't think that was it. I think you were about to tell me everything you know about the Dyad so that I don't call the Major back and give you to him."

"Wouldn't that be a bit awkward?" I asked. "He'd know that you were holding out on him."

"He knows that now," said Qethar. "Nothing would change except that I would have handed over a criminal he badly wants to get hold of. You've really nothing to bargain with except information, so you would do best to make my little misdirection of the ever-loyal Graf worth it."

I filed that last bit away without remarking on it. "What if I don't have anything useful to tell you?"

"Then you really won't like the way the Elite go about asking you the same questions I want answered now. They won't take no for an answer and they won't be gentle in the way they ask, not with Thauvik taking a personal interest in the matter."

The way he said "Thauvik" made it sound like a curse word. Whatever he had against the king it was more than just business.

Qethar continued, "I'm giving you a chance to walk away unharmed. You'd do well to take it. Your own species will not be so merciful. They never are."

"All right." I needed to buy time while I figured a way out of this. "But how do I know I can I trust you?"

"You don't and you can't, but if I'd wanted to harm you I could already have done so."

The earthen walls around my little hole squeezed in for a brief instant, trapping my arms at my side and pressing the air from my lungs in a great gasp. Then they relaxed again, and I could breathe.

"Point taken." I used the sound of my own voice to cover the faint scrape as I drew a knife from the sheath at my hip. "I'll tell you everything I know."

I tipped my head back, scanning the darkened area above me, trying to decide which crack to drive my knife through for best effect if it should come to that. I didn't think I'd get more than one chance, and I was in a lousy position for delivering a killing blow, but I thought it'd make a marginally better opening move than a burst of magelightning that would mostly get soaked up by the planks. Maybe it would be better to just have Triss garrote him. . . .

"Do put the knife away," said Qethar. "It wouldn't get through my armor."

I didn't remember any armor, just a light tunic and trousers, with a cloak thrown over the top. How had I missed something as bulky as armor?

He continued, "Even if you did manage to kill me, you would only die a moment later. My sister holds you in the palm of her hand and she would crush you in revenge."

His sister? Oh, right, he claimed kinship with the earth around me. That changed things. I didn't know whether that was some sort of Durkoth mystical gobbledygook way of talking about their own special magic or if he meant it literally. If it was the former, a quick enough kill might still get me out of this in one Aral-shaped piece. But if it was the latter, I'd have a problem of the fatal variety. Not a question I wanted to settle the hard way.

I was rapidly running out of good options. I didn't want to give up what little I knew about the Dyad, and even if I did turn nose on her, my meager information was unlikely to satisfy the Durkoth. Which meant I was going to have to bluff my way out of that hole in the ground.

"It's hard to know where to start. . . ." I began.

"Start with the Kothmerk. Has the Dyad recovered it?" Qethar asked impatiently, betraying the first sign of emotion I'd yet heard from him. "Did she have it with her?"

I wished once again that I had some idea what the hell the Kothmerk was. This was going to be damned hard to pull off without that knowledge, and I couldn't be too obvious with my fishing. "Well, I didn't exactly *see* it. . . ."

Which was the truth—when you're spinning a lie it's always best to steer as close to the truth as possible where you can manage it. It's much harder to get tripped up later if you keep things simple, and nothing's simpler than the truth.

The Durkoth caught my implication. "But you do think she had it, don't you? I can tell." More impatience, and just a touch of eagerness.

So, whatever it was, a person could conceivably carry it concealed. Small enough to fit in a pouch, then. What else could I get? "I don't know," I said. "She seemed mighty nervous. She could have left it hidden somewhere."

"No." Flat and cold. "If she's recovered it she won't have let it out of her sight. Not after her great failure earlier. Where is she now? Tell me! If you can help me catch her, you're a free man."

"If I tell you, what's to keep you from killing me?"

"Nothing at all. You have no power in this situ— Ack! What?" he asked, his voice going suddenly harsh and tight. "How are you doing that?"

The walls suddenly pressed in sharply all around me, pushing my pack into my back and driving the air from my lungs. Spots of white light started to eat away at the edges of my vision.

"Stop it or I'll crush you!" husked the Durkoth.

I wanted to tell him that I would happily stop whatever it was if I could, but I didn't have the breath for it. I didn't have the breath for anything.

Then, faintly through the roaring in my ears, I heard Triss saying, "If he dies, you die. Back it off right now."

"I don't know what you are, familiar, but if I kill your master, you die, too, and that frees me."

"No," said Triss. "I have set my will. If you kill me, I behead you as I die. Everybody loses."

"So be it," replied the Durkoth. "My life means nothing."

4

"My life means nothing," repeated the Durkoth. "Not when weighed against my sacred duty to the Kothmerk . . . but I can't find it if I let you kill me."

As suddenly as it had come, the pressure around me eased, and I could breathe again. I wasn't aware that I had started moving until the night opened up around me when the earth very gently spat me out onto the street.

Qethar was sitting on the stoop of the old tenement perfectly motionless. If I hadn't known what he was, I would have taken him for a particularly bizarrely placed piece of public art. A Chang Un masterpiece sitting unguarded in one of the city's worst shitholes.

Qethar's expression was cruel and hard, making a sharp contrast with his relaxed, almost indolent, pose. He sat with his upper body leaned way back, supporting himself on his elbows as though he had settled in for a long spell of watching the street go by. He wore the loose flowing trousers and sleeveless shirt that is the summer uniform of the people of Tien—every detail seemingly rendered in impossibly clean white marble—fully visible now that he had shed his concealing cloak. That garment had fallen away to lie across the rough planks like a carven shroud. His bare feet were firmly planted in a patch of dirt that sat amidst the hard cobbles like a sunken island.

I imagined the plaque that would have gone with the apparent sculpture saying something like "the god of dark passions watches the death of the maiden," or some other equally disturbing fancy. The only thing marring the image of a statue at rest was the thin loop of utter blackness that wrapped his neck like a shadowy hang-man's noose, its tail trailing down to disappear between the cracks in the porch.

It should have been invisible there in the deep dark of the empty streets. But the Durkoth was so pale that he seemed almost to glow with an inner light, and that cast the slender loop of blackness bind-ing his throat into stark relief. The shadow looked so fragile and insubstantial against the heavy stonelike weight of the Durkoth. Even I, who knew exactly what Triss was capable of, could hardly credit the danger that dark thread represented.

"Well played," said Qethar through lips that didn't so much move as jump from one position to the next without passing through the intervening stages. It was unnerving. "You have me at a fatal disadvantage. What are your demands, Blade?"

"Start with not repeating that last word," I replied, suppressing a pinch of worry over having my identity exposed yet again. With the death of Namara I had lost so much, not least the freedom from complication. At least the street was empty. "The Blades are as dead as their goddess."

The Durkoth said nothing, but he knew he had scored a hit, and his expression shifted without actually seeming to move. One in-stant he looked worried and angry, as though he had always looked that way. The next, a feral smile turned up the corners of his lips, and again, it looked as though it had always been there. It made me want to slap him. Instead, I leaned in close to tap a finger against the base of his throat, just below Triss's shadowy presence.

"I don't know what your game is . . ." But I trailed off as I touched him.

I'd been expecting him to feel the way he looked—flesh like marble, cold and smooth and lifeless. Instead, his skin was fever-ishly hot and softer than silk. The contact jolted through me like a tiny charge of magelightning and I couldn't help imagining what it would feel like to take him in my arms and . . . I shook my head, trying to clear away the images that had arisen there seemingly of their own volition.

"Are you quite sure?" asked Qethar and I realized his voice wasn't cold and hard, but rather crystalline—pure and perfect as a finely cut diamond.

"Wha'?" My own voice sounded slow and thick, slurred, a very poor second to the beauty of the Durkoth's.

"You're shaking your head 'no,' but your eyes are saying 'yes.'

And you haven't moved your hand away. Quite the contrary. Which is the real impul—gluk!" he choked mid-sentence as Triss tightened the noose.

"I . . ." Even then I found it hard to focus on anything but the place where my palm now rested against the skin of his throat and chest. "I . . ."

A sharp pain caught me across the cheek as Triss slapped me. I staggered back involuntarily, breaking the contact between me and Qethar. It felt like I'd stepped straight out of an Aveni sauna and plunged into an icy pool. The fuzz in my head burned away in the sudden fiery cold, and I recognized it for what it was.

Glamour.

But even knowing what was happening, I had a hard time keeping myself from moving forward to touch the Durkoth again. The feelings had been so intense. I much preferred women to men as bed partners, but Qethar was so very . . . This time *I* slapped myself. It hurt. That was good. It helped remind me that it wasn't me thinking those thoughts. It was the glamour. There'd have been nothing wrong with the impulse if it were mine. But it wasn't.

"I don't like it when people mess with my head," I said quietly. "Cut the glamour magic."

"It's not magic, it's just me." His voice was still cold, but edged now with bitter contempt and loss. "Your Emperor of Heaven bound our magic after the death of his predecessor in the War of the First. *None* of the First may use magic beyond the borders of the Sylvain. We had to choose between magic and our ancient home under the mountains. Is not the history of the First still taught in your schools?"

"He's not *my* Heavenly Emperor. And, yes it is." But the Others— or, as they generally called themselves, the First—were so rare here in the lands beyond the wall that it had never seemed all that important. More mythology than history.

Besides, I wasn't sure that it really mattered what you called what the Others did. No human could hope to *persuade* the earth or to cast a glamour without using magic. From my point of view the only real difference was that Other magic didn't register in magesight. If anything, that made it *more* powerful than the human variety.

I wondered then how Siri had handled the glamour when she had been tasked with executing the Sylvani demigod whose death had made her the Mythkiller. But I pushed the question aside for now. It might matter later, if I had much more to do with the Durkoth, but at the moment I needed to focus.

"That's not important right now," I said. "I don't really give a damn about First history. What I want to know is what's between you and the Dyad. That, and more about the Kothmerk. So start talk—" I stopped as Qethar burst into wild laughter that made his whole body shake.

It looked *wrong*. A statue in the grips of an earthquake. Except there was no earthquake. It made my head hurt to watch him.

"What's so funny?" I asked when the first tremors had passed.

Between aftershocks, Qethar forced out, "You say that you don't give a damn about First history, then in the very same breath demand that I tell you about the Kothmerk." He lost control again for a moment before continuing, "The Kothmerk *is* First history. The one can no more be separated from the other than the moon from the tides. At least not for the Durkoth, though others among the First might argue the point, particularly the accursed Sylvani. It is a part of the soul of my people."

"Could you give me the short version then?" I asked. "What is so important about this Kothmerk?"

"It's a magic ring," said a familiar voice from my right. Captain Kaelin Fei.

I winced. Partially that was because I'd let myself get so distracted that someone had been able to sneak up on me. But even more it had to do with *who* I'd let sneak up on me. Captain Fei was an officer of the watch and the perfect model of a corrupt cop. A sometime employer, sometime ally of mine, I'd been avoiding her for months because I owed her a really big favor. Several actually.

I sighed and turned so that I could see the captain—who emerged now from a gap between the tenement and its nearest neighbor—while still keeping an eye on the Durkoth. Fei was a big woman, broad shouldered and fit, a jindu master as well as a street fighter of ugly reputation.

You couldn't see it in this light, but pale eyes and a spray of freckles marked her out as having non-Zhani blood in her ancestral line. That was probably why she'd turned into such a good brawler; the Tienese streets were hard on those of mixed parentage. Her face was round and would have been almost too pretty for playing the strong arm if not for the deep knife scar on the left side.

She bobbed a nod at me. "The Kothmerk is a ring, carved from a single massive ruby and magically hardened to make it tougher than steel. It's priceless."

Qethar hissed at that. "It is neither carved nor was it *magically* anythinged."

"Yeah, I know." Fei rolled her eyes. "One of your supersmith gem cutter forebears "persuaded" it to assume its present form back before the dawn of history, or some such crap. Well, that's more than close enough to magic for a simple old street cop like me."

I snorted. The captain was anything but simple. If there was a significant shadowside operation anywhere in Tien that she didn't have her fingers in, I had yet to hear about it. She was as crooked as crooked could be, and somehow she'd convinced her bosses all the way up to the king himself that it was all for the best. Where most watch captains had a regular district assigned to them, Fei's beat was the whole city. Her job was peacekeeping in the sense of making sure the criminal element didn't significantly inconvenience anyone important.

"What does this Kothmerk do?" I asked. I didn't like the direction this was going. Magic rings tended to attract nine kinds of trouble.

"Nothing," said Qethar.

"It starts wars," replied Fei.

"It *does* nothing," said Qethar. "It simply *is*. The Kothmerk is nothing more nor less than the living heart of the Durkoth." Fei raised an eyebrow at Qethar, who conceded, "Though, sometimes, that is enough to start a war."

"Well, it is not going to start one here," said Fei. "From what I've been able to find out, the damned thing leaves a trail of bodies wherever it goes. The massacre at the Gryphon's Head is only the latest and gaudiest killing since the thing hit Tien. I want that fucking ring out of my city, and I want it done yesterday."

"There we are in agreement," said Qethar. "I want to find the Kothmerk as quickly as possible and return it to its rightful master."

Fei turned a hard look on me. "Which is where you come in, my jack friend. Large scale incidents of slaughter like the Gryphon's Head are *very* hard to explain to my bosses. So, I'm calling in a favor. Make the problem go away."

"You want me to find the ring for you?" I asked. This was going to complicate my dealings with the Dyad, I could just tell.

"If that's what works, great. But I really don't care how you do it. All I care about is that it stops killing people on my streets. You understand me?"

"I think so. How long do I have?"

"Like I said, I want this thing done yesterday." Fei sighed. "But I know that shit like this takes a while. I'll give you a week."

"You expect me to wrap this up in just eight days?" I asked, and Fei nodded. "Not a lot of time. I may have to cut some corners. . . ."

"I don't care if you have to cut throats. Just get it done."

"I thought you didn't want any more bodies found in the streets," I said.

"So make sure they don't end up there, Aral. Or, are you going to try to convince me that you can't make a body or two vanish if you need to?"

"I can help you there," said Qethar. "I can make any body vanish forever."

"Why would you do that for me?" I asked.

"Because we're going to be working together, of course. We do have the same goal now, don't we, human?"

I looked a question at Fei, who shrugged. "Like I said, I don't care what happens to the damned thing as long it stops being my problem. If swapping sweat with the Others is what it takes, by all means swap away."

Qethar looked at me and raised a stony eyebrow the tiniest fraction of an inch. I shuddered.

"I think I'll pass," I said to him. "I don't trust you. I don't like you. And, I prefer to work alone."

"Funny definition you've got of alone." Qethar touched the shadow at his throat.

"Fine, then let's say that I already have a partner, and leave it at that. Either way, I'm not working with you."

"You'll never find the Kothmerk without me. Even if you did, what would you do with it? If you want the killings to stop, it has to go back to my people. It is the most precious thing we own and it should never have come anywhere near your filthy human hands. You can't get it where it must go without dealing with me or another of my kind. You need me."

I turned to Fei. "How about if I make and get rid of another body right now?" Qethar was really beginning to irritate me. "Would that be all right?"

"You'd better not," said Fei. "He's got something going with the Elite right now. And he's well known in certain circles here in Tien. If he vanishes, it'll generate the kind of heat that would get a lot of light shone into a lot of shadows." Fei shrugged apologetically. "I might even have to remember what you look like if that happened. I wouldn't want to, of course, you're too valuable to give away if I can possibly avoid it. But business is business."

I nodded. I wasn't happy about it, but I understood. "All right, I'll let him walk away, but you can't make me work with him. Triss."

The noose slipped from Qethar's neck and my shadow resumed

the appearance of a plain old shadow—all but invisible in the darkness. Qethar rose to his feet and tipped a bow my way.

"This one is yours, human, but rest assured that we *will* speak again. You do need me." He reached into a pouch at his side and pulled out a small white pebble. "When you see it my way, crush this under your heel and I will come to you."

He held out his hand with the stone on his palm. I would have preferred to simply turn and walk away at that point, but I knew he might be right. Reluctantly, I reached for the stone. As I took it my fingertips brushed the hot silk skin of his palm for the barest instant, and I had to fight to finish the original gesture instead of taking his hand between my own. Qethar raised an eyebrow at me again. Then the ground at his feet opened up and swallowed him whole. A moment later, the cobbles closed over the bare earth, erasing the last mark of where he'd stood.

"Now"—I turned a sharp eye on Fei—"tell me more about this ring." I could feel Triss's interest, though the Shade stayed hidden.

"Not much to tell. You've seen Durkoth work, intricate, beautiful, inhuman. Unmistakable. Especially when we're talking about a ring carved from a ruby as big as your eyeball."

"What about the bodies? You said this thing has killed more people than the ones at the Gryphon. Tell me about those."

"The official count is four incidents, though I'm thinking it's really five, maybe more." Fei sniffed loudly and glanced around as though double checking that we were alone. "First, two dead Durkoth just inside Northgate, throats cut. Outsiders, you can tell by how they dressed. You'll have noticed Qethar's gone native. So have the rest of the locals. Nobody heard or saw anything, of course."

"Of course."

"Second, and this is my maybe," continued Fei. "Anonymous teenage girl, young, very well dressed, took a crossbow quarrel through the left eye right out in the middle of the square on Sanjin Island. Nobody saw the shooter. Very professional job. High-end black jack work, if not government."

"Government?" I asked. "Whose?"

"That's where it turns into a maybe, at least formally. Two off duty Elite just happened to be walking across the bridge from the palace when it happened, a captain and a lieutenant. The official report says they hurried over to see if they could help the girl but found her already dead, and then they searched her to see if she was carrying anything that could be used to establish her identity."

"Which she wasn't."

"Nope, at least nothing our good Elite friends wanted to share with the rest of the children. The watchmen who first arrived on the scene didn't want to push them on that, or anything really. I wouldn't even have their names if Sergeant Zishin hadn't happened on the scene before they could get away. Maybe wouldn't even know they'd been there."

"Ah, and what did the good sergeant find when he searched the girl?" Zishin was Fei's right hand man.

"Well, under the fancy clothes she was half starved and dirty, though her hands and arms were freshly washed. The only other thing he could find was a purse with twenty-five gold riels in it. No other possessions whatsoever."

"The Elite didn't seize the cash and write up a receipt?"

"Nope."

"Then they weren't off duty."

Twenty-five gold riels was a lot of money. Like a year's rent on a house in a decent neighborhood kind of money. The Elite were incorruptible and that sort of money on an anonymous corpse with no obvious next of kin would normally have had them pulling rank on the watch. They'd have gone all official about the whole thing so that the money didn't vanish into the watch's pockets, which it would have. No question. Leaving it like that was tantamount to offering the watch a bribe to forget they'd ever seen the pair of Elite.

"So you think the Elite killed this girl?" I asked. "And that it was on orders from someone higher up the feeding chain?" The Elite don't do anything without orders, and those orders generally come down from the king one way or another.

"You tell me." Fei lowered her voice. "The next official death was an officer of the Elite, throat slit in his own home. The same lieutenant who found that girl's body. The captain was reassigned out of Tien about four hours after that. I never got a chance to talk to him. That makes four dead Elite now, which is going to have the Crown sounding like a kicked-over beehive very shortly."

"At the least. Now, that's three of your murder incidents. You said you had five at least. Who are the others?"

"Another foreign Durkoth," said Fei. "Dagger from behind. Between the ribs and into the heart, as neat as could be. Professional, but not in the same way as that girl. The last one that I feel sure about is a half dozen street toughs who thought that damned Dyad looked like easy meat. It's how we found out she was here. I'm inclined to think of that one as mass suicide. If the ring weren't involved I wouldn't even care."

"And the ones you aren't sure about?" I asked.

"I haven't really got anything there but a feeling. An unusual number of minor fish from the night markets have turned up dead or simply gone missing in the last week and a half, cindersweeps, banksmen, scuttles. You know the type."

"And you're thinking that dead night marketeers might have something to do with a priceless stolen Durkoth artifact. I can't imagine why."

Fei chuckled. "I guess I'm just suspicious that way." Then her face went suddenly serious. "I'm under a lot of pressure here, Aral. Someone way up the chain ordered that raid on the Gryphon, and they did it without me hearing a thing beforehand. Things are going to get really ugly. Fix it. I don't care about how. All I care about is that you do it fast and that no one finds any embarrassing bodies. Now I need to get back to the center of things before I'm too much missed."

Fei turned away then, heading back toward the gap through which she'd arrived. As she was about to step into the deeper dark, she paused.

"Oh, and Aral, while we're on the subject of embarrassing corpses . . ."

"Yes?"

"I know you're not the type to think this way, but if it ever crossed your mind to get me out of your life by making one more body vanish, well . . . just don't. I've left instructions for what should happen if I suddenly disappear. One of those things involves a wanted poster for Aral Kingslayer. It's the only one of its kind with an actual likeness of the elusive Blade on it."

"Captain," I said rather stiffly, "you know I'd never do something like that."

"I do. Your goddess trained you too well. Your mind just doesn't work that way."

"Then why set me up like that?"

"Because mine does."

Fei sniffed audibly at the entrance to the little gap, almost as though she were taking a scent. Then she was gone, too, and I was free to go about my business.

"So, now what?" I asked my shadow.

"How about we get off the street, for starters."

He had a point, but I noticed just then that the Durkoth had left behind his marble-white cloak. It lay crumpled carelessly on the planks like the carven lid of some fanciful sarcophagus. On impulse

I reached to pick it up, thinking it might come in handy later. I nearly broke two fingers when it turned out that the illusion of marble was no illusion at all.

Heavy stone met my outthrust hand. Cold and motionless now, though the garment had moved and flowed like the finest wool when Qethar wore it. I poked it again, more gently. It must have weighed close to what I did, and there was no good way to move it.

Triss murmured something impatient then, so I left the stone cloak behind, though not without a couple of backward glances as I climbed the wall of the tenement. When I hit the roof, I turned in the general direction of the place I'd told the Dyad to meet me and looked around for a spot to lay up for a little while. I needed time to think about what Fei had told me and everything that had happened with Qethar.

I chose the top of a small private water tower—popular in a neighborhood where the city was slow to fix things like the aqueducts when something went wrong. The tower—cobbled together from whatever lumber the builders could beg, borrow, or steal—looked more than a little ramshackle. But it was plenty sturdy. It had to be to support the several hundred gallons of water it held when full. I settled down into the low well of the collector and eyed my shadow, barely visible now in the light of the half-full moon.

"I ask again, now what?"

The shadow shifted into the shape of a small, winged dragon. "Go after the Dyad, of course."

"Of course."

"You don't sound convinced, my friend." Triss canted his head to one side. "Given the circumstances, what else could we do?"

"Given the circumstances, I don't know, and that bothers me. We've been doing nothing but reacting since I first went over to talk to them . . . it . . . her?" I shook my head. "I'm not even sure what to call our new friend, much less how to deal with her. I don't like the way this whole thing is going. We've got no plan, and no fallback. That's a recipe for disaster."

Triss slid closer and placed his head in my lap. "I'm sorry. I didn't know it would all go so bad so fast."

"It's all right." I reached down and scratched his spinal ridge. "You were trying to do what you thought was best for me . . . for both of us. You were even right. They did need help, just not the kind it *looked* like they needed."

Triss made a happy little growling sound and wriggled to let me know I should keep scratching. Pushing my worries aside for a little while, I smiled and obliged, working my way down from the back of his head to the always itchy spot between his wings. His flesh felt warm and comforting in the cool night wind blowing in off the ocean. The eye might only see a flat lizard-shaped shadow, but my fingers brushed along soft scales and the ridge of lumps where his vertebrae pressed up against his invisible skin.

It made for a strange contrast. One that seemed stranger still knowing that when he shifted back to aping my form, he lost all texture. Master Alinthide had explained it to me once, going on for some time about elementals and how they manifested themselves in different ways under different circumstances. But even though I more or less understood the difference intellectually, it always *felt* like a mystery to my scratching fingers.

Finally, Triss sighed and went limp under my hand. "You can stop now. I feel better. Much, much better. I also know what we should do." He turned his head and looked up at me—at least, I think he did. It's hard to tell with a shadow.

"Good, tell me about it."

"We should go and find the Dyad." His voice was firm and matter-of-fact.

"I thought that was what we *had* to do, given the circumstances."

"It is, which makes it doubly nice that it's also what we *should* do."

"I'll bite. Why *should* we do it?"

Triss held up a front paw and poked out one claw. "First, because it's the only real option."

I raised an eyebrow at him, but he continued, extending another claw. "Second, Captain Fei wants us to solve the problem of the Kothmerk, and there is no doubt that the Dyad is involved. If we want to learn more about that we'll have to talk to them. And the good captain even gave us free rein to solve things however we want, which means we just might be able to make *everyone* happy."

"Conceded. The part about needing to talk to them at least. The making everyone happy bit seems much iffier to me. What else."

Another claw. "Third, they need the help. They're foreigners here, alone and hunted by the Elite, the Durkoth, and who knows who all else. They have a major problem."

"I'm not sure why that means *we* have to help them, but go on."

"Fourth, I liked them. Even if we did only spend a little time with them, they struck me as good people. I want to help them."

"That's the best reason I've heard so far."

He held up the last claw on that paw. "Fifth, I'm curious and this is fascinating. I want to know how this ends. Don't you?"

"Truth be told, yes, though not enough to risk my life over it."

"Finally"—Triss closed his paw into a fist and held it up in front of my face—"and this is the real reason we should—no, *must* go meet the Dyad. It is the *right* thing to do. The Kothmerk is dangerous. Tonight, without even making an appearance, it killed people at the Gryphon, which has been our home since we arrived here over six years ago."

He growled low and harsh, then continued, "It hurt people we know, forced us to kill an Elite, lost us our home. That's wrong and it has to stop. Namara may be dead along with most of her followers, but *you* are ever and always a Blade. A rusty one at the moment perhaps, but a Blade still, the living tool of Justice, and I am your partner. It is our duty."

A year ago I'd have laughed at a call to duty, and it would have been a bitter, broken laugh. The laugh of a man pretending he wasn't drinking himself to death, while every day he sank a little further into the bottle. Things had changed since then. My goddess was dead, yes. But Justice lived on. The ideal Namara had once personified survived beyond the death of its champion. I had felt its touch, like the benediction of a ghost. Triss was right. As long as there was still a hope of doing some good, I couldn't turn away from my duty.

5

———◆———

"**Y**ou win." I hopped up into a crouch and looked out over the edge of the water tower. "We'll go after the Dyad."

"Only because I'm always right," said Triss, fanning himself with one wing.

"But Triss . . ."

"Yes."

"You do realize there's a possibility that this Dyad you like so much is the villain here, don't you? What then?"

He sighed. "The same as before, the same as always. We do our duty." Then he slid upward, enveloping me in a thin skin of shadow before expanding outward into a cloud of obscuring darkness and releasing his consciousness into my care.

This time, I had more leisure to settle myself properly into my familiar's skin. With my vision subsumed within the Shade's radically different way of perceiving the world, paying attention to my other senses becomes more important. I took a moment now to focus on each one individually. Hearing, smell, touch, taste, each has its uses.

It's a discipline the masters started teaching us on the first day— even before we knew which of us would be chosen by the Shades— running us through lightless tests in the deeps below the temple. They would send us into mazes where all the clues and warnings were designed to force us to think with our ears or noses, or the tips of our fingers.

Once you know how to do it you can find a pit by the changing echoes of your own footsteps, or follow a scent trail marked out with dots of perfume. Your fingers can show you things hidden from the eye, subtle differences in wall surfaces that betray the presence of hidden doors or traps. Even taste can serve, if less directly, telling you things about what your targets eat or wear, things that can be used to craft the perfect poison or deliver a drug.

When I was ready, I climbed to the edge of the water tower. Then I spread wings of shadow, leaped into space, and soared. For perhaps a dozen heartbeats I glided above my city, heading west and north toward the place I'd told the Dyad to meet me. It should have been a much shorter flight, but I prolonged the sail-jump by pulling nima from the well of my soul and using it to push myself that extra bit higher on launch.

It was a dangerous choice, because it involved a brief flare of magic that would mark me out if anyone with magesight happened to be looking in the right direction at the right time. Doubly so, since there isn't enough of Triss to both cover me and provide me with wings.

But sometimes I just can't help myself. I love it too much, this time, where I get to break the bonds that tie me to the earth and play the bird. No matter that I must risk exposing myself to hostile eyes to do it. No matter that it uses the least of magics—the brute manipulation of forces. No matter even that it paints me for what I am, or once was—the "flight" of the Blades plays a prominent part in the stories they tell about us.

Sometimes I just need the release that only comes from dancing with the sky.

All too soon, my feet touched down on a ridgeline, divorcing me from the heavens. A story-and-a-half building, it was the sort that usually housed a little business of some kind—workshop and storefront below, tiny apartment above. Pulling shadow around me once again, I ran lightly from one end of the roof peak to the other. I hopped from there to a narrow balcony that peered out from the back of a dilapidated tenement much like the one where I'd met the Durkoth earlier. Using window frames and cornices I quickly climbed the six stories to its flat roof.

I had to slow up a little then and ghost my way across, stepping lightly to keep from waking sleepers who'd sought escape from the summer heat by laying their ragged blankets on the roof. Drop two stories to another aging tenement. Roll out of the fall and step up onto the low wall that circled a rooftop whose lack of sleepers warned of a rotten roof. On and up to the next. Avoid stepping on the human carpet once again.

Over, under, sidewise, down.

I made my way across the roofs of this twistiest of Tien's slums,

heading for a rendezvous with two women who together made up
something not quite human.

"**I** don't think he's coming," I heard Vala say from just above where
I lay hidden within my concealing shadow, her voice barely more
than a whisper.

The Dyad had picked a good temporary refuge, a tall slender
corner tower on a much larger building. In addition to the view afforded by the extra height, it had a sloping roof that would discour-
age any residents from sleeping up there. Vala's position, lying flat
atop the little shack that housed the stairhead, allowed her to keep a
lookout while remaining hidden from most watching eyes. She had
set herself up facing back toward where they'd last seen me, scanning the rooftops while idly twirling her wands in her fingers.

"Good." Stel sat propped against the little shack on the side opposite Vala's lookout and the door, to give them a complete view of
the surrounds. Her voice was likewise soft. "We're better off without him."

"Don't start that again," the Meld said, speaking out of Vala's
mouth. "He knows the area. He took down an Elite. He has resources we don't."

"We don't need help," growled Stel.

"Said the lady with the broken ribs." Vala glanced upward as if
asking for strength. "If he hadn't pitched in when he did, there's a
good chance we'd be dead now."

"I'll be fine," said Stel. But she didn't look it. She had one arm
pressed against her tightly wrapped ribs, and was using the other to
stay upright. "Just give me a couple of days to rest up."

"Counting the time we spent tracking the thief here to the city,
we've been at this for nearly a month." The Meld again, speaking
through Vala. "We don't have any time to waste. I say we're taking
his help. That's final."

Stel's back stiffened briefly at that, but she shut up. It was fascinating to watch, this three-way argument between the different
facets of the Dyad. It sounded more like the kind of back and forth
I'd have with Triss than the perfect two-minds-one-body supersol-
dier of the Dyad legends. I wondered whether that meant my Dyad
was unusual, or if they all talked to themselves like this when they
thought no one else was around. Maybe the myth and the reality
had less in common than I'd believed.

Unfortunately, the Meld's declaration seemed to have ended the out-loud portion of their conversation. After several minutes passed without another word, I decided eavesdropping wasn't going to give me anything else. That made it time to make myself known. But not without some setup first. I slipped silently back off the edge of their roof and climbed down to street level to look things over.

The streets were still eerily silent and dark, but I didn't find any guard presence within the two block circle I checked before returning to the rooftops. Nor, thankfully, given the unusual darkness and quiet, any restless dead. Once I returned aloft, I found a secluded corner and dropped my shroud before releasing my hold on Triss. Then, careful to make a little noise to draw Vala's attention, I started back in the general direction of the Dyad's hiding place. As I went, I made a show of looking for the pair.

I was on a slightly lower roof and just starting to go past their perch when Vala hissed like a cat. I stopped then and glanced up in her direction, and she waved a hand over the edge of the roof. I nodded and jumped across the gap, catching hold of a terra-cotta drainpipe that vanished into the building a few floors below—a supply for a kitchen garden in the courtyard, probably. From there it was the work of seconds to pull myself up beside Vala.

I flattened myself out a few feet away from Vala. Close enough to talk quietly, far enough away to let her know that was all I wanted to do. "Stel?"

"Behind us, against the back wall." Vala had tucked her wands away before she waved me over, but kept running her fingers through the twirling motions.

"How's she doing?"

"Grumpy as a manticore that's stung itself in the back of the neck." Her smile flashed in the darkness, and I thought of Jax again. "Which means she's practically her normal self again."

"I heard that," said Stel.

"You were supposed to," replied Vala. "Through my ears, if nothing else. Consider it a subtle hint."

"Subtle. Right, that's you all over."

I slithered around on the roof and stuck my head over the edge to look down at Stel. "Speaking of subtle. What the hell were you thinking back there when you launched yourself up onto the roof?"

She dropped her shoulders a little bit. "I wasn't and Vala chewed me up real good on that one already. I was in pain and I just wanted to get somewhere that I could collapse in a heap." Her voice dropped even lower. "This is our first real mission outside of Kodamia. I made a stupid choice. I'm sorry."

"I couldn't ask for a fairer answer than that." Well, I *could*, but not without playing the hypocrite. "It's not like I haven't done more than my share of stupid things over the years." Triss gave me a quick slap on the back that I took for hearty agreement. "So, how about we get you someplace where you *can* collapse for a bit?"

"I'm certainly all for it." Vala rubbed her own ribs, and I remembered that Dyads were supposed to be able to feel each other's pain.

Stel just nodded.

"Where is this place?" the Meld asked via Vala's lips. "How sure are you that it's safe?"

"No place in Tien is completely safe for anyone who was involved in what happened at the Gryphon tonight, but my fallback's as good as you're going to find. There's an abandoned brewery about a quarter mile from here. I sealed off one tiny section of the attics. The only way in is to go down an old ruined chimney." I had an even better fallback, but it was farther away and I wasn't willing to take a stranger there.

"What's to keep some other squatter from setting up shop?" asked the Meld.

"The chimney is capped with a ceramic pipe not much bigger around than your arm."

"So, how do you get in?"

"There's a catch down here," I said half an hour later as I stuck my arm into the chimney pipe.

Out of sight of the Dyad, Triss extended himself down the chimney another three feet to release the latch. Then I pulled my arm out and pivoted the chimney's top cap aside. The opening thus exposed was narrow and dark, barely big enough to fit a person, especially with a bamboo ladder eating up some of the space.

"I have some surprises set up for unwanted visitors, so I'd better go first." I slipped off my pack and used a line that I pulled from one of the side pouches to lower it into the darkness before climbing into the gap myself. "The ladder's on the fragile side and won't hold two. Wait for me to call up to you before you start down. Oh, and the ceiling's low. Be careful."

Stel came second, with Vala following after. Once they were down, I told them to wait quietly just a little bit longer. Then I had to slither my way back up to close and latch the lid. When that was done and I'd dropped a thick light-blocking curtain over the opening I'd cut into the side of the chimney, I finally started to relax.

"Half a minute more," I said while I dug in my pack for the intense little magelight.

I'd intended to bring it out slowly to give everyone time to adapt, but it tumbled out onto the floor when I moved a shirt, and the light stabbed at my eyes. Vala swore, and even Stel, who had her back pressed firmly against Vala's so she was looking away, grunted unhappily at the reflected brightness.

The room thus illuminated was long and low, no more than five feet at the midpoint that ran beneath the roof peak, and sloping down from there. It was a sort of secondary storage space above the main attic over the southern wing of the brewery. When I'd first found it, it'd been full of rotting bits of ancient brewing equipment, most of which I'd scattered on the level below. It was maybe fifty feet by fifteen at the floor level.

If you didn't mind rats and bats and slinks, the complete lack of air flow, and an ever present risk of death by fire due to the nature of the downstairs neighbors, it was actually nicer than my room at the Gryphon had been.

"Is that magelight going to draw attention?" asked a still blinking Vala.

"It shouldn't." I picked it up and wedged it into a gap in the bricks of the chimney, which gave us better light—though the chimney itself now shaded a good third of the room. "The ceiling in the room below is plastered over and doesn't leak light, and the roof is shockingly sound."

"What about noise?" After carefully helping Stel lower herself to lean against an upended half barrel, Vala started to prowl around the room. She looked into every corner and crevice.

"Noise shouldn't be a real problem as long as we keep it down to a reasonable minimum," I answered her.

I crossed to the corner where I'd left a half dozen big amphorae. Sealed properly, the clay jars make for cheap vermin-proof storage. Add a few simple spells and they'll keep food and other perishables in good condition for years. These days I generally buy mine off the back of a wagon that collects empties from local taverns. There's always some breakage, so the foreman at the firm that recycles them turns a blind eye to the pilferage as long as he gets a cut.

"Downstairs neighbors?" interjected Stel. "I presume you've got 'em in a building this sound. What are they like? Can they get up here?"

I could tell that I wasn't going to get any peace until I reassured my guests, and that "trust me" just wasn't going to do it. If our positions were reversed I'd have been the same way. Rather than play twenty questions, I decided to give them the full run down.

"Floor below us is another, much larger, attic. There used to be a ladder up to a trapdoor from there to here. I pulled the ladder—it's in the chimney now—and nailed the trapdoor shut. I also plastered over the hole from beneath and aged the plaster to match the surrounding ceiling."

"How?" asked Vala from somewhere off in the dark beyond the chimney.

"Trade secret." I wasn't willing to admit to magic yet, though I knew they figured me for a mage. "Anyone who looks up from below and actually thinks about it will know there's a void up here, but a couple of factors play against them bothering or doing anything about it.

"First, the floor of the main attic below is thoroughly rotten and likely to drop anyone wandering around up there onto the main brewery floor. The fall's thirty feet and there are enough uneven surfaces on the old brewing gear to make that a fatal height. Second, the ground level of the brewery houses a caras seed-grinder. She keeps her little band of skull-crackers well and truly dusted up, which makes them paranoid, intermittently homicidal, and pretty damned slow on the uptake. It also keeps everyone but her dustmen the hell away from the building."

"Sounds like the perfect neighbors for something like this." Stel nodded approvingly, and for the first time she sounded something other than hostile and suspicious of me.

"Pretty much. As long as we don't make any more noise than can be easily explained away by the rats, bats, slinks, and nipperkins, plus the various critters that hunt them, they won't give us any trouble.

"Now, who's hungry?" I'd just finished cracking the spelled seal on two of the amphorae to expose the rations within, mostly salted pork wrapped into neat bundles in the one, and bags of rice cakes in the other. "It all tastes like the inside of an amphora, of course, but it'll keep skin and bone together in a pinch."

"Sounds . . . delightful," Vala said in a tone that suggested she was trying to convince herself. "We'd love some."

I tossed her a bag of rice cakes and slid a greasy bundle of pork over to Stel, then went on to the next amphora. It held blankets and a large bottle of Kyle's, the six year. It was drinkable but nowhere near as good as the fifteen I kept at my main fallback—a necessary

economy given the state of my purse. I set the bottle aside and divided up the blankets.

"You won't really need them in this heat, but they'll give you
some padding against the floor. I tried keeping a straw pallet up
here for a while, but it didn't work out. Even a good strong mix of
fleabane and worrymoth won't keep the rats and nipperkins away
after they've gotten into the caras seed."

The next amphora held water skins, and I passed one to Vala to
carry back to Stel. There were more supplies in the remaining amphorae, but I didn't want to breach the spelled seals if I didn't have
to. Both for convenience's sake and to keep them preserved against
future need.

Reluctantly, I left the Kyle's unbroached as well, both the six and
the smaller fifteen from my pack, and grabbed myself a water skin
instead. The salty pork and bone dry rice cakes needed a lot of
washing down. Now, with basic amenities taken care of it was time
to move on to other, more dangerous, necessities.

Moving casually, I crossed to another broken-down half barrel
and took a seat. It lay midway between the magelight and Stel, and
my shadow fell across the lower half of her body—a deliberate
choice on my part. I might like the Dyad, but I was still a long way
from trusting her, and putting Triss there made for cheap insurance.

"We need to talk," I said quietly.

Somewhere behind me, Vala stopped her inspection of the room.
I half turned, so that I could look at both halves of the Dyad. Vala's
farther hand was out of sight, concealed behind her hip, though I
guessed that it now held one of her battle wands. I didn't blame her;
casting my shadow across Stel's legs was a very similar tactic, though
they didn't know it. Or, at least, I hoped they didn't.

"Yes, we do." The Meld spoke through both of her mouths. "Why
don't you start."

Though in this case it was quite obvious, I'm not entirely sure
how the Meld made it so clear when she was speaking instead of
Vala or Stel. Something about body language as much as tone perhaps? Certainly, Vala moved less in those moments when the Meld
came to the forefront, but that didn't explain the obvious differences
in Stel's demeanor. It was clearly much more complicated than the
stories had led me to believe.

"It's pretty clear that you have a problem," I said. "A big one,
and one that puts you in opposition to Tien's charming authorities.

I'm a shadow jack. My job is helping people with exactly that kind of problem. . . ."

Stel frowned and Vala sighed. Then, the Meld spoke. "Something was stolen from us. We need to recover it. How much would you charge to help us find it?"

"That depends on a couple of things. The value of the item. How dangerous the job is. How long it takes. Etc. Oh, and I don't work in the dark. You tell me everything you know or think you know about the job, and you do it up front."

"How do we know we can trust you?" asked Vala, who had resumed her pacing.

"You don't. If you had time and knew the city, you could ask around about my rep, but that's not a luxury you have, not with the amount of heat you've already generated."

"I wouldn't be so sure about that," said Stel. "We might surprise you there."

"That's certainly possible, but the impression I've gotten is that in addition to the heat coming from the guard, you're under a lot of time pressure on this thing."

"What if we tell you what you want and then you decide you don't like the odds?" asked Vala.

"Easy. If I don't like the job, I won't take it, but I also won't slink you out to the guard. That's one of the things you'd know if you'd had time to check me out."

"Actually," said Vala, "that reputation is exactly why we came looking for you at the Gryphon's Head, Jack Aral."

I blinked several times then, and Triss jerked sharply, but only a few tiny fractions of an inch. If the Dyad noticed either gesture of surprise, neither of her faces betrayed it.

"That's an interesting statement," I said after a slightly too long silence. "If you were at the Gryphon looking for me, why didn't you say so in the first place?"

"Say that we were of three minds about it," the Meld said from both sides of me, "and you will hit close enough to the mark."

"I didn't like the idea," said Stel.

"I wasn't thrilled with it either," agreed Vala, "though I thought it worth investigating."

"But I . . . felt we needed some sort of help," said the Meld.

I noted the choice of "felt" as opposed to "knew" or "believed," and could tell there was something interesting going on there, if not what. "It sounds like there's some major significance to the way you phrased that. Or am I mishearing?"

"You have a good ear," replied the Meld. "I . . . or in this case, *we* had not reached a formal decision about whether to consult with you in your professional capacity. We had hoped to spend some time observing you in your natural surrounds before doing anything more. Several days, perhaps. But circumstances got away from us and now we are come to the choice prematurely."

"I don't know. In many ways you've had a better look at what I'm capable of than most of my clients ever get. I don't normally let on that I'm up to dealing with Elite problems, if you know what I mean." Nor would I have allowed that information to get out this time, if I'd had much in the way of a choice about it. "In fact, I generally flat refuse any job that would bring me in close contact with the king's personal bonebreakers."

"That's only made the decision harder," said the Meld, speaking through Stel. "Before, we thought you no more than a common jack. Now, you are revealed to be much more than we expected. But exactly how much more and in what ways is still a dangerous mystery. So, Aral, what are you?"

"Funnily enough, that's a question I've been asking myself a lot lately."

Anger flashed in Stel's eyes and Vala stiffened. "We didn't come here to play verbal games!" said the Meld.

"No, you came here because you need me." I jumped to my feet and walked toward Stel, keeping her firmly in my shadow. "I offered you the best hope of a temporary refuge and redress for your problems. You made that choice after checking me out as much as you could from a distance and then you kept me in the dark about your intent until now. If I've got doubts about the arrangement, they're no less valid than your own, so let's not get all high-horse about things, shall we?"

Behind me I heard Vala quietly shifting to the side, presumably so that she could blast me without putting Stel at risk if she had to.

Without turning, I continued, "For starters, that means that your Vala mote stops pointing those wands at my back, Dyad, and you start trusting me at least a little bit. That or you take your best shot and only one of us walks away. Which is it going to be?"

6

I tried not to let my tension show in any way as I waited to find out whether I was going to have to kill the Dyad. I had no doubt that I could, even if she decided to attack first. I just might not live through the experience.

"Well, I'm going to have to vote for shooting you in the back," said Stel, her voice perfectly calm. "No offense, but there are a lot of jacks in this city. We can find another, one who doesn't present so many unknowns and risks. And, I don't see any way that we can lose the fight. Vala?"

"I'm leaning that way as well. But I am wondering why our jack friend here isn't acting all that worried about the possibility."

"Is that concern the only thing that's keeping you from attacking me from behind right now?" I asked. "Because, if it is, then we're never going to establish the kind of trust that we're going to need to make this work, and we might as well get this over with."

"No, it is not the only thing," said the Meld, speaking through Vala's mouth. "That would be me. I have chosen to overrule the thinking of my motes."

And how did that work? I wondered. Clearly there was more to the Meld than just the sum of its parts. There were definitely three distinct people sharing the two bodies.

"So far you've done us nothing but good turns," continued the meld. "Most recently, giving us the chance to have this conversation, instead of simply killing Stel when Vala drew on you."

"What?" Stel looked shocked. "He's empty-handed. Even if he's a mage, he hasn't so much as pointed a finger in my direction."

"Yeah, I'd have blasted him before he could even begin to get off a spell," said Vala. "What haven't you told us, Valor of Steel?" Vala sounded indignant, and I had to assume she was addressing the Meld by its formal title, a thing I'd heard rumored but never confirmed.

"He is a Blade," said the Meld, speaking through Vala's mouth. "Some would say *the* Blade, if I'm not wrong in my guess at his identity. You *are* the Aral known as Kingslayer, are you not?"

I nodded slightly, but said nothing. I don't really think of myself as the Kingslayer anymore, but this weird conversation was far too fascinating to interrupt.

"I still don't understand," said Stel. "A Blade is just another type of mage, no matter what the legends say. What makes you think he could kill me before Vala could stop him?"

"You're sitting in his *shadow*," said the Meld, and exasperation crept into her voice. "His Shade holds your life in the palm of its hand, and has since before this conversation started. Honestly, motes, I sometimes wonder how I manage to think half so clearly as I do when it's your minds I have to use to do all the work."

"Oh," said Stel, her voice gone suddenly very small, while somewhere behind me Vala swallowed audibly.

"You both know about Shades," said the Meld. "I know you do because I can see the lessons about Blades in your memories. But apparently it's never occurred to either of you to actually *think* about them. Not even when you've got one with its fingers wrapped around your throats."

The Meld's eyes looked out at me through Stel's face. "I've turned the battle wands away, Kingslayer. Now I'm going to bring Vala over here so that we're all where you can see us. At that point I'd take it as a gesture of good faith if you'd step out of the light."

Again I nodded without saying a word. Creaking boards warned me of Vala's approach. She paused as she passed, laying the battle wands on the ground in front of my feet without ever looking at me. Then she went to take a seat on Stel's barrel with her back turned to both of us, thus preserving what I had already come to think of as the quintessential Dyad posture—looking both ways.

"My turn," I said. "Though there's no need to actually physically move out of the light. Triss?"

My shadow slid to the left and up onto the ceiling, uncovering Stel. Then it shifted shape, assuming the familiar outline of a small dragon and his normally concealed identity.

"Aren't you going to introduce me?" he asked, his voice strangely diffident.

"If you like." I wondered at the formality, but now wasn't the time to ask him about it. "Triss, this is Stel, her bondmate, Vala, and their Meld, Valor of Steel . . . At least I believe that's how the Meld should be addressed—please correct me if I'm wrong."

The Meld interjected, "VoS will do, actually. Valor of Steel is a formal thing worn only for formal moments. It is also, more rightly, the name of our Dyad, a sort of formalized rendition of the names my motes assumed when they bonded. I also answer to 'hey you.'"

"My pardon. Triss, meet Vala, Stel, and VoS, collectively the Dyad Valor of Steel."

Stel nodded, which was as much of a bow as could be managed in her present position and condition. Vala waved. The Meld repeated both gestures, somehow making them distinct from the originals.

"VoS, Vala, Stel, this is Triss, my familiar, and one of the finest Shades ever to grace our world of Gram."

Triss tipped his wings back and bowed from the waist. "I'm very pleased to finally meet you all. I'm sure that Aral and I will be able to help you recover the Kothmerk."

"What!" Vala spun half around, her hands reaching for the empty wand sheaths at her hips.

"How did you know about that?" demanded Stel, half drawing her fighting rods.

"Very clever." VoS turned Vala back around and resheathed Stel's rods. "You're going to have to tell me how you know about that."

"I'll trade you," I said. "You tell me how you realized who and what I was, and the story of how you ended up here, and I'll tell you what I know about the Kothmerk and how I learned it."

"Deal." The Meld nodded both of her heads. "Oh, and in case you hadn't guessed. You're hired."

"Aren't you going to ask me how much I cost?"

"No. This is a matter that touches on the honor of the Archon. If we recover the Kothmerk, my government will pay whatever is necessary. If we don't, it will be because we're all dead. In which case, money is *really* no object."

I chuckled. "I'm glad you've got such confidence in my dedication to your cause, though I'm not sure how you arrived there."

"Start with the Shade, then," said the Meld. "And with my half of our exchange of notes. A few moments ago, when Vala mentioned that we'd come to the Gryphon specifically to find Aral the jack, your shadow moved of its own accord. I didn't register it at that moment, since I was too busy watching your expression and posture. But later, when you showed such confidence in the face of what seemed overwhelming odds, I knew that you had to be much more than you seemed, so I replayed all our memories of you.

"The movement of your shadow then was the clue I needed to make sense of the chaos at the Gryphon when my motes somehow lost track of you. You didn't *seem* to vanish then, you did vanish, and without using magic. Therefore, you had to be a Blade."

"Makes sense." I nodded. "But it still doesn't tell me why that makes you trust me so much."

VoS looked at me like I was speaking a language she didn't understand. "You are the Kingslayer, Blade of Namara, the living hand of Justice. And our cause is just. What else could we possibly need to know?"

She said it so simply and with such conviction that it felt like I'd taken a knife to the heart. My eyes burned with unshed tears as I remembered what it felt like to have that kind of unalloyed faith in the goddess and the cause I served. Not to mention in myself and my fellows.

That was all gone now; my faith in all things godly had been swept away by the Emperor of Heaven's murder of Namara. Its remains were buried in the ruins of her temple by the Emperor's chief priest, the Son of Heaven. My faith in my fellow Blades had gone into the grave when I found out that some few of my companions lived on, having cut a deal with the most abhorrent of new masters, that self-same Son of Heaven.

My first impulse was to tell the Dyad that, to warn her that we who had once been Blades were just as broken and betraying as anyone else, but somehow I couldn't do it. She had a faith in me and my kind that I had long since lost, and I couldn't bear to take that away from her. Not when I knew how much its loss had cost me. Perhaps because of that, I found myself wanting to help them more than anything I had wanted in a very long time, to see myself as I had once been, if only for a little while and through the eyes of another.

And if somewhere in the back of my head there was a cynical voice reminding me that appearances were not always what they seemed and that the Dyad might turn up on the wrong side of justice, and another voice pointing out that I had already promised to help Fei and that the Dyad's goals and Fei's were not necessarily in alignment . . . well, that was probably all to the good.

Vala might remind me of Jax, but she wasn't Jax. She was part of a Dyad; a creature as alien as you could possibly find inside of a human skin. And long after she had returned to Kodamia, I would

still be dealing with Fei. My life would never again be as uncompli-
cated as it had been when I lived to obey my goddess, and there was
no point in pretending otherwise.

"You've gone very quiet over there, Aral," said Vala. "And you
look so sad. I hope we haven't brought you pain." Her voice was soft
and sympathetic and it cut all the deeper for that.

"No, it's all right," I said as Triss slid down from the wall and
laid a comforting wing across my shoulders. "I need to remember
sometimes."

And that was true. My old, simple faith might have died with
my goddess and my fellows, but over the last year I had finally started
to build something new atop the ruined foundations of what I had
once been. I might not be a Blade of Namara anymore. Too much
gray had spilled across the black and white of my old worldview for
that, but I could still serve justice in my own way. And maybe
even—on the good days—serve Justice as well.

"You were going to tell me a story," I said.

"It's a long one."

"Then I'd better lay out my blanket and get the whiskey." Triss
snapped his wings disapprovingly at me, but I ignored him this
time. I needed something to take the sting out of the blow VoS had
unknowingly dealt me.

"Let Vala get the bottle," said the Meld. "She's going to go crazy
if I don't allow her to get up and move around soon anyway."

"That works for me."

Before I'd finished my sentence, Vala had bounced to her feet
and said "Oh, thank the Twins!" A reference to Eyn and Eva, the
two-faced goddess at the center of the Kodamian branch of the
church. "And now I can take off this damn armor, too."

She shimmied out of the heavy leather vest and then practically
bounced over to the place where I'd left the Kyle's six beside my
blanket. "Here you go." She flipped the bottle to me like a juggler's
club, following it a moment later with the balled up blanket.

"Thank you." I uncorked it and took a long swig. Then I started
to drag over the half barrel I'd been sitting on earlier, noting, "It'll
make it easier to pass the bottle back and forth."

"Don't bother," the Meld said through Stel's mouth. "I won't be
drinking until after I've finished my story. It tends to blur the edges
between the three of us, and I'd rather not have that interfere with
the telling."

"Well then," said Triss, rather acerbically, "why don't we all just
drink water for now? It tends to blur Aral's edges as well."

I rolled my eyes and took another sip. The harsh peaty burn of the six felt wonderful, but I could see how much my taking a drink upset Triss. So I recorked the bottle and set it aside, gesturing for him to fetch me my water skin—which he was quick to do.

"Familiars, what can you do?" I said with a shrug, and it was only after I'd spoken that I realized that the age-old mage complaint about our companions might play differently with a Dyad. "Begging your pardon, if that strikes you ladies as offensive."

This sent both—or perhaps all three—of the Dyad's component personalities into gales of laughter. I took the opportunity of them recomposing themselves to fold my blanket into a pad and take a cross-legged seat with my back against the half barrel.

"I take it I said something funny?"

Stel, who was wiping tears from her eyes nodded. "Oh yes. You see, one of the biggest running jokes among the Dyadary has to do with exactly who is the familiar and who is the master, and thus who it is who suffers whom. The mages usually say it's us 'muscleheads' since that's the way the mage/familiar bond works. We claim it's them, because, after all, we're the ones with the familiar gift. But . . ."

"But what?" I asked.

"But," sighed the Meld, "when really pressed on the topic, both sides will pick on their poor Melds." She crossed all four of their arms in a deliberately prissy manner. "Which is silly since I don't actually exist in any physical way. I maintain that I am simply a figment of their conjoined imaginations."

"The bossiest figment in the history of ever," whispered Vala, and Stel nodded vigorous agreement.

I decided at that moment that everything I'd ever heard about Dyads was probably as wrong as the crazier stories about Blades, and that I had no real clue how their thought processes worked. And the only way to find out was to observe them in action.

"Tell me about the Kothmerk." I slapped a couple of pieces of pork on a rice cake and took a bite—I could eat and listen.

"All right," replied the Meld. Then she began, switching back and forth between voices as best suited the moment or allowed one or the other of her halves to eat.

It started when the Archon called us into the high office. I'd never been up there before. It's a round room on top of the tallest tower in the Citadel with the Archon's desks sitting opposite each other against the outer walls. They seated us back-to-back between them so that we would be able to face them and still feel comfortable.

"I hear very good things about you from Master Sword," said the Meld we refer to as the Archon. He spoke through both mouths then, as he did throughout the entire interview—adding authority and weight to his words. "Master Wand is also quite effusive about the combat side of your magical training, if somewhat less so about the rest."

I blushed at that. I've always been better with the more, shall we say, active *magics.*

"I'll work harder on the rest," I began. "I promise to—"

But the Archon was already waving that off. "I am not at all displeased. In fact, your martial skills are why I've called you in today. I intend to assign you to your very first real field mission, beyond the bounds of Kodamia even."

"But Master Book says I won't be ready to go out among the singletons for years." And I must admit that I wailed a bit here since I'd never even met a real singleton like you—the solos who live in Kodamia are different. "Not at the rate I'm currently advancing, at least. He says I couldn't fool a drunken mercenary in search of a tumble into believing that there were actually two of me."

The Archon laughed a good natured sort of laugh. "Well, since this mission doesn't require you to tumble any singleton mercenaries, or even to pretend to be anything other than a Dyad, that shouldn't be a problem. I have to send something very valuable to the Durkoth of the north and it needs the best protection I can send with it."

That's when the half of the Archon that faced Vala pulled out what looked like a small block of gold, maybe two inches on a side and covered in intricate etching too delicate for any human hand to have made. The designs reminded me of the patterns frost will make on steel high in the mountains, only more deliberate, as if some thinking hand had stolen winter's brush to paint with.

"What is that?" I asked through Vala's lips.

The Archon pulled lightly at the top and bottom of the little block. It opened like a jeweler's box, though I could see neither latch nor hinge, nor even a seam twixt the two halves. I've held it several times since then and I still have no idea how it can open. Inside was a lining of some black stone like richest velvet. It held the Kothmerk as a mother holds her babe, firm yet soft, with care against any slip or mishap.

The Archon had to tip the box upside down to get it to release the ring. Then he raised the Kothmerk so that the sunlight streaming in through the window at his back shone through the stone.

"What did the ring look like?" asked Triss.

He'd slipped down from his perch on the wall and laid his head in my lap and now I was idly running a finger up and down the ridge of his scaly neck, letting my fingers find nuance where eyes saw only undifferentiated shadow.

VoS answered Triss as she continued their story.

It was a king's signet in general shape, though no king of men ever wore so fine a seal on his finger. Nor one carved whole from a single ruby. The band is etched inside and out with more of that thinking winter's frost, deeper than that on the box, though no less delicate. It rises spiral-like to the crown of the ring, then leaves off at the edge of the seal proper.

That, you will know from seeing it here and there on Durkoth work, is the circle that eats itself set round the Durkoth character for the evernight. It seems a simple signet, and too easy to counterfeit by far, until you look close and see that both circle and symbol are themselves etched with a fine pattern like the veining of leaves. It was the most beautiful thing I'd ever seen, and as I leaned forward I stilled my lungs so as not to fog it with any touch of my breath.

"This is the Kothmerk," said the Archon, "living heart of the Durkoth and a necessary piece in the recrowning of the King of the North that happens at Winter-Round this year."

"I don't understand," I said. "Neither the recrowning, nor why we hold the ring." I knew little of our relationship with the Durkoth and less about the people themselves.

"Many years ago there was a war fought between the Durkoth of the northern mountains and their southern cousins. Mostly they fought in the deep ways of the earth, far below Gram's surface. But one great battle was fought here aboveground in the gap that splits the mountains and holds Kodamia at its heart. For reasons lost in history the then Archon came to the aid of the King of the North and helped him and his people drive the southern armies from the field. She even personally saved the king's life and with it his throne.

"In token of the debt he owed her, the king gave the Kothmerk into the keeping of the Archon and her heirs. It was to be held against the time of our greatest need, when the Durkoth of the North kingdom will redeem it by fighting at our side. We have held it unused for seven centuries, bringing it out of the vaults only for the recrowning ceremony once every two hundred years when we send it back to its rightful master."

That's when I realized why the Archon had called me into his tower. "You want me to take the ring to the Durkoth?" I asked, and my voice squeaked when I spoke.

The Archon laughed. "Yes, though not alone by any means. There will be a round dozen of the Dyadary in attendance upon the ring and all of them, but you and Edge of Persistence, are the hoariest of *veterans. But I'm a little short on fully trained death-spinners at the moment, what with the trouble in the Kvanas."*

I interrupted VoS then. "Death-spinner? What's that?"

Vala spoke, indicating herself and her bond-mate. "We are. Different Dyads have different specialties. We're given extensive testing soon after the pairing to determine where our first-order aptitudes lie. My birth sister and her bondmate went to study under the research sorcerers. Ours was close-in combat, so we went to the spinners."

Having seen the Dyad take on a pair of Elite I couldn't say I was surprised. "And you stay with that for the rest of your lives?"

"No," said Vala. "When we're older, they'll assign us to learn a second specialty and then maybe a third."

"That's assuming we get any older," grumbled Stel. "And that we get the Kothmerk back. If we don't manage that, we'll probably end up as the only Dyad ever permanently assigned to mucking out the stables."

"We'll get it back," said Vala. "We have to."

"And we'll help you," said Triss. "But please continue the story."

VoS nodded.

The Archon put the ring back in the box and closed it. "Based on the recommendations of Sword and Wand I'm going to brevet you to field status for the duration of this mission. If you do well, the promotion will become permanent and you can move out of the cadet quarters, though I'll want you to continue your training with a new master in hopes of expanding your range beyond death-spinner and the mere cracking of skulls. An important and necessary skill, but only a first step into becoming a full Dyad."

The next several days passed in briefings and logistics. Maps, packs, and orders, none of which is all that important. So I'll skip over all of it except for one tiny detail, the secondary staff. On any major expedition with multiple Dyads involved, there are bound to be a number of solos needed as well. Drivers for the wagons, cooks, porters, and grooms to name a few.

Among the crowd on this particular trip was a little slip of a girl who worked in the stables, fourteen, maybe fifteen years old. Her name was Reyna and she was a refugee from some disaster south and west, though no one could ever get her to talk about the details. She'd arrived a year or two before and went to work mucking out the stalls in exchange for meals and a spot in the loft. She was so good with the horses that she was quickly given a job as a groom with actual pay and a tiny room that she shared with the other girl grooms. For all that, she was very easy to forget. Stay with me, she'll be very important later.

We departed the Citadel on foot and in the middle of the night and met up with the wagons and animals a full two days later on the Zhani side of the border. They'd been sent out a few at a time and gathered at an isolated spot in the hills to wait for us. There had been problems moving the Kothmerk before, and the Archon didn't want to give any signal that something so important was on the road. That's why it didn't go straight into the Durkoth tunnels that come out near the Citadel either. The trouble's been much on their end of things.

You see, whatever great noble holds the Kothmerk on the morning of the recrowning has the right to ascend the throne, till the next time around. So we were going to haul it up through western Zhan and Kadesh and hand it over to the Durkoth at Hurn's Gate pass. Since the Durkoth don't like it up on the surface, the Archon and the King of the North figured it'd be safer to send it with us by wagon.

They were wrong.

7

———◆———

*I*t *happened while we were in deep forest. I was riding lookout about a half mile ahead of the wagons. That's the only reason I'm alive to tell you this story, Aral, that I drew the straw for forward scout that morning. It's almost funny. The first couple of days had gone smoothly enough, well-kept road all the way, and no cause for alarm. It looked like we'd slipped out of the Citadel clean.*

There was nothing at all to mark the day out as special, though you'd think there would have been. So many Dyads lost, and not just mere cadets, but high lords at the peak of their power and fame. A couple of them were practically legends in the Dyadary. And the numbers . . . more Dyads lost at one time than have fallen anywhere else short of the great battles.

VoS's voice burned with pain and loss as she spoke now.

There really ought to have been a red sun rising, or a falling star, or a flight of black eagles. Something more to mark their passing than a bright morning that ended in blood and the smoke of a mass pyre.

I couldn't have been more than a mile ahead at the utmost when the attack happened—and that far only if I'd badly misjudged the little caravan's speed—but I heard nothing. Nothing. I didn't even suspect anything had gone wrong till the sun hit noon and my relief didn't show. I reined in my horses and waited then, nearly an hour, figuring that things had just gotten a bit distracted. But time passed and no one came and I began to worry. I didn't want to send up the alarm signal—a red smoke spell kept always to hand and set to trigger in the event of my sudden death. There was nothing wrong on my end and I didn't want to give away our presence.

Finally, Vala convinced me and I let her send up a column of bright blue smoke—a standard signal requesting orders—though not one that had been authorized for this mission. I expected a royal chewing-out to come along with my response. None came, nor any answering smoke, nor any signal at all. Finally, I turned my horses around and rode back to meet the wagons. I was worried by then, but not yet afraid. What could possibly happen to a dozen well-trained Dyads and forty support staff? I was about to find out.

My fears started to rise after I'd covered a second mile without encountering any of the wagons. It was possible they'd fallen farther back than that due to some delay, but I'd have expected a signal if so, and none had come. Three miles, and I started to panic. I drove my horses hard after that, pushing them to a very fast trot for the last couple of miles. The attack had come early in the day, not long after I'd ridden out judging by the distance I had to cover to get back to the site of the attack.

They were all dead, Dyad and solo alike, or that's what I thought then. All those bodies . . .

VoS closed both of her sets of eyes then and shuddered. I could see she was fighting tears, so I didn't say anything, just scratched Triss behind the ears and waited for her to recover. After a time, her breathing smoothed and she nodded.

I couldn't believe it for the longest time. Not even with their corpses there in front of me like so many discarded dolls. They were strewn randomly along the road and off into the forest for a few yards on either side. Nothing could have done this. Nothing. I think the multiply repeated dichotomy of bloody ruin and apparent peace was the worst.

She canted her Stel head to one side and looked a question at me.

I don't know if you've ever seen a fallen Dyad, but it can happen like that if death comes fast enough. One half shot in the back of the neck and the other dead without a mark on her. . . .

Dagger in Waiting had been the leader of our expedition, the best eavesman and nightcutter Kodamia has produced for at least three generations. Or spy and assassin if you want it spelled out plainer. Impossible to surprise and a deadlier close-in fighter than many a spinner. His Watt half looked like it had been crushed between great stones, covered in blood and with all the bones broken. Dag, his other half, was lying peacefully on his back not five feet away, as though he'd just lain down for a quick nap. If not for Watt's shattered corpse, I might even have tried to wake him to ask what had happened.

Seven of the ten Dyads that had ridden out with the Kothmerk that morning had died that way, killed too quick to respond to whatever slaughtered them. Three more had gone down fighting, leaving both halves badly injured. Several of the fallen had been crushed like Dagger in Waiting. Others had been torn asunder or sliced up. Malice in Mysticism had been run through by something the size of a fence post. Clash of Remorse, who was the trailing rider, had come late to the battle and almost certainly better prepared. He had all four weapons drawn. But it hadn't helped. He suffered a double beheading before he'd made it forward of the last wagon.

There was even something of that weird mix of destruction and peace to the battlefield itself. Perhaps for the same reason of a quick end. Kodamian bodies lay everywhere, along with tipped over wagons and their wildly strewn contents. All the horses were dead as well. But the road itself, where most of the action had taken place, looked remarkably clean and unmarred. It had none of the rucking and ridging I'd come to associate with a battlefield. But that observation was driven out by another and even stranger one.

What about the enemy fallen? That was the question that really got my mind going again. Curiosity is a powerful force and acted now like spurs on a reluctant horse, forcing me to move.

There wasn't an enemy body to be seen. Not one. Yet I was sure there must have been casualties, because Malice in Mysticism's blades were covered with dried blood, so dark it looked black—you don't lose that much and walk away. Not even with a good combat healer ready to hand. And his weren't the only weapons that had spilled blood; it spattered the grass in places where none of my people lay.

So, where were the enemy bodies? And, since I was asking questions, what about the Kothmerk? Had any of our solos survived? Their bodies were scattered amongst the fallen Dyadary, but I hadn't yet taken their number. What right did I have to stand around like an idiot when there was a mission to finish?

That last I heard in my head in Master Sword's voice, and it galvanized me as only your first drill instructor can. I had work to do, and a damned lot of it. I had to figure out what had happened, see to the bodies in an honorable fashion, and recover the Kothmerk if possible. Gawping wasn't an option and mourning would have to wait for later.

I looked for the Kothmerk first, as that was the whole point of my mission. Dagger in Waiting had been carrying it in a small, locked, chainmail bag fixed around his Dag waist and hidden under his shirt. The bag was still there but it had been neatly opened and the Kothmerk was gone. Not a surprise, but it got through the numb I'd been feeling and made me angry enough to gut someone.

A quick check of Dagger in Waiting's person revealed that was the only thing taken, and the same was true of every other body I checked. If anything, that made me angrier, all this death for one damned little trinket. I mean, there must have been a couple of thousand gold riels' worth of jewelry and equipment there, plus the mission purse and personal coin.

I think that's when I realized that it must have been the Durkoth who killed them. That, and how very inhuman the Others really are. No human, solo or Dyad, would have left all that money just lying around for the next person who came along to pick up. We're simply not made that way. Even I couldn't do it, and they were my friends and companions, though I only took the mission purse and that for emergencies. The rest, the durable personal items and individual purses, went into a spell-dug hole for later recovery and return to the heirs.

I went back and took a closer look at Malice in Mysticism's swords then and the blood on them. I hadn't noticed before because it was dried and I was in a hurry, seeing what I expected to see, but it was more purple than red, the color of royalty, not humanity. Then I started gathering bodies and piling them up for a mass burning, not having the leisure for proper individual pyres. I worked fast and hard and I burned through my nima like a maniac, but night had long since eaten the sun by the time I dropped the last of the fallen onto the heap.

I had numbered the fallen several times by then. Each time, I'd come up one short, Reyna, the girl groom. I hoped that she'd escaped, of course, and that I could find and question her. But if she had gotten away, she was almost certainly long gone into the hills. If she were still alive and around, she would certainly have come out by now. But I hadn't the energy left to do anything about that, much less the more urgent task of going after the Durkoth.

So I called fire down upon the dead and collapsed there beside the burning bodies of my companions. Exhausted beyond bearing, I slept only a little less deeply than those I'd just bid on their way to the wheel of judgment.

It turned out to be a good thing I'd waited to leave, for the morning brought me fresh eyes. When I looked over the battlefield one last time, hoping for some sign of the missing girl or the departing Durkoth, I found the dead spots I had missed the night before. They were about seven feet long and three wide, loosely diamond shaped, board flat, and completely devoid of any plant life.

They lay perhaps twenty feet off the road, in a small clearing in the wood, well beyond the main area of the battle. The four of them formed the radiating points of a star. When I touched the bare earth of the nearest, it felt wrong somehow, as though the dirt had been fused

*into something approaching the consistency of stone. I couldn't break it
with my fingers, and jabbing at it with a dagger left by one of the fallen,
barely made any mark at all.*

*I went and got a shovel, and dug down several feet along the end of
one of those diamonds, but I couldn't find a bottom to the fused area. I
had no other evidence for it, but they* felt *like tombs to me, and I believe
that they were Durkoth burial sites. Somehow that made me feel better.
Knowing that they'd paid a price for what they had done to my people.*

*There was a very clear, if very strange, trail leading away from
the graves and on up into the mountains, as though a dozen or more
of the raiders had gone that way. So I hobbled my horses and I headed
up the path on foot—they'd have made noise I didn't think I could afford,
the trail was that fresh. I don't know how they do in their element, deep
under the mountains, but out in the woods the Durkoth are apparently
shit at covering their traces.*

*They'd followed a deer path up into the hills. And, while they'd left
no actual footprints, the trail of bent and broken branches along the
way would have led the blindest hunter to their camp. But that wasn't
the odd part. No, that was the way the trail itself looked as though
someone had come along with a fine-tipped calligraphy brush and removed every trace of irregularity from its surface.*

*A deer path is generally a rough thing. It widens and narrows and
bumps up and down, even grows the odd bit of foliage. But this had
none of that. This trail looked as though it were maintained by a team
of deer engineers with a fetish for precision.*

*It reminded me of the state of the main road, which I now realized
had shown some of the same signs of smoothing and evening out. Normally, at the site of a battle the road gets churned up by the action. You
get scars and clods and horrible red mud from the spilled blood. It's
awful and ugly and you can tell something terrible has happened there
just by looking at it. But not this one. I still don't know why, but the
Durkoth seem to abhor the sight of torn earth. Knowing that's saved
my life a couple of times since then.*

*The trail they'd left was my first luck. The second was finding sev-
eral of the Durkoth still at home. They had shaped a cavern out of the
living rock of a cliff face maybe two miles from the place of the ambush.
I don't know whether they'd waited for the caravan there for a couple of
days, or if they just casually move rock around like that for a single
night's camp. Whatever the case, they'd scooped out a space the size of a
small manor house, with what looked like multiple rooms, many of
them with windows.*

They were arguing when I arrived, and loudly, or they might have spied me before I spotted them. Like an idiot, I'd walked practically up to the cliff face before I realized what I was hearing. I'm only middling fair at woodcraft on my best day, and I don't speak much Durkoth. Though I'd been studying my heart out since I'd gotten my orders for the mission, I just didn't recognize it at first.

Spoken fast and angry, as they were speaking it, Durkoth sounds more like the weirdest cat fight you ever heard than anything a person might say. Eventually though, I did realize what I was listening to. I threw myself down under some brush then, about three feet from what turned out to be the nearest window.

"What were they fighting about?" Triss asked VoS.

The Kothmerk, but you'd probably guessed that part already. More importantly, they were arguing about whose fault it was that the thing had gone missing. One of 'em swore up and down that he'd felt a little human girl running off into the woods right before he discovered the thing missing—and maybe one of those ishka-ki Kodamians had survived.

The others thought that was ridiculous and just an excuse for his failure on guard duty. How could any human, much less a young one, have possibly gotten into their krith without someone seeing her? And why would a human thief leave the ring box behind when she took the Kothmerk? But even with that, a bunch of them had gone off along the durathian road—whatever that was—to try to get ahead of the possibly mythical girl, and they'd only just left a short while before. I felt a nasty little chill at that, thinking how lucky I was that they'd taken some other route than the deer path.

Now, I was only getting maybe one word in three, if that. So, it took me quite a while to make sense of it all. But when I finally did, and heard the bit about the girl, I immediately thought of the missing young Reyna. So I slipped away from there right quick. Then I turned around and hurried back down the path the way I'd come.

VoS clenched four fists and briefly shut as many eyes, and it was easy to see that the memory hurt her.

It wasn't what I wanted to do. No, not by a long haul. What I wanted to do was rush in and kill the lot of them. I probably would have tried, too, if I'd thought I had any real hope of managing it, but these Others had brought down eleven Dyads already and with only a loss of four of their own number. I knew that any attempt I made then might as well come with a suicide note.

Even that might not have been enough to stop me if it weren't for the girl. What if it was Reyna? What if she had the Kothmerk now? Maybe I could still finish out the mission. Maybe I could make all those deaths matter.

When I got close to where I'd left my horses, I slowed down and started moving extra quietlike. I still didn't know what a durathian road might be, but if they were trying to get ahead of the girl and they thought she was one of ours, they might well have come back to the battlefield looking for her. It was a good thing I did, too, because I found three of them standing around one of my horses looking angry and jibbering their jabber.

I listened long enough to determine that the rest had gone off, a-hunting after my second horse and the girl who'd taken it. Following the tracks or something, it sounded like, though I can't say for sure. There were a lot more strange words involved and a good deal of pointing and what sounded like swearing. I figured that was all I needed to know, so I got my angles lined up and I used my battle wands to punch nice big holes in all three of them at once.

They're the toughest bastards I've ever seen, I'll give them that. The two I got through the heart made it halfway to me before they went down for good. And the one I'd only drilled through the lungs was practically on top of my Vala when Stel beheaded her. Thumb-sized hole running from armpit to armpit and she was still going strong right up till the second she lost her head. I wanted to ride then, but figured I couldn't afford the noise, so I took the mission purse and as much food as I could carry, unsaddled my horse, loosed the hobbles and headed out very quietly.

The dead Durkoth had all been pointing back along the road, so that's the way I went. I'm not sure how the Others were traveling, but they left an obvious enough trail, a series of parallel lines running lengthwise along the road where the grade was smoother and straighter than any human would ever have made it. I also don't know how fast they were moving, or Reyna on my stolen horse either, but I kept along at a nice steady march from a couple hours after sunup till near nightfall without catching anyone up.

I was just dropping off to sleep when it occurred to me that with the timing and all, the girl would pretty much have had to pass me on that trail I'd followed to the Durkoth krith. That meant there was a good chance she'd seen me coming up, and had decided not to flag me down. That, plus the fact that I hadn't seen her, even though I was looking out for anyone coming my way, left me feeling more than a little hollow.

Add in that she'd gotten past the Durkoth guards to steal the Kothmerk from them, and the way she'd somehow managed to avoid getting killed during the battle, and you had to start asking questions. How did she get past the guards? How did she avoid getting killed in an ambush that had taken the lives of nearly a dozen of the finest Dyads I knew?

*And, further back: Where had she really come from? What exactly
was the disaster she'd fled in the southwest? How the hell had she gotten
this far without either the Durkoth or me catching her? Etc.*

*I didn't sleep very well that night, and the next day only added
more questions. I found my missing horse after about an hour's walk.
She was lying dead in a little clearing off to one side of the road with
her saddle and bags in a heap not too far off. There were smooth neat
lines running along the ground all over the place, and two of those
weird burial diamonds. My first thought was that the Durkoth had
caught up with Reyna, and by some miracle she'd managed to take two
of them with her.*

*But a quick look around changed my mind. First off, there was no
crumpled little body, and if the earlier battlefield had shown me anything, it was that the Durkoth didn't much care what happened to human corpses. Second, I followed flies to a couple of huge purple blood
patches about forty feet apart. Both had the look of ambush killings,
like someone had gotten their throat slit or the big artery in the groin
opened up without ever getting a chance to fight back.*

*Once I was finished with looking around the clearing, I went back
to the road. There was another set of lines leading onward. Since I was
pretty sure I'd fallen behind, I resaddled my horse and mounted up,
with Vala riding pillion. About midafternoon I hit a crossroads where
all the trails turned and headed toward Tien. As you've probably
guessed, I never did catch up to the girl, though I did run into two
wounded Durkoth on the way to Tien—too hurt to travel I think—and
one of those nearly did for me before I gutted her.*

"You really believe one young girl managed to kill two Durkoth
and do all those other things?" asked Triss. "How?"

VoS shrugged Vala's shoulders. "I have no idea. Nor how she
survived that first battle, or any of the other fantastic things I've
ascribed to her. But I'm pretty sure that's what happened, and what
evidence I've found has tended to support the idea. I may not have
found Reyna, but I did turn up ten more Durkoth graves scattered
along the roadside between there and here, along with the corpses
of a score or so of what looked to be innocent bystanders."

"Maybe it wasn't Reyna that did all that," I said as I wrapped up
what was left of my dinner. "It could have been a third party as yet
unknown." I couldn't help but think of the dead girl that Fei's sergeant Zishin had found—the one with a couple of Elite standing over
her corpse—and wonder if that wasn't the missing Reyna.

"A third party who just happened along at that exact moment?"
asked VoS. "One who sounded to the Durkoth like a little girl

running away? Who also removed Reyna's body from the battle-field, or did something else to get rid of it? And all without leaving any other clues to point to his or her existence?"

"There is that," I said. "Maybe she was a mage of some sort, or had help."

I didn't say it, but killing from ambush like that would be right up the alley of one of my kind. And now that I'd encountered Devin, I knew a number of my brethren had turned their coats at the fall of the temple and might well be willing to take on that kind of job. But I didn't want to share any thoughts on that just yet, not till I had more information. Not about that and not about the dead girl. Not till I was absolutely sure about who was on the side of justice here.

"A mage I'd be more willing to believe," said VoS.

"We've discussed it amongst ourselves," said Vala. "Stel likes the unknown allies theory, but I don't see it. There's never been any evidence for her being anything other than alone. I think she might have been a much older mage just pretending to be a girl."

"How would she manage that?" asked Triss. "Illusion's all right if you're dealing with the mageblind, but I've never heard of a Dyad having that problem."

"We don't," said Stel. "If Reyna was wrapped in an active spell Vala would have seen it, or if not Vala, one of the other mage-halves."

"But there is a way . . ." Vala started, but trailed off when Stel gave her a hard look.

"We are *not* going to talk about that," said Stel.

8

―――•◦•―――

"**T**alk about what?" I leaned forward on my half barrel curiously, but Stel just gave me a stony look and stayed clammed up.

"Might as well just tell him," said VoS, after a dozen or so heart-beats. "It's not like he doesn't know more than enough to get us court-martialed and hanged if he wanted to already."

"But no one outside the Dyadary is supposed to even know the spell exists," protested Stel. "It's a state secret."

Vala shrugged. "And one we're almost certainly going to have to use after the disaster at the tavern. Even if we waited till Aral left to do something and then worked the change, it's not something we'd be able to hide from him. Not if we're going to keep working together."

"All right," said Stel, "but for the record, I'm really not happy about this."

Vala winked at her bond-mate. "So write me up when we get home. Maybe they'll let you roam free while they've got me locked in the stockade."

Stel rolled her eyes in a way that suggested this was a common tease between the two of them. Then she shrugged and gestured for Vala to continue.

"There's a spell we use in the Dyadary that will permanently alter your appearance." Vala grimaced. "We call it the bonewright, because that's what it does. Within certain limits that is."

"By which she means to complain to the unjust gods that there's no way to make her significantly taller," Stel said with a little smirk.

"I've never heard of anything like that," I said. "But that's probably not a huge surprise. While the goddess lived, she clouded the minds of those who saw her Blades, so that we could neither be drawn nor accurately described. There was never any need for us to significantly alter our appearance, or even to think about it."

"I don't think *anyone* knows about this outside of Kodamia," said Vala. "It's extraordinarily painful for the one experiencing the change, and losing control of the process is usually fatal, and always disfiguring. Most mages simply couldn't manage it. The only reason it's come into regular practice amongst the Dyadary is that we sorcerers can cede control of our bodies over to our lovely and charming familiars."

Stel raised her eyebrows. "I think you misspoke there. Don't you mean, oh familiar-mine, that your masters can control your puny little bodies, while you do the petty conjuring?"

"My bond-mate might be right," said Vala. "About my making a mistake, I mean. I'm afraid I have to retract the *charming* part of the description of our familiars, at least in Stel's case. Though she is still lovely." Vala blew Stel a kiss.

"You're not trying to say that Reyna is one half of a renegade Dyad, are you?" Triss lifted his head from my lap and looked more closely at the pair. "Because that makes no sense whatsoever."

"No, of course not," replied VoS. "But it's possible, however unlikely, that some other sorcerer got hold of the bonewright and had a familiar that could handle half of the process. One of the greater dragons or a vampire perhaps. Something with a lot of power and a good mind at any rate. Or, maybe there's some sort of familiar that has some way of mitigating the agony."

"Or," interjected Vala, "—and this is my theory—it's possible that a sufficiently disciplined mage could simply handle the pain. That they wouldn't need help from their familiar to manage the thing."

Stel put a hand up and pretended to whisper to me behind its cover, "She has delusions of mage-grandeur sometimes. Just pretend to agree with her."

Triss flipped a wing up in a perfect mirror of Stel's gesture. "Mine does that, too. Do you think it's a flaw inherent to those born with the mage gift? Or is it learned somehow?"

"I don't know about Aral, but poor Vala's *always* been a little off, if you know what I mean."

"That's too bad," said Triss. "If they'd learned it, there might be some way to train them out of it. Snacks for better behavior, or a sharp swat on the nose whenever it happens, or something. . . ."

Vala marched over to me, slipped her hand through my elbow, and tucked herself in tight against my side. "I've never been so insulted in all my life." She was short enough that she hardly had to stoop to make the connection, though I was sitting. "Take me away from all this, won't you please?"

My sense of humor might be a bit rusty, but it wasn't yet dead, so I grinned and nodded. "Of course, my lady. Where should we go?"

"Be careful there, Aral," said Stel. "She's a dangerous one once she gets her hooks into you. Deadly cute, and too smart by half. I should know."

"Oh, I would never do anything to hurt Aral," said Vala, laying her head on my shoulder and blinking up at me faux-adoringly. "For he is a fellow mage and, like me, he clearly suffers under the crushing burden of a too-insolent familiar."

With Vala pressed so close, I couldn't help but notice the smell of her hair and the warmth of her body. It was the first time that I'd really thought of her as a human woman rather than half of a Dyad, which was the next thing to some sort of exotic creature from another dimension in my book. It was a rather alarming realization, and I felt my face flushing.

I decided to brazen it out and pretend nothing had happened, but the rather smug look that suddenly appeared on Vala's face suggested that I was perhaps pulling it off less well than I'd hoped.

"But I promised to tell you how I came to know about the Kothmerk," I said.

"You did at that." Vala didn't relinquish her hold on my arm, choosing to sit on the edge of the barrel with me instead. "Let's hear it."

I was somewhat distracted as I rattled off my encounter with Qethar, and I wondered if that wasn't exactly the Dyad's intent. But I still managed to tell the bulk of my tale in a reasonably lucid manner. Lucid enough that VoS and company didn't seem to notice the gaps where I omitted things like the pebble Qethar had given me, or the appearance of Captain Fei, both of which incidents I thought better to keep to myself for the moment. Oh, the joys of trying to serve two masters, and justice besides.

When I finished speaking, Vala hopped to her feet and began to pace—the only one of us short enough to manage it in the confined space of the attic. "I don't like the sound of this Qethar even a little bit. Do you think he's one of the group that we followed to the city? Judging by the marks in the road, there were at least a half dozen left by the time they got here."

"I doubt it." Mostly because of things Fei had said about Qethar being well-known in certain circles in Tien, but I couldn't very well tell the Dyad that. "He seemed to know the city like someone who lived here, and that Elite major treated him more like a well-known pain in the ass than a visiting VIP."

"That reminds me of a thought I wanted to mention about the major," said Stel. "You say his dog was practically on top of you when it suddenly turned away?"

I nodded, which stretched sore muscles and reminded me of how very long the day had been already. "Yes. I thought sure it had us there, and then nothing. It was strange and Qethar later implied it was his doing, but I don't see how."

"Maybe he can persuade the stone dogs in the same way he persuades the stuff of the earth itself. They are elementals, after all."

Triss reared back. "Oh, I don't like that thought, not one bit."

"But do you think it's possible?" I asked him through a sudden yawn.

Triss was our resident expert on elementals—being one himself.

"I don't think you could do it to one of us," he replied, his voice low and worried, "but then there are no Others who have a history of alliance with the shadows. And, well, how can I put this kindly? The stone dogs aren't the smartest of the elementals. Much smarter than a dog, certainly, but not even as smart as most men."

I gave him my best raised eyebrow. "Thanks for that vote of confidence, partner."

"Oh, you're significantly smarter than most of your breed . . . about some things at least. And that makes you nearly as smart as the average Shade. But neither you nor I have anything like the mind of one of the great water dragons. A shinsan or a kuan-lun, say."

"He's got a point," said VoS. "You humans are smart enough in your own way, but you're a long way from the brightest lights around."

Vala sighed. "Is she going to go into her thing about how much smarter she is than we are again?"

"It sure sounds like it," said Stel.

"It's not that I'm smarter per se, it's just that I have twice the thinking power, so I can do things both faster and better than either of you could alone."

"Not if I knock back this bottle of whiskey." Vala picked up the Kyle's. "And I've got to tell you that's what this whole line makes me want to do. What do you say, Stel?"

"I'm in . . . if this whole superiority spiel goes on much longer."

VoS snorted through both of their noses. Then she sighed and shook her heads. "Fine. I'll stop. Now, what's next on our agenda?"

I got up and hunched my way over to the chimney, sticking my head through the curtain and looking up. A clear patch of pale rosy gray sky showed at the top.

I closed the curtain again. "I don't know about you, but sleeping is getting pretty high on my list. I've been awake for something like twenty hours straight and on the run for more than half of that. I'll be a lot more useful for planning in the morning."

"That sounds like a damned fine idea to me," said Stel, and for the first time since we'd gotten her settled, I remembered how badly injured she was. "I'm all in."

"Fair enough," said Vala. "I'm pretty knocked down as well." She looked at the bottle a bit wistfully. "Though I wouldn't mind a nightcap if any of you wanted to join me."

I was quite tempted, and because I was tempted, I shook my head. "Maybe tomorrow."

Stel had already slid down the barrel to lie fully prone and closed her eyes.

VoS said, "Save it. You were right about the spell earlier. We're going to have to make some alterations to our appearance before we can show our faces out on the street again, and that means the bonewright. You don't want a hangover for that, and after, we'll all three need a drink or five."

Vala grimaced and set the bottle aside. "We will at that. Aral, this is your aerie. Do we need to set a guard?"

"No, the main risk is a fire started by our downstairs neighbors and sitting up worrying about it won't make one jot of difference as to whether that's going to happen. Beyond that, there's Triss."

My little dragon nodded and spread his wings. "Even with the sun coming up it'll stay pretty dark in here. Once the magelight's out, I'll be completely free to roam around the attic and even to slip down through the cracks once in a while to check on the caras-heads."

"Don't you sleep?" asked Vala. Stel had already started to snore faintly.

"Mostly I nap, and much of that in the day, while I'm dragging along in Aral's shadow, going bump-bump-bump down the street and pretending I don't exist. I'm wide awake now and will be for hours yet."

"I guess that covers everything." Vala looked at me. "Do you want me to do something about the light since I'm up?"

"I was just going to toss it in an amphora and tamp the lid down. You're welcome to the duty if you want it."

She nodded and took down the light. The shadows, all but Triss, danced wildly around as she followed my suggestion. Then it got very dark and I had to follow her progress by ear. First, grabbing up her blanket. Then, laying it out and settling herself.

I'd expected her to put it down beside Stel's, but she actually chose a place on my farther side, bracketing me between her and her bond-mate in a way that I found a bit discomfiting. Especially as she took a spot rather significantly closer to me than Stel was—just the other side of the little half barrel where I'd been sitting.

"Aral?" she said after several minutes had passed.

"Yes."

"I wanted to wait till Stel went to sleep and took VoS with her before I said this. I'm glad we found you. I don't think we could do this on our own. Thank you."

I heard a faint noise from her direction, but couldn't figure out what it was until Triss whispered in my ear. "She's reached her hand out along the left side of the barrel. I think she wants you to squeeze it."

So I did. "You're welcome."

She squeezed me back, then withdrew her hand. "See you in the morning, Aral. Sleep well."

"You, too, Vala."

I woke to the sound of chalk scratching across rough boards, and rolled up onto my side to find Vala busily scribbling diagrams on the floor at the far end of the room. The attic felt breathless and baking, like the inside of a huge and dusty oven, and I guessed it must be getting near sundown. I wiped sweat off my face and took a second look at the huge splash of multicolored chalk Vala was creating.

"That kind of spell, is it?" I mumbled. I've never been much for high magic, especially not the intricate stuff with all the fuss and bother.

"Hush." Triss shushed me from above.

He had climbed high up on the angled ceiling to get the best view of the process. This put him in a very strange position relative to me and the glow of the magelight. Vala had pulled it out and fixed it on the back of the chimney so that it lit her end of the room and left me mostly in shadow. Which meant Triss was just about 180 degrees from where a natural shadow would have been.

I ignored his admonition and kept talking. "I don't suppose anyone's made porridge and toast, or even some of that awful fish soup the locals favor for breakfast?"

"Nope," said Stel from somewhere behind me. "You've got your salted pork, your rice cakes, your salted pork between two rice cakes, or, if you're feeling all bold and experimental, your rice cake between two slices of pork. That one's kind of messy."

I looked over my shoulder. Stel was sitting up against the half barrel with her head leaned back and her eyes closed.

"Ribs bad?" I asked.

She nodded very slightly without moving otherwise. "I took a look under the bandages this morning. It looks like I've been rolling around in raw indigo."

"You want me to get you the whiskey?" I knew how much cracked ribs can hurt.

"No, I can't afford to dull my wits now. Not right before we attempt this damned bonewright trick."

"Maybe you should wait till you're feeling better," I said.

She opened her eyes and met mine, shaking her head slightly. "Without a real healer that could take weeks, and we can't go see a healer until we do something to lower our profile."

"I know a couple of backstreet wound-tailors who will forget they ever saw you if the fee is high enough."

"And how do we get there without running the risk of being seen?"

Stel's face shifted as VoS came to the fore. Even after listening to her tell the long story last night, it was still jarring to watch the shifts in expression and manner when the Meld inhabited one or the other of them. It made the person I'd just been talking to feel like nothing more than a mask to be put on or taken off at the convenience of the creature that ruled them both.

"More importantly," said VoS, "what happens if the Durkoth offer a reward for anyone with information? Will your friends stay bought if they can make ten times as much by turning us in?"

It was my turn to shake my head. "They aren't really friends, and even the most honest of them would probably sell his mother for parts given the right incentive. That doesn't change the fact that Stel's injuries are going to keep her from operating at anything like her best. If this bonewright is that dangerous . . ."

"It is," VoS said flatly. "But we still have to try it."

"Partially *because* of Stel's injuries," Vala tossed over her shoulder, entering the conversation for the first time. "I think that if I work her transformation right I can mend her ribs myself as part of the process."

"Really?" asked Triss. "It's not all cosmetic?"

"No." Vala rose from where she'd just finished a line and turned to face Triss. "Or, at least, it doesn't have to be. If you want to really change the way someone looks, you need to restructure the bones of the face, at least a little bit. That's why it hurts so much. VoS and I don't see any reason why we shouldn't be able to extend that to knitting Stel's ribs back together."

"I'm still not entirely sold on that part," said Stel. "The spell is complex enough without trying something that's not a standard part of the routine. Even the best eavesmen usually don't do much more than surface work below the neck, and you've only ever drilled with this spell."

"It'll be fine," said Vala, but I could see she was worried.

"Wait." I held up a hand. "Are you saying you've never actually performed this bonewright thing before?"

Vala's chin came up. "Not to completion, no. But I can handle it. The structure of the spell isn't that difficult to manage. It's just the pain factor that makes it dangerous, and Stel and I have had a lot of practice dealing with pain. I'd expect spinners like Stel and I to be much better at this than those wimpy old eavesmen."

"But you don't *know* that," said Stel. "And it's dangerous to mess with the big bones. That's what Pride at Valerian said when you asked about making yourself taller."

"That was only because you can't actually add or subtract anything, just move it around. Unlike fat and muscle, there's no good way to make extra bone. If I made myself significantly taller I'd have to thin out my bones so much they'd be as brittle as old porcelain."

"You know, I'm beginning to think I should have taken you up on the offer of a drink," said Stel. "If I passed out we couldn't try this hob-brained scheme."

"You know VoS wouldn't let you do that," said Vala.

"Some days I just want to whack her one," replied Stel. "Unfortunately, the one who'd get hurt would be you."

"And you, through the echo," said Vala.

"That, too." Stel sighed. "Do you have all the chicken-scratching done, Vala?"

"I do."

"Then let's get this over with one way or the other."

Vala crossed to her bond-mate and helped her up. "It'll be fine. I promise I'll take good care of you."

"I'm not worried about that so much as whether I'll be able to do the same for you. I'm not at my best right now."

"That's why we've got to do it, and you're first."

The pair crossed to the chalked up area of the long low room, with Stel leaning heavily on her smaller companion. I got up as well. I wanted to take a closer look at the diagram. I don't *do* ritual magic if I can avoid it, but I was taught the basics, and it was always good to learn new things. Triss flitted along the ceiling above my head, moving in to get a better look as well.

The main figure was a pair of large hexagons that shared one side in common. Sketched in and around the points were great bunches of the usual glyphs and sigils. I'd just started trying to work out the general gist of the structure, when Vala completely snarled my line of thought by the simple expedient of slipping off her shirt, about three feet in front of me.

Her breasts were small and perfectly formed, with nipples like dark coins. She was thin, but not so much so that I could count ribs, and very muscular—an athlete. Before I could even think about turning away or otherwise offering her greater privacy, she skinned out of her pants and underwear as well, exposing a lovely pair of legs and the patch of raven hair at their juncture.

"Uh . . ." I began, but couldn't for the life of me think of anything to say next.

Vala grinned. "I take it you like what you see, then?" She showed not the slightest sign of body modesty and I was reminded that at the Kodamian games, the athletes mostly compete in the nude.

"I think he's actually drooling," Stel said, rather dryly.

I turned toward her, initially delighted at being offered a distraction from staring at the naked Vala. But apparently the spell required nudity for both partners, because Stel was also stripping. Because of her injuries, she'd only just managed to get her shirt off, exposing large full breasts. Beneath were loops and loops of bandages that acted rather like a corset, lifting them up and forward. At that point, I closed my eyes and turned around while I tried to reclaim my composure. Behind me, Vala chuckled low and wicked while Stel snorted amusedly.

"Ah, he's blushing," said Stel. "That's kind of sweet. The legends never mentioned that the Kingslayer was shy."

I wanted to growl at her. For a number of reasons. First off, I'm neither shy, nor am I normally thrown off my stride by the naked female form. Not if I'm somewhere I'd be expecting it, say in a Tienese bathhouse, or on a Kodamian field of sport. But I originally come from a culture where nudity is strongly associated with sex, and if I don't have time to think ahead, that's where my mind goes. Especially with Vala reminding me of the first great love of my life. Though Jax would probably have been more shocked right then than I was. She came to the temple from Dalridia, an even more modest culture than Varya.

Second, there's the whole Kingslayer thing. That guy isn't me. Not anymore, at least. I was him once, but that was before my goddess died and took the Blade part of me with her, the better part of me, really. These days I'm just a jack living in a world of shadow.

I shrugged and turned back around to face the pair of naked women. They were still both attractive, and a part of me couldn't help but react to that, but this time I had it under control.

"I tell you," I said, "you kill one lousy king, and pretty soon people are buying you hats that are three sizes too large with the word 'Kingslayer' writ large across the brim. Don't listen to the stories. I'm no legend, I'm just Aral. What you see is what you get."

Triss had visibly started at my initial comment and now his mouth was half hanging open. "Wait, was that a joke up there at the front?"

"Might have been," I said defensively. "Why?"

"Because it's been an awfully long time since you made one for real, and I'm kind of hopeful right now."

"Didn't have much to laugh at," I replied. "Or, no, that's not it. Say rather that I didn't have much to laugh with, and it'll be closer to the truth."

"And that's changed?" Triss asked, and his voice made it sound like he was trying to keep a particularly tricky spell from exploding in his face.

"Some. Maybe. I don't know for sure, but maybe."

"I'll take that," said Triss.

I turned my attention back to Vala. "Sorry about my silence there a minute ago. The answer is 'Yes.' I do indeed like what I see. You're a very attractive woman." Now Vala blushed, and I turned to Stel who was just peeling off the last of her bandages to expose a huge patch of bruises. "So are you, I might add. Though I think you'd look better without all that black and blue."

Stel didn't blush, she smiled. "It's really not my color scheme. The yellow and green that will come later, on the other hand . . ." She put her fingers to her lips and made a smooching sound.

"Tell me more about this bonewright," I said.

"It'll be easier to just show you and answer any questions you have left after," said Vala.

Vala turned and headed over to help Stel down into a cross-legged position in the nearer of the two hexagons, before settling herself in the farther. The two faced each other, with Stel's back to me.

Vala looked at me over her bond-mate's shoulder with a wicked glint in her eye. "Which do you prefer, Aral, brunette or redhead?"

"Raven, why do you ask?"

"Sweet of you to say," said Vala, whose hair was already black. "But that wasn't one of the options. Brown or red?"

"Then red." Jax was a brunette, and I really didn't need Vala hitting my weak spots any harder than she already was. Not if I was to have any hope of honestly finding the justice in this situation.

"Done." She lowered her hands to rest on her knees with the palms turned up, then began the bonewright.

9

The bonewright was a subtle spell, with no overt gestures or chanting to start things off, just a lot of concentration on the proper sequence of the glyphs and their naming. I could follow along with my magesight, as long multicolored threads of light slid from the tips of Vala's fingers outward to connect to first one ideogram, and then another as she named them. Soon she sat in the middle of a cat's cradle of light: green and gold and scarlet and violet and azure and peach.

Techniques learned long ago helped me make sense of the process, and to store enough cues away that I could probably even hope to remember how it was done later, if someone wanted to know. At that thought I felt a little lead ball form in my heart, because for me there was no one left to tell. The art of mapping a spell was something I'd only ever really used when making reports to the masters and priests at the temple, and now they were all gone into the grave. Triss and I were alone in the world.

I was so distracted then that I almost missed the start of the next stage, when Vala raised her hands to touch her face. More threads of light rose from the glyphs then, connecting themselves to Stel's head and chest, mirroring the structure that centered on Vala. Making tiny, subtle motions, Vala ran her fingertips along her own cheekbones.

In response, the lights touching Stel dug into her face, stretching and twisting, reshaping bones and flesh. Stel grunted like she'd taken an arrow to the chest, and tears began to stream down her cheeks. Though she was clearly in agony she neither screamed nor tried to move away from the threads. Drops of blood broke out here and there on her face, prickling up in the wake of the moving threads.

Her cheeks broadened and thickened at the same time that her lips narrowed. Deeper chin, teeth that shifted to give her the faint hint of an overbite, higher thicker eyebrows, a stronger nose, eyes that went from deep brown to shimmering green, hair lightening from black to a chestnut brown. When Vala finished, Stel was still a pretty woman, but a very different one.

Now Vala's hand moved down, cupping her breasts and squeezing and shaping, shifting from there to her sides and ribs. A tiny high-pitched noise escaped from Stel's lips, like the dying squeak of a mouse, as her breasts grew higher and smaller, their nipples lightening and shrinking. The changes left more blood in their wake, mixing with the sweat that sheeted Stel's skin. She whimpered a little as the color began to fade from her bruises, and I could see her ribs shifting and knitting from ten feet away.

Finally, mercifully, Vala finished. Stel sagged forward as the light left her. But now it was Vala's turn. The threads that had fallen away from Stel snapped back to connect with their counterparts on Vala, collapsing into themselves and doubling in size. For a couple of heartbeats nothing more happened.

Then, Stel's face took on a look of intense concentration as Vala's hand began to move again. The motion was different this time, no less smooth or clean, just much less *Vala*. Though I couldn't have proved it, I could see that Stel had taken control of Vala's body. The fingers that slid along Vala's jaw drawing lines of blood, moved in a firmer, more matter-of-fact way than they had earlier. Still graceful, but a warrior's grace now instead of a dancer's.

It was simultaneously fascinating and repulsive, this obvious invasion, and I wondered briefly if that was how another Shade might see things when I took control of Triss to perform a spell or sail-jump. I wanted to turn away, and yet, I found that I couldn't. It was too fascinating. The process flowed along in just the same sort of way it had for Stel, though Vala made no noise at all.

Features shifted first: jaw lengthened, lips fattened as if by bee sting, cheeks hollowed out under freshly razor-edged cheek bones, eye sockets deepened. Blue eyes became an exotic amber, streaming tears. Short straight black hair shifted to a thick curly auburn, and dropped to hang below her shoulders. A faint scar appeared at the corner of her right eye like the echo of a tear. When her hands moved down, her breasts became fuller and farther apart, though no less firm. A stroke across her pubic hair changed it to match her hair, and that was it below the neck. They made no deeper changes to Vala's body, just shifted the areas that attracted the most attention.

When they had finished, Stel released Vala, or so it appeared, as Vala suddenly sagged forward like a string-cut puppet. For several heartbeats she sort of hung there, looking empty. Then, slowly, she put her hands on her knees and forced herself back upright. Sweat and blood and tears stained her face and chest. She looked like she'd just run an endurance race as she sat there gasping for breath.

"Fuck," she whispered as she began to loose the threads of her magic, letting them fall away one by one. "I hate it when that happens."

"What?" asked Triss.

"I prove Stel right."

Stel, who didn't look like she felt any better than Vala, blinked several times, and said, "Could you repeat that?"

"I said you were right. Are you happy now?"

"I'd be happier if I knew what I was right about."

Vala laughed, or tried to—it sounded harsh and forced. "That bit earlier where I said that a sufficiently disciplined mage might be able to handle this spell on their own. There's no fucking way. If you hadn't been moving my hands I could never have managed to keep hold of the magic. I could *feel* my bones being reshaped—like someone chopping off bits and gluing them on again in less comfortable positions." She suddenly hugged herself, covering her breasts with her crossed arms. "And what it did to my tits . . . never again."

"I'd think a lone mage would need more tools, too," I said. "Like a mirror for starters."

"I don't think so," said Stel. "I wasn't really looking at Vala while I was working with her hands. It's much more about imagining the result you want than it is making conscious visual choices in the moment."

By then Vala'd dropped the last of the glowing threads, and now she simply fell over onto her side without otherwise changing position. Stel was apparently made of tougher stuff. That or she was just more bullheaded. In either case, she forced herself up onto hands and knees and started crawling toward her clothes. Triss, quicker of wit than I was, slid down the wall and picked them up to carry over to her.

"Thanks." Stel crawled into her shirt, then flopped over onto her back to drag her pants over her hips. She tossed her underwear in the general direction of her bandages, then closed her eyes and let her head fall back against the boards with a gentle thud. *"Now we drink."*

Somewhere along about then it occurred to me that I should probably be helping, so I picked up Vala's clothes and brought them to her.

"No way," she said when I set them down in front of her. "I know where those have been." She sighed. "But I suppose I don't have much choice at the moment." Still, she didn't move.

"You could borrow one of my shirts," I said. "I've got a complete change of clothes or two stored here. They're pretty threadbare, but they're clean, and with the size difference it'd just about make a dress for you."

"Yes please."

Stel opened one eye and glared at me balefully as I passed her on the way to the appropriate amphora. "And where were you with your offers of clean clothes a minute ago when *I* was in need?"

"Sorry," I said. "It hadn't occurred to me yet. You're welcome to the other set." I tossed a pair of aging pants and an old threadbare shirt her way. "It'd just about fit you."

She poked at them with a finger. "Ah, you just want to see me naked again. I'd even indulge you if I didn't think changing would hurt more than it was worth. Maybe after I've had a couple of drinks it'll sound like a better idea."

I had no good answer to that, so I just hauled the better of my two spare shirts over to Vala. It fit her more like a tent than a dress, with the too-wide collar continually falling off her shoulder to expose a distracting amount of pale flesh, including the top of a much fuller breast than the old Vala's. And it only covered her to the tops of her knees, a scandalous length in any court in the eleven kingdoms of the east.

That, however, was far less distracting than the changes to her face and hair. I'd only just started to get to know the old Vala, and here she was looking like a whole new person. She didn't even look Kodamian now, more like an Aveni or Osian, though the only place I'd ever seen amber eyes like that was in the mage lands.

"And it's permanent, you say?" I asked as we all moved back over to where we'd created a rough sort of sitting room with the barrels.

Vala nodded and her new red curls tumbled down around her shoulders. "That's going to get really old, really fast." She swept her hair up back off her face, twisting it into a knot on the back of her head for about the fifth time. "I may have to find a pair of scissors before the day gets too much older."

"What if you want to go back to looking like the old you later?" I asked. Triss kept sliding back and forth along the ceiling to get a better look at both Stel and Vala. He'd just slipped around behind them when I asked my question.

Vala took a careful sip of the Kyle's, holding it in her mouth for a couple of beats before swallowing, then passed the bottle over to me. I imagined what it would be like to kiss her then, with the whiskey fresh and sweet on her tongue.

"The bonewright's really not that precise," said Vala. "Between the vagaries of memory and the lack of fine control on the spell, about the best you can hope for is to get to a place where you look like a sister to the old you."

"Some of the older eavesmen probably don't even *remember* what they originally looked like anymore," said Stel. "They've changed their face so many times. Names, too. It's a strange sort of life. Why didn't you change your name, Aral? I'd think here of all places that would have been the easy thing to do."

I took a long pull on the bottle while I thought about how to answer that. It wasn't my first drink, and the bottle was already looking a lot emptier than it had when we opened it. It had been a while since I'd had this much alcohol this fast, and it was hitting me hard. I brought the bottle away from my lips and started to roll it between my palms, just under my nose, letting the rough peaty smell waft over me. It wasn't an easy question, and all the answers I had were hard ones. Triss had frozen when Stel asked it, and now he was peering worriedly my way from behind Vala's back.

It was him I addressed when I spoke next. "I'd like to say it was stupid or habit or some other mistake on my part, but that'd be a lie. I guess the honest answer is that I *wanted* to die. I was away on a mission when the other gods decided to destroy Namara. When I came home, I found my goddess murdered, my friends dead or taken, the temple that was my home pulled down, the grounds sown with salt. . . ." I could feel tears burning down my cheeks and my will breaking, so I took another drink—this had needed saying for a long time, though I hadn't realized it until then.

Triss slid down from the ceiling, and came to curl around my ankles.

"At that moment I thought that everything I'd cared about or believed in had failed, that there was no point in going on. I wanted more than anything to have died in defense of my goddess. At least then I would have been with my friends . . . no, my family. It was almost worse that I'd been successful in my assignment, because it seemed like such a pointless victory. There I'd been, in Gat, satisfied at having performed my duty to my goddess, happy even, when I should have been in Varya fighting to save her. If not for Triss I'd have probably opened my veins beside the sacred pool, a last offering to a dead goddess."

Vala leaned forward and touched my knee. "I'm sorry we asked, Aral. I'm sure Stel had no idea. . . ."

Stel turned around so that both of them were facing me, a very rare occurrence. "I'm sorry, too." Her voice was small and quiet, contrite. "I guess if I thought about it at all, it seemed kind of romantic. Aral Kingslayer, last Blade of Namara, still fighting for justice and the right, refusing to hide his identity even in the heart of enemy territory. What I should have been thinking about was what I'd feel like if I came home to find the Citadel a smoking ruin and all my friends and family dead. I'm a fucking idiot."

I shook my head. "It's all right. It wouldn't have been even a year ago, but it's all right now." And it was, a fact that surprised me. The wound was still there, but it was no longer actively bleeding. "It's a reasonable question. It's not your fault that it doesn't have a reasonable answer. I did it because I wanted to die but couldn't just kill myself because of what that would mean to Triss. I couldn't even admit to myself that was what I wanted without betraying our bond."

I shrugged. "Maybe lying to myself like that is part of why it took me so long to crawl out of the bottle. Speaking of which—" I handed the Kyle's to Vala and dusted my hands together. "You can have the rest. I want it too much to dare drink any more."

I did, too. I could feel the ache in my chest at letting the bottle go. It cost me. The only thing I wanted more was a nice hot cup of efik, but I knew if I started down *that* road again, I'd never get off.

Vala sighed. "It's not very nice of you to go all responsible like that. It sets a terrible example. Fortunately, I'm immune." She lifted the bottle to her lips then froze.

"How much have you two had to drink?" a very muzzy sounding VoS said through Stel's lips.

Vala, or more likely, VoS corked the bottle and put it on the floor. "I take one little nap and I wake up to find my heads packed full of cobwebs spun by tipsy spiders."

"We didn't drink *that* much!" Stel sounded rather like a teenager caught behind the shed with a bottle of cheap sake. "We were going to wake you up soon, weren't we, Vala?"

VoS turned her Vala head my way and rolled her eyes. "You'd think they'd learn how very silly it is to try to lie to the voice in their heads, but somehow they never do."

Triss lifted his head off my lap and looked the Dyad over quizzically. "I don't understand."

"You're wondering how I can be asleep when they're awake?" said VoS. "It's the bonewright. Nasty, nasty spell."

"I can feel Stel's pain," said Vala.

Stel nodded. "And vice versa. In theory, I could also feel Vala's pain at feeling my pain, and so on in an infinite recursive loop that would incapacitate both of us. Part of the reason the Meld exists is to act as a coping mechanism to shut those loops down."

"Now I'm a coping mechanism," muttered VoS. "I like that."

Stel gave VoS in Vala a hard look.

"Oh, all right." VoS shrugged Vala's shoulders. "It's true enough as far as it goes, which isn't even halfway to encompassing all that I am."

"What that means," said Stel, as if VoS hadn't interrupted, "is that VoS sometimes gets a double or even triple dose of what Vala and I are feeling. Because of the level of magical and mental commitment that the bonewright takes, Melds can really get hammered as a side effect."

"When the spell was finished, so was I," agreed VoS. "At least for a little while."

Vala winked at me. "Which is how we came to enjoy a half hour of uninterrupted peace, and a couple of drinks with a handsome Blade."

Then she snorted, or rather VoS did, and shook her head. "Motes, can't live with 'em, can't Meld without 'em. But downtime is over now. We need to get back to work." She looked at me. "You're the expert on Tien, Blade. Where do we go to find the girl, Reyna."

"It's 'Jack' these days," I replied, "not Blade. And this is where the legwork starts. If your Reyna really does have the Kothmerk, as seems likely, and she doesn't want to keep it for her very own, she's going to need to find a buyer." Again, I thought of Fei's corpse, and wondered if she hadn't already tried—there was only one way to find out. Footwork. "I'll start by talking to a few of my night market contacts in case I get lucky." I had my doubts about how much I'd get from them, but I figured I'd give it a go before I brought that up.

VoS nodded both of her heads. "Then, let's go." She started putting on her leather vests.

"You're not going anywhere. Also, I'm going to need some cash to buy drinks and grease palms."

"You're wrong you know," said VoS.

"About what?"

"We are coming with you."

"One, it's too risky. You've only just changed your appearances and now you want to be seen with me again? Two, I'll get better information if I'm alone."

"I'm going with you," said VoS. "We can always do the bone-wright again if we have to." She sounded absolutely firm and calm, though both Vala and Stel winced at that suggestion. "We can have a huge time-consuming argument about this, but the results are going to be the same either way. I'm coming with you."

"Give me one good reason."

"You just told us how much trouble you had giving up this bottle." She held it up. "Now you want me to hand you a large sum of money to go fishing through the bars of Tien. Don't you think that would be better done with a little bit of extra backup?"

I thought about her earlier protestations of absolute faith in who and what I was and how this new argument showed a distinct loss of some of that faith. Then I looked at the bottle, and thought about how much I wanted another drink.

"You might have a point," I said.

So, the Dyad no longer trusted me completely. That was only fair. I didn't fully trust her either.

Stel reached under the tail of her shirt and pulled out a heavy purse, tossing it over to me. "Then lead the way."

"**Look,** Ashelia, I know this isn't your dodge, but I thought you might be able to tell me who to touch for that kind of thing these days."

The smuggler leaned in close as she patted me on the cheek. "Aral, you know I love you, right? You've been a great runner for me in the past, but right now? You're pure fucking poison. The Howlers have your picture up on every wall from here to godsdamned Kadesh and the price on your head would buy a house in a good neighborhood."

"I need this—" I began.

But Ashelia cut me off. "I don't even want to be seen talking to you, much less give you anything that could be traced back to me. I'm sorry, but it's just not going to happen. In fact, in about two beats I'm going to throw my drink in your face. If you ever want to work with me again, you're going to play along by swearing at me as I walk away."

So I closed my eyes and my mouth and breathed out through my nose when she threw the rice-white in my face—you really don't want that shit in your sinuses—and then I hissed obscenities at her back as she sashayed away. After that, I wiped myself off, picked my drink off the Busted Harp's bar, and crossed the common room to sit down at a small table that backed the one where Vala was fending off her third proposition in as many minutes.

This time she used a well-placed boot and a flashed knife to get the message across. It seemed to deter the rest of the crowd as well, at least for a little while, because a space opened up around her and stayed open. Stel had taken up a standing position by the bar so she could back me up if I had any trouble with Ashelia, and there she remained for now. We were doing everything we could to make it look like Vala was with me if she was with anybody and that she and Stel had no relationship to each other.

"That went well," Vala whispered to me as I leaned back in my chair so that our shoulders were only a few inches apart. "If I'd known you were so popular, I might have picked a different jack."

"If you'd picked a different jack, I wouldn't be having these problems." The Harp was the third tavern we'd hit that night and Ashelia was the fifth shadowside player who'd frozen me out. "It's the Howlers that are the sticking point. If it was just the Stingers that wanted me, I'd be getting somewhere. Stinger attention's just part of the price of doing business."

"Stingers? Howlers?"

"Sorry." I chuckled. "When I slip on my shadow-jack face for the locals I tend to fall into the argot. Howlers are the Elite, named for their stone dogs and the way they pursue their prey like a hound. And the city watch wears black and gold, like wasps or bees. Hence, 'Stingers.'"

"All right. So no one will talk to you right now because of the Howlers. Is that going to get any better as we go along, or do we need to try a different approach?"

"Maybe. I thought I might get somewhere with Ashelia, since she's been a bit sweet on me in the past. But apparently that's not enough. What I need is to find someone who owes me big for past favors. Clubfoot Tan or Monkeygirl would have to talk to me, but I wouldn't bet on them knowing what I want. Issa Fivegoats would be perfect since he's a sell-cinders himself."

Stel gave me a quizzical tilt of her head, so I elaborated. "A sell-cinders is someone who deals in hot merchandise. Fivegoats is mostly a low merchant, but he knows people who deal with the serious rarities. He's definitely my best bet for information."

"Great," said Vala. "Where do we find him?"

"At this point? Probably under a rock somewhere. He'll be hiding from me."

"He will?"

"Yep. People have seen me out and about. With the size of the price on my head, that'll get around." I couldn't see Vala's response, but Stel's head turned my way at that. "Oh, don't worry, I'm being careful about which dives we visit. Nobody around here's going to run to the Howlers, because none of 'em want the Howlers to have a reason to remember their faces. But that's not going to keep the word from getting spread."

"I thought you said this Fivegoats guy owed you?"

"He does. That's why he's hiding. If I can find him I can call in the note, but if I can't, he's off the hook. Since I'm poison right now, he's not going to want to be seen with me. Hell, if he can stay out of my way until the Howlers pinch me, he's got a good chance of writing off the debt all together. Nobody shadowside owes nothing to the heads hanging above traitors gate."

"That's a pretty ugly way of looking at things. And these people are your friends?"

"Not really. In Tien, shadowsiders don't really have friends, or at least not many. What we have is professional relationships and debts. Even where there's some genuine affection, business trumps emotion. Take Ashelia. She's let me know more than once that she'd like to have me as a long-term bunk-mate, and I've been more than half tempted from time to time. But the main reason she talked to me tonight was to find out what I want. Then she can sell my questions to anyone who'll deal for them."

"So how are we going to get anywhere?" It was VoS speaking this time, and she sounded really disheartened.

"By digging Fivegoats out from under his rock." I grinned and raised my drink in Stel's general direction. "One of the reasons I'm not being a whole lot quieter about my questions is exactly so that word gets out and scares people like Issa enough to make 'em pull a fadeout."

"I don't understand. . . ."

I chuckled. "I know Issa pretty well, and that includes knowing which rocks to look under. By scaring him into hiding, I'm actually cutting down the number of places I have to look. I'd say it's had enough time to take effect. So, let's go turn over some rocks."

10

———

Because of my newfound notoriety we kept to the chimney forest as we made our way across the city, alternately walking and jumping from rooftop to rooftop. We had to take a slightly different route than I would have alone since VoS had no Shade to sail-jump her across the broad canyons made by the bigger thoroughfares. But there was an easy enough solution to that, as generations of thatch-cutters and other shadowtraders had crafted plank or pole bridges that could quickly be laid in place across all but the largest of streets.

We saw quite a few other chimney runners along the way, since it was a cloudy night, and perfect for a quick bit of second-story work or clandestine delivery service. We pretended not to see them, of course, and they extended us the same courtesy. So no one got hurt. The lack of a moon also could have provided hunting opportunities for the odd urban ghoul or nightghast that had crept in from the countryside, but we saw none of the restless dead in our journeys.

We finally caught up to Fivegoats at a warehouse he used to store particularly hot items while he waited for them to cool down enough to resell. It was a big old stone building on the Royal Docks side of the harbor that had been broken up into numerous smaller stalls that were rented out individually. Regular watch patrols went past at least once an hour, and the only two entrances had attendants who wouldn't let you in unless you showed them your key.

"I don't get it," Stel said to me. "What's a two-kip fence doing in a place that's so upmarket?"

I grinned in the darkness. She was picking up the argot. Fivegoats had just passed by below us on his way into the warehouse—he was easily identifiable even at that distance because of the magelights at the entrance. He'd been carrying three skins and a case that probably held a couple of days' worth of cold trail rations. He was clearly planning on bedding down in his tuckaside while he waited for the Howlers to catch up with me.

I leaned in close to Stel's ear—Vala was about twenty feet behind us, crouched in the shadow of one of the building's light wells. "It's much safer storage than anything up by Smuggler's Rest and the free docks. The Stingers pretty much leave it alone investigationwise, because several important nobles have stalls that they don't want anyone official looking in on. That's why a lot of the smarter night marketeers and smugglers keep stalls here if they can afford the rent. Put on a nice set of clothes and pack your coals in a fancy box and the various minions of the king pay you no mind."

"Coals?" asked VoS.

"Stolen goods so hot they'll burn you if you're not careful," interjected Triss.

"Thanks. Why here, though? If this place is really so high pocket he's got to be running some serious risks by camping out here. That can't be something they normally allow."

I smiled again. "It's not, and the bribes are probably murder. But with the Howlers looking to nail my skin to a tree, staying out of my way is going to be worth a touch of silver—I'm sure Fivegoats thought he'd be safe from having me show up here. He keeps this place quiet enough that I'm probably the only one of his regular runners that knows it even exists.

"And honestly, if I were only what I pretend to be, I *wouldn't* know about it. On top of that he probably figures that if I did know to look here, I'm too hot to risk showing my face in a neighborhood this well patrolled. Now, let's go show him just how wrong he is."

With Stel trailing behind, we slipped back toward the light well where we'd left Vala. The warehouse roof was plenty secure enough to fend off your average thatchcutter or ghoul. It was part of a line of buildings that stood a good story and a half above the surroundings, with twenty feet of empty air between them and their nearest neighbors. The low wall that topped the complex had enough jagged-edged potsherds affixed to it to cut any grappled line.

But they hadn't stopped there. The light wells, which provided a cheap source of illumination as well as much needed ventilation, were covered over with a fine metal mesh that had alarm glyphs threaded through it. They were also narrow and topped with low hanging rain guards, making it just about impossible to get down one. It was a really good system, as far as it went. But it hadn't been designed to keep out a Blade, or any of the other high-end mages for that matter.

That kind of security simply wasn't cost effective for anything short of the layered protection that surrounded kings and great nobles. Even that could be circumvented with the right preparation and a little luck, which is why they'd started calling me "Kingslayer."

I asked Triss to stretch himself out along the edge of one of my swords. As he did so, he opened a door in his soul and became a blade-thin gate into the everdark, the dimension from whence his kind had originally come. With Stel leaning hard on the bricks so that it wouldn't sag and bind the back of my sword, cutting the light well free of the roof took scant minutes. Then we were able to lay the whole thing neatly down, leaving us a nice-sized hole through which to make our entrance. If we'd tried it during the day, the added light would have given us away, but here again the dark and clouds worked in our favor.

Looking down through the hole, we could see a narrow aisle four floors in height with walkways running along the sides to allow access to the storage stalls. Dim magelights provided just enough light for the owners and staff to find their way around at night. I knew from an earlier exploration of the facility that the storerooms ranged from closet sized on the top tier up to a space big enough to park a good-sized coach down on the bottom. Fivegoats had a windowless third-level stall maybe four feet by ten on another aisle.

I lowered myself through upside down and hung by my knees while I extended my arms so that Triss could use them to anchor the great shadow wings he now shaped from his own substance. A guard patrol was passing by on the bottom floor, but they didn't look up and wouldn't have seen much of anything if they had, between Triss's shadow and the starless sky above. When I let go, we flipped over and glided neatly down to the top-level walkway.

VoS tossed me the weighted silk line we'd used to get them onto the roof in the first place. I fastened my end to a rail, while the Dyad anchored hers to the roof with a spell. Then she slid down to join me—first Vala, then Stel. A moment later, the magic faded and the rope dropped free of the light well and I stowed it away in my trick bag.

Fivegoats had stuffed a bit of cloth across the bottom of his door to prevent light from leaking out, but he'd missed the vent along the roofline. He'd chosen to rent a bottom-end Durkoth lock from the warehouse owners. It would have served him well enough against the shadow-jack I was supposed to be, but with Triss able to flow into the keyhole and shape himself into the perfect skeleton key, it didn't even slow us down. As I unlocked the door and pulled it open, Stel leaped through with fighting rods drawn.

By the time Triss had gone back to playing the shadow and I followed her through a moment later, Stel had Fivegoats pinned to the floor with one iron-tipped rod pressed firmly into the hollow of his throat. Behind me, Vala closed the door and took up a position outside, where she could watch for anyone coming our way.

"Hello, Issa," I said in the sweetest voice I could muster. "Did you know that I've been looking for you all over town?"

Fivegoats was not a pretty man, short and stout, with a distinct penchant for fatty kebabs that left him with a permanent grease stain in his ratty little beard. He looked even worse than usual now with sweat popping up along his hairline in big oily beads.

"Aral, my friend," he said, his voice hoarse from the pressure Stel was exerting on his throat, "it's so good to see you looking so well. And such a surprise to find you here at my little tuckaside."

"Looks more like a fallback to me." I poked at one of the skins with my toe. "And like you were planning on staying here for a while. Perhaps there was someone you didn't want to see?"

Fivegoats was sweating more and more by the second. "Of course not. I was just having a small libation and letting it get a little darker before I hauled a couple of rarer items back to my shop."

"Really?" I lifted the lid on what I had taken for trail rations earlier. It was full of oiled paper packages of salted meats and dried fruit. "You don't say. Because, if someone was to ask me about my good friend Issa Fivegoats—who just happens to owe me his miserable skin—I'd have to say it looked like he was trying to slither out from under one of his debts. That he was hoping to stay out of someone's way until that someone's head went up over the traitor's gate. That's what I'd say."

Fivegoats closed his eyes for a moment. "Please don't hurt me, Aral. It's just that I'm not a brave man and you're not long for this world, and I really, really don't want to leave it with you. You *know* me. I'm a coward. Right now it's dangerous to even be seen near you, much less give you any help. I'm happy to pay my debts. I just don't want to die for them, and it's not only the Howlers after your hide. There are Others looking for you, too, though they're very tippy-toe about it."

"You don't say. . . ." That was news to me.

Fivegoats lowered his voice. "Yeah, I don't know what you did to piss off the Others, but I hear that there's a small fortune available for anyone who drops a whisper on you to any Durkoth in the city before the Howlers can get their teeth in you."

"That wasn't so hard, now was it, Issa? I think we can deal. You want to pay your debts and you don't want to die. I want a little of what you owe me, and I don't want to kill you. I'm no black jack and I'd rather not start building that reputation by killing an old friend. So, talk to me. Where'd you hear about these Others?"

"It's not up on any posters, if that's what you mean. But it's definitely starting to get around the night markets. Some Durkoth that calls himself Chetha or Karath or something like that's been showing that poster around and asking about you real quietlike. Says he wants you alive and unhurt."

"Qethar?" I said, emphasizing the throaty "hch" sound at the beginning of the name.

"Could be, yeah. Rumor says people that piss him off get buried, and he's not real picky about killing 'em first. Fucking scary, them Others."

That was *very* interesting. Especially the bit about wanting to keep me away from the Howlers. I wondered what he had learned since our last encounter that had him so eager to find me again.

"Good stuff, Issa. A real solid start." I waved a finger at Stel and she removed the rod from Fivegoats' throat and the boot from his chest, moving back to lean against the door. "Now tell me something else I want to hear. You're getting real close to walking away with all your bones intact."

Wisely, he chose not to move, remaining on his back. "What else do you want to know, Aral, my old friend?"

I gave him a hard look and he flinched and held up his hands between us. "All right, all right. Maybe I've heard a few things about the questions you've been asking on the street. I don't know where you can find this girl you're looking for. I also don't know anything useful about a"—he paused—"'very valuable bit of Durkoth sparkle that she might be trying to hawk.' Though I *have* heard she's still trying to find a buyer, or was three days ago."

There went my theory that Reyna was Fei's corpse. At least if Issa's information was good. *"Really?"*

I tried not to let any of what I was thinking show in my face, but Issa flinched at something he saw there anyway. "No, Aral, it's true. That's absolutely all I know. What I might know is who *would* know something. I don't deal with the really big stuff, and Other artifacts are a complete mystery to me. You know that if you know me at all. But I do hear things. If you wanted to move an item like that quietly—and I *would* have heard if someone tried to auction something that hot on the open market—you'd go to Miriyan Zheng in Goldsmith's Lane in the Highside. She's the expert, talk to her."

"I hate to have to do this—" I began, bending down to reach for his collar.

"Wait, wait." Fivegoats held up his hands again. "I told you the truth."

"Maybe. But you know I can't go anywhere near Highside with the Howlers looking for me. I might just as well saunter up the road a piece from there and hand myself in at the palace. Tell me something I can *use*, Issa. I promise it won't get back to anyone who'd take it the wrong way."

"All right, all right. Miriyan does most of her work out of the Highside place—she's a very fancy bit of business. But if you want to move cinders in Tien you've got to have a toe in dockside. I can put you on to her roost in Smuggler's Rest. It's run by a guy named Coalshovel Shen, and *he's* got a little caras problem that you could maybe use to pry a bit of news loose."

I smiled at Fivegoats and offered him a hand. "There, you just bought back a piece of what you owe me with no blood spilled. Not so hard, see."

He took my hand, and I pulled him upright. "Then you're *not* going to hurt me?"

"It's not something I ever *wanted* to do, Issa. And now I don't have to."

Fivegoats edged backward to sit against the wall. "Then toss me that skin, if you will. I really need a drink."

Stel hooked the cord with one of her rods, and flipped it through the air to Fivegoats. He opened it, filling the room with the floral bite that accompanied the better rice wines. It smelled wonderful. After taking a good pull off the skin, he offered it to me.

Regretfully, I shook my head. "No thanks, Issa, I've got business in Smuggler's Rest just as soon as I get an address."

"The place is down in the luff, next to a kip-claim and three doors to the right of the Spliced Rope. It's got the usual sign in the window, and you never heard nothing from me, right?"

"Not a word, Issa, not a word." I touched my finger to my lips.

"You're a good man, Aral, and not so hard a jack as your reputation."

I let my smile fall away. "Don't you believe that last, Fivegoats, not for a minute. If I'm soft with you today it's because you've given good value. I may not play the bone-breaker when I don't have to, but when I have to, I can be a very hard jack indeed. Never doubt that, and you'll get to keep wearing all your bones inside your skin."

Fivegoats looked at me, swallowed hard, and took another long pull at his wine. He didn't say another word as Stel and I departed, and neither did we. We collected Vala and were just heading back for the little trapdoor we'd made of the light well, when a sharp whistle came from that general direction, followed by the ringing of an alarm bell.

"I think they just closed the back door," said Triss.

"Now what?" asked VoS—the Meld had visibly taken complete control the moment the alarm sounded, pushing Vala and Stel down beneath the surface.

As a matter of reflex, I'd started cataloguing escape routes while we were on our way in. Assassins, even godly ones like Blades, spend an awful lot of time running away. Keeping one eye on the exits is nearly as deeply ingrained as breathing.

"How well do you swim?" I asked.

"Good enough to compete at the Kodamian games, but nowhere near good enough to medal." VoS sounded as though that latter disappointed her.

"That's better than me." I reversed our course, heading for the nearest set of stairs up to the top level. The bay was a long way from the building and the Dyad would need more altitude to make the jump. "I don't suppose you happen to know a good fast charm for breathing underwater that doesn't need a bunch of diagrams and suchlike?"

"Actually, yes."

I gestured for VoS to precede me up the stairs. "Excellent! Turn right at the top of the stairs and start running."

Somewhere below and behind us another whistle sounded. A moment later, a quarrel thunked into the bottom of the stairs.

"Triss, cover me."

My familiar pooled briefly around my ankles, then slithered his way upward, surrounding me in a cool, silken skin of shadow. When we got to the upper walkway, I turned and knelt with my hands on the stair supports. Taking full control of Triss through the bond we shared, I focused my nima and released a blast of magelightning into the wooden stringers. With a deep tearing noise and a shower of splinters, the stairs fell away beneath me. The smells of dust and freshly sawn wood filled the air.

VoS anticipated me, and by the time I caught up to her, she'd destroyed the stairs at the other end of the fourth floor walkway and moved on to the end wall. Several more quarrels thumped into the wooden planks beneath us as we ran, but the guards hadn't yet thought to climb the opposite stairs to get a decent shooting angle. I was just about to tell VoS we needed to make a door when she raised Vala's battle wands and let loose an enormous burst of magical force.

Masonry exploded outward from the point of the blast, sending a huge chunk of the wall crashing out into the dockside street below. The walkway sagged alarmingly as it lost its end supports, but the cantilevered beams that stapled it to the stalls kept it from collapsing. I spared a moment to hope that VoS had planned ahead for that and not just blown the wall apart without thinking about it. I stuck my head through the cloud of powdered mortar and shattered sandstone that marked the demise of the wall, and looked down. There was maybe forty feet of street and dock between us and the bay. Way too far for a normal jump.

"Can you make that?" I asked, but VoS was already moving, tossing one of her battle wands to Stel as she quickly backed up.

Before I could so much as hazard a guess as to VoS's plan, Vala had already taken a running jump through the hole in the wall. Turning in midair, she aimed her battle wand at the building below me and let fly with another burst of energy. The backlash of the blast pushed her out and away to splash down in the bay. Stel followed her a moment later, using the borrowed wand and leaving me to summon up wings of shadow and bring up the rear.

Mine was a gentler descent. I glided out and down, crossing over the docks perhaps thirty feet above the water's surface. I was trying to spot the Dyad, when a pillar of ochre light like a giant's staff drove up from a spot maybe a hundred yards away along the bayside street and swung around to meet me. Firespike! The spell caster led my course perfectly, Elite work if I was any judge. He would have batted me neatly out of the sky, if not for Triss wrenching free of my control and collapsing his shadow wings to send us plunging toward the dark water below.

Even so, the swinging pillar of orange light slid along my chest, and clipped the side of my head as I turned away from the burning pain of that contact. It felt like I'd been grazed by the fiery tongue of a gigantic hunting salamander. I was already dazed from the sudden severing of my deep-channel connection with Triss when he'd broken himself free of my command. Now the added pain and shock sent me to dance along the edge of unconsciousness as I tumbled through the air.

The surface of the bay slapped the right side of my body like the cold dead hand of a drowned titan but I barely registered the impact. Polluted water rushed into my nose and mouth as the weight of my equipment dragged me under, but somehow I couldn't bring myself to care. Fortunately, Triss was on the job and before I'd sucked down too much of the dreadful stuff, shadow hands pinched my nose shut and clamped down over my mouth.

Somewhere a million miles away, I thought I could hear Triss shouting at me. But for some reason I couldn't make out the words. My chest hurt both inside and out, and I lost all track of direction as I kept feebly trying to turn my face away from the burns on my cheek. I couldn't breathe and I couldn't think, and more than anything I wanted to sleep. Just a little nap, a few minutes of blessed darkness to put me right again, but Triss wouldn't let me sleep. I could feel him yanking at the connection that bound our spirits, like he was shaking my soul. Or maybe that was just the tug of the currents.

Then things changed, though it took what felt like several thousand years to register the difference. I'd stopped moving, or maybe the world had. It was hard to tell, because it was all fading farther and farther into the distance. Triss was still trying to keep me with him, but it mattered less and less.

11

I had just about surrendered to the sea and the night when the lightning fell on my lips. It jolted through my face and ran down my throat to ignite my lungs. I screamed and tried to turn away from the pain, but it was already inside me. In the wake of the scream, foul water rushed in, freezing the fire and filling my lungs. I was drowning. Only, I didn't die. Instead, the awful stuff that now gurgled inside my chest brought cool relief and the first flush of returning awareness.

As my thoughts began to flow again, the strangeness of the situation slowly wrote itself into the pages of my mind. I was lying in the dark with thick cold slime pressing against my back and sides. It provided a marked contrast to the warmth that lay along my chest and thighs. I was blind, too, or nearly so, seeing only a few dim and scattered lights through my magesight. The nearest were slender lines like paired worms, with a pair of dots above them. Breathing felt *wrong*, as though the air had gone thick and gelid, but at least I *was* breathing. In and out, in and out, the rhythm of life.

I concentrated on that, focusing first on breathing, then on its implications. I was alive. Alive and underwater. On the bottom of the bay by the feel of the ooze that held me tighter than any lover. And I was breathing. But how? I blinked and blinked again trying to make sense of the lights I saw with mage's eyes. Worms became lips and nostrils. Vala's, a few inches from my own and Stel's farther away, up and back, behind Vala. The spell that allowed them to breathe had lighted the portals of the lungs.

In turn, that meant the warmth that lay its length upon me was Vala's body, and the spell that had saved me was hers as well. I pulled my arms up and out of the clutching muck and slid one hand up along her side and neck to touch those glowing lips—a question, though not voiced. She smiled and leaned in to give me a quick kiss, and I felt the faintest echo of the lightning that had touched me there before. Then she put her hands on my chest, pushing herself up and back, freeing me to rise.

I wanted to follow her, but I was weak and weary and couldn't at first break myself loose of the grip of the mud. Fear shocked through me then, as returning coherence brought with it memories of our situation and a renewed sense of urgency. I began to thrash. I hadn't been without air for long, or I wouldn't have been able to come back from the land that borders death, but every second counted right now.

The Elite who had tried to burn me out of the sky would not willingly follow us into the bay—water was no friend to the stone dogs. But he could send that hound down and under the bay's floor. Even now it might be rising up through the layers of sodden earth beneath me, jaws agape.

Before I could panic, I felt Triss's reassuring presence as he slipped around underneath me. Pressing himself against my spine, he pushed, forcing me up and out of the muck. Long habit made me check my swords and trick bag then, making sure I hadn't lost my most important tools to the horrid stuff. But now what? We had to get up away from the bottom without rising so high as to become visible to the inevitable Elite presence on the shore and docks above.

"What now?" It was Vala, echoing my own question, though it took me a moment to recognize the distorted words for what they were in that medium—still, it was clearer than I would have expected. An effect of the magic, perhaps.

"Up a few yards and out where it's deeper." Tien's bay was a deep one and dredged regularly to keep it open to the largest ships, but this close to shore the water couldn't be much over twenty feet, not enough depth to hide in if they managed to light us up. "We need sea room. Beyond that, I don't know."

"Follow me." Triss tugged at my hand to let me know where he wanted me to go. "We'll cross the bay in deep water."

As I started swimming in the indicated direction, I called up a tiny bit of magic, the precursor to a spell, and let it play about my hand to provide a guiding light for VoS. Swimming a level course with all my gear was hard work. I don't think I could have managed it without the occasional push or pull from Triss. It didn't help that I was still more than a little dazed, and that the side of my face where the spell had touched felt like someone had taken a hot vegetable grater to my skin.

We had gone perhaps a dozen yards when I thought I felt something big moving from right to left down below us, a presence almost more imagined than sensed. At first I hoped that it wasn't a stone dog. But then, after thinking about what else might be moving around in the dark waters, I decided that maybe I hoped that it was.

A few moments later, a brilliant and now familiar pillar of ochre light stabbed down through the waters off to my left—the direction I thought the stone dog, or whatever it was, had taken. The spell briefly lit up the waters around it, but then the bubbles from the steam it created blotted out everything. In the instant of clear sight I got a hazy impression of something big and dark and sinuous getting hammered by the firespike. Something that had been looking our way with an open mouth and lots and lots of shiny white teeth.

My first thought was a shark, or maybe one of the smaller sea serpents that had been spied in the bay from time to time. For an instant I was almost glad to have the Elite up there trying to kill us if it meant he'd saved us from whatever that was. That's when the pressure wave hit, sending me tumbling back and away from the thing the spell had touched, and slamming me into Vala.

I got the confused sense of something vast and pissed off rising up from the floor of the bay.

Then Triss yelled, "Water dragon!" and started tugging me frantically back the way we'd just come.

I realized then that what I'd seen in that flash of light was just the head of a *much* bigger creature. The upside of that was that the Elite on the docks above was about to get a lesson in how bad an idea could be. The downside was that after the dragon was done with them it might decide to blame us for the incident, and that was a very big downside indeed. Because angry dragons are about the worst news there is. Especially if the dragon in question was *the* Dragon, Tien Lun, ancient guardian of the city's bay.

But even if it were merely the least member of the mighty Lun's court, it would be more than sufficient to make an end of us, there in its element, if it wanted to. So I swam like mad, and hoped that the dragon chose not to see us as a part of the problem. Hoping that it hadn't noticed us, or that it couldn't eat the Elite and still catch us before we got out of the water seemed a bit too much like hoping that the Emperor of Heaven would descend from the Celestial City to personally pick us out of the water and set us ashore.

We had gotten about back to where we started from when an

enormous banner of golden light rolled through the water in front of us, cutting us off. It came from our right and lit up a good acre of the bay. Turning toward the source of the light, I found myself facing a dragon that compared to the one we'd seen a moment earlier as a gryphon does to a gryphinx. All I could see of it was the head, but that must have been thirty or forty feet long, and eight feet from top to bottom with whiskers like harpoons.

Its massive jaws were spread wide and golden light poured forth, like flames from the mouth of one of its winged cousins. As I hung there slowly treading water, I couldn't for the life of me think of anything to do or say. Vala and Stel, who paced me on either side, seemed just as incapable of any useful response as I. Only Triss was not frozen. My shadow slid forward between me and the great dragon, his wings spread wide in my defense.

He looked like a toy. Fear filled me as I imagined the great dragon turning that blast of liquid light upon my best friend, and I had to stop my hands from sliding back to draw my swords. Any attack I could make would act as little more than a provocation. But instead of destroying us as it so easily could have, the water dragon closed its mouth and cocked its head to one side, as though trying to get a better look at Triss.

The great banner of light that it had spewed forth did not disperse. Rather, its near end hung in front of the giant face, as though it were anchored there somehow, while the long tail of it curled around to encircle us with light, like some sort of huge fishing net being drawn tight around an interesting catch. The increase in light was painful for Triss—I could feel the echoes of it through our link—but he neither flinched nor backed away from the great dragon.

The creature fixed me with one enormous green eye and I felt a terrible pressure in my head. Intense but brief, it ended with a tearing sensation as something seemed to break suddenly free, and a voice spoke into my mind, *Whither go you, oh Blade? And why come you into my domain?*

I found myself answering in like style. *I come out of necessity, fleeing the forces of Tien's master.* It didn't even occur to me to try to lie. *I would not have intruded if I could have avoided your realm. I wish only to pass from here to the far side of the bay where I have business with a trader in stolen goods who knows things I need to.*

Is your cause just?

I paused at that. Was it? What would my goddess think of what I was doing now if she could see me? Would she be proud? Disappointed? Appalled? That I didn't know the answer to that hurt me. That I could never know the answer . . . there were no words.

I hope so. It was the best I could do. No, it was the best I would ever be able to do.

The eye blinked, then shifted to fall on Triss as the great mind voice spoke again. *What say you, my little cousin of the shadows? Is the cause just?*

I couldn't hear Triss's answer, but whatever it was, the great dragon nodded his head. *Then, so let it be.*

Its nostrils flared and the banner of light flowed backward into them, leaving us once again in darkness save only for the dull green glow of that gigantic eye. For a few heartbeats more it hung there, then an eyelid the size of an Aveni war shield blinked slowly closed.

Before I could think of what to do next, a mighty current sprang up and seized us, dragging us willy-nilly across the bay. If I'd had any doubts about the source or shape of that current, they would have been dispelled in the moment before the current let us go. Just for an instant, I saw that great green eye again, one of a pair hanging unsupported in the water on either side of us as though the dragon carried us in its mouth. Then they wavered and dissipated as the dragon let go of its mortal shape to become one with the waters once again.

The last vestige of the current rolled us into a calm spot at the base of one of the many little piers that dotted the bay and was gone. I didn't have to swim so much as a stroke to put my hand on the bottom rung of the slimy wooden ladder fastened to one of the pilings. I started to pull myself upward, and everything was going fine until my head broke the surface of the water.

The wind across my spell-burned cheek and ear felt like fingers of fire sliding along my skin. When I gasped at the pain, I drew more fire down my throat and into my lungs, and lost my grip on the ladder. The cool water instantly put out the fire in my throat and chest and soothed but didn't completely erase the pain in my face. Vala swam in close then and touched my lips.

"Fool," she said into my ear, though her tone sounded more affectionate than exasperated. "Let me unspell your breath before you try that again."

I nodded and she moved in even closer, pressing her lips against my own. The kiss shocked through me, sending tendrils of what felt like gentle magelightning down my throat and into my chest. There was no denying that it hurt, but in no bad way—more like a lover's teeth nipping at a tender spot. The electric feeling lasted for a few bittersweet seconds then faded away.

Vala's lips left mine. As she drew away, I felt as though someone had seized my lungs and started squeezing from the bottom up, like a parched man trying to get the last few drops out of his water skin. The pressure rolled up through my chest and throat, forcing me to open my mouth as all the water I'd breathed in burst forth like a drunkard's one too many.

Suddenly, I ached for real air again. Putting my hand once more on the ladder, I pulled myself up and out. This time, when the air burned across my injured face, I was ready for it and kept my grip. By the time I reached the top of the pier and dragged myself out onto the wooden planks, I'd grown used to the pain. There were no lights on the smugglers' docks, and it was as dark as the inside of a troll up there. Ostensibly that was because the docks were closed at night, though the real reason was that every time the city tried to put lights up, they mysteriously went missing.

I cleared the way for the Dyad to follow me, then flopped down on my back for a moment. I felt like I'd swum the width of the bay rather than being carried, and I badly needed to catch my breath. Triss must have felt much the same, as he sank down into the shape of my shadow without a word. Even then, hours after the brutal summer sun had gone away, the boards felt warm against my wet back, and the night breeze had no bite to it.

Stel followed me out and lay down a few feet away as well, panting lightly. "I don't suppose we can call it a night now and skip visiting this Coalshovel fellow?"

VoS shook Stel's head. "No, of course we can't."

"Yeah, didn't think so," said Stel.

It was odd how natural that exchange seemed already, where under normal circumstance hearing someone arguing with themselves in two different voices like that would have had me moving quietly away. Somehow, without my really noticing it the Dyad had become a part of my world, a friend even.

I wanted to be happy about that, to take pleasure in the simple comfort of companionship, but the great dragon's question about justice kept echoing and reechoing in my mind. Was my cause just? I looked at Stel and hoped that it was, and that someday I might even be sure of it. But until and unless that day came I had nothing but my own badly flawed vision of the world to guide me. For now it would have to do. Just as I would have to hope that my promise to help the Dyad wasn't going to come into conflict with my promises to Fei.

Vala climbed up to collapse on the edge of the pier then, hanging her head over the water and vomiting noisily. "Eyn and Eva but I hate the way that spell ends." She rolled onto her back and up against my side, giving my thigh a squeeze.

"It didn't seem so awful to me," I said. "I never knew a kiss could pack that much punch."

"Honey," said Vala with a touch of her usual fire, "that part wasn't the spell. That's just me."

I squeezed her back. "Then we'll have to try it again sometime."

"You're on. But it'll have to wait till after I get something to clean out my mouth. The spell might not be so bad for you and Stel, but I get both ends of the chain and it doesn't open or close with a kiss."

"I could use a palate cleanser myself." My mouth tasted of bay. And since the bay was the ultimate end of Tien's sewer system . . . and well, I didn't like to think about that. "Now, I just need someone to carry me somewhere so I can get it."

"Not going to be me," said Triss from his spot in my shadow. "I'm done for the night. First that river dragon scared me halfway back to the everdark. And then Tien Lun her own self shows up." I felt him shudder beneath me. "You can get your heavy butt up on your own this time."

"*River* dragon?" I asked.

"Yes," replied Triss. "You can tell by the feel of them, though what a freshwater dragon was doing out in the bay and wearing its physical form I have no idea."

"Whatever the reason," said VoS, "it turned out to be a good thing for us. We might have done all right on our own, but you never know, and the dragons ultimately saved us a lot of swimming."

Vala rolled up onto her shoulders and then flipped herself from there to her feet. "We've wasted too much time here already and I *really* need to get this taste out of my mouth."

I turned my head to look at Stel, though it made my cheek hurt. "Is she always like this?"

"You have no idea. In school the other Dyads threatened to sleepspell her every other night. Perky is *not* a standard operating mode for our kind. Not even VoS can keep her under control all the time. Ouch!"

"What?" I asked.

"She pinched herself when I wasn't expecting it. That's just mean, Vala."

"And telling tales on me out of school isn't? Here, let me give you a hand up." There was a scuffling noise as the Dyad got her other half upright, then she approached me. "It's your turn now, Aral."

She extended her small hand to take mine and then pulled me upright with a great deal more ease than I'd have expected, even knowing what good shape she was in. She was so tiny it was almost impossible to believe she could be that strong. I suppose I shouldn't have been surprised given my experiences with Jax back in the day. *She'd* saved my life once, too.

I remembered long distant kisses then and almost against my will found myself comparing them against the way Vala's lips had felt against mine—the magic of a spell vs. the magic of first love. . . . I blushed and shook my head. It was an unfair comparison, to both women.

Together, the four of us headed up the pier toward land. By mutual consent we decided to find a tavern and get a drink to wash away as much of the . . . stuff we'd all been breathing as could be managed. Likewise by mutual consent—with one abstention from Triss—we'd decided it should be a sterilization-strength drink. We passed quite a number of people in the immediate area of the docks, mostly carrying darkened magelanterns and pretending that they couldn't see us.

We extended them the same courtesy, of course, it being Smuggler's Rest. That's how you kept out of the sort of conversations that substituted the club and the dagger for hellos and good-byes. Farther in, we started to pass more legitimate traffic that carried its lights with the shutters open.

Mostly yellow and white depending on whether they could afford magelight or needed to rely on fire and oil, though there were a number of lanterns whose gaudy green glass announced the bearer as open to negotiations where virtue came into play. Some of those were quite elaborate, with filigree on the lens casting intricate shadow patterns that told the streetwise that the bearer was into more . . . exotic sorts of play. Several of those swung their lanterns wide, to play across our feet and legs by way of invitation when we passed.

There were just enough of the poor and reckless out to prevent our lack of lights from marking us as anything too out of the ordinary. I had a tiny thieveslamp in my trick bag, but no one carried those openly. I considered conjuring a temporary light onto a bit of rock, but I'd have had to carry it bare, and that *would* have been even more unusual.

The first obvious tavern we came to had a pair of dim torches out front lighting up the sign of a seaweed-encrusted ship's wheel. Vala went in first—crossing quickly to the bar to place an order, then turning back our way—with Stel and I trailing behind. For this one brief appearance we figured it would be all right to be seen together.

As we came through the door, Stel let out a little gasp, and said with Vala's intonation, "Aral, you should have told me how bad you got clipped by that firespike!"

Then she grabbed my arm, spun me around, and shoved me right back through the door before following after. As soon as we were outside she dragged me off the street and into a gap between two buildings.

"What are you doing?" I asked.

"The side of your face looks like a nightmare, blood and mud and blisters everywhere. I couldn't see it till we got into the light there, but Holy Twins, Aral! You must be in some kind of pain. And that doesn't mention the front of your shirt, which is a scorched ruin. I'm half scared to peel it off of you in case your hide comes with it."

I put a hand on my chest. The shirt was a wreck all right and there were definitely some scrapes and blisters underneath, but nothing too awful. My dip in the bay must have helped stave off the worst effects there.

"That's not too bad, but yeah the face definitely feels like I've been to the wars. I suppose the upside of that is that no one's likely to recognize me at the moment."

About then, Vala reappeared carrying a brown bottle. "Tell someone next time!" she growled at me. "I shudder to think what all that shit floating in the bay has already done with the open wounds on your face. I'm going to have to get pretty drastic with both the magic and this—" She raised the bottle to pour some on my cheek and I winced in anticipation.

"Let's go a little deeper into the dark," said Triss. "That'll let me cover you better and muffle any yelps."

After, we found a bathhouse that catered to the night trades, and I bought the shirt off a passing workman's back for five times what it was worth. Then we headed for the sign of the Spliced Rope and located Coalshovel's offices next-door to the kip-claim under a tiny plaque that said Dry Goods.

We settled in atop the roof of a small unmarked building across the way while we checked the place out and talked through our strategy. This wasn't going to be like asking questions of old comrades in a bar. Coalshovel didn't know me, though he might have heard of me . . . or seen the wanted posters. He wasn't going to want to talk to me about anything half so hot as the Kothmerk, so this was going to be more like a raid on potentially hostile territory.

We decided I should go in first with Vala, who looked basically harmless, to say nothing of distractingly sexy. She'd find someplace to perch that put her eyes on the door, while Stel would keep a lookout from up here. That was the initial plan anyway. But that was before we'd spent the better part of an hour up on the roof without seeing any sign of life from the shop front across the way, despite a number of passersby rather furtively trying their luck with the bell-pull. I began to get a bad feeling about the thing.

"Does that place look a little *too* quiet to you?" I asked quietly.

"I don't know," responded VoS. "I've never done anything like this before. It's a cloudy night and they're smugglers, aren't they? Maybe somebody's out on a run?"

"It's possible, but if that were the case, I'd expect them to have left some muscle behind to keep an eye on the store. If they do any business at all out of the offices, there's bound to be a strong room for larger valuables plus a chest for cash storage. It's not like a legitimate business. They can't give bank notes to their clients. Triss?"

"Something's wrong. The shadows over there look empty and dead. I can't say for sure without thoroughly tasting them, but that's the impression I get from here. The building's been abandoned."

"So what do we do?" asked Stel.

I shrugged. "To borrow a smuggler's terms, what we *should* do is cut our lines and run for the open sea before the law arrives. But that'd leave us as much in the dark as we are now. It's risky, but I think I'd better go in and have a look around."

"You mean *we'd* better go in and have a look around," said Vala.

I snorted. "Sure, but let's not go in through the front door, shall we?"

"Roof?" asked Stel.

I nodded. "Around back first, I want to check the back door before we try anything. Then up the wall and we can cut our way in."

12

A s it turned out, the sellcinders didn't have a visible back door.
What they did have was a rabbit run that exited through a trapdoor on the flat lead roof of the office. It was butted up tight against
the building's nearest neighbor, a taller structure with a series
of bricks removed to make a ladder for the run. So, in event of
emergency: out and up, then over and off onto the chimney road.

The trapdoor was sealed from below with a heavy bolt, but after we'd spent a while listening for activity below, Triss was able to
slip between the cracks and draw it for us. The door opened down
into a narrow space bordered on two sides with rough lath and studs,
implying plastered walls. The bricks of the neighboring building
made a third wall, while a wooden panel with a latch on our side
provided an exit. VoS was sensible enough not to dispute my going
first. She couldn't make herself invisible after all.

The wooden panel folded in the middle like a decorative screen,
so that it could be slid to one side without taking up much space either in the rabbit run or the large cupboard it backed. Maybe five
feet deep by three wide, the space was lined with cedar and full of
hanging bundles of expensive cloth. The cloth gave a good illusion
of a packed space while still allowing for quick and quiet movement, front to back. Light leaked in from a broad crack at the base of
the cedar cupboard's front door, so I spent a few anxious moments
waiting while Triss edged his nose under the door.

"Empty," he whispered after a while.

I slipped the latch on the door and eased it open. The room beyond was filled with the sorts of items you would expect to find in
the back of a legitimate dry goods dealer, if perhaps a little too rich

for the neighborhood. It was lit by a single dim and aging magelamp hung from the ceiling. As I slid forward toward the nearer of the storeroom's two doors, I heard a faint scuff from the cedar cupboard and knew that Vala had started down behind me per our agreed upon timeline.

The door I checked first opened into a narrow front room with a counter dividing it. The second door, at right angles to the first led into a small office with a desk and two more doors, one of which had been reinforced with bands of iron and a heavy locking bar that had been chained in place. The other opened on the front room. That was it. No people, no noise, no sign of occupation beyond the piled heaps of goods.

When I checked the front door, I found it not just locked but also barred from within. Like the strong room, it had been reinforced with heavy iron bands. That gave us an empty building with all of its entrances barred from within. The easy answer was magic, which could drop or raise a bar from without, but that felt wrong somehow.

Still, I checked the front door and the rabbit run and found that the building's owner had gone to the not unexpected trouble and expense of having them tamper-warded. A really good mage-thief could still have opened or shut them without tripping the spells, so that wasn't conclusive, but it was more than a little suggestive. VoS joined me as I was making the check, peering over my shoulder with Stel's eyes.

"Interesting. Do you think there's another way out? Maybe through the strong room?"

"Not the strong room, but there's almost certainly another exit. We need to find it and check, but I'm willing to lay a bet right now that it's all bolted up, too."

"Don't take the bet," said Triss. "The shadows here taste like death, not abandonment. It reminds me of a tomb, except there are no bodies."

A little while later Vala called out low and soft from the storeroom, "Found the back door. It's hidden behind an empty crate and heavily bolted. I agree with Triss. This place feels like death. I'm going to see if I can't crack the strong room without making too much noise. I think I'd better go through the wall from back here. Stel, give me a hand?"

While they worked at that, Triss and I prowled around the building, looking for any further exits. No luck. And the strong room held nothing but coin and bits of expensive flotsam. I leaned one hip against the counter while I tried to find an angle on the thing that I liked. We needed to get out of there, and soon, but I hated to walk away with nothing. Triss slid back and forth across the floor behind the counter in his version of pacing.

"It's way past time we left," said VoS after several long minutes had slipped past without any further discoveries.

"You're right. I just feel like we're missing something obvious and important. It's possible that Coalshovel and his people are all just out for a walk, but that feels wrong. Doubly so since he's a front man for a big sellcinders up in Highside. There's a small fortune in the strong room. You don't just walk away and leave that unguarded when you've got a boss. Not in this business, not unless you're in a mood to watch someone take your skin off an inch at a time."

"You think this is about the Kothmerk?" asked Vala.

"It's got to be. This doesn't fit the way things normally work in Tien. Especially not down here in Smuggler's Rest. No blood. No bodies. Unguarded money left for the first neighbor bold enough to check out the silence . . ."

"So," said Triss, "say it is the Kothmerk. How does that change the equation? What's different?"

Then I had it. "Durkoth. The Durkoth are what's different."

"I missed a step there," said Stel.

I ignored her. "Triss, check the floor. Look for anything strange, any boards that have been moved, anything."

But Triss was ahead of me, shooting across the floor to a spot at the end of the aisle behind the counter. It was on the very edge of the area where he'd been pacing.

"Fire and sun, but I should have seen it earlier. The boards here aren't seated quite the same as the ones around them. I noticed it before, but I thought it was old work because the nail heads are just as rusty as their neighbors, which they wouldn't be if they'd been recently hammered in again."

"But if they weren't hammered down, but rather persuaded from underneath . . ." I said.

"Exactly." Triss slid down through the gap between two boards, only to reemerge a few seconds later. "There's a big patch of dirt under here that looks like it's been smoothed out by a cobblestone layer. No roach tracks, no nipperkin spoor, no fresh fallen dust. It's a subtle thing. A human would need good light and a suspicious mind to see it, but it's there."

"Want to bet the Durkoth ghosted the lot and our missing bodies are down below somewhere?" I wasn't expecting any takers and I didn't get any.

"Sounds like a lot of digging for not much return," said Vala. "Especially since there's no telling how deep the Durkoth would think is deep enough. I wonder if your friend Qethar had anything to do with this. Fivegoats said he was burying people."

I shrugged. "Could be, but I haven't got any answers. This whole mess makes no sense."

"Time to leave?" Vala didn't wait for an answer, just headed for the rabbit run.

I motioned for Stel to follow her and fell in behind.

"**So,** where does that leave us?" Stel was perched on a little dormer with her back to me, looking out over the harbor—she sounded depressed.

"I'm not sure," I replied from my spot up on the widow's walk. The more I learned about this whole thing, the less sure I was of anything. It was a lot like the way I felt about my life.

We'd taken up a roost on one of the larger houses in the nameless little neighborhood between Smuggler's Rest and Dyers Slope. I find that houses with servants are less prone to check out the occasional odd scuffing noise from above. There's always someone else to blame them on and not a lot of communication between the social layers. Given the location, the place probably belonged to a well-off smuggling captain, which meant there was probably also a fair amount of night traffic that no one was supposed to talk about or pay too much attention to.

"What happened to Coalshovel had the look of the Durkoth snipping off loose ends," I continued as the timesman's bells rang one. "Which means that your Reyna probably *did* try to fence the ring through Coalshovel's boss. I wonder if Miriyan Zheng's dead, too, or if she cut a deal."

"Dead." Triss had taken up a perch on the railing—a gargoyle's shadow without the gargoyle. "There's no way she'd have agreed to what happened back there."

I blinked. "You're not suggesting her heart's too pure to betray her own people, are you, Triss?"

"Don't be silly. If she's a typical sellcinders, the question isn't 'Yes or no?' It's 'How much?' I have no doubt she'd sell Coalshovel and whatever muscle might have heard the wrong things. What she wouldn't do is leave the goods in that strong room unguarded for so long. Counting the time we spent on the roof, how long were we there? An hour and a half? Two hours? Plus whatever time it was empty before we showed up."

"Point," I said.

Vala frowned. "Does that mean that the bad Durkoth have the ring now?" She leaned on the railing beside Triss, keeping an eye up the Kanathean Hill behind the house.

"No," I said. "Well, probably not. For that matter, we don't know which Durkoth are the bad Durkoth. Not beyond the ones that attacked your caravan. Nor if there are any *good* Durkoth for that matter. Take Qethar. I have no idea whose side he's on, beyond his own. He *could* be working with the ones who killed your friends. Or he could be an agent of the rightful king trying to recover it for his master."

"I hadn't thought of that," said VoS. "When did it occur to you?"

"It's been kicking around the back of my head for a while, but it wasn't until you said 'bad Durkoth' that it really gelled. Basically, I know shit about Tienese Durkoth politics. They don't have an official embassy or anything but there are as many as a couple of dozen in the city involved in various businesses. But I couldn't tell you if they're all affiliated somehow, or if they're divided into factions, or hate each other's guts, each and every one. I know even less about how they might interact with the broader Durkoth world, about which, in turn, I know practically nothing at all."

"*That's* reassuring," grumbled Stel. "Do you have any other happy thoughts to share?"

"Well, I think it's a sage bet that your little Reyna's still got the ring, at least if she ever had it to begin with . . . and if she's still alive, of course." That was a tough call. I no longer believed that she might have been Fei's corpse, but a lot of people had a lot of reasons to ghost her. "If she's not, it's probably lost. Maybe for a good many years."

"What makes you think that?" Both Dyad heads swiveled to give me a pointed look. "Or that the Durkoth don't have it for that matter? It seems to me the cleanup operation we just stumbled on is the sort of thing the Durkoth would do once they found the ring."

The rare dual scrutiny gave me an uncomfortable feeling in the pit of my stomach. "Because of what she's got. The Kothmerk's pretty much impossible to fence properly, and the scene we just left illustrates that. Touching it can seriously get you dead. If Reyna hopes to get even a tiny fraction of what it's really worth, she needs a buyer who knows what it is. But anyone who knows what it is will also know it's hot death on a platter to handle the thing."

"I'm with you so far," said VoS.

"Assuming she's not a sort of master mage-thief who had everything planned out, that poses a major problem for her."

"But how can you make that assumption?"

I frowned at them. "Isn't it obvious? The only sane way to steal something like the Kothmerk is to do it on commission for a specific buyer who already has a plan for what they're going to do with it. Make the lift, deliver the goods, get the hell out of town. Maybe change your name and learn a new language. What happened to Coalshovel suggests rather strongly that he was involved, which means it wasn't that kind of deal. But there's another piece as well, and that's the Elite."

"Now I'm lost."

Triss said, "The Kothmerk is too big a headache for anyone in Tien to hold onto short of King Thauvik wanting it for something political. Thauvik would be a great choice for a villain in this piece except for one thing. If *he* was the buyer, the Elite wouldn't be running around making a lot of noise and drawing attention to the fact that the ring's in Tien like they did with that raid on the Gryphon." Which was further evidence against the dead girl being Reyna—more likely someone hired to deliver information and then ghosted for her troubles. "They'd be quieter than the neighbors of your average graveyard on the night of the hungry dead."

"What about someone other than Thauvik?" asked Stel. "Surely there are a few rich collectors around who'd want the thing."

"Not if they have even a shred of sanity." Triss turned to face her. "If you fail, is the Archon of Kodamia going to let it go? Or the King of the North?"

"Of course not," replied VoS. "The King of the North might well send an army after it."

"Exactly." I nodded. "Whoever gets a hold of this thing has to know that they're going to spend the rest of their lives looking over their shoulder. No collector with even a shred of sanity is going to sign up for that. For that matter, no sane thief would take such a commission for pretty much the same reasons. The payback's going to be eight kinds of hell on this one."

"Now," I continued, "you can never completely rule out an insane motive on someone's part, but it's such a wild card that you pretty much have to throw it out when you're placing your bets. No, what I think is much more likely is that Reyna is mostly what she looks like, a kid in the wrong place at the wrong time who saw an opportunity and didn't think about the consequences."

"But how could an ordinary kid have done what she's done?" demanded Stel. "I just can't buy that."

"I didn't say anything about ordinary," I replied. "At a guess, she's a mage of some sort, and a powerful one, but not properly trained. She couldn't be, not as young as she is. Probably she's a Natural."

"Or a Founder," added Triss. "If she's summoned up a brand new type of familiar, she could have resources no one else has even imagined yet."

That was an ugly thought, but it might fit the circumstances. Mostly the mage and familiar-gifted get nosed out early and routed into one or another of the existing mage-schools, but every so often one slipped through the cracks. At that point what you have is a magical accident waiting to happen. Talent is going to come out eventually, and if it's a big talent, it's going to come out in a big way, especially under stress.

If it's a big mage gift, what you end up with is a Natural— powerful magic bonded to whatever familiar-receptive creature is closest to hand. A cat, say, or a lesser air spirit. Some creature from a line that's got established ties to some school of magery, in any case. But if it's a big familiar-gift you might get a Founder. Someone who cries out for help and is answered where no one has ever been answered before.

That's how the Blade association with Shades began, before the school was co-opted by Namara, back in the days of Dain. Really, it's how most of the mage-schools started, with one previously unbound familiar forming a bond with a budding mage in a moment of need.

"All right," conceded Stel. "Maybe she's a wild talent who did just get lucky. That doesn't explain why you think she's still got the ring."

"Or that it's lost," I said. "Don't forget that possibility. She may not know exactly what she's got, though I wouldn't bet against her knowing a lot more than she was supposed to. Anyone who can sneak into a Durkoth krith and lift the ring in the first place is more than capable of listening in on any discussions your Dagger in Waiting had with his under-officers. And she certainly has to know that it's incredibly dangerous to touch; look at the trail of dead Durkoth she left behind."

"True enough," said Stel.

"So, she's talented, smart, and knows a bit about what she's got.

If she's not on commission, and we've got good reasons to think she wasn't—in the shape of those dead sellcinders—then she needs to find a buyer and not get dead in the process. We know from Five-goats that she didn't just offer it up on the open market. We can infer from the raid on Coalshovel that she found out who she should talk to and went to them. That means she does her homework."

"Still with you." Vala was looking more interested and less angry, which I took as a win.

"Given all that, there's no way she just waltzed into Zheng's place and offered up the ring. That'd be the same thing as handing herself over on a platter. So, she sets up a meet somewhere she can control and shows the goods. Zheng's not stupid either, so she's not carrying anything like enough cash to make the deal. Neither one of them wants to be there long, so they set another meet where they can talk things over. Someplace public with neither of them carrying the goods."

I got up and started to pace. "Zheng either recognizes the item, or looks it up after the first meet. In either case, she runs straight to her Durkoth connections and they have collective conniptions. At that point, if they were thinking straight they'd have quietly bought the thing from Reyna. But I don't think that's what happened. I think they tried to grab the girl at the meet and it went bad." Which would be another way to explain the dead girl—a decoy hired by Reyna. "Either she got away—good chance, given what we know about her—or they killed her and found out she'd stashed the ring in whereabouts unknown. That's when they started leaning on the Elite and all hell broke loose."

"But why kill Zheng's people? Isn't she on their side?"

"She might be," said Triss. "But they know there are other players interested in the Kothmerk, the Elite for example, and they know she can be bought. If they want to make absolutely sure that no one else can find out what they do or don't know, they need to cut down on the number of potential leaks."

"That's why I think the ring's still out there on the loose somewhere," I said. "If they had it, they'd be halfway to the mountains with it by now and they wouldn't need to get rid of past allies who might come in handy in the future. That kind of thing'll cost you on the street later when you're trying to find fresh partners."

"Alternatively," said Triss, "Coalshovel was ghosted by a different faction among the Durkoth to cut off Zheng's friends from potential allies."

"That's possible, too. The main thing is that there's still too much happening aboveground for me to believe the ring's in Durkoth hands yet. That means Reyna, or her tuckaside."

Stel turned and climbed up to join us on the widow's walk. "I'm still not entirely sure that makes sense, but the whole reason we went looking for local help in the first place was because we were out of our depth here. I'm going to vote that we trust you on this one and move on to the next important question on the agenda."

"Where do we look next?" asked Triss.

"That's an important one, too, but I'm more focused on an even shorter term goal, getting something to eat. We've had nothing but aging trail rations and rotgut this side of the day before yesterday and it's really starting to catch up with me. I want to get some real food into my stomach. Is there anywhere around here we can get a good meal?"

I smiled; the client wants dinner, the client pays for dinner. "I know just the place. It's a tavern called the Spinnerfish and it's only a couple of blocks from here. Dinner's on you."

Stel frowned. Then VoS nodded her head for her.

The Spinnerfish was one of the city's better restaurants in one of its worse neighborhoods. Smuggler's Rest brought a lot of money into Tien through the night market. That ready cash explained part of the success of the Spinnerfish. The rest belonged to the cook, Manny Three Fingers—who could turn fresh fish into heaven on a platter—and to his boss.

Erk Endfast used to make his living as a shadow captain in Oen in the magelands. Before that he was a black jack, or an underworld assassin, if you prefer bluntness. He'd ended up in Tien after the Magearch of Oen ordered his execution. When he arrived, he'd bought up a burned-out lot lying at the intersection of three of the city's shadowside territories and built the Spinnerfish. Now he ran it as the ultimate in neutral ground and enforced that by the threat of sudden death. He'd been a very very good black jack in his day.

Anyone, shadowside or sunside, could come in and have a great meal knowing that no one sane would try to cause them any trouble. Even the Elite would be reluctant to take a shot at us there. Great food and neutral ground made the Spinnerfish *the* place for meets of all kinds. It also meant Erk could charge an arm and a leg for the fancier dishes and no one so much as blinked. I normally had the special, but with the government of Kodamia picking up the tab I figured I'd splurge this time.

We approached the front door carefully, picking a roost in the chimney forest and surveying the entrance before descending to street level. Enforced neutrality inside did not equal enforced neutrality on the street out front, though Erk had been known to make exceptions. It had been years since the last time anyone got ghosted within sight of the front door, though I'd come pretty close to breaking that rule on a previous job. Fortunately, it was a dark night and raining at the time, so visibility sucked.

Tonight there was a fair pile of muscle hanging around outside dicing and drinking while they waited for their various bosses, liege lords, and owners, but no watch and no Elite. I was reminded again that summer was the hunting Blade's ally as it meant all the windows and doors were propped open, showing the tavern to be equally devoid of the forces of Tienese officialdom.

I took a moment to refresh my memories of sight lines, with an eye for sitting someplace where a bounty hunter with a crossbow and a copy of my wanted poster would have more trouble making his shot. I didn't think they'd survive Erk's response to that kind of violation, but it'd be hard to appreciate the payback from the bottom of the lime pits where Tien dropped the corpses of its criminals and paupers.

Once we hit the street I took Vala in on my arm with Stel loitering along nearly a block behind and playing the loner. Normally I like to get to the Spinnerfish early because that's the only way to get a good table, or, in this case, any table. A lot of heads turned when we came in the door. They always do at the Spinnerfish. What was instructive was how many of them turned back around just as fast. Especially among the faces I knew. Nobody likes to play with poison.

Erk himself appeared from the back within a minute of my placing an order for our drinks, a bottle of expensive white wine for Vala, and a tucker of Kyle's twenty year for me. I wasn't about to drink out of anything but a sealed container anytime soon. Not even at the Spinnerfish.

"Aral," Erk whispered when he got close, "what the hell are you doing here?"

13

————•+•————

"I'm just looking for a fish dinner," I told Erk, "and yours are the best in town."

The owner of the Spinnerfish looked less than happy to see me, which came as no surprise. If the price on my jack's face was high enough to buy a house for the bounty hunter that brought me in, the price on my Blade's face would cover a grand old country estate with all the trimmings. And Erk was one of the half dozen people in the city who knew what I really was. Though he'd made it very clear that he valued his neutrality much higher than the price of my head, having me around always made him a little nervous. Present circumstances would compound the hell out of that sentiment.

"I should throw you out on your ear," he said. "You're a very expensive grade of poison at the moment. Especially with your face all beat up like that and drawing extra attention." Then he sighed. "But that'd violate my neutrality. I don't suppose you're enough in funds to afford a private booth?" he asked none too hopefully. He also knows what I make as a jack.

"Actually," said Vala, who had started to look a bit nervous herself, "I think we can manage that."

Erk raised his eyebrows. "New dance partner?"

I shook my head. "Client."

Vala grinned wickedly. "Why not both?"

Before I could think of anything clever, Erk said, "Why don't you follow me."

As we headed for the back and the private booths, Stel came in the door behind us and wedged herself at one end of the bar. Erk led us into a maze of twisty little passages lined with shimmery green gold curtains. The unintelligible buzz of dozens of conversations filled the air. Somewhere near the back of the building he pulled one of the curtains aside to expose a shallow alcove with a table just big enough for two and a pair of chairs.

Vala shook her head. "We want a three seater."

"Costs more," said Erk, but he didn't argue, just led us forward a few yards and opened a different curtain, exposing a tiny U-shaped booth. "Suits?"

Vala nodded. "Suits."

"Should I be looking to direct a third back here?" Erk asked as we slid into the booth.

"Just don't stop the big brunette when she heads back from the bar," I said. "She'll be able to find her own way."

Erk didn't say anything, just nodded and let the curtain drop, but I caught his eyes flicking to Vala as he did it. He was a damned shrewd man and I had no doubt that he'd just made the right guess. Still, him knowing was safer than leaving Stel out in the main room with no backup.

"Am I really just a client to you?" Vala asked with a sexy little pout. "There's no chance for a . . . *dance*." Her voice dropped low and husky on the last word.

I blinked several times. "I . . . uh . . . well—" Then Triss flicked me playfully on the ear, and my mouth snapped shut as I realized I was being teased.

"Not nice," Triss whispered to her over my shoulder. He hung against the back of the booth in my shape, just as the light would have placed him. "But well played."

"Oh, it's not *all* play," said Vala, dropping her voice into a husk again. "All this cloak-and-dagger stuff does set a spark to the kindling, if you know what I mean." She started to reach across the table toward me, then froze as her posture shifted subtly.

"Can we talk so openly here?" asked VoS. "That curtain seems awfully thin and I could hear a lot of people talking on the way here."

"Did you actually hear any words?"

"No, but Vala wasn't listening that closely."

"Wouldn't have made any difference. Erk protects his clients' privacy. This whole area is protected by anti-eavesdropping magic. Though it has no effect on other sounds." Footsteps could be heard coming toward us from beyond the curtains as if to illustrate my point—distinct but not obtrusive. "Take a really close look at the curtains."

She did. "The shimmer's actually a bit of spell light."

I nodded. "Yep, if you've no magesight, they look like dull cut-rate velvet, which is what they're made of. That's why the booths back here are so expensive."

The footsteps stopped and Stel pulled the curtain aside. "How expensive are they?" Her voice was sour as she slipped into the booth, pushing Vala around the curve of the table so that her knee pressed tightly into the side of my thigh.

I laughed. "Expensive enough that there's no point in economizing on the fish."

A frown touched both faces. "Stel was being extra careful to be quiet on her way here. I tried to make her even more so when I heard her coming through Vala's ears, but it seemed to have no effect. Another part of the magic?"

"Yes," Triss said from behind me. "The chances of someone trying a raid in the Spinnerfish are very low. Erk knows where too many bodies are buried. But the clientele here tends to the paranoid and violent, so Erk made sure they'd have plenty of warning if anything untoward started out in the halls. The curtains block sound going one way and amplify it going the other."

"I think we're going to be very glad we took the mission purse with us when we came south after the Kothmerk," said Stel.

Just then another set of footsteps announced the approach of our waiter, who tapped on the wall beside the curtain before pulling it aside. He had my Kyle's and Vala's wine as well as a small chalkboard listing the day's fare. After he took Stel's request for a second wine glass, he vanished.

"What do you recommend?" Stel asked rather resignedly. "We don't get a lot of sea fish in Kodamia, and none that isn't packed in salt."

"If you're all right with spicy, you'll want the grilled spinnerfish with salamanda sauce. It's the house specialty."

"I adore hot, Aral," Vala said while giving me a look that smoldered more than a little itself.

Stel rolled her eyes at her bond-mate. "Don't you think you're laying it on a little thick?"

"We're on a compressed schedule for everything else while we're here. Why not the flirting?"

Stel ignored her and turned to me. "What's in the sauce?"

"No idea, it's one of Manny's secret recipes, though I feel confident in saying that no actual salamanders were harmed in the production of the stuff."

"Oh, just get it, Stel," said Vala. "I'm sure you'll love it." She turned my way again. "Don't let that gruff exterior fool you. She's at least as adventurous as I am. She just feels she has to play things serious now that we're in the field."

"Well, you're certainly never going to do it," countered Stel. "I figure it's VoS's job. That's what Melds are for, right?"

VoS sighed but let it pass. When the waiter came back we ordered up three plates of the spinnerfish for dinner and a small bucket of unicorn scallops for an appetizer. We had just started to dig into the main course—a lovely flaky white fish lightly kissed with a spicy-sweet green sauce—when a distinctly bootlike tromp sounded in the hall outside. In response I drew a dagger from my own boot, an action that instantly drew Vala's attention since the proximity of her leg to mine meant the back of my hand slid along her calf in the process.

"What's happening?" she whispered as she pulled out her battle wands and laid them in her lap.

"Not sure," I responded. "But the only people who wear those sorts of boots in this weather all work for the Crown."

The clomping stopped right outside our booth and a knock sounded on the wall. If there was going to be an assault it was certainly shaping up to be a polite one. I held up a hand to signal the Dyad to wait. The knock sounded again and a hand pushed the edge of the curtain aside.

"Aral, you in there?" The voice was low, barely above a whisper, but it sounded familiar.

I reached out and tugged the curtain fully out of the way. A man in the yellow and gold of the city watch stood in the hall. He had a sergeant's triple sword insignia on his shoulder patches.

"Hello, Zishin." I nodded the faintest of bows. "What does Captain Fei want?"

"A meet." He set a folded slip of paper on the table, then turned and walked away without another word.

I reclosed the curtain, then picked up the slip. It had two words on it, a place and a time.

Stel raised an eyebrow at me and I handed it across. "Nonesuch?"

"It's an alley-knocker." The eyebrow went up again.

"An illegal tavern," interjected Triss. "It's on the western edge of the neighborhood we call Uln North or the Magelander's Quarter, right where it bumps into Little Varya."

Uln North centered on the wedge where the Channary Canal

met the Highside Canal, a mile and a half or so east of the Palace Quarter. I knew the alley-knocker well because they'd started to sell efik there, and even though I had no intention of ever going back to the stuff, I kind of kept an eye on the trade. I wasn't sure whether Fei had discovered that I went there, and was trying to send me some sort of message, or if it was just unfortunate coincidence, though I suspected the former. Not much gets past Fei, and why else would she expect me to know where the place was?

"How far away is it?" asked Stel, tapping the paper.

"If we take the chimney road, something over an hour. We could get there faster by taking a boat and using the canals, but if we ran into a customs cutter we'd have to fight our way out."

"Are we going?" asked VoS.

"I don't know about you, but I'd better. Fei's . . . well, not quite a friend, but more than an ally of convenience. She's important to this city." And I really really hoped my business with her wasn't going to get in the way of my business with the Dyad.

"That matters to you?" The Meld sounded casual, but I noticed Vala had a forkful of fish hanging halfway to her mouth and had for some time.

I paused to ponder the question. I hadn't really thought about it that way before. I'd originally come back to Tien in search of my own death. I could admit that now. After the destruction of the temple, there wasn't any place in the eleven kingdoms that I could have gone where there wasn't a price on my head simply for having been a Blade. But here in Tien there was a second, much larger reward because I was the Kingslayer. The current king hadn't cared for his half-brother any more than anyone else did, but he also didn't much like the *way* I'd opened the throne for him to take the seat.

"Tien does matter to me," I finally said.

"You sound surprised." Vala's fork still hung in the air.

"I am. I hadn't expected to be here half so long as I have. I guess that somewhere along the line it turned into home."

I turned and looked over my shoulder to see what Triss thought of that, but all I saw was my own shadow. If Triss had an opinion, he wasn't in the mood to share it just then.

"So we need to go meet this Fei," said Stel.

"I do, but you're free to meet me at the fallback if you'd prefer. I owe Fei a major favor or two, *and* she's got a ton of leverage on me if she chooses to use it. I can't ignore this meet." I didn't mention that I could get there faster without them, though whether that was because I wanted the company, or just because I didn't feel comfortable with them out of my sight, I couldn't have said.

Vala sighed. "Guess we'd better eat fast then. It's a shame, because this is really delicious."

The closer we came to the Nonesuch, the unhappier I got about the whole thing. The Magelander's Quarter was well outside my normal haunting grounds. I'd made a point to learn the streets, and this particular alley-knocker was a place I'd visited before, but that wasn't the same as really knowing the place. For that matter, I didn't think Fei spent much time in the neighborhood either.

Unlike her beat-bound fellows, the captain's assignment covered the whole of Tien. But it focused on the trouble spots, and I'd never heard of the local contingent of Magelanders causing anyone any problems. The rest of the watch was supposed to stop and investigate crimes—that whole protect and serve thing. But Fei and her comparatively tiny force had a different job. She was supposed to keep the peace using whatever means were necessary.

In her case, that meant keeping a piece of every major illegal operation in town. If you worked the shadowside of the street, Fei knew your name. If you worked the wrong play in the wrong place, or made a ruckus in a rich neighborhood, she put your name on her list. Then you'd get a visit from Fei's Mufflers—so called because they kept things quiet. If the play was a minor one, you might only get a couple of broken fingers out of the deal. If it was a big one of the sort that drew noble attention or killed the more upright type of citizen in any numbers, you could end up floating out to sea in a nailed-shut barrel.

The Magelander's Quarter wasn't Fei's kind of place any more than it was mine, and it was a damned sight closer to Highside and the palace beyond than I wanted to be while I had the Elite out looking for me. It was nearly five bells when we finally set eyes on the Nonesuch, and the coming sun had painted the scattered clouds over the ocean a pale shade of coral. It was certainly not cool out, but not yet hot either—the best you could hope for at this season. We'd made our way to the top of a tower on a temple to Shan about two blocks down the street from the Nonesuch. I wanted to give the whole area a look over before heading in and Shan's timekeepers built high towers.

Down in the narrow streets, the last of the night people were wending their way home, marked out by the lights they still carried slowly along like ten thousand exhausted will-o'-wisps. But the first of the morning people had come out as well. Carters and delivery-men brought in the country milk and a bewildering variety of fresh produce for the city's breakfast. Laborers and craftspeople hurried to get to work. The day watch were in the process of replacing the freaks and ne'er-do-wells who populated the night shift. Most of the newcomers hadn't bothered with lights, relying on the early sunrise of summer to see them on their way.

I watched for patterns in the moving crowds around the None-such, voids that could mark out hidden Elite or other frightening individuals, places where the human current moved faster to get away from something that spooked them, or slowed down too much because of a choke point. Like most of Tien's neighborhoods, the Quarter got steadily more residential as you moved deeper into its heart. Traffic reflected that, with more big oxcarts circulating around the edges on the large thoroughfares while the in and out mostly happened on foot.

The Nonesuch lay in the borderland between the Quarter and Little Varya, about a block from the main road that ran between them, where the two types of traffic mixed most heavily. There were plenty of little voids and eddies in the turbulence that created, but no more so than anywhere else in sight of our position and I had to conclude that my misgivings had no evidence to support them.

"Looks like we go in," I said.

"You don't sound very happy about it," replied Triss from within my shadow.

"I'm not, but I can't put my finger on why. I just feel uneasy." I looked at the Dyad. "Maybe you should stay back here while I go in with Triss."

"I don't think so," said VoS. "This has to be about the Kothmerk, and I'm not getting shut out."

I shrugged. "You're the client."

As VoS slipped back into the depths behind the faces of Vala and Stel I couldn't help but wonder how much of their reactions and emotions reflected on their Meld. VoS was clearly more cautious of me than Vala, who looked somewhat embarrassed by VoS's com-ments. Stel was harder for me to read, but I think she now trusted me more than VoS did as well, though she'd started out leaning the other way.

Who was my client, really? Vala? Stel? The pair of them? The Meld? All three? I couldn't sort that out in a way that satisfied me, but the better I got to know the Dyad the more I knew that I didn't think of them all as one unit. Which was maybe craziness on my part, but true nonetheless. They had different wants and needs and possibly even slightly different agendas.

Triss nudged me then. "Let's get this done before the sun finishes coming up. It's going to be a bitter-bright day and that will limit what I can do for you. Besides, we're almost past Fei's meeting time and she's going to be pissed if we're late."

In seeming response to Triss's words, the great bells in the tower below us began to toll the hour. I made a "follow me" gesture to the Dyad, and headed for the back of the tower where we'd climbed up.

As had become our habit, Vala accompanied me to the door of the Nonesuch, her hand tucked into my elbow, while Stel trailed behind pretending she wasn't with us. It put a distance between the bond-mates that they found uncomfortable, but Stel was actually the one who'd originally suggested it. The Elite were looking for Aral the jack, and/or the female Dyad he'd last been seen with. The fact that Dyads virtually never came in mixed sex pairs meant that the simple act of having Vala and I play the couple, with Stel substantially out of the picture made us all much less visible.

The sign over the narrow door showed a chimera-like creature made up of impossibly mismatched parts. Six legs, each from a different animal and each a different length—horse, lion, spider, monkey, rabbit, and a seal's flipper. Four heads on four contrasting necks—hippo, salamander, raven, and mole. Two tails, one a snake, one an elephant's trunk. The body of an enormous aardvark. The Nonesuch. I opened the alley-knocker's door and exposed a rickety set of steps leading down into the dark—more ladder than stairs.

Vala eyed them dubiously. "There's really a tavern down there somewhere?"

"A pretty big one actually. There's another door at the bottom and it opens into a series of galleries that were a part of the old sewer system before they hired in Durkoth to dig the whole thing deeper down into the bedrock."

"And they serve food there? In the sewers?"

I laughed. "It's been high and dry for five centuries, plenty of time to clean things up. This is one of the few parts of the city where basements make any sense because we're above the water table but not yet so high that they have to be cut out of stone."

"All right." She started down the ladder. "But I'm glad we ate before we came, and I'm not drinking anything that doesn't come in a sealed bottle with a familiar label."

"That's always a good idea at an alley-knocker," I called down, having decided it was better not to test the steps with two people at the same time. "You never know when a shadow-side distiller might decide to cut the product with a little wood alcohol or add in some of the more interesting sorts of mushroom."

She looked back up at me. "Well, *that's* reassuring. Why don't—" Vala's expression went suddenly far away.

Her voice shifted and it was VoS looking through her eyes. "Aral, it's a trap. Durkoth. They've grabbed Stel." She whipped out one of her battle wands and pointed it straight at my face.

Before I could move, she'd blown the ceiling out of the little staircase. "Run!" she cried and then the earth opened beneath her.

I leaped straight up and caught the jagged lip of the floor above, hauling myself up into someone's parlor. I didn't want to leave her behind, but the familiar link meant that if they had Stel, they had Vala, too. All that my staying would do was add another name to the list of prisoners. Triss slid upward, sheathing me in shadows as I looked around for my next step, a door leading to the stairs perhaps.

A chair toppled over as the building began to shake. It felt like a giant was pulling at the foundations. I opened my hands and pointed my palms at the ceiling. Triss handed me the reins of his will, and I let loose a burst of magelightning, shattering plaster and lath and opening another hole. Up I went. And again. Through an attic crawlspace and onto the roof with a red summer sun rising over the bay. Its angry rays turned the water to blood. Flames fell around me as a sorcerer of the Elite ran out into the street in front of the Nonesuch, lashing at me with his magic. Major Aigo!

Triss screamed and my shirt began to smolder where the fires had touched it. I felt the heat like a slap along the injured side of my face and had to fight down the urge to strike back—more for Triss's sake than my own—because we couldn't afford the delay. Instead, I pushed Triss outward to form a cloud of shadow around me and I ran, leaping across a cramped wynd that ran between the Nonesuch and its nearest neighbor to the southwest.

Fire bloomed red and raging in the roof of the building that held the Nonesuch, sending smoke clawing skyward. A fountain of sparks went up somewhere behind me and whistles began to sound, calling the watch and any other forces the Elite might have in the area. A stone dog howled its deep hunting cry.

The shaking that had battered the Nonesuch followed me to the next building over and I stumbled, almost missing my jump across the narrow street that divided the block holding the Nonesuch from the next one that bordered on the main street between the Magelander's Quarter and Little Varya. I turned more south there, knowing I couldn't make the leap across to Little Varya without spinning shadow wings and exposing myself to any eyes that chanced to look up. I wanted more distance between me and my pursuers before I took that kind of risk.

People screamed and ran this way and that in the streets below me as the very surface of the earth heaved and twisted beneath their feet, shaping itself to the will of the Durkoth moving in the deeps. The smoke from the burning building rose ever higher, telling a tale of fire unchecked in the face of panic. My impressions of the world, filtered through Triss's unvision, read even stranger than usual, faded as they were by the hammering of the sun.

I traveled through a war of the elements. Air was my ally, buoying me up as I made one mad leap after another across the rooftops. Earth and fire bayed at my heels, closing off the north and west. Shadow held and hid me from the rising light in the east as it tried to betray me to my enemies. Time blurred away into a series of distinct but somehow unconnected moments, as I moved south. Before I knew it, I was racing toward the edge of a building with an unbridgeable gap beyond. I sped up, throwing out wings of shadow as I leaped into space.

14

The war of the elements continued. Out and down I fell, dropping through empty air until water enfolded me when I plunged deep into the Channary Canal. Full morning had come and the stagnant waters of the canal were a madness of boats of every size and description. I swam a long way through foul water before surfacing in the shade of a small pleasure boat—some noble's fancy, fast and fit and heading out to the river proper. I sank a shadow-pointed dagger silently into the hull well below the waterline to provide me a hold.

I pulled a length of my broken-down blowgun from my trick bag then and put it in my mouth with my free hand. Submerging myself in water and shadow, I clung to the boat like a lamprey battened on the side of some fat sea serpent, letting it drag me along beneath the surface. Breathing quietly through my slender length of reinforced bamboo, I left my enemies behind. Earth and fire and light momentarily defeated by darkness and deep water.

I had a lot of time to think there in the warm shadows beneath the little yacht. About what had just happened and what came next. About the betrayed look on Vala's face as VoS cut me an escape route—another vision of failure to add to the many that haunted my nightmares. About Fei and Sergeant Zishin, and whether I'd been set up by one or the other, or if they'd been betrayed as well.

The answer to that question was the next thing I had to find out. I needed to find and free the Dyad as quickly as possible, but I couldn't do that until I knew who had her and why. Until then, I would force myself to box up my concerns for her and lock them away in the back of my mind. I had to. Whether it was just or not, the Dyad had come to matter to me, especially Vala, and I'd failed her.

If I didn't put that aside for the moment, the guilt and distraction might kill me, and that wouldn't do her any good at all. So, when the canal disgorged itself into the Zien River, I pried my dagger loose and swam to a barge heading upriver toward the Palace Quarter and Fei's office, focusing wholly on what I had to do next instead of why.

Moving out into the main river was a huge relief at first. Tien had good sewers and horrendous penalties for not using them, but people still dumped trash and chamber pots into the waters from time to time. On the river the ordure was quickly swept out to sea by the currents, but the waters of the canals were still and stagnant, and the waste lingered there stinking things up.

In summer, the sun made the canals blood warm, and that heat had combined with my exhaustion to spin my head full of cobwebs. The colder waters of the river came as a relief at first, bringing me back to full alertness. But I'd already been in the water for quite a while by then and it didn't take long for the chill to start seeping into my muscles, bringing a deep ache and shivers with it. Ironic to be so cold with brutal summer lying barely a foot away, just the other side of the interface between water and air.

Though Triss remained deep down in the dream state necessitated by the various feats of magic that had allowed us to escape, I could feel a growing sense of impatience from him. It was rare for me to keep him under for so long, but we were still in too much danger of discovery for me to give up my moment-to-moment control quite yet. I tried to think him a message of reassurance, but couldn't be sure it got through. The difference in the minds of Shades and their human companions was such that we'd always had to rely on the spoken word for most of our communication, a fact that had frustrated the sorcerers of my order for centuries.

Just a little longer, my friend, I thought, *just a little longer.* But of course, there was no response. I patted myself on the shoulder in the vague hope that he would feel the reassurance somewhere down there in the depths of my dreams, but I didn't have much faith in the effect.

A few hundred yards after my barge passed the palace docks, I slipped free once more and swam to the western shore, maybe half a mile below Westbridge. The river had cut away the base of the Palace Hill here, exposing the underlying bedrock in sheer bluffs that prevented the estates above the palace complex from spilling all the way down to the river's edge. I took a risk then by climbing the dark limestone cliff in broad daylight, trusting to shadow to shield me from all but the most dedicated observer.

It must have worked, because there was no hue and cry raised, nor any greeting party waiting for me when I chinned myself on the low wall that crowned the bluff and peered over the top. That wall marked the practical boundary of the estate of the Duchess of Tien, titular ruler of the city. Even though it looked down on the river from the top of a hundred-foot bluff, someone on the ducal staff had made sure to keep the wall's defenses in beautiful condition.

The stones were all clean and well laid, the joints freshly tuck-pointed and nearly seamless. One of the predecessors of the duchess had even gone to the expense of having the top liberally studded with silver nails, a sovereign protection against both the restless dead and intruders who couldn't glove their hands in an armor of shadow. They'd interspersed them with a smaller number of iron spikes, an unusual precaution in a great city like Tien where the creatures of wild magic rarely ventured.

I wondered if that was down to tradition, or if it was meant to address the proximity of the river, which provided one of the few conduits for the wild ones to enter the metropolis. In either case, I thought them a bit much. There were simple alarm wards as well, but the maintenance sorcerer had done inferior work there. They were so obvious that even a mageblind burglar could have avoided them if he were halfway competent at his craft. I loosed Triss briefly then, signaling for him to withdraw the enshrouding shadow from in front of my face.

The morning sun that now rode high in the sky behind me had more than half blinded Triss's unvision. I needed to take a look with my own eyes before committing myself to the next step in my plan. I also wanted to give him a chance to voice any concerns that he might have. I hung there for perhaps ten minutes without spying any patrols or having Triss collapse himself down to a speaking shape, though I could feel something like a silent grumble coming through our magical link.

Up and over, and down and drop, and I was in. The ducal estate was huge, second only to the palace complex itself in scope, just as the Duchess of Tien was second only to the king in practical authority. At the moment, she was also second or third in the succession, depending on how you counted things.

Among the many outbuildings that dotted the acres of mani-cured groves and formal gardens of the estate were several dedicated to various functions of the city watch, which held the duchess as its ultimate commander and liege lady. Temporarily reasserting control over Triss, I moved quickly from the wall into the shadows of a large and carefully kept stand of bamboo. As I slipped deeper into the estate, I made sure to stay under the trees as much as possible, avoiding the numerous groundskeepers and the several small groups of household guards that I passed along the way.

At one point, I walked through a stand of flowering pears, and after that I had stolen fruit to munch on. After all the energy and nima I'd expended to escape the ambush at the Nonesuch, I was hungry enough to ignore the fact that the fruit was still well short of ripe. Eventually, I arrived at my destination, a suite of offices and meeting rooms ceded to the watch on a more or less permanent basis.

The duchess rented them the building so that she had a place she could confer with her officers without having to leave the bounds of her estate or allow the cruder functions of the watch to impinge on her residence. Conveniently for me, the goal of reducing the visual presence of the watch on the estate included planting a dense silverthorn hedge around the building to help hide it from delicate noble eyes. Once I slipped into the space between the planting and the wall, I was thoroughly masked from the broader estate, and could almost have let Triss slip back into dragon shape.

All of the city's watch captains kept offices there, as did several of their more important lieutenants. I peered in the window of Fei's first floor office, the largest of the lot, just in case, but was unsurprised to find it dark and empty. That wasn't why I'd come. Assuming a low crouch I moved carefully along the outside wall, peering through basement windows into the closet-sized offices assigned to minor officers until I found what I was looking for. It was child's play to slip the lock and wriggle through the window—no one breaks *into* a watch office. Especially not one that's in the center of a guarded estate and only intermittently in use.

Once we were safely inside, Triss slid down off my skin, puddling briefly on the floor before reassuming his dragon form and taking up a position covering the door. He flicked his wings back and forth angrily. Since it was impossible for him to really communicate with me in shroud form, this was the first chance we'd had to talk since the attack at the Nonesuch. He was obviously upset about it.

"Care to tell me what the plan is?" the little dragon growled quietly. "Or is that too much to ask from my bondmate?"

"I'm sorry, Triss. Truly. I didn't have one at first, not beyond getting away. Then, when I started to look at next steps, the situation was such that I couldn't have talked to you no matter how much I might have wanted to. Being underwater limits one's conversational options, I have to say."

Triss stopped fussing with his wings and cocked his head at me quizzically. "If I didn't know better, I'd swear that was the second attempt at a joke in as many days." Then he shook himself. "But don't think that's going to get you off the hook, my friend. What are we doing on the Duchess of Tien's estate?"

"We need to free Vala and Stel," I said. "That means finding out who took them. There was an Elite presence at the Nonesuch, if only a small one, and they started whistling up the watch the second I slipped the net. That implies official ties for the snatch, and that means that we were set up, though I'm not yet sure whether it was Fei or Zishin. Which, in turn, means I need to have a word with one or both of them. I don't know where Zishin lives, and if it was Fei, she's smart enough not to go home."

"I can see that, but I'm not making the jump to why it's a good idea to break into the estate of the Duchess of Tien."

"If it's Fei, she's going to be holed up in her office and surrounded by a sea of Stingers. Since my face is up on wanted posters all over this city, I figured that I'd do best to gather up some protective camouflage before trying to sneak into watch central."

"Which brings us into this room right here why?"

I pointed at a little silk pillow tucked unobtrusively on a high shelf above the door.

"Still not following you."

"The lieutenant who belongs to this office keeps a real pillow here, and an expensive one by the look of it. The only reason to do that is if he occasionally sleeps here, and not just naps. Which means . . ." I opened the little cabinet behind the desk and reached inside to pull a neatly folded watch uniform off the shelf.

Behind it I saw a small bottle of brandy. My stomach cooed like a mating dove and cool beads of sweat broke out along my hairline as I imagined taking a long sweet drink.

"Are you all right?" asked Triss.

I nodded because I didn't trust a mouth suddenly gone dust dry to get the right words out. My hands shook as I flipped the uniform open to check the fit. A little big, but not so much so as to draw suspicion. I focused on that. One nice thing about being only middling tall for a man and likewise of average build was that most clothes fit me. Add in that Tienese dress tended to the loose and flowing and I could almost always steal an appropriate outfit when needed.

"What do you think?" I asked Triss, when I could speak again.

"That's pretty clever, actually," said Triss. "You chose the offices here because they were not far out of the way and rarely in full use?"

"That and because the guards here are mostly on the outer perimeter, not in the building. You sound surprised."

"I guess I'm still not used to you thinking like the old Aral. Not after spending so much time with the pickled version the last few years." His voice was dry and acerbic.

"I'd like to say I don't deserve that. But the fact that I'm absolutely dying to have a drink from the bottle of brandy that's in there suggests that you might have a point. It's funny, I can ignore it most of the time when I've got something else to keep my attention, but every time I see a bottle . . ."

"You can do this," Triss said quietly but firmly. "I know you can. I shouldn't have made that dig. I'm sorry."

"It's all right, Triss. I'll take a hard truth over a pretty lie any day."

There was a formal dress jacket of polished silk in the cabinet as well. But that would only draw unwanted attention where I was going, so I let it lie. I did take the broad-brimmed hat the watch sometimes wore in the summer, both for sun protection and because the shadows it made would help hide my face. Especially since I intended to have Triss give them a little hand. At other times when stealing clothes I'd left a couple of riels to pay for their replacement, but I didn't bother this time. I didn't owe the Stingers anything.

I quickly stripped out of my still damp clothes, wincing at the sting as I dragged the shirt over the fresh scabs and bruises on my face. The Elite had done a number on me there, though Vala thought it would heal without scarring after her spellwork.

Then I changed into the uniform. It felt wonderful to have fresh clean fabric against my skin. It was raw silk instead of the cotton of a duty uniform, but the rough texture of the fabric meant you'd have to look close to notice. The biggest problem was the badges on the upper arms. The paired fans of a ranking lieutenant would draw more attention than I wanted. But that could be fixed with a sharp knife and a bit of creative magic to replace them with a sergeant's tripled swords. I'd have made myself a corporal or a private if I could have, but neither would ever wear a uniform as nice as mine.

I still had the problem of my double-draw sword rig and trick bag, both of which were profoundly nonstandard equipment, but I figured I could manage that by stealing a long tool sack from the groundskeepers. My wet clothes went into that as well since I didn't want to leave behind anything that could be used by a tracker, magical or otherwise. The sack fell outside the realm of standard watch equipment, but everybody ends up hauling around an extra bag from time to time so I didn't think it'd draw too much attention my way.

And I was right, though not for the reasons I'd expected. The Mufflers offices were normally very quiet, in keeping with their special mission. But today when I arrived at the little building on the Highside/Palace Quarter border, it looked like an overturned hornet's nest. Gold and black watch uniforms buzzed around everywhere and a sort of haze of suppressed fury hung in the air, though I didn't know why. I kept my head down and my hat pulled forward as I slipped through the crowd.

I'd expected to have to do a certain amount of fancy footwork both verbal and literal to get where I wanted to go, but nobody even noticed one more Stinger in the midst of that angry swarm. I was able to go right in the front door and through to the small latrine off the front room without being challenged.

Under normal circumstances I'd have pulled up a few floorboards and slipped into the crawlspace beneath the offices. Like many of the newer buildings in Tien's wealthy hillside neighborhoods, it had been designed with plenty of room for airflow beneath, both for summer cooling and winter heating using one of the hypocaust furnaces imported from the Sylvani Empire. The under-floor space provided the perfect route for moving about unseen if you ignored the potential problem of the Durkoth coming at you through the bedrock that lay only a few inches below the surface here. Not something I was willing to do after what had happened to Coalshovel and later at the Nonesuch.

Instead, I climbed up onto the bench and examined the narrow, bamboo-framed mulberry-paper panels separating the attic from the rooms below. The rough unbleached paper of the ceiling was another marker of a newer building, one expressly designed to be easily switched from one sort of use to another.

I much preferred older, more solid ceilings as did the thatchcutters and other shadowtraders who made illegal entrances via the roof. The mulberry paper was far too easy to rip, and it amplified any noise like a drumhead, but I had no other good choice. Sighing, I pushed up the panel closest to the wall, and poked my head into the space above. It felt like I'd opened the door on a fresh-filled drying oven, as hot damp air smacked me in the face.

I lifted my bag through, laying it carefully across a couple of rafters, then followed it up as quickly as I could manage. Pausing only long enough to have Triss reach down and open the latch on the latrine door, I reset the panel behind me. I had to hope no one would enter for the few minutes it took for the heat I'd just let in to dissipate. I didn't want anyone wondering about that.

Sweat drenched me in seconds, though I hadn't even started moving yet. If I wanted to get to Fei's office, I was going to have to crawl on hands and knees along the rafters with my sack slung awkwardly in front of me because the roof hung so low it nearly scraped my back. Working slowly and carefully despite the stifling heat I got moving. The bustle and buzz below would cover most of the noise of my passing, but too loud a creak or a slip that ripped one of the paper panels and I'd be fucked.

I had to pause repeatedly to mop the sweat off my face and out of my hair just to keep it from dripping and spattering on the paper panels below. It was a public building and not some noble's fancy, so the panels were inferior paper, very rough and often stained, but the Mufflers were a lot sharper than your average watchman. One of them might actually notice a series of fresh wet spots drawing a slow line across the ceiling and decide to check on the problem with a woldo or some other spearlike object.

Normally, Triss would have caught the drops for me, but a dark shadow sliding along the translucent paper would make an even worse tell than the sweat, especially with the light coming up from below. After crawling for what felt like a thousand years and three hundred miles, I ended up over what I hoped was Fei's office.

I'd only been there once before, and that very reluctantly, to collect a payoff for a small courier job I'd done for the captain. Then, she had occupied a big open room in the building's back right corner which was where I was now. The relative quiet and dark of the room below was reassuring, suggesting closed windows and a place where even watchmen treaded lightly.

I lowered my head into the space between two rafters and lifted a ceiling panel a few inches, giving me a narrow view of part of the room. I recognized Fei's desk. It was covered in a light scatter of writing paper, but the seat behind it held nothing. I lifted the panel higher, listening carefully all the while. Nothing. I poked my head down into the room and looked around. Empty.

I moved a couple of yards to my left and lifted out the panel directly above Fei's desk. That allowed me to lower myself onto the raised top and avoid the noise of a drop to the floor. A quick glance through Fei's papers didn't turn up anything useful, though I did notice there was nothing dated from the last two days in the scatter. Looking around, I spotted a small set of filing shelves. All the most recent reports and paperwork were stacked neatly on the top shelf, implying she hadn't had a chance to look at them yet.

I was just deciding what to try next, when a faint courtesy knock sounded at the door. It was the sort of knock an underling makes when they know that no one is home, but don't want to violate protocol in case they turn out to be wrong. The hinges were on this side of the door, so I stepped into the blind spot that would be created by its opening. I drew one of my swords and waited. A second knock followed, this one even fainter than the first. The door opened a heartbeat later.

A tall, slender man in the uniform of a watch corporal stepped into the room carrying an extra-large sheet of paper rolled up like a scroll. Corporal Anjir—I knew all the Mufflers by sight. As he started toward the file shelf, I pushed the door gently closed and raised my sword. The corporal froze as the latch clicked shut, but he didn't turn around.

"Captain Fei?" he said, very quietly.

"Nope."

Anjir's shoulders slumped. "Didn't think so. I presume that I'll get something sharp and fatal between the shoulder blades if I make any loud noises or sudden moves."

"That's very perceptive of you, Corporal. Keep thinking that clearly and there's an excellent chance you'll get out of this room alive."

"Best news I've had in the last thirty seconds," said the corporal. "Should I keep standing as I am, or would you prefer me to move someplace?" He sounded almost calm, but I could see the trickles of sweat starting to run down the back of his neck.

"Just stay there if you please. I've got some questions for you, and I'd rather you didn't see my face."

"You could bind my eyes if you like. I'd really prefer not to see your face either. Improves the odds of you leaving me alive and all."

It was a good idea, so I signaled Triss to put a hood of shadow over his head.

The corporal twitched a bit when Triss first covered his eyes, but then seemed to relax. "Nice little spell that, thank you."

I leaned back and put my ear against the door behind me. There was a distant clamor from the front of the building, but it didn't sound like anyone was moving around in the hall. That meant I probably had a little time. If anyone had seen the corporal come into Fei's office and close the door, and found that at all suspicious, he'd already been in here long enough to draw more focused attention. Now it was a question of how long it would be before anyone missed him doing whatever he was supposed to do next.

"You're welcome," I said. And then, because I was curious, "You don't seem nearly as alarmed as I would have expected."

"I work for Captain Fei. This isn't the first time I've had my head bagged on the job. It's always come out all right in the past."

"Speaking of the good captain; where is she?"

"No one knows. She's been missing for two days. That's why the office is in such an uproar."

"That's funny. I talked to Sergeant Zishin no more than eight hours ago and he acted like he'd seen the captain recently."

"Maybe he had," said the corporal. "But if so, he hasn't told the rest of us about it."

"Do you know where the sergeant is now?"

"I imagine he's at home."

"And where is home for the sergeant?"

"Somewhere on the Kanathean Hill, though I couldn't tell you closer without looking it up. I don't suppose you'd be willing to let me go out to the front desk and ask, would you?" He didn't sound hopeful and I didn't bother to answer.

I snarled mentally. So far I hadn't gotten anything useful out of a very dangerous game and I was running out of time fast. The sand in the hourglass had started to empty the moment the corporal came through the door.

"I presume the captain's house has been searched?" I asked.

"Several times, and there are men stationed there now waiting for her to come home."

That was something at least. My original plan had called for me to try Fei's place next if I didn't get anything here, and that removed a stop from my list. I decided to allow myself about three more questions before I put the corporal to sleep for a while and got the hell out of there. No Fei, no Zishin, and no hope of finding either one easily. So, what to ask next?

"What do you know about the operation at the Nonesuch?" I was guessing the answer was nothing, but it was the next most important thing on my mental list.

"Only that it happened and that it failed to get its primary target. At least, that's what the gossip is saying. That was an Elite operation, Major Aigo's people with some unofficial help from the local Durkoth. The Howlers don't much like us down here at Silent Branch, so rumor's the best I can do there."

I felt a little slithering spot of cold moving upward along my spine, like someone running an icy feather across my skin.

"If the Dyad wasn't the primary target, who was?"

The corporal half turned and held out the scrolled paper, opening the roll with a flick of his wrist.

There, looking back at me was as nice a likeness of my face as I'd ever seen this side of a mirror.

15

———◆———

"The main target was the famous assassin, Aral Kingslayer, of course," said the corporal. "Captain Fei found him!"

I took the poster. It had a much better drawing of me than the one the Elite had put on the posters for my jack face. Fei had clearly paid serious money for her sketch artist. Guessing from the level of detail, she'd also arranged for them to spend some time watching me at the Gryphon's Head. The reward was much higher as well, having doubled my old Kingslayer numbers. I was now worth fifty thousand gold riels. Or, my head was anyway. All you had to do was deliver it to the palace with or without the body attached.

That was enough to buy a palace and staff it. A single gold riel would have paid the rent on my little room over the stable for half a year, or bought ten fancy dinners at the Spinnerfish with drinks and dessert. The king was offering *fifty thousand* for my head. It was hard to even conceive of that kind of money, much less imagine it being paid out for my death. And now that the poster was out there with my old name attached, the likeness would spread.

Before you knew it, the Aral Kingslayer reward posters that the Son of Heaven had up all over the eleven kingdoms would have a picture of me on them as well. If a bounty hunter could figure out some way to deliver my head to both secular and religious rulers, they could add another ten thousand to their potential take—the high church of the eleven kingdoms being a bit more parsimonious than Thauvik IV. I had a brief wild moment of wondering how one might go about that, since I didn't think either one of them would want to part with my head. There was too much cachet to be had by putting it up on a spike somewhere. But that way lay madness, so I pushed the thought away.

"How do you know that's really the Kingslayer?" I asked.

"You'd have to ask Captain Fei. Funny thing really. It turns out the Kingslayer's been hiding here in Tien since the true gods put down his crazy goddess. Just pretending to be a plain old shadow jack, if you please."

I'd already overstayed my time, but I couldn't help ask one last question. "So, no one knows how Fei figured it out?"

"No, though it's supposed to have been quite a recent discovery." He dropped his voice. "They think he probably killed Fei when he found out she'd identified him, and that's why we can't find her, though we're acting as if she'll be coming back. That's why I came in here, actually. Leaving the captain a copy of this new wanted poster the Elite have been putting up everywhere since the thing at the Nonesuch went bad."

I needed to get out of there. "I'm going to have to put you to sleep for a little while now, Corporal. Don't struggle, and I promise you'll wake up. If you do struggle, or make any loud noises, I won't have time to do anything but kill you. Now, turn around."

He tensed, but then nodded and did as he was told. Reaching into my trick bag, I opened a small brass case and pulled out a robin's egg. It was filled with a powdered mixture of efik and opium, which made a powerful and fastacting soporific. I set my sword aside and wrapped my free arm around his neck. Again, he tensed briefly before relaxing.

I squeezed hard, lifting him off the ground and cutting off his air. He instinctively tried to fight me then, but Triss had slipped down to pin his arms, and there wasn't a lot he could do. I could easily have broken his neck. Instead I let off the pressure after only a few seconds. When the corporal took a deep gasping breath, I slapped the little egg against his face, shattering it and sending the powder deep into his lungs. Within seconds he went limp in my arms. Nothing short of magic would wake him for at least several hours.

I draped him artistically across the desk, where anyone looking in from the doorway couldn't possibly miss him. Then I unlatched Fei's window before climbing back up into the ceiling. From there, I gave the window a shove, opening it wide. Next, I made my way across the rafters to a place just in front of the door. Sticking my head back down into the room, I screamed like a man being murdered.

I barely had time to drop the panel back into place before a half dozen officers of the watch crashed into the room below. From their hurried shouts, I could tell they'd made the obvious connection with the open window and sent men leaping out to see what had become of the corporal's attacker. While that was going on, I hurried across the rafters to the office opposite the captain's and flipped up a ceiling panel. As expected, it was empty now, so I dropped down into the space behind the wide open door.

By then, the pandemonium had grown to such a degree—with Stingers running every which way—that it was a trivial matter for a man in a sergeant's uniform to slip out through the front offices and into the street. As I made my way down through the Highside toward the river and the Magelander's Quarter, I found myself losing track of little stretches of time. One moment, I would be looking toward a familiar landmark like the King's Head tavern. The next, I'd find I'd passed it without noticing.

I was operating on nerves and nothing more and I desperately needed to get off the street before I got myself killed. Death by stupid is a terrible way to go. Somehow, I managed to keep things together long enough to get down off the Palace Hill and into the streets of Little Varya without falling asleep on my feet or getting caught. At that point, my watch uniform started to draw more attention than it deflected. Since I'd already seen more than a dozen copies of the Kingslayer poster, that meant it was time I ditched it. I couldn't afford to have anyone looking at me too closely. So I turned into the first tailor's I passed and walked straight up to the woman behind the counter.

"I need a change of clothes," I said. "Something simple."

Her face went unnaturally pale. "I . . . uh . . . yes, my lord. Anything you say, my lord."

I rubbed my forehead. "Since nobody wearing a sergeant's swords on his sleeve has any right to a 'my lord,' can I assume that you've seen the wanted posters?"

She swallowed and nodded miserably. "Please don't kill me, Lord Kingslayer. I'm only a poor tailor and I promise no one will hear you've been here from me. No one. You did us a great service by putting the sword to old King Ashvik, and that's no mistake. I've said that afore now, and I'll say it again."

"You're as safe with me as you would be in your own bed," I said as gently as possible. "I swear it. If you know who I am, you also know what I am. No Blade kills the innocent. Not if there's any way to avoid it. But I can't have you running off to the watch the second I leave, and I can't trust your word that you won't, so I'll have to tie you up before I go. Hold on a moment."

I crossed back to the shop's entrance and flipped the little sign to closed before shutting and latching the door. When I turned around, the tailor was already pulling out several suits of clothes and laying them out on the counter. I chose a loose sleeveless shirt and pants of a second grade silk, blue bordering on gray, and I paid more than they were worth. I also bought a nicer bag for my swords and other gear, something more appropriate to the clothes I was wearing. It was all on Kodamia's kip anyway, so what the hell.

I left the shop a few minutes later with my fresh change of clothes on my back and the tailor unbound behind me because I couldn't bring myself to do the sensible thing. Not in the face of so much fear. And especially not with Triss whispering in my ear about it.

The streets of Tien had never seemed so crowded nor the people so curious and prone to stare. Every water seller and kebab vendor from the Weavery to Backpast seemed to have wedged themselves into the Magelander's Quarter intent on getting me to stop and buy their wares. And every one of them seemed to have set up under another copy of that damned wanted poster. I moved as fast as exhaustion would let me, fending off the hawkers and gawkers with an occasional thrown up hand and a frequently barked series of "nos."

I also kept my hat low, risking the telltale of having no personal shadow in order to keep an unusually heavy one across my face. Triss stayed wrapped tight around me in case we had to fight. I figured the crowds were so dense that my shadow never would have touched the ground anyway, so the chances of anyone noticing it when I didn't block a share of their sun were pretty slim. At least, that's what I told myself, and in my ragged state I believed me.

Whether it was true or not, I did eventually make it across the Zien on the Low Bridge, which led to the Stumbles and Smuggler's Rest. And I did it without getting bagged by the Stingers, the Howlers, or some freelance bounty hunter. That put me back on my home ground, where I knew every nook and every cranny. There it was much easier for me to fade into the background, even with all the damned posters nailed up every which where. But I was pretty much out on my feet by the time I made it to the best of my fallbacks, a gutted out old tenement that had been ravaged by fire.

The inside of the ruined building was an unstable maze of broken rubble and charred debris. I normally went up the one remaining outside wall that still had any structural integrity, but there was no way I could have climbed it in daylight without being seen. Not even fully shrouded. Instead, I slipped through a trick board the local kids had rigged, and risked life and limb by threading my way across the shifting wreckage inside on my way to the back tower.

Looking up into that chimney-like void, it was impossible to tell that the very top floor of the old tower was still sound and in place eight stories above. In fact, the careful enlargement of a couple of windows on the floor below increased the light in ways that made it seem as if there was nothing but shattered beams and a scrap of old roof between the ground floor and the sky.

I hopped lightly over the ruin of a door that lay on the floor just inside the tower's entrance and crossed to the far wall. The slab of charred wood covered a big hole where the floor had collapsed into the sewers. I'd long ago burned away what little strength the original fire had left the door, so that the weight of anything much bigger than a cat would break it in half.

It took me more than an hour to make my way up the well of the tower, a route I'd only ever been forced to use once before. I had to take frequent rest breaks, perching on rotting window ledges or the stubs of old beams, and I'd never have made it at all without Triss's ability to make me fingerholds no normal human could have used.

Eventually, I climbed up to just beneath the top floor. There, rather than take the risk of being seen slipping out a window and up the last few feet, I got Triss to unlatch the trapdoor I normally used for a privy so that I could crawl through from below. The tiny room above was an oven, so I cracked the shutters as wide as I dared—too much obvious change might draw attention to the tower. Then I stripped off my outer clothes and flopped down on the old straw mattress.

When I woke, the sun had moved the shadows a few feet, making it early afternoon. My rough sheet was soaked with sweat and I had a pounding headache, but no one had beheaded me in my sleep, so I had to count that as a win. The two or three hours of shut-eye I'd gotten weren't nearly enough, but hunger kept me from just rolling over and trying for a couple more. It'd been ages since the Spinnerfish, and I'd long since run off all of my dinner. When I blearily sat up on the narrow mattress, Triss flowed out from under me and up onto the wall.

"What now?" he asked.

"Breakfast, or lunch. Whatever the hell meal you have when you wake up groggy at . . . What time is it?"

"A bit past the second afternoon bell," said Triss. "And don't think I didn't notice the way you dodged the question."

"It wasn't a dodge so much as a delaying tactic while I wake up and think things through. I don't suppose you want to fetch me that breakfast?"

Triss sighed, then slid down the wall and across the floor to the place where my amphorae were racked. For a moment, the nearest was covered in shadow, then the big ceramic stopper thudded gently to the floor. Two beats after that Triss pulled out a small clay pot and brought it to me before going back to open another amphora.

I broke the seal and pried off the lid, exposing a dense brick of a cake and filling the air with the smell of orange liquor. The cake was mostly made up of dried fruit and nuts baked in just enough rice flour to hold it together, then steeped in liquor to preserve it. As long as you left them in the pot they came in, the things would last virtually forever. Or, for traveling, you could wrap them in oiled paper and stow them in the bottom of a pack and expect it to still taste pretty good after a month or three of bouncing around.

I broke off a piece and started chewing. Heavenly stuff, but expensive. Which is why I hadn't had any at the other fallback. While I was munching on my orange cake, Triss brought me a jar of excellent small beer and a tiny ham wrapped in oiled paper—likewise much better fare than I had been able to offer Stel and Vala. That thought gave me a little pang of guilt now. But the only thing I could do about it at the moment was to get out there and find them, and eating a good meal would put me in a much better state to achieve that.

Triss didn't open the amphora that held my Kyle's twenty, and I didn't ask him to, though I would very much have liked a sip or two of something stronger than small beer and the liquor in my orange cake. I'd finished about half of the ham and all of the cake when Triss suddenly whipped his head around and looked sharply at the open trap door.

"What is it?" I asked.

"I'm not sure, hang on."

Triss slipped down through the door, leaving only the thinnest thread of darkness to connect him back to me and the place the sun would have put his shadow. I set the ham quietly on the floor and reached for my clothes. My hand had just touched the rough silk of my pants when I felt a thrum of alarm run back along the line of shadow that linked us. It was the most urgent sort of warning, so instead of putting my clothes on, I just hooked them through the carrying strap of my new bag and grabbed my boots.

Triss reappeared through the trapdoor as I pulled the first boot on. He came up slowly and carefully, slithering over the edge rather than popping back up. I opened my mouth to ask what was wrong, but before I could speak he touched my lips with one claw and shook his head. Then he handed me my remaining boot before wrapping my bag in shadow and lifting it silently to my shoulder for me while I slipped on the boot. For the first time I realized how quiet the world outside my tower had gotten. Shit.

As I rose into a crouch, I lifted my head back and mimed a wolf howling. Triss nodded and held up five fingers, making a circling gesture to let me know they were all around us. That meant we couldn't sail-jump, especially not mid-afternoon when Triss would be at his weakest. I pointed down through the trapdoor and he nodded. This was going to get seriously nasty.

A very quiet scuffing sound, as of someone stealthily climbing a stone wall, came in through the window. I leaped and caught hold of one of the cross beams, quickly swinging my feet up so that I could hang by my heels and free my hands. Triss wrapped himself around me as I pointed my palms at the edges of the floor, submerging his will within my own. I drew a deep breath, then closed my eyes and released the lightning as I let it out. The blast chewed through the wooden planks, igniting them at the same time it severed the two main supports for my little aerie.

With a terrible rending noise, the whole floor fell away beneath me—a burning wheel dropping into darkness. The tower shook, and clouds of dirt blossomed everywhere as bits of brick shattered and burst under the stress, but it didn't collapse. Not quite. I counted to three then let go of the beam, following the floor down into the dense pall of smoke and dust. Extending my arms, I shaped the shadow-stuff of my familiar into huge twinned claws, pushing them out to drag along the walls, slowing my fall while simultaneously adding to the general noise and destruction.

Using that touch point to tell me where I was relative to the height of the tower, I was able to let go and draw the shadows back in a few feet from the ground, dropping free for the last few feet. That was my intent anyway, but the fall was longer than I anticipated. This latest abuse had been too much for the floor. The whole thing had caved in, collapsing into the sewers below. I hit hard, and had to ditch my bag as I rolled across the debris to soak up some of the impact. Rough edges jabbed at my bare back and legs, opening ragged cuts and driving splinters deep into my flesh.

If Triss had been free, he might have armored me from the

worst of it. But I had chosen to keep control, reaching for his senses in the same moment that I wrapped him around me now. That saved my life, because it meant that I felt the presence of the Durkoth a split second before he spotted me. Two staggering steps, pivot, and a flick of the wrist as I extended my arm. The dagger in my right wrist sheath slid into my hand and I continued the swing, dragging the edge of my steel across the Other's throat.

Blood hotter than any human's fountained across my hand and sprayed my face and chest. Deep purple according to VoS—the same as their Sylvani cousins if the stories Siri had told me about them were true, and she ought to know after the assignment that earned her the name "Mythkiller." She'd also told me that Others were damned hard to kill and the Durkoth proved her point by not going down immediately as a human would have.

Instead, he lurched forward, slamming into me and knocking me over backward. As I fell, I remembered Qethar's stone cloak and willed my wrapping of shadow-stuff into a stiff, barrel-like configuration to protect my chest and ribs from the impact. But instead of landing on hard debris as I'd anticipated, we plunged into the main flow of the sewer.

I felt a moment of disorientation as our progress slowed. Then the crushing pressure of five hundred or more pounds of dying Other and long stone robe—this one was dressed in foreign manner—pushed me deep into the muck at the bottom of the channel. For a few instants I could feel the stone fabric of his robe writhing against my shadow armor, trying to catch and crush me.

Then the Durkoth went limp and his clothing froze in place—the half-open hand of a stone giant gripping my chest. I hadn't had time to draw an extra breath before we went in, and now I thought my lungs might burst before I worked my way free of that great weight. Only the fact that my shadow armor had kept the grasping stone from getting a tighter grip saved me. I had just enough room to slither free of the dead Other, though I lost some skin doing it.

When my head broke the surface, I drew in a huge lungful of air, then swam to the side of the channel. It ran deep and fast here under the Stumbles, where the many outflows off the Sovann and Kanathean Hills came together before making their conjoined way out to the bay. I dragged myself up onto the narrow access ledge and released my hold on Triss, letting him go as I collapsed onto my side.

For a good minute I just lay there in the dark, gasping raggedly and trying to recover. The stench should have been unbearable, but after my recent time without any air at all, the simple fact that I could smell *anything* made it seem almost sweet. An occasional dull crash or sudden splash spoke of the continued disintegration of the tenement above. I found that vaguely reassuring since I didn't think the Elite would be in any hurry to enter a building in the midst of collapse.

Triss slipped away up channel, moving back toward where we had fallen in for reasons he didn't bother to share. Just as earlier, he left a thin thread of shadow to connect us, and just as earlier he hadn't been gone long when I felt a thrum of alarm run back along that connection.

"Aral, downstream, now!" Triss's voice rang out shrill and harsh from the darkness up channel, riding over a sudden increase in the noise coming from above.

Reflex rolled me off the ledge, and long years of training designed to keep my body moving well past the point of physical endurance got me paddling, though my arms felt like lead and my soggy boots kept trying to drag me under. But I couldn't have gone more than a dozen strokes before the world fell on me.

It began with a sound like chained thunder, or the hands of a god beating a mad dance on the drum skin of the sky. Then came the dust, a great, blinding, choking wall of it that rolled down the tunnel from behind me like an avalanche filling a high pass. It clogged my nose and rimmed my mouth with mud in an instant, forcing me to close eyes against the grit. I ducked my head under the surface of the sewage-filled water and scrubbed at my face to clear the worst of it, because it was that or suffocate.

That's when the wave hit. Somewhere behind me the old apartment had given its final gasp and fallen in on itself, dropping nine stories of brick and stone down into the sewer all in an instant. Tons of water and the waste it carried were suddenly displaced, a veritable river of sewage thrown out and away from the point of impact all in an instant. It hit me like a liquid hammer, tumbling me over and over until I lost all sense of direction or self.

16

The hissing registered first, a low dangerous stream of sibilants like the world's largest asp venting its rage. It should probably have frightened me, but it didn't. Instead, I found it comforting, and so I focused my fragmented attention on the sound. Slowly, it shifted from senseless noise to words spoken in some alien vernacular . . . the language of the Shades. Triss! Angry or frightened or perhaps both, and swearing violently in his native tongue.

Something was wrong then, beyond the fact that I had no idea where I was or how I'd gotten there. I knew only that it was dark and chill and that I felt as though someone had stuffed me into a barrel half filled with rocks and rolled me down a long and bumpy slope. I struggled to sit up, realizing only in the moment of action that I had been lying down. Before I could get much more than half-way upright, the top of my head smacked into something hard and I let out a tiny yelp.

As I fell back I threw out both arms, striking curving stonework on either side of me. I was in some sort of stone pipe, probably a side run into the main sewer where my last memories left me. That would explain the smell. . . .

"Don't move," hissed Triss. "You're safe, but only if you hold still until I've dealt with the nightghast."

I froze. The words came from somewhere beyond the ends of my feet and I did as Triss ordered. Nightghasts ate human flesh when they could get it. They weren't the worst of their kind, not by a long road. But even the least of the restless dead could be plenty dangerous and they didn't have to kill you outright to make an end of you. If the nightghast clawed or bit me I might well survive the immediate damage, but succumb a few days or weeks later to the curse that animated it, becoming one of the restless dead myself.

There came a sudden scuttling sound in the dark beyond my feet. Triss answered with a sharp hiss and some large movement that I could feel through our link though I couldn't see anything. That was followed by a thud like a dull blade hitting old meat, and then a long wailing shriek.

"That's done it," said Triss, coming closer. "It won't be bothering us again soon."

"Thanks, Triss. What happened? The last thing I remember is you telling me to swim for it."

"The apartment building came down and collapsed part of the sewer. There was a big wave, and you got knocked around quite a bit but I couldn't find anything broken. How do you feel?"

"Like the shit I've been swimming in, but I'm basically all right. Next question. What happened at the fallback? I didn't get the chance to ask you anything before we had to bolt."

"Elite, a half dozen of them led by Major Aigo, with a company of Crown Guard in support."

"And Durkoth below. I don't like that alliance at all, not even if it's just a sort of truce of convenience." My hand went reflexively to the hilt of a sword I was no longer wearing. "I don't suppose you managed to save the bag with my gear in it?"

"I did," he said, his voice more than a little smug. "I was bringing it back to you when the roof fell in and I hung onto it as our link dragged me along in your wake. I had to drop it when I fished you out and put you in here, but it's on the bottom not far from here. You haven't been out long and the nightghast has been occupying my attention. Should I fetch it now?"

"Please. Any idea where we are?"

"Somewhere under Smuggler's Rest," he called over his shoulder. He was back a short time later with my bag. "If you crawl up the pipe behind you, you'll come to a storm grate pretty quickly."

I'll skip over the details of getting clean—relatively, and finding yet another set of new clothes—lifted but paid for, and move straight to the next stop on my tour of undiscovered Tien.

Sergeant Zishin was collecting the Mufflers' share of a little sell-cinders operation when I caught up to him just after sunset. I waited for him to finish his business and walk past the mouth of a tiny alley before I let him know I wanted a word with him. The polite thing would have been to give him a call as he went by, but I was fresh out of polite.

What I did instead was shroud up, slide out, grab him by belt and collar, and toss him head first into the darkness of the little snicket. I also kicked his feet out from under him as he went by, just for good measure. A jindu fighter and Fei's longtime sparring partner, he reacted fast, turning the fall into a roll and spinning and drawing his boot dagger as he came to his feet. He dropped his watchman's lamp somewhere in there and it fell at his feet, painting him with bright light while leaving me in darkness.

"Come on, bastard," he said, "step into the light and I'll gut you."

But I didn't have the patience for a dance, so I set Triss on him. Shadow teeth sank deep into a flesh-and-blood wrist, drawing a high sharp scream and forcing Zishin to drop the blade. Before he could even think about recovering it, Triss shifted shape and became a noose around the sergeant's neck, lifting him half off his feet. As Zishin clawed at the shadow wrapped tight around his throat, I kicked the lamp away down the alley. Then I stepped in close and touched the tip of my steel to the spot just below the point of his jaw.

"You've got your choice, Zishin. You can stop making a fuss and maybe get to walk away, or you can piss me off. Which is it going to be?"

He froze. "Aral?" There was real fear in his voice.

"Call me Kingslayer." I still hated that name, but it was out there now, and I had been trained to use all the tools at hand. "You fucked me, Zishin, and that's going to cost you."

"I don't know what you're talking about, Aral."

"That'd sound a lot more convincing if your voice weren't shaking, Sergeant. Let me refresh your memory. Me, you, a message supposedly from your missing boss . . ."

"Swear to Shan, Aral, that wasn't a play. I know Fei's supposed to be belly up in the bay somewhere with your knife in her back, but she isn't. She was alive to give me that message I gave you. She's got some kind of game going, but I don't know what it is. Maybe the big retirement strike, or maybe something for the king. Whatever it is, she didn't cut me in. Swear to Shan, Aral, that's the straight. Swear to Shan."

He was terrified of me, that was plain enough, and he sounded sincere. But I'd been lied to by frightened men before. That's the problem with going hard on someone. If they were scared enough, or hurt enough, they'd say just about anything to make it stop even for a minute. It didn't help that truthsay is all kinds of tricky, like any mind magic. Zishin was no sorcerer, which was the biggest confound, but I figured Fei had probably paid to have him counterspelled. Question was: how much protection had she laid out for, and could I break it in the time I had?

"Triss, I need you. Zishin, move and die. You know what I am, you know it will happen."

Triss let go of Zishin's neck and flowed back into my shadow. Then up and around, wrapping me in the thinnest skin of darkness, like the first skim of ice on the surface of a pond in fall. As his will faded into an extension of my own, I put my free hand on the back of Zishin's neck. He shivered at the cold of my shadow-gloved hand, but didn't move otherwise. He wanted to live, and that held him long enough for my magic to take hold.

I hated to go quick and dirty, but I didn't have a lot of choice. Extending the penumbra of my shadow, I covered Zishin's head with a hood of living night and whispered a word of command. Light flared under the shadow, and I felt a brief but sharp burn across the skin where my palm rested on the sergeant's neck—the charm of conditional silence coiled around the root of his tongue rising to the surface to strike at me. Zishin whimpered and a brief convulsion rippled the length of his body from head to feet, but that was all the movement my hood allowed him.

The charm that sealed his lips against unbidden truths was strong, but not strong enough. Now that I knew how much opposition I faced, I knew the cost of breaking the spell. I spoke the word again, louder. This time, when the burn came, it felt as though someone had wrapped my entire arm in a fiery blanket, and the pain lasted much longer. When Zishin whimpered and convulsed, I whimpered with him. Closing my eyes, I took a series of deep slow breaths, forcing the pain to bend to my will.

As it faded away, I braced myself for what was to come. I was pretty sure that I *could* have unraveled the charm if I'd had a bit more time, and I desperately wished that I'd had the leisure for the less painful option. But even here in Smuggler's Rest, tossing a watchman into a darkened alley would draw comment and, eventually, investigation.

Bracing myself, I repeated the word one last time, yelling it this time. The world dissolved in fire and pain drove me to my knees. Zishin followed me down, bound as he was by my magic. I managed to hold onto consciousness, Zishin, and my knife, though I only barely kept my grip on that last. My point nicked the sergeant's skin just above the big artery in his throat, drawing a tiny trail of blood droplets in its wake like a scarlet inchworm.

"Tell me true," I said. "Did Fei send you to me with that note?"

"Yes." The sergeant's voice sounded weak and thready. "Or, if it wasn't her, it was one like enough to be her twin."

"And why didn't you let any of your fellow watchmen know about that?"

"She made me promise not to tell anyone, not even the rest of the Mufflers, and you don't cross Fei if you want to keep breathing." His face twisted into a frown. "I think she might have been afraid of something. But that's really all I know."

"Thank you," I said, then struck him across the base of the skull with the pommel of my knife.

The blow was gentle, barely enough to stagger a healthy man. But the sergeant had just suffered through the breaking of a spell housed inside his own head, and now his eyes rolled up and he slumped to the ground. He would be out for a good hour if I was any judge of spell backlash.

I held onto my control of Triss, using his shadowy fingers to find extra holds amongst the stones of the nearest building as I ascended once again into the chimney forest. Then I shrouded up and put some distance between me and the unconscious Zishin. The rooftops were crowded, thick with sleepers and creepers both.

I finally found us a nice secluded little perch at the intersection between a corner post and a huge beam nine stories off the ground in a tenement going up in a lot cleared by fire. In this part of town, that probably meant arson and insurance fraud. And, judging by the sloppy work on the joins and the fact that none of the beams looked like they'd been properly cured, neither the owner nor the construction crew was planning on this building lasting beyond the next convenient fire.

It made me wish I had the time and freedom to track down the bastard. I didn't much care about the insurance company getting screwed or the property damage, but I'd never yet seen an apartment fire that didn't kill someone poor. That shit pissed me off royally. Nine times out of ten, the kind of owner that would burn a building like this had been born to money and claimed blood as blue as the sky. Not that they sullied their precious noble hands with the actual details of things. They usually did all their business through agents and cutouts.

That was a good part of the problem, really. They didn't know a thing about the lives their tenants lived, and they didn't really see them as people, just silhouettes, ghosts of the lower classes. That was the true tragedy of Namara. With the death of my goddess, the people who didn't matter to the mighty had lost their divine champion, the one member of the Court of Heaven who was willing to see justice done on the nobles and landholders. I salved my guilt at surviving my goddess's fall with a promise to look into this if I lived through the next couple of weeks.

When I finally released Triss, he stretched himself out into dragon form on the beam at my feet. Then wrapped around it snakelike, curling back to look at me. "Tell me what the sergeant had to say."

So I did.

"What an interesting conversation," he said after I'd finished.

"Wasn't it just," I agreed.

Zishin was no mage, so it was possible he'd been played by someone using an illusion and pretending to be Fei, but that felt like the wrong answer to me. It'd be one thing if Fei's body had turned up, but failing that, I would be very reluctant to count her out of the picture under any circumstances. After hearing what Zishin had to tell me, I was going to assume she was still with us. But what was her play in all this?

"Do you think Fei set us up?" asked Triss.

"I don't know. I'd like to believe she didn't." Triss cocked his head to one side skeptically, and I continued. "Oh, not because I'd put something like that past her. Just because I'm having a hard time seeing her angle. If all she wanted was to bag the reward for turning me in, she could have done it any old time. No, there's something more going on here, and we need to find out what."

"That's not going to be easy, not with the entire city knowing exactly what you look like now. The whole of Tienese officialdom is going to be yammering after us like they haven't since the week right after you killed Ashvik. Add in that every single one of our shadowside acquaintances will be measuring you for a coffin and counting the various rewards up, and that we've lost our best fallback, and I'm thinking we're real close to having to head for parts elsewhere."

"What about our Dyad friends? And all that talk about duty?"

Triss shrugged his wings. "You've just named the only reasons I haven't been pushing hard to leave town since we first saw that damn poster. But frankly, I'm at a loss as to how we can help the Dyad when we can't even find out who took her. I'd hate to abandon VoS, but I don't see how us dying for her without accomplishing anything advances her cause any. Or our duty for that matter. I'm willing to sleep on it and see what we can come up with, but if nothing occurs between now and tomorrow night, I think we may have to walk away."

I didn't like it, but he had a distinct point. We didn't know who had VoS and Vala and Stel, much less where they might be keeping them. Or, if I was going to be completely honest about the whole thing, even if they were still alive. It had been twenty hours since the ambush at the Nonesuch, plenty of time for the worst to have happened.

I rubbed at my burning eyes and tried to think of a decent counterargument, but I had nothing. Possibly because I'd gotten all of three hours' sleep since the ambush, and little enough in the twenty-four before that. Exhausted, covered in cuts and bruises, still stinking of shit despite my best efforts to get clean . . . I was all out. Once upon a time I could have relied on my faith to carry me forward when wit and will had failed me, but that faith had long since failed me, too. Maybe it *was* time I gave up.

"Maybe you're right, Triss, but I hate the idea."

"So do I, Aral. So do I."

There didn't seem to be anything more to say at that point, so I dragged myself upright. Much as I would have liked to go to sleep right there on the beam, I needed to get under cover before the sun came up, ideally someplace where I could find a drink. With my face glaring out of posters on every wall in the whole damned city, the harsh light of day had become as much my enemy as it was any vampire's.

Unfortunately, I was running mighty thin of good places to lay up and sleep, a fact that was hammered home when I reached the location of my third-tier fallback, a ruptured water tank atop a condemned tenement in Quarryside. The whole building should have been leveled long since, but the owners had gotten tied up in legal battles, and squatters had taken over until things got settled.

It was a shitty spot, both in terms of the state of the tank and the fact that if the owners ever solved their differences the place would be gone in a matter of days. But I no longer had temple funds covering my fallback expenses, and that meant I had to live with squats.

I'd placed a couple of minor aversion spells on the tank when I parked my cache there. That had kept anyone more desperate than I was from moving in. What the magic hadn't done, as I now discovered, was prevent some of the more enterprising squatters living on the floors below from simply knocking the thing off the roof and putting up a new tank on top of the old supports.

"Now what?" I asked Triss. As if to emphasize my question, a single drop of water plinked free of one of the freshly tarred seams on the new tank and splattered itself across my forehead. A momentary kiss of cold soon lost in the muggy summer night.

"I don't know. I don't like any of the one-nights under the circumstances."

I didn't either. A silk hammock hung high in the branches of an ancient oak in the royal preserve might provide a decent place to grab a few hours' sleep on a dark night when Triss could be relied on to keep watch. But full sun and high summer would render Triss mostly blind, and the place would be teeming with petty nobles taking to the park on the Sovann Hill as a refuge against the city's heat. That would seriously increase the chances of someone deciding to climb the wrong tree.

The one-nights in Backpast and down behind Spicemarket weren't much better, and all three were far enough away that we'd be doing most of our traveling under a new-risen sun. There was only one place I could think of that was close which might serve as a refuge.

"What do you think of going back to the brewery?" I asked reluctantly.

"I hate it," he grumbled. "But I hate it less than cracking into someone's attic and hoping they don't notice or laying up in the sewers with the Durkoth hunting us."

I sighed. None of the neighborhoods within dark-time traveling distance were affluent enough for the attic option to have any real chance of success. Only the well-to-do could afford the amount of empty space that play needed to succeed, and Triss was right about the sewers. We simply didn't know enough about Durkoth capabilities to make that a safe choice. I ran through the options in my head again and finally nodded.

"That's pretty much where I'm at." Going back to a fallback that was known to someone who'd been scooped by the enemy was the worst sort of tradecraft, but sometimes you have to go with the least bad option.

In this case, I figured the brewery would be safe for a few days more. It would take at least that long for anyone to crack the Dyad, assuming they could do it short of killing her. Like a Blade or one of the Elite, Dyads were protected from magical questioning and thoroughly trained to resist the more mundane sort of interrogation. She couldn't hold out forever if her interrogator was good enough, but she didn't have to for our purposes. She just had to keep her mouths shut for a day and a night. Then we could abandon her safely if we had to. . . . Yeah, I didn't think much of me just then either.

I turned away from the water tank. "I was really hoping you'd come up with a better alternative, my friend. As far as I can see, it's the brewery or the Ismere, and I'm not willing to involve Harad in my business when I'm this toxic." The Ismere was an independent library, and Harad, its head librarian, was one of the only people in the whole world who I could still call a friend.

"No," agreed Triss. "I'd rather we chanced a one-night than bring our poison into the house of a friend. Let's go scope out the brewery and see what's what. It's that or give up on the city and our Dyad client right now, and I'm not quite ready for that."

"It's getting light," said Triss.

I nodded. It was, and, as far as I could tell, the brewery remained undiscovered and abandoned. Or, at least, I couldn't spy any watchers, and the dustheads who squatted in the lower levels weren't acting any more paranoid than usual. After working our way completely around the building twice, we'd settled in atop a nearby tannery to give things a longer eyeball—businesses that stank tended to cluster in the worst neighborhoods.

"We need to get under cover," Triss said. "Now."

I nodded again, but maintained my perch in the angle where two sections of roof came together. Everything seemed all right. It even *felt* all right, but going back to a snug that might have been burned really rubbed me the wrong way. I ran through the alternatives in my head for perhaps the dozenth time, but none of them looked any better from this angle than they had earlier.

"I really don't want to do this, Triss."

"Neither do I," he said. "But the sun's coming up and the city is against us."

"Aral Kingslayer?"

The voice that whispered in my ear was so gentle and quiet I barely registered it at the conscious level, but that didn't stop my hands from flying to my swords. I drew them in the same motion that spun me out and away from my perch, bringing the blades up into a guard position between me and . . . nothing. There was no one above me on the roof and no obvious opening in the tiles through which the voice could have come.

"What the . . ." I trailed off as I turned slowly around again.

"There's no one here, Aral," hissed Triss. Then, before I could respond, "But I heard it, too. Show yourself!"

"You *are* Aral!" Right in my ear again, and louder, but still little more than a whisper.

This time as I spun I sliced the air with my swords, but air was all I cut.

"My mommy sent me to find Aral! And I did. I found you right where you were supposed to be! She'll be *so* happy with me."

"Your mommy?" I asked.

"Aral, I'm sorry about yesterday morning. I had no choice." This time the voice sounded firmer and stronger, urgent but still little more than a whisper. "They forced me to it." It also sounded *very* familiar.

"Fei?"

"My mommy!" The weaker voice again.

"I think it must be a qamasiin," said Triss. "One of my cousins of the air, sometimes called the whisper on the wind."

Oho! "And Fei's familiar, if I don't miss my guess. Which would explain a great many things about our captain." An unfaced sorcerer with an invisible familiar could learn an awful lot about all sorts of things in a city like Tien, things that would do someone in the captain's business a world of good. "Fei *is* your mommy isn't she, little one?"

"Uh-huh. Scheroc found you for Mommy Fei. She will be so happy with Scheroc."

"Found us for what?" I asked.

The qamasiin squeaked in alarm, then said, "Bad Scheroc! Bad! Forgets to deliver rest of message." The voice shifted to mimic Fei's once more. "The Elite have me and your Dyad friend VoS. They've got some foreign Durkoth helping them."

Another vocal shift. "Aral, Triss, I think you can trust the captain, at least until we're out of this." It was Vala's VoS voice. "She's not been treated well down here."

Back to Fei. "Get me out of this and all debts are paid. Hell, I might even owe *you* one. Scheroc can carry a message back to me and—shit! Guards are coming back—Scheroc, go!"

Well, well, well, Fei must have been all kinds of desperate to send Scheroc to ask me to bail her ass out. It was pretty much equivalent to putting a noose around her own neck, handing me the other end, and hoping I wouldn't pull it tight. Being an unfaced mage in Crown service was very nearly as dangerous as being a hidden Blade. The Crown didn't like officers who kept secrets.

"That's all Scheroc has." Scheroc sounded sad. "Will you help my mommy?"

"I might," I said, flicking a hand signal to forestall any interruptions from Triss. "But I need to know some things first."

"Anything!" it said.

"How did you find us?"

"Scheroc went right where the two-faced lady told him to and waited. Scheroc waited and waited and waited, but you never came!" The qamasiin sounded quite cross about that. "No one came, and it was boring. But then Scheroc saw you slinking around the edge of the place, and Scheroc came to listen for the voice of the Aral. You spoke in that voice, and Scheroc thought it must be you, but you were not where you were supposed to be, so Scheroc asked. And Scheroc was right!"

"That's good, now—"

"Aral," interrupted Triss. "If we don't get off this roof in the next few minutes, the sun is going to finish coming up and then we're going to have a hell of a time getting into the brewery unnoticed."

"Point. Were you waiting for us over there?" I pointed at the brewery.

"Yes," said Scheroc. "Where the big magic drawing is. It was empty and boring."

"I guess we'll have to count that as verification that it's still uncompromised. Come on, Scheroc, we'd best finish this conversation inside, out of the light."

17

I leaned my head back against the half barrel and closed my eyes. "Triss, have I told you recently what an absolute treasure you are?"

"I take it you're getting tired of trying to draw sense out of our little qamasiin friend?" Triss dropped his head into my lap with a sigh.

I idly scratched the divots behind his ears. "You could say that. Or you could say that I'm just getting tired. How many times has it had to go back to Fei to get us an answer now?"

"Believe it or not, this is only the third, but I'm sure there'll be more. Spirits of the air are neither very focused nor interested in the dealings of the fleshed, not even the mightiest of the mystrals. Scheroc is a qamasiin, a minor eddy born of a lesser breeze, barely one step up from the natural winds of the world."

I opened my eyes just to keep from falling asleep. "I understand that, but it would make things so much easier if it could at least . . . I don't know, tell us exactly where Fei and the others are being kept."

"It has, and in some detail. It's just that neither you nor I can make any sense of its referents. If I tried to tell you how to get some-place using only a shadow's view of the world I don't think you'd get much out of that either. For all that Scheroc speaks the tongue of Zhan, I don't think it actually understands much of what it's say-ing. So it's no surprise that it makes no sense to us."

"Which is a long way of telling me to suck it up and get ready to spend tonight following an invisible spirit who cares nothing for the limits of the fleshed as it makes its weird way across the palace compound, right?"

"That's about the size of it, yes. Don't forget the part where we have to break into what Fei called 'an impregnable fortress buried deep under the roots of the palace' and fight our way past the Elite guarding the place."

"No fight!" came the sudden whisper in my ear.

"Oh, good, you're back." I sat upright again, though I'm sure the qamasiin wouldn't have cared if I'd been hanging by my ankles from the ceiling. "What do you mean, 'no fight'?"

"Mommy says no fight, guards will kill her and the Dyad. Aral must bargain them out."

"Yeah, I'm having trouble seeing how that's going to work. We've got nothing and nobody to bargain with."

"Crush the pebble, summon Qethar." This last was said in Fei's voice. "You can trust Qethar. They hate him here. Offer him the Kothmerk and he can make us a back door. It's the only way to get past the foreign Durkoth I've seen around the place."

"In case your mommy hasn't noticed, I don't *have* the Kothmerk. I've got no leverage, and if I do crush the pebble, I'm pinpointing my location. Not smart when half the city is looking to turn me over to the Howlers and pick up the reward. Doubly so when I'm not sure whose side Qethar's really on, no matter what Fei says."

"Scheroc doesn't understand, what does Aral want?"

"What I want is out of this fucking box that fucking Fei's fucking poster put me in." I started to rise, remembered the height of the ceiling, and settled back to the floor with a growl. "Dammit dammit dammit, I feel like a wolf caught in a trap, with those wanted posters out there everywhere. No. Worse. If I were a wolf at least I could gnaw my leg off and get free. Gnawing your own face off is a much harder . . ."

"What are you thinking?" demanded Triss. "I don't like it when you go all quiet like that."

But I barely heard him. My eyes had fallen on the diagram left behind by Vala and Stel, the remnants of the bonewright spell. "Maybe I *can* gnaw my own face off." I rose to hands and knees and made my way over to the edge of the nearer hexagon.

"That's madness, Aral." Triss put himself squarely between me and the diagram, spreading his wings wide in warning. "You heard what Vala had to say after they finished performing the spell, how painful it was, how no ordinary mage could hope to handle it alone."

"I am no ordinary mage, Triss. I am a Blade. Fallen perhaps, but still a product of the temple of Namara. From my first days in the order I was taught how to master and control my pain through will alone, disciplines of mind and body that no other school of magery ever taught because they simply didn't have to."

Triss didn't move.

"Other mages have always had their magic to fall back on, spells to heal and spells to numb. But we could never be certain that magic would be an option, not when magesight might spy a spell's light. You know I'm right, Triss."

"No. I don't."

I raised an eyebrow at him.

"Yes, you're far better trained to deal with pain than nine and ninety other types of mage, but that still doesn't mean that you can handle this. You're talking about a spell that rearranges your very bones!"

"Several of them have been rearranged before. With less warning and to no good effect. I lived through it when Devin broke my wrist, and when that guard in Öse shattered my shoulder blade, and both times I got the job done despite the pain."

"I don't think this is a good idea. . . ."

"I don't think it's a good idea either. Frankly, it's a terrible idea and I hate it, but I don't have a better one that solves the problem the posters have made for us. Think about it, even if we can get from here to where Fei and Vala and Stel are being held without those posters getting us killed, I'll still be exposed."

"Help Fei?" said Scheroc.

I pushed myself back and up to squat on my heels, ignoring the qamasiin and focusing all my attention on Triss. "Even if we successfully bust them loose and somehow find the Kothmerk, return it to its rightful owner and then leave Tien, I'm going to have to deal with the problem of my face at some point. That likeness is going to spread to every one of the eleven kingdoms. I'll never be able to show this face anywhere again safely."

"I know but . . ."

"But what, Triss? As long as I look like this"—I touched a hand to my cheek—"I'm fucked. The bonewright gives me a way out. And not just once either. The goddess no longer protects my identity. Say we manage to change my face some other way—and we're going to have to, or I'll never be able to go out again—well, the next face I put on is just as vulnerable as this one. If it's exposed somehow, I'll be right back in the same trap. I know it's dangerous, but if I can make the bonewright work for me, I'll always have an out. I think that's worth the risk."

Triss's wings slumped. "It might be at that, but do we have to do it right now?"

"Not this minute, no. We're both too wrung out to try it short of a couple of hours' sleep and a good meal, but I don't think we can wait much longer than that. If we're going to try it, then sooner is much better than later, because it increases our chances of succeeding at what's going to be a damned hard job under the best of circumstances."

Triss hissed grumpily. "All right. We'll do it after breakfast, but I reserve the right to say 'I told you so' if you end up with your face twisted into a pretzel."

"So noted."

"Save Fei?" Scheroc sounded awfully pathetic.

I nodded. "Soon, little one. Soon." At least, I hoped so.

I was actually a lot more pessimistic about our chances of making any of this work out than I'd let on to either familiar. Especially the bonewright, since I've never been much for high magic. A fact I was reminded of in ways both obvious and subtle as I worked to duplicate Vala's spinning of the spell threads. Sitting in the middle of one of the hexagons that she had drawn and decorated with symbols, I moved through a slow recreation of her spell, while Triss offered up encouragement and corrections from his place in the other figure.

If Triss and I hadn't watched the whole thing with an eye to reporting how to recreate it at a later date, it would have been utterly hopeless—thank you, Master Urayal. As it was, I had to check and recheck each colored thread of light as I set it in place with my will and the naming of the corresponding glyph, hoping that I had managed both the proper intent and intonation. What the Dyad sorceress had done with ease and verve in a matter of minutes took me over an hour to painstakingly set in place. But I did eventually get there, or at least I hoped that I had.

From within, the spell looked even more challenging than it had from the sidelines. The web of magic was all around me, a continually shifting net of color and light that I could only ever see a part of, since it lay as much behind as in front of me. But even more than the appearance, the *feel* of the spell daunted me. I could sense each of the connected glyphs as a presence anchored in my flesh—the ends of the lines were far more than just dots of light dappling my skin.

Each thread created an almost unreadably tiny replica of its master glyph, a replica that went ever so much farther than skin deep. I could feel the glyphs scribing themselves inside me. Most wrote themselves on the muscles and tissue lying just beneath my skin, others anchored themselves in sinew or bone, while some few drove deep, etching their meaning in heart and mind. It felt as though I were being illustrated from within, a living manuscript in three dimensions.

As I worked through the spell, I kept telling myself that the sensation would probably stop when I finished naming the glyphs, or at least that I would get used to it. Wrong on both counts. The threads of magic never quit moving and I never stopped feeling it as they wrote and rewrote their meanings within the medium of my flesh. It didn't hurt, but it was the creepiest sensation that I'd ever experienced. Perhaps this was how the dead might feel could they be made aware of the worms burrowing through their nerveless flesh. Sensation returned somehow beyond pain, but not beyond the ghost of imagination.

"Are you all right?" Triss asked, and I realized that some long but unmeasured slice of time had passed since I set the last of the lines in place.

"I don't know," I replied a few heartbeats after I should have. "It's a question with no simple answer. Say that I am unhurt, and you will strike as close to the mark as matters at the moment. This is a most disturbing sort of spell, my friend."

"It's not too late to call the whole thing off," he said, his voice low and worried.

"No, but I'm not sure I'd be able to make myself assay the thing again if I aborted it now, and all the arguments I made before are still true. Much as I would prefer to take another path, I don't see any way to get from here to where we need to go without passing through the gates of the bonewright."

And so, before Triss could argue further, I began. Raising my hands to my face, I touched fingertips to cheekbones, sliding them back and down . . . into agony!

When I was thirteen, Siri clipped me beside the eye with a spinning backfist. She was wearing a pair of cestuses at the time, and the iron weight over her middle knuckle cracked the orbit of my eye socket. My whole head filled up with the most excruciating sort of pain, and I'd thought that I could almost feel the line of the fracture, like a ribbon of hot wire dragging along the bones of my skull. This was like that, only more so, a red hot chisel carving away at the planes of my face.

I shrieked and jerked my hands away from my cheeks. I couldn't help myself. Triss responded with a hiss like a whole kettle of tea spilling into a roaring fire as he leaped forward to the very edge of the hexagon that held him. The necessities of the spell kept him there on the other side of the line, but I could see how badly he wanted to come to me.

Shifting to the Varyan that was his first human language, Triss barked my name, "Aral! Aral! Get it under control! You can't make that kind of noise here, not with the carassnuffling maniacs who live below."

He was right, of course, and I forced myself to inhabit the pain, to own it and make it mine. Make pain a part of you instead of an outside enemy and it becomes your own, a possession that you can put aside for a time instead of an invader you have to fight. My face still burned, but I was in control again . . . for the moment. I knew that I had a lot more work to do and I didn't think I'd be able to suppress the screams when I got to it. Which meant I needed to take precautions.

So, while holding the main structure of the bonewright firmly in my mind, I spun a second spell. Simpler, weaker, freestanding, something that I had learned long ago at the feet of Master Kelos—a zone of silence that would contain my anguish. As I finished, Triss nodded his approval, though I could tell from the set of his wings and the twitching of his tail that he was still deeply upset and worried.

So was I.

Not to mention frightened and hurting. It took an enormous effort of will to bring my hands back up to my face. This time I set my fingertips against the still raw-feeling lines of my cheekbones, and then stroked down from there with my thumbs to the hinges of my jaw. It felt like someone was hammering spikes into my jawbone as I swept my thumbs forward—shifting flesh and bone as I went. This time I didn't scream. I didn't dare, not while working on my jawbone. But oh how I whimpered.

It was the corners of my eyes that did me in. I'd wanted to reshape them to make me look less foreign. I'd never make myself look truly Zhani, not without much better sculpting skills than I possessed, but I'd hoped to at least split the difference between my Varyan roots and my Zhani home. But the nerves in my eyelids were simply too sensitive for what I was trying to do and I started to black out.

I could feel my control of the spell slipping away as I went under and I tried to hang on, but I just couldn't keep it together. The glyphs under my skin started to pulse and jump as the spell backlashed and my muscles convulsed in response, driving my fingers

deep into the flesh of my face. I felt my bones bend and twist in response to the magic and knew that I was seconds away from tearing
my own face in half.

That's when the voice came into my mind. *You are a Blade of
Namara. The* last *Blade. You will control yourself as befits a servant of
the goddess, and you will overcome this.*

The voice was firm and cold and genderless, but strongly familiar, and my only thought was that somehow, beyond hope or prayer
or death Justice herself was speaking to me. The thought was reinforced by the feeling of a second ghostly pair of hands closing over
my own, weakly tugging at them, trying to move them back and
away from my face. In that moment I believed that my goddess had
returned to give me one last command.

And I obeyed.

How could I not? I reached through the agony and the backlash
and the convulsions and I took control of my actions and my pain
once again. I followed the guidance of the ghostly hands and stopped
my own from tearing at my face. I'd never known pain like I felt
then as I slowly and carefully smoothed out the damage I had inflicted on myself. It made me want to curl up and die, but every time
I thought I had nothing more to give, the voice would speak again
into the darkness of my mind.

*You are Aral Kingslayer. You will not fail. You cannot fail. I love
you and I will not let you fail. You will do this. You will survive and you
will triumph.*

And somewhere in there I realized that it was not the voice of
Namara I was hearing. It was Triss. The hands that guided mine
were cold and silken, wisps spun from the shadow that connected
us even across the uncrossable lines of the diagram. It should have
been crushing—a sort of second losing of my goddess—but it wasn't.
It was deeply comforting.

Never in all the long centuries of my order had Blade and Shade
communicated that way, words spoken clearly mind-to-mind. To
have it happen now in this moment of dire need, was, quite simply,
a miracle. My goddess might be dead, but there was no other power
but Justice that would grant a Blade that beneficence. Not after we
had been damned by the Court of Heaven itself. Somewhere, somehow, the ghost of Justice lived on and had given me what I needed
when I most needed it.

With that to hold onto and Triss to guide me, I completed the
difficult task of redrawing the lines of my face. Again, how could I

not? When I finished, I released the threads of the bonewright, then
bowed my head briefly and whispered into the void.

Thank you, Namara, wherever you may have gone.

Triss flowed up and around me then, enclosing me in his wings
and his love. *She is in our hearts, as she has always been. You knew
that once, though for a time you may have forgotten how to listen for
her voice.*

I looked inward, focusing my mind on the problems I now faced,
and listening for the voice of my goddess to tell me what to do about
them. But I could hear nothing but silence. I would have expected
that to hurt me, like a new hope snatched away before it could fully
form, but it didn't. Namara might not have answered me in the way
I would once have expected her to, but somehow that was exactly as
it should be.

Because Triss was right, but he was also wrong. Namara did
live within us, but not in our hearts. She lived on in the ideal of justice and our duty to see it done. But justice was not the simple thing
I had once believed it to be. In my youth I had seen Justice as a sort
of divine idol in the shape of Namara. I had worshipped that idol
and served her as best I could, and that was right for the boy that I
was. But many things had changed in the years since then and not
all for the worse.

In my youth I had believed not just in my goddess but in the
idea of the gods, that they were our rightful overlords and that they
always held our best interests in their hearts. I had seen Namara as
a part of something greater than the base strivings of those who
walked the surface of our world. Because of that, the death of my
goddess at the hands of her fellows had very nearly killed my soul.

It had also rewritten my identity far more thoroughly than the
bonewright ever could and in ways that I was only beginning to
understand. For one, the gods were us. Whether our evils and petty
cruelties were a reflection of those who created us, or whether in
some way we had created the gods we deserved through the power of
our belief didn't matter. What mattered was that the Court of Heaven
held no more claim to true justice than did the courts of men.

While I might still agree with Namara's ideal of justice, I was
starting to understand that in simply handing my conscience over
to the goddess of justice, I might not have made the justest of
choices. It wasn't merely that I no longer saw the world in the stark
black and white that I had as Namara's Blade. It was more that by
falling into the place where the grays dominated the scale, I had

finally started to understand the importance of all that lay between the extremes.

The world was no simple place, and in becoming more complex myself I had begun to see the complexity of that world. It was not a comfortable feeling, nor one that lent itself to the simple act of listening for the echo of the goddess in my heart. I had to *think* my way to the right answers now, an entirely more daunting proposition. Where *was* the justice in my present plight? And with it, my duty?

Aral?

Triss's voice in my mind startled me out of the world of ideas and back into the one where my problems wore uniforms and carried death warrants with my name on them.

Yes?

Triss had shifted, leaning back so that he could look into my eyes. *When are you going to drop the silence spell? This thinking words at you is much more work than speaking them would be.*

Is it? And in asking the question I realized that it was. Mind speech must have something of magic to it, because using it felt a bit like spell casting and drew energy from the well of my soul.

With a thought and a gesture I dismissed my dome of silence. "Better?"

"Much." Triss visibly relaxed, lowering his head back to rest on my shoulder. "How are you?" The words came out low and urgent, yet soft, as though he were afraid I might shatter.

How was I? I ran my palms over my face, feeling for deformities or other surprises. It felt good, smooth skin and stubble. Though I wouldn't know what I looked like until I found myself some time and a mirror, it felt pretty much like my old face. Even the scabs and raw patches from my burns were gone. Externally I was doing fine. Of course, internally I felt like I'd been dragged behind a delivery cart for eight hours. It was a strange mix of wrung out and renewed.

"I'll live," I finally said.

"Good. I had my doubts there for a while."

"How did you do it?" I asked.

"I don't know really. It was like breaking down a barrier within my own head, a barrier made from my own substance—pain and blood, and nightmare giving way suddenly to wakefulness. I wanted so badly to reach you. I was beating at the invisible wall of the spell with my wings and claws, trying to cross into your half of the diagram with everything I had."

Triss squeezed me with his wings again, hard enough to take my breath away. "But I just couldn't get through, not even by following the line of shadow that always connects us. I was watching you die and I couldn't bear it, and suddenly I thought of the way Tien Lun had spoken into my head. How she had torn something in my mind. I looked for the place she had opened and though I didn't find it, I did find a new place to push. I can't really describe it further than that except to say that it lay at the heart of what makes you and I an us. Somewhere in the interweaving of familiar bond, shadow link, and love there was a barrier that is no more."

I'm glad, I thought at him.

So am I.

"Now can we help my mommy?" asked Scheroc.

"I don't know," I said.

Where *was* the justice in this situation? I didn't know that either. Nor who really deserved to get their hands on the Kothmerk. All I knew for certain was that justice wasn't on the side of the people who'd imprisoned Fei and used her to set a trap for me and my Dyad friend. That, and that I wanted to get the damned ring out of my city.

"I don't know," I said again. Then I pulled Qethar's pebble from my pocket. "But there's one way to find out."

"But not here," said Triss.

"No, of course not. For a number of reasons. I was thinking of someplace high up and close to water. I want the Durkoth out of his element and off balance for this conversation, and I think I know just the place."

18

"**H**ow do I look?" I asked.

Harad leaned in close. "Different enough that I'd not have let you in if you knocked on the front door of my library."

I grinned. "Then it's a good thing I broke in like usual."

"Yes, my wards knew you where I would not. This is, I presume, your response to those rather distressing wanted posters that have gone up all over the city. It seems a little drastic. . . ."

I nodded grimly, and felt a faint cool stirring across the back of my neck at the motion—Scheroc had insisted on coming along and I couldn't think of any way short of a binding to keep the little elemental spirit from doing whatever it wanted. Since bindings range from uncomfortable to excruciating for the bound, depending on their natures, that'd be pretty much tantamount to declaring war on Fei. Not really an option I wanted to pursue even if she was locked up in a royal dungeon somewhere.

I was just trying to decide whether I should mention the creature to Harad, and if so, how much I should tell the old librarian, when he preempted me. "Did you know that you have Kaelin Fei's familiar trailing along at your back?"

"Uh, yes?" Good answer there, Aral.

"That's a story I'll want to hear more of at some point. But I suppose that if you're all right with having it following you around, it's not a problem for me. Just keep it away from the stacks and any loose paper. The things make a dreadful mess."

I suppose I shouldn't have been surprised that Harad would be aware of the qamasiin. He was, after all, one of the most powerful sorcerers I'd ever met, and the Ismere Library was both his passion and his home. I did wonder how he knew about its relationship to Fei—that was a story *I* would have loved to hear more about.

Founded nearly four hundred years ago by a Kadeshi merchant-adventurer who had headquartered his operations in Tien, the Ismere had grown to house one of the finest collections of books and scrolls anywhere north of the Sylvani Empire. We stood now in the third-floor reading room, my usual point of entry into the private lending facility—via the roof of the neighboring Ismere Club and a little pick work on the balcony door locks.

The Ismere was much better stocked than the Royal Library of Tien, in large part because it had never fallen foul of the sorts of censorship and purges the latter facility had faced over the years. More than one Zhani king or queen had tried to censor the Ismere as well, but they'd never managed to get far, mostly destroying inferior or badly damaged copies the library had intended to get rid of anyway. It's hard to force one of the great mages to do anything they don't want to do, and being a great mage was one of the minimum—if secret—qualifications for becoming chief librarian of the Ismere.

"While we're on the topic of interesting stories, Aral," said Harad, "what *have* you done to yourself? And how? I don't think I've ever seen anyone manage that sort of bone-deep facial reshaping before, short of a full-on shape change, though I can see several ways that one might attempt it."

"Actually, I'm not entirely sure about the what. It's dark out there and I haven't exactly had access to a good mirror. The how's a longer tale than I have time for if I go into the level of detail I know you're going to want. So, if you don't mind, I'll save that part for a later date. In the meantime"—I pointed at my face and smiled—"I don't suppose . . ."

Harad nodded. "I think I can manage that."

With a sweep of his hand and a mumbled word, Harad conjured a full-length mirror clearer than the finest silver. The librarian was an old friend, my oldest in one way, at a shade over six hundred years. His span had been greatly extended by his bond with whatever slow-aging familiar companioned him—the life of a mage and his familiar always tend toward the longer of the two. I didn't know the nature of Harad's familiar because he'd never volunteered that information, and I knew better than to push, but I had no doubt it was something at least as rare and exalted as one of the great dragons.

"Thank you." I stepped up to the magic mirror and gave myself a careful looking over.

We hadn't done too bad a job, Triss and I. The face wasn't the

one I'd been born with, of course, but it did all the things my old
one had, if that makes any sense. I've always been a bit boring
where it comes to looks, medium brown hair, medium brown eyes,
skin somewhere between the dark side of light and the light side of
dark, features neither ugly nor particularly handsome, medium
build. . . . I *am* a touch on the tall side, and certainly my training
has put a lot of muscle on that frame, but really, barring the wanted
posters, I'm not the type who draws a lot of second looks.

The temple masters had often noted that very lack of distinction
was one of my greatest assets as a Blade. The face looking back out of
the mirror at me now fit that same old bill in a new and equally boring sort of way, which is exactly what I'd hoped to achieve. The exact
details aren't terribly important, but I was pleased with the way we'd
managed to tone down the Varyanness of my appearance without really making me look too much like I came from anywhere else either.

If I'd had to make a guess at my apparent ethnicity, I'd have said
my new face belonged in the Magelands where there was a lot more
blending of bloodlines than almost anywhere else in the eleven
kingdoms. Anyone from anywhere could claim Mageland citizen-
ship if they tested positive for either of the mage's gifts. An awful
lot of refugees from conflicts and purges in the other ten kingdoms
had ended up there because of that.

It made for the densest population of sorcerers anywhere in the
east, though there were plenty of citizens who had no magical gifts at
all, both native and immigrant, as there were other paths to citizen-
ship. It also meant that mostly the rest of the world left the Magelands
the hell alone. It wasn't smart to piss off a population that could throw
a thousand and one kinds of spells at you on a moment's notice.

"Well?" Triss asked after a while. He sounded nervous. "What
do you think?"

"That we did a good job, my friend."

He let out a sigh of obvious relief. "I'm so glad. I was worried
about the parts that I did. I don't see you like your fellow humans
see you, and I didn't know if that was going to make for some horrible mistake that you would never forgive me for."

I laughed. "Triss, there's nothing you could do to me that I
couldn't forgive after all we've been through, though I am glad you
didn't put my nose back on upside down."

Harad smiled. "I don't know. It would lend you some of the
character that you've always lacked."

"In my business, character is a dirty word, and you know that,
old man."

"And yet, your Master Kelos with his eye patch and tattoos was quite the visible one in his day. And that beard . . ."

Harad had, once upon a time, been brought in as a teacher of the art of deception for my order. That was nearly three hundred years ago, when he'd been involved with an acting company in Varya, one in a long line of careers that he'd taken on over his more than half a millennium of life. It was that association with the Blades which had prevented him from frying me like a bug the first time I broke into his library some eleven years in the past. Well, his wards really, as they'd been keyed to allow the entrance of anyone companioned by a Shade, a condition since narrowed to be specific to me.

"Don't go waving Kelos around as an example at me," I said. "You know very well that he always put in a glass eye, covered his tattoos with makeup, and shaved off the beard when he went out on a mission. The more flamboyant aspects of his appearance were something he used to draw attention to what he wanted people to look for when they thought he might be stalking them. It was a stage magician's trick, one I imagine that was originally drawn from the tool bag you created for the order."

"There is that. But come, you've said you're short on time and I think you've done sufficient homage to the niceties. What is it that you want from me in such a hurry. Questions answered? A banned book to read, like the one you needed when you got sucked into the Marchon affair? Is it something that we can work out over a drink? I've picked up a bottle of that whiskey you favor since you won't drink my tea."

"I'm afraid I'll have to pass on the drink." Though I felt a distinct pang of regret at the thought. "And it's neither answers nor a book that I'm hoping you can provide."

"Well, if it's not information you want, I have to say a library is a strange choice of venue. What *are* you here for?"

"I am looking to have a little talk and learn a few things. Just not from you. I need to speak with a Durkoth and I wanted to borrow your riverside grand balcony for a bit."

Harad blinked several times, the only real exhibition of surprise I'd ever seen him make. "It seems an odd place at an odd time, but I think it can be arranged. Do you mind if I ask, why here?"

"Aral thinks we might have to jump in the river and swim for our lives," Triss said in a dry tone. "Which would be the third time in as many days we've done something of the kind. It's getting to be almost as much a habit as the whiskey, and about as good for him."

Harad nodded. "Ah, you want to oppose earth with water

and air. A sensible precaution, and one that answers half my question . . ."

"Yours is about the only balcony around that both overhangs the river from such a height and doesn't require us to focus at least half of our attention on keeping an eye out for the rightful land-lords. I've only just shed the face on the wanted posters and I'd rather not have a new set drawn up because I've been spotted on some baron's private balcony. I know it's an imposition and not without some risk. . . ."

"Tell me a bit more about this Durkoth," said Harad.

I was impatient, but if I wanted Harad's help, I knew I had to give him what he wanted. I quickly filled him in on my earlier en-counter with Qethar and as many of the surrounding events as I could manage in a few minutes. More than once during that time an impatient Scheroc tugged at my hair or the folds of my shirt. At the end of my explanation, Harad asked to see Qethar's pebble, so I handed it over. He examined the small stone closely, going so far as tasting it before finally giving it back to me.

"No magic there, but then I didn't expect any. Do you really think this Qethar won't figure out who you are?"

I shrugged. "I honestly have no idea. He's got to know I don't trust him. That means my cover story of being a go-between from the real Aral should be plausible enough, as long as Triss stays out of sight. I guess if I'd thought it through I might have waited to use the bonewright spell till after we'd had our conversation. But then again, I might not. There's some real advantage to be had in con-vincing him I'm someone else."

"Hmm." Harad stroked his beard. "All right, I haven't had much to do with the Durkoth, though I know their Sylvani and Vesh'An cousins well enough. Whatever happens, it should be quite interest-ing. I'll set the grand balcony up for you if you don't complain about my keeping a scrying eye on the whole thing from a safe distance."

Triss snorted. "Does anything happen in this library that you don't keep an eye on?"

"No."

Setting the pebble on the limestone floor of the Ismere's grand bal-cony, I put the heel of my boot on it and . . . paused. Now that the mo-ment had come, I found myself very reluctant to take the next step. In my mind's eye I pictured Qethar's pale inhuman perfection and shiv-ered. I really didn't want to face him and his glamour again. But then,

I didn't have a whole lot of choice, not if I wanted to break my associates out of durance vile and solve the problem of the Kothmerk.

Fucking magic rings.

I pushed down hard, expecting resistance, but the heavy little stone broke as easily as if it were a blown-glass bubble. While I waited for Qethar to appear, I hopped up to stand on the sweeping stone rail of the huge half-moon balcony. I wanted nothing between me and the river but air. I didn't have to wait long either.

Within ten minutes, Triss gave me a gentle tap on the heel of my right foot. *The corner of the building. Something's happening there. I can feel movement in the shadows.*

The library's foundations had been built right at the river's edge so that it seemed as though the stone wall grew straight out of the flowing water below. For a brief instant, the corner of the building seemed to ripple in sympathy with the water. Then Qethar was there in all his white marble glory, having simply slid around the corner on a narrow stone projection that grew out of what had been a smooth stone wall only moments before. He stood perfectly still, looking for all the world like the statue of some important past library patron. Though he faced me, the blank white orbs of his eyes could have been looking anywhere.

Like a low wave sliding in to break on a sandy beach, the Durkoth's little ledge rolled up the wall, leaving unmarked stone in its wake. When it reached the level of the balcony, the wave changed direction, sliding across the wall to a place just beyond the balcony's rail. Qethar inclined his head in my direction and stepped forward onto the balcony, passing through the railing as though it were merely the ghost of a barrier. Behind him, the ledge sank back into the wall around it, vanishing as if it had never been.

Though I'm sure he could have persuaded the stone of the balcony to bring him to me, he chose to walk instead. I suspected it was because he knew just how much it unnerved humans to watch his kind moving, and he wanted to throw me off balance. It was a ploy that I was quite sure he'd employed to excellent effect any number of times in the past, and not one iota less effective for the realization.

I couldn't take my eyes off him, or forget how his too-hot skin had felt against the palm of my hand. The smile he threw me when he finally came to a stop a few feet away was almost terminally self-satisfied—call it *Portrait of the God of Hauteur in Marble* by Sebastian Vainglorious and you could have sold it to any art collector in the eleven kingdoms.

I wanted to slap myself for the gut-level reactions I felt for him, both the unease and the desire. If I was going to have to work with Qethar to get Fei and the others free, I needed to break the . . . not a spell exactly, since the Others had no magic. Glamour or geas or simply the human fascination with perfection. Whatever you called it, I needed to figure out a way to neutralize my fascination with its object. As had so often happened at times of trouble in the past, the words of one of my teachers at the temple spoke to me out of memory.

In this case, I heard Mistress Alinthide saying, *"The key to solving any problem is understanding it. Observe, identify, analyze. Think!"*

Start with observation. Qethar looked like a statue, or really, the realized ideal of a statue; gorgeous, permanent, eternal. It was, I suspected, that illusion of eternality that lay at the heart of the Durkoth's weird mixture of allure and repulsion. The senses revolted against the idea of that which should not move moving.

That thought touched a chord in my memory. I'd felt something like it before. When?

Neither of us had spoken yet and now Qethar raised a sardonic eyebrow at me, but I ignored him. I had to if I wanted to regain and retain my equilibrium in the face of his glamour.

Find the memory . . . there. I had it. Walking through one of the Emperor of Heaven's temples as a very young boy—maybe even before I was given to Namara. It was a midnight service for Winter-Round. In honor of the solstice the temple was lit with torches rather than the brighter and steadier magelights used for most worship.

The gallery that led to the inner sanctum was lined with statues of Heaven's Court, gods and goddesses looking nearly as beautiful and haughty as the Durkoth glaring at me now. In the flickering torchlight the carven deities had seemed to shift position between eye blinks. I never actually caught a statue moving, but every time I looked, I felt as though something had changed from the last time.

It was one of my earliest memories. One that had lived on in the nightmares of childhood, and one that Qethar echoed simply by existing. Statues shouldn't change position. So, instead of seeing Qethar move, my mind registered a series of discrete and apparently unrelated poses, each of them feeling as though the Durkoth had *always* been in that position. That was profoundly creepy all on its own, but there was more to my response than that if I could only ferret it out.

Before I could pin it down, Qethar spoke. "I presume you summoned me for something other than a staring contest, Blade. What do you want of me?"

I was still badly off my game, but I couldn't let that pass. "I think you've got the wrong man. I'm no Blade." I turned so that the light from the windows fell more fully on my face. "Though I've come at the word of one."

Qethar's face didn't move but somehow I got the impression of a frown. "Are you daft, Blade? I told the pebble to only break for you. There's no way I could have been summoned by anyone else. Even if such were possible, your shekat does not lie. I can see that you're the same human I contended with in the street the other night. The one since identified as the Kingslayer."

"My what?" I'd never heard the word "shekat" before.

"Your soul-fire, human, your nima."

"You can see nima?" I'd never heard that about the Durkoth.

Qethar seemed genuinely surprised. "Of course, far more clearly than I can see the evanescent housing of flesh in which it resides. In the deep dark under the mountains, the essence of a thing is infinitely more important than how it might look under the light of sun and sky. Yours is an especially strong shekat for an ephemeral, perhaps because the shadow that lives within your shadow has strengthened your lifeline by tying it to his own."

And with that I had the final piece to understanding my response to Qethar. It was in his soul or apparent lack of one. Among my strongest and dearest memories is the day my goddess made me a Blade.

Namara is . . . or rather, *was* the Soul of Justice. *Was.* It's such a simple word and so sad—it stabs my heart every time I have to remember that she is gone. *Lock it away, Aral, focus on the Durkoth and what you need to do about him.*

Namara had manifested herself on this plane as a great granite idol sunk deep within the temple's sacred pool. When she made new Blades, she would come to the surface to test the initiates and to give them their swords if she found them worthy. Like the Durkoth, she never seemed to move, though her position changed. But with my goddess, there had been one incredibly vital difference.

The goddess didn't *feel* like a statue. The statue that was my goddess had a soul. No, the mightiest of souls. When you were in her presence you could feel that with every fiber of your being. You couldn't *not* feel it, whereas the Durkoth felt dead to me. If he had any soul at all, it was hidden deep under stone, reinforcing the illusion of untouchable statue.

But he wasn't a statue and he wasn't untouchable, a fact demonstrated by his obvious and growing irritation. "I have very little patience left for your kind, Blade. I gave you the pebble so that you could call me when you decided you needed my help to find the Kothmerk, and that is the most important thing in your entire stinking human city. If you've summoned me just so you can play games, it will go very hard with you."

"Don't threaten me, stone face. I've been threatened by the best. Push me and you'll just be one more name on the very long list of the dead I have to answer for when I face the lords of judgment. You won't get very far in the quest for the Kothmerk if I kill you, Qethar."

Triss spoke into my mind, *Let me handle this please.* Before I could answer, he reversed his position, moving against the light so that my shadow briefly stretched toward the bright windows behind Qethar.

Then he shifted, becoming the dragon. "Qethar, you want to find the Kothmerk. So do we. At the moment, your best chance and ours is to work together. Once we have it, then we can argue about what to do with it."

"I knew you'd see it my way," he said rather smugly. "Where do we start?"

"With Captain Fei and the Dyad," replied Triss, which was a hell of a lot more diplomatic than what I'd have said. "The Elite and some of your out-of-town cousins have them locked away in the deeps beneath the palace. We need your help to get them out."

Qethar went perfectly still. For perhaps forty heartbeats there was absolutely nothing to distinguish him from the statue he so resembled.

"The Elite have the Dyad?" he asked when he finally spoke again, and the only thing that moved were his lips. "How did you discover this?"

"I have my ways," I said. I sure as hell wasn't going to tell him that Fei was an unfaced mage.

"And you say that the creature is being kept in the hidden vaults beneath the palace?"

I nodded. "You know of them?"

"I do."

"That's good because my source is a bit hazy on the exact location. And it's not just the Dyad, but Captain Fei of the watch, too. I need your help if I'm going to get them out in one piece, and that's the first step toward finding the ring. What do you say?"

"If I help you with this, you will help me to recover the Kothmerk?"

"I'll work with you to find it." Which wasn't quite the same thing, but I felt pretty sure Qethar wasn't being completely straight with me either.

"Then, let us go and see what we can find out."

19

"**A**ren't you worried they'll be able to sense us here, so close, Qethar?" Triss breathed the question as he slid off my skin to peer through the narrow slit of the air shaft.

We stood in a sort of bubble in the rock with only a thin curtain of stone between us and the cavelike kitchen where several Crown Guards sat quietly drinking tea and chatting under the eye of the Elite officer commanding them. His stone dog lay against the far wall, a few feet from the doorway, where a quietly scowling Durkoth stood like a sculpture dedicated to the personification of disapproval. He wore robes rather than local garb, so I assumed he belonged to the raiders who'd attacked VoS's people. Another Elite could be seen down the hallway beyond him.

"No," replied Qethar in a voice softer than any whisper. "Several may be near kin of the earth as well, but none are so dear to her as I. She will not betray our presence. Not even to my cousin of the North kingdom."

Meanwhile, I kept my mouth shut and tried to hang onto my breakfast. I am not easily frightened, but our passage through the silent deeps of the earth had left me with the feeling that I had blind and many legged things crawling all over my skin. I almost wished that I had not borrowed Triss's senses for the trip, for my eyes would never have shown me what his unvision had made all too clear.

With silent tugs, wafted scents, and gentle brushes, Scheroc had led us to the place where a narrow and cleverly concealed air shaft emerged from the stone face of the riverside cliffs just north of the palace. Qethar had asked me to take the lead as he wasn't sure where in the complex Fei and the Dyad might be, and it was clear I had sources he did not. I'd worried at first that the simple little spirit might accidentally reveal itself to him in the process, but I needn't have bothered.

Scheroc's years with Fei had long since taught it the subtle art of communicating without betraying its presence. And now I better understood the captain's frequent habit of sniffing the air. Her bond with the qamasiin had probably given her a nose like a bloodhound's— the nature of the familiar always shaped the power of the mage— and the sniffing was a way of communicating with her invisible companion.

That's when things had taken a disturbing turn. Qethar had reached out and touched the rock wall a few yards to the left of the shaft. In response, a narrow tongue of stone had extended itself down to the nearer thwart of the rowboat we'd rented, like a sort of limestone gangplank. Qethar had gestured for me to precede him, so I stepped onto the projection and moved up as close to the cliff as I could get. Or I thought I had, at least.

But then Qethar stepped up behind me, saying something about the durathian road. I felt the stone moving beneath my feet as it slid back to once more become part of the wall and took me with it. Instinctively, I threw up my hands to protect my face when the hard surface came toward my eyes. It's difficult to describe the sensation as my palms touched the stone and moved through and into it. And I don't even like to *think* about the way it felt as the skin of my face sank into the stone.

Imagine a giant vat of rendered pork that's congealed. Thick, viscous, cold, filled with bits and pieces that you'd rather not know any more about. Now dump in some sand to give it grain, as though you wanted to make a scouring soap. Push your hands into the mess, your face, your whole body. Then, just as you realize that you really don't want to have anything to do with the stuff and start to pull away, it comes to life and pulls you under.

Every tiniest particle of this slurry has suddenly developed the power to grab and hold and push, and now it's moving you along through itself wholly against your will. You shouldn't be able to breathe, and yet you can. There is a sort of void around your mouth and nose that gives you a pocket of cold, dank, earth-smelling air to breathe.

In the first instants, Triss wrapped himself around me, providing a sort of silken armor that insulated me from the worst of it. But in my sudden panic at the situation I foolishly reached out and borrowed his senses, giving me something of a view into the matrix that held and moved me. Though mostly what surrounded me was solid rock—or as solid as could be, given the circumstances—here and there were veins of thinner stuff, sheets of aggregate and earth where water worked its way through from higher ground.

And these were filled with life. Worms and slinks and worse. Things of flesh and things of magic, the blind crawling creatures of the deep places. Through Triss I could feel them pass, and though I shall never forget them, I will not speak of them more. Eventually, after what felt like years, we arrived at the far end of the air shaft and Qethar opened a broader space for us to stand in while we watched and listened. Several minutes on and my heart was only just slowing back down to something like its normal rate.

"Come," Qethar breathed into my ear, "we need to find your friends and they're not here. The excavation moves away both to right and left. Let's move on."

I really really wanted to say, "Let's not." Instead, I chewed on my tongue and nodded.

We didn't have nearly so far to go this time, and a few awful moments later we were peering out through another ventilation slit. Three or four inches tall and a little over a foot wide, it offered a good view into a large domed chamber with two passages and several doorways leading off in various directions. It held a surprisingly opulent sort of miniature throne room, complete with dais, tapestries, and several large and expensive magelight chandeliers. The only current occupants were a pair of Crown Guards standing watch at the largest of the doors with bared woldos.

"Where are the cells?" I asked Qethar.

"There aren't any. This place was built as a refuge for the king and his closest advisors in the event of a major magical attack on the palace or a coup, not as a dungeon. Ashvik ordered it excavated, and hired my people to do all the work at great expense. I supervised the project."

"So where are the prisoners kept?" asked Triss.

"I don't know," replied Qethar. "There are many small chambers that could be hiding them. Guestrooms, storerooms, closets . . . Can't you use the same method that led you here in the first place to find them now?"

I shrugged. We'd lost Scheroc when we entered Qethar's durathian road. The air spirit was either unable or unwilling to ride along with me. I couldn't blame it. If I'd known what I was getting into, I wouldn't have been willing or able to ride with me. I'd hoped that it would follow us down the air shaft, but so far we'd had no such luck.

"I seem to have lost my fix on their location," I said. "Can't you just persuade the earth to tell us where they are?"

"My sister doesn't pay all that much attention to the quicklife that lives upon her surface and burrows into the shallowest layers of her skin. All she can tell me is that there are perhaps a hundred of your kind scattered throughout the complex. If I could point to one and ask her to keep track of that one, then for a time she would hold them in her attention and I might follow in their footsteps. But without me or one of my people to point up the scent in advance, I'm afraid we're out of luck."

Just then, there came a booming knock on the door where the guards stood. One of them looked through a slit in the thick bronze and then waved at the other while she went to work on the bolts. The second guard pulled out a small silver whistle and gave it a good hard blow. By the time the first guard had the door open, the Durkoth, Elite, and Crown Guards we'd seen in the kitchen earlier had spilled out of one of the open hallways.

As the door slid open, another Durkoth stepped through, this one wearing Tienese garb. She was followed by a lieutenant of the Elite and her stone dog. The latter had a limp human form tied face-down across its back, long dark hair a-drag on the ground. Though I couldn't tell for sure from there, the shape of the unconscious fig-ure's shoulders and hips suggested a young woman.

"Is that her?" asked the Elite from the guardroom, a male cap-tain.

"I certainly hope so," responded the lieutenant. "But we won't know for sure until Roketh here makes an identification." He jerked his chin at the foreign dressed Durkoth who stepped in close to the unconscious girl now.

While the Durkoth was looking the prisoner over, another door opened, this one off to our left. A third Elite peered into the room—another lieutenant, this one male. "Have you got her, finally?" He started across to join the others, his huge stone dog trailing behind.

"That's definitely the girl who killed Merqa and Thelat," said Roketh. "I recognize her shekat. I presume that she didn't have the Kothmerk on her when you took her."

So that was our Reyna. Beside me, Qethar made a low hissing noise, but otherwise remained still and quiet.

"Of course not," said the other Durkoth. "Do you think we'd have bothered to keep her alive if we'd gotten what we needed from her? After all the lives she's cost us?"

A faint breeze cooled the back of my neck and tugged my hair in the direction of the door the male lieutenant had emerged from. Scheroc had returned to point the way to Captain Fei.

"That's it then," said the captain. "We've no need of the other prisoners anymore." He made a throat cutting gesture toward the male lieutenant. "Time to clean up loose ends."

The lieutenant drew his sword, half turned toward the door he'd entered by and then stabbed Roketh as neatly as could be. At the same time, the two woldo-carrying guards brought the heavy blades of their sword-spears down on the shoulders and neck of the other Durkoth, and kept hacking away as she collapsed to the floor.

Several things happened all at once then: The three stone dogs threw their heads back and howled like demented wolves. Qethar snarled something unintelligible and reached out to open the stone in front of us, parting it like a curtain. Reyna, apparently having returned to consciousness at some point, lifted her head ever so slightly from where it lay against the side of the dog she'd been tied to and looked around. Roketh wrenched himself free of the sword that had skewered him and fell to the ground, crying out something in the Durkoth language.

"Tell Fei we're on our way," I said to Scheroc, and felt the little qamasiin dart away from me.

Triss was swearing at Qethar in Shade as he enclosed me with a skin of shadow once again. I couldn't blame him. This was *not* the way I'd have chosen to go about things if I'd been asked. But I'd been trained to work with what I had and not what I wished I had, and I was drawing my swords as I stepped out into the room on Qethar's heels.

Leave me a view, Triss.

Done.

As he expanded into a cloud of shadow, he left a thin slit open in front of my eyes. Functionally invisible, I started forward. I identified the Elite lieutenant with his drawn sword as my first target and aimed myself that way, though I tried to keep an eye on everyone in the milling chaos that had exploded in the wake of the murder of the two Durkoth. I would have liked to go straight for Fei and the Dyad, but leaving live Elite at your back was a mistake I would never make again. I'd learned my lesson on the day I killed Zhan's king.

But before I'd gone a dozen feet, the floor underneath my chosen target rose up on either side of him like great stone jaws and smashed him to pulp. And there they froze as Roketh finally died. None of the others had yet noticed us, and I shifted direction slightly to angle toward the captain. Meanwhile, Qethar was riding a moving section of the stone floor toward the remaining lieutenant.

That's when I saw something that sent my heart into my throat. The ropes that bound Reyna's hands to her feet under the belly of the still howling stone dog fell away as if they'd been neatly cut. Then she slid forward, touching down with her palms and cartwheeling to her feet, before vanishing as a cloud of shadow exploded outward from her skin. A moment later, a lacuna of darkness flowed briefly between me and the captain. Then the Elite was clutching at his freshly opened throat as the life gushed down his chest.

It was beautifully done, a perfect realization of one of Master Kelos's favorite moves, and I froze as everything I'd heard about Reyna the thief suddenly rearranged itself in my head. Suddenly everything she'd done made perfect sense. She wasn't working with a Blade as I'd once thought was a possibility. She was one of our lost apprentices, the last children of the house of Namara. That made her my responsibility as surely as if she were my own daughter. I started to move forward again, only then noticing that I'd stopped.

Triss!

I know, I saw. Blade trained and Shade companioned. We've got to catch her, find out who she is, where she's been. . . .

I reached the remaining group of Crown Guards just as Qethar dropped a foot-thick pillar of stone from the ceiling and crushed the last of the Elite. Within seconds, the fight was over and all of the enemy lay dead.

"Reyna!" I yelled, though I didn't think that was her real name. "Where are you? We need to talk."

Faint and far up the hall I thought I heard, "I'll find you, King-slayer, someday. I promise."

Closer, Qethar said, "The little witch has vanished, and she knows to mask her feet from the earth, so I can't tell exactly where she went. I'm going to try to cut her off!" A low stone wave rose from the floor and Qethar surfed it toward the door.

"Qethar!" I yelled after him. "That girl's important to me. If you harm her, I'll cut your heart out and feed it to you."

I didn't know what her name really was, or had been, but I damn sure intended to find out. I just hoped she wasn't one of Devin's traitors. More than anything I wanted to follow Qethar and find those answers right now. But I didn't know who or what else might be left down here with me—Qethar had said there were a hundred or so humans in the area, and if I abandoned Fei and the Dyad now, they'd probably die.

Duty before desire.

Swearing bitterly, I put aside thoughts of the girl and turned to run for the door the qamasiin had indicated earlier. As I went, I forced myself to let go of my awareness of the girl, to put those worries and concerns in a box and lock it away deep in my mind. I was on a mission now. Letting myself get distracted could easily kill me. That wouldn't do her any good at all.

As I passed through the doorway, I heard shouts behind me and glanced over my shoulder to see more Crown Guards rushing into the room from the other passage. I kept going. Hopefully, Qethar's presence in the entrance passage would prevent them getting a message to the surface and the palace any time soon, but I wasn't going to bet on it. Time was about to get very short and unless Qethar came back, my exit strategy was well and truly fucked. In light of which, yelling a death threat after him might not have been the best of tactics, but too late to worry about that now.

The throne room door opened into a broad open hallway with heavy wooden doors facing each other every twenty feet or so, all of them closed—quarters for personages of importance not directly related to the king at a guess. The Elite who'd come out of here couldn't have been too far away or he wouldn't have heard the whistle, which meant what I was looking for had to be close. I scanned for signs of occupation and noticed that the corridor got a lot cleaner about three doors down, which suggested not much traffic beyond that point.

Triss, check under those two doors. I pointed as I passed them.

Done.

While Triss collapsed back down into dragon state, I turned and put my back against the wall just beyond the doors. I wanted to keep watch both ways while simultaneously remaining as inconspicuous as possible. It wouldn't be long before the Crown Guard and their inevitable Elite officers got around to looking in on the prisoners. Triss slid his dragon's nose under the door now on my right, then vanished completely, leaving only a slender thread of shadow back to me.

Nothing here and no signs of occupation. I'll try the other side.

The thread contracted, and my familiar returned briefly before sticking his nose under the other door.

This is it. Noble's suite. Audience chamber. Table with scattered cards and a few kips on it where someone's been gambling. Two inner doors. One for the master, one for the servants. Two guards in front of the latter. It's close enough that if I stretch myself thin I can slip past them to take a look.

That sounds pretty risky. I'm not sure it's such a good idea.

No, it's all right. As long as I stay behind and under the furniture and keep myself on the pale side, I should be—ooh nasty.

What have you got, Triss?

Tiny anteroom, basically a large closet with doors on all four walls. Crude peepholes mounted on three of the doors. Destruction wards on two of them and the guards literally a half step away. We'll have to do this fast and clean.

Not to mention soon.

I'd been lucky so far, with no one coming to look down my hallway, but that wouldn't last. Now I had even more reason to hurry. Destruction wards were ugly business and I didn't know what orders the Elite lieutenant had given before heading out to the throne room. Not that I was particularly surprised to find them under the circumstances. I wished I could get a look at the wards through Triss's eyes, but I can only borrow his senses when he surrounds me. Still, I didn't dare move till I knew a bit more.

Tell me about the wards, Triss.

Drawn in blood. Fire, multiple triggers. Magic, breach, door, pull patches for the guards, maybe more.

I nodded though he couldn't see the gesture. That much I'd expected. There weren't a lot of ways to imprison a mage. If you had plenty of time and skill you could build a special cell with all kinds of passive wards that would cause the mage's own magic to rebound on them. But that kind of thing took constant maintenance from specialists, and really worked best on the lesser sorts of mage.

For quick and dirty yet effective you'd do something like the destruction ward, where any breach of the cell, magical activity—keyed to the blood—or even an unauthorized opening of the door would rain major league destruction down on the inside. Some seriously overpowered version of magefire was the overwhelming favorite for stone rooms, the sort of thing that leaves a fine coating of glass on all the surfaces because the heat is so intense. Really, the only surprise was that they'd warded Fei's room that way, too. It seemed like overkill if no one knew she was a mage, and if they did know, they'd have done something about binding her familiar. Someone was being awfully cautious.

Death-key? Or anything like it?

Hang on, sent Triss. *I'll look.*

A lot depended on exactly how they'd drawn the things and what, if anything, would happen when we took out the guards. Worst case was a death-key or some other trick that would trigger the wards if the guards died. But that sort of thing usually only happened in serious, cover of darkness, deny all knowledge, espionage kinds of situations. And, if they'd been going to use one, I'd have expected it to be keyed to the Elite lieutenant.

I'm not seeing anything too drastic, Aral. I think if we can just keep the guards away from the wards until we drop them, everything will be fine. Plan?

Can you keep that door closed? All I need is a few seconds.

Sure, but I'll have to stay here and hold it.

Do it.

Sometimes subtle and complex is the answer, with all kinds of distractions and reconnaissance and careful efforts to not harm the innocent. Sometimes you just pop the damn door open and cut some heads off, because that's the only choice you have. This was one of those latter times.

Though I generally preferred not to kill guards if I didn't have to, it actually felt pretty good. Maybe because this pair was keeping people who mattered to me locked up. By the time I was opening the inner door to the improvised prison, Triss was sliding across my back trail to close the one that led into the hall.

Still no interest from the direction of the throne room, he sent as he used a shadow claw to click the lock into place. *But that won't last.*

I'm working as fast as I can.

A double check of the wards reassured me that I wasn't going to kill anyone by opening the doors. Scheroc blew out of the peephole on the right as I was making my check, and started tugging frantically at my clothes. So I opened that door first.

Fei was waiting on the other side, her face bruised and bloody, with a long slice across her right cheek mirroring the old scar on the left. "It's about time you got here, Bl—Wait, who the hell are you?" The look of surprise on her face reminded me of the look of somebody else on mine.

"Aral." I was already turning to the other door. "The new look is your fucking fault, and it nearly killed me, so I don't want to hear any shit from you on the subject. There are two dead Crown Guards out there." I jerked a thumb over my shoulder as she came out. "Grab one of their swords and go keep an eye on the front door. We're a long way from out of this. Oh, and you're welcome."

"Thanks, Aral." She squeezed my shoulder. "I owe you big." Then she went to do as I'd asked.

Stel and Vala were also waiting when I opened their cell—handy little messenger, the qamasiin. They both looked the worse for wear, though not nearly so much so as Fei had.

This time I spoke first, tapping my cheek. "Bonewright. We can talk about it later."

Vala grinned and rose onto tippy-toes to give me a kiss on the cheek. "You look delicious."

Stel kissed the other one. "Don't know if I'd go that far, but I have to say that circumstances do make you look pretty damn fine. Thanks for the rescue, Aral."

I followed them out into the audience chamber. "Don't thank me too much just yet. We're still way down deep under the palace, and the Durkoth who was supposed to be our ride out of here has gone missing."

20

"**W**hat do you mean, Qethar's gone missing?" Fei growled the question from the position she'd taken up just to one side of the door.

"Come on, Fei, it's not that hard a concept. Last I saw of Qethar he was vanishing up the exit passage on a stone wave. He spotted something he was more interested in and left us in the lurch."

"Like what?" she demanded. "I thought I told you to offer him the Kothmerk. What's more important to him than that?" The look she shot me lay somewhere on the edge between defeated and outraged.

"You offered him the Kothmerk!" said VoS, turning both Vala and Stel's heads to glare at me. "Aral, how could you?"

I know you told them not to thank you, but I didn't expect the turnaround to be quite this fast, sent Triss.

Me either. Then, aloud, "I didn't promise Qethar anything other than mutual cooperation in locating the Kothmerk, and I'm pretty sure he understood that to mean that we'd probably end up at odds over what happened to it afterward."

"That was stupid," said Fei. "Why not just lie to him?"

"That's not how I work, Fei, and you know it. So does every other shadow captain in Tien. My word is good. But even if I'd lied to him, I think going after the thief who stole the ring might have ranked higher on his list than getting our asses out of trouble. As far as I can tell, he doesn't much like humans."

"Wait, Reyna is here?" This from Vala.

"She was," said Triss. "Very briefly before killing an Elite and bolting."

"Little Reyna killed an Elite, and you saw it happen?" Stel sounded incredulous. "How'd she manage it?"

"Pretty much the same way she killed all those Durkoth, I imagine." Then I held up both hands because I didn't dare let myself think about the girl yet—I had to hold it in a little longer. "But I'm done answering Kothmerk questions for the moment. We have more important things to worry about, like how we're going to get out of this hole."

"And what to do about the soldiers I hear out in the passage right now?" asked Fei.

"Yeah that'd be right up there. Triss, take a peek, would you?" He snapped his shadow wings down, launching himself across the floor and slipping under the door. "Stel, Vala, why don't you check the other chamber back beyond the anteroom there, see if maybe they were dumb enough to keep your gear close by."

"They weren't," said Stel. "That's where they conducted their interrogations. We got to see a lot of it in the last couple days." Her expression didn't invite further inquiries or discussion on the subject, so I just nodded.

"I guess we'll have to do without your battle wands then."

Vala scowled. "They broke them in front of me."

Triss reappeared from the hallway. "They're not coming down this way yet, but they've put two guards on the passage and there's at least a score of Crown Guard milling around the throne room."

"Elite?" I asked.

Triss shrugged his wings. "Probably, given where we are, but there was too much light in the hallway. I didn't dare try to slip past the guards to look."

"So, basically, we're screwed," I said.

"Then it's a good thing I came back for you when Fei's familiar begged me to, isn't it?" Qethar stood at the door to the inner suite. "Quite a surprise actually, since I hadn't even known the good captain was a mage." He directed a smile at Fei that made me want to smack him.

"The girl got away then?" I asked in my sweetest tone—I couldn't help myself. Though I was using every trick I'd ever learned to keep my concerns for Reyna down below the level of conscious thought, she kept bubbling up to the surface of my mind, and Qethar was really starting to piss me off.

For just an instant, the Durkoth's mask of perfection slipped, and his expression shifted from smilingly predatory to something twisted and ugly and utterly inhuman with startling swiftness. But then he got himself back under control and directed a too-serene look my way—the sculpture once more.

"Why yes, she did. Does that mean you *don't* want me to make you a back door, Blade?"

Aral . . . Triss sounded worried.

I'm fine, Triss. "Not at all. I think we both saw what happened back there, and I wanted to establish just how much you need us before I let you carry me through any more walls. Lead the way."

Fei shot me a "What the hell did I miss there?" look after Qethar had the floor turn his back to us. But I ignored her and followed the Durkoth. I would have loved to turn him down, if for no other reason than because I desperately wanted to have a go at following Reyna's shadow trail. But there was no way I could get out past an even halfway serious opposition when I'd have to pass through a bottleneck like the long narrow passage to the surface.

The trip back through the stone to the place where we'd left our boat was every bit as unpleasant as the trip down had been, and the less I have to think about it the better. Even the wet heat of summer slapping me in the face like a bucket of soup didn't improve my memories of the trip, however cool and dark it might have been.

The boat was gone, of course. Tying it up would have risked drawing unwanted attention to the place of our entry. Not that I thought your average guardsman would have been able to make much of the newly aligned granular structure of the rock wall, if they even noticed the slight change in the dark. All of which meant that someone had to go and fetch us a new boat before the sun came up. One look at the various injuries of the women and the attitude of the Durkoth told me which someone got swimming duty.

As we were looking around the nearby palace docks for a boat to steal, Triss alerted me that we'd crossed Reyna's shadow trail. Unfortunately, it led straight into the water, where it vanished. Given infinite time before sunrise and equally infinite stamina, I might have been able to pick it up again wherever she returned to shore, but with my comrades counting on my return and dozens of miles of shoreline to search just within the city, I had to let her go for now.

We'll find her later, Aral.

I know. We have to.

So, *Reyna,* I sent Triss as I ducked into Fei's privy.

This was the first chance I'd had to talk to him alone since we'd arrived at the captain's fallback, a town house in the Spicemarket.

Even now, we couldn't talk out loud. Not with Fei's qamasiin flitting about.

Scheroc had been very quiet since we got the wind spirit's bondmate free of the complex under the palace. But even without the odd little breezes that caught at my hair from time to time, I wouldn't have forgotten it was around and no doubt monitoring everything we said and did. Because of that and because I had business to do I dropped my pants and took a seat.

Triss slid up the wall to face me. *Reyna's not her real name.*

Of course not. I don't suppose you got enough of a fix on her Shade in the midst of the fight to identify her.

Afraid not. We did pass across her shadow trail long enough for me to get a good sense of her—he mentally hissed an unfamiliar Shade word—*but I didn't recognize the one it belonged to.*

I raised an eyebrow. *The girl does have to be one of ours, doesn't she?*

Almost certainly. But she's young, somewhere between thirteen and sixteen at a guess, which makes her somewhere between six and nine at the fall of the temple. We would have been on active field duty for much of her initial training and I just didn't pay that much attention to the little ones back then.

Do you think she's with Devin? I absolutely loathed the idea but I felt I had to broach it.

My one-time best friend among the Blades had turned traitor when the temple fell, along with some unknown number of the others. They'd set themselves up as the new order of the "Assassin Mage," or some such pretentious garbage, and now when they weren't doing favors for the Son of Heaven, they rented their skills out to the highest bidder.

At least, that's what Devin had told me. That and that they were going to become the power behind every throne. But I had no way of knowing what he'd told me was truth and what was lies, and I trusted Devin about as much as I trusted Qethar at this point. Maybe less. The idea of our lost and found apprentice falling into his hands made me want to vomit.

I doubt it, Triss said after a long pause. *If she had that kind of organization backing her up, I think there'd be a lot less chaos in the picture and a lot fewer bodies left where people could find them. That's sloppy craftwork under the circumstances.*

She moves like someone who studied under Kelos and Kaman, I added, *which suggests she's not a wild card who just happened to hit on a Shade when she summoned up a familiar.*

No chance.

*Just exploring all of the possibilities, partner. That would put her
name on the wanted posters along with the rest of the Blades that escaped the fall of the temple but didn't go over to the Son of Heaven.*

Though they'd become fewer and farther between over the
years since then, all I had to do to pull up the image of that poster
was close my eyes—the thing was burned into my soul.

*Let's see. Remove me, Loris, Jax, Siri, and Kaman. That leaves five
masters, all almost certainly dead, and all too old for our girl.*

So are the journeymen.

That left a dozen or so names. Remove the boys, and you had
five of the right age. One of those was Aveni, a pale blonde—rare
and hard to forget. That brought us down to four. Omira, Jaeris,
Faran, Altia. I named them to Triss.

*Not Altia. Her companion was Olthiss and I'd have recognized
that one, very sweet . . . nor Jaeris.* He slid back and forth across the
floor in front of me, pacing. *Ssithra, it could have been Ssithra, very
easily.*

Which girl? I sent my question with a force far greater than I'd
intended—this *mattered* to me at some level down below the conscious.

Triss pulled his head back in startlement. *Faran. It's got to be
Ssithra, and that makes it Faran.*

I tried to picture her. The name was Kadeshi, but that didn't
necessarily mean anything. There were Farans aplenty in northern
Zhan, southern Aven, the Magelands, even a few in the Kvanas. But
none of those sounded right for some reason. Radewald maybe?

Yes, that was it. She was from up north, by Dan Eyre, right on
the edge of the wastelands where things went strange. I got a brief
flash of the girl's face, laughing at something, a fall maybe. Laughing, but with a hard determined edge underneath.

Yes . . . on the obstacle course. She'd missed a tricky jump trying to take a shortcut and nearly broken her neck. But she'd laughed
about the incident instead of crying. A smart girl and determined. I
didn't know her at all really, but it was easy to imagine the girl who
laughed like that surviving where so many others had died.

We have to find her and take care of her, I sent. *She's one of ours
and we owe it to Namara's memory to do what we can for her. But how
do we do it?*

*I don't know. It's damned hard to find any Blade who doesn't want
to be found. It took the Elite weeks to catch her and they had the entire
weight of the Crown behind them. She's got to be very very good to have
survived the fall of the temple and to go on to do what she's done.*

Whatever mistake delivered her to the Elite last time, you can bet she won't let it happen again.

"You all right in there, Aral?" It was Fei's voice coming from the other side of the privy door.

"Yeah, just finishing up, sorry." *We'll talk more about this later.* I stood and cleaned up, then closed the lid that covered the hole in the marble bench with an audible bang. It was a nice privy, voiding directly into one of the faster running sewers, and with a good tight seal on the lid.

"We thought you might have fallen in," she said when I opened the door.

She gave me a suspicious look as I stepped into the hall, but didn't say any more, just went in and closed the door behind her. I had no doubt she'd sent Scheroc in to check on me, and was wondering what else I'd been doing in there besides the obvious.

"**Not** bad, Fei," I said as I looked around the sitting room maybe half an hour later. "Not bad at all. And you're sure no one can connect this place to Captain Kaelin Fei?"

She frowned at me over the lip of her ale pot—the expression pulled at the stitches in the big slice on her cheek. "Do I *look* dumb to you, Aral? Or have you just developed a need to spew pointless insults?"

I threw up my hands. "Sorry, it's just awfully fancy for a fall-back by my standards. I can't afford to keep a house as my *main* snug and you've got one you can just throw away on us? The corrupt cop gig must pay better than I'd imagined." It sounded snippy, even to me—this Faran thing was really throwing me off my game.

Fei's expression turned sour. "Oh, I'm not real happy about having to burn the place this way, but having the Elite turn on me like that means I need to stay officially dead, at least for the duration of this Kothmerk thing."

What she didn't say was that with the Elite involved she might need to stay officially dead forever. In which case, she'd have to abandon her Tienese real estate along with her job, any assets she couldn't carry away easily, and probably her name. The king's pet killers can really hold a grudge.

While an individual Elite might fail in his loyalty to a given king, if never the idea of the Crown, there was no fucking way that setup under the palace had been anything other than a Crown operation. Oh, given the politics involved with the Kothmerk, Thauvik would certainly deny his involvement to a degree that would include denouncing and executing the participants if they fucked up badly enough to embarrass him. But if he didn't know *exactly* what they were doing down under the palace, I'd eat one of Qethar's marble shirts.

The Durkoth himself was sitting in the corner on a stone chair he'd shaped from the flagstones he'd drawn from under the rugs. It looked rather like a throne, and probably irritated Fei no end. He hadn't moved or spoken since we'd arrived a good hour earlier. I couldn't say whether that was because he just needed some time to think after the raid on the underground fortress, or if he simply had no interest in the very human tasks that had occupied us since we got to Fei's place.

Food and drink had topped my list after my talk with Triss, while the ex-prisoners had all been in a rush to make use of the house's remarkably expensive and extensive bathing facilities after they took care of things like Fei's stitches. Stel and Vala had yet to return from an extended date with the biggest tub I'd seen this side of a palace. I'd never have guessed Fei for a secret sybarite, but her bathing room belonged in one of the more modern great houses.

I took another sip of my whiskey. It wasn't Kyle's, or even Aveni, but it wasn't bad and it was definitely soothing my raw nerves. It came from a Magelands distillery I'd heard good things about but never had the chance to try before. Sharper and sweeter than an Aveni, but with a really nice layer of smoke left on the tongue after the drink was gone. Fei kept a good liquor cabinet.

Despite a couple of very pointed looks from Triss, I was just starting on my third round. It'd been a while since I'd let myself take a third drink, but I didn't regret it this time. Traveling Qethar's durathian road had left me with a bad case of the creepy crawlies. Between that and my worries about Faran, I really needed something to take the edge off the impulse to try to beat some answers out of our Durkoth friend. I had no doubt he knew more than he was sharing.

"Why don't you just walk away now?" I asked Fei. "We both know what that place down there meant. Say you do solve the Kothmerk problem in a way that doesn't put you permanently on the wrong side of your king. Would you honestly be willing to go back to serving a man who'd use you the way Thauvik just did?"

Fei's expression went from sour to angry and she set aside her beer as she put both hands on the table and leaned toward me. "Don't go all sanctimonious on me, Blade. I'm not the one who walked away from the fall of the house of Justice to become a two-kip jack of shadows."

That hit me harder than any slap in the face, and much harder than it would have if I didn't have Faran on my mind. I'd walked away from her and the other apprentices as surely as I'd walked away from the temple, though I hadn't realized it till now. I set my drink aside as well, instinctively clearing my hands for a fight.

But Fei kept right on going. "My job's never been about the bastard who wears the crown, and I've never had the luxury you temple-raised hothouse flowers did of sitting in judgment over the ass that sits on the throne. Nor do I get to stick to the pretty bits of the city like the shining knights who run the regular watch. My blood's never been Zhani enough to get me that kind of job. Hell, I was barely able to talk my way onto the night watch in the Stumbles back when I started out. These days I'm the one stuck with keeping the fucking peace amongst the monsters and the mobsters any way I can.

"I know a lot of people look down on me because my hands are dirty from all the shadowside shit I have to touch in the course of my job. I want to save lives and keep the shadow wars from eating this city alive, and that means I've had to play kissy face with every kind of leech and lawbreaker imaginable. I understand what that makes me. But I will not take condescension from Aral fucking Kingslayer on the subject of crossing moral lines. I may be a crook in the service of keeping the worse crooks from doing too much harm, but I don't see how there's a whole hell of a lot of difference between that and black jacking for the gods."

I expected to feel outrage when she finished yelling at me, and I could sense Triss worrying about my response—his emotions were coming through stronger and stronger since we'd developed the ability to speak mind-to-mind. In some ways I would have welcomed outrage. It would have been easier, less painful. But it just wasn't there. Not after my experience with the bonewright and the thinking I'd had to do afterward.

What I felt was sympathy and shame. Though I'd never realized it before, Fei and I had a hell of a lot in common. We were both the end result of the corrosion of an idealist. So, instead of getting in Fei's face the way she'd gotten in mine, I just nodded.

"Point."

"What?" Fei collapsed back into her seat, deflating like a gaffed puffer fish. "Aren't you going to go all self-righteous on me and talk about how much better your goddess is than my king?"

"Nope. My goddess is dead, Fei. I can't serve her anymore. I realized that recently." I took another sip of whiskey and noticed the glass was empty. "I can still do my best to serve justice, and I've been working to get there again, though it's shit for paying the bills. But that's not really the same thing. Because, no matter how sure I am of my interpretation of justice, I don't have a mandate from Heaven anymore and I can't *know* I'm right. Quite the contrary. The Heavenly Court hates my guts."

I shrugged. "Maybe they always did. Maybe we Blades never had that mandate we believed we did. Maybe Namara's idea of justice was just as subjective as mine."

Triss slid up against my back, wrapping his wings around me protectively. *Are you all right?*

No. But I think I may finally be heading there. Thanks for hanging in there all these years.

"You're a strange one," said Fei. "Are you saying you don't believe in Namara anymore?"

"Say I don't believe in authority anymore and you'll be closer to the truth. Not temporal, not religious. Maybe not even moral. It's funny. I loved my goddess and I obeyed her without question. Her followers were and are my family. I killed who she said I should kill and spared those she wanted spared. I'm not at all sure that was right, but if you managed to bring her back from the grave somehow, I'd probably do the same again. Though I'm starting to hope that I'd have the strength not to."

Triss leaned forward so that his head came into view on my right. He looked worried. "Where are you going with this, Aral?"

"I'm not entirely sure, but I think I'm giving up on the idea that having a goddess—or anyone else—define right and wrong for me is a good idea. I—we, have to find our own way to justice now, Triss, and duty, and that's actually a good thing." I turned my gaze back to Fei. "That's pretty much what you do every day, isn't it?"

She snorted. "Hardly anything so high flung as all that, Blade. Justice would probably throw my ass in a cell. I'm just trying to keep my city from drowning in its own shit." She tossed back the rest of her beer and went to the liquor cabinet. "Think of me more as one of those poor bastards whose job is to unblock the sewers, and you're much closer to the truth."

Yeah, right, I thought at Triss. It seemed kinder than keeping Fei on the spot. *She can tell herself that all she wants, but she gave herself away earlier. She's as bad as I ever was in her own way.*

Bad? Not at all. At the moment I think you're both rather wonderful.

Whether Fei wondered about my sudden blush, I would never know, as Qethar chose that moment to reinsert himself into the conversation. "Will you two stop blithering about pointless philosophical piffle and get back to thinking about how we can recover the Kothmerk. Every hour that it remains in human hands is another hour one of our most sacred relics is profaned."

Since Qethar had pretty much blended into the background for me by then, I just about rolled backward out of my chair when he spoke. Maybe that's what the still and silent treatment was all about, another little way of dicking with the humans.

We're just not very good at paying attention to stuff that doesn't move at all over periods measured in hours. Didn't matter that he was strikingly beautiful. Didn't matter that no ordinary house would have an expensive statue of the sort he now resembled more than ever. Didn't even matter that I'd trusted snakes more than I trusted Qethar. After a while, I simply lost track of him.

I hadn't yet decided how I was going to respond to Qethar's comment, when I heard Fei say, "Well, and fuck you, too, Durkoth. As much as I appreciate the rescue, I don't work for you, and I don't think Aral does either." She stepped over and poured another couple of fingers of whiskey into my glass before I could protest.

She pointed the bottle at Qethar now. "So, if you want my help, stone man, you can damn well be polite about it. You can also wait till I've had a little bit of time to recover and think. I haven't had two hours' solid sleep in the last three days, and I had the shit beat out of me a couple of times in there, too." She touched the tip of the bottle to the long slice on her cheek and winced. "You want something from me, ask me nicely when I wake up, and then we'll see. I'm going to bed." She headed for the stairs.

That's when I realized just how tired I was, too, not to mention how much satisfaction watching Fei jerking Qethar's chain had given me. "You know, that's got a lot to be said for it." I raised my glass. "Here's to sleep."

Fei turned and looked back at me. "Blankets in the closet at the top of the stairs. Couch is next to the stone asshole." She jerked a thumb at Qethar. "There's a second bedroom upstairs. You and the Dyad can wrestle to see who gets that if neither of you wants to bed down next to his marble haughtiness."

"Or we could just wrestle for the fun of it and then all bed down together," Vala said as she came out of the bathing room. She was toweling off her hair, and now she threw me a suggestive grin.

But I wasn't in a mood for banter. "No, it's all right. I can just

sleep on the floor in the upstairs hall. It'll be more comfortable than
my brewery fallback ever was." I turned to the Durkoth and lifted
my drink in a mock salute before draining it. "See you in the morning, Qethar."

The ugly inhuman thing I'd seen earlier looked back at me out
of his face for a few brief heartbeats and I found myself wondering
how that inner ugliness could coexist with the outer beauty. Then
his face slid back to a neutral expression and I found it hard to believe I was looking at anything living.

At the top of the stairs Vala waited for Stel to go into the bedroom, than gave me a kiss. It made the world spin. Well, spin more.

"When this is all over, if we're still alive, I want to . . ." She
trailed off and looked suddenly thoughtful and serious. "I'm actually not sure what I want to do. I like you, Aral, maybe more than I
ought to considering what you are, and what I am. I'd like to try
something more than a quick tumble with you, but I don't know if
that can work."

I didn't know how to answer that. I liked her a lot, too, but I had
other responsibilities, and the one to a girl named Faran seemed all
too likely to come between us, to say nothing of what I owed Fei.
Before I could do or say anything though, Vala's normal mischie-
vous smile came back, and she gave me a wink.

She squeezed my arm. "So, I guess we'll just have to start with
the tumble and see what develops from there." Then she gave me
another kiss, this one rather more serious than the previous one,
and followed Stel.

That left me alone on the landing except for Triss. So I sat myself down with my back against the wall in a position that allowed
me to keep Qethar's feet in sight and my head from spinning. I really *wanted* to bed down, but I wanted to have another quiet word
with Triss even more.

What do you think? I sent, before he could take me to task for
my drinking.

He snorted grumpily but let it pass without a lecture. *About
what? Vala? What you talked about with Fei? Faran and Ssithra?*

*All that, I guess. I don't know what our next move should be. I'm
having trouble seeing how we can make this all work out without betraying someone, or several someones.*

I know. So what's most important?

My heart says Faran and Ssithra.

*We don't even know them, Aral. What if they've gone as bad as
Devin?*

Why do you always ask the hard questions, Triss? I don't know. They're just kids really, and the closest thing we've got to family. I don't want to believe they're anything like Devin, but then, I didn't want to believe it about Devin either.

What does your head say?

The Kothmerk. If it doesn't get back to its rightful owner soon, there's liable to be a war. No matter how much I want to make the girls my first priority I can't put them over that.

Good, then we're on the same page.

I closed my eyes and leaned my head back for a moment. The world lurched underneath me. I *needed* sleep.

I'm done for now, Triss. Keep an eye on Qethar, won't you? I have to let go for a while, but I don't trust him and I want to know if he moves from that chair.

Sleep. I've got it.

I think I managed to actually stretch out before I was gone, but I wouldn't bet money on it.

"**Aral,** you surprise me again." Stel set her napkin aside and belched. "I had no idea a person could do so much with a bit of rice, some fresh fish, and a few dried beans and pulses. That was a damn fine meal. I'm impressed. Doubly so, given what you had to work with."

"Fei's spice cabinet is almost as well stocked as her liquor cabinet, and that's a good part of the battle."

"I would never have imagined they'd teach you to cook like this at assassin school," said Fei.

I smiled sweetly. "If you don't know a lot about how to make food taste exactly like you want it to, it's very hard to slip poison into someone's dinner. Or their breakfast, for that matter."

Fei's eyes went very wide for a moment, then narrowed. "That's not funny, Kingslayer."

"That's because I'm not joking."

It's been so long since you joked regularly that I'd forgotten how evil your sense of humor could be. Triss sounded more amused than scolding.

Unlike this morning when he'd been very unkind about my hangover. An overreaction, I thought, since it was the first time I'd been really hungover since the mess with Marchon had made me take a firm look at my drinking. It was just the once, and now I'd been reminded not to do it again. I was in control of this thing.

I waited a few beats and then threw a broad wink at the table.

"But, more seriously, I wish I could have taken the risk to go farther afield and find some fresh vegetables. Unlike my luck with the fish cart there haven't been any to be had in sight of your front door, Captain." I started scooping up plates, then paused before taking them into the kitchen. "Vegetables always make for a better meal. To say nothing of the way adding more color improves the palette of toxins you can use."

Fei growled. "You're a bastard, Aral. You know that, right?"

"It's all in the spicing," I called over my shoulder. "I don't normally bother to cook . . . like that, but you're special, Fei."

I heard Vala laugh behind me and felt that I'd been fully rewarded. The interchange made a nice break from the frustrations of the moment. We'd been back and forth all morning—afternoon really, but who's counting—trying to figure out how to find "Reyna" and the Kothmerk. It wasn't going very well, and it didn't help that I hadn't yet told the rest of them what she was, or that I knew her real name. Which was something I needed to do soon if I was going to do it at all.

How the hell do we find Faran, Triss?

My shadow shrugged his wings. *I don't know that we can. It's too bad we can't make her fulfill that promise and find us.*

I froze. *Now there's a thought. . . .*

21

—◦—

"**T**hat's insane, Aral!" Triss had placed himself on the wall behind the empty chair at the foot of Fei's table so he could more fully participate in the discussion. "You nearly killed yourself with the Dyad's face-changing spell not two days ago, and now you want to risk exposing your new identity to the Elite?"

"Not at all, my friend. I'm talking about spreading a rumor, not putting up fresh wanted posters with my new face on them."

Triss lashed his tail but didn't say anything further.

"I think I missed a step in there somewhere," said Vala. "Why would telling people that Aral Kingslayer had been tracked down to what's left of the Old Mews neighborhood bring Reyna there? Wouldn't she want to stay as far away from the manhunt as possible?"

"There's something Aral hasn't told us, Vala," said VoS, choosing, rather disconcertingly, to speak through Vala's own mouth. "He's got a secret he's reluctant to share, though I haven't figured out what it is yet."

"Is that true?" Vala asked.

"Yeah, I guess that it is." There was no good way to do this, so I figured I might as well go for bald and bold. "Her name isn't Reyna. It's Faran and she's . . . well, not a Blade—as Namara died before she was old enough to confirm—but she is Blade trained and raised. Up to the age of eight or nine."

Vala jerked in her seat, almost as if she'd been slapped.

"That would explain a lot," said Stel after a long pause, though she didn't sound happy about it.

Fei nodded. "That *does* change things. You think that if we can get shadowside buzzing loud enough about where to find the Kingslayer, that'll make her come running to you for protection and help. Clever."

"But you *aren't* going to take her under your protection, are you?" This from VoS, via Stel. "She stole the Kothmerk and it clearly wasn't to return it to the Archon. She was going to sell it, forever staining the honor of Kodamia."

"It's not that simple," I said and Triss nodded his agreement.

"How is it not?" demanded VoS, this time speaking through Vala. "We took her in and sheltered her, gave her a home, responsibilities. Then, as soon as she got the chance, she betrayed us all."

For the first time since I'd known her, Vala looked genuinely uncomfortable about what VoS was saying through her mouth. Interesting.

It's probably not *the first time Faran did something like this,* Triss sent my way.

Just the first time she got caught. That thought had occurred to me, too. A girl with Faran's skills and talents had no need to play at being a groom to earn her keep. If nothing else, she could simply steal everything she needed. *Let's just hope none of* them *think of that.*

They will. In fact, Fei probably already has. Look at the way she's pretending to be part of the wall.

That made me glance at Qethar as well. He'd moved his stone chair in close at the beginning of the conversation but had played statue thereafter. Whatever his thoughts were on the matter, I couldn't read them from his face. And I was growing increasingly inclined to believe that any illusions I'd had earlier about doing so were pure fantasy, that all resemblances between human expressions and his own were deliberate manipulations on his part.

"Do you have any idea what this girl's been through?" I asked, as much to keep VoS too busy to think about what I was thinking about as for anything. "I do. When the other gods murdered Namara and had their followers tear down the temple, they tore down my life, too. I lost everything and it broke me. Completely. I crawled into a whiskey bottle and damn near drowned there, and I was a full Blade, an adult with five years of field duty. The Kingslayer. It nearly killed me. Faran was eight."

Nine I think, but close enough.

"Eight years old, VoS, and every single adult in her life was murdered. All of her teachers, her priests, even the servants who cleaned the halls. Most of her friends died, too. Everyone she knew and counted on was murdered along with her goddess. Everyone she cared about. Her family." I slammed the table with both fists, pushing myself to my feet and realizing as I did so that I was actually shaking with anger. "There were six hundred people living at the temple of Namara at the time of the fall. Over five hundred of them died, probably while Faran watched.

"An eight-year-old. And that's only what we know about. She showed up on your doorstep, what a year and a half ago? The temple fell more than six years ago. Who knows what happened to her in the interim? A little girl, with no one to protect her, her name on wanted posters in every town and city in the eleven kingdoms. Don't you dare judge her till you've been through half of what she has!" I was bellowing by the time I came to the end of my speech.

Neither Vala nor Stel would meet my eyes, though I saw Vala glancing uncomfortably at Triss.

I think you might have made a mistake there, he sent. *With the Meld if not the motes. They're embarrassed, but she's going to be thinking very hard about what you just said, and it's not going to take her long to start wondering about how little Faran was keeping body and soul together during the missing years.*

You think she was spying in Kodamia? I crossed to the liquor cabinet and poured myself a large glass of Fei's Magelander whiskey. My throat felt like I'd eaten a bottle instead of drinking from one.

I do. Though whether she was freelance or someone's Crown agent I couldn't say. It's the perfect job for someone like her. That or thieving, and she wouldn't have stayed so long if all she wanted to do was make off with a few choice items from the Citadel. Oh, and just so you know how I feel, it's far too early for whiskey.

I agreed with him, but that didn't stop me. I needed the help in calming down.

"You realize that none of that matters, don't you?" Once again Qethar's entry into the conversation startled the piss out of me— this time I slopped whiskey all over my hand.

"The only important question is whether the idea will work or not," continued Qethar. "Whether the girl lives or dies and who ends up with her if she does is immaterial. Only the Kothmerk matters. It's the most important thing in your whole world." He turned his hard blank eyes on the Dyad. "Your Archon would surely say the same thing if he were here now, Valor of Steel."

Vala and Stel went very still at that. "How do you know our name?" she asked through both mouths. It was a deceptively quiet question.

"I know the names and specialties of all the Dyads that set out with the Kothmerk as well as the pass codes for your mission. I would have thought the reason was obvious. My king sent me that information when the delivery went bad. It went out to all of his chief agents in every city that lay within a couple of week's travel of the ambush. You didn't really think your failures would go undiscovered by the rightful King of the North or that he'd trust humans to get the Kothmerk back for him, did you?"

"Why should I believe you?" asked VoS, again through both of her mouths.

Qethar pulled a thin plate of rock loose from the arm of his little throne and placed it on the table in front of him. Seemingly of its own accord it slid across to Stel.

"Flip it over," said Qethar. "Look at the other side, but show it to no one else if you don't want your Archon's precious secrets leaking out to the rest of the world. No offense, Captain Fei, Blade Aral, but you're both known shadowside operators and Valor of Steel never should have trusted either of you."

"None taken," said Fei as Stel lifted the stone. "We all know what I am, and I'm sure Aral feels the same way."

"Those are the mission pass codes, all right," said Stel. "I guess you are what you say you are." She set the stone back on the table and slid it back to Qethar. "We really are all on the same side."

"Of course we are, and if you'd been more than just muscle for your delivery mission you'd have known enough to send word to my offices when you got into the city instead of bringing in the broken Blade here. Though, now that you've finally hooked up with me, I might be inclined to overlook your failures in my report. Assuming, of course, that we can recover the Kothmerk and get it back to its rightful owner."

"That's very kind of you," said VoS through Stel. She sounded completely sincere, too, though I couldn't help noticing the way Vala's knuckles had gone white as she clenched her hands together out of sight of the Durkoth. Somehow, I didn't think they trusted him any more than I did. "I look forward to working together more closely to make sure that happens."

"Good," said Qethar. "I'd offer to shake on it, but my recent . . . contact with Aral has reminded me of the way my touch affects you children of the later gods."

Qethar turned a smile on me then, a beautiful smile full of promise that I felt all the way down to my knees. It made me simultaneously want to take him in my arms and punch him in the face.

"I *am* sorry about that and the other awkwardness at our first meeting," he said to me, "but I didn't know what your true place in all this was then. I still don't trust you, of course, but I do see the merits of your current plan and how much we need you. I'm sure that my government will agree with me when I say that once this is all successfully concluded you can expect a very handsome reward from the Durkoth."

This is an interesting development, sent Triss. *Do you believe a word of it?*

I don't know. A good deal of it fits in with the facts that we have available, but somehow I can't help but feel there's one sure sign he's lying.

What's that?

His mouth is open and words are coming out.

Triss chuckled knowingly in my mind. *There is that.*

While we were having our little side discussion, Qethar looked at Fei. "There will be a reward for you as well, Captain. Never fear. It's clear to me that Aral's plan will require the extensive use of your contacts in the shadow world if we're going to make it work, as well as my own, since Aral's are denied to us by his . . . loss of face. Shall we get started?"

"There's one little problem," said Fei. "I'm officially dead, and I need to stay that way for a bit."

"That is a problem," I said. "But not an insurmountable one. I figure the easiest way to start the rumors we need is for me to trot over to the Old Mews and let myself be seen, repeatedly."

"Aral!"

"It's all right, Triss. I'll be wearing a hood, and a mask of shadow. No one's going to see my actual face, just a man who can vanish into a cloud of darkness. Though it would be nice if we could use Fei's contacts to amplify the effect on the shadowside and get it to spread faster there. That would allow me to take fewer risks."

"Oh, I think I can manage that," said Fei. "I didn't mean to say I wouldn't help, just that it wouldn't be simple. I'll have to work through an agent. Aral, can you deliver a message to Sergeant Zishin and then escort him to someplace private for a meeting with me? I can't send Scheroc without revealing what I am."

I nodded. "Let's get to work."

My entire back itched in that way it does when you're expecting someone to put a big fat arrow between your shoulder blades, and the sweat trickling down my spine didn't help. I'd been at this for a week and two bottles of whiskey, and the neighborhood had filled up with Crown officers and bounty hunters of both the professional and amateur variety. To keep the rumors going, I had to keep sticking my hand in the bear trap.

It didn't help that even a year on, the Old Mews still stank of smoke and ashes. The faint sickening miasma kept swirling up to my perch atop Tien's newest temple to Shan—why is it that the temples always come back first? Fresh reminders of the fire that had murdered the entire neighborhood were kicked up every day, as the long slow work of rebuilding broke open the old scabs of burned-out building after burned-out building. Somehow the optimistic smells of fresh-cut lumber and raw plaster just couldn't make up for the occasional whiff of burnt meat and charred bone. At least for me.

Even knowing I'd killed the woman responsible for that fire was cold comfort. It wouldn't bring a single one of the dead back. Nothing would. I shivered then and wished I could pull Triss more tightly around me, or at least talk to him. But once again circumstances required that he sink himself into the dream state that gave me maximum freedom to use both his powers and my magic.

I was lonely and miserable and it would have been better on an emotional level if I'd picked any other neighborhood. But the combination of burned-over rubble fields scattered amidst all sorts of new construction and temporary structures created an ever-changing maze that made it much easier to lose even the most determined pursuit. That had saved my ass more than once as the number of hunters had gone steadily up over the last couple of days.

I could see at least a dozen different groups and singletons from my current location, every one of them out for my blood. Most notable was the Elite mission under Major Aigo, who had temporarily evicted a well-off merchant from his new mansion to set up headquarters.

There was nothing official to mark the place out as belonging to the Elite, but the constant stream of Crown Guards running in and out in their civvies at all hours of the day was unmistakable. I'm not sure what it is about the military mind that thinks that dressing career soldiers in civilian drag is going to somehow make the arrow-straight backs, battle scars, and drill field muscles invisible, but I've seen it time and again.

The *official* Crown Guard presence had taken over a three-quarters-finished apartment building a few hundred yards up the road, and it was particularly funny watching the out-of-uniform folks ostentatiously not saluting their officers as they went by. The bounty hunters were more circumspect, mostly taking rooms at nearby inns or squatting in burned-over basements. The number of genuine civilians had dropped off steadily starting on day two. Most of the lanterns moving about on the streets below belonged to one faction or another of the hunters now.

About the only set of lights down there that didn't belong to someone who wanted to sell my head to the king were the green lamps that marked those selling their asses to the hunters. Given the character of the new neighbors, there was plenty of work down there for the sex trades. Which reminded me, it was about time for me to dangle my own ass out in the breeze again.

"How's my route look?" I whispered to the wind.

"Give it two minutes from when you hear this, then go," the wind whispered back after a bit.

The ability of the qamasiin to blow words halfway across the city was coming in very handy for our little operation. In this case, the wind sounded an awful lot like Vala, who was down on the streets, carrying an intricately inscribed green lamp. The shadows it cast suggested that what she was offering was very specialized and staggeringly expensive.

That helped keep the number of customers she had to turn away to a minimum, but Stel, who had taken on the character of a bounty hunter, had still had to cover for her bond-mate by getting rid of two bodies. The corpses in question belonged to individuals who'd rather forcefully refused to take a whore's "no," at least until it was delivered with the crude battle wands Vala had created to replace her old ones.

After I'd counted off the requisite number of heartbeats, I dropped down the back of the tower and made my way along the spine of the temple. At the end I jumped across a ten-foot gap and down a story to land on the roof of a partially rebuilt tavern. As I moved on from there, I opened a tiny hole at the top of my shroud to give Scheroc a way to find me, the first of many such instances. Since the tactic exposed only the top of my head and that only to someone looking straight down from the skies above it seemed a small enough risk.

After about a four-block run across the hot rooftops, I reached the outer edge of the neighborhood and released Triss. It would have been safer for me if I could have kept control over him through the whole exercise, but Triss needed to be fully awake for the next bit since he would be the one doing the real work. Working carefully and quietly, we made our way back and forth along the perimeter we'd established for our operations, dancing an intricate and risky snake-step with the many hunters who were also quartering the area.

As we went, Triss kept "tasting" for any traces left by another Shade. We worked both on the rooftops and the streets below since I had no doubt that if Ssithra and Faran came a-visiting they'd do it fully shrouded. That was all part of the plan. When a shadow was strengthened by the presence of a Shade within it, it left behind what Triss called a "flavor" in the shadows it passed over and through. Fire and sunlight quickly destroyed such traces, as did moving water, but at night, one Shade could always tell where another had recently passed.

The more present a Shade was in the shadow, the stronger the flavor and the easier it was to both trace and identify. Full-on shroud mode left the strongest trace short of some sort of shadow-magic work, and that's what we'd been looking for since day one. So far we'd found shit, which was pretty damned disheartening considering how much we'd all risked to try to lure Faran here.

Dammit, I thought at Triss, as we came to the end of our run. *This is getting us nowhere, and it's getting more dangerous with each passing hour. I'm starting to think Faran's not coming.*

I was shocked at how much that thought depressed me considering that a mere two weeks ago I hadn't spared so much as a passing thought about her, or any of our lost apprentices for that matter—I imagine I felt a bit like a man who suddenly finds out years after the event that he's a father.

I think you might be right, Triss replied glumly. *But I don't have any ideas for what we might try next if we have to give up on this.*

I don't either, so I guess we'd better get ready to let some idiot bounty hunter get a look at us again. If we don't keep showing our colors, everyone's going to assume we've gone elsewhere.

"Hide!" The whisper in the wind was in Scheroc's own voice this time. "Elite coming this way!"

As if in punctuation of the qamasiin's warning there came the distinctive howl of a stone dog on the hunt. The labyrinthine nature of the Old Mews construction came to our aid once again, as three long steps took us from the center of a recently cleared and cleaned street to the edge of a large pit. There, charred debris from all over had been mounded up, filling in much of what must once have been a huge and multilevel cellar. A gap between two blackened beam ends was just big enough for me to slip through on my belly, though I tore a long rent in the hip of my pants in my haste.

A few yards farther in I came to a place where I could worm my way down into the deeper levels below the street. I would have preferred to make my escape up and out with the stone dogs involved, but haste had directed a different choice. With Triss to guide me, I made my way down toward the sewers and the bedrock where I could break another of Qethar's pebbles to summon him if I needed a pick-up. At the cost of several more rips in my clothes and a couple in my skin, I finally reached a floor grate that opened into a large pipe, which, in turn, presumably led down into the sewers.

That's when Scheroc whispered in my ear again, "Go quickly-quietly. Stone dogs sniffing above."

Fuck. I really didn't want to have to summon Qethar. I'm not sure whether that was more because I didn't trust him, or because calling him would mean another trip along the durathian road. I'd had to rely on him for a rescue twice since I'd started trailing myself like a lure through the Old Mews, and each time I'd come to loathe the passage through the earth that much more. That didn't keep me from pulling the pebble out of my pouch and slipping it into my mouth, where I tucked it between teeth and my cheek before proceeding. If I needed that pick-up, I'd need it fast.

Just above where it opened into the sewer, I ran into a partial blockage of the old stone pipe. I don't know what it was, but it felt like several hundred pounds of cheese that had gone bad, and it smelled worse. For once, I found myself profoundly glad that Triss's unvision didn't work the same way as my eyes, because I really didn't want to know any more about the stuff than I learned by dragging myself through it. I dropped the last four feet face first and landed hard when my attempt to roll out of the fall ran into another heap of drain cheese.

The winds tugged at my hair. "Stone dog has stuck his head into the ground above."

"Thanks, Scheroc." I spat the stone into my hand. Time to—

Don't break it, she's here!

"What?" I said aloud.

"Scheroc doesn't understand your question." The qamasiin sounded both sad and confused. "What does Aral want?"

Before I could answer, Triss spoke into my mind, *Tell it to go up and keep an eye on things. A Shade has been through here recently, and I'd like to investigate before we tell the others anything.*

I didn't ask Triss why he wanted me to do it that way, just tucked the pebble back into my pouch and sent Scheroc away. It wasn't the first time we'd looked for Faran in the sewers, but it was the first time we'd found any trace of her. I didn't trust any of the others where it came to dealing with our young Blade either. Not even the Dyad. Not with so few of my kind left. The stakes were too high to let anyone but Triss and I handle this.

Is it Ssithra? I asked once I'd sent the air spirit on its way again.

I think so. I didn't get a good enough taste of her—he hissed something in Shade—*at the palace to be absolutely sure, but it tastes much the same. Turn left and hurry. She's moving down and away from the Old Mews.*

The pipe wasn't big enough to stand in, so I kept low and ran, using Triss's senses to look out for any obstructions. At least it was dry—like many of the Old Mews sewers its upstream end was still clogged with debris from the fires.

"Stop," Triss said suddenly as we reached a junction where our pipe met another, larger one. Then, "Ssithra"—before he shifted into a long hissing string of Shade.

A moment later he was answered in kind from off to the left. I looked that way, but if Faran and her companion were there, they remained enshrouded.

Aral, we've found them. Step out onto the accessway in the main passage. Do it slowly—they're both terrified.

"Master Aral?" The voice was low and throaty but feminine, and there was a strong undertone of fear. "Resshath Triss? Is that you? Have we really found more survivors after all this time?"

Unshroud us, Triss.

"It's me," I said as he did so. "And if we're right in our guesses, you must be Faran?"

"Oh, thank Namara!"

She hit me with something midway between a hug and a tackle, pushing me back into the curved bricks of the wall. I wrapped my arms around her more or less instinctively, and suddenly we were both hugging and crying, and I was making vague reassuring noises. It didn't matter that we'd had practically nothing to do with each other back at the temple, or that we were of different generations. What mattered was that we shared a past now lost to us, a past that so very few people could ever even hope to understand.

Without my asking him to, Triss drew on my nima to conjure up a very faint magelight, setting the temporary spell in one of the bricks of the wall, so that I could look at Faran with my own eyes. For a long time, all I could see was the top of her head and the tangled and dirty brown hair that spilled down her back, and that was enough. Even the smell from the turgid flow in the central channel couldn't dent my joy at finding her alive.

"I'm in so much trouble," she said into my chest after the first storm of tears had passed.

"I know. We'll fix it. We just need to get the damn ring back to its rightful owner and everything will be all right. I'll see to it."

"Really?" She peered up at me and I got my first look at her face. There was hope there. Hope and fear, and lines made by the sort of pain no fifteen-year-old should ever have to bear.

"I promise. First we need to get you out of here, then we can arrange for you to hand over the ring and I'll take care of everything."

Her face fell. "Can't I just give it to you now?"

I was genuinely shocked. "You mean you've got it with you?" Judging her path from the outside, she'd looked so smart for so long, it seemed insane that she'd risk everything now by carrying her only insurance into the heart of enemy territory.

"Of course not. It's in the everdark, but Ssithra can retrieve it anytime."

"What!" Triss and I spoke as one. "How?"

"It's a spell I thought up on my own, based on something Master Siri once said about folding shadows and moving things through the everdark."

That triggered a memory of Siri doing something impossible with moving from one shadow to another and then trying to explain to me why it was both dangerous and too impractical to use. She'd gone into a whole lot of gabble about advanced magical theory and mathimagics, and the conversation had made my head ache. I hadn't asked again.

"Wait," said Faran. "It'll be easier for me to show you than to tell you about it. I don't really have the right words. But I'll need better light. Ssithra?"

For the first time I looked around for Faran's Shade. I found Ssithra on the curve of the far wall, where a shadow phoenix sniffed noses with Triss's dragon shape.

Ssithra shifted now to mirror her human companion's form as Faran stepped away from me, moving a few yards up the accessway. I increased the flow of nima to our temporary light—basically a controlled application of the same sort of low magic used in magefire. The long-lasting kind took a much more elaborate sort of spellwork and a good deal of power to create.

It revealed a badly eroded sewerscape with bricks missing from the walls in many places. The central channel looked more like a dried-up creek bed than a properly kept sewer. Though whether that was because of some blockages upslope in the Old Mews, or due to some failure of the water source they used to keep this part of the system flowing, I didn't know.

Faran stood up straight, then extended her arms out to the sides. In response, Ssithra relaxed into her partner's natural shadow, allowing Faran and the bright light to direct her movements. With my magesight I could see a glow of magic building within Faran as she folded her arms and then squatted down so that her shadow formed a rough ball on the wall across from her. Her inner spell-light slowly brightened, sending out streamers that tied her to the passive Ssithra. As she worked the lights changed color, becoming a rich green gold, like sunlight in the deep forest.

Soon the ball of shadow was threaded all through with spell-light, a dark package tied up with strings of magic invisible to the mageblind eye. Faran stood up then and stepped to one side. I expected to see her shadow mirror her motions again, but it did not, remaining as a ball bound with spell-light. More light flew from Faran, wrapping around the slender tail of shadow that connected her to the dark ball.

Then a bulge appeared in that tail and quickly grew into a second shadow, mirroring Faran's shape and movements once again, as Ssithra somehow disengaged from the binding Faran had laid upon her while simultaneously leaving something of herself behind. As that happened, the ball slowly shrank, until it was no bigger than a fist.

Now, Faran knelt to one side, reaching out toward the ball of shadow so that Ssithra, still mirroring her, did the same. The shadow of Faran picked up the shadow of a ball and began unfolding it like a paper artist uncreating an elaborate piece of origami. When she finished, a thin sheet of shadow-stuff lay on the shadow-Faran's hand with lines of spell-light marking the creases where folds of shadow had come undone. In the middle of the sheet sat a ruby ring, which the shadow brought to Faran.

In turn, Faran stepped toward me, extending her hand as she did so. "Here it is, Master Aral, and you have no idea how happy I am to get rid of the thing. It's nearly killed me a dozen times."

She lurched leftward suddenly, stumbling toward the open channel for no reason I could see. I lunged forward and grabbed her wrist before she could go over the side, but the Kothmerk fell from her hand in the process, dropping toward the noisome muck. But Triss was there, diving to catch the ring and close it tight in a fist of shadow.

"I saw that," he hissed. "Move the floor again, Qethar, and I'll send this thing back to the everdark in a way that will make it completely irretrievable."

The wall across the way rippled and flowed aside, forming an alcove where Qethar stood, his arms crossed, a cruelly beautiful smile on his face. He looked calm, but I thought I could sense something almost like panic underlying his expression. He was *really* concerned about the safety of the Kothmerk, if I was any judge. Which, of course, I might not be.

"Don't be a fool, Shade," he said. "And don't think I'm one either. If you destroy the Kothmerk it will mean war between Kodamia and the King of the North. I know you don't want that, so if you'll just pass me the Kothmerk, no one has to get hurt and I can finish with this hideous human dance I've been dragged into while trying to rescue a sacred trust."

Faran let out a quiet little eeking sort of noise as she saw Qethar and I put a protective arm around her. Ssithra moved, too, shifting back into phoenix form and putting herself firmly between the Durkoth and her bond-mate.

"It *is* you," said Faran, and something about her tone prompted me to put my free hand on one of my sword hilts.

"You know Qethar?" asked Triss, his voice low and worried.

"Of course I know him, though this is the first time I've heard his name. He's the Durkoth who led the raiding party that killed all the Dyads back in the forest!" She turned her head to look at me. "You're not working with him, are you Master Aral?"

I drew my sword and leveled it at Qethar. "Not anymore, no."

Qethar held out his left hand and made a clenching motion with his right. In apparent response to the latter gesture, the walls of the sewer flexed briefly inward.

"Give me the Kothmerk now and no one else has to die, Aral. Defy me and I'll destroy you all. And don't think killing me will save you either. I've asked my sister the earth to collapse this space if I die here."

"What's your play, Qethar?" I didn't have a lot of options, and I needed to buy some time. "There's no reason to do this, not if you are what you say. Or was your claim to be the King of the North's chief agent in Tien a lie?"

"Lying to ephemerals is beneath me," he replied. "I am the right hand of the *true* King of the North in Tien. I just haven't put him on his throne yet."

The ugly inhuman thing that lived within Qethar glared out at me again. "I am a high lord of the Durkoth. I was prince consort to the current occupant of the throne for four hundred years before he used some trumped up treason charges to cast me aside in favor of a prettier and more biddable model some twenty years ago. In exchange for handing over the Kothmerk, my new king has promised to restore me to my rightful place at court, if not to the consort's chair."

For at least the hundredth time in the last two weeks I wished I had a better grasp of Durkothian politics, this time to help me keep Qethar talking. As it was, I had no idea what question I should ask next. So I decided to go with what I did know, the Tien end of things.

"Why didn't you hand me over to the Elite when you first brought me down under the palace?"

"Why would I bother?" asked Qethar. "Your petty human squabbles bore me. I want the ring and a return to my rightful place among my people. Once I have them, I will leave the surface forever. Zhan's king and his creatures were a temporary expedient, just as you were, a means to an end."

"Looks like you and Thauvik are two of a kind then, after the way he had your people murdered." I hoped that a reminder of his fallen fellows would jab his conscience.

"He saved me time and effort," said Qethar. "The local Durkoth are all petty criminals and outcasts, unworthy to share my coming triumph, and the soldiers my rightful king lent me would only have served to dilute the honors that belong to me. But enough of this, your time is up. Give me the Kothmerk now or die."

I dropped a few inches and almost fell as the stones underneath my boots tilted me sharply toward the central channel which now flexed, assuming the aspect of a great mouth ready to bite and rend with the jagged bricks of its teeth.

"Aral!" Faran had slipped with me, and she sounded more than a little panicked. "What should I do?"

"Harm them and I destroy the Kothmerk!" shouted Triss.

An incredibly intense burst of blue light slashed across my vision from left to right, striking Qethar and temporarily filling my eyes with burning stars. Somewhere in the blurry darkness beyond my tears, the Durkoth let out a shriek. In response, the whole world lurched and then began to shake erratically like a caras snuffler entering the first throes of withdrawal. I stumbled and went to one knee as the floor leveled itself again, losing contact with Faran as I did so.

"The next one that moves dies!" snarled a new voice.

Aigo, Triss said into my mind as the earth continued to shake. *He's come in through a new opening in the roof of the main pipe along with another Elite. There are more Elite above, along with Crown Guards, but I can't see any stone dogs—maybe hiding in the walls around us.*

Qethar? Faran?

The Durkoth is down for the moment, but he's not dead or he wouldn't be bleeding so much. Faran's shrouded up and no longer close enough for me to touch her and Ssithra, but their trail leads straight toward the Elite.

My vision was starting to come back and despite the dust shaken loose by the ongoing quivering of the earth, I could now dimly see the haze of preset spells that hung around the two Elites—they were armed for dragon. *Toward?*

I'm afraid so, though I couldn't say whether she's going for Aigo or just trying to get out past him.

We've got to give her some cover either way, make a distraction....

I looked around, sizing up my options—I didn't have many. The space was too tight to give me any real room for maneuver. The only real cover was the alcove where Qethar lay in a slowly spreading puddle of dark purple blood.

But as Triss had said, he wasn't dead. He might get back in the game at any moment. Might already be on his way even, as a piece of stone had torn itself free of the floor and was now crawling slug-like up his arm toward the huge bleeding gash where his neck met his shoulder. I really didn't want to be standing over him when he reentered the fray.

When we move, Aigo's going to rain hell down on this whole tunnel, sent Triss.

Of course, but if there's anything at all to this idea of being a Blade without a goddess, it's this moment right now. Faran and Ssithra are family. I won't let any harm come to them.

So, what's the plan?

There's nowhere to run, and nowhere to hide, so it's going to have to be a frontal assault. Give me the Kothmerk, then shroud me up.

I don't think that's such a ... it's gone! Ssithra must have lifted it off me when the two of them bolted.

"What?" I said aloud.

Then something small and red and shiny hit the wall next to the Elite and went bouncing off into the darkness behind them before splashing into the muck at the bottom of the channel.

As all eyes turned that way, Faran's voice called out, "Was that what everyone's looking for?"

"I've got it!" Aigo jumped down into the channel and went after the ring. "Keep an eye on the Durkoth and the assassin."

Before Aigo had gone five steps, the second Elite let out a gurgling cry as Ssithra tore her throat out. I could tell it was Ssithra because she had to thin out a lot to manage both the kill and the shroud, and I got a flash of Faran's boots as she leaped up and caught the edge of the hole the Elite had come through. Aigo whipped around then and unleashed one of his preset spells.

In magesight it registered as a wave of sickly yellow light that rolled down the tunnel, breaking over the collapsing Elite and quickly beginning to dissolve her. Clearly it was aimed more by hope than any planning, because it slid past the hole well below the place where I'd last seen evidence of Faran. However, it didn't stop there, but came straight on toward me. Out of the corner of my eye I saw Qethar forcing himself up onto hands and knees then. The bleeding of his neck had been mostly staunched by a bandage of stone, and the increasingly violent shaking of the ground seemed to have no effect on his equilibrium.

Then the world went dark as Triss enveloped me in a cloud of shadow. I leaped forward and to my right, landing neatly in the middle of Qethar's back just as the stone slab that floored his alcove started moving upward toward a brand new hole in the roof. Behind me, a spike of violet energy stabbed through the place I had been standing. A moment later, I leaped again, launching myself from Qethar's back up and out onto the street.

I hit rolling just as a stone dog breached the surface of the street, throwing itself into the air like a leaping dolphin. It would have smashed Qethar to a pulp if it hadn't twisted suddenly in the air when it saw him, torquing itself around in the manner of a dropped cat trying desperately to get its feet under it. The maneuver worked, but only at the cost of the dog making a hard landing on its side. The ground lurched under the impact of the elemental, and several cobbles shattered. Then it reasserted control of its element and sank into the stones.

The street was in utter chaos. The ongoing and steadily worsening quaking of the earth had brought several nearby buildings down, though from what I could see, the effect extended a few blocks at most. Crown Guards were running to and fro, shouting madly and brandishing their weapons. Several Elite exchanged spells with what I guessed to be Vala and Stel sniping from a couple of nearby buildings—the incoming blasts looked an awful lot like the discharges

from the former's wand. Thick clouds of dust from the falling buildings were clumping heavily around the Elite and any remotely organized looking group of the guard in a way that strongly suggested
the intervention of a wind spirit.

Faran and Ssithra's presence made itself known by the rather
large number of soldiers bleeding out through opened throats. The
pair were both very good and completely ruthless, a combination
that went a long way toward explaining how they had survived the
fall of the temple when so many others had not. I was trying to sort
out where the pair might have gone by the simple but gruesome expedient of extrapolating along the line of dead they'd left in their
wake when Aigo came up out of the ground a few feet in front of
me. He was riding the back of his stone dog Graf, like a horse.

"It was a fake. The bitch assassin's still got the ring!" he yelled,
though the only reason I could hear him over the general sounds of
mayhem was that he was so close. "She went that way!" He pointed
with his sword. "Find her! Kill her!"

Neither he nor Graf even looked my way, just charged off in the
direction I'd already decided on myself. As I started after them, I
couldn't help but notice Qethar sliding in to follow in their wake as
well. He was still atop the stone slab from the sewers, riding it along
the surface of the street like a one man raft. I moved in close behind
him, but didn't kill him yet. I might need the distraction he could
provide.

He remained on hands and knees, nose up like a pointer and
utterly focused on Aigo and Graf and whatever lay beyond them. It
was easy enough to remain unnoticed even from just a few feet
away. Faint threads of purple continued to leak out from under the
stone bandage on his neck, and though he remained marble pale he
had lost the look of perfection. His flesh seemed to be collapsing in
on itself. None of which prevented him from going very nearly as
fast as the racing stone dog. It was a pace I was hard-pressed to sustain, and neither of us was making any gains.

As we moved onward, the tremors traveled with us, bringing
down more buildings. A huge stone temple crashed down practically
on top of us, filling the street with a wall of rubble and crushing a
half dozen Crown Guards who'd rallied behind Aigo. It would have
gotten me, too, I think, if I hadn't been so close to Qethar. The falling
and bouncing stones seemed to avoid him with uncanny prescience.

We made it another couple of blocks, with me slowly losing
ground on Qethar and the gap between him and Aigo also growing
steadily wider. I'm not sure what happened then, because Aigo was

around a corner somewhere in front of us, but I heard a sudden shriek from up ahead, followed by a terrible angry hissing.

Ssithra! sent Triss.

And Faran. I pushed harder, finally passing Qethar.

I could have killed him then, but it would have cost me seconds I wasn't sure I had. Instead, I gathered my nima and sent a sheet of magelightning flashing down the street in front of me. I hadn't a chance of hitting Aigo or Graf, but I could hope to draw their attention away from the girl. I heard Qethar snarl something behind me about saving the Kothmerk. Suddenly, the whole street on which I was running started to move with me like a horizontal avalanche. More buildings fell as I accelerated toward the corner and whatever lay beyond.

I drew my swords and readied myself. Just before I reached the corner, I threw one high into the air ahead of me as a decoy. Then I dived forward low and fast, rolling as I hit the moving cobbles. Some sort of really nasty blue-green spellburst briefly converted the flying sword into a burning metal torch before it exploded above me, but better it than me. Tiny drops of molten metal flew everywhere. Some of them struck my back and legs, burning deep holes in my flesh that stung bitterly as I rolled across them and up onto my feet again just beyond the mouth of the street.

Faran lay crumpled at the foot of a statue of some longdead general, her hair half burned away and blood streaking her face. She wasn't moving, but Ssithra was still there and unfaded, which meant she was alive. Major Aigo and his stone dog stood between me and her, the former facing me, while the latter repeatedly reared up on his hind legs and then drove down with his front paws like twinned sledgehammers, striking again and again at something on the cobbles.

The major whipped his head back and forth, scanning the darkened and dusty street, his hands raised high and strung with ready spells. That's when Qethar came around the corner, riding his little stone slab. Aigo brought his hands down sharply, sending long strands of spell-light snaking toward the Durkoth like dozens of snapping whips. That distraction was the opportunity I'd been waiting for, and I dashed across the short distance separating me from the Elite.

Aigo must have seen something out of the corner of his eye, because he turned midcast and tried to wrench one hand's tail of streamers sideways away from Qethar and toward me. But the spell had a lot of inertia, and he was only able to redirect a few of them with any hint of accuracy. Add in the ongoing shaking of the earth and my lacuna of shadow, and those few arcing trails of spell light that did come my way went wide enough of the mark that I never did find out what they would have done to me.

I heard Qethar's hoarse grunt of pain from somewhere behind me in the same moment that I brought my remaining sword around in a two-handed stroke, separating Aigo's head from his shoulders. I didn't even pause long enough to watch it bounce, but raced straight on past him to the place where Faran had fallen. Dropping to my knees beside her, I checked her breathing and pulse—both ragged but still going. I wanted to sweep her up into my arms and get her the hell out of there. But I knew better than to move someone with unknown injuries, for fear of making things worse.

I was just reaching around to check her neck when she opened her eyes and looked up at me. "Master Aral?"

"I'm here, Faran. Don't move. We don't know how badly you're hurt."

She smiled and shook her head. "I've had worse. Much." Then she laughed that same hard little laugh I had first heard from her so many years ago on the obstacle course, and levered herself up onto her elbows. "What happened to the Kothmerk? Please, I have to know."

"I don't know," I said, "and I don't care." But I did. I had to—even now the cursed thing could still start a war.

She opened her mouth to speak again, but I shook my head. "No, you're right. I have to find out, and quickly. We can't stay here for long. Bide a moment."

But Triss was ahead of me again. "It's here, shattered," he called from somewhere behind me, and his voice sounded like it was coming through six feet of grave dirt. "That's what the stone dog was doing. Destroying the ring so that Thauvik can have his war between Kodamia and the Durkoth."

And then, presumably, he could sweep in and pick up the pieces afterward and own the gap of Kodamia and the gateway to the west. I swore.

Faran's expression went cold and flat. "Show me."

I helped her to her feet, and with Ssithra trailing along behind, we followed my own shadow trail to where Triss was waiting. The stone dog had fallen on his side, leaving behind a deep divot where he had driven one cobble some inches below the level of its fellows with his hammering paws. The Kothmerk had taken a lot of breaking, carving a roughly ring-shaped hole in the hard granite paving stone, a hole that was now filled with shimmering red dust and shards of ruby. Blood stone it was called sometimes and now blood would come of it. We had failed.

I turned away, looking back toward the fallen major and Qethar. The latter lay broken and bleeding atop his shattered raft of stone, as ruined as the ring he'd tried to steal. I thought he was dead at first, but then his hand moved and reached out. Catching the edge of a cobble, he dragged himself a few inches along the shaking ground in our direction, then reached for another cobble.

I raised my sword and pointed it at him. Though it was already far too late to do anything to protect the Kothmerk—Graf's great stone paw had seen to that—I still didn't trust him or his purpose.

"Let me through," he whispered as he dragged himself closer. "Please, I must get to the Kothmerk."

"It's gone, Qethar, utterly destroyed. We all failed. Everyone except Aigo and Graf, and they're dead."

"No." Qethar closed his eyes and hissed in pain, then opened them and dragged himself a few feet farther. "I failed my king. My ambitions. Myself even. But I will *not* fail my honor. The Kothmerk is the soul of the Durkoth and the soul of a Durkoth can restore it. Please, badly injured as I am, I could still save myself if I let the earth take me into her heart and hold me sleeping for but a few years. I would live then, but my honor would die. Let me keep that and spend my life instead. Let me make right the horror you and your kind have wrought upon the Durkoth. Let me through so that I may give my life to the sacred Kothmerk."

What can it hurt? Triss whispered into my mind. *The ring is shattered.*

I sheathed my sword and reached to help Qethar, but he ignored the hand I extended him. Faran looked like she wanted to argue at first, but then she shook her head and moved aside. Qethar thanked us with his eyes, though no words passed his lips. It took him a good minute more of agonized crawling to reach the place where the broken ring lay on the scarred cobble.

He reached out his bloody right hand and laid it in the deep hole Graf's blows had driven in the street. With an effort that must have cost him a lifetime's worth of pain, Qethar pushed himself up onto hands and knees, keeping his right hand firmly in place in the hollow that held the shattered ring.

The stone bandage fell away from his shoulder and he began to shake in rhythm with the ground as the rich purple blood rolled down his arm from the great wound in his neck and shoulder.

Somehow he held himself there as it slowly filled the indentation, rising to cover his hand and the destroyed ring.

When it began to overflow the print, Qethar closed his eyes, drew a deep breath, and rattled off a long string of the Durkoth language, rich in Q's, Ch's, and Th's. The only words I recognized were the two that began and ended the phrase; Kothmerk and Durkoth. As Qethar finished speaking, something seemed to go out of him and he collapsed, falling onto his side and then slumping to lie on his back within the curve of Graf's great paws. Dead, or at least that's what I thought.

The hand that had covered the shattered Kothmerk had fisted up as he fell, coming free of the blood-filled paw print. Before I could decide what I should do next, Qethar's eyes fluttered open.

"It is done. Now I can die." Qethar's hand relaxed as life left him and there on his bloody palm lay the restored Kothmerk.

I knelt and closed the dead Durkoth's eyes. "May the lords of judgment show you mercy." Then I took the Kothmerk from his hand and held it up in the moonlight.

It was the first time I'd really gotten a look at the ring that had brought us so much fear and doubt, and I couldn't help but feel that VoS's description was a pale shadow of the reality. The moon shining through the great ruby transformed the ring into a shining eye that burned with a deep cold flame, and it no longer seemed a strange fate that such a small thing could bring so much harm to so many. Here lay a spark that could light whole kingdoms afire were it given the chance.

"But not this time," I said aloud. Then I closed the ring tight in my fist and turned to Triss. "Now what?"

"Now you hand over the ring and the girl," said two voices speaking in perfect unison. "Then we pay you your fee, and you're done."

I turned around to find VoS standing behind us, wands and rods at the ready.

Triss, tell Ssithra to get ready to shroud up. Oh, and not to hurt the Dyad.

"The ring is yours, VoS, but you'll take the girl over my dead body." I looked straight into Vala's eyes. "You don't want to do this."

"No, I don't," she replied.

"But it's not her decision," continued VoS through her mouth. "We can't let the girl just walk away after what she's done."

On my count, Triss. I shifted the Kothmerk within my hand. *Three. Two.* Without any warning I threw the ring underhand, fast and about three feet to the left of Vala—just out of the reach of those short arms. *One.* She had to lunge forward to catch the ring, and for a brief instant both wands and eyes left me.

That was all the leeway I needed, as both Faran and I vanished into shadow. VoS was very good, turning Vala's lunge into a cartwheel that allowed her to both catch the ring and send a blast of magic my way. It clipped the edge of my shroud as I dove forward, and Triss let out a low grunt as the magic punched a hole in his substance. Not a bad injury, but it pissed me off royally and increased my resolve for the next step.

Before Vala could get off another blast, I'd drawn my sword and bounced to my feet with my blade's edge against Stel's throat.

"Don't make me kill you," I growled. "Drop 'em."

Stel let her rods fall to the ground and Vala her wands.

"You win this round, Blade," said Vala.

"But only because one of my motes betrayed me," continued VoS, through both mouths, and she sounded wholly disgusted. "Don't think I didn't notice you resisting me like that, Vala. You could have had him, but you let your feelings get in the way."

"I did," said Vala. "Because it was the right thing to do. We've got the ring back. That's all that matters. That's all that ever mattered, and it wouldn't have happened without Aral's help. Without the *Kingslayer's* help. You know what relations were like between Kodamia and Zhan back when Ashvik was king. Without Aral Kingslayer acting as he did then, there'd have been a war with Zhan." She held up the ring. "And without Aral Kingslayer acting as he did now, there would have been a war with the Durkoth."

"Not to mention that you would have died." Faran faded back into view behind Vala, a long slender dagger in her hand. "Aral asked me not to harm you, but if you'd killed him I'd have sliced your throats and thrown the damn Kothmerk in the ocean." There was no threat in her tone, but no mercy either, just a statement of fact.

"Maybe you're right." VoS looked at Vala through Stel's eyes and spoke through her lips. "Maybe he did save us a war. But this girl committed a crime against Kodamia. Probably more than one, and that I can't forget or forgive. It's not in my nature."

She turned both her heads toward me. "Good-bye, Aral. Here's your fee." She threw a heavy pouch at my feet. "Take the girl and go to hell."

"I'm sorry," said Vala. "I so wanted to make at least a try of it."

"I'm sorry, too," I said.

Then they turned and walked away.

Faran looked at me and the cold killer that had spoken a moment before seemed to fade away, replaced by the scared teenager I had briefly glimpsed earlier. "Were you and Vala really . . ."

I shrugged. "I don't know. Maybe, given time. I don't think it would have worked, but it probably would have been good for me to try."

Her eyes slid to the ground. "I always liked VoS and her motes. They seemed a lot more human than some of the older Dyads. I'm sorry you had to fight over me."

"That's funny. I can't think of anything I'd rather fight over."

She looked up, startled. Hopeful. "I don't understand."

I wanted to tell her that it was because just this once, I *knew* where justice lay, but I didn't think it would make any sense to her.

Instead I said, "Nothing's more important than the future." Because that was true, too, and because I could see the future, a future where Aral Kingslayer was no longer the last Blade of Namara. "And that's what this fight was about."

Epilogue

Captain Fei's private table at the Spinnerfish had space to seat ten, though it only held two at the moment. Two people anyway, and neither Triss nor Scheroc took up any space.

Fei reached out and almost touched my cheek. "I can't get used to the new you."

"It's your own damn fault," I growled.

She dropped her hand and looked down at the table. "Yeah, I know. I didn't mean it to work out that way. The guy who was supposed to hand the poster over to the watch and make all my other arrangements was also supposed to make damn sure I was dead first."

"Other arrangements?" I asked.

"Let's just say you're not the only one who's pissed off at me. I'm going to be catching shit from his fuck up for a long time to come."

"I hope you explained to him how much trouble he's caused."

"I did. I used short words and a long knife. He got the point." She drew a thumb across her throat.

"So, what happens next time you turn up dead?"

"I haven't worked that out yet, but I can promise it doesn't include a wanted poster for Aral Kingslayer."

"Good."

"Look, Aral, I'm sorry. I fucked up big time and now I owe you double." When I didn't say anything, she awkwardly changed the subject. "Where's Faran now?"

I decided to let her off the hook for now. "Damned if I know, but she's supposed to meet us here."

Fei raised an eyebrow.

"Don't give me that look. You think it's easy to suddenly inherit a teenage daughter?"

"Oh, come on. How hard can it be for the great Aral Kingslayer to keep an eye on one young girl?"

"I guess it depends on whether the girl is a Blade-trained thief and spy who survived six years on her own with a five thousand riel price on her head."

"So she really was spying in Kodamia? For who?"

"Whoever happened to be the highest bidder of the day," said Faran as she suddenly appeared in one of the empty seats—Fei just about jumped out of her skin, but I barely twitched. I was starting to get used to her comings and goings. "Mostly that was Thauvik, which is why I trusted him further than I should have."

"How the hell did you get in here without either of us noticing?" demanded Fei.

"By arriving ahead of you and hiding under the table," replied Faran, sounding more than a little disgusted. "You shouldn't always insist that Erk give you the same table, Captain Fei. It makes things too easy."

Triss, did you know she was here?

No, there was no Shade trail at the entrance. She must have come in quite early and unshrouded, though I've no idea how she could have gotten past Erk like that.

Damn but the kid is good.

"What did you mean about trusting Thauvik when you shouldn't have?" asked Fei.

I knew the answer to that one already, but I wanted to see what Faran would tell the captain.

"After I sold Thauvik the information about the movements of the Kothmerk, he sent me a message promising a hundred thousand gold riels if I got the chance to steal the ring and bring it to him."

Fei whistled. "That kind of money is enough to cloud anyone's thinking. What happened?"

"I was supposed to deliver the ring to a pair of Elite on Sanjin Island in exchange for an anonymous draft from a Magelands bank."

"The dead girl," said Fei. "The one Zishin found those two Elite searching. You sent her in as a decoy. But I thought you said you'd trusted Thauvik too much. Am I missing something?"

"Qethar and the rest of the Durkoth," I replied. "Thauvik had cut a separate deal with them. He figured he could have it both ways. If Faran stole the Kothmerk and brought it back here, he could destroy it and start a war between the Durkoth and Kodamia, which latter is the biggest obstacle to his ambitions. But if Qethar succeeded, the new King of the North would owe his throne to Thauvik."

"And," said Faran, "as a side benefit, if Qethar succeeded, the only one who knew about the other plan, namely, me, would die in the attack on the Dyad caravan. He won either way."

"Right up until he got greedy and tried to get the ring from your decoy without having to pay the fee." Fei looked very unhappy, and who could blame her? Thauvik was her boss again now that she'd returned to the Mufflers. "Stupid bastard."

"More a panicked one, I think," said Triss.

"I think I missed a step," said Fei. "Why would Thauvik panic?"

"Because Faran, good as she is, wasn't able to shake the Durkoth off her trail. That meant that everyone knew the Kothmerk had come south and that the loss might get wrapped around his neck instead of the Archon of Kodamia's."

Fei nodded. "And that could have started the wrong war."

"Exactly."

"So, why did Aigo destroy the ring?"

"Trying to salvage the original plan maybe," I said. "I imagine Aigo knew he didn't have much chance of getting away from me and Qethar both under the circumstances. With Qethar firmly in opposition to Thauvik now, he went with the surest choice. If he'd managed to kill Qethar as well, it would have worked."

There was a long pause, then Fei spoke again. "I heard that the King of the North has been recrowned, and that a Dyad by the name of Valor of Steel was awarded Kodamia's highest honors for service to the realm."

I nodded. "I heard that, too."

Another pause. "I'm sorry, Aral. I know you and Vala were . . ."

Fei looked into my eyes for a long moment and then stammered to a halt, while Faran did everything she could short of shrouding up to fade into the background.

A little intense there, Kingslayer. You might want to back it down a notch.

What do you mean?

The face you're wearing now could blister paint.

Oh.

I took a deep breath and forced a smile. "It's all right. I made the only choice I could and so did she. Sometimes that's just the way things work. Besides"—and now I looked at Faran and my smile turned into something real—"as I've told Faran several times, it was the right choice, the just choice."

Out of the corner of my eye I saw Triss nod his approval. I might have lost whatever I had with Vala, but I'd found a piece of myself, and that seemed a fair trade. More than fair.

No story ever ends, but we all have to leave it sometime. I left this one as I had entered it, sitting in a bar, with a glass of good Aveni whiskey in my hand. Though now I raised it in a toast.

"To things lost and things found."

Terms and Characters

Aigo, Major—An officer of the Elite.
Alinthide Poisonhand—A master Blade, the third to die making an attempt on Ashvik VI.
Alley-Knocker—An illegal bar or cafe.
Altia—A onetime apprentice Blade.
Anyang—Zhani city on the southern coast. Home of the winter palace.
Aral Kingslayer—Ex-Blade turned jack of the shadow trades.
Ashelia—A smuggler.
Ashvik VI, or Ashvik Dan Pridu—Late King of Zhan, executed by Aral. Also known as the Butcher of Kadesh.
Athera Trinity—The three-faced goddess of fate.
Balor Lifending—God of the dead and the next Emperor of Heaven.
Black Jack—A professional killer or assassin.
Blade—Temple assassin of the goddess Namara.
Bontrang—A miniature gryphon.
Calren the Taleteller—God of beginnings and first Emperor of Heaven.
Caras Dust—Powerful magically bred stimulant.
Caras Seed-Grinder—Producer of caras dust.
Caras Snuffler—A caras addict.
Channary Canal—Canal running from the base of the Channary Hill to the Zien River in Tien.
Channary Hill—One of the four great hills of Tien.
Chimney Forest—The city above, rooftops, etc.
Chimney Road—A path across the rooftops of a city. "Running the chimney road."
Coals—Particularly hot stolen goods.
Cobble-Runners—A gang in the Stumbles.

Dalridia—Kingdom in the southern Hurnic Mountains.

Devin (Nightblade) Urslan—A former Blade.

Downunders—A bad neighborhood in Tien.

Dragon Crown—The royal crown of Zhan, often replicated in insignia of Zhani crown agents.

Drum-Ringer—A bell enchanted to prevent eavesdropping.

Durkoth—Others that live under the Hurnic Mountains.

Dustmen—Dealers in caras dust.

Eavesman—A spy or eavesdropper.

Elite, the—Zhani mages. They fulfill the roles of secret police and spy corps among other functions.

Emberman—A professional arsonist.

Erk Endfast—Owner of the Spinnerfish, ex–black jack, ex–shadow captain.

Eva—With Eyn the dual goddess worshipped by the Dyads.

Everdark, the—The home dimension of the Shades.

Eyespy—A type of eavesdropping spell.

Eyn—With Eva the dual goddess worshipped by the Dyads.

Face, Facing—Identity. "I'd faced myself as an Aveni bravo."

Fallback—A safe house.

Familiar Gift—The ability to soul-bond with another being, providing the focus half of the power/focus dichotomy necessary to become a mage.

Fire and Sun!—A Shade curse.

Ghost, Ghosting—To kill.

Graf—A stone dog, familiar of Major Aigo.

Gryphon's Head—A tavern in Tien, the capital city of Zhan. Informal office for Aral.

Guttersiders—Slang for the professional beggars and their allies.

Hand of Heaven—The Son of Heaven's office of the inquisition.

Harad—Head librarian at the Ismere Library.

Hearsay—A type of eavesdropping spell.

Highside—Neighborhood on the bay side.

Howler—Slang name for the Elite.

Ishka-ki—Durkoth oath.

Ismere Club—A private club for merchants.

Ismere Library—A private lending library in Tien, founded by a wealthy merchant from Kadesh.

Issa Fivegoats—A sellcinders or fence.

Jack—A slang term for an unofficial or extragovernmental problem solver; see also, shadow jack, black jack, sunside jack.

Jax—A former Blade and onetime fiancée of Aral's.

Jerik—The bartender/owner of the Gryphon's Head tavern.

Jindu—Tienese martial art heavily weighted toward punches and kicks.

Kaelin Fei, Captain—Watch officer in charge of Tien's Silent Branch—also known as the Mufflers.

Kaman—A former Blade, crucified by the Elite, then killed by Aral at his own request.

Kanathean Hill—One of the four great hills of Tien.

Kelos Deathwalker—A master Blade who taught Aral.

Kip-Claim—Pawn shop.

Kodamia—City-state to the west of Tien, controlling the only good pass through the Hurnic Mountains.

Kothmerk—The original signet ring of the first king of the Durkoth.

Krith—A Durkoth word for a cave dwelling.

Kuan-Lun—A water elemental, one of the great dragons.

Kvanas, the Four—Group of interrelated kingdoms just north of Varya. Sometimes referred to as the Khanates.

Kyle's—An expensive Aveni whiskey.

Little Varya—An immigrant neighborhood in Tien.

Loris—A former Blade.

Magearch—Title for the mage governor of the cities in the Magelands.

Mage Gift—The ability to perform magic, providing the power half of the power/focus dichotomy necessary to become a mage.

Magelands—A loose confederation of city-states governed by the faculty of the mage colleges that center them.

Magelights—Relatively expensive permanent light globes made with magic.

Magesight—The ability to see magic, part of the mage gift.

Mage Wastes—Huge area of magically created wasteland on the western edge of the civilized lands.

Malthiss—A Shade, familiar of Kelos Deathwalker.

Manny Three Fingers—The cook at the Spinnerfish.

Maylien Dan Marchon Tal Pridu—A former client of Aral's.

Miriyan Zheng—High-end sellcinders specializing in Durkoth art.

Mote—Dyadic term for their constituent halves, mote and Meld.

Mufflers—Captain Fei's organization, so known because they keep things quiet.

Namara—The now-deceased goddess of justice and the down-trodden, patroness of the Blades. Her symbol is an unblinking eye.

Nightcutter—Assassin.

Nightghast—One of the restless dead, known to eat humans.

Night Market—The black market.

Nima—Mana, the stuff of magic.

Nipperkins—Magical vermin.

Noble Dragons—Elemental beings that usually take the form of giant lizardlike creatures.

Old Mews—An upscale neighborhood in Tien that burned to the ground.

Olen—A master Blade who taught Aral.

Oris Plant—A common weed that can be used to produce a cheap gray dye or an expensive black one.

Others—the various nonhuman races.

Palace Hill—One of the four great hills of Tien.

Petty Dragons—Giant acid-spitting lizards, not to be confused with noble dragons.

Qamasiin—A spirit of air.

Qethar—A Durkoth outcast living in Tien.

Rabbit Run—An emergency escape route.

Restless Dead—Catchall term for the undead.

Riel—Currency of Zhan, issued in both silver and gold.

Risen, the—A type of restless dead, similar to a zombie.

Sanjin Island—Large island in the river below the palace in Tien.

Scheroc—A qamasiin, or air spirit.

Sellcinders—A fence or dealer in hot merchandise.

Shade—Familiar of the Blades, a living shadow.

Shadow Captain—A mob boss.

Shadow Jack—A jack who earns his living as a problem solver in the shadow trades.

Shadowside—The underworld or demimonde.

Shadow Trades—The various flavors of illegal activity.

Shadow World—The demimonde or underworld.

Shan Starshoulders—The god who holds up the sky, current Emperor of Heaven.

Shekat—Durkoth word for the soul, which they see far more clearly than they do faces.

Shrouding—When a Shade encloses his Blade in shadow.

Silent Branch—The official name of the Mufflers.

Siri Mythkiller—A former Blade.

Skip—A con game or other illegal job, also a "play."

Sleepwalker—An efik addict.

Slink—Magical vermin.

Smuggler's Rest—The unofficial name of the docks near the Spinnerfish.

Snicket—Alley.

Snug—A resting place or residence.

Son or Daughter of Heaven—The title of the chief priest or priestess who leads the combined religions of the eleven kingdoms.

Sovann Hill—One of the four great hills of Tien.

Spinnerfish, the—A shadowside tavern by the docks.

Ssithra—A Shade.

Stingers—Slang term for Tienese city watch.

Stone Dog—A living statue, roughly the size of a small horse. The familiar of the Elite.

Straight-Back Jack—A shadow jack who gets the job done and keeps his promises.

Stumbles, the—Neighborhood of Tien that houses the Gryphon's Head tavern.

Sunside—The shadowside term for more legitimate operations.

Sunside Jack—A jack who works aboveboard, similar to a modern detective.

Sylvani Empire—Sometimes called the Sylvain, a huge empire covering much of the southern half of the continent. Ruled by a nonhuman race, it is ancient, and hostile to the human lands of the north.

Tailor's Wynd—An upscale neighborhood in Tien.

Tangara—God of glyphs and runes and other magical writing.

Thauvik IV, or Thauvik Tal Pridu, the Bastard King—King of Zhan and bastard half brother of the late Ashvik.

Thieveslamp/Thieveslight—A dim red magelight in a tiny bull's-eye lantern.

Tien—A coastal city, the thousand-year-old capital of Zhan.

Timesman—The keeper of the hours at the temple of Shan, Emperor of Heaven.

Triss—Aral's familiar. A Shade that inhabits Aral's shadow.

Tuckaside—A place to stash goods, usually stolen.

Tucker—Tucker bottle, a quarter-sized liquor bottle, suitable for two or for one heavy drinker.

Twins, the—Eyn and Eva, the patron goddess or goddesses of the Dyads. Sometimes represented as one goddess with two faces, sometimes as a pair of twins, either identical or conjoined.

Uln North—The Magelander's Quarter of Tien.

Underhills—An upscale neighborhood in Tien.

Vangzien—Zhani city at the confluence where the Vang River flows into the Zien River in the foothills of the Hurnic Mountains. Home of the summer palace.

Warboard—Chesslike game.

Wardblack—A custom-built magical rug that blocks the function of a specific ward.

Westbridge—A bridge over the Zien, upriver from the palace and the neighborhood around it.

Worrymoth—An herb believed to drive away moths.

Wound-Tailor—Shadowside slang for a healer for hire.

Zass—A Shade, familiar of Devin.

Zhan—One of the eleven human kingdoms of the east. Home to the city of Tien.

Zishin—A sergeant of the watch answering to Captain Fei.

CROSSED
BLADES

For Laura, simply because I love her.

And in memory of Lee Perish, friend, aunt, fan—
you will be missed.

Acknowledgments

Extra-special thanks are owed to Laura McCullough; Jack Byrne; Anne Sowards; my mapmaker, Matt Kuchta; Neil Gaiman for the loan of the dogs; and cover artist John Jude Palencar and cover designer Judith Lagerman, who have produced wonders for me.

Many thanks also to the active Wyrdsmiths: Lyda, Doug, Naomi, Bill, Eleanor, and Sean. My Web guru, Ben. Beta readers: Steph, Dave, Sari, Karl, Angie, Sean, Laura R., Matt, Mandy, April, Becky, Mike, Jason, Todd, Jonna, and Benjamin. My family: Carol, Paul and Jane, Lockwood and Darlene, Judy, Lee C., Kat, Jean, Lee P., and all the rest. My extended support structure: Bill and Nancy, Sara, James, Tom, Ann, Mike, Sandy, Marlann, and so many more. Lorraine, because she's fabulous. Jackie Kessler—she knows why. Also, a hearty woof for Cabal and Lola.

Penguin folks: Kat Sherbo, Anne Sowards's fabulous assistant; production editor Michelle Kasper; assistant production editor Jamie Snider; interior text designer Laura Corless; publicist Brad Brownson; and my copy editor, Mary Pell.

1

Today I saw a ghost in an old lover's eyes. I hadn't realized how much I would miss my face until the moment Jax looked at me and saw a stranger.

I was sitting in the Gryphon's Head, as I have so often in the past, and drinking too much whiskey—likewise. Only it wasn't my usual whiskey, and I wasn't my usual self. The bells of Shan had just sounded the sixth hour. The sun slanting in through the open windows of the tavern was still hot, but the first touch of evening had started to steal the worst fire of its bite. I'd taken a seat far from my usual table and ordered the Magelands whiskey instead of my favored Aveni to reinforce my recent loss of face.

I recognized Jax the instant she stepped into the Gryphon, though she had the sun behind her and shadow hid her face. First love is like that. It writes itself into your heart and your memory in letters that can never be erased.

Or can they?

The look Jax gave me when our eyes first met cut as deep as any sword could. Not for what it said, but for what it didn't. There was no recognition there, no hint of what had once been between Jax Seldansbane and Aral Kingslayer. No love and no loss, just the cold assessment of a professional killer sizing up a room for threats.

She gave me a single measured glance, alert for any trouble, then moved on when she didn't see it, just as I would have in her place. I should have expected that, should have remembered what I had become, but I hadn't, and that indifference from one I had once loved tore at me. I was invisible to her, a ghost in her eyes.

It's all right, Aral. Triss's familiar voice spoke directly into my mind, sweet and clear and wholly reassuring. *It's you who have forgotten your face, not Jax.*

As usual, my familiar was right. I felt a pressure on my shoulder like a friend's hand, squeezing briefly and then gone. I glanced at the shadow that stretched out behind me and gave it a wry smile. Him really. Triss is a Shade, a creature of living night. He lives in my shadow, quite literally.

Thanks, my friend, I sent back. *Even a month on, it's hard to remember what the bonewright did to my face.*

I reached up, rubbing a rueful hand down my cheek and across my chin. Not that different from my old face, really, not from the inside anyway, and not to my fingers. But I knew that no mirror would show me the face of Aral Kingslayer ever again, nor even the somewhat more haggard and haunted version that I'd worn for my years as Aral the jack. A *jack*, one of the underworld's all-purpose freelancers. Packages delivered, bodies guarded, the occasional contract theft. All in a day's work for that Aral, and oh what a very long fall from the days when the world had called me Kingslayer and the unjust had shivered when they thought of me.

I took another long pull on my whiskey, smoky and strong, just what I needed. Then, I reminded myself that my changed appearance was for the best, considering all the wanted posters showing my old face. I kept telling myself that, and until the instant Jax's eyes had passed me over unrecognized, I had mostly even pretended to believe me.

I've never had a particularly distinguished sort of face. Medium brown everything, from eyes to hair to skin. Not too pretty, not too ugly, the kind of face that's easy to ignore or forget. The masters and priests who raised me to be an assassin in the service of a goddess now dead had always told me it was one of my strongest assets.

My new face shared all the best aspects of my old face, improved on them even. I had deliberately reshaped skin and bone in a way that removed most of the markers of my native land, worked at making myself look like the product of a mixed heritage. It was the sort of face you might see in any of the eleven kingdoms of the East—never a native, but not a clear foreigner either. In so many ways it was the perfect face for what I had once been. Aral Kingslayer, Blade of Namara, the goddess of Justice. How ironic then that I put it on only after the murder of my goddess, her temple's destruction, and the death of all but a handful of my friends and fellows.

Easy. Triss squeezed my shoulder again—a shadow's touch—

this time in warning. *Remember where we are and control yourself. They are hunting us still.*

Again, he was right. The Gryphon was a public place. One where I was known to have spent a good deal of time, before my second life as a jack of the shadow trades was exposed. Looking around the room, I could spy several tables worth of potential trouble. The place in the corner that I used to consider my regular spot, for example. A man and a woman sat there, both with their backs to the wall, both exhibiting the alert calm of the waiting hunter.

She was slender, tall, and long limbed yet muscular, and far from fragile. Ice blond hair and white skin marked her out as foreign, as did her hard blue eyes. Her quick precise movement made me think of some sort of giant praying mantis. The man was also tall, but broad where she was slender, with heavy muscles showing through the thin silk of his long-sleeved tunic. He was as dark as any of the locals, but the angles of his face and his thick black beard suggested a Kadeshi background, as did the short broad-bladed axes he had tucked into his sash.

He caught me looking at him and raised an eyebrow ever so slightly, touching one of his axes in a way that told me he thought I was a thief. I pretended to be intimidated, swallowing heavily before looking down into my drink, and he snorted and went back to talking to the woman. Trouble averted easily enough, but dammit, I shouldn't even be here. I should have walked away and found a different bar to haunt, a new place to start building myself a new identity to go with my new face.

But I was deadly tired of running, and somehow I just couldn't walk away from the old me that easily. Not even the drunken wreck of a version that had earned his bread as a shadowside jack.

Which brought me back to Jax. We had grown up together at the great temple of Namara. She had entered the service of Justice a year after I did, barely four. A tiny girl with long dark hair, pale skin, and a winsome smile that had grown into a wicked one as the years transformed the girl into a beautiful young woman. Though she had never grown all that much in physical stature, she had more than made up for it with her skills as a sorceress and assassin in the service of Justice, coming third in our generation for the quality of her kills, after Siri and me.

Why had she chosen this moment to walk back into my life? I didn't make the foolish mistake of thinking her presence in the one place in all of Tien I was known to have frequented was any kind of coincidence. I also wondered where she had been hiding during the six years since the temple fell. Not in Zhan, I guessed by the lack of color to her skin. Nor anywhere else with brutal sun, unless she had become a creature wholly of the night.

Aven perhaps, or back home in Dalridia or the mountains of the Magelands. One of those, almost certainly. She would have had to hide someplace she could blend in, and someplace close enough that she could have reached Tien in four weeks or less. That ruled out Öse, Varya and Radewald.

The news that the Kingslayer had been unmasked would have flown fast and far on wings of magic. Everyone in the eleven kingdoms with any sort of governmental or shadowside connections would have heard *that* message within a week, two at most. Unless she wanted to spend a lot of money and draw the sorts of attention that one of our kind couldn't easily afford, Jax would have had to travel by more mundane means. No ship or horse could have brought her here from any farther afield so fast.

I knew that right after the fall Jax had spent time in the grip of the Hand of Heaven, the human instrument the gods had used to destroy the temple and Namara's worshippers. As the magical enforcement arm of Shan's archpriest, the Hand was known for its willingness to employ torture and the stake to achieve its aims. That, no doubt, explained the dozens of thin scars that threaded Jax's face and arms, white on white like fine lace on a marble table.

But where had she been since her escape? What had she been doing? Her clothes told me nothing. Like anyone both sane and in-purse who found themselves facing Tien in summer, Jax had opted for a vest and loose pants in the thinnest of silks—gray in this case. She had eschewed the more common sandals for light boots of the same sort that I wore for roof-running. The short, curved swords she wore in a double sheath on her right hip looked vaguely Dalridian in design, but they could have come from anywhere. No clues there. No clues anywhere really.

I wanted to go to her, to take her in my arms and tell her who I was and how very happy it made me to see her alive. But six years as a fugitive had taken its toll. I would wait and I would watch, and only when I was sure there was no trap would I make a move. Even then, caution must come before trust.

For several long minutes she chatted quietly with Jerik at the bar, obviously asking questions, though I couldn't make out specifics. He kept shaking his head no and shrugging, despite the fact that she flashed several heavy gold coins at him. Finally she seemed to give up, flipping her hair back with an angry snap of her neck that

I'd seen too many times to count in the short, tumultuous year we
had shared a bed. Without another word she stalked straight out the
front door of the Gryphon.

It should have been funny watching hardened shadowside bonebreakers twice Jax's size getting quickly and prudently out of her way
as she gave them *the look.* But she'd caught me so off guard with the
suddenness of her departure that I barely had the leisure to notice. I
was far too busy trying not to *appear* as though I was following her,
when I knocked back my drink, and then rose to do just that.

What's the plan? Triss asked silently. *I thought we were going to
take this slow.*

*That was before she left so quickly. We have no way of knowing if
she'll ever come back, and I want to know why she's here.*

Point. How shall we play it?

*Cross her shadow. Tell Sshayar to let Jax know to meet us some-
where private at midnight. Walk away.*

It was an old Blade trick for passing secret messages one to another. Shades had a means of silent communication that would allow Triss and Sshayar to exchange basic information. Unfortunately,
with the exception of my newfound ability to communicate with
Triss, no Shade could bespeak their Blade companion mind-to-
mind. That was another legacy of the magic that had reshaped my
face, the breakthrough that allowed us to do what none of our kind
ever had before: mindspeak. But it wasn't something that could be
taught, so we would have to fall back on the older method of passing
the message Shade to Shade for later verbal relay.

Great plan in theory. In practice . . .

I hate it when we do that, I thought at Triss. *Where the hell did she go?*

That way, replied Triss, unobtrusively nudging my right foot. *I
can taste Sshayar's essence on the street, but only very faintly. She's
hiding deep in Jax's shadow and the sun is strong today, burning away
the traces of her passing. We'll have to move quickly if we want to keep
track of her.*

Jax had been barely forty feet ahead of me leaving the bar, but
by the time I got out the door, she'd vanished into the crowd. Some
of that was simply height. At a hair under five feet, Jax stood a head
shorter than the average citizen of Tien. Thousands of whom were
out wandering the streets in search of dinner.

The Stumbles, where the Gryphon is located, is one of Tien's
worst neighborhoods. The streets are narrow and poorly kept—there

are cobbles down there somewhere, but you have to dig through a lot of filth to find them. At the moment it was hard even to see the filth beneath the swirling mass of people that filled the street.

As was so often the case with slums, the Stumbles was also one of the city's most heavily populated neighborhoods. The accommodations mostly varied from miserable to inadequate, but rooms and parts of rooms could be had for a few kips a day, and that meant that people who'd have been sleeping on the street in other parts of the city could put a door between themselves and the night while they slept. That meant a lot, especially in a place like the Stumbles.

As I threaded my way through the crowds, guided silently by Triss, I kept an eye out for Jax. But between her height and the fact that almost everyone in that poor neighborhood wore light browns and middling grays, I never caught sight of her. I did spy a half dozen pickpockets and cutpurses, and had to warn two of them off with a look when they got too close to me. That last was a shock. Another painful reminder of my lost face—people knew Aral the jack in the Stumbles and would have known better than to even consider picking his pocket—but they didn't know me.

No one knew me. Not the petty criminals, not Machim the beggar, nor Asleth the noodle vendor. No one. That should have made it easier for me to pass through the crowds, as people who would normally have wanted a piece of my time ignored me. It didn't. Aral the jack was a dangerous man, a drunk maybe, and down on his luck, but people knew to get out of his way. Nobody knew to get out of the way of . . . who?

I stopped in the middle of the street as the weight of that question hit me. Who was I, really?

Aral Kingslayer had died with his goddess. The man who wore that name had crawled into a bottle and not come out again. In his place a new Aral had emerged, Aral the drunk who had paid his bar bills by playing the shadowside jack. Doing things for money the earlier Aral would never have contemplated. Petty little illegalities, and all freelance, so that there was never a chance he'd owe any loyalty to anyone ever again. Never anyone he'd have to care about.

That had all changed a bit over a year ago when a woman named Maylien had found an echo of the old Kingslayer hiding under the skin of the jack.

For a little while I thought I'd found a new purpose in life, a new Aral who might have a chance at doing some good in the world again. That was the plan anyway. I'd even thought it was working, right up till the moment I realized how much of me I'd lost with my face. I didn't even have a name anymore. Not really. Not one I could wear in public. If your only name was a secret, was it even really a name?

Aral! Come on, we're losing Jax. Triss gave me a sharp slap on the side of my foot and I got moving again.

But I'd lost my hunger for the chase and I hardly even blinked when we lost the trail as it left the narrow streets of the Stumbles and plunged into the human river of Market Street.

Fire and sun! Triss growled into my mind. *It's gone, and I can't tell whether that's an effect of the sun or if Jax did something clever to break her trail.*

I found it very hard to care about the answer when what I really wanted was to go back to the Gryphon and drink until the world went away. I couldn't tell Triss that though, not with the way he felt about my drinking. Instead I just stood and stared at the passing parade, full as it was of walkers and riders, carters and rickshaws, even the odd palanquin. Sandals and boots and hooves and wheels, all of them grinding away at the dust and dirt and . . .

Wait. Back up. Think, man!

There it was. So simple and elegant I had no idea why it hadn't occurred to me before.

My guess would be she got into one of those. I pointed at a passing oxcart. *If she made sure that her shadow didn't spill over the edge of the bed, a cart would make a very good getaway vehicle. That or one of those closed palanquins. Hell, she could even have had a covered rickshaw waiting for her here.*

I'm an idiot. Triss sounded shocked. *The idea of a shadow trail is new enough to you that I can understand why you wouldn't have thought of that before now. But, why didn't it ever occur to me?*

For the same reason it didn't occur to me, probably. Blinkered thinking. We both knew fire and sun and running water can break a shadow's trail, so it didn't occur to either of us to think beyond the big and flashy to simpler means.

So now what? Triss asked me.

The Gryphon, I think. Maybe Jax will come back. Triss didn't say anything, but I could feel his disapproval as he thought about me having another drink. *I could also use some dinner, and it's Jerik's cooking or go home where we'll have to deal with Faran and Ssithra. . . .*

I guess one more whiskey won't kill you.

I thought you might see it my way.

Faran was almost sixteen and a problem and a half. She'd been eight when the temple fell. A combination of talent, smarts, luck, and utter ruthlessness had allowed her to escape an attack that killed most of her peers and teachers. For six years she and her familiar, Ssithra, had lived completely on their own, spying and thieving their way across the eleven kingdoms to stay alive. Her last assignment had gotten away from her in a way that would probably have killed her if it hadn't also brought her to my doorstep. I'd had to abandon my old face as part of fixing that mess.

Now she'd become my . . . apprentice? Ward? Surrogate daughter? Faran and I were still working out the details of what we were to each other. So far, the process involved a lot of snarling and baring of teeth and I desperately wanted a little break before I faced the next round. Though Triss's relationship with Ssithra was harder to parse, the level of hissing in Shade that went on between the two of them suggested to me it wasn't any less fraught. In any case, the Gryphon sounded a hell of a lot more like home to me right at the moment than the rented house we shared with Faran and her familiar.

The Gryphon had started to fill up by the time I got back. Jerik just grunted and pointed me toward an empty seat at the end of the bar when I called out my order for whiskey and a bowl of fried noodles topped with shredded whatever-happened-to-fall-off-the-back-of-the-cart-today. His indifference stung a bit, since I was used to being treated like a regular. A few minutes later, he dropped off my bowl and a small loaf of black bread that I hadn't ordered along with my glass, then turned away before I could say anything about getting my order wrong.

I was tempted to throw the bread at his retreating back, but just sighed and took a sip of my whiskey instead. It tasted smooth and silky, like liquid magic. Kyle's eighteen, the special cask reserve if I knew my whiskeys. Nothing like what I'd ordered. As I paused before taking another drink, Jerik spun around to drop a beer in front of the smuggler sitting three stools to my right. I raised my glass ever so slightly in Jerik's direction as well as an eyebrow. Jerik responded with something that could have been the faintest ghost of a wink or perhaps nothing at all.

I took another sip. It was top shelf Kyle's all right, the spirit old Aral the jack had drunk whenever he felt deep enough in the pockets. Since I'd ordered nothing but Magelands whiskeys at the Gryphon since I changed my face, and the Kyle's wasn't sitting somewhere you'd get them confused, I had to figure the switch was intentional.

Which meant he'd recognized me, and wanted me to know it. I would have liked to believe that was impossible, but he'd been my landlord and bartender for five years and knew me as well as anyone in the city. It was hard to disguise a walk, and harder still if you were drunk.

But why was he letting me know about it now? To cover my confusion I took another sip of my excellent whiskey and then followed
that with a mouthful of noodles. The hot pepper sauce almost covered
the aging vintage of the fried bits of meat and vegetables. Almost.

I considered my bread then. Jerik makes a hard black loaf that
will keep you alive for a long while if the effort of chewing it doesn't
kill you first. It's cheap and awful, and over the years I've spent
almost as much time living on it as I have avoiding it. This loaf
looked more battered than most of its fellows, with several dents
and dings and a wide crack splitting it nearly in half along one edge.
Hmm. I jammed a thumb into the crack, then broke off a tiny corner of the loaf when I felt a bit of paper shoved deep into the bread.

As I was twisting the scrap of bread in my pepper sauce, Jerik
slid back past me. "Tab?"

I nodded and he left. Jerik only runs a tab for serious regulars,
and the face I was wearing now simply hadn't been around long
enough. I suppose I shouldn't have been as surprised as I was that
he'd recognized me.

Jerik's a damned clever man. He used to hunt monsters for a living, and mostly on crown lands, which adds dodging royal patrols
to the list of dangers involved in the trade. The dumb die quick, and
the smart can get rich if they live long enough. There's a good deal
of money to be made by selling the bits off to various magical supply
houses, and Jerik was at it long enough that he really didn't need to
work for a living anymore.

He retired from the business after the gryphon he ultimately
named his bar for ate about half of his scalp and one of his eyes.
The scars are terrible and a good part of the reason he keeps the
lights low, but I think he missed the thrill of it all. It wasn't too many
years after he got mauled that he first opened the Gryphon's Head
and nailed the damn thing's skull up behind the bar. I've always
figured he bought an inn down here in the Stumbles among the
shadowside players, when he could have afforded a better location,
because he missed spending time around dangerous predators.

Despite a burning desire to read my little note right then and
there, I knew better. Instead, I just nibbled another corner off my
bread and took a long slow sip of the Kyle's. Golden, though I still
missed efik. More now with the recent presence of another Blade to
remind me of things left behind. Brewed or chewed, the effect of
the beans was so much smoother than alcohol's. Of course, if I
hadn't given it up I'd be dead by now. Or worse, a sleepwalker sitting in some alley and slicing my arms so I could rub powdered efik

into the wounds for a bigger better ride to the place where nothing matters.

I pushed the thought aside. Thinking about efik made me want it, and that was the road to ruin. After I finished my noodles and carefully rationed out the rest of my Kyle's, I scooped up the loaf and headed out into the Gryphon's yard. I used to rent a room over the stables back there. Now, I took advantage of long familiarity to slip into the lower level and find an empty stall, before I cracked open my bread envelope.

By the time I'd gotten it split in half, Triss had defied the conventions that light normally enforced on shadows, by sliding up the wall to a place where he could read over my shoulder, and changing his shape. Most of the time, he pretends to be nothing more than light would make him, a darkened copy of my own human form. But when we're alone, he will often reshape his silhouette to assume the outline of a small dragon complete with wings and a tail. When he does that, he assumes some of the other aspects as well, and now I reached out to give him a light scruff behind the ears, where his scales always seem to itch.

He made a happy little noise at that, but then shrugged me off and jerked his chin at the tightly rolled piece of paper I held. *What's it say?*

Unrolling it revealed a folded sheet with a small blob of black wax sealing it. There was no imprint in the wax and no name on the outside of the letter, but magesight revealed the faintest glow of magic on the seal. I held it up to Triss and he reached out with one clawed finger and touched the seal. There was a hiss and the wax dissolved. I raised an eyebrow at Triss and he nodded. As I had expected, it responded only to the touch of a Shade. Any other attempt to open it would have resulted in the whole thing burning instantly away to ash.

I opened the letter. Inside it said: *Ashvik's tomb. Two hours past midnight. The anniversary of the day you broke my heart.* And that was all. No names. No signatures.

Clever, just a location, the time, and a date no one but I would know. The day I told Jax I wasn't going to marry her. The fifth of Firstgrain, one week in the future. The whole thing was smart, and I wondered how many of these she had handed out, hoping one would get to me. There had been six kings of Tien with the name Ashvik, and their tombs were scattered widely through the royal cemetery. Anyone who intercepted the message and didn't know it was intended for me would have to guess not only the date but which one was the intended meeting place. The tomb of Ashvik VI, the man who had died to give me the name Kingslayer.

2

My earliest memories are filled with darkness. When I entered the service of Namara at the age of four I stepped into the shadows.

From my very first day, I trained in the lightless depths below the temple, learning to operate without sight to guide me. By the time I turned seven I was at least as comfortable in utter blackness as I was in brightest day. Then I bonded with Triss, and a shadow became my closest friend.

Most people think of darkness as the simple absence of light, but we who share our lives with Triss's kind know that it can be a living presence. A Shade can take many forms. He can be a substanceless wraith hiding in the shadow of his bond-mate. He can command that same shadow, reshaping it to reflect his will, as Triss does when he assumes the form of a dragon or gives me claws to climb with. He can even become a thick cloud, like a black mist, and wrap his companion in a lacuna of darkness—the form Triss currently held.

The greatest advantage any Blade has is his familiar Shade. On the most basic level, the mage gift needs a familiar to act as a focus if it is going to function at all. A mage without a familiar who wants to cast a spell is in much the same position as a bird without wings who wants to fly. Beyond that, familiars shape the power of their bond-mates' magic. If you want to wield fire, it helps to have a salamander to back your play.

Then there's the power a familiar wields on its own. If you want to pass unseen in a world where any mage can see the glow of your invisibility spell, if not the person hiding within it, a familiar who can cloak you in shadow is the best bet going.

"Bide a moment," I whispered into the darkness that surrounded me.

"Why?" Faran's voice came from behind me, low and angry.
"What are you worried I'm going to mess up this time?"

I wanted to bang my head on the rock face to my right. Instead,
I released Triss from the dreaming state that allowed me to use his
powers and senses as my own. It was possible to make use of the latter even when he was awake, but if I needed to use magic or shift
the substance of his being around, I could do things *much* faster
and more cleanly when I had direct control.

I replied, as calmly as I could manage, "I'm not concerned for
you, Faran. I just want to look things over before we go in. It's been
a long time since I tried to sneak past palace security."

"And I've been doing practically nothing else for the last few
years. The Zhani variety doesn't look any worse than Kodamia's, at
least not from up here. Why can't we just *do* this?"

"Because it's abysmal tradecraft," Triss said in a much sharper
tone than I'd have used. "The target could be a lone shepherd asleep
in the middle of an open field, and it would still be foolishness to
charge in without thoroughly assessing the situation. Did you learn
nothing from the masters at the temple?"

Faran let out a very noisy, very fifteen-year-old sigh, but she
didn't argue. For some reason she took reprimands from Triss far
better than she did the ones I gave her.

Thanks Triss. Could you uncover my eyes now?

If you wanted to see, you had to risk being seen. That was one
of the first lessons a Blade learned. The enshrouding darkness a
Shade could provide wasn't quite invisibility, though it came damned
close in all but the brightest daylight. One of the few disadvantages
was that while no one could see in, neither could I see out. Not with
my eyes anyway.

The senses I could borrow from Triss when he surrounded me
included a sort of otherworldly cousin to human sight, but it was
so differently focused that even with years of training and practice
it couldn't quite substitute for the real thing. It really paid to use
my own eyes as a double check on what I was getting through my
familiar.

Consider it done. Triss rearranged himself so that the shadows
thinned away to nothing in front of my face, allowing me to look
down on the night-wrapped city.

As so often happened when I got my sight back, the first thing I
noticed was how beautiful the world could be. Immediately below

me, the palace sparkled like a great triangular crown studded with a thousand jewels glowing in every color imaginable. Even at this hour, the magelights shone so thickly on the lanes and winding paths through the gardens that they almost erased the night in places. In the wealthy neighborhoods immediately beyond the palace to the east, the lights made a looser net, outlining the streets in ribbons of white and blue and bright green.

As you moved farther away, the effect took on something of the nature of a patchwork quilt. While richer areas made extensive use of magic's shining answer to the night, the bright hard points of mage-lighting became few and far between in poorer areas. Frequent thefts kept strapped neighborhood councils from using the expensive lights to illuminate their streets. But even in the true slums like the Downunders and the Stumbles there were lights. Small, dim, and too often the cheaper and more dangerous flickers of oil lamps or torches, but lights nonetheless.

What beauty the slum lights lacked in power they made up for with movement, flitting and flickering like ten thousand fireflies. When there were no streetlamps, people had to carry their own lights with them. Between the restless dead and the more common human predators, no one wanted to be without light. That necessity transformed static nets and ribbons of light into slow-moving streams where the sparks danced to the whims of the current and rippled with the wind. The lights of the city made a colorful contrast to the dimmer white stars in the lightly clouded sky above.

Regretfully, I pulled my focus back down onto the palace complex below us. Faran and I perched on a narrow horizontal lip of stone, high up on the bare broken slope that stood behind and above the palace. In terms of a straight military assault this approach represented the palace's biggest weakness.

The top of the slope, which separated the spur of rock that held the palace compound from the taller Palace Hill behind it, lay a good fifty feet higher than the walls of the palace below. If you could get siege equipment up there you could bombard the compound with relative impunity. Of course, you'd have to fight your way through miles of one of the densest cities in the world to get there, and the royal family would long since have retreated to the island citadel or moved upriver to the great fortress of Kao-li.

The palace had been designed with the comfort and convenience of the Crown in mind rather than brute projection of power. The ruling family of Zhan had long preferred to keep their brass knuckles hidden inside elegant gloves. That didn't mean that defense of the palace was neglected completely, just that it was geared much more toward keeping out thieves, assassins, and the occasional peasant uprising. In the case of the back slope, that meant constantly burning off any vegetation that tried to gain a foothold among the rocks, and doubling the height of the wall.

Further protection was afforded by the fact that the slope was bounded on the upper edge by the extremely well-guarded estates of several of Zhan's greatest nobles including the Duchess of Tien. That was half of why I had chosen to come in this way. The combination of the massive rear wall and powerful neighbors who firmly supported the Crown meant the guards tended to pay less attention to this side of the compound.

Add in the fact that the royal cemetery stood tight against the wall—with many tombs actually burrowing down into the bedrock on which it stood—and you had one of the few places in the palace compound that a Blade could get inside with relative ease.

Which is exactly what we proceeded to do once I'd resumed control of Triss and his senses. Down the slope. Then wait for a gap in the guard patrols. Collapse the shroud to about half the optimum size. That freed up enough of Triss's substance to spin myself finger and toe claws out of hardened shadow. Up the wall using cracks and crevices no unaided human could ever have hoped to find. Fully reshroud, and down the stairs from the battlements. Then up and over the low stone wall of the cemetery to drop into the shadows behind a free standing mausoleum, with every step mirrored perfectly by Faran and Ssithra.

"Told you it'd be easy," Faran said as we briefly settled against the dark granite wall of the tomb—the meeting wasn't supposed to happen for almost two hours yet, but I'd wanted to have plenty of time to scout and prepare the ground.

Triss's senses provided a full circle of view, so I didn't have to turn my head to look at Faran. Not that I could see her. Even a Shade's . . . call it unvision, couldn't see through the lacuna of another Shade. Faran and Ssithra simply registered as a deeper patch of shadow in a darkly shadowed world. Though the royal cemetery wasn't wholly devoid of illumination—each tomb had a small magical flame burning eternally on the altar on the right side of its door—it was one of the darker parts of the compound.

Still, I could imagine the smug look she now wore on that slightly too-angular face. Faran was going to be beautiful once she grew into her bones and put an adult's flesh on that lanky frame.

Brown hair and eyes, skin a shade paler than my own, and nearing my own height. When people saw us together in the market they assumed she was my daughter.

"I never said that I expected it to be hard, Faran. Triss was absolutely right back there. A smart Blade practices caution even in the simplest of assignments, because it's the unexpected difficulties that will trip you up."

"With the exception of what happened with the Kothmerk, I've done all right for myself these last few years." She sounded defiant, edging into angry. "Certainly better than you have, playing the jack here in Tien's shadow world."

I sighed. The Kothmerk was a big exception and one that had led to three different governments all trying to kill Faran and Ssithra. But give Faran her due. "Yes, in many ways you have." After the fall of the temple she'd become a freelance spy, selling other people's secrets to the highest bidder. "Certainly you made more money in your years on your own than I have in my entire life." Which was why Faran was the one paying the rent on the small house where we lived on the skirts of the Kanathean Hill.

"Doesn't that bother you?" For the first time that evening she sounded like she was asking a question she didn't know the answer to.

"Not really. Before the death of the goddess I never cared about money. It was simply a tool the priests supplied me with when I needed it for a mission. Afterward, I didn't care about anything except for Triss and where my next drink was coming from."

I continued, "I don't know what all you went through when the temple fell, or in the days immediately after."

Faran didn't say anything. She'd been nine at the time, a child trained in the arts of killing and not much else. From the way that her eyes narrowed and she changed the subject every time it came up, I knew she'd suffered. But I hadn't ever pressed, and I wouldn't now. The world can be a very bad place for a lost child, especially a little girl. If she wanted to tell me about it she would.

"I only know what I went through," I said. "Almost everyone I'd ever cared about died that day along with my goddess and my faith. It hurt me that I wasn't there to die with them, that I was spared when so many I loved had died. With my goddess dead I wanted to die, too." Though he'd heard me talk about it before, I was still glad Triss was deep down in dream state for this conversation. It caused him a lot of pain when I spoke about it. "I'd probably have killed myself then if it wouldn't have killed Triss, too."

"That's why you started drinking, right? Because it eased the pain."

"That, and I rather hoped it would kill me, though I didn't even admit that to myself until quite recently."

Faran took a deep breath. "I got drunk once, maybe three weeks after the Son of Heaven's soldiers killed everyone. I knew the priests of Namara were against alcohol, but I'd run out of the efik I took with me when I ran away, and I didn't have anything else to dull the pain. And it hurt so very much to be me right then. I was hiding out in a charcoal burners' camp while I tried to figure out what I should do next. I stole a bottle of rum and I drank until I passed out."

Faran stopped speaking and there was a long silence, but I didn't think she was done, so I let it run.

"There was a man at the camp, older, kind. He'd been feeding me, though I had no way to pay for it. He found me there asleep and he touched me."

Faran made a tiny little choking noise, but then continued. "But not in a bad way, that would almost make what happened bearable. I was having a nightmare you see, about the soldiers at the temple and all the blood, and he was trying to wake me up. That's what Ssithra thought anyway. He was just trying to wake me up. I seized control of Ssithra and I tore out his throat with claws of shadow. I didn't mean to. I was still drunk and I was scared and . . . dammit!"

I heard the dull thud of a fist hitting a thigh, then there was another long silence.

"I'd never killed a man before," she finally said. "I had the opportunity several times when I was escaping from the temple. I could have slaughtered half a dozen of the people who killed my friends. I wanted to, but I was too afraid. I was too afraid I'd get caught and killed myself. I was too afraid that I'd do it wrong. But mostly, I was too afraid of what killing them would do to my heart. So, instead, I killed the first good person I met outside of the temple."

I didn't know what to say to that.

"It's almost funny how much that first death hurt me, when you consider how many I've killed since," she said after a moment.

"I'm sorry, Faran. I . . . just . . . I'm sorry."

"It's not your fault, Aral, nor any of the Masters, though you all made me what I am. I blame the man who calls himself the Son of Heaven. He's the one who sent the soldiers who drove me out into the world before I was ready, and someday I'm going to kill him for it."

While I sincerely hoped she got that chance, a sudden feeling of presence from somewhere off to our left kept me from saying anything about it. Instead, I just leaned in close and extended my shroud to overlap Faran's—a long established warning signal among Blades—so that she would know something was up.

I'm not sure what it was that aroused my suspicions. Certainly nothing so blatant as a scuffing sound or a change in the light, but I felt certain we were no longer alone. Reaching through the shadows that separated us, I found Faran's shoulder and squeezed it once, before pressing gently to let her know which direction I wanted her to go.

Moving with all the exquisite caution that my years of training and experience could bring to bear, I rose and started moving toward that feeling of presence. Through Triss's senses I could see the deeper patch of shadow that was Faran and Ssithra vanishing around the back of the tomb behind me, following my signal. When I got to the front edge of the tomb, I stopped and spent a long couple of minutes doing a slow scan of the area.

I focused all of my senses as well as Triss's on the task, devoting a part of my attention to each sense in turn, as well as to the collective picture they painted. Touch was nearly useless at the moment, telling me little more than the hang of my clothes and gear or the way the carefully manicured lawns pressed into the thin soles of my boots. What it did give me was the direction of the faint and fading sea breeze—about a quarter turn to the right of directly into my face. And that led to smell.

Most of the news my nose brought me had to do with things rotting in the harbor and several hundred thousand people packed tightly together in the late summer heat. Underneath it all though was a strange and subtle touch like a ghost from some spice markets past. I rolled my tongue, trying to bring up the memory of a taste, but couldn't quite establish it.

Hearing brought me a much more densely layered picture. Farthest and faintest I heard the sounds of the city proper, muted now while most of her denizens slept, but still there in the occasional scream or deep bellow. Closer in, the palace noises carried more nuance; the scuff of a guard's boot on the wall above, a low moan that suggested an assignation in the shadows behind a convenient hedge, the metallic click of a groundskeeper's shears as they tried to fulfill the impossible charge of keeping things perfect, while never getting in the way of their betters. Nearer still came the faint tinkling of the tiny fountains on the left side of each tomb's door, balancing the altar fires on the right—part of the traditional display of the elements signifying that the very stuff of nature mourned the passing of each of Tien's rulers.

The final piece of my collage view of the world came from Triss. Shades "see" in full round. They use a sense organ we don't even have a name for, to pick up on changes in the texture of darkness in every direction. Bats "see" with their ears, screaming and listening for the echoes, or that's what I was taught anyway. What Shades do is closer to that than any human sense, but it's a passive process, with the dark-echoes provided by the interplay of light and shadow.

Each individual shadow takes on a sort of depth that isn't quite color, but still possesses all the subtle shading of that palette. Where my own eyes might have perceived a simple block shadow where the edge of the tomb across the way cut off the light from several altar fires, I now registered a whole gradient of shadow flavors. It gave me an extremely precise sense of things, like the way the three magical tomb-fires that cast the bulk of that shadow sat, and how their intensity varied over distance and with the flickering of the flame.

No single part of my mosaic of the senses was enough to give me what I needed, but together . . . together was a different thing entirely. As I moved deeper into the graveyard, flitting from shadow to shadow, I followed my nose and that faintest hint of exotic spices until a change in the quality of the light drew my attention to a particularly tall tomb. There, the flames burned a little brighter in the reflection off a couple of faint scuff marks where the moss on the fountain had been displaced. Moving around the back, I put an ear to the wall and waited . . . there, the quietest of grating sounds came through the stone. Unless the tomb's primary inhabitant was moving about, there was a lurker on the rooftop.

I squatted down to make an even smaller target and released my hold on Triss's will. *Wake up, my friend. We've got company of an unexpected nature.*

As I filled him in on what I'd learned so far I double-checked all of my gear. The pair of short straight swords I wore on my back in a custom built hip-draw rig hung light and loose. All I needed to do to release either of them was pop the catch with a thumb and let the blade drop a few inches to free the tip. Wrist and boot daggers were likewise properly aligned and ready to go, as was my little bag of tricks.

Who do you think it is? Triss silently asked me when I had finished both narrative and preparations.

I can't say for sure, but I've got a suspicion. It's the spice scent. I've only ever smelled it secondhand myself, but Master Kelos mentioned once that some of the Hand of Heaven's sorcerer-priests use a special ritual soap. It's supposed to help keep them pure in the face of the corrupt world out here beyond Heaven's Reach.

Triss let out an angry mental hiss when I mentioned a possible Hand presence. *Should I slide up and take a look? Maybe tear out a throat while I'm at it?*

Much as I'd love to let you, I don't think we can risk it yet. If there's one finger of Heaven's Hand trying to push the scales down here, you can bet there are more close by. Killing this one could all too easily alert the others.

Point. So, what's the plan?

Finish scouting. If it is the Hand, I want to know how many more of them are around and where they are before I make a move. I just wish we had some way to warn Faran. She's damn good, but the Hand are the people who destroyed the temple. They've killed a lot of Blades.

Faran and Ssithra survived then, they'll be all right now. When she's playing it smart that girl is one of the most promising young assassins I've ever seen.

And if she's not playing it smart?

Triss just hissed. Faran was good, but also ruthless and prone to kill first and worry about the consequences later. And she *hated* the Hand. It was a bad combination, but we couldn't do anything about it without giving ourselves away. Not for the first time, I wished that my kind had better methods of communication. But our powers simply didn't work that way, which was part of why Blades had always worked solo far more often than in concert.

What if it's not the Hand? asked Triss.

It would still be nice to know if there are more of them around before we start slitting throats. Either way, we'll have to come back and pay a quiet visit on our friend up there before we head down to meet Jax. What do you want to bet that rooftop has a clear view of Ashvik's tomb?

You know it does. Triss sent back, and there was a strong undertone of anger to his mind voice. He didn't like the way this was going any more than I did.

I'd rather say that I'm sure *that it does, but yes, I agree with you. Somebody set us up. The question is who and why. I have a hard time imagining Jax doing something like that, but two years ago, I'd have told you Devin would never turn away from the order or our friendship either. Look where trust got me there.* My best friend's betrayal of everything I'd ever held dear was a wound that would never stop bleeding.

I took control of Triss again and went hunting. But while I did verify the sight lines to Ashvik's tomb and my meeting place with Jax, I didn't turn up any more signs of watchers on the tomb-tops over the next twenty minutes. Nor anyone else for that matter. Whether that was because my first target's companions were that much better at concealing their presence, or because there was only the one, I couldn't say. Process of elimination wasn't much help either, there were just too damn many tombs with good sight lines for our meeting point.

I had circled most of the way back around to my starting point, so that I could make sure of my original target and that I hadn't hallucinated my initial impressions, when I crossed a Blade's shadow trail heading toward Ashvik's tomb. Two actually. Bringing Faran into my life had given me the opportunity to use my borrowed senses to focus on what was—for me—a newfound Shade skill, as we practiced trailing each other around the city.

But I wasn't yet good enough at parsing the nuances of Triss's shadow-tasting ability on my own to identify these traces fully, or tell which came first or how far apart in time the two had been made. I was pretty sure one at least belonged to Faran, and I guessed the second was Jax, but I had to call up Triss to verify my assumptions.

Faran and Ssithra, with Jax and Sshayar trailing along behind— probably following the youngsters, though there's no way to be sure, Triss opined.

I still didn't know what Jax might be up to, but the fact that she was on Faran's trail worried me. Doubly so in light of our unexpected guest on top of the tomb, which meant it was time to make a ghost of the latter. This was going to be that very rare kill that I could truly take pleasure in. After what the Son of Heaven's people had done to mine, I felt not the slightest bit of pity for any of them. I planned my approach as I hurried back toward the tall mausoleum.

I was nearly there when a rather sharp darkening of the skies above drew my attention. Great reefs of cloud began to form in the skies above, blotting out the stars, while the wind from the sea kicked up sharply, cooling the steamy air over the city and bringing with it the lightning-burned air smell that always came with the truly brutal thunderstorms. If I was any judge, we were all going to get very wet before the night's business got much further along.

It might just have been the weather shifting with that shocking speed you sometimes get in coastal areas, but I made a dash for the tomb at that point because of the other possibility. The elementals most commonly known as the Storms or the Heavenly Host. They took a myriad of shapes, lightning bladed swords, lucent wheels, whirling cones of darkness, but they all shared two features. They all had dense wings of cloud, and they only ever companioned the priests of the Hand.

The polished black granite blocks of the tombs were tightly fitted with no finger or toeholds. I could still have climbed the back or side walls of one if I reduced my shroud. But I thought it better to keep it at maximum extension under the circumstances, so I took the same route the Hand had: fountain, door-frame, entablature, lip of the roof.

I chinned myself on the edge at that point, peering across the flat top of the tomb before moving forward. My target was right where I had expected her to be, kneeling in the shadow of the low wall that encircled the rooftop, and she was indeed a member of the Hand.

There was nothing particularly distinguishing about the loose dark robes the slight figure wore. Nor the long spell-lit rod she held like a crossbow, braced on the wall and sighted in on the front of Ashvik's tomb in the distance. But the cord holding her ponytail in place was tied with the ritual knot of those who served the Son of Heaven, and she had a Storm at her side.

This one took the form of a huge gemstone, like a star sapphire with wings the exact green of the swirling clouds that gave birth to whirlwinds. It was of middling size for the breed, with a central body maybe three handspans wide by five long. Its wings were furled at the moment and most of it lay concealed below the level of the parapet.

That would slow the thing down if it spotted me before I could kill its master, which was good since I didn't know how well my shroud would hide me from it. It had no eyes and no obvious way for me to tell which direction it was facing, but I knew from my training that its most important senses belonged to a family other than sight anyway. A creature of sky and storm, it relied primarily on the movement of air currents to bring it information.

I was downwind, which would help conceal me, and was another reason I'd chosen to come in from the direction I had. But I didn't honestly know whether that would be enough. Silently, I slipped over the edge of the parapet and started toward the Hand.

That's when I heard Jax's voice, low but clear and sounding far too close. "Aral, is that you?"

Reflex put my hands on my swords as I shifted my attention from the Hand's back to focus my unvision beyond her to Ashvik's tomb. Jax stood there, silhouetted by the altar flames just to the right of the door, her shroud lowered to pool around her feet. Dammit! What was she thinking?

With a flick and a twist I released my swords. Dropping them down and around to point at the roof just in front and to the outsides of my smallest toes. That kept them within my shroud but ready to use on the instant.

Jax spoke again, and I realized that the Storm must be picking up noises from the area of the tomb and making them louder somehow, or I could never have heard her that clearly. "I see a Shade there," she said. "Just beyond the fountain and—"

I never got a chance to hear what Jax would have said next. As the Hand in front of me started to shift her aim toward the place Jax had indicated, a slender lance of brilliant white light speared out from somewhere off to my right. It punched a neat hole through Jax's left side before it carved a deep pit in the granite face of Ashvik's tomb.

3

Love may burn away to ashes, but it never lets us go. Despite all the years and all the pain that lay between us, it felt like I'd taken an arrow in the chest when Jax let out a quiet little cry and crumpled to the ground.

The sapphire Storm snapped its wings then, popping straight up into the air before diving toward Jax, and Ashvik's tomb. That was an opening I'd never expected, and I leaped forward to take advantage of it. But even as I moved, the Hand whispered a word of power.

The long rod she cradled in her arms flared and sparked in my magesight, briefly surrounding itself with a blazing azure halo. As I brought my right-hand sword around in a beheading stroke, the rod spat forth a lance of fierce white light, like lightning smoothed and shaped into the form of a bright spear.

In the distance I heard Faran's familiar voice yelp and say, "Motherfucker!" And then, "Somebody's gonna die for that."

I continued forward. Blood fountained from the Hand's neck as her head fell free, bouncing off the lip of the low wall before dropping to the grass below. It splashed my left leg, hot and sticky, as I leaped past her slumping body and put one foot on the parapet before launching myself out into the darkness beyond.

A giant flash of lightning ripped the air between me and the tomb, temporarily blinding my unvision in midleap. The death spasm of my target's familiar as its life spilled away with its master's. It left a brutally painful afterimage burned into my borrowed senses; like a splintered crack in the very stuff of the universe. With no other choice, I tore aside the veil of shadow in front of my eyes so that I could see the ground.

I touched down briefly on the balls of my feet before letting my knees go loose as I collapsed into a forward roll to bleed off some of the speed of my fall. Holding onto a pair of drawn swords added a significant element of risk to the maneuver, but with at least one more priest of the Hand about, I didn't dare let them go. Fortunately, the turf of the royal cemetery was deep and exquisitely tended. Instead of the badly ripped up knuckles and separated shoulder I half expected, I came back to my feet with little more than grass cuts and a few fresh bruises.

I'd taken barely two steps when a lance of white light speared past my head. The smell of burning hair filled my nostrils and I felt Triss shriek in his dreams as the light tore a hole in his substance. I threw myself sidewise into a cartwheel that cost me my left-hand sword when it stuck deep in the earth and I was forced to let it go.

More lightning hammered down from the sky, half blinding my mortal eyes at the same time that it burned away my returning unvision for a second time. Another cartwheel put the edge of a tomb between me and the source of the white beams—another Hand obviously. This one more powerful by far than the one I'd killed.

"Faran!" I yelled. "Get Jax clear!"

Then I turned and dashed along the wall of the tomb, sheathing my remaining sword as I went, to free my hands. The bastard clearly knew where I was, shroud or not. I needed to make my next move fast. I was just getting ready to dive into another roll when shouts came from the compound wall above, and the palace alarm bells began to ring. Not unexpected, but damned inconvenient. I froze for a moment. Go back to help Faran with Jax? Or ghost the remaining Hand and clear the field of at least one of the opposing forces?

That's when the wet hand of a god smashed me back against the wall of the tomb. Rain and wind as I had never even imagined them wiped away vision and unvision alike, blinding me utterly even as they deafened and washed away all scent, leaving only touch and memory to guide me. I turned back the way I had come, abandoning any hope of finding the priest as I dropped my shroud and my control over Triss.

He let out a series of sharp hisses, swearing in Shade as he awoke. *Fire and sun but that hurts. What happened? It feels like I had a starshine chewing on my left wing.* I couldn't see Triss in the darkness, but I imagined him stretching out on the wall beside me, obviously wincing as he extended his wings.

One of the Hand clipped you with some kind of tightly focused lightning blast or something, but we don't have time to go into it or go after him. We need to find our way to Ashvik's tomb. I pointed in the direction I'd last seen Jax. *I'm utterly blind in this, the alarms are going off, and the Crown Elite are certainly on their way.*

The Elite were warrior mages whose stone dog companions could swim through earth like a fish through water. The storm wouldn't even slow them down, and we had minutes at best to get clear of the area before they arrived along with several hundred of the less magical but more numerous Crown Guard.

Go.

Trusting Triss to guide me, I began to lope in the direction I hoped was the right one, moving quickly, though I had to bend nearly double to fight the wildly shifting patterns of the buffeting winds. Through our bond, I felt my shadow stretch out ahead of me, spreading himself thin as he searched out the path. I hated to go unshrouded like this, but I didn't have a choice.

Stop, Triss mindspoke. *Bend over, your sword's a few inches to the left of your forward foot.*

I reached out a hand and found the blade. I cut my finger in my hurry as I slid it along the wet steel, searching for the hilt in the still blinding downpour. As soon as I had a grip I started moving again. Faster now, as Triss spoke directions into the silence of my mind.

Left a bit, or you'll hit a tomb. You've a free twenty yards in front of you, go. Watch out, there's a divot here where the gardeners missed a slink's burrow, jump. There, just ahead is the line of the cliff where Ashvik's tomb lies. Let me slide left and right to find the way . . . got it! Jax is gone, but there's a shadow trail.

Lead on.

We caught up with Faran and the unconscious Jax atop a long low tomb built half into the wall of the bluff.

"Faran," I called, "I'm coming up, try not to stab me."

I dragged myself up beside them, fighting against the teeth of the wind all the way. Jax lay in a heap on her side, her face pillowed on her limp arm—presumably to keep her from drowning in the rapidly puddling water that was overwhelming the drains in the low parapet.

"She's alive?" I asked.

"Barely," replied Ssithra, invisible in the darkness. "The lightning lance pierced the bottom of her lung. Sshayar is very worried. We need to get her someplace warm and dry."

"First, we need to get the fuck out of the palace compound before the stone dogs show up," I said.

"That's why we're up here," said Faran. "I thought they might have more trouble spying us out through the elemental muddle of the tomb."

"Good thinking," said Triss.

It was, too. The stone dogs were creatures of earth with powers of and over their element. The Zhani custom of invoking all the elements to honor their fallen mighty created a multielemental barrier between the earth under the foundations of their tombs and the air above. Fire and water came in the shape of the altar flame and the fountain; air and shadow surrounded the bier where the embalmed bodies lay in their sarcophagi within their tombs. Of the six great elements only light was not included separately, though light's great ally, fire, made sure it was not totally excluded. A stone dog would have to be right underneath us to sense us through all that, an all too likely circumstance if we didn't get out of there fast.

"Sshayar," I said. "It's Aral. I have to get Jax out of here unless moving her will kill her."

"You do not look as I remember you, but there's no mistaking Triss." A barely visible patch of darkness lifted itself up from Jax's side and I knew from long experience that I now faced a shadow tiger, its stripes formed by subtle difference of shading and texture— Sshayar. "It's good to see you both alive after so many years when we had feared you dead. Do what you have to do, I will see to Jax's wounds. They aren't nearly so bad as I first believed, but I still need to pack them with cool shadows if they are to heal as quickly as possible."

Then the shadow collapsed, falling back down to wrap itself tightly around her stricken mistress. I bent and lifted Jax onto my shoulders, glad of how tiny she was. With her wounds, I would have preferred to cradle her like an infant, but that would have left me defenseless. None of us could afford that.

"Faran, you're going to have to lead the way back to the wall and over." I opened my trick bag and started digging for a couple of leather straps to bind Jax in place. "Kill anyone who gets in the way."

"Of course," she said, and a feral smile flashed briefly in the rain. "I've already ghosted my first ever priest of the Hand tonight—I think that's when the storm started. It sure as hell got worse when you killed that second one. Maybe I'll get lucky and bag a third to give us a triad. Let me just make sure the first stage is clear. I'll have Ssithra signal you when I'm ready." She dropped over the edge of the tomb and vanished in the dark and the rain.

I'd barely gotten Jax fastened in place when Triss spoke into my mind. *Faran says to follow now and hurry. She doesn't want to get too far ahead of us in case a stone dog comes up from below.*

That was a sentiment I could heartily support, though the steady worsening of the storm helped us there. The brutal pounding of the earth by wind and rain—or water and air, if you preferred to think in magical terms—would do much to cover both our passing and our trail. It made an unanticipated but welcome secondary payoff for eliminating the two Hands and their companion Storms.

I nearly sprained an ankle jumping down from the tomb with Jax on my shoulders, and had to drop to one knee to prevent it. Forcing myself back upright I pushed on into the storm, with Triss whispering words of encouragement and guidance into my mind. Even with all of her gear, Jax couldn't have weighed much more than a hundred pounds. But a hundred pounds gets heavy fast when you're jogging along with it on your shoulders in a giant thunderstorm.

By the time we reached the low wall separating the cemetery from the palace gardens, I was sweating despite the cold rain. Climbing up that wall with Jax on my shoulders made me feel about twice my age, as did climbing back down the other side. I normally would have jumped, but I'd learned my lesson there.

Maybe fifteen feet on, Triss had me edge over against the palace compound's outer wall to avoid tripping on the bodies of a pair of fallen Crown Guards Faran had slain. They lay at the base of the stairs leading up to the ramparts. By luck or fate or Faran's skill, those were the only agents of the Crown that I encountered. The first pellets of hail started hammering down around me soon thereafter, stinging when they hit scalp or skin.

Faran was waiting for me at the great tower that marked the corner where the wall bent sharply to the northeast, as it followed the spur of rock that footed the compound, a denser shadow in the murk of the storm. "You sure you still want to go out this way?" She'd already slung a rope over the outside wall.

"No," I replied, "but I don't think we've got a good alternative."

I glanced over the edge. Somewhere down there in the darkness was the river Zien. The plan had always been to make our exit via the Zien, though I'd originally expected to sail-jump off the wall and glide down to the river on shadow wings. The running water was supposed to do double duty, helping us to shake off any possible pursuit by the Elite and their stone dogs as well as breaking our shadow trail in case Jax had taken up with Devin and the other rogue Blades. Now . . .

"There's no way she can swim like this," said Faran.

"No," agreed Sshayar, speaking up for the first time since the tomb, "but I can keep her face out of the water and cover her nose and mouth when needed if you can tow her along behind."

"I still don't know," said Faran.

"I suppose we could—"

"Stone dog!" yelled Ssithra, cutting me off. "Coming up through the wall. Go!"

Dammit!

I leaped up onto the nearest crenellation and jumped outward, spreading my arms as I cleared the wall. It was that or face a stone dog biting and clawing at me through the stones while I tried to climb down a wet rope in a thunderstorm. Triss spun himself into great dark wings, extending outward from my arms. It was only the second time I'd ever attempted a sail-jump while carrying a passenger—a dangerous proposition—though at least I was able to use my arms to reinforce my wings this time.

As I glided clear of the palace wall, I heard a faint roaring coming from below and realized it must be the river, angry with all the water pouring down off the hills of the city. Again I regretted the necessity that drove us to this escape route.

Fresh lightning splintered the air less than a spear's throw in front of me. I was still blinking away the afterimages when the lightning came again, closer. This time it very nearly struck Faran, who let out a startled yelp, followed by swearing.

"Fucking Storm!"

It wasn't until the next bolt fell between us and I saw the cloud-winged scythe, hovering above like some blade-headed ibis, that I realized Faran had spoken of the elemental rather than the elements. The last Hand must have set their familiar to hunt for us, and when we entered the heart of its domain it had found us. Much easier here, since sail-jumping kept us from shrouding up—there simply wasn't enough Shade to manage both sail and shroud. More lightning fell around us and Faran folded her wings, dropping away into the roaring murk below.

Hoping that we had cleared the riverbank I mindspoke Triss, *Let us fall, it's our only hope of shaking the damned thing off.* Then we, too, plunged into darkness.

We fell perhaps forty feet before the snarling of the river filled the world and the waters swallowed us up. We plunged deep, cutting straight through the icy surface currents generated by the storm into the blood-warm waters washing off the sun-bitten plains beyond the city. Slowing but still moving down, we passed into the cool shadowed depths the sun never warmed, coming to a stop only when my feet hit the bedrock beneath the half yard of muck that floored the great river. I felt the impact all the way up to my teeth, but pushed off again immediately.

Having Jax across my shoulders ruined my swimming stroke, making it all but impossible to control my motion. The wild flood currents tumbled and torqued me around until I lost all sense of direction. If not for Triss's constant tugs and nudges guiding me in the right direction I would never have found my way back to the air. As my head broke through the foam-frothed surface, I felt Sshayar cut the ties that held Jax to my shoulders and briefly panicked at the thought of losing her in this madness. I twisted wildly, trying to catch her as she slipped free.

It's all right, soothed Triss. *Sshayar and I have her. You just worry about getting us out of the river in as few pieces as possible.*

Then Sshayar looped some of her substance around my chest and shoulders, snugging Jax in tight against my back like a trader's pack.

I nodded my thanks. *Triss, can you see Faran at all?*

In this? Are you crazed?

Point.

Between the winds, the rain, the hail, and the whirling masses of flotsam and jetsam that the storm had swept off of the streets and out of the sewers, the normally placid river had become a wave-wracked demon.

Most of the floating debris fell into the repulsive but harmless category of dead dogs and human waste, but there were bigger and more dangerous items to be avoided as well, like a jagged-edged broken cartwheel that nearly impaled me. I'd only been in the water a couple of minutes and I was already exhausted. The cold and the extra weight of Jax made for a punishing combination as I fought toward shore.

The huge stone pier came at me so fast I didn't even have time to try to avoid it. I just threw my arm across my face and hoped for the best. A big eddy caught me at the last possible second and twisted me around and down, briefly sucking me under before it spat me out again beneath the bridge where the growling of the sharply narrowed waters echoed and reechoed like an angry dragon.

It wasn't until the current spat me out the other side that I realized I'd just passed the foundations of the Sanjin Island bridge. I'd covered half of the distance from the north side of the palace to the bay, well over a mile, and faster than a galloping horse. I needed to get out of the water fast if I didn't want to end up swimming home from Kanjuri with my ex strapped to my back. Actually, that sounded an awful lot like some Kadeshi vision of hell. But no matter how hard I swam across the current I couldn't seem to get any closer to shore. Not compared to how fast I was heading for the bay. I started to worry more and more about which way the tide was running. If it was in we had a decent chance of making one of the piers. If it was out . . .

I think we may be well and truly fucked, my friend, I sent to Triss. *Unless you've got something?*

I don't know, replied Triss. *I'm doing what I can to keep us afloat, but this isn't my element and the effort's draining me, especially after that hit I took from the Hand.*

A few moments later I started tasting salt in the water. I also had my first cramp threatening—my left calf where the scars I'd picked up along with the name Kingslayer ran deep.

It seems almost funny, I sent.

What does? Triss's mind voice sounded weary and worried.

Between the Son of Heaven and the King of Zhan the price on my head's over sixty thousand gold riels, enough to buy a palace with all the trimmings. That's without mentioning all the other folks who'd pay to see me dead, and you with me. Or Jax and Sshayar for that matter. Literal armies of people have worked to kill us all, and here it's going to be a storm that does the deed.

We're not going to die here, Sshayar and I can keep us all afloat for quite a while. The words sounded confident, but the mental voice behind them came through weak and thready.

It doesn't have to be drowning. This water is cold, and there's always exposure. Beyond that there's sharks, sea serpents. . . . My mind was starting to drift. Very bad sign. *I just hope we wash up where someone who really deserves the money can find the bodies.*

Stop that!

What? Triss sounded madder than he had since the last time I went on a bender. Speaking of which, I could really use a drink. *Kyle's. That's what I want right now, a big glass of Kyle's. Or better yet, a hot pot of efik or a couple of beans . . .*

Namara-dammit, Aral!

That cut through the fog. In our nearly twenty-five years together I'd never heard Triss use the name of our goddess to swear. I realized that I'd stopped swimming somewhere along the line and

was just idly treading water as the swells rolling in from the deep
water rocked me up and down.

You're better than this, Aral. Come on, don't give up on me.

Sorry, Triss, I'll try.

I dunked my face to clear out the cobwebs. Somewhere along
the line we'd transitioned from salty river water to actual saltwater.
The water had warmed a little, too. Not enough to stop it from killing me, but enough to slow it down. The hail had tapered off as well.
I thought about Faran then and worried, but survival had to come
first.

*Shadow me up, Triss, I want to use your eyes and I need to try a bit
of magic.*

I won't be able to help keep you afloat. . . .

It won't be long, and out here in the bay—I hoped I was still in the
bay—*the saltwater will help. Do it fast though, I don't know how long I
can stay focused.*

I could tell he wanted to question and argue, but all he said was,
I trust you.

We settled in the water as Triss went incorporeal and stopped
pushing from below, but Jax's head stayed above the surface. Then I
felt him sort of sink into my skin along the interface between us,
and slowly spread outward from there.

Normally it felt a bit like someone wrapping me, head to toe, in
tight silk, cold and sleek and vaguely sexy. This time it burned like
sealing wax straight from the edge of the flame. He trickled his way
along my skin under my clothes. Whether I had gotten so cold that
Triss felt hot, or the nerves in my skin had just taken so much
abuse that ice and fire met in the middle now, I couldn't say.

I welcomed the sensation, any sensation. My mind was drifting
and unseated, and the pain would help keep me in my head. Even
the most minor sort of magic requires intense focus and real energy,
and I had very little of either left to give. The well of my soul was
nearly drained.

That meant it was time to place my final bet, and it was a long
shot. I had no prepared spells for something like this, no long practiced tricks to fall back on, just my entirely inadequate magical
skills. Unlike some of my peers, I'd always preferred the sword and
the shadow to the word and the wand. I was going to have to improvise and that's why I had Triss playing second skin.

Blade magic of any high order worked best when it was guided
by a single will and executed within a cloak of shadow. We had now

reached the point where I'd normally have centered myself with deep breathing and an attempt to wipe away all my cares. Instead, I just yanked out the long dagger that hung at my right hip and balanced it on the palm of my hand.

I picked the dagger because it had a teak grip as opposed to the slimmer knives at wrist and ankle with their simple leather-wrapped metal hilts. I wanted maximum sympathy. Focusing what little nima I had left, I strengthened and thickened the shadows on my palm. The dagger lifted free of my hand, floating within a ball of liquid darkness, as I pictured a lodestone seeking a mate.

The dagger slowly rotated widdershins until it pointed toward me and Jax and our sheathed swords—wood and steel together, and not unexpected. I shaped that finding into my working, made it a part of the sympathetic structure of my spell. The dagger's point slid away from my chest, continuing to rotate slowly leftward until it had made a full circle. Another. I had to use my other hand to brace the raised one to keep it from shaking as both physical and magical reserves started to fail me. A third rotation. I couldn't do this much longer.

The fourth round began and I didn't think I'd be able to manage a fifth. The dagger bobbled. Stopped. Rotated back the other way an inch or two and froze. It was pointing somewhere ahead and to my right. If I'd done everything right there would be a ship lying along that line. If I was also lucky, it would be close, and lying at anchor instead of drifting with the tides. If I wasn't lucky we were all dead. I released Triss and the dagger sank back down to rest on my palm.

Do you think you can keep us pointed in that direction? I asked.

I can try.

Good. I dropped the dagger and let it sink because I didn't want to waste the time to put it away.

Is there a ship there?

I sure hope so.

4

---✦---

Pain is a hone. Give it a chance and it will keep grinding till there's nothing left but dust, but properly wielded it can create the sharpest of edges. I was starting to feel awfully gritty.

Every stroke of my arms or kick of my legs grated like stone rasping on stone and I knew that if I stopped I'd never start again. I'd been swimming a quarter hour at the most, but the rain and the cold and bearing the weight of the woman I'd once loved on my back had taken their toll. Soon, very soon, I would stop struggling, and that would be the end of me. But not yet.

Not quite yet.

Once again, I dragged an arm up out of the water and forced it forward, reaching out to take my next stroke. This time, something changed. I smashed my hand into rough wet planks, a ship's hull. My hand was so cold I had to flex my fingers and check it with my other hand to see how badly I'd hurt myself. It was stiff and I'd jammed a knuckle but I didn't think I'd broken anything—one small benefit of my exhaustion, I just wasn't swimming hard enough to cause much damage.

Triss.

Nothing. He was tired and hurting, too, worn out from keeping me afloat and the hit he'd taken at the cemetery, though I knew he'd never have admitted it.

Triss!

What? Wait, we're here?

We are.

I'd pushed myself out and away from the ship's side so that I wouldn't scrape up and down against the rough surface with every lift and fall of the swells. Despite the still brutal wind, the waves weren't bad. Probably because the storm had blown up so quickly right on top of Tien rather than rolling in from the deeps. It hadn't had the time or impetus to build the sort of waves that a big ocean blow brought with it.

Now we need to find a way aboard, I mindspoke. Just for a little while really, until the storm blew itself out and we could return to Tien.

Looks like they lost the anchor, or cut it loose, Triss replied. *So the easy way's out.*

Damn. I couldn't see that well through the murk, but had no reason to doubt him. *Maybe we can use the rudder somehow.* I turned and forced myself to swim slowly toward the back of the ship.

Namara had never sent me to the islands, so I didn't know a lot about ships. I mean I knew the things everybody knows, like the pointy end goes in front, and right and left were called starboard and port. Beyond that my knowledge was spotty, a mix of the simple stuff you picked up hanging out in dockside bars, and the esoterica one gleaned from the odd courier job for smugglers.

It was a three-masted junk, and the thought of smugglers gave me another idea. On the big ocean-going junks like this one, there were often compartments, fore and aft, designed so they could be rapidly flooded to help the boat stay upright in strong winds and big waves. They called them ballast tanks or something like that, and the design was very different from the southern ships that came up out of the Magelands and the Sylvani Empire.

I'd been in and out of ships of both sorts while dealing with smugglers, and the tanks were great for that kind of work. If you put a secondary watertight compartment inside the big main one, and kept that main compartment flooded when you sailed into port, it made a perfect hidey-hole.

As I slipped around the back end of the ship, I was very happy to find a couple of flood ports at the waterline, along with a whole series of fist-sized ports slaved to the larger ones with magic. The main ports were just big enough for a man to slip through. They sat on each side of the rudder, just above a set of sailor's wards. Of those, the only one I really recognized was the one to prevent fires, though I could guess at a couple of others since they were variations of the sorts of protections you'd see onshore for repelling vermin and the like.

Two questions remained: Was this a smuggling boat? And, did I have the strength to get both Jax and me aboard? On the first, I figured the odds were pretty good. Despite the storm, there wasn't a light showing. Add that to the fact that it must have been lying at anchor out in the harbor instead of tied up at the docks, and the case was pretty damning. Either it was waiting for a fast cutter to come unload it, or it wanted to ride the tide out to sea before the sun rose. As for the latter question, there was only one way to find out.

Triss, hold us steady while I see if I can't get the ports open.

I sank in the water while Triss shifted around, but then he got a grip on both me and the ship and lifted me partway free of the swells. A band of solidified shadow like a crescent moon now passed around my waist between me and Jax, then extended itself forward to sink its horns into the tarred seam between two planks. By bracing my boot tips against another seam lower down, I was able to position myself quite steadily in front of the nearer port.

The port looked like a giant's closed eye. Starting at what would have been the outside corner of the eye, my magesight showed a line of silvery light running upward to the deck far above. Somewhere near the ship's wheel it would connect to a tiny glyph. A simple thing, so that even the least of hedge witches would be able to close and open the port. The trick would come in activating the spell without also lighting up the glyph for anyone with the eyes to see.

I could cut the line, but then the glyph above would wink out and that would be almost as much of a problem. If I had time, tools, and energy—or really, any two of those—I could have managed it a dozen different ways. As it was, I had to go for an ugly little improvisation. Flicking my right wrist, I dropped the knife sheathed there into my hand . . . where it slipped straight through numbed fingers and vanished into the depths of the harbor.

Well, fuck. Moving more carefully, I reached across and very gently pulled the knife out of my left wrist sheath. Then I stabbed it into a plank so that the edge just touched the line of silver light.

"Sshayar," I whispered, "can you take over for Triss for a moment?"

For a heartbeat or two there was no response, then Sshayar responded just as quietly, "If it's brief. Between packing Jax's wound and everything else, I'm very close to my limits. Holding the two of you up for any length of time is going to hurt."

I'd partnered Triss long enough to read the subtleties in a Shade's tones, and I could hear deep exhaustion and pain in Sshayar's. But I didn't have a lot of choice. "Do it."

Triss, I need you to let me take over again as soon as Sshayar's in position.

You don't sound much better than Sshayar, he replied. *Are you sure you can handle this?*

No. But it's this or climbing the rudder, and there's no way we're going to manage that without being spotted.

Triss sighed in my mind. *I suppose we can't just yell for help and trust to the goodness of people's hearts. Not with the likelihood that our soon-to-be hosts are smugglers, at least.*

To say nothing of the combined prices on my head and Jax's. Trust isn't something any former Blade can afford.

Not even with each other, Triss sent sadly.

No, not even that.

Then Sshayar was in place, and Triss vanished into dreams so that I could go to work. Placing my palm firmly against the center of the port, I reached for the well of my soul and found it . . . well, not exactly empty, but drained below the place where I could safely draw from it. Too bad I had no other choice. I could feel the drain in the deeps of my soul as I pulled energy from my core and fed it into the shadows that held me, extending the stuff of Triss's being to cover the port.

I pushed it further, forcing a line of shadow up the line of the spell to the place where my knife stood out from the planks. My ears began to ring and little sparks danced around the edges of my vision. It felt like taking a deep cut in a fight, the kind where the blood comes out in pulses and you can bleed out in a matter of minutes if you don't plug the hole.

I had seconds to act, and I did so, forcing the hatch with a brute application of magic. That sent a spike of light racing up the line of the spell toward the glyph above, light that burned away shadows, burned away the substance of my familiar, if only a little bit. When it hit the knife I forced it to shift course, forced it into the knife. There was a bright flare in my magesight, and the whole world went white for a moment as the knife softened and bent.

I lost control of my body and slumped forward, my feet slipping free of the planks. If not for Sshayar holding me up, I'd have smashed face-first into the ship's hull and that would probably have been it. But Sshayar held onto me, and I held onto consciousness. Only barely, but barely was enough. I released Triss and he slid down my skin, collapsing into my natural shadow.

Sshayer collapsed, too, dropping us back into the water, but not before I reached out with one flailing hand and caught the lip of the port. As I dragged myself up and in, Jax slid free, staying in the water behind me. My back felt suddenly cold and unguarded. Necessary but scary—I'd never have fit through the opening with her there, but for the next few heartbeats I had no way of knowing if Sshayar had let go of me because she wanted to or simply because she'd reached her breaking point.

After I slid my hips through the gap I twisted myself around, so that I could bring my legs inboard without letting go of the port. I didn't know how far up the inside wall the port would lie, and wasn't up for jumping games. Then I pivoted and hung over the edge, reaching out and down toward the water, hoping I would find Sshayar waiting there, ready to catch my outflung hands. A swell rolled in first, dipping my hands in the water then raising them high into cold air and the rain.

Nothing. Nothing. Noth—

"What the hell!" A harsh whisper came in a familiar voice.

"Hussh!" Sshayar hissed. "Just reach where I guide you, Aral's going to pull you up."

A hand met mine. Jax! Another. I eeled backward off the lip of the port, losing some skin and nearly dislocating my elbows in the process. Turned out, the port was a bit higher than my shoulders, a fact I discovered as my feet splashed into calf-deep water. Up came Jax. I let go as her hands reached the lip, and fell back onto my ass with a splash. Jax hung for a moment on the edge of the port above me, still more out than in. Then another swell came along, and shoved her through, along with about a hundred gallons of saltwater. She landed beside me swearing. We were in.

"Where in Namara's name are we?" Jax demanded in a whisper—even injured and disoriented she knew better than to make too much noise before she knew how the shadows lay.

"On board what I very much suspect is a smuggling vessel. Or," I amended, "at least one with a smuggling compartment or two. We're stuck till the storm's over."

"All right. That's one. Here's two: Why do I feel like pan-fried shit on a stick?"

"Because the Hand of Heaven put a very neat little hole in your left side. Luckily they used a self-cauterizing spell of some sort or you'd have bled out before I could even get to you."

I heard something like a hand sliding along wet cloth. Then, "Son of a bitch, that hurts. The who did what now?"

But another swell slopped a big bunch of cold water in through the port just then. "Answer you in a minute. I need to close that before any more of the sea comes in to join us." I dragged myself back upright and grabbed the lip of the port.

Standing hurt. Everything hurt. I could feel my teeth wanting to chatter in my aching jaw.

"After that, we'll see if there's a nice dry smuggling compartment around here where we can collapse for a while," I said over my shoulder. "If not, I'm going to cut a hole in the nearest bulkhead and we'll figure it out from there."

"Triss, you still with me?" I asked aloud because I didn't want to let Jax know about our newfound ability to communicate silently. A part of me might still love Jax, but I knew damn well better than to trust her.

His voice was weak and came after a brief pause, but it came, "Yeah, I'm here. What do you need?"

"Can you reach out there and pull what's left of my knife free?" I asked.

In response, a tentacle of shadow slid past me. If I'd done this right . . . The hatch blinked itself shut like the great eye it had been painted to resemble.

I yanked my hands back just before it would have crushed my fingers. My knees buckled as I staggered back, and I went down hard, falling face-first into the water and sucking in a noseful. I came up gasping and coughing, glad it still barely topped my calves. Much deeper and I might have drowned. The irony didn't escape me.

"You all right, Aral?" asked Jax.

"Not really. No. I feel pretty much like I came out of that deep-fried shit pan you mentioned a minute ago. But we can't stop just yet."

I wasn't ready to stand, so I stayed on my knees as I pulled my trick bag around front and dug around inside. Everything water could hurt was a loss. So was some of the stuff I'd have expected to be fine. Fortunately, that didn't include my little thieveslamp. Slightly smaller than a closed fist, it was basically a metal box with a shutter on one side and a dim, red, magelight inside. The mechanism didn't much like all the time it had spent submerged in saltwater. It squeaked its unhappiness when I forced it open with my thumb, but it did open.

That revealed a large, flat, boxlike space with no apparent access other than the ports. Considering the size of the ship and the height of the ceiling, I didn't like the odds of a smuggling compartment being concealed up top. Underfoot was possible, but unlikely as it would be easier to intuit from a quick glance at the hull and much harder to keep dry. That left the forward bulkhead.

"I don't see anything," said Jax.

"That's kind of the point," I replied. "Now be quiet and let me concentrate. I need to do this before I keel over, and I don't think I've got a lot of time." With some reluctance and a great deal of difficulty I forced myself back up onto my feet and stumbled my way over to the bulkhead.

"If you'll tell me what we're looking for, I'll help." Jax was heading for the other end of the bulkhead on hands and knees.

"I don't know exactly. A loose joining peg maybe, or a knothole that can be pulled out, if we're lucky. If not, something completely invisible and devilishly clever."

Turned out to be a loose peg high on the starboard side of the bulkhead. Push it in hard and it popped back out far enough to reveal a release. Pull that and it exposed a gently glowing glyph. A moment in shadow's skin and a word of opening and a large section of bulkhead swung out and down, becoming a short set of stairs leading up into darkness. I poked my head through the opening. The compartment was about four feet in depth by eight high and it probably ran the width of the ship. I couldn't say for sure because they'd packed it tight.

"Here." I helped Jax up onto a seat on the steps to get her out of the water and handed her my light. "Hold this.

"Triss, see if you can't slip back into the depths and check for anything dangerous." I started pulling out enough of the stuff right around the hatch to make room for Jax and me, as he slithered through gaps that would have stymied anything bigger than a nipperkin. "Looks like they're on their way out of port."

"How can you tell?" asked Jax.

"This." I dropped a small bale of exceptionally fine silk regretfully into the water sloshing around the bottom of the bigger compartment. "And this." I added a tiny crate of tea stamped with the seal of the Duke of Jenua—everything had to be packed small enough to fit through the flood ports.

"I think I must have missed a step, Aral."

"You don't smuggle tea and silk *into* Zhan. Though *this* they might." I pulled out another small crate labeled with a familiar distiller's mark and set it on the top step—Aveni whiskey, though not my favorite Kyle's.

"How do you know so much about smuggling?" she asked as I pulled my remaining hip dagger out and jammed the tip of it under one edge of the crate's lid.

I pounded on the pommel with the heel of my hand. "I don't know what you've been doing since the temple fell, but I needed something to pay my rent and my bar bill." I leaned gently on the dagger—I'd lost three knives already tonight—and the lid started to lift. "Turns out the smugglers will pay pretty well for a courier who never gets stopped by the Stingers."

"Stingers?"

"City watch. That's what the underworld types call them because they wear gold and black. And . . . oh, there we go." I lifted out a bottle of Skaate's finest eighteen, sliced the seal, and pulled the cork with my teeth. "Beautiful."

And so very delicious. I took a long swig off the bottle.

"Aral, that's disgusting! Don't you remember what the priests had to say about alcohol?"

I pulled the bottle away from my lips and looked down to meet her eyes. With the way she was holding the thieveslight I couldn't see them clearly, but the way her lip curled spoke to the contempt I couldn't see.

"Every word, Jax. Every word." I lifted the bottle and took another long drink—damn but I needed that. "I also remember how much good all those words did when the Hand of Heaven came knocking on the temple door. There was a lot the priests didn't know."

"Aral's a little bitter," said Triss from the mouth of the smuggling compartment. "In case you hadn't guessed."

"So am I," said Jax. "But drinking that way? How could you?"

"I'll show you." I took my third drink in as many minutes.

I hadn't drunk like this in a while—Triss hated my drinking and I tried to control it for him even when I couldn't for me. In my better moments, I succeeded. This wasn't one of my better moments, and that felt fucking wonderful, though the booze hadn't hit me nearly as hard as it should have. In fact, I'd burned so much nima that it felt like it was mostly just vanishing. Too bad. Sticking the cork back in the bottle I set it beside Jax.

"It's there in case you want some." Her jaw tightened in an all-too-familiar anger. "Before you throw the bottle across the room, or start yelling at me, I've got two things to say. One, we're trying to stay hidden here. Two, 'spirits for the drained spirit.'"

"What the hell are you talking about, Aral?"

I was pleased to note that despite the obvious anger in her voice, she kept it low and quiet.

"Nima," Triss said to Jax. "It's something we learned from . . . another mage. If you've overtapped the well of your soul—as Aral did getting us all here alive—you can temporarily recover some of what you've lost by drinking. That's why Aral hasn't fallen over yet, neither from exhaustion, nor from drinking half a pint of cask-strength whiskey."

Jax's expression calmed and she bit her lip. "Really?"

"I take it there's nothing back in there that we have to worry about, Triss?" My question came out a lot grumpier than I'd intended and I knew the reason for that.

It hadn't escaped me that in the years after Jax and I stopped being an us, she'd continued to get along beautifully with Triss, and vice versa. I resented that, though it made me feel petty. When Triss didn't answer me, I went back to making space.

"That seems an awfully useful thing to know," Jax said after a while. "Why wouldn't the priests have told us about it?"

"Because it only works when you've pushed yourself too far," replied Triss, his voice low and worried. "And, if you do it very often, it'll hollow you out like a piece of old bamboo. Pretty soon you'll start to feel like the only thing that can fill that void is more booze. It works in the short term, and sometimes I'll even say it's a good idea, but what drink does to your kind, over time, is ugly."

I closed my eyes and bit back my instinctive response. Then I pulled out one last crate of expensive tea and dumped it in the water.

"And there we go. Your bower awaits, Master Jax."

She looked up at me and I was shocked to see tears on her cheeks. "I'm sorry I didn't come looking for you earlier, Aral."

"Why do you say that?"

"I waited until I needed your help. And because of that, I think I missed the time when you needed mine."

I felt my throat go tight, but I didn't have any good answer for that, so I turned away. I wanted to yell at her. Not because she was wrong, but because she almost certainly wasn't. Eight years on from the mess we'd made of what should have been the best thing that ever happened to me, and she still knew me better than I'd ever known myself. Two sentences and she'd cut straight through all the armor and all the cynicism and drawn blood. She had no fucking right to still be able to do that to me. Not anymore.

When I finally turned back around, she'd crawled up the stairs into the smuggler's stash, though I hadn't heard her move. A glance through the hatch showed her curled tightly in a hundred silver riels worth of silk and dead asleep. She'd left just enough room for me to stretch out beside her like I had so many times before.

I looked up at the shadow tiger keeping watch on the wall above Jax's head. Sshayar's subtle stripes just barely showed in the red glow of the thieveslamp. I knew she was looking back at me, but not

BLADE IN SHADOW

even a Blade can read the expression on a shadow's face, so I didn't know what she was thinking. I reached for the bottle and took another deep drink. This one I felt all the way down to my toes, which was good. I needed it to get me to put my foot on that first step. But it wasn't quite enough for me to take the rest of that short walk.

If it weren't for the fact that I'd probably drown if I stayed out there, I don't think all the whiskey in the world would have put me in bed with Jax again, even if it was only for sleeping. I raised the bottle again, then paused with it against my lips as I noticed the shadowy dragon take a spot on the wall beside the tiger. I looked into the place where his eyes would have been, for several long seconds, then raised one brow in question. I knew I couldn't trust my judgment on the booze, so I left it up to him.

Triss looked down at Jax, then back at me, and finally he nodded ever so slightly, though I could see it cost him.

I took another drink.

5

Intentions are ice. Results are diamonds. Both can be hard and cold or sparkle and shine, but intentions only matter as long as the heat doesn't melt them away to nothing. Results can't be gotten rid of half so easily. You can split them or polish them, even burn them in a hot enough fire, but you have to work if you want to change them.

Waking up with your ex and a hangover when you'd only intended to have a quiet conversation with her will bring that point home with stunning clarity. More so if you wake up wedged into a tightly enclosed space the gods have decided to use as a dice box. At least, that was how it felt, between the way the world had started to roll and pitch and the stuffiness of the air. Things had gone completely dark back when I closed the thieveslamp, so my eyes were useless unless I dug it out again. The heavy smells of tea and sweat and old whiskey in the air made me long for a fresh breeze.

Triss, how long have I been out? And what the hell is going on?

Maybe four hours. The storm's still hammering us. If anything it's gotten worse. We're getting serious waves now.

I hope Faran made it out of the river all right. There was nothing I could do about it now or anytime soon, but that didn't make me feel any better.

I'm sure she's fine, sent Triss. But he didn't *sound* sure.

I forced the thought aside, burying it in the back of my mind for the time being—mental discipline had always been at least as important as physical for a Blade, and *much* harder. I lifted my left arm—Jax was asleep on my right shoulder—and felt along the wall, finding the hatch closed tight.

What happened? I asked Triss.

When the big waves first started to hit, the captain or somebody opened up the outer ports to let the compartment flood. The back of the ship was practically underwater at the time and it came in so fast Sshayar and I barely had time to get the stairs closed. The seals are tight enough that not even a shadow can pass, but as far as I can tell the ballast tank is still full of water.

I nodded. *So, for the moment at least, the only way anyone is getting in or out is by cutting through the forward bulkhead into the hold. Not my first choice, but I guess I can live with that. Though it's a good thing I don't mind enclosed spaces, and that I'm not prone to motion sickness.*

The hidey-hole I'd hollowed out for us up at the top of the stowed contraband couldn't have run much more than two feet high by four deep and seven long.

I took a deep breath by way of a test. *I notice the air isn't getting any worse.*

The planks between us and the ship's inner hold are pretty tightly fitted, but the caulking's only good enough to make it look *like a water-tight bulkhead. Sshayar and I popped some of the seams to improve the air.*

Sounds like you've got everything covered and I can go back to sleep.

I really needed it, but both the pounding pressure at my temples and a growing thirst that the whiskey would ultimately only worsen gave me doubts. The fact that Jax had put my right arm to sleep and that the whole world was pitching about like I'd had six drinks too many didn't help. I might have managed to get past all the physical discomfort anyway—I'd slept with worse—if only I could have quieted my mind.

But now that I was awake, the questions had started. Both proximate: where was the ship going and how were we going to get off without being noticed? And, more remote: What had really been going on back at the cemetery? Could I even trust Jax? I massaged my forehead, but it didn't help, either with the pain or the thinking.

After a minute or so I gave it up only to have my hand replaced by a sudden cool pressure running from temple to temple like a damp cloth—Triss, doing what he could to ease my pain with a shadow's touch. That surprised me. It had been years since he'd been willing to help with any of my bottle-born and self-inflicted wounds.

You hit the booze pretty hard last night, on top of all the things that hit you. Triss's mental voice sounded cautious and worried, not at all his usual bitter morning-after demeanor. *How do you feel?*

I did a quick mental inventory, comparing the ache in my head and the rot in my gut to the cold and the exhaustion of the night before and came up with a mostly positive balance.

Less like I'm about to die, but more like I might be happier if I did, I teased.

That's not funny.

No, I suppose it's not.

Jax stirred against my side, then drew a sharp breath—probably when she felt the pain in her side. "Aral?"

"I'm here."

"Why is the world moving?"

"Storm."

"Then we really are stuffed in some tiny little smuggler's stash on board a ship somewhere off the coast of Zhan?"

I nodded in the darkness. "Yes."

"Damn. For a few blissful seconds there I thought I'd just had the longest and worst nightmare in the history of dreaming. But the goddess is still dead, isn't she?"

"Would that it *were* a dream."

"And you and I are not a we?"

"No. Not for a very long time."

Jax drew a ragged breath. "Well at least that's one small mercy, though I think getting back together would have been worth it if it erased all the other bad stuff."

"Jax!" I growled. I so didn't need this shit.

She gave my ribs a squeeze. "I'm sorry, Aral. I was joking. Well, not really joking so much as desperately trying to keep myself from going quietly mad. It's an ugly habit I picked up from Loris when the Hand had us. Laughing was the only thing that really seemed to put the torturers off balance. They hurt us all the more when we did it, but they didn't enjoy it half so much."

What do you say to that?

"You've changed," is what finally came out, though it seemed both inadequate and obvious. I thought briefly about digging out the thieveslight, but somehow the dark made it easier to say the things that needed saying. "And I guess it's my turn to be sorry. I wish there was something I could have done. . . ."

"You've changed, too," she said.

More than she could imagine. Another small grace of leaving the light closed was that it meant we didn't have to talk about my face quite yet.

"I think the old Aral would have tried to match my joke with one of his own," continued Jax. "Perhaps the Hand did something of a transfer there. If I got your sense of humor, what gift did the Hand give you?"

"I can't think of a single thing." It came out harder and flatter than I'd intended, and I felt Jax stiffen against my side.

"Rage," Triss said quietly—it was hard to hear him over the noises of the tossing ship.

"What?" I asked in the same breath as Jax.

"Anger is a terrible gift," said Triss. "It cuts the hand that wields it every bit as deeply as its target, but I think you needed it in the years right after the temple fell. Without anger, we would not have survived."

Sshayar let out a low growling chuckle somewhere in the darkness. "If so, it was a good choice. Jax has always had plenty to spare."

"Hey now," started Jax, but then I felt her shrug against my side, and then wince and put a hand to her wound. "I guess you may have a point there."

"Of course I do," replied Sshayar. "It's ironic really. If you had possessed more humor or Aral more anger, you might even have stayed together."

I didn't know how to respond to that, it came like another punch in the gut. I closed my eyes, though it didn't matter in the dark.

"I doubt it," said Triss. "They were too much of an age to do well together."

"There is that," said Sshayar. "She does not fight with Loris half so much as she did with Aral, or with Devin for that matter."

"You're with Loris now?" I asked before I could stop myself.

Jax drew a deep ragged breath, then let it go as she pulled away from me. "I am. Our experiences in the dungeons of Heaven's Reach gave us a close bond. After we escaped, it grew from companionship into something more."

I couldn't see, but from the sounds of things, I guessed she'd taken advantage of her diminutive size to wedge herself in the far corner, probably in the cross-legged pose she'd always favored. I didn't say anything right away, because I needed time to process the idea of Jax with Loris.

It really shouldn't have surprised me. Loris was perhaps twenty years older than Jax, a large gap for the general run of humanity, but like all the greater mages, Blades measured their lives by the span of our familiars. A dragon-bound mage might last a thousand years if they were lucky enough. The longest I'd ever heard of a Blade living was three hundred years, but it wasn't old age that killed her, it was a bodyguard's sword. When Blades died, we died by violence in action, and mostly we died young.

Lifespan was part of the reason Blades tended to form partnerships across generations rather than within them, but lifestyle had a lot to do with it, too. Jax and I had literally grown up together. From the age of four on we had spent much of our waking lives together. What lay between us included every childish mistake and every adolescent cruelty as much as it included our onetime love. Little surprise then that it hadn't worked out, that it almost never worked out.

Thinking about it, better by far Loris than Devin. I wasn't looking forward to being the one to break the news of Devin's betrayal to Jax if she hadn't already heard it. I reached for the whiskey bottle, though I didn't yet twist the cork free.

"That's why I'm here, actually," Jax said, finally breaking the long silence. "The Hand has Loris."

"I'm sorry," I said. "That's terrible. Do you know if he's still alive?"

"I believe that he is, but I can't know without going after him . . . them actually, and I don't want to do that until I'm ready to break them out. I need your help."

"You'll have it," I said, there could be no other choice. There were very few situations that I could imagine where Jax would need help from anybody, but taking on the people who'd destroyed the temple and murdered so many of our brethren was definitely one of them. "But back up a moment, I think I may have missed a step. 'Them'?"

"After we broke out of Heaven's Reach, Loris and I tried to gather as many of the escaped journeymen and apprentices as we could find. We've been bringing them back to a sort of fallback we set up in Dalridia at Cairmor. It's a minor castle my brother owns."

"Your brother?" I asked. "I don't remember you ever talking about your family when we were together."

Jax sighed. "My father was the younger brother of the King of Dalridia. It never seemed like a great thing to bring up among a group of people dedicated to enforcing justice on the royalty of the world. Between my induction into the order and taking my journeyman's swords, the priests and masters made sure I had no contact with my family, nor heard any news of them. After though, I had the freedom to seek out that news, or even my family, I went out of my way to avoid it and them."

I could understand that. Though my own family had been

merchants of some sort and lived within sight of the temple, I'd never sought them out, nor talked to them in the city those few times I encountered them by accident. It was simply not the way things were done.

"Then the temple fell," I said.

"Exactly. After Loris and I escaped from the Hand we needed a place to lie up and heal. Loris comes from the Kvanas where the Son of Heaven's word is as good as any of the great Khans, so Dalridia and my family seemed like our safest option. When we arrived, I found out my uncle and father had both died. That left my brother King of Dalridia, since my uncle had chosen to honor the commitment he'd made to his prince consort rather than succumb to the pressure to produce an heir, and thus had no children of his own."

"How did your brother feel about taking in a fugitive from the Son of Heaven?"

"It's been ten generations since Namara had to send a Blade after a noble of Dalridia, though not a few noble heads have fallen to the royal executioner. My family takes pride in that record. My brother, Eian, was likewise proud of me and what I'd become."

"But," said Sshayar, "after what happened to the temple, Dalridia must be cautious about being seen to be in opposition to the high church of the eleven kingdoms. Eian was glad to see us and to offer us shelter, but politics forced him to ask us to keep as low a profile as possible."

"That's why he put us at Cairmor," added Jax. "It's a royal retreat high in the mountains at the southwest end of the kingdom, far from the major passes and any foreign influence. The villagers are personally loyal to my brother, and no else ever comes there. It's served us admirably as we've slowly gathered up what we could of the surviving Blade trainees."

Jax shifted in the darkness, then let out a little gasp of pain. "Damn, but this hole in my side hurts. Cairmor is nothing like what we had at the temple, but we've made it more than just a place of refuge. We're trying to teach the old skills so they won't be lost . . . though I'm not sure if that can ever matter again."

"How many have you brought there?" asked Triss, and I could hear the eagerness in his voice, the longing.

The destruction of the temple and our years in hiding had been even harder on him than on me. I might have lost my friends, my goddess, even my faith in myself and my mission in life, but at least I still lived in my own world among my own kind. The familiar bond could only be severed by death. When Triss had tied himself to me, he had left behind the quiet deeps of his home in the everdark, never to return.

Here in the sunlands, his only possible connection back to the life he had been born to came from congress with his fellow exiles. We'd only encountered three other Shades in the past few years, and never since the fall of the temple had he had a chance to talk to more than one of his fellows at a time.

"There were twenty-one of us at Cairmor before this latest attack by the Hand." Jax's breath and speech sounded more labored now.

"And all were taken?" demanded Triss.

"No. The attack came in the city of Tavan, during a mission, not at the school. They got Loris and four of our eldest journeymen—they'd be masters by now if Namara had lived to name them so, Maryam, Leyan, Javan, and Roric."

That hurt. I didn't remember Javan or Maryam very well, but Leyan was a wonderful girl, and very good with the garrote. Too young for me to have spent much time with her, but I very much liked what I'd seen of her. Roric, too, a huge bearlike boy who still managed to move with a cat's grace.

"What were they doing in the Magelands?"

"We'd heard of a daring young thief and spy working out of Tavan, and it sounded like it might be one of our last four lost apprentices. Loris and the others went to see if they could find out more, but ran into a cohort of the Hand instead of the missing apprentice."

"Ugly," I said. "When did this happen?"

"A few weeks ago. I'd been considering trying to break Loris free with the help of our three remaining older journeymen, but I couldn't make the odds work no matter how much I wanted to. This is the Hand, the force that destroyed the temple and more than a hundred Blades. My students aren't ready to face that. They simply haven't had the real-world experience in dealing with the problems that kind of raid would encounter. That's why, when I heard about your presence here in Tien, it seemed like a sign sent by a kindly fate."

"Do you know where they're being held?" asked Triss.

"When I left to come find you and Aral they were in a large abbey in the plains east of Tavan." She spoke a brief spell and then drew a quick glowing map in the air between us.

"About here." She touched a spot. "There's a good chance they're still there. I'm sure the Hand wants them in Heaven's Reach, but moving religious prisoners around the Magelands is going to be damn tricky."

I nodded, though she couldn't see me. The council of Magearchs may pay lip service to the High Church and the Son of Heaven, but they're a nation founded by, and for, magical refugees from various sorts of persecution.

Sshayar spoke now: "Outside of the abbeys and their temple-cum-embassies in the cities, the forces of the Son of Heaven are probably weaker in the Magelands than anywhere in the eleven kingdoms, save only Kanjuri. Tavan is particularly tough, squeezed up against the border with the Sylvani Empire like it is. The Others hate our gods with an immortal passion, and would cheerfully skin any of the Hand they could get their hands on."

I looked at Jax's map. "I think you're right. There's no good way for the Hand to get them out. Tavan's on a river, but the outflow goes right past the Sylvani capital. Upstream runs into the mountains and ultimately Dalridia."

"The Son's greatest strength is all in the north," said Triss. "In Zhan and Kadesh on this side of the mountains and Aven, Osë, and the Kvanas to the west. The Hand's only reasonable option is to get the prisoners on a ship, send them north to Kadesh, and then over Hurn's Gate and down through Aven. That's going to take some doing."

"Huh," I said as a thought hit me.

"What is it?" asked Triss.

"I just realized something. The current Son of Heaven has really expanded the power of the church, but he's strongest in the kingdoms where mages are weakest. Zhan, where the rules and customs make it very hard for mages to hold a title of nobility. Kadesh and the Kvanas, where the mage gift will automatically get you disinherited. Aven and Osë don't have any formal antimage rules that I know of, but I can't think of a single major noble house that's headed by a mage in either."

"I never thought of that before," said Jax, "but you're right. My brother is a mage, if a minor one, and so was my uncle. Varya's nobility is lousy with them. So are Radewald's and Dan Eyre's. In the Magelands and Kodamia you have to have magic to hold a title at all. Kanjuri's the only odd one out. They have no true mages, but the High Church is all but disbarred from the islands."

"Maybe it's got more to do with familiars than magery," said Triss. "Any Kanjurese peasant who exhibits the familiar gift is automatically raised to the peerage, and they disbar those nobles who are born without it. But none of that will get Loris or the others free. We need to focus on the task at hand."

"Not at hand," said Jax. "Not yet anyway. We've got to get off this ship. Then we have to get to the Magelands, and none of that's happening in the next couple of hours."

"First, we have to get back to Tien," I added. "I have things I need to take care of before I can leave." For reasons I couldn't really articulate, I didn't want to talk to Jax about Faran yet.

"Ah, your hidden Blade," said Jax. "Who was that at the cemetery with you?"

Before I could even start to dissemble, Sshayar spoke, "It was Ssithra and Faran. I spoke to them while you were unconscious."

"She's alive then!" Jax sounded delighted, which made me feel the worse for doubting her but didn't remove the doubts. "How is she? How long has she been with you? I don't remember a second Blade being mentioned in any of the stories that made their way to Dalridia."

"She only joined me recently, and we've gone out of our way to keep her presence a secret."

There was obviously no point in my trying to conceal her name, not when Sshayar knew it. But I still couldn't shake the feeling that talking about her with Jax was a betrayal of some sort, which made me wonder what my hindbrain wasn't telling me about Jax.

"That might be harder than you think," said Jax. "Do you know about the shadow trails?"

"Or the apostate Blades?" Sshayar added with more than a bit of a growl in her voice.

"Apostate Blades?" I asked, though I thought I knew who she was referring to.

Sshayar coughed like the angry tiger she could so easily become, and I couldn't blame her. Damn, but I needed a drink, and there it was at my side. I pulled the cork and took a sip.

"Bastards and traitors," said Jax. "When they took us prisoner at the fall of the temple, the Son of Heaven offered us a deal through the senior surviving officer of the Hand. Any Blade, trainee or master, who would agree to serve the will of Heaven from time to time was offered the chance to walk away free and clear. I refused, as did Loris and many others. That's when the torture started. Every so often they would come by and ask again, though I don't know how they could have believed we could ever be trusted if we said yes."

"Spellbound oaths, I assume," I replied. "That or the Son of Heaven believes that torture works and the switch of allegiance from Namara to Shan can be reliably achieved with coercion."

Jax made a rude noise. "Was that last a joke? Because if it was, it's almost funny. If it wasn't, I have to say that the drink's starting to affect you. As for spellbound oaths, you know as well as I do that there are a thousand ways and one to twist them around if you've got the incentive."

"Maybe even more than that, but it also depends on the oath, and the Son of Heaven has resources beyond the normal. Do you know how many of our brethren took the deal?"

"It's hard to say. I only know of one for sure, Kayarin Melkar. She and I were chained together immediately after we were taken. She agreed to the bargain, right there in the yard with a dozen slaughtered journeymen and priests lying within a stone's throw. If I could have moved I'd have strangled her on the spot, but the enchantments on the manacles barely left me the strength to breathe through the pain."

"Speaking of which"—Jax let out a sharp little noise. "Does alcohol work as well as efik for pain?"

"Better in some ways. It doesn't numb things up, but you care a lot less. You've got to be more careful about dosage, and the side effects get uglier faster. On the other hand, it'll help restore your nima, at least temporarily, and that'll help both of you."

"Hand it over." She put a hand on my knee, so I'd know where to pass the bottle.

I did, and I heard her take a long drink that ended in a rough gasp. "Stuff tastes like horse piss, how do you stand it?"

"It grows on you."

"Not if you're lucky," grumbled Triss.

Jax took another drink, shorter this time. "Still piss, but yeah I can already feel it taking the edge off. Thank you."

"You're welcome." I licked my lips, and managed not to ask for the bottle back, just. Even if she finished it, there was probably more around.

She continued, "Later, I saw Kayarin's name listed among the dead on that obelisk the Son of Heaven had erected outside the main gates of the temple. I'm not sure if that means she recanted or if the traitors are all listed among the dead or what, though I suspect the latter. I do know that there are at least a half dozen of the apostates running around loose. We've encountered their shadow trails a couple of times."

You have to tell her, Triss said into my mind. *He was her friend as much as yours. Maybe even more. They were lovers for years after the two of you called it quits.*

"I can't speak to Kayarin specifically," I finally said. "But I can say for certain that at least some of those listed as dead are alive and well and making a great case for the twisting of spellbound oaths."

"You've encountered some of them, then?" asked Sshayar.

"I have, or one of them anyway. That's how I learned about the shadow trails. He used ours to set us up for a deathspark."

"A deathspark?" asked Sshayar. "Why didn't your sacred blades protect you?"

"For starters, they're sitting on the bottom of a lake beside the stone corpse of the goddess. I returned them to her when I left her service."

"What happened after you got 'sparked?" Jax's voice sounded low and dangerous, angry.

"I ended up on a big wooden glyph thing they called the 'pillory of light.' The straps bound me and the glyph bound Triss."

"They beat him," said Triss. "They hurt him and I couldn't stop them. Later, I killed them all, but I couldn't do anything about it until a friend rescued us." Even a year later Triss was slurring his sibilants in a barely controlled rage.

Jax put a hand on my knee again. "I'm sorry, Aral. I know a thing or two about being bound to the pillory. If I could have, I'd have come to get you."

"It wasn't anything like what you faced. I wasn't even there that long."

"Four days, though you *were* unconscious for much of it," Triss interjected in a voice made icy by anger.

"You said that you knew some of the names on the obelisk belonged to the apostate instead of the dead." Jax sounded just as hard and cold as Triss. "I assume that means that you know who set you up."

"I do."

"But you haven't said a name yet. I know you, Aral, and I know what that means. But you can't possibly hurt me anywhere near as much as I've already been hurt. Stop trying to protect me and tell me the bad news. Who set you up?"

"Devin."

"Oh." I heard the bottle tip back again, for a very long time, then a small cough. "Damn but that's awful stuff. Did you kill him?"

"No. I could have, but I chose not to. I let him walk away."

"I wouldn't have," said Jax, and there was no give in her tone.

6

Love and hate are two edges of the same sword. The hilt can twist in your hand in an instant, and suddenly the sword cuts the other way. It's a simple twist, simpler than anyone can imagine until it happens to them, simpler by far than putting the sword aside, or letting it rust away to nothing. All the strong emotions are like that, easier to reverse than to transform or put aside, and every one of them can cut you to the bone.

Jax was bleeding now. I could hear it when she talked about Devin. Quiet and cold, barely audible above the noises of the ship fighting the storm. Again, I was glad that neither of us had chosen to unshutter our thieveslights. I didn't want to see the pain that went with that voice.

"You should have killed him, Aral."

"You loved him once," I said.

"So did you. I got over it long before the temple fell. Why didn't you? If not in the years before the fall, when he started treating you badly, then later, when he arranged to have you and Triss tied to a rack?"

"Because I looked at him and I saw what he used to be," I replied. "There was a greatness there once."

"No, Aral. There never was." I drew a breath to respond, but Jax preempted me. "Don't. I knew him better than anyone, I think. Better than you did, certainly."

Jax took another long drink—I could hear the sweet gurgle of whiskey leaving the bottle. "I *heard* the things that he'd never say to you, the bitter things he whispered in the dark, his angers and his envies, and how very much he resented playing the second sword to 'the great Aral Kingslayer.'"

That stung. "I know that it was hard for him to have me as a best friend after I killed Ashvik. I can't blame him for resenting the attention the masters gave me."

"Not just the masters," said Jax. "The whole world."

I felt my face heat. I never much liked the renown that came with killing a king. I was proud of what I'd done, ending the life of a monster in a crown. Proud, too, of my ability. I'd managed an execution that three senior masters had died attempting. For a little while I was the world's best . . . assassin—I still found that word uncomfortable. It wasn't what the goddess called us, nor how we'd thought of ourselves, but now, looking back, I had to admit it was what we were. I'd loved the work and knowing I was good at what I did, but I'd never felt comfortable with the adulation.

"He couldn't stand all the attention you got," said Jax. "He hated that you were Aral Kingslayer and he was plain old Devin Urslan. He hated you."

"I can't believe that. Envied yes, I know that. I'd have to be an idiot not to, but hate? No. He may have said things he didn't really mean, but that's all."

"Why the fuck are you defending him? He betrayed Namara and he betrayed the order. But long before that he betrayed you. He's a traitor through and through." Jax shifted and then drew in a harsh pained breath. "He told me how much he hated you, Aral, more than once, and he meant every fucking word of it. That's what drew us together in the first place."

"I—"

"No. Let me finish. This needs to be said. Just give me a moment."

Jax took another drink and I found myself wishing for the bottle again. I started quietly searching around for another and hoping Triss or Sshayar would get involved in the conversation, though I understood why they didn't. This was a human thing, between me and Jax and Devin.

"It's true, Aral. The whole damned order thought you walked in the shadow of the goddess. Everybody but Devin and, later, me. After you and I broke up, we both hated you. That's what put us in bed together. I thought it would hurt you more than sleeping with anyone else would. And Devin . . . well, Devin's motivations were more complex. I think he wanted to be you as much as hurt you, and he figured fucking me would serve for both."

"I was happy for the two of you," I said.

"I know, and damn but it pissed us off. It's funny really. You were what brought Devin and I together, but you were ultimately what drove us apart as well."

"How so?"

"I hated you for what you did to me. Devin hated you for what you were. Somewhere along the line I realized that as much as you'd hurt me, you hadn't done it because you wanted to cause me pain. You did it because you figured out we were never going to work as an us. And, quite simply, you were right. It took me longer to get there than it took you, but if we'd stayed together I'd have come to the same conclusion at some point. Probably a hell of a lot sooner than I did by being with Devin."

She chuckled ruefully and took another drink. I didn't remember my reasoning as being anything like that clear-cut, but I wasn't going to argue with her, I'd done that more than enough when we were together.

"Once I understood why you left me when you did, I fell out of hate with you. Devin noticed and it didn't sit at all well. We started to fight, a lot. More than you and I did even. And whenever we fought, there you were being sympathetic and trying to help out your friends. It reminded me of why I'd loved you in the first place. Though I was smart enough not to fall *in love* with you a second time, I ended up loving you all over again. That was absolute death to my relationship with Devin."

Devin had the chance to kill me when I'd encountered him last, more than once. He hadn't done it. Part of that was clearly self-interest—I was potentially valuable to him in his new enterprise. But there was more to it than that. Even if Jax was right and Devin *had* hated me for years, I think he still loved me, too. We'd been best friends for almost fifteen years before I killed Ashvik and I never had reason for a moment's doubt of our friendship in all that time. It wasn't until I became the Kingslayer that I first started to notice a distance growing between us.

No. It wasn't as simple as Devin hating me for what I had become. But again, I didn't want to argue with Jax. Hell, that was the main reason I'd left Jax a month before we were to be married—I didn't want to argue with Jax ever again. Nine years on, and the whole not-arguing-with-Jax thing *still* felt good.

"Damn." Jax sloshed the whiskey in her bottle. "This stuff is brutal. Here, it's all yours." I felt the bottle pressed against my thigh. "I need to take a little nap."

Jax let go and the bottle tipped, but if anything spilled out I couldn't tell in the dark and the damp of the smuggler's compartment— even with the tight seals around the hatch and between the planks there was no avoiding the wet salt air. By the time I'd picked Jax's whiskey up and wedged it upright between a couple of bolts of cloth, she was snoring. Sleep sounded like a good idea, so I closed my eyes and was gone.

The next time I opened them my head felt like someone had bent a hot iron poker around my skull at eyeball height. I started groping toward the bottle.

"There's a good idea," said Triss in his normal sharp, morning-after voice.

Apparently, I'd used up all of my drinking grace with Triss— not that I blamed him. Mostly, these days, I managed to keep the whiskey from dominating my life the way it had a few years ago, but I was a drunk. The murder of my goddess had broken some-thing in me, something that nothing and no one would ever be able to fix. I had a hole in my soul where my faith had once lived.

Sometimes, on a good night, if I poured enough whiskey into that hole, it felt liked I'd filled it up. Like maybe I'd finally stopped losing bits of me down that hole. But it never lasted. I'd go to sleep and the booze would drain away, leaving things exactly the way they were before I started drinking. That's because there was no bottom to the hole, and all the whiskey ever did was hide that fact for a while. The next morning always came along and shoved the truth in my face so hard it hurt.

Even knowing that, I found myself grabbing Jax's bottle and drinking off a good solid inch of the whiskey before setting it aside. It didn't do a damn thing for my hangover.

"It's a terrible idea, Triss. Nine kinds of stupid and more, but today I needed it, and that's all I'm having." That's when I realized we weren't moving. Not at all, and we were sitting at a funny angle. "What happened to the boat?"

"We're aground somewhere east and north of Tien."

"What! When did that happen?"

"A couple of hours ago. It was surprisingly gentle. I've been slip-ping through into the hold to listen to the common sailors. I've only been getting dribs and drabs, but as I understand it we lost the rud-der at the height of the storm. They tried to make do after that with something they called sweeps, but it wasn't really working and they were deathly afraid of running into some bad patch of reefs. So when they hit a lull in the storm, they beached us."

"What happens now?" I hadn't the vaguest idea of how they might handle something like that.

"Once the sun's up, they're planning on emptying the holds and refloating the ship. Then they're heading on to Kanjuri."

"Which means that even if they don't open up the smuggling compartments, we need to get ashore. I have to get back to Faran. What time is it?"

"Judging by the taste of the night, it's a few hours before dawn."

"So, thirty hours since the fight in the cemetery, more or less." I reached out a hand and touched Jax's ankle. "Time to get up."

She jerked at my touch, then said, "Ow! Shit, my head feels worse than my side. Is that normal?"

"It is if you drink like Aral," said Triss.

"Then why does anyone drink like Aral? Aral excepted, of course, because he's obviously a fool and madman. He'd have to be, to give up efik for this stuff."

"I have no idea," replied Triss, sounding entirely too smug.

"The priests were right. Drink is a demon. This is the worst I've felt short of actual torture. I'm never doing this again."

"Entirely sensible," said Triss.

"Then why in the name of all that's holy did you tell me it could be a good idea? I'd never have even tried the stuff if it was just Aral saying it."

"When did I say anything like that?" asked Triss.

"Right after Aral said 'spirits for the drained spirit.'"

"Oh right. Sorry about that, but it really can help under a very specialized set of circumstances, save your life even."

"Hmph, I think dying might be less traumatic. Never again. Hey, the boat stopped moving. What's happening?"

Fifteen minutes later, we were slipping out through the half-flooded ballast tank to the still-open ports. Half an hour after that, we were holed up in a patch of thornbushes on the shore—the best defense against the restless dead we could find there in the middle of nowhere. I was just telling Jax to wait and rest her wounds while I went to see if I could find us some sort of transport back to Tien, when she reached up and touched my cheek.

"Aral, what have you done to yourself? I *thought* you looked a little odd when we were trying to get the hatch open to get into the compartment back there, but I'd assumed it was exhaustion and the hole in my side making me see things. But it's not, and that's more than makeup."

"It is. The last job I took exposed my face to the whole . . . well you know all about that. The stories and wanted posters that came out of that mess are what brought you up here to look for me. Fortunately, the same job also gave me the tools I needed to reshape the bones of my face."

"I didn't even think that was possible." Jax ran a finger down my cheek to my jaw and then back up the other side, pressing at the corner of my mouth and the orbit of my eye before suddenly pulling her hand back as if she'd burned it. "I'm so sorry it came to this. There's hardly any of the old you left in your face."

There wasn't much of the old me left on the inside either, but I didn't have the heart to say it. "Things are better this way. It gives me a chance at a new start."

But Jax just shook her head. "I expected you to have taken on some sort of disguise—you'd have to—but I was sure I'd recognize you no matter what you tried. I was wrong. I could have looked you straight in the eye without ever knowing you."

"You did, at the Gryphon's Head. I was—"

"Sitting at the table in back by the door into the courtyard. You had your back half exposed to an open window—how could you stand it. I saw you there, marked you as a killer even, but I didn't see it was you. That's . . ."

"Remarkable," said Sshayar, "and potentially very handy."

"Awful," said Jax. "It's awful."

"You'll have to tell us the story," said Sshayar.

"After I see if I can find us a cart or something. You shouldn't be walking or riding with that side."

"**When** and where should I meet you?" Jax asked as we abandoned the cart on the outskirts of Quarryside.

From here on in, the city got steadily busier and it was going to be easier to walk. The hole in Jax's side was going to take weeks to heal fully, even with the spells we'd spun to help, but it wasn't much bigger around than an arrow puncture, and far cleaner. Not much fun for walking but not impossible either.

"I need to pick up my things and attend to a small matter or two before I can leave for the Magelands," she continued. She didn't invite me to come with her.

That was fine. I didn't want her coming with me either. I wasn't ready to trust her, or anyone else who knew who and what I was, with the location of my current snug. Especially not with Faran there—at least, I sure hoped she was there. I had no intention of exposing the younger Blade to any risks I didn't have to. Honestly, I suspected courtesy on that front was half of why Jax wanted to split up for the moment.

"How about we meet back down by the docks." I pointed south. "There's a tavern called the Spinnerfish in Smuggler's Rest. It's as safe a place to meet as any in the city. The owner runs it as neutral ground where sunside and shadowside can meet without any worries about ambush or betrayal. People who bring their outside fights inside end up dead. Also, the fish is as good as you can get in Tien. Say, a few hours before sunset tomorrow? That'll give us time to find a ship that's headed for the Magelands with the next morning's tide."

Jax rolled her eyes. "Oh goody, my last ride on a boat makes getting on another one sound like the best idea ever."

"Not my first choice either, but if time's a concern it's a hell of a lot better than riding. It's not like we have the resources to pay for the fastest magical transport anymore."

"Tell me about it. I had to borrow money from my brother to pay my way up here." She looked up then. "This is my turn. See you tomorrow."

I tossed her a wave and angled right while she turned left and headed south along the waterfront. When I got to the Kanathean Canal, I hired a boat to take me out to the river and up to Bankside. That took me a long distance out of my way, but a shadow trail can't be followed on running water, and sitting in the little boat gave me plenty of time to watch for tails.

By the time I hopped the fence and stepped up to the back door of the little house I shared with Faran, I was quite certain I'd lost any potential hangers-on. I hated to be seen entering the place in my working rig, especially during daylight hours when it was harder to fudge the details. But it had been three days and I just couldn't wait any longer to find out what had happened to Faran.

I pretended to pull a key out of my trick bag and bring it to the keyhole, but Triss did the real work, slipping a portion of himself into the lock and triggering the spell points there to release the mechanism. I kept lock and hinges carefully oiled, so the only sound the door made was the faint scuff of wood on wood as it slid across the threshold. Beyond lay a short hall with a second locked door at the other end, rather than the more typical direct entrance into the kitchen—part of the reason we'd chosen this house.

I took a short step inside then closed the outer door and locked it behind me without going any farther. Concealed now from the outside world, Triss slid up and around me, dressing me in a second skin of cool shadow. As he released his will, I took control, raising my arms and extending yards, long tendrils of shadow from the palms of my hands.

I reached down through the cracks between the floorboards, splitting the tendrils so that I could simultaneously touch the glyphs marking a dozen short steel posts distributed randomly through the space there. This temporarily disarmed the spells on the posts so that I could move forward to the next door without triggering the magical death that lay in wait for any trespasser. Just as with the outer door, the inner answered to the shadows of my familiar instead of a key.

When the lock clicked open, I reached up my finger, now free of shadow, and slipped it into a hole drilled above the frame on the left. It was invisible to anyone shorter than the door itself. Pushing down and twisting, I released the purely manual trigger on the heavy blade waiting to split the skull of anyone who relied on sorcery to get them past our defenses. Only then did I twist the handle and open the door to the kitchen.

Faran was waiting for me, no doubt alerted by the spell glyph carved into the top surface of the outer door. My profound relief at seeing her alive and in one healthy-looking piece lasted the two seconds it took to register the look on her face. Grim and cold, the controlled anger of the professional killer instead of the wild fury of the wronged teenager. Faran was both, and when the teenager lost the argument to the killer things were bad.

"What's wrong?" I asked.

"Besides you falling into a storm-wracked river and then vanishing utterly for half a week?" She spat the words out one by one, but I recognized it for the play it was.

"Yes, besides that." I kept my voice perfectly calm because I knew that would annoy her, and being annoyed might put her off stride enough to listen more carefully. "You're wearing the wrong face for the worried apprentice."

She snorted and a tiny bit of the grim went away. "I suppose I am, though I'm that as well. I really do care about you, despite all our arguing, and I *was* very worried."

"So was I."

Then, without really intending to, I stepped forward and caught her in my arms, squeezing her hard. For a long moment she remained stiff and angry, then she relaxed, dropped her head against my shoulder and squeezed me even harder.

"Terrible old man," she whispered.

"Dreadful little monster," I growled back.

We had a strange relationship, Faran and I. Part master and apprentice, part surrogate father and adopted daughter, part opposing duelists. We'd barely known one another at the temple and hadn't seen each other for five years after its fall. During those years I had diminished, going from being one of the two or three most feared professional killers in the world to a broken down jack who delivered smuggled goods for drinking money. Faran had grown from a terrified and half-trained eight-year-old into a professional thief and spy who killed with far less regret than I'd ever shown.

When I rescued her from a job gone horribly wrong, the adolescent who'd lost every shred of family she'd ever owned had wanted nothing more than to turn over the reins and the hard decisions to a respected authority figure dimly remembered from her past. That child's desire for security sat very poorly with the professional killer who had taken one look at our respective records over the last few years and found me wanting.

My own feelings weren't any easier to parse. I'd never wanted children. In fact, like many in the order, I'd chosen magical sterilization rather than risk any future potential conflicted loyalties between family and goddess. And yet, there was something about having Faran in my life, in the role that a child of my flesh might have held in a different world, that felt so very right. It didn't make for an easy relationship.

Time passed and Faran's death grip on my ribcage eased. I could feel the tension returning to her back and shoulders, so I gave her one last squeeze and then stepped back and away from her. On the wall behind her the dragon and the phoenix watched us as silently as shadows, reminding me that we were a family of four.

"Where the hell have you been, old man?"

"Shipwrecked," I replied.

"Seriously?"

"It's a long story," I replied before giving her the three-minute version.

"We have a major problem," Ssithra said when I'd finished. "Faran and I found it while you were gone."

I turned my gaze back to the girl. As I watched, the child faded away and the killer settled back into the place behind her eyes.

"Tell me about it," I said.

"I'd rather show you," replied Faran, "and the sooner the better. I had trouble believing it myself."

"Lead on."

7

Legends cast the longest shadows. From the day I killed Ashvik onward, I never had any hope of slipping free of the shadow of the Kingslayer. The name carried so much more weight than the one they'd given me as a child, that sometimes I could barely stand the load.

But even so, I wasn't the most famous of Blades. Mythkiller outweighed Kingslayer, and Deathwalker had eclipsed us both when he was in his prime. Kelos Deathwalker, two-hundred-year-old lord of assassins, a legend and an inspiration before he died with the fall of the temple. He had taught me more about the arts of death than all my other teachers combined. His death had felt almost as impossible as Namara's. Without hers, it would have seemed completely unbelievable.

That's why the scene in the room below our hiding place cut straight through my heart. Legends died, they didn't turn their coats. Yet there was Master Kelos, alive and well and practically bending his knee to a woman whose robes declared her the Lady Signet, Nea Sjensdor, preceptor of the Hand of Heaven. She was tall and slender and she moved like a praying mantis . . . just as she had in the Gryphon's Head on the day that Jax had walked back into my life, though I hadn't recognized her then.

I felt a little shiver at the memory. It was Kelos she'd been sitting with then—had to have been—though I hadn't recognized him at the time either. Not even when he made eye contact and warned me off. I wondered if he'd known it was me despite all the changes to my face. There was no clue in his gaze, and Jax hadn't, and she and

I had been as close as I'd ever been to anyone other than Triss. But somehow I couldn't make myself believe I'd fooled Kelos.

Fucking legends. I knew exactly how hollow they could look from the inside, and yet I couldn't make myself stop believing in the Deathwalker's. Not even now when I saw him playing lackey to one of the people who'd destroyed us. How could I not have recognized him?

The Signet I could understand; I'd never seen her face before. This Signet had been promoted to replace the three layers of officers that had died in the fall of the temple. We'd made the forces of Heaven's Reach pay a price in blood for destroying us, especially the Hand and the Sword, but it hadn't been enough. It could never be enough.

Breathe, Triss whispered into my mind. *Tell me what you see.*

Sorry. Give me a moment to get myself back under control.

Faran had brought along both a hearsay and eyespy, so we were able to listen and watch without actually getting in close. I lifted my gaze from the big glass half sphere of the eyespy now to meet Faran's gaze—the device didn't work with Shade senses so we both had our faces unshrouded.

"Later," I whispered, "you're going to have tell me more about how you found your way here."

"Not much to tell. Ssithra picked up Malthiss's shadow trail and we followed it."

I didn't ask how they'd recognized who the trail belonged to. There wasn't a member of the order who hadn't studied under Kelos and Malthiss. Legends, dammit, and for good reason. Look at our little spy post.

The Hand had set up temporary headquarters in a riverside warehouse just above the Royal Docks. Judging by the seals on the crates where Faran and I had taken up our perch, it was owned by the Crown. That meant the Hand was there with the King's blessing. Which made me curious about why they had chosen not to set up at the high temple of Shan or one of its satellites. But there could be a dozen or more reasons for keeping their presence unofficial, not least of which was my known presence in the area.

Most of the huge warehouse was simply a giant open room studded here and there with pillars to support the roof. One large section in the corner had been partially cleared of crates in an obviously hasty manner to make space for the Hand to set up their operations. At the far end, where we were, a series of open lofts had been built against the wall, allowing for the segregated storage of goods that couldn't be stacked very high or that needed to be off the ground.

Our perch was on the second loft from the top in the corner farthest from the Hand. The crates there climbed to within a few inches of the bottom of the level above us except for one small gap. The angled supports coming off one of the pillars holding up the lofts had forced them to leave an opening, and that's where we were.

Someone—almost certainly Kelos—had cut a trapdoor from the much more sparsely packed level above to allow access to the niche, hiding it under a couple of crates. The route into the building was equally clever.

It involved a really challenging roof-run, a brutal spider walk, and a barred clerestory window that had been invisibly converted to a pass-through, among other things. None of it would have been impossible for a mage with the right skills, but all together it would be damned hard for anyone but a Blade to manage. Even most Blades would never have stumbled on it by accident.

That was why I wanted to talk to Faran about how she'd done so. It didn't *feel* like a trap, but the good ones never do. I'd have been more worried about the possibility, if whoever set up the spy hole hadn't also put together a damned fine emergency exit. That involved a series of shadow-triggered destructive spells that would open a half dozen bolt holes. I couldn't really test it without giving us all away, but I had very little doubt it would work as I expected it to.

Aral!

Sorry. On it.

I looked down into the eyespy again, and began to describe the scene below to Triss. The cleared space was divided into three unroofed rooms by walls of crates. The main living area held a couple of couches and tables where three of the Hand were studiously ignoring the score of Swords taking up most of the space. A sort of bunkroom with a bunch of pallets held about another dozen Swords and one Hand, all asleep—probably the night shift.

A smaller office and sleeping area stood off to one side, separated from the living area by a heavy velvet curtain. The room contained a platform with a proper mattress on it, several chairs, a cabinet for papers, and a desk with an intense mage-light of the sort favored by those who dealt with large amounts of correspondence. A loose ball of white fluff, like an afternoon cloud fallen to earth, lay curled on the mattress, the Signet's Storm familiar. I couldn't be sure, because it was mostly hidden under one wing, but the Storm's head looked to be the blade of a scythe.

The Signet sat behind the desk, glaring up at Kelos, who had perched himself on the open side panel of a high crate. He was squatting on his heels, a pose that would allow him to move in any direction on an instant's notice, and one that I knew he could hold for hours if he chose.

Kelos had ditched the bushy black beard for an equally false red goatee, and swapped his glass eye for the leather patch he used to wear back at the temple. His arms were bare, showing off the deep black scaled tattoos that slithered around his arms and torso like a great snake endlessly curling back on itself. There was no obvious sign of Malthiss, which meant the Shade had chosen to add a few extra loops to the tattoo as he so often had in my memories. The sudden appearance of the Shade's head rising into a striking position from amongst the inky coils that beautifully camouflaged his presence had given more than one apprentice Blade nightmares.

"I still don't see why you insist on perching above me like some great vulture," said the Signet.

"I like the light here," Kelos replied in that deep bass growl I remembered so well from my youth—his training voice. He'd used a lighter, sweeter tone with those he considered his peers.

"Clever," said Faran, and I had to agree, though I didn't like the implications.

Kelos had chosen a perch where both the dying light from the windows and the bright lamp on the desk would only paint his shadow across the boards beneath his feet or into the mouth of the open crate behind him. At a guess, that opening led to some sort of passage that would allow him to come and go from the Signet's office without casting any stray shadows where another Shade might taste them.

That meant he was concerned about the possibility of other Blades finding out he'd been there. But who was he worrying about? Me? Jax? Someone else? He'd been careful at the Gryphon's Head, too, or Triss would have tasted Malthiss's shadow there. Was that because I was known to spend time there? Or because he'd seen Jax and followed her there? Or just on general principle since he was supposed to be dead? With Kelos it could have been any of those, or all of them, or something everyone else had missed entirely.

"It's disrespectful," snapped the Signet.

"How so?" Kelos grinned, exposing big white teeth. "You command the Hand of Heaven, I lead Heaven's Shadow. I'm pretty sure that makes us coequal in rank."

"I am the Son's chosen successor and you should treat me with the deference my eventual ascension demands."

"The Son looks mighty healthy to me, and you have a dangerous job. I wouldn't bet any money on you outliving him."

"Is that a threat, Deathwalker? Because you don't scare me."

This time, Kelos laughed. "Tell it to someone who gives a damn, Signet. I don't care whether you're too brave to be scared of me, or if anybody else is for that matter, haven't in more than a century. What's in your head is your problem, and threats are for villains in children's stories. I don't bother. Why deliver a warning, when it's just as easy to deliver a foot of steel?"

The Signet leaped up from behind her desk, but the curtain snapped open before she could say anything. A short man wearing the livery of the king barged in. Looking beyond him, I could see that the Swords on duty at the entrance to the warehouse were not happy. I didn't blame them. If the king's envoy pissed the Signet off, she was likely to take a piece out of their hides for it. But short of starting a war with their hosts in Tien, there wasn't a whole lot they could do about a king's envoy playing things hard.

I didn't recognize the man, but I recognized the type, a glorified message runner with delusions of grandeur. Every court has a few— officials of sufficient rank to be taken seriously when you send them to run an errand, but limited enough ability that a king can afford to leave them sitting around and waiting for orders most of the time. Lesser nobles of dubious intelligence were ideal for the purpose.

"The more the king learns about that mess you created at the royal cemetery the less happy he becomes," the envoy snapped without prelude. "What were you playing at there?"

"Playing?" growled the Signet. "Is that what you think this is? A game? Because this is a deadly serious business. I lost two officers of the Hand the other night, if you hadn't noticed. We're trying to bring down the Kingslayer and—"

"Doing a terrible job of it," said the envoy. "When His Majesty agreed to your presence here, he assumed you knew what you were doing. Since that's clearly not the"—the envoy glanced up at Kelos, apparently noticing him for the first time. "What's this, have you acquired a pet monkey?"

"Ook," said Kelos, his voice deceptively mild as he made a show of scratching under one armpit.

"Insolent," said the envoy. "And you're not wearing the Son of

Heaven's badge, monkey. Does that make you some local creature that the Lady Signet has picked up for some reason? Or what? Come down here where I can take a better look at you."

"I think I'll stay where I am," said Kelos.

"That wasn't a request, monkey, it was an order."

I saw the Signet's back tense at that, but Kelos just shrugged and silently held his place.

"Who do you think you're dealing with?" The envoy stomped closer to the crates as he spoke, pointing from Kelos to the floor imperiously. "I'm Heela Sharzdor, personal representative of King Thauvik the . . ." His words trailed off and he froze for a moment before making a little squeaking sort of noise.

"Sorry about the mess," Kelos said to the Signet.

It took me a moment to figure out that the envoy had stepped between the magelight and Kelos, so that his shadow now fell across the old assassin and the crate, making it quite obvious that Kelos cast no shadow of his own. At that very moment, Kelos's neck seemed to lift and broaden as Malthiss's cobralike head slid out from under his bond-mate's collar and rose into the air above Kelos. Before the envoy could do much more than let out another squeak, Malthiss opened his wide mouth and spat.

A thin amber stream of venom struck the envoy in the face and eyes. Sharzdor let out the faintest of whimpers, went completely rigid and toppled over on his side. He landed with an audible clunk, still in the exact position he was in when the venom struck, falling more like a statue than a man. The illusion grew stronger as his skin took on a distinct stony gray cast within a matter of seconds. Malthiss dropped back onto Kelos's neck, sliding down to vanish among the tattooed coils.

The Signet sighed and looked up at Kelos. "Now, what am I going to tell the king when he asks about what happened to his envoy?" She sounded more annoyed than angry.

"Tell him the Kingslayer did it."

"The Kingslayer? Really? How could he possibly get in here without us catching him?"

Kelos let out a low chuckle. "Aral's a damned resourceful Blade. You'd be surprised where he could get without you ever knowing he was there."

He knows we're here, Triss whispered into my mind. *And he's playing the Signet.*

How could he know about us? But I couldn't help but think Triss

was right, about both things. Malthiss could have moved much
faster had he chosen to, I'd seen him do it.

The Signet just shook her head. "*Of course* he could. Or at least
that's what I'm going to have to sell the king now. That and that the
Kingslayer poisoned the envoy? Do you think he'll really believe
poison? That seems a bit out of character."

"More than a bit, but that's not what you're going to tell Thauvik.
You'll say that Sharzdor here was beheaded, the way Aral ghosted
your priest in the cemetery the other night."

The Signet stiffened briefly, then shrugged and visibly forced
herself to relax. "What makes you so sure that killing was the Kingslayer and the other wasn't?"

"Slitting throats isn't really Aral's style. That'll be the third
Blade they had with them, the unknown one." Kelos jerked his chin
at the fallen envoy. "You'd better chop his head off soon."

"Why me? And why does it matter?"

"I'm not coming down there, so it's going to have to be you. And,
the longer you wait, the harder it's going to be to conceal the fact that
it was basilisk venom that killed him. You've got maybe five minutes
before it starts to go from plain old paralysis to genuine petrification.
At that point not only does the process become pretty difficult to
conceal, but it'll blunt your edge when you make the cut."

"He'll actually turn to stone?" The Signet sounded dubious.

"He will. The venom acts as a magical catalyst. It uses the victim's own life force to transform flesh into something very like
granite."

"Well then, hang on a moment." The Signet drew her sword of
office—a long straight blade that glowed bright blue in magesight
from all the spells it bore.

Bringing it around in a precise vertical cut, she beheaded Sharzdor without scraping her sword's tip on the floor scant inches beneath his stiff neck. Blood fountained across the flag-stones and she
had to hop aside to keep it off her boots.

"He bleeds like he's still alive," she said.

Kelos nodded. "Of course. If the venom killed its victims outright, there'd be no residual life force to drive the petrification. For
the magic to work, the victim has to stay alive right up to the point
where they finish turning to stone."

"Is it painful?"

"The turning to stone part?" Kelos shrugged. "Once the magic
sets in fully there's no known antidote or countercharm, which

makes it a little hard to ask the victims. As for the poison? It burns like a motherfucker, but if you can rip your eye out fast enough you can stop it before it takes effect." He tapped his eye patch. "That stings a bit, too, but it's better than the alternative. Any more questions?"

The Signet blinked several times, looking genuinely non-plussed for the first time, then nodded. "I've got two, since you seem to be in a cooperative mood. First, why does everyone claim that basilisks kill with their gaze?"

"Myth. The venom works best if it hits you in the eyes, so basilisks usually kill face-to-face and at some distance, as Malthiss just demonstrated. It's a pretty short jump from there to the whole deadly gaze thing. What's your second question?"

"Malthiss isn't really a basilisk. He's a Shade. So how can he spit basilisk venom?"

"Trade secret." Kelos smiled a very alarming sort of smile. "Now, don't you have an explanation to fabricate for the king?"

"Thanks to you."

"Then I'll leave you to it, as I've things to deal with as well, now that the sun's finally down. Also, unless I miss my guess, you'll be receiving another visitor shortly. One I'd rather not meet." He slid back into the open crate, pulling the side he'd been perched on shut behind him.

We should get out of here, said Triss. *We don't want him getting around behind us.*

"I think that's our exit signal," whispered Faran.

"You might have a point," I said, starting to rise. Then I took one last glance at the eyespy and swore.

The warehouse door stood open with Jax on the threshold.

What is it? asked Triss.

I told him, and he let out a series of angry mental hisses in Shade.

"Faran, Ssithra, can you play lookout? I hate to ask, especially when it's Kelos you'll be looking out for, but I need to see what's going on between Jax and the Hand, and I won't get a chance like this again."

"Isn't it obvious?" demanded Faran in an angry whisper. "Your ex is another fucking traitor."

"Probably," I agreed, though it hurt me to say so. "But I still want to know the details. Will you watch for Kelos? Because if not, we have to go right now."

Faran's face twisted angrily. "Yes, dammit, but under protest."

"Thank you. If you see any sign of him, any sign at all, activate the glyph that brings the house down and run for it. Don't hesitate for even one second. I'll be right behind you."

She didn't say another word, just shrouded up and vanished. I turned my attention back to the eyespy. In the meantime, Jax had crossed the distance to the Signet's office where she now waited between a pair of the Hand. A third Hand had stepped through to have a quick and whispered conference with the Lady Signet. Though none of them spoke a word, the tension between the Hand and Jax was so palpable I half-expected to see steel come out of scabbards at any second.

Before that happened, the Hand in the office waved Jax in and then, with obvious reluctance, stepped out and let the curtain close behind him. The Signet had returned to her place behind the desk. Her Storm, quiescent all through the discussion with Kelos, rose now to hover above and behind her left shoulder. Its scytheblade head bobbed angrily as it glared eye-lessly down at Jax.

"I'm not happy about what happened at the cemetery," said the Signet, "not at all."

"Fuck you." Jax stepped over the corpse of the royal envoy to put both hands on the desk and lean down over the Signet. "*You're* not happy! You change the plan without consulting me. You show up unannounced at a meeting you promised you would let me handle my way, and alone. You personally mage-blast a hole in my side, knocking me completely out of the game. Then you have the fucking gall to tell me that *you're* not happy? I ought to kill you right now."

The Signet didn't so much as blink, though her familiar angrily flared wings which had shifted from fluffy white to storm-cloud gray.

"Are you done yet?" asked the Signet.

"You'd better pray to your stinking god that I'm not," said Jax. "Because the second I decide this is over and there's nothing more I can do, I'm going to cut your heart out and burn it in front of your eyes."

The Signet shrugged and continued as if Jax hadn't spoken, "I'm not happy and your lover will suffer for it."

"What are you going to do? Torture him extra hard?"

"I promised that Master Loris and your captured journeymen would remain unharmed as long as you cooperated with me, Master Jax. Thus far I have kept my promise."

"Of course you have. However could I doubt the head of the Son of Heaven's personal inquisition? Maybe because I've been in your dungeons before, and I know what sort of people you are. You may have ordered your people not to leave any fresh marks, but like hell you're not hurting them. No, you can tell me all you want that you've called off the torturers, but I know how much your precious word is worth."

"I can always rescind the order to leave no marks. I lost two fingers of Heaven's Hand because of that debacle at the cemetery, and then afterward you vanished for three days! You should consider yourself lucky that I kept sending the daily messages to keep them alive while I waited for your return."

"You didn't *lose* any priests, you murdered them yourself when you changed the plan without consulting me. Did you think all you had to do was get Aral out in the open and then you could throw me away and do this yourselves? He's the fucking Kingslayer. Even if he's turned into a drunken wreck, he's still one of the half dozen most dangerous killers in the entire world. How stupid are you to think that barging into that cemetery wasn't going to explode in your face?"

The Signet moved like coiled lightning, leaning forward and backhanding Jax so hard that she staggered back and tripped over the corpse. As she went over backward, Jax twisted and put a hand on the floor, turning her fall into a cartwheel that ended with her on her feet halfway across the room with both swords drawn. The Storm rose high into the air and buzzed toward Jax, only to try to sheer off at the last second as a shadow tiger leaped to meet it. But Sshayar was faster, catching the Storm with both front paws and dragging it down toward the floor.

The Signet jumped to her feet and shouted, "Call your familiar off, Blade! Do it now, or there's no message and Loris and the apprentices die in the morning."

Jax twitched, but she didn't otherwise respond.

8

Choosing not to die can be the hardest thing in the world. Sometimes life puts you in a place where all of your options are bad. No matter what you do, you're going to make things worse. It's easy to let despair rule you in a moment like that, or rage, or simply the desire to let go of your problems and let everything fall on someone else's shoulders.

I'd been there myself, more than once, and quite recently. I was starting to climb out of hell now, had gotten a good way up the ladder even. But I could still see the fires below waiting for me to slip. I knew how easy it would be to fall back into them. I woke up some mornings imagining how much simpler things would be if I didn't ever have to open my eyes again. But then I thought about what my death would do to Triss, and I dragged myself out of bed and forced myself to keep moving until the urge to die faded.

I could see Jax fighting with that same suicidal impulse right now. Faran's eyespy was a damned good one. I could read the rage and despair in Jax's expression, could almost hear the voice in her head telling the Signet to go fuck herself, could feel her longing toward the peace of oblivion. The balance between life and death held for three long beats, and then Jax's eyes fell.

"Damn you. . . ." she said. And then, a few seconds later, "Sshayar, let it go."

The shadow tiger turned her head toward her bond-mate. "Jax . . ." But then she loosened her claws and the Storm popped free. "She's just going to betray us in the end. You know that, don't you?"

Jax nodded. "I do. But until that moment comes I still have a chance of finding us a way out of this." She turned back to the

Signet. "I'm going to kill you. It might not be today, it might not be next week, but I promise you the day *will* come. I will be the instrument of your destruction."

The Signet just smiled. "You keep telling yourself that, my dear. As long as it doesn't interfere with what I need you to do, you can harbor whatever little fantasies will get you through the day. Now, I need you to set up another meeting with the Kingslayer as soon as possible, and this time we'll get him."

"No."

"No?"

"No. We're going to do things my way this time, the way I told you it had to work from the very beginning. That is, unless you *want* to kill a bunch more of your people? Because I could go for that, too. Every time one of you dies it makes the world a slightly better place. If that's really your choice, just say the word. Otherwise, I'm going to turn around and leave now, and I'll see you again in the Magelands in a couple of weeks where we will do this my way."

It was Jax's turn to smile, and if I'd been the Signet I'd have been backing away. But then, I'd seen that exact expression on Jax's face in the past and I knew how much spilled blood it portended.

"Fine," said the Signet, "we'll do it your way, but if it goes wrong, the consequences will all be on you. Now, get out of my office. Oh, and have my leech patch up that hole I put in your side. I'm going to need you in top condition for this."

"Fuck that, and fuck you. I got enough of that hurt us and heal us crap last time I fell into the grip of the Hand. At this point I'd rather die than let another one of your butchers touch me."

"If that's how you want to play things, it's your lookout. You won't find a better healer anywhere in Tien than mine, but you *will* find a healer and get that side patched up. I don't give a damn about you as a person, but as an asset I need you in good health. Now, get out of here."

Without another word, Jax turned and stalked toward the exit. As she reached for the curtain, the Signet called after her retreating back, "Report in to the chief officer of the Sword of Heaven at Shan's temple in Tavan when you arrive. She'll have instructions telling you where and when to meet me after you contact her."

Jax threw a rude gesture over her shoulder and stepped through the curtain. The instant it fell behind her, I snatched up the eyespy and hearsay and tucked them into my pouch.

"No sign of Kelos?" I asked Faran as I joined her at the clerestory pass-through a few seconds later.

She indicated the glyph designed to bring the house down. "Does it *look* like I blew up the warehouse?"

"No."

"There's your answer."

"Awful child."

"Old monster."

I half expected her to demand that I give her a complete recap of what had happened then and there, but the professional killer had pushed the angry teenager aside once more. She didn't say another unnecessary word between the warehouse and Jinn's, a small cafe near the Ismere Library. It took us almost three hours to cross the two miles between the two because we more than doubled the distance traveled in an effort to prevent anyone from following us.

By the time we sat down on the riverside rooftop, I'd used every technique I'd ever learned to shake a hound off my back-trail. Of course, the hound I most feared had taught me the bulk of those tricks. It made for an itchy feeling right between the shoulder blades. That was half the reason I'd chosen to head for the cafe. Better by far to lead any hound there than home.

Jinn's had its own tiny dock, and we'd arrived by hired sampan—our third boat ride of the night. That easy access to the water was one of the reasons I liked the cafe. Another was the rooftop seating, four stories up with a lovely view of the river. From our table, five running steps and a long drop put you in the water. Ten steps and a short jump in the other direction carried you up onto the chimney road.

A lot of Jinn's custom came in that way, though the staff pretended not to notice since roof-runners mostly walked the shadow-side and valued their privacy. The food ranged from good to damned good, with most falling in the latter range. Faran ordered a plate of fried rice with clams and scallops and a pot of tea. I opted for gingered whitefish served on a bed of noodles, and small beer. I wanted something stronger, but my recent indulgence had reminded me of where that would lead, and besides, it would take my edge off. Damn but I missed efik at times like this, when I wanted to calm down but stay sharp.

Faran rubbed her biceps through the sleeves of her gray silk shirt. "Do you think he followed us?" She looked even more paranoid than I felt. "That he's out there somewhere watching us right now?"

"No. I don't think so, no matter what my gut keeps telling me. The man's good, none better, but even he's not so good that he could have followed us through all that."

Care to bet your life on it? Triss whispered into my head.

Haven't I? Then, *Why, have you seen something I missed?*

No. I even think you're right. It's just . . . Malthiss, and Kelos. How can I not worry about them?

"You're doing it again," said Faran.

"Doing what?" I replied.

"Going away into your head. You do it a lot, and sometimes when you come back you know things that you didn't before. You're talking to Triss when you do that, aren't you? Mind-to-mind."

I blinked several times while I tried to figure out how to answer that. As far as I knew, Triss and I alone among our peers had developed the ability to mindspeak. Certainly, the temple masters had always taught that such communication between human and Shade was impossible.

"Don't try to deny it," said Faran. "Ssithra and I have been discussing it for weeks now. That's the only answer that makes sense."

I nodded. "I guess I should have known you'd figure it out eventually." Faran *had* become a quite successful spy after the fall of the temple. "It's not exactly a secret." It's just that I didn't entirely trust anyone but Triss.

"How did you manage it? And why not tell us about it?" She held up a hand. "No, wait. I want to hear about what happened with Jax first. That's more immediately important, though I'll want to know everything about the mindspeech, too. If you could teach us . . ."

"I doubt it," I said. "The circumstances were *very* unusual, but you're right, Jax comes first. But even before that, I want to know about how you stumbled onto Kelos's trail."

"You think he set me up to find that warehouse, don't you?" said Faran.

"I don't know, but if he put together that observation post he went to a hell of a lot of trouble to make it hard to spot. That he then left a shadow trail leading right to it strikes me as potentially suspicious."

Faran shook her head. "I don't think it was a setup. You saw the route we had to follow to get in. Three sail-jumps and a couple of spider walks, and none of it on main paths through the chimney forest. Kelos repeatedly went a good deal out of his way to cast no shadows on commonly trafficked rooftops."

"So, how did you stumble across it?"

"It was the night after you vanished. I was searching along the edges of the river on both sides, hoping to find the place where you and Jax had come ashore. There'd been pretty brutal sun all day, so

I didn't have much hope of picking up the trail at that point, but I figured that with two Shades there was a slender chance."

"What time was it?" I asked.

"About three hours after sundown. I'd wanted to go right at dusk, but Ssithra wouldn't let me."

"Why not?"

Faran blushed. "She insisted that I needed to get some food and a nap before I went back out."

"Back out?"

"I'd spent some of that day looking around, too." On the table, the shadows cast by Faran's hand shifted subtly, and she jerked, letting out a small "ouch" sort of noise. "All right, I'll tell it your way, there's no need to pinch me."

She looked down at the table and her blush deepened. "I hadn't eaten or slept since I lost you in the flood. The only way Ssithra talked me into taking a break then was by pushing hard and insisting that with the sun gone, any trail would wait for a while."

She glared at her shadow. "There, happy now?" Ssithra didn't respond, but then, considering the relatively public nature of our current circumstances, the fact she'd done so much as pinching Faran was quite unusual.

When Faran looked up at me, I raised an eyebrow and she blushed yet again. The food arrived then, and we both went quiet for a few minutes—it'd been a long time between meals for both of us.

When she'd finished most of her plate, Faran continued, "Sorry. Where was I? Oh, right, sneaking along the riverbank practically under the Royal Docks, maybe a quarter mile on from where I'd left off earlier. Under any other circumstances we'd probably have missed it, but we were going over every inch of ground and paying extra attention. It was such a tiny scrap of shadow trail, no bigger than a silver riel, and not connected to anything."

"Then how did you follow it?"

"We didn't. Not at first anyway. We searched all around that first trace and couldn't find anything, but Ssithra swore up and down that it had come from Malthiss. So we didn't dare let it go. We didn't want to leave off the search for you either though, so after about an hour of scrabbling around on the bank there, I marked the spot for later investigation and we went on looking for your trail."

"But I'd been washed out to sea, so you didn't find that either."

"Exactly, though we kept on looking all through the next day. It was getting close to sundown then when we pretty much decided you and Jax had drowned." She swallowed hard and reverted to looking like a frightened teenager for a few heartbeats before re-composing herself. Then she gave me a very hard look. "And don't you *ever* scare me like that again, or I'll cut your throat in your sleep and bury you out back just so I know where to find you."

I smiled at her. "I'll see what I can manage."

"Don't think I won't do it," she growled, but smiled shyly a moment later. "Anyway, we were just coming back past the place where I'd left that stone when it occurred to me how a bit of trail might have gotten out there on the riverbank all by its lonesome—it fell from the rooftops above. The long shadows made by the falling sun gave me the idea."

She paused as our waiter brought us a plate of sweet butter biscuits for dessert.

She ate one while she waited for him to get out of earshot, then nabbed a second and continued, "We had to pinpoint where it came from, but that was easy enough once I'd figured out the mechanism. There was a gap between a couple of chimneys that lined up nicely with the sun and the stone."

She paused. "You're looking worried again."

"It just seems like an awfully stupid mistake for someone like Kelos to make."

"I don't know. I looked around the rooftops there. It was a really tiny slip. You have to practically crab walk to get past that point without rising above the level of the roof peak, and the gap's less than an inch wide. All it would have taken was for the back of his collar to flare the tiniest bit as he ducked past."

"We're talking about Kelos. His shirts probably address him as sir and ask before they wrinkle."

"There's that," Faran said ruefully. "But how would he know I'd find the trail from a patch that tiny? It was already mostly faded when I got there."

"Kelos *Deathwalker*."

She sighed and nodded, then laughed. "He's probably listening to this entire conversation, isn't he?"

"I wouldn't bet my life that he wasn't, but you've got a point. If we don't at least pretend that he's not that good, we're never going to sleep again, much less go home. All right, the man's not perfect. He slipped up and it led you to that warehouse, which gives us a chance to get ahead of our enemies. So what do we do with it?"

"Depends, what happened with Jax?"

So I gave Faran everything that had happened at the warehouse after I sent her to keep an eye out for Kelos. Then she wanted me to tell her about what happened between Jax and me on the boat. I'd given her the brief version earlier, but she wanted the whole thing now. I skipped some of the more painful details about my conversations with Jax, but sketched in enough so that it didn't feel like I was lying to Faran by omission.

"I guess that leaves me with one question," said Faran.

"Which is?"

"Do you want me to kill Jax for you?"

I stopped with a biscuit halfway to my mouth. "What?"

"Well, she *was* your fiancée once upon a time. It seems awfully harsh to make you do it."

"Nobody's going to kill Jax."

Are you sure of that? Triss asked me.

Faran raised an eyebrow. "What does Triss have to say about that?"

"Never mind what Triss thinks. I'm making the call here, and no one is killing Jax. It's that simple." But really it wasn't. So, I added, "At least not anytime soon. She's not working with the Hand because she wants to, that's for damn sure. I don't know what Kelos's game is here either. And, even if it *is* a setup, somebody has to free Loris and the journeymen. Maybe we can find a way to make it all work out."

"Do you really believe that will happen?" Faran spoke with all the corrosive cynicism of a girl who'd had her entire life destroyed at the age of nine.

"I'd like to."

"That's all the answer I need." She touched the long dagger at her right hip. "Just say the word when the time comes."

I put my biscuit back on the plate. I was no longer hungry. When the waiter came by again I ordered a small bottle of sake. Neither Triss nor Faran said a word about it.

Jax turned and opened her mouth to say something to me, a smile on her face. That put her back to Faran, a fatal mistake. My apprentice stepped in silently and drove a short broad-bladed dagger into the place where Jax's skull met her neck. She collapsed at my feet, turning as she fell, so that her dead smiling face looked up at me.

Wake up! Triss shouted into my dreams, and I did.

For the fourth time in as many hours, I lay panting in my sweat-soaked bed, as out of breath as if I'd just finished a ten mile roof-run. I couldn't say which variation of the nightmare cut deeper, the one where Faran made the kill perfectly, or the one where she stepped on a squeaking board and Jax turned and neatly split her skull.

In either case, sleeping any more sounded like a terrible idea. My room occupied the eastern half of the second floor of the little house Faran had rented for us. Even through the thick mud-brick of the walls the heat of the morning sun had started to drive the temperature up toward unbearable. Without getting up, I cracked the shutters in hopes of catching an ocean breeze. The bright light drew bands of hot gold across my bed. For a moment it touched the shadow of a dragon stretched out atop my sheet, his chin on my chest, then Triss hissed and slipped around behind the headboard.

"Warn me next time," he said from his place in the dark. "This time of year the sun stings when I'm not ready for it."

"Sorry, old friend. I wanted to chase the nightmares away, not you. Thanks for waking me up."

"You're welcome, but it was self-defense. The images are so vivid they're spilling over into my dreams." He poked his head over the back of the headboard and peered down at me. "I find it deeply weird looking at the world as you humans do. You see things very strangely, and I may be the only one of my kind ever to view it so."

His wings popped into sight as he flapped them agitatedly. "This two-way mindspeech is not an unmixed blessing. I'm glad I only get the images when you are dreaming or intentionally projecting them. I'll have to discuss it with Ssithra now that she knows that you and I can mindspeak, see what she thinks of your bizarre view of the world."

"Just don't tell her about the contents of this particular dream. The more I think about it the less I like the idea of Jax and Faran spending two weeks in close proximity shipboard. I'm going to have to figure out a way to leave Faran here. That'll be plenty hard enough without Ssithra giving her any reasons to be suspicious."

Triss shot out a long forked tongue, touching the top of it to my forehead. "It's funny, you don't *feel* feverish."

"What's that supposed to mean?"

"Do you really think Faran is going to agree to anything that prevents her from coming on this trip? She's a teenager. She's deeply devoted to you, even if she pretends not to be most of the time. She doesn't trust Jax, and has already offered to kill her for you. There's nothing you can possibly say that will convince her to meekly wait here for you."

"You're right. Which is why I to have to trick her into missing the boat somehow."

Triss sighed. "This isn't going to end well. You know that, right?"

"But you'll help me, won't you?"

"No, I don't think that I shall. Not this time. I see no reason to put myself in a situation where I have to apologize to Ssithra and Faran for trying to implement a plan so obviously doomed to failure."

"But I've got to keep Jax and Faran apart. You see that, don't you? I can't let Faran kill Jax, and I won't let Jax endanger Faran in any way."

"This is not the temple, you have no authority over Faran other than that which she chooses to give you. I know you want to shield her from the cruelties of this world, but she's nearly a grown woman and you can barely take care of yourself."

"She's fifteen!"

"And you're not yet thirty, and more an older brother than a father figure to her, no matter how you see things. She survived six years all by herself in the hard cold aftermath of the temple falling. Thrived even. She and Ssithra managed a hell of a lot more than we did in those years."

"But I've got to protect her. I've got to protect both of them."

"Jax is your age and twice as responsible as you ever were and I've already said all I intend to about Faran. Leave the job of protecting the women to the women. Or, if that's not enough of an argument, leave it to Sshayar and Ssithra. It's their job, not yours."

"But—"

Triss just shook his head and dropped down behind the bed again. "This is exactly the same sort of sentimental nonsense that kept you from killing Devin. You can't save the whole world from itself, no matter what they taught us at the temple. Now, I'm going back to sleep. Wake me when you get out of bed or come to your senses. No. Scratch that latter, I'd prefer to wake up sometime before the end of the century. Wake me when you get out of bed."

I reached for the book I'd borrowed from Harad, the librarian at the Ismere, but gave it up after a few pages when it became clear that reading wasn't going to be enough to push the nightmare images away. Still, I remained in bed. I had about fifteen hours till my meeting with Jax and I needed to figure out how to get Faran out of harm's way between now and then.

*   *   *

It's amazing how fast a day can pass when you would rather it
didn't. I'd spent practically the whole time trying to find an answer
to the problem of keeping Faran and Jax away from each other. Yet
here I was walking into the Spinnerfish for my meeting with the
latter without so much as a clue's ghost.

About the only thing I could claim to have accomplished on that
front was convincing Faran to play the hidden ace to my faced jack.
Instead of sitting in on the meeting, Faran and Ssithra were dancing
a slow circle around the Spinnerfish looking for the Hand. I didn't
think Jax would have changed her mind about how she wanted to
run things with the forces of Heaven's Reach, but I trusted the Signet to keep her word even less than I currently trusted Jax.

My stomach twisted around on itself like a knotsnake with an
itch. That I even had to think this way about someone I'd nearly
married at one point was so beyond fucked, it made me want to
crawl into a whiskey barrel and have someone hammer the top shut.
At least I'd have a little fun before I drowned that way.

I half expected Erk Endfast to slide out from behind the bar
when I came through the front door of the Spinnerfish and tell me
to turn right the hell around and march back out. A onetime black
jack, he'd given up the blood trade when he left the Magelands one
step ahead of an official execution order. He said he'd had enough of
living shadowside after that, but it didn't keep him from making a
ghost of anyone who threatened the peace of his establishment.
And, whether I wanted things that way or not, I threatened the
peace of the Spinnerfish just by walking in the door.

But Erk just nodded hello and kept on puttering away at something below the level of the bar top. He'd known my old face back in
the days before ever it got pasted up on wanted posters across the
eleven kingdoms, but my new one didn't belong to anyone who mattered. I was finding that I liked being a ghost even less than I liked
being a legend. When I got closer to the bar, Erk smiled vaguely.

"You meeting Captain Fei again?"

I'd been in maybe a half dozen times since the change, mostly to
have dinner with Kaelin Fei, Tien's number one corrupt cop and
one of the very few people in on my secret.

I shook my head and spoke with a deliberate husk, "Afraid not,
but I will need a private booth for two. I'd prefer not to be seen
while I'm waiting."

"You know your way back. Take the third table past Fei's on the

right. I'll send your guest back when they get here. Who should I be
on the lookout for, the kid?" Faran had joined Fei and me on a couple
of occasions.

"No. A woman, tiny with pale skin and long brown hair. Pretty,
too."

"Anything really distinctive about her?"

"Besides her height? She's got a net of thin scars on her face and
arms like finest lace. She'll probably be wearing two swords in a
double sheath on her hip. Oh, and if you get on the wrong side of
her she'll give you a look that'd cut diamonds."

"Two swords, huh?" Erk gave me the second look he hadn't earlier, though his expression didn't change. "I knew a man who used
to carry two swords once. About your height and build actually. I
haven't seen him around in a while, and that's too bad. Dangerous
man, but a good one on his sober days. I liked him." He smiled now.
"If you see him, give him my best."

"Doesn't seem likely, but I'll keep it in mind." I started toward
the back room.

"Hang on," said Erk.

"Why?"

"I think your friend's just arrived."

I looked over my shoulder and found Jax heading my way.

"Jax," I said quietly as I went to meet her. "Your timing is perfect, as always."

"Aral." She caught my hands in her own and pulled me down to
give me a kiss on the cheek.

I couldn't help but glance at Erk out of the corner of my eye to
see whether he'd heard her name me. But if he had, he didn't give
any indication of it. Still, I frowned. What was Jax's play there? I
didn't make the mistake of believing she'd slipped. She was better
than that.

I pulled one of my hands free of hers and guided her around me
with the other. "We've got a private table waiting. It's this way."

Like all of Erk's private tables, ours sat in an alcove off one of
the many little halls that made a maze of the back of the Spinnerfish. Designed to seat no more than two people, the narrow table
had built-in bench seats on either side. I let the shimmering green
gold curtains fall behind us as we settled in across from each other.

Jax touched the fabric. "It's subtle, but these are spelled."

"For privacy, nothing more, part of why I chose this place."

"Nice. How did your business go?" she asked.

"Just fine. Yours?"

"Much the same."

Then, forcing the words to come out smoothly despite the tightness in my throat and back, I asked, "Anything I should know about?"

It was a test. Like all Blades, Jax had been trained to lie smoothly and seamlessly, but she'd never been good at lying to anyone she cared about. Not in the old days.

She smiled and looked me straight in the eye. "Not really. Routine stuff all, though I can go into it if you're worried about it." There wasn't so much as a flicker of her eyelashes out of place.

"No, that's all right," I lied back at her, though probably not half so well. "I'm more interested in planning for what comes next. This is going to be very dangerous, too dangerous for a half-trained girl like Faran. I want to leave her in Tien, and I'm going to need your help to make sure she stays here."

9

The rising sun spilled blood across the waves, red and wrathful and full of portent, like the dreams that drove me out into the light. I am a creature of the night, an assassin and companion to shadows. The morning sun is my enemy. I do not seek it out, it hunts me. Today it caught me high in the rigging of the *Fortunate Lamia.*

I had come looking for the winds, hoping they would blow away the thick cobwebs of my nightmares. I found only melancholy and the burning edge of morning. For perhaps the hundredth time I rubbed at my eyes, trying to scrub away the images of Jax and Faran, each dead at the other's hand. Even leaving Faran behind hadn't been enough to banish my dreams. Maybe because I still had no idea how to deal with Jax, much less evade the trap that was waiting for me, and get Loris and the others free. I couldn't see any way to make things come out right.

Things had been so much simpler before the temple's fall. I never had to figure out what was the right thing to do, the Just thing. My goddess told me what needed doing, and I did it. The world was black and white. Or, at least, it had looked that way at the time. Among the many things I had come to understand since then was that the world was rarely as simple as I wanted it to be. A fact that was very hard to forget with Jax and Faran murdering each other behind my eyelids every night.

I never thought that I would miss my old nightmares, I sent to Triss.

Excuse me? His mind voice sounded muzzy and unsettled—he likes the morning even less than I.

Usually, I dream my failures or the dead face of the goddess.

And that's better how, exactly?

I prefer the scar that aches to the fresh cut that has yet to start bleeding. These nightmares remind me of how much I have left to lose.

Not how much you have left to save?

I shook my head. *Since the temple fell my glass has always been half empty.*

Is that *why you keep adding whiskey?*

I snorted. *Perhaps it is, the need to fill that which can never be filled.* Then I shrugged. *I don't know.*

The lookout is very nervous about you being up here, Triss sent, tapping my arm by way of pointing at the man.

I'd taken a perch on the rope strung along below the yard of the big junk's foremast. The one the lookout atop the big mast had referred to as the "footrope" when he called out for me to use that instead of trying to walk the yard itself, "for Orisa's sake."

I snorted. *There's barely a wind and the swells can't be running much over three feet. I'm in no danger of falling.*

I know that, and you know that, but the poor lookout is practically in hysterics. The captain doesn't look any too happy either.

The captain? When did he come out on deck?

Just now, he's having some very harsh words with the steers-woman, and his face is beginning to turn red.

I suppose we ought to get down before he orders us down. That would be awkward, since I've no intention of setting the precedent of obedience. Maybe if we show him we're in no danger it'll help calm him.

Before Triss could argue, I braced hands and feet and vaulted up onto the yard. Then I ran lightly back to the mast and jumped to one of the ropes that ran from it to the deck, quickly hand-over-handing my way down. The *Lamia*'s captain, a small round fellow, was there to meet me when my feet touched down, his face red and swollen with anger.

He opened his mouth, presumably to start yelling at me. I gave him the look that I used on the occasional footpad foolish enough to follow me into an alley. It was something I'd learned from Kelos, and the captain, who had been leaning forward, closed his mouth and took a small half step back.

"What do you think you're doing?" he said a moment later, but it sounded more plaintive than demanding.

"Getting some exercise. I woke up too early and needed to work out the kinks before I get in a practice duel with my partner." I arched my back and put my hands on my hips inches from the hilts of my swords—I'd put them on as a sort of talisman against the nightmares. "Why, is there a problem?"

"You gave me a bit of a start is all. I thought you'd fall and hurt yourself, or mess something up, but you seem to know your way around a ship's rigging. I didn't know you were a sailor."

"I'm afraid that I'm not really."

"Then where'd you learn to climb like that?"

"You really don't want to know." I smiled a predatory smile and the last of his color faded.

He looked from my face to the well-worn sword hilts at the base of my spine and jumped to what was almost certainly the wrong conclusion. There'd never been that many Blades to begin with, and now we were all but extinct. "Maybe I don't at that."

That wasn't very nice, Aral.

No, it wasn't.

You don't sound sorry.

I'm not. Oh, I didn't really want to step on him, but it was that or take a lecture and stay out of the rigging thereafter, and I'm already feeling trapped enough on this damned boat.

I suppose it's better than having you hitting the bottle again. I winced as Triss's mental voice scored a direct hit.

While I talked to Triss, the foredeck quickly cleared as the captain and what crew were awake found things to do elsewhere. I was just wondering if I might not be able to go back to sleep when Jax came up the ladder from the lower deck. The sun highlighted the scars on her cheeks and I felt a little stab in my heart. She still looked every bit as wild and appealing as she had when we were together, but the gentler side of her beauty was gone. Her face was a battlefield, gorgeous still, but marked forever by blood and pain.

"Was that wise?" she quietly asked me.

"Probably not, but I'm in no mood for an argument."

"From him? Or from me?"

"Either, both. If I'd thought about it, I might not have climbed up above, but it felt damned good, and I'll certainly do it again. I had a rough night and I wanted to get away from my dreams."

"Feeling guilty about leaving Faran behind?" Jax asked with a lift of her eyebrows.

"No. That's one of the few things I actually feel *good* about. I don't want her involved in what's coming. This business is going to get damned ugly."

Jax turned away when I said that, walking to the rail to look out over the sea. "Yes, I'm afraid that it will."

Was she ever going to stop lying to me? But I couldn't ask her that, so instead I asked, "How much of my little chat with the captain did you hear?"

"All of it. I don't sleep so well myself these days." She turned back to me, resting a hip against the railing. "You woke me when you climbed out of your bunk. I followed you out of the cabin after I saw you put on your swords."

"Worried about what I'd do?"

Jax frowned. "No. More about what you might have heard that made you feel you needed to arm yourself." Her expression slid into something more melancholy and she hugged herself. "You have night-mares?"

I pictured her smiling corpse lying at my feet the way my dreams had painted it so many times in the last few days, and I nodded.

"I get them, too. Almost every night. The torturers coming for me, the fall of the temple, dead friends cursing me for living when they didn't—all my failures." She shook herself and forced a grin. "Were you serious about a practice duel?"

"If you're interested, yes."

"Good, it'll give me something to think about besides evil dreams." She drew her swords, one overhand, one under and slid forward into a guard position.

I reached for my own, then froze with them half out of their sheaths. It was the first time I'd seen Jax draw her swords since she'd come back into my life, and I simply wasn't ready for the sight that greeted me now. The hilts and hip sheath had betrayed me into believing she had chosen to put aside the swords of Namara and make do with lesser steel, as I had. But those were temple blades in her hands.

"Are you all right, Aral?"

I nodded, completing my draw. "You had them rehilted." The words came out harsher than I'd intended, angry.

Namara's swords had simple oval guards that divided blade from hilt, all of it enchanted by the goddess to never break or wear. The guards were faced with lapis so that looking at them point-on you saw what appeared to be a blue eye widely opened—the unblinking eye of justice. Jax had replaced the oval guards and black sharkskin grips with traditional Dalridian style basket hilts. The cups and guards were shaped of bent steel, the grips surfaced with braided bronze wire.

But the short, lightly curved blades with their distinctive smoky blue steel that absorbed light rather than reflecting it, and their absolute unmarred perfection of line, were unmistakable. The swords of the goddess didn't look so much forged as wished into existence.

"Of course I did." Jax shifted a step to her right, and raised her right sword to point at my throat. "I couldn't bear to see the old hilts every time I looked down, and these are much less obtrusive in Dalridia. Would you prefer to spar with wood? I'm sure the captain must have some practice blades around here somewhere."

I snorted and shook my head, recognizing it as more of a tease than a serious offer. We'd both trained under Master Kelos, and while he might prefer that the apprentices and journeymen didn't cut each other to ribbons, he'd always been adamant that there was no substitute for working with live steel for the expert. With a practice weapon you always knew that a fuckup wouldn't really cost you. That changed the calculus of attack and response for the worse. It made you more likely to take stupid risks or deliver imprecise attacks.

"Do you want to do this or not?" I asked.

"Whenever you're ready then."

I feinted a cut at her left wrist, she parried and tried to catch my blade in a bind that I slipped. She flipped her underhand blade to an overhand grip, spinning in close as she did so with a cut that would have taken my feet off if I hadn't hopped over it.

"Not much of a jump," she said, as she flicked a thrust at my forward thigh. "The old Aral would have gone a good foot higher."

I parried and forced her sword down and out, opening up a line on her biceps. "The old Aral would have been wasting his energy." As I attempted the cut, she followed her out-of-line sword into a spin that put her arm out of my reach while bringing her other sword around to slice at my collar bone.

"Why should I move even a half inch more than I need to?" A strategy I implemented by twisting just out of reach of her blade. As I riposted toward her heart I found myself wondering whether I ought to stop my thrust if Jax didn't.

But she beat my blade neatly aside, and delivered a heel tap to the top of my forward foot. "That would have broken your foot if I'd followed through."

"Point," I said.

Stung by the ease with which she'd taken the point, I jumped out of the way of her next thrust, leaping back and up onto the rail that separated the foredeck from the drop to the ship's waist. Then, before Jax could adjust to my higher position, I did a front flip over her, slapping the flat of my left blade against the back of her neck as I went past.

"Point," replied Jax, "and much more the old Aral."

Nice, added Triss.

In other circumstances, he and Sshayar might have joined in with our sparring, making it a partners match. Or, Jax and I might have taken control of our respective shadows to attempt maneuvers impossible to the Shadeless duelist. With the ship's crew watching, that wasn't really an option, so they stayed out of it. Even though our reduced circumstances dictated that Faran and I practice without our Shades as often as with, it felt strangely lonely to do so against Jax.

Now we really picked up our game. Lunge, parry, thrust, block, cut, bind, spin, flip, thrust again, cartwheel, slice, kick, and so on. I picked up a half dozen nasty bruises and three minor cuts in the exchange and inflicted a similar bill of damage on Jax. We kept it up for a good ten minutes before simultaneously throwing up our blades and stepping back. I think I scored more points, but I was gasping like an asthmatic dragon by then, and felt as though I'd just run the roofs from Westen to the Spicemarket and back without a break. Jax was sweating and breathing heavy as well, but she didn't look half so blown as I felt.

"More?" She flashed me that wicked smile of hers, daring me to pretend she hadn't run me into the ground.

"How about I take a turn," said a smug and all-too-familiar voice from behind me.

"Faran?" I wheezed, more than half in shock.

Not that anyone but a Blade could have hidden themselves in the tiny triangle of space at the front of the ship, or that I had any doubt who that voice belonged to. But she couldn't have picked a better moment to lay me out with a few words.

"Of course. You didn't really believe I was going to let you out of my sight that easily, did you, Master Aral?"

The "Master Aral" waved all kinds of warning flags. The only times she'd called me that since I first found her in the sewers of Tien was when she was well and truly pissed off.

I was still trying to find the wind to come up with a good response when Jax spoke up. "Oh, very nicely done, Faran! I presume you've been here this whole time, but I didn't catch so much as a hint of your presence. Later, I'd love to hear how you managed to get aboard at all. I'd swear no one else was riding that sampan Aral hired to deliver him to the ship right as we sailed out of the harbor."

"Maybe if you ask nicely, I'll even tell you," said Faran, and I could hear the hard cold undertone to her words.

"If you're half as good with your steel as you are with your shadow-slipping then you'll be a damned worthy opponent. Come on, give me a try."

"Done." Faran stepped past me to face Jax, and there wasn't a damned thing I could think to do about it.

Faran held a pair of cane knives instead of swords. She much preferred the heavy, forward-curved blades that fell somewhere on the range between a long dagger and a short sword with a side order of hatchet. The weapons had come out of Kadesh originally, where they used them to harvest cane and bamboo, as well as the occasional enemy head. They weren't a traditional weapon for the servants of Namara, and Faran had never talked about how she'd come to pick up a set, but she used them with a brutal efficiency that often scored points against my longer and more elegant Zhani dueling swords.

Now, as she squared off against Jax, I couldn't help but feel that I'd stepped right out of the real world and into one of the scenes from my earlier nightmares. I wanted to stop them, but couldn't come up with any way to manage it short of physically stepping between them. Worse, exhausted as I was from my bout with Jax, I didn't know if I'd be able to do anything about it even if I tried.

I was still dithering when Faran dropped into a crouch and spun a reverse kick at Jax's shins. Rather than hop over the attack, Jax simply sank one of her swords into the deck. I winced. She placed the sword flat on to Faran's kick, rather than setting it up for a sliced hamstring, but it was still going to leave a hell of a bruise.

Only, it didn't. Somehow, Faran shifted her kick, lifting it from a low sweep into a heel strike aimed at the big muscles in Jax's thigh. At the same time, she interposed one of her cane knives flat on between her calf and Jax's sword. Striking there, just below the hilt, the impact of Faran's kick forced Jax to let go of her sword rather than have it ripped out of her hand. That collision between blades slowed the heel strike enough so that Jax was able to hop back out of the way, but it left her leaning too far forward to avoid Faran's follow up a moment later.

I drew a sharp breath as Faran's second knife slid up and under, drawing a line straight toward Jax's throat, but there was simply nothing I could do but watch. If Faran decided she wanted to kill Jax right now, Jax died. Though I hated myself for it, I couldn't help but think of how much less complicated my life would be if she followed through.

"Sorry about that," Faran said, an instant later, when the tip of her second knife skidded across the skin under Jax's chin, leaving a bleeding gash. "I didn't turn the blade fast enough. You look taller than you are."

"Point, and I'm tempted to call it two," Jax said ruefully as she retrieved her sword from where Faran's blow had thrown it. "Or am I wrong that you *chose* a disarm over breaking my wrist?"

Faran smiled wolfishly. "You're not wrong. I couldn't slow my kick down at that point, so I decided I'd better not aim for flesh."

"Two then, and very well done. I wouldn't have believed how fast you move those heavy knives around if I hadn't seen it." Jax dabbed at the blood dripping off her chin and looked up at me. "She's good, Aral, she's . . . are you all right? You've gone awfully pale. And you haven't put your swords away. Did I push you too hard earlier?"

I shook myself. "No . . . I'm fine really. Just the lack of sleep catching up to me." I flipped my swords around and resheathed them—not sure why I hadn't done it before. What was I going to do with them, kill one of the women to prevent her from killing the other? "Nicely done, Faran."

"No worries about me losing control then, Master Aral?" She spoke sweetly, her voice making a sharp contrast to the anger in her eyes. "I did mark her pretty good, after all."

"An accident," said Jax who turned away from the main part of the ship and any watchers among the crew before applying a very minor sort of spell to staunch the bleeding. "And, hardly an uncommon one for live steel practice. Hell, I'm already oozing blood from four places where Aral nicked me today, and I've had much worse from him in the past." She laughed. "Remind me later, and I'll show you the scar that Aral gave me back in the days of our youth—it's nowhere I care to expose in public."

"I'll do that," said Faran. "Master Aral is concerned about my control, and it would be nice to see how well he did when he was my age. In the meantime, shall we continue?"

Jax nodded, before simultaneously cutting high and thrusting low. Faran blocked both blades, but had to twist hard to her left to manage it, leaving herself open for the elbow Jax drove into her right kidney as she stepped past her younger opponent. It wasn't a full force blow, but it still sent Faran staggering forward, allowing Jax to turn and tap her on the back of the head with the flat of her sword.

Faran growled, "Point." Then she pivoted to face Jax, assuming a low guard position.

There's really not a whole hell of a lot I can do here, is there? I asked Triss.

No. I don't like it either, but short of spilling blood or confronting Jax about the Signet, there's no way to keep them from what should be a friendly sparring match. Honestly, doing the latter's as likely to set them at each other's throats for real as anything. He sighed mentally. *Jax would already be dead if Faran wanted to kill her right now, so I think you have to let it go.*

While I reluctantly agreed with Triss, that didn't make it any easier to watch as the pair exchanged several more passes. Faran was more cautious now, and less vicious, and Jax was likewise taking extra care now that she knew her young opponent was no tyro. The pace increased as the two felt out each other's style. As the cuts and ripostes grew steadily faster and more potentially lethal, I had to practically nail my feet to the deck to keep from turning away.

But somehow I managed to keep watching. It was a rare chance to study Jax's present style from the sidelines and, as much as I hated to admit the possibility, I might well need any advantages I could get against her later. Faran drew blood again after a bit, though not as much this time. Then Jax put a huge slice in Faran's shirt, and a much smaller one in the skin along the lower edge of her ribs.

"Point." The growl was gone from Faran's voice, replaced by a cold flat emotionless delivery that worried me far more than the earlier anger had.

"Sorry," said Jax. "I twisted my grip a touch too late."

"Don't be. The mistake was mine. I let you in too close. I promise you I won't do it again. Ready?"

I really didn't want the bout to continue with Faran in this mood. Then, as if in answer to the prayers I could no longer make, the arrival of one of the *Lamia*'s officers gave me the perfect opportunity to end things. The man had climbed the ladder from the lower deck and poked his head up over the edge of the foredeck but looked deeply unhappy at the idea of getting any closer to the two women and their bared steel. I couldn't really blame him.

I waved at him and stepped between Jax and Faran. "Hello, can we do anything for you, Master Sendai?" The ship's Kanjurese sailing master and first officer was a good-looking man, slender and tall like most islanders—though it was unusual to see one of them outside the archipelago.

Sendai swallowed but nodded and climbed the rest of the way up onto the foredeck. "Begging your pardon, sir, but we're just about to clear the mouth of the gulf, and the captain sent me to ask that you take a brief rest while we treat with the Vesh'An."

"Of course." Jax flipped her left hand sword back to an under-handed grip, then sheathed it and its mate. "Can't let the Vesh'An go waiting."

The tall man smiled a very fetching smile. "Thank you, ma'am. Much appreciated. If the three of you would like to watch, I'm sure the captain would be happy to have you as his guests for the wan-dersea ceremony."

"Wandersea?" asked Faran, who hadn't yet put up her weapons. "What's that like? I've heard the name, but I've never been out on the open ocean to see one before."

"It'll be easier to show you than to explain it," said Sendai.

"Fair enough." Faran slid her cane knives into the crossed sheathes on her back. "Show away."

The captain came up on the foredeck. A burly sailor followed along behind him carrying a pair of large brandy bottles. My mouth went dry as I stared at the bottles going by. A drink would make dealing with Faran and Jax so much easier.

As the captain climbed up onto the platform at the end of the foredeck, Sendai directed us to the portside rail for a better view. A few minutes later the ship cleared the headland that marked the mouth of the Gulf of Tien and entered the open ocean. Three fins broke the surface, veeing the water beside the ship.

"They look just like the dolphins I've seen in the fish market, except for the black and white markings," Faran said quietly.

"You won't *ever* see these dolphins in a fish market, nor any-thing else with those markings," Jax replied just as quietly. "No sailor would be insane enough to try to net or spear a Vesh'An."

"Even if a sailor was crazy enough to try, they'd never make it back to shore alive," I added.

"It's strange seeing them in the flesh like this after hearing about them all these years," said Faran. "Will they really shift?"

Before either of us could answer, the captain trilled out some-thing in a strange liquid tongue that sounded more than half like a series of whistles. It was nothing like what I'd heard of the lan-guages of their Durkoth and Sylvani cousins, but the Vesh'An were the strangest of the Others who shared our world. The leader now leaped high out of the water and trilled imperiously back at the cap-tain. He bowed deeply and responded in kind.

They went back and forth like that two or three times before the captain reached back and took the first bottle from the crew-

man. With another trill, he tossed the bottle far out over the side.
The Vesh'An who'd been trailing along to the left of the leader shot
forward and leaped high out of the water. Right at the top of its arc
it shimmered and transformed into a woman, naked and inhumanly perfect, though still marked like the dolphin in black and
white. She caught the bottle in one hand and plunged back into the
sea in a perfect athlete's dive.

For another few heartbeats she streaked along beneath the surface in a woman's form. Then the shimmer came again, and she returned to dolphin shape, diving deep and vanishing. When she was
gone, the captain repeated the trilling phrase and threw the second
bottle. The Vesh'An who caught the tribute this time was male and,
if anything, prettier than the woman had been. The captain bowed
to the leader and spoke a final trilling farewell. The Vesh'An returned it in kind before disappearing beneath the waves. The captain left then, too, without so much as a nod for his passengers.

"The foredeck is yours again," Sendai said to us as he started
after the obviously uncomfortable captain. "Please try not to scar it
up too much." He flicked a glance at the deep gouge left behind
where Faran had kicked Jax's blade. "He'll be ever so much easier
on all of us if you don't." Then he winked at me.

"I'll see what I can do," I said quietly as he went down the ladder.

Good luck with that, Triss said into my mind.

"Do they always use brandy?" asked Faran.

Jax shook her head. "No, though it's almost always alcohol. What
kind depends on what the local clans have been asking for. That'll be
part of the exchange with the captain. When he next comes into
port up this way, the captain will leave word at the harbormaster's
office so that other ships will know what to bring."

"Why alcohol?" asked Faran. "That stuff is nasty!"

"There we are in perfect agreement." Jax gave me a speaking
look. "But the Others invented distilling along with brewing and
fermenting back in the days before the god wars, and it's one of the
few things the Vesh'An can't do for themselves very easily in their
watery halls. Since they've never lost the taste for it they need a
source, so they get it in tribute from us or trade with the Sylvani."

Jax stretched and rolled her shoulders. "And now, I'm thinking
that I should leave you and Aral alone to argue out your unexpected
arrival. Hopefully, cutting me up has taken the worst edge off of
both of your tempers, and you can do it without further bloodshed."
Then she vaulted over the rail and dropped the eight feet to the
deck below before heading back to our shared cabin.

594   BLADE IN SHADOW

"She's as nice as I remembered her," Faran said once Jax had closed the door behind her. "I see why you don't want to kill her." Then she turned back my way and her eyes went hard and cold. "Which definitely means I'm going to have to do it for you."

As she walked away, I found myself wondering where the captain stored those big bottles of brandy and how long it would take before anybody missed one.

Don't, Triss sent.

Don't what?

If you get drunk right now, you're not going to be able to stop Faran.

Just one drink ...

It won't be one. Not when you're this worried, and you know how that'll end.

He was right but . . . "Fuck." I scrubbed at my eyes, trying to erase the vision of a big beautiful bottle of booze tumbling through the air, as though I thought it might work.

10

Every assassin knows that beauty and death sometimes walk hand in hand. It's there in the perfection of the smith's art expressed in deadly steel, or in the night sky like a scatter of diamonds on velvet, seen from the side of a castle tower. Even spilled blood has a terrible beauty to it, rich and red and royal.

So it was with the oncoming Vesh'An hunting party that passed us on our tenth day at sea. Most of the clan's warriors slid through the seas in dolphin shape, leaping in and out of the water, weaving a wild pattern in the waves. A few, including the lord and lady and their leading knights, rode in human form astride the backs of great war-whales. There were ten of the black and white beasts, looking for all the world like giant brutish cousins to the dolphin-formed Vesh'An that danced around them. The nobles rode bareback, armored in seaweed and shell. They carried shining swords and deadly lances carved from the bones of dragons. Harder than iron, their edges shone green and gold and blue and silver—all the myriad colors of the sea.

The sailing master ran out onto the bow platform and waved at the Vesh'An as they raced past, calling out "Good hunting!" The lord bobbed his raised lance in response, and one of the knights blew a conch horn. Master Sendai must have seen my curious look, because he crossed to where I was leaning against the rail.

Though the rest of the crew continued to avoid us, and the captain mostly pretended we didn't exist, Sendai had seemed almost fascinated by us, going so far as to watch our sparring practices from the foot of the bow platform the last few days.

"That's Clanarch Ekilikik and his people. They've done us a

good turn more than once. They're going after one of the great sea serpents or a kraken by the look of their gear, which means some of them likely won't be coming back. The Vesh'An are the only reason the outer lanes stay open for shipping. Without them, we wouldn't dare sail beyond sight of land. If they pass again on the way back to their home waters around Ar, we'll throw them a couple of bottles of our brandy, though protocol doesn't demand it."

"How long till we reach Ar?"

I was slowly going crazy trapped between Jax and Faran on the tiny island of the *Lamia*. I wanted off that boat, but at the same time, our arrival in the Magelands would bring the moment when I had to make a final choice about what to do about Jax that much closer.

"If the winds stay as good as they've been so far, we'll hit port late tomorrow," said Sendai. "That's where you leave us, right?"

I nodded. "It is."

"That's too bad. I'm actually going to miss having you aboard."

"Your captain won't."

"No, but he's far too much of a traditionalist to be happy with landsmen who run the rigging like old hands. To say nothing of the fact that you frighten him. Hell, you frighten most of the crew."

"But not you?"

Sendai laughed. "Oh, you frighten me, too, but mostly in a good way. I'd love to get to know you better. . . ."

He let it hang there for a long moment, long enough to make sure I understood the offer underneath. I had to admit I was tempted, at least a little bit. He was an attractive man, both physically and emotionally. I generally preferred women, but had slept with a few men over the years, and Sendai appealed to that part of me. Also, it had been a long time since Maylien, and I hadn't shared a bed with anyone since.

But finally, I smiled and shook my head. "I'm sorry, we won't get that chance."

"Already committed elsewhere?" he asked lightly, though I could read disappointment in his eyes. "Or just not inclined my way?"

"Neither, actually. I've got no commitments and no objections, but my life's too tangled up at the moment for me to want to add another twist."

"I guess I can understand that, but you can't blame a fellow for trying."

"No, and another time I might have said yes."

"Well, if another time comes round at some point, look me up.

We mostly make the coastal run back and forth between Tien and the Magelands." Then he turned and left me at the rail.

As I watched him walk away, I couldn't help but smile. There was something preciously normal about the exchange. No one trying to kill me or anyone under my protection, no one I needed to kill, just a simple proposition and no hard feelings when it didn't pan out. He waved at Jax and Faran as he passed them on the lower deck. The pair were perched atop a stack of barrels in the shade of the mainsail, quietly talking.

I was still smiling when Faran got up a few minutes later and came my way. Climbing up the ladder to the foredeck, she crossed to stand in the exact same place Sendai had.

"Did you know that Jaeris and Altia are alive?" Faran asked without any preamble.

I nodded. When Jax and I had been trapped by the storm, she'd told me the names of all the surviving apprentices and journeymen she and Loris had taken in.

"They were my best friends at the temple, along with Omira and Garret." Faran said rather wistfully. "Jax says she doesn't know what's happened to Garret but that Omira turned up on the list of the dead. She's really dedicated to her students."

"Having second thoughts about killing her?"

"No. The only reason I haven't killed her *yet* is that I don't want to have to deal with a body on the boat." Faran's voice came out flat and hard, but it didn't match her eyes. There, I could see the teenager wrestling with the killer.

"You know," I said quietly, "it's all right if you are having trouble with the idea. Better, really. I know that the priests taught us to kill without regret or remorse in the name of the goddess, but times have changed. If you do kill Jax, it won't be because the goddess ordered you to, it will be because *you* decided that you had to do it."

Faran opened her mouth, but I touched a finger to her lips. "Wait, let me finish. That decision, should you have to make it, might even be the right one for the moment. But it's not a choice you should make easily or lightly or without second and even third thoughts. In fact, nothing has ever been as simple as the priests told us."

Faran looked genuinely shocked. "Are you saying that the order was wrong to do what it did?"

"No, and yes. It's complex." I stood up from the rail and leaned toward Faran as I tried to organize my ideas into something I could express—ideas that would once have been bitter heresy, but had increasingly come to dominate my thinking over the past year.

"I don't think that Namara ever ordered me to kill anyone who didn't need killing. King Ashvik, in particular, was a monster, and killing him was certainly justice. But that's not *why* I killed him. I killed him for the simple reason that my goddess told me to. And that's not enough. Or, it shouldn't be."

Faran frowned. "I don't think I see the distinction. Namara was Justice personified. If she wanted someone dead, surely that meant that they should die. It seems pretty simple."

She's right, you know. Triss sounded almost as confused as Faran, which is part of why I hadn't been talking with him about this. Despite his shadowy nature, Triss didn't really think in shades of gray.

No, she isn't. I sent back at him.

Aloud, I said, "I imagine that the destruction of the temple and the mass murder of our order seemed a right and simple thing to the forces of Heaven's Reach." Faran let out a little gasp of outrage, but I shook my head. "No. Really. Think about it. Speaking through the Son of Heaven, the great god Shan himself, Emperor of Heaven, declared our damnation and ordered our annihilation."

"That's different," Faran said aloud at the same time as Triss declared, *But he was wrong to do so!*

"How *exactly* is it different? Their god, who also happens to have been our goddess's liege lord, told them what they should do, and they did it. You and I and every other servant of Namara may believe that what they did was wrong, but as long as the word of a god is all that it takes to define what is right for anyone, it's simply one god's followers against another's. The only way to make what the followers of Shan did wrong is to accept that there is more to making your choices than the word of any god."

"I guess I never thought about it that way before," said Faran.

In my head, Triss remained silent.

I plowed on, "Some days I miss the simple view and I want nothing more in the world than for things to go back to the way they were when Namara was alive. Then, I only had to think about how to kill someone, never why I was doing it. Other days, I wonder what I would do if Namara were somehow resurrected. Is it possible to go back to certainty? Even if it were, would it be *right* to do so?"

"Do you regret killing Ashvik?" asked Faran.

"No. Not at all. He oppressed and murdered his people, and even killed members of his own family. He slaughtered thousands of Kadeshis for no apparent reason, and tried to start wars with Kodamia and the Magelands. Ashvik deserved to die."

"Then why does the distinction matter?"

"Justice is rarely such a simple thing, no matter how much we might like it to be," I said. "Most killers aren't monsters. They're people who made the wrong decision for what might have seemed at the time to be perfectly good reasons. That's why we have laws, and why in places like the Magelands there are courts and juries who try to interpret those laws."

"But the courts can't or won't touch the high nobles in places like Zhan, or even the Magelands sometimes," countered Faran. "And there are no courts in the Kvanas or Kadesh, only the word of the khans and warlords."

"Which is where we come in, or did."

"I thought you just said you didn't want to go back to the way things were," said Faran. "You're not making any sense."

"Maybe I'm not," I agreed. "I'm not entirely sure what I want or don't. I believe that the world needs a way to handle the Ashviks and the dukes of Seldan, and I think that almost has to look something like what the Blades of Namara once were. But I also believe that doing things just because the gods tell us to has to stop."

"And what does all this have to do with whether or not I kill Jax?" Faran asked, looking more than a little frustrated. "Her working for the Hand seems pretty straightforward to me."

I raised an eyebrow. "You're smarter than that, Faran. The situation here is the most tangled I've ever had to deal with. Jax is my friend and was once much more than that. I care about her deeply."

Faran looked away, so I put my hands on her shoulders and gently turned her so I could look her straight in the eye. "I also care about you. I don't want to see the two of you in conflict, but I also understand that ultimately what Jax chooses to do in the face of pressure from the Hand is on Jax. She may put you, or me, for that matter, in a position where killing her is the only answer. I don't want that to happen. I understand that it might."

"You're trying to make me think again, aren't you?" she demanded. "Well, it won't work. And I won't feel bad about it if I do have to kill her." She sighed. "You really are a horrible old man." But then she gave me a hug.

"I try, my young monster. I do try."

Faran pulled free of my arms. And then, with a very thoughtful look on her face she crossed to the nearest section of the rigging and went aloft. I wasn't sure if I'd really gotten through to her, or if it would change anything even if I had, but at least she seemed to be considering it.

What do you think? I asked Triss, since it was the first time I'd run most of it by him as well.

I think that if the goddess were still alive you would be facing a heresy trial.

Nicely dodged.

He hissed something in Shade that sounded obscene, then sighed. *I don't know. Some of what you say makes sense, at least from the human perspective, but I'm not so sure that justice is as difficult as you make it out to be. We were right to do as Namara ordered. The goddess was just as well as Justice.*

What does that make Shan?

A legitimate target.

That made me blink. *Shan is a god, Triss. Even if I agreed with the sentiment, I think that Namara's death pretty well demonstrates that he is beyond the reach of justice.*

Some said the same about Ashvik after he killed the first Blade that came for him. More said it after he killed the second. Most agreed when he killed a third. That did not stop us from making an end of him.

Are you seriously suggesting that we try to kill Shan? I asked. *Because that sounds more like suicide than justice.*

No, I am not, but if the opportunity should ever present itself . . .

I'll keep that in mind, but now I'm confused about your position on gods.

It's simple. Namara was good because what she wanted to see done was good. Shan is bad because what he wants to see done is bad. Why is that hard to understand?

Who makes the decision?

Me. You. Anyone. The fact that they are gods only tells us that they are powerful. It says nothing about whether they should be revered or reviled.

I'm beginning to think that I'm not the only heretic in this partnership.

No. My thinking is perfectly normal for a Shade. You, however, are a very strange Blade, and a rather odd human on top of that.

I laughed, though I couldn't tell whether or not he was joking. Triss and I have been together so long that I sometimes forgot that he's not even remotely human. It's always something of a shock when I'm reminded of the fact. I was trying to decide what to ask him next when I noticed Jax coming up the ladder from the lower deck.

"Hello." I nodded as she got closer.

"That was very well done," she spoke cheerfully enough, but her expression was troubled.

"What was?" I asked.

"How you handled Faran, just now."

I felt my stomach clench. I hadn't seen any evidence of Jax pointing a hearsay our way, but I'd been too intent on paying attention to Faran to even spare a glance for Jax. Stupid. Really stupid. The kind of stupid that would have Master Kelos spinning in his grave . . . if he weren't still alive and a traitor. How the hell did my world get so fucked up?

Jax was giving me a very strange look now, so I opened my mouth and said, "I . . ." But that's all the further I got. What did she know? What should I say?

Jax laughed. "What a look, Aral. You'd think I'd caught you plotting to murder someone's puppy. No"—she waved me off before I could continue—"it's all right. I don't know what the two of you were talking about and I don't want to know. She's your apprentice and the two of you need a private space for that to happen."

"I'm confused. If you don't know what *we* were talking about, then what are *you* talking about?"

"I've spent most of the last six years gathering up and teaching the surviving students of the temple. It's not at all how I'd planned to spend my life, but I've found it enormously rewarding. I've also learned a few things about how to handle the youngsters."

"I have no idea where you're going," I said, feeling ever more lost.

"Faran is right on the line between child and adult and that's a very hard place. Not just for the child either, but for everyone around them. I couldn't hear what the two of you were saying, but I could see how you were saying it. She was upset after I told her about Omira and Garret, that was obvious. So she went to you. Am I right so far? I don't want details."

"Yes."

"You gave her your full attention and you treated her with complete seriousness. I don't know what you told her, but I could see from over there that you were talking about things that mattered to you. I could also see that Faran wasn't entirely happy with what you had to say, but that it made her think. The hug at the end reinforced that you care about her even if you don't always agree. In short, it was everything I try to do with my students."

"So why do you look so torn up?" I asked, though I thought I knew at least part of the answer, or hoped I did anyway. I didn't want to believe that the Jax I had once loved could be anything but torn up over the idea of betraying me to the Hand.

She looked away from me, then down at her feet. "Because I'm here, doing"—she flung her hands out to the sides—"this! I should be back in Dalridia taking care of *our* students, not feeling more than half jealous about you and yours. Fuck! I hate this."

"Jax . . ." I put a hand out to touch her shoulder, but she shrugged it off.

"I'm sorry, Aral. I should never have gotten you involved in this." She looked up into the rigging at Faran. "Either of you. She's good, Aral. Really, really good. She reminds me of the way you and Siri were at that age. But she's fey and fragile, too, poised on the edge of disaster with only you between her and . . . I don't know what exactly, but nothing good. It's easy to see how many scars the fall of the temple left on her, but not so easy to see how she's going to deal with them."

"You're not making a lot of sense," I said.

"I know, and I'm sorry for that, too. This whole thing with Loris and the journeymen just has me all messed up."

"Tell me about it, maybe I can help." I put my hand on her shoulder again.

This time she left it there for several beats before shaking her head and slipping free. Without another word, she walked off.

I think she almost told us just then, Triss sent.

But almost isn't enough.

No. It's not.

I don't want to have to kill her.

Neither do I, but if it comes to it, I'd rather it was us than Ssithra and Faran.

Sendai tossed a bottle to the Vesh'An just before we entered the harbor at Ar, and I hated that I couldn't look away as it sank into the water. Hated the way I was backsliding on the booze in general. I was better than this. I could control my drinking. I'd proved that over the last year, and more than once. But dealing with Jax and Faran and all the lies and tension in the confined spaces of the boat had me thinking about drinking all the damned time again.

I shook my head. It wasn't me, it was the situation. I just needed to get off the fucking boat and it would all be fine. But somewhere in the back of my head, a little voice was saying, *Yeah, you just keep telling yourself that, Aral.*

Jax joined me at the rail as we came into the dock. "Ready to go?"

I nodded. "Packed my bag an hour ago. Is there a plan? Or are we winging it from here?"

"I've got a snug on the west edge of town by the last of the river docks. I'd like to hole up there for a day or two while I check with a few local contacts about what's been going on in the month I've been gone. Then we hop a barge heading upriver."

"I'm getting awfully tired of boats, Jax."

"You and me both. I'm a mountains girl, both by birth and, more recent, experience. But in this case it beats walking. Come on, let's get our gear."

Faran was already grabbing her small bag out of the cabin when we arrived, and a few minutes later all three of us were crossing the gangway down to the dock. It felt damned good to be back on solid ground. I was going to walk back to Tien when this was all over. Assuming I survived the next couple of weeks, of course. No sure bet there.

I hadn't been to Ar in years, and I'd almost forgotten what a bedlam it could be. The Magelands had a more disparate population than the rest of the eleven kingdoms to begin with—since anyone from anywhere could become a citizen if only they possessed one of magic's gifts. Add to that Ar's status as the largest and most populated human port on the outer sea, and the kaleidoscopic whirl of people alone would be more than enough to bewilder the average traveler.

But there was more to it than that. Much more. Ar was a mage city, built around the magical university that both provided its reason for being and its government. In Tien or Kadeshar, or even Dan Eyre, one person in a thousand might have some modicum of the mage gift, and most of those were hedge witches at best. In Ar or Uln or Tavan it was closer to one in twenty. Magic was everywhere.

In magesight the streets of Ar flashed and twinkled in every shade of every color of the rainbow. Walking through the city felt like walking through the middle of the annual fireworks display Tien put on for the king's birthday. Windows bore charms that kept them forever clean. Canopies of light protected restaurant patios from the worst depredations of rain and sun. Even the sewer drains had glyphs inscribed on them to keep clogs from forming.

Much of the magic was ephemeral, minor spells that required constant renewal to keep them going. Permanent magic needed both expertise and significant expenditure of power. But the city had minor mages in plenty, and part of the training of young scholars at the university included maintaining the service spells that helped keep the city functioning. Nowhere but in the great university cities of the Magelands was magic so cheap and plentiful.

I had already developed a headache, but I knew from past experience that both the pain and the confusion would pass once my inner eye had a chance to adjust to the feast of light. Still, the visual cacophony of it almost made me wish I could shut down my second sight. Nor was I alone in my discomfort. A sidelong glance showed me that Faran was squinting as well, though Jax seemed more inured.

She leaned in close to Faran and said, "You'll adapt faster if you look around for the biggest spells and brightest lights and stare at them a bit. It makes the rest of it a bit easier to bear."

"I've been here before," Faran snapped back at her. "I know what I'm doing. I'm not one of your poor little lost apprentices." Then she stormed forward.

"Dammit," Jax said to me, "I didn't mean it that way."

"I'd better have a word with her," I said.

But Jax shook her head. "No, if we're going to be working together, she and I need to sort out our differences. I need to talk to her myself. Why don't we make the best of this. If you let us get a block or so ahead it'll give you a chance to see if we attract any undue attention."

"Start with a block, then go two and three, split and double-round?" I asked.

"Even better," said Jax. "It does double duty. If I tell Faran she's given us a great opportunity it'll make it easier for her to accept my apology. And a split and back around will definitely tell us if we've got a hound nosing after us. Keep going straight up this street till you hit University Way and then take a left. If we get separated we can meet back at the dock where we landed at sunset."

"Fair enough."

So, as Jax speeded up to catch Faran, I slowed down a little bit. One of the easiest ways to spot a hound is to split up. The hound has to decide who to follow, which makes the job much harder. It also gives you lots of options for circling around each other, and putting the hound in a trap. A good hound knows all that, but it leaves them with very limited options.

I didn't want to be too obvious about what we were doing, so I pretended there was something wrong with my boot. As I knelt to adjust things I did a quick top of the eyes scan of my surroundings. Perhaps inevitably, I spotted the nearest alehouse. As I stared longingly at the place, a magic light flared on the rooftop of the low building.

I probably would have missed it among all the visual noise if not for the fact that it was a very distinctive shade of orange pink— not a common color for magic, and one I'd been trained to look for from the age of six. I glanced up, and there, crouched in the shade of a narrow dormer, was Master Kelos. He held up a hand, palm out, and magical light flashed again, this time drawing words, "Here Midnight Alone."

11

———◆◆◆———

The past is never dead. It lives inside us, no matter how hard we might try to cut it out. As a child my parents gave me to the temple. Not long after that the temple gave me to Master Kelos. I had other teachers, other masters—we all did—but more than anyone else it was Kelos Deathwalker who shaped me into Aral Kingslayer.

Each of the children who went through the temple had a special master they answered to. For Siri and me, that master was Kelos. He taught me how to hold a sword, how to walk in shadow, how to kill. On the day the goddess made me a Blade and sent me after Ashvik, there were only two people at the temple who knew what I planned. Devin was one. He tried to convince me not to go. Kelos was the other. He wished me good hunting. I loved the man as you can only love the idols of your childhood.

Maybe that was the reason it didn't even occur to me to try to follow him. Or maybe it was simpler than that. Maybe it was fear. Kelos didn't want to see me right now, and for all that I had done in the years since I entered the temple, I was still afraid of making him mad at me because I knew all the way down to my bones that he could take me.

After sending his message, Kelos had nodded to me and walked away over the peak of the roof. I nodded back and I watched him go. And then, after he'd left, I walked away myself.

Are we going to do it? Triss asked as we followed Jax and Faran up the road in the general direction of the university.

What?

Meet Kelos tonight.

I stopped dead. It was only in that instant that it even occurred to me that I *could* decline to show up. Somewhere deep down below the level of conscious thought, I had simply assumed that I would meet him. Master Kelos had summoned me. Period. Nothing after that involved a choice on my part.

Only, it did. It's hard to describe what happened inside my head when I finally realized that. Even though I had seen Master Kelos talking to the Signet and heard him acknowledging the Son of Heaven as his master, it hadn't really sunk in. It didn't matter that I'd been filled to overflowing with a toxic mix of fury, betrayal, and a half dozen other awful emotions at the time. Somehow, down in the deeps of my soul, Master Kelos was still *my* Master Kelos.

In the hierarchy of my life it had always gone from Namara to Kelos to me. The high priestess of Justice had barely even entered into it. Now Namara was dead and Kelos was . . . what? A traitor certainly, but beyond that, he was no longer *my* master. Somehow, that was so much worse than things had been when he was simply dead along with my goddess.

Despite Triss's companionship, I suddenly felt alone in a way that I never had before, like I'd lost a layer of protection between me and the void. Maybe this was what it felt like for a normal person to lose a parent. I don't know. I wanted to scream or cry or send a pillar of magelightning blasting into the heavens.

I did none of those things. I couldn't. Discipline held me back and got me moving again. Bitterly, ironically, even poisonously, the very discipline drilled into me by Kelos Deathwalker kept me from acknowledging the pain now inflicted by that same Kelos Deathwalker.

Aral? Triss spoke into my mind, but I couldn't answer him because I wasn't really there.

I was walking through the past at the same time I walked up the street. The day I summoned Triss was the very same day the priests gave me to Kelos. I was seven.

"Greetings, young Aral." Always a big man, Kelos had seemed a giant to me, but one who now crouched down to put our eyes on a level. "The priests tell me that your bonding ceremony was successful." He extended his hand. "That makes you my brother as well as my student. Welcome to the order and our mission, young Blade."

I wasn't truly a Blade yet, merely an apprentice, but Master Kelos was treating me like a man and his brother. Kelos Deathwalker! The Blade that all the other Blades used as an example.

Heady stuff for a child raised by the priests to believe nothing was more important than our sacred mission. I extended my own hand to shake his, trying as hard as I could to mirror the way that he had offered his.

"Greetings, Master Kelos." I wanted nothing more in the entire world than to justify the serious way Master Kelos treated me as he shook my hand and then released it. "The priests have informed me that you are to be my master and teach me the ways of the Blade."

"I am that, son, as well as your brother."

"I will try to justify the honor Namara has done me by giving Triss into my care today and me into yours."

My shadow shifted then, for the first time since the summoning ceremony ended, as Triss took on his dragon shape and folded his wings and bowed his head. "Masster Keloss, mosst honored Resshath Malthiss, I—" Triss's continued in Shade then, as he seemed to have exhausted his knowledge of the tongue of Varya.

Malthiss changed, too, assuming the form of a great basilisk coiled around Kelos's neck and shoulders. "Triss, Aral, welcome. We have much to teach you."

"And that ends the formalities," said Kelos, with a grin. "Now, let me get you a pair of proper swords and show you to your new room."

I half expected him to pick me up then, but he never treated me like a child. Oh, he gave me hugs when I needed them, as well as the occasional hiding. But from the very first day I entered his care to the moment I placed my Kila in the great orb of Namara and became a full Blade, he always accorded me the respect due to one of his full brethren. Perhaps more importantly, he was one of the very few who didn't treat me any differently after I became the King-slayer.

Oh, he was proud of me, none more, and he told me so the very first chance he got. But that didn't keep him from pounding me in the salle the very next day, or scolding me in exactly the same way as he always had when I fucked up. It was a blessed relief, especially compared to the way the younger trainees started treating me after I killed Ashvik.

The funny thing was that it didn't occur to me until years later that he probably would have loved to have someone who treated him as just another Blade. Not until shortly before the temple fell, in fact. But he was still *Kelos Deathwalker* to me at that point, and I never quite worked my way up to it. And now, I never would.

Are we going to meet Kelos? Triss sent after a time. *You never answered my question.*

I shrugged. *I'd give you an answer if I had one, Triss, but I don't. I just . . . don't.* I didn't want to, but I wasn't at all sure that we had much of a choice.

"**Nice** place," I said to Jax.

The snug was a large open attic room on the top floor of a warehouse. It stood just above the river docks on the western edge of the city. Not a bad location, but not a prime spot either, not even for a warehouse. Most of those lay on the far side of the city, along the harbor front where you could easily shift things from the sea-going ships to river barges. But there was a secondary hub here where a spur of the Great Coast Road made a loop around the back of the city to give wagons and livestock a route that didn't run through the heart of the university district.

For reasons known only to the original builder, the place stood seven stories tall, which was two more than any of its neighbors. No one sane hauls crates up above the third floor even with a crane. For that matter, there was no real call for that much space, that many stories off the ground, so far out from the center of the city. All of which meant that Jax's brother had been able to pick the place up for about half what the floor space might otherwise have justified.

In addition to being the main port of the Magelands, Ar and its river provided the only real route for goods to move from the coast inland to Dalridia. That meant that the Dalridian Crown, in the person of Jax's brother, had significant interests in the city. Those included wanting some unobtrusive storage space for the odd bit of goods, or royal sibling for that matter.

Jax had taken over the entire southwest corner of the top floor, which mostly consisted of a big open room with lots of shuttered windows and a trapdoor that provided roof access. At the moment, the shutters were all flung wide, providing a beautiful view that took in the river, a good chunk of the coast road, and miles of farmland. The furnishings were sparse, a couch, a couple of chairs, a table, and a couple of rolled-up futons for sleeping.

Fully half the high-ceilinged room was empty save for a dozen or so large and badly mildew-stained rugs that provided some padding for falls in what was obviously an improvised salle. The sanitary facilities consisted of a closetlike room with a porcelain bucket and a small balcony that allowed it to be emptied unobtrusively into the river—as illegal here as it would have been in Tien. Baths could be had at a public bathhouse across the way, a fact Jax had mentioned to Faran as we passed the place.

I walked over to the nearest window and leaned out. "Really a nice place." Though what I was thinking was, "How the hell am I going to get out of here without having Faran and Jax follow me?"

"You mentioned that already." Jax gave me a rather suspicious look. "Are you feeling all right? Because you've seemed a little dazed ever since we left the waterfront area."

"I'm sorry. I don't generally like boats, but I'm finding it shockingly hard to get used to ground that doesn't rock back and forth under my feet."

"Right. Well, I need to go out, and I don't think I'll be back till well after dark. There's food and drink in the amphorae along the back wall. Is there anything more you two need to know before I leave?"

"It's barely past noon now," said Faran, joining the conversation. "What's going to take you so long?"

"Mostly a lot of very boring business for the Dalridian Crown, though there's also the odd bit of spymastering. Part of the way I pay my keep and that of my students is by helping out Dalridian intelligence. In service of which, I need to talk to a couple of people at the university, as well as a few at the docks. After that, I have to stop in at the Dalridian embassy to see what our local eavesmen have picked up."

Jax smiled. "You're welcome to join me for most of it, if Aral will allow it."

I raised an eyebrow.

"Oh, I couldn't bring you along, Aral. That would be out of character, but I've dragged my students through the city often enough that no one will remark on Faran if she wants to come." She turned back to Faran. "Of course, you'll have to wait outside for several of my stops."

"It's fine by me," I said. It would provide the perfect opportunity for me to step out without having to explain myself beyond a note on the table saying that I thought I'd seen something.

"I don't think that would be a good idea," Ssithra said quietly from within Faran's shadow.

Faran nodded. "Point. Besides, I already know all that I need to about the eavesman business."

Faran had made an extremely good living the last few years playing the independent spy for a number of Crowns and services. Without knowing in advance who Jax's contacts were, she'd be running the risk of bumping into past employers. Or worse, competitors.

Jax shrugged. "Makes no nevermind to me. Now, if you'll excuse me . . ." When neither of us argued, she waved good-bye and left.

We'd had lunch—mushroom and sausage kebabs from a street vendor—on the way across town, otherwise I'd have sent Faran off to find us food while I had a look around. I was just trying to think of some other way to get Faran out the door when she preempted me.

"I'm going to that bathhouse Jax showed us, and I'm going to take a good long soak," she said. "Two weeks of nothing but cold saltwater for washing up is two weeks too many. Do you want to join me? You need it."

"No, I'll get a bath in later." Faran gave me an odd look, and I realized that I needed to explain a bit more.

"I know I stink, but I don't trust Jax and I want to give this place a really thorough going over before we settle in. I also want to check out escape routes. All of that's likely to involve a lot of dirt and sweating. No point in having to take two baths in one day." All of which was true, though not primarily for the obvious reasons.

"Suit yourself. I'm gone."

That gave me something in the neighborhood of an hour alone. I spent it crawling all over the upper floors and roof of the warehouse and coming to one inescapable conclusion.

"We're going to have to tell Faran about the meeting with Kelos." I was looking out over the river from the southern windows for the third time as I said it.

A sail-jump would carry me down to the roof of one of the near continuous stream of passing barges. From there I could get aboard a water taxi to bury my shadow trail. It was a good plan . . . for stage two of my little trip to talk to Kelos, and it wouldn't work this side of sunset. Unfortunately, stage one—getting out the window without having either Jax, Faran, or their Shade companions see me go was a nonstarter.

"So, we're going then?" He didn't sound happy.

Neither was I, and I still wasn't certain, but I didn't see a good way to avoid it. "I expect that we are, yes."

Triss sighed, but he didn't try to argue with me—not then anyway. "If we're going, why don't we just leave now?" He had taken dragon shape, though he stayed on the floor beside me, where the sun would have put him.

I sat down on the window ledge. "If we go now, Faran will come looking immediately, no matter how clever a note we leave. We can't sail-jump in broad daylight without flashing a sign that says 'Blade here' for anyone who knows how to read it. So the chance she won't find our trail approaches zero. You saw Kelos's message when he signaled us down by the harbor. He told me to come alone, and he might react violently if I don't. That could get very ugly very fast."

"Then, leave from the baths in a couple of hours. Find some reason to put off bathing till the sun's almost down. Faran's already soaked for nearly an hour, she's not going to want to go back so soon. That would give us a good half hour's head start. If we can't make that work for us, we're so far past it that we shouldn't even be in the game anymore."

"That might work, but there's also Jax to consider, *and* what happens if we leave Faran alone and vanish for hours. I don't think it's a good idea to have Jax show up and run into a Faran who's maybe thinking something bad has happened to me."

"Then, better yet, don't go. We don't have to meet Malthiss and Kelos at all. They have embraced the evil that destroyed Namara. They have no right to ask anything of us. You know that, right?"

"It's not that simple, Triss. We don't know what Kelos wants out of this whole situation and he's far too dangerous to ignore. I'd much rather run the risks involved with dealing with him face-to-face now, than skip out on the meeting and wait for him to show up behind us somewhere later."

Triss flicked his wings angrily. "I do not like this."

"I don't like it either, I'm just speaking of what is." I shrugged. "We have two options. One, we can deal with him now."

"When he and Malthiss have had plenty of time to get ready for us," interjected Triss.

I laughed. "Like they need it. Or, are you seriously suggesting they wouldn't be able to take us without a lot of set up?"

Triss turned his head away. "No. Even at our very best we could not have beaten them in a straight fight, and we have fallen a long way since then."

"Which brings us back to my original point. Now. Or later, after we've pissed him off. Those are the choices."

Triss sighed and slid closer, reaching up to put his head in my lap. "I guess we might as well get it over with."

I scratched behind his ears, in the place where his scales were thinnest. "Then we have to tell Faran. Speaking of which . . . Why don't you come in off the roof?"

There was a snort from above, and Faran's face suddenly appeared upside down at the top of the window. "How'd you know I was here? I swear I didn't make any noise."

"No, you didn't. But neither did you go to the bathhouse. I made sure to be on the roof on that side of the building when you should have been crossing the street. That meant you were either following Jax, or hanging around here for some reason. Once I knew that, I just had to watch the right shadows to see if any of them were a touch too dark."

Faran reached down and caught the lintel of the window, flipping herself around to land neatly on the ledge. "I could have been sneaking off to do something entirely different. Maybe meeting up with some of *my* old spying contacts."

"Possible, yes, but given the circumstances, not likely."

"So the whole conversation you just had was entirely for my benefit?"

I shook my head. "No. I needed to convince Triss, too, and Ssithra for that matter. We have to meet Master Kelos. We have to do it tonight. We can't let Jax know about it, either before or after. And, we have to do it alone if we don't want Kelos thinking it's a double cross. For this to work, I need all three of you on my side."

Faran's shadow shifted, so that a phoenix now joined the dragon. "I am convinced," said Ssithra. "What is our part?"

Faran held up a hand. "Not so fast, Ssithra. I want to know more about Master Kelos's message."

"There's not much to tell," I said before giving her the details.

"All right," said Faran. "I don't like it either, but I think you've got to go to that meeting. So, what do Ssithra and I have to do about Jax?"

"Besides not trying to kill her while I'm gone? Not much. Just tell her that I was up on the roof about half an hour before she got back and that I thought I saw something suspicious. So I went to check it out. Then, when I get back, find a way to let me know when it was I'm supposed to have left."

"Really, that's it? You think she'll buy it?"

"If she asks for more than that, I'll tell her it was just a couple of none-too-clever thatchcutters looking for an easy nut to crack. After I warned them off, I followed them till they tried and botched a shutter job and then I headed home. On my way back from my meeting with Kelos, I'll break a set of top-story shutters a mile or two from here and do it loud and stupid enough to get the owner screaming for the watch."

Faran nodded. "Then if Jax has her people ask around there'll be a nice clean trail to corroborate you. That should work nicely. All right, now that I know what you're up to, I can go and get my bath."

"One question before you do," I said. "How did you know I was up to something?"

"You agreed to let me go off alone with Jax way too easily, considering how hard you've been working to keep me from killing her. The only reason I could think of for you to do that was that you wanted to get me out from underfoot."

"Point. I screwed up there."

"No wonder, you are getting awfully oooold for this stuff."

"Brat."

"Geezer."

The university bells were ringing a quarter past ten when I dropped from the dormer onto the patch of roof where I'd first seen Kelos. I'd spent the better part of an hour circling around the place and looking for any signs of a trap, but I hadn't found anything. No surprise. Not with Kelos involved. If he were laying a trap for me I wouldn't see it till the jaws closed.

Damn but that's clever! Triss said into my mind.

What?

Kelos has left us a message that only a Blade could read.

Oh, how?

Kelos got Malthiss to concentrate himself completely on the tip of one of his fingers. Then he used that finger to write a shadow-trail message on the roof here.

That is clever. Why didn't we think of that?

No need for it, I suppose. I wasn't allowed to tell you about the shadow trails before the fall of the temple. It was a secret between the Shades and the highest masters. Afterward, I didn't have any reason to think about it, not until we ran into Devin. Now that we're dealing with other Blades again, I'm sure we'd have figured it out eventually.

What does it say?

Triss swore in Shade for a moment.

What? I asked.

"Aral, quarter after ten? If so, then you're exactly a quarter of an hour behind me and I still know you well enough to predict some of your actions. I've left a trail for you starting on the round stone tower directly north of you. You should just be able to see it from where you're standing. Follow it. I know you don't trust me, and I don't expect you

*to. That's why the trail will take you someplace where we can talk
without you feeling you have to keep looking over your shoulder."*

He signs it, "Your brother and onetime teacher, Kelos."

"He has no right to call me brother," I said in a shaking voice.
"Not anymore." I closed my eyes then and clenched my fists so hard
I half expected my nails to tear the skin of my palms.

We can turn back. Triss's mental voice was barely louder than a
whisper.

No. We still need to do this.

I didn't know the chimney forest of Ar half so well as I knew
Tien's, so getting around was just flat slower than it would have
been back home. But the trail that Kelos had left me was clear. It led
directly toward the university, which struck me as a little bit odd. As
a rule, Blades avoid other mages where we can. Magical power is a
huge wild card in any game, and going anywhere near a Magelands
university is like playing cards with a whole roomful of people holding nothing but jokers. Even Kelos has to tread carefully around
such people. So, I was more than a little surprised when the trail
brought me straight to the university wall, without turning aside.

Are you sure? I asked Triss.

*There's an arrow here at the end of the trail pointing straight
across to the university. Also, I don't think you can see it with your eyes,
but there's about a foot of black silk rope trailing over the wall by the
pillar there across the way.*

*I'm surprised you can pick it out against the dark wall. Normally
you don't do well with that sort of minimal contrast.*

*The rope has been treated so it stands out to my senses. I've never
seen anything like it before, but it would be difficult for a Shade to miss.*

*A foot, you say. Is it tight against the wall? Or is it hanging out
where I could grab it easily at the end of a short sail-jump across this
alley here?*

It's an easy grab, but you knew it would be.

I did, because it was there for me, and Kelos wanted to make
things easy. I wondered what he had done about the wards. The
entire top of the wall glowed with intense spell-light, every inch of
the surface crawling with alarm and attack glyphs, including the
area directly above the rope. I had no idea how Kelos had managed
to leave the wards intact and unblocked there and still left a hole
that I could pass through. But I had no doubt that he had.

At that point, even if I hadn't had other reasons to make the
jump, curiosity would have driven me to it. I wanted to know what
he'd done. So I asked Triss to give me control for a bit, took three

running steps, jumped . . . and nearly fell out of the air when a huge bang and a flash happened at ground level about fifty feet to my right. I had just enough presence of mind to keep my wings out and make my grab when I hit the wall.

What the fuck was that? I thought.

Of course, Triss couldn't respond from within his dream state, so I got no answer. Swearing quietly but continuously to myself all the while, I reshrouded myself and hung quietly from the rope while I waited for my pulse to return to normal. I also tried to figure out what had happened. A couple of locals had gone to look around the area where the noise had come from.

"Looks like someone blew up Snurri's rain barrel," said the first.

"Damned university prank," said another. "There oughta be a law."

"Wouldn't do any good with these youngblood mages," replied a third. "They'd just see it as a challenge."

"That's the truth," said the first. "Guess Snurri'll have to complain to the proctors at the university. Won't catch the prankster of course, but maybe the administration will at least replace his barrel."

There was more grumbling over the next few minutes and much speculation as to whether the university would replace the barrel, but I shut it out. I knew damned well that no student had done the deed. It was Kelos providing a distraction for any watchers who might otherwise have chanced to look up and see me gliding across the alley.

When the neighborhood chorus left, I braced my feet on the wall and very carefully raised my head enough to look at the top of the wall where the rope ran. A thick piece of leather-backed black felt lay across the wards and spikes. They had done the latter up fancy with silver and steel both, not that any of the restless dead or creatures of wild magic were likely to attempt to enter a mage university. I poked at the mat with a fingertip. It was obviously a custom wardblack, but unlike any I'd ever seen before.

Normally, to make a wardblack, you lay a piece of enchanted silk across the top of the wards you want to fool and let it soak up a copy of the guard spells. Done right, it almost never sets them off. Then you attach that to a chunk of spelled felt that effectively mutes the wards for as long as you leave it in place atop them. In most circumstances, that's all you need. Either you cross the warded area fast and pull up the wardblack behind you. Or, if it's in a not terribly well-traveled space, you leave it in place for a cleaner and faster exit on your way out.

But most wards aren't attached to a university with literally thousands of mages inside. Here, the spell-light of the wards was almost as much protection as the wards themselves. If you left a wardblack in place for any length of time, someone would be bound to notice the dark patch it created. Kelos had gotten around that by sewing a bunch of fake wards into the top surface of the felt and enchanting them with a simple charm to make them glow in magesight. Add in the leather to provide a protection against the spikes, and you had a temporary doorway through the university's security that you could leave open behind you.

It was the easiest thing in the world for me to pull myself up atop the wall and then, following another shadow-trail arrow, drop down inside and head across the lawn. The trail led me from there to . . . *You're not serious. The fucking proctor house? He wants me to meet him on top of the offices of the university police department?*

Apparently, sent Triss. *Apparently.*

12

Sometimes words cut deeper than any blade. Sometimes it doesn't even matter which words, only who says them.

"Hello, Aral." Master Kelos stood with his arms crossed and one hip leaning casually against the proctor house chimney. He was dressed in the full ritual clothing of the Blade—loose and flowing grays in a half dozen shades. "It's good to see you alive."

Without thinking about it, I found my hands on the hilts of my swords, my thumbs on their release catches.

"Don't." He said it quietly, not an order, nor even a serious request, but somehow I couldn't resist, and my hands fell away from my swords. "Oh, good, you're going to be sensible. I'd hate to have you start a fight up here. With a university full of mages around it wouldn't go well for either of us."

"What makes you so sure I wouldn't be willing to die if it meant taking you with me?"

"Nothing at all. In fact, I suspect that if you were sure that's the way things would play out, and if that was the only price, we'd already be fighting. But there's Triss to consider, and Malthiss. As well as all the many, many things that could go wrong along the way. That's why you weren't there at the fall of the temple, actually. Nor Siri either."

"What?" The word fell out of my mouth, barely loud enough for even me to hear, and it left behind a feeling of cold that made my jaw feel numb and useless.

"You don't think it was a coincidence that our best and most-talented young assassins were a thousand miles away when Heaven's

Hand and Sword arrived at the temple, do you? You were both far too valuable to waste and too dedicated not to force them to kill you if you'd been there."

"But the goddess chose us for those missions. . . ."

"She did, yes. But she did so in consultation with the shadow council, her most senior priests and Blades. I requested that you and Siri and a few others receive assignments that would put you out of harm's way, in hopes that someday I would be able to bring you back into the fold."

"You knew they were coming? But that means that . . ."

"I betrayed Namara. Yes, it does, and it was the hardest decision I ever made."

The numbness in my jaw had spread to my whole body by then. I felt like I no longer had any real control over my limbs or actions. Sometimes, when you're drinking, there's a moment where you stop feeling like it's *you* that's drinking, where you feel completely disconnected from yourself. It's like you can see what's happening to you but it's not you that's doing it. This was like that, only without the alcohol. Without any drugs at all, just my own shock and betrayal slowly poisoning me from within.

So, it was doubly startling when Triss suddenly changed into dragon form and lunged toward Master Kelos. Kelos didn't so much as twitch, but before Triss had gone three feet, Malthiss was there, wrapped around Triss like a constrictor. The older Shade moved so fast I didn't see it, didn't see anything beyond a blurred impression of the shadows around Kelos's neck and shoulders flickering. It made a sharp contrast to the casual, almost leisurely way he'd acted against the envoy back in Tien.

The world blurred and flickered again, and I was standing a few feet from Kelos, my swords drawn, one point inches from his throat, the other hovering in front of his heart.

"Tell Malthiss to let Triss go, right now."

Kelos still hadn't moved. "Don't," he said in the exact same tone he'd used earlier. "I'd rather not have to hurt you."

"Kill him," said Triss. "It'll be worth whatever it costs."

I . . . couldn't. I tried, or at least I intended to, but the arm that I wanted to thrust the blade through his throat wouldn't move no matter how hard I thought at it that it should.

"Sensible," said Kelos. "I'm almost surprised. Perhaps the years have taught you some of the things that I never could. Now, I want you to move back to where you were standing before.

Then Malthiss will let Triss go, and we can continue our conversation."

"I don't think so," I said. "You let Triss go first, and then we'll discuss the rest."

"I'm afraid it doesn't work that way," said Kelos. "Do be sensible again. We'll both be happier for it."

"No."

"Your choice."

Now, Kelos moved. I knew he was going to. I was ready for him. It didn't help, not even with my swords already in a position to strike. It was almost as fast as what happened with Malthiss. One instant Kelos was leaning casually against the chimney, arms crossed. The next, his arms drove forward and apart, using the knives in the wrist sheaths under his shirt as armor against my edges. He struck the blade of my swords, pushing my right sword to the left, and my left to the right as he slid toward me, putting my arms into a cross-bind.

I tried to backpedal, but he moved faster, shoving my own arms back into my chest with the weight of his body. Before I could recover in any way, I felt Kelos hook a foot behind my ankle and ride me to the rooftop. A moment later, I was flat on my back with Kelos kneeling on my chest and arms, gasping. He took the swords from my hands almost casually and flipped them around. Cold steel kissed my wrists as he slowly forced the blades down through the straps of my wrist sheaths and deep into the lead and planks of the roof, pinning me.

The most shocking thing about the whole maneuver was how quiet it had been. Even my fall had been controlled to minimize noise. If someone was in the room directly below us, the sword tips coming through the ceiling would have been much more likely to draw their attention than my landing.

"There," he said, "that ought to illustrate my point nicely." Then he was off me and stepping back to retake his place against the chimney. "That was very badly done, Aral. Once you drew steel you shouldn't have stopped to threaten. You should have gone for the kill. I might have been forced to hurt more than your pride, but you would at least have had a fair shot at spilling some of my blood in the process. This was beneath you."

Another flicker and a blur and Malthiss snapped back to peer at me over Kelos's shoulder as he had so many times in the past. With an angry snarl, Triss moved sideways to crouch on my chest, though he didn't try to attack either Kelos or Malthiss again. Instead, he just sat there, quietly but steadily hissing at them.

"But none of this is why I brought you here," said Kelos. "Jax intends to betray you to the Hand."

"Yeah, I'm on top of that. It's not going to happen. I won't let it, though I'm hoping she'll choose to come to me and talk about it rather than force me to stop her. And, yes, I do understand exactly how ironic that sounds coming from me to you right now."

Kelos smiled sadly. "It's not what I wanted, you know, not what I would have chosen if I could have seen any other way. Much like what I am doing now."

Triss's hissing rose and Malthiss leaned forward over Kelos's shoulder. "Triss, desist." Then he added something scathing in Shade, and somewhat to my surprise, Triss shut up.

"Why?" I didn't know whether I was asking about the temple or the current situation. I just knew that I wanted answers.

"Eleven years ago, you killed Zhan's king, Ashvik the Sixth. You were the fourth Blade to make the attempt and the first to survive the experience. Yes?"

I nodded and used the opportunity of that movement to shift my arms so that my sword's edges began to cut into the straps on my wrists.

"What good did it do? In the long run?"

I shifted to look Kelos in the eyes, working at cutting the straps with the same motion. "I brought him Justice. Isn't that enough? Isn't that what you taught me? That we have to show the people that not even kings are above paying for their crimes?"

"It's not enough, Aral. You know that Thauvik took the throne when his brother died, right?" I nodded. "Do you think he's one whit less of a monster than Ashvik was?"

"Well, I certainly haven't heard of him invading Kadesh, or murdering his own sons." Though Maylien had told me he was doing plenty of harm.

"That's true, but it's not because he's a better person. It's not because he learned that he mustn't do evil. No. What he learned is, 'don't get caught.' His first murder happened within hours of taking the throne, and he's quietly killed hundreds since."

"Thauvik being too scared to become a full-blown and highly visible monster means we've failed?" I demanded. "That we shouldn't even try? I don't see that."

"Oh no. That's not what I'm saying at all. Thauvik's stance

means we were never allowed to go far enough. We were never allowed to go all the way."

"What are you talking about?" asked Triss. "Isn't killing a king going all the way?"

His talking now reminded me that Malthiss hadn't said a word since he told Triss to quit hissing. Though he'd never been the most talkative of Shades, this seemed more of a speaking silence. I just wished I knew what it was speaking of.

Kelos shook his head in response to Triss's question. "The pair of you weren't the first to kill a monster King of Zhan. I killed Ashvik's great-grandfather, who was a damned nasty piece of work, and Alinthide killed *his* niece when she played regent to Ashvik's grandfather and polo with servants' heads. In the service of the goddess I killed seven rulers and hundreds of lesser nobles and generals. But no matter how many times I administered Namara's justice, new monsters just sprang up to take their places."

He squatted down so that our eyes were closer to the same level. "It never gets any better, Aral. Not in any meaningful way. I've lived longer than almost any other Blade, and what I've seen is that when you stomp out evil over here, it just springs up again over there. Or it comes back again a few years or decades later. Killing kings isn't enough. I told Namara that more times than I can count, but she would never agree to do more."

"Like what?" I'd cut through the straps on my wrist sheaths by then. Though the swords still pinned my sleeves, that wouldn't hold me. But I still didn't move. Kelos clearly had more to say, and he was the one who'd taught me never to do something that will shut up a source of information until you absolutely had to.

"Get rid of the damn kings completely."

That was an argument I could almost agree with. "And replace them with what? Rulers elected from among the elite, like in Kodamia or the way the Magearchs of the universities are chosen here in the Magelands?"

"Why would I want to replace it with anything? The whole idea of one person having any kind of ruling authority over another is corrupt at its roots. I want to tear the whole system out of the ground and burn it. Injustice stems from inequality. The only way to eliminate it is to level the field so that no one person sets themselves up above the others."

"I'm not sure that's going to work," said Triss. "Your people seem to have a natural drive to rule over their fellows."

"That's why the order of the Blade will have to continue for at least a little while after we take down the nobility. We'll need to chop down those who would become kings until a new system of self-government can arise on top of the ashes of the old autocracy."

Part of me thought that what Kelos was saying had some merit, if only in a purely abstract sort of way. But I didn't believe it would work any more than Triss had. Real people didn't act the way that Kelos seemed to be saying they would. No, at the moment, my real question was whether Kelos believed any of it or if he was playing me. He certainly sounded serious; calm, collected, intense. But then, he always sounded that way. And still, not one word from Malthiss.

While Kelos *might* believe every word he was saying, there was no way for me to know that, this side of his implementing his ideas. He was perfectly capable of acting as though the total destruction of the ruling classes of the eleven kingdoms was his goal right up until whatever his real plan was needed him to act otherwise. I was very tempted to ask him how betraying the goddess to the Son of Heaven served any of those goals. But I thought I had enough now to make some good guesses, and time was passing. I had other, more important questions, and Kelos seemed in an answering mood.

"And what you're doing now? How does that serve your plans? Why did you set that trail for Faran to find?"

"You figured out that I left that for you? Excellent. I tried very hard to make it look like chance, but I needed you to see what was going on with the Signet and Jax. I got very lucky when you and she arrived so close together on the very first attempt. By the way, you might as well slice yourself the rest of the way free. It's not like you're going to take me by surprise when you do. But I would appreciate it if you left your swords where they are for now."

So I did, both. "I still don't know *why* you wanted me to know what's going on with Jax and the Signet."

"Because I need you to free Loris and the others without getting yourself or Jax killed in the process, of course. I've lost too many of you already. There were almost four hundred Blades and trainees once. Over three hundred of those died at the fall, with more killed since then. The Signet set this play up on the sly, so I didn't have a chance to block it in advance. If she had her way, every single one of us would be dead. I can't let that happen. I need all of you alive to help me once I take the system down."

"Why not simply kill the Signet yourself?" asked Triss. "Why involve us?"

"I . . . can't do it myself for a number of reasons. Not least of which, it would interfere with my longer-range plans. And I can't get Jax to do it. She's not ready to know that I'm alive again yet, not after what the Hand did to her and Loris. It would distract her too much."

"Don't you mean what *you* did to her and Loris?" I asked furiously.

Kelos's expression didn't change. "Not at all. I thought they'd been killed in the battle for the temple. It wasn't until months later that I discovered I'd been lied to. As soon as I found out where they were and what was happening to them, I arranged an opportunity for them to escape."

"How very nice of you to do that after arranging for the temple to fall in the first place."

"Don't be ridiculous, Aral. I didn't do it to be nice. You should know me better than that. Nice isn't a part of my character. I did it because I wanted them out and alive so that I could bring them back into the fold later, once they'd had some time to let the memories fade a bit. Neither did I *arrange* for the fall of the temple. The Son of Heaven was going to move against Namara one way or another. What I arranged was a way to salvage something from the ashes of our collective ruin."

What could I say to that? What could I do? When I was twenty-one, a building came apart around me in the middle of an escape. I got clipped upside the head by a chunk of falling beam in the process. It'd left me seeing double for a while and screwed up my thinking for days afterward. I felt that same sick confusion now, but instead of pain in my head I felt a vicious gnawing void in my chest and gut.

Aral? Triss spoke into my mind, and he sounded every bit as anguished as I felt. *What do we do?*

I don't know. I'm lost. One second I want to cut out his heart and feed it to him. But the next, I remember how much he did to make me who I am, and I want so desperately to have a reason to forgive him that I can almost believe that the only way he could save any of us was by betraying Namara.

Kelos reached into the trick bag at his side and pulled out a small package tightly wrapped in black silk. "I know you don't trust me. You shouldn't. You have no reason to. But I have to go now, and I don't know whether I'll get the chance to see you again before you have to deal with the Signet's ambush. You're going to need this. Here." He tossed it over.

As I caught it, Kelos shrouded up, vanishing into shadow. For a few beats I could still pretty much guess where he was by a combination of experience, intuition, and observation. But that quickly passed, and Triss and I were alone.

Silently, I opened the package and found two items. The first was a Shade stick—a short length of thick wooden rod with numerous holes drilled through it at a variety of angles. It would hold a message or, more likely, a map readable only with the help of a Shade. I put it aside for later perusal.

The second item was a small silver box with a piece of parchment across the latch that said "Do NOT remove the ring." Flipping it open, I exposed a gold signet ring still on the finger that had once worn it. Though I wanted nothing more than to close the box and throw it away—I've killed plenty of people, but the idea of keeping trophies turned my stomach—I forced myself to look at it closely. Where it had connected to the hand someone had attached a thick disk of bone or antler. Both the ring and the disk glowed brightly in magesight. There was a second, much smaller Shade stick tucked in next to the finger.

Grisly little package. Triss extended a tendril of shadow. *Let's see . . . the big stick's a map. The little one's a note about the ring, but I can't tell more without doing this properly and this is neither the time nor the place.*

Shaking my head, I carefully closed the box and rewrapped the little package, tucking it away in my trick bag. We needed to examine the contents more closely, but Triss was right. Then I stripped off my wrist sheaths and dropped them into the bag beside the package. Tomorrow, before we got on the boat I would have to buy some leather so that I could make new straps.

I'd have to be careful not to let Jax see them or the package, or she'd want to know what happened. That would pose a problem, since I wasn't yet willing to tell her about Kelos and didn't think I'd be up to making something up anytime soon. Next, I moved to pulling my swords out of the roof, which proved harder than expected. Kelos was an exceedingly strong man, and I ultimately had to get Triss to help me.

My final Kelos-delivered surprise of the evening came when I tried to pull the wardblack off the wall behind me. It was a clever piece of work, and I wanted to stash it somewhere for later study. But, as soon as it came free of the wards it had kept muffled, it became briefly too hot to touch, and then came apart in a puff of ashes when I dropped it.

All my elaborate planning with Faran went for nothing when

Jax didn't make it home till after I'd gotten back. I told Faran enough of the story to satisfy her curiosity, though I omitted any mention of the finger. Before I could show her the map, Jax came in, deliberately making noise as she opened the roof hatch to let us know she'd arrived. After the others dropped off to sleep, I pulled out the tucker bottle of Kyle's that I'd picked up on the way home and got quietly drunk. Triss didn't say a word.

The day to day of travel is really only interesting to the participants. The riverboat gave the three of us more time to spar and train together, which was going to be key to making things work if Jax ever came clean, or to dealing with her if she didn't, for that matter. It also gave us plenty of time in too-close quarters to get on each other's nerves and inflict loads of mutual misery.

I drank more than I should have and obsessed about Kelos and his mysterious package—which I still hadn't gotten a chance to examine privately in any detail. Jax spent much of her time sinking into an ever more visible slough of despond. Faran sharpened her knives and spent a lot of time staring at the back of Jax's neck. The Shades quietly talked amongst themselves, enjoying the trip far more than their respective bond-mates. Whenever I asked Triss what they were talking about he told me I wouldn't understand. Mostly, I believed him.

It took us nearly three weeks to travel against the current from Ar to the landing stage where the road to Tavan met the river at Fi Township. There, we rented a mule to carry our gear and started walking south. Since horses are my next least favorite way to travel after boats, walking was just fine by me. The road ran between low rolling hills covered with small copses of trees and long stretches of farmland. This part of the Magelands provided the bulk of the food consumed in the big university cities: Ar, Gat, Tavan, Uln, and Har.

Periodically a small town or village straddled the road, and even here, several days travel from the nearest of the universities, magic sparkled and shone a hundred times more densely than anywhere in Tien. The spells were mostly small ones, just as the local mages tended to be hedge witches and petty wizards. But every lock had a keytrue charm and every window a shatternot.

The first night off the boat we stayed at an inn, delighted to have separate rooms and more privacy than at any time since we'd left Tien. That's when Triss and I finally got a chance to examine the package in detail. We started with the big Shade stick.

First, I doused all the lamps in the room but one. Then I held the stick up to the light at an angle that cast its shadow on the wall precisely six feet away. Turning it slowly, I worked until I got the alignment just right, with light passing through two larger holes at either end to make pinpoints of brightness in the shadow. Then Triss flowed down my arm, completely covering the stick in darkness.

Projecting himself into and through the holes, he made cross connections following some formula only the Shades knew, and sketched out a three dimensional line drawing in the air. At its center stood a large multistory building with a half dozen major outbuildings around it, the whole enclosed by a high wall.

Looks like an abbey, I sent rather than said, in case one of the others was listening through the wall.

Yes, almost certainly the one where Loris and the others are being held. We'll have to memorize it.

I nodded. *Is there anything else?*

Yes. He shifted and the abbey faded away to be replaced by densely written text in Kelos's hand but the language of the Shades. *Looks like a list of the abbey's inhabitants, and another of the Signet's current entourage. Do you want me to read it to you?*

Later, after I've got the layout memorized.

Do you want to work on that first? Or should we look at the message that came with the finger?

Finger. Better to get it over with.

I shuddered at the thought of the thing Kelos had given me. Though I knew of a number of peoples who made trophies of their fallen enemies—skulls for cups and the like—it was not something that Blades did. Not sane ones anyway. Knowing Kelos, I doubted that was its main purpose, but I still really hated the idea of touching the thing. With extreme reluctance, I retrieved the box from my bag and opened it.

I can lift it out of there if you'd like, Triss offered.

No, I'll do it. I'm going to have to touch it sometime, and I might as well get it over with now.

I reached down . . . and promptly dropped both box and finger, spilling the latter on the ground along with the smaller Shade stick. I managed not to let out a shriek, but only just. The finger was still warm. Somehow, against all logic and reason, and after three weeks of riding around in my bag, it was still warm.

In fact, it felt exactly as if it were still attached to a living hand.

13

Fear touches everyone. The soldier who panics at the sight of snakes, the torturer afraid of the dark, the murderer who abhors the deep blue sea. No matter how hard you think life has made you, no matter how many lives you've ended, no matter how many darkened alleys you've walked down, you have a breaking point. Apparently, a severed but still living finger was one of mine.

Aral! Triss wrapped himself around my shoulders, a cool but firm presence. *Are you all right?*

I nodded. *I will be. I just wasn't expecting it to still be warm.* I pushed at the finger with my boot tip.

I'm sorry, I should have warned you. I felt it when I first touched it.

It's all right, Triss. How is it . . . no, that's silly. It's magic, of course. But why?

Breathing deeply as I had been taught—by Kelos, ironically—I forced myself to relax. *Calm the body and the mind will follow.* He must have told me that a thousand times.

Once I felt like myself again, I reached down and picked up the finger. It felt disturbingly alive, and it took every shred of discipline I had to turn it so that I could look at the bone disk instead of flinging the damn thing across the room. I was so going to need a drink after this.

A silver nail head centered the disk, presumably driven through and into the bone of the finger on the other side. It was surrounded by a tracery of tiny glyphs and a single word carved in the runic alphabet of Aven—Kelos's name. I had to suppress another shudder at that. Though I hadn't yet parsed the spell's specifics, I instantly knew the only possible reason for Kelos to include his name like that. He had tied the functioning of the spell to the magical force of his own life, his nima.

The vast majority of magic happens in the moment, for the moment. What we call "low magic"—things like magefire, or summoning an item across a room—is the simple manipulation of forces. But even most high magic is temporary. Wards, for example, require regular renewal—weekly or even daily. Things like my thieveslamp or a window's shatternot are longer lasting. They might survive a year or more depending on who casts them, but those, too, will fade without regular renewal.

Permanent enchantments take a lot of power. Far more than any one spellcaster can muster in a single session. They need to be built one step at a time over days or weeks, layering in spell after spell to achieve the desired results. That's for the simplest of things. Greatspells take months or even years to build, though the most powerful sorcerers can collapse the process somewhat and a god can do even more.

Namara had created my temple swords in a seeming instant and those embodied multiple greatspells—though again, there were limits even to what a goddess could do. It was a rare year that saw more than a half dozen Blades become masters. That many usually died as well and their swords returned to the goddess, so she was able to use the power from the old to create the new, more often than not.

There are other ways around the time constraints, for those who are willing to find the price. Blood magic in all its forms is the most obvious. At the darkest extreme of that scale lies necromancy, which uses stolen life force to fuel magic out of all proportion to the caster's strength. What Kelos had done lay at the other end of the same line, tying his own life to a spell in a small but steady draw that would last as long as he did. No one was harmed by it except for Kelos, but it was still blood magic and fundamentally unclean.

Unicorn horn, said Triss.

What?

The bone plug on the end of the finger. It's a segment of unicorn horn. It's been carefully polished. But you can still see the spiral structure if you look closely at the edges, especially down in the bottoms of the glyphs carved around the outside.

I whistled low and quiet. Unicorn horn is fucking expensive, right up there with dragon bones and salamander blood. The original owners are magical creatures of enormous power and homicidal disposition, and they do not look kindly on corpse robbers. Still, I could see why Kelos had chosen it, no better medium existed for spells of vitality. It would make what had been done with this finger much easier to pull off.

Aral! Triss voice rang loud in my mind.

Yes?

Look at the ring.

I'd almost forgotten about it in my revulsion at the thing that wore it. Now, I turned my gaze on the gold signet . . . and nearly dropped the damn finger again. It was a starkly simple design. The band was watermarked in a cloud pattern, but otherwise unremarkable. The seal itself was an oval surrounded by a jagged band of lightning and imprinted with a six-fingered hand—the emblem of Heaven's Hand.

Is this what I think it is? I asked Triss.

I'm pretty sure that it is, but let's see what the Shade stick has to say.

We repeated the process we'd used earlier. This time there was no map, just a page or so of text in Shade. Triss read it, translating for me as he went along.

"Aral,

"This is the ring and finger of Eilif Uvarkas, Signet to the Daughter of Heaven and master of Heaven's Hand in the year 3130. I took his life of my own choice rather than at the command of Namara, though I think she would have ordered his execution soon enough had he lived. He abused his power and he deserved to die.

"This finger is the reason I could not wait for Namara's sanction. Had his life fallen to her decree, his body would have been left as a warning for others and the loss of hand and ring might have come to light. I refused to allow that to happen, sending the body into the everdark and burning a castle to hide its loss. Otherwise, the least response of the Daughter of Heaven would have been to change the spells on all the locks of all the temples of Shan, and that would not have suited my plans.

"As long as this ring stays on this living finger, the bearer has a key that will open any lock in Heaven's mortal kingdom. Do not let it fall into the wrong hands. Do not show it to anyone. I expect its safe return at the end of your present mission for me.

"Kelos."

I looked at the ring and finger again. Kelos had been holding onto this magical skeleton key for almost a hundred years. That led to a whole mess of questions. Like, why did he make it in the first place? And, what was he planning on doing with it when he got it back from me? Or, why trust me with it now?

I didn't think I'd much like any of the answers, though I knew that ultimately I needed to find them. Without saying another word, I put both ring and finger back in their box. The accompanying note from Kelos I destroyed. Then I asked Triss to show me the map again. The abbey was large and complex, and my memory was not what it once was. I knew it would take some hours over several sessions to really set it in my mind.

Fortunately, we spent the next couple of days traveling through populated country and our nights at inns, which gave me the time I needed. Our fourth day on the road found us high on a spur of foothills that came down off the Hurnic Mountains to the west. With so much good land north and east, no one had bothered to colonize these stony ridges, and we were, ourselves, alone and far from any inns or houses when the light started to fail.

The weather was fine and we had nothing to fear from bandits or any but the most fearsome of beasts. So, when we came to a small oak wood, we turned off the road and looked for a good place to lay in a fire and camp for the night. While I got the fire going, the women went out a-hunting. Faran and Ssithra killed a good sized huddle bird, and Jax and Sshayar turned up some lovely fat mushrooms and a few apples that we could roast along with the fowl.

The fire was merry and the Shades took delight in slipping in and out amidst the flickering shadows it created, playing a sort of dancing game of tag—phoenix, tiger, and dragon. The meal was excellent, and wanted only a bottle of wine or whiskey to make a real feast of it. But the small beer didn't taste half bad. After most of a skin—neither Jax nor Faran would touch the stuff despite how weak it was—I felt very nearly relaxed for the first time in more weeks than I cared to count.

I think Faran felt the same way, and we bantered back and forth for quite a while before I noticed that Jax had gone silent. When I shot her a questioning look, she quietly backed away from the fire and shook her head.

"Are you all right?" I asked.

"Stomach's not sitting quite right." She put her hand to her mouth. "I need to go off a bit and deal with it." Before I could say another thing, she turned away and hurried into the darkness beyond the fire.

Faran sat up and looked after her. "Do you think she's going to be all right?"

"No," said Triss. "She's poisoned herself, though it's not the mushrooms she fed you that did the job. It's bottling up fear and guilt and six years of unrelenting anger. I hope she figures out how to let it go before it kills her."

Faran cocked her head to one side. "Can something like that really kill you?"

Triss looked at me in a way that made me very uncomfortable before he spoke, "Oh yes. Not directly perhaps, but there are as many ways to die as there are stars in the night sky. If a person starts looking for their own death, they're bound to find it eventually."

Faran's face creased with a pain I'd seen there too often these last few months, and she turned to stare into the fire. Fifteen and full of bitter memory. I hated to see her hurting but I was too wounded myself to believe anything would help her but time.

She nodded lightly toward the flames. "They started with fire, did you know that?"

"No. I saw the scorch marks in the rubble, of course, but by the time I got there it was far too late to make any sense of the mess." I didn't have to ask what she was talking about—the fall of the temple was still a raw wound for me six years later. "The buildings were all shattered and the rubble had been pushed into the cellars. They'd plowed up the fields and sown salt in the furrows."

Faran nodded. "I saw all that when I went back a year or two after." She closed her eyes tight as a fist. "It started with lightning all around, igniting the orchards and the wheat in the fields. The Storms, of course, though we didn't know it at first. They came at noon and late in the summer when the sun is strong and the Shades are weak. The whole complex was ringed with fire in minutes, miles and miles of fire."

"That's why we couldn't take the little ones to safety," whispered Ssithra. "Between the fire and the sun, the heat and the light were simply too intense for us to do much of anything but hide in our bond-mates's shadows."

"Then the lightning started to fall inside the walls," continued Faran. "Master Tamerlen was leading a few of us toward the main building when she was struck. Her hair caught fire and her eyes boiled. I see it again and again in my dreams. . . . I don't think I'll ever be able to unsee it."

I got up from where I'd been lying with my feet to the fire and walked over to kneel beside Faran, putting a hand on her shoulder. "I'm so sorry I wasn't there." Faran didn't reply, but she did lean her head against my forearm.

"You wouldn't have changed anything, Aral." Jax's voice came from behind me. "You'd have died with so many of the others . . . if you were lucky. If you weren't you'd have been taken by the Hand."

I turned to look over my shoulder, but couldn't see Jax in the darkness. I realized that if Master Kelos were there right now, I wouldn't have hesitated to kill him. How could he have done this to them? To us?

I shook my head and started to answer Jax, "But—"

"But me no buts," she said quietly but firmly. "I know what I'm talking about. I dreamed about how things might have gone differently if you'd been there to help. You and Siri and Kaman. We were short a dozen of our very best that day."

A darker shadow slid out from between the trees, and Jax continued, though she didn't yet show herself. "When they had me on the rack I fantasized about how you all might have changed things, and I hated each and every last one of you for not being there for us."

My throat constricted. "Jax, I . . ." What? What could I say that would make the slightest bit of difference?

"It's all right, Aral. Even then, I knew I was lying to myself, that your presence would have done nothing but increased the body count. I needed the lie then. Needed it for years afterward. I couldn't have done . . . well, a lot of things over the time since then without it. Most especially I couldn't have done what I've been doing since that day at the Gryphon's Head."

She dropped her shroud as she got closer to the fire and to us. "Without lying to myself, I couldn't have lied to you. But I'm done with the lies now. We need to talk."

"It's about damned time!" Sshayar twisted herself out of Jax's shadow and into the shape of a tiger slipping around in front of her. "I thought sure you were going to force Faran into killing you. Or worse, Aral."

"What?" Jax looked completely flabbergasted.

"Oh, Jax, I do despair of humans sometimes. You know how good Aral is, and you've seen a bit of what Faran can do. Did you honestly think that one or both of them wouldn't figure it out given time? I didn't even have to tell them, they already knew."

Jax looked from me to Faran and back again, her expression shocked. "You know that the Hand is using Loris and the others as hostages to force me into betraying Aral to them?"

I nodded.

Jax rolled her eyes. "Then why in the name of all that was once holy have you been sitting here with your faces to the fire and your backs to the shadows and me? And why did you let me feed you mushrooms of unknown provenance?"

I smiled at her, though it wasn't a happy smile. "Because I thought I owed it to you to give you the chance to do what you're doing right now."

"You are a complete and total madman, and infuriating to boot. You do know that, right?"

Triss said, "If he doesn't, it's not for lack of hearing it from me. But really, in this case I agree with him. Sshithra and Sshayar and I have been talking it over, and contrary to Sshayar's worries, none of us would have let you harm each other. We've been quietly trying to figure out amongst the three of us if there wasn't some way we could get you to just get on with your confession so we could start working on a real plan."

"For that matter," said Faran, "we didn't let you feed us strange mushrooms. I very carefully watched you pick them."

"How did you manage to do that without me spotting you?"

Faran grinned and winked, burying her darker side under the brash teenager. "I thought we'd already established that I'm very, very good."

When she'd first appeared in my life I'd wondered which of the two was the mask. But the more time I spent with her, the more I realized that the two faces were equally real. Now I wondered if she'd ever be able to integrate them, or if one must inevitably give way to the other. Then Jax plopped herself down on the ground on Faran's other side and I pushed the question aside.

"All right," said Jax. "I give up. I'm apparently a lousy conspirator and a fool on top of that. So, now what?"

Sshayar put one large paw on Jax's lap and gave her a very hard look.

Jax blushed. "Oh, right. Thank you, Sshayar. Aral, Faran, I'm sorry. I should never have lied to you. I . . . I'd like to make excuses for my choices, but then it's not really an apology. Suffice to say, I fucked up completely."

"Apology accepted for my part." I grinned. "I knew you were a fuckup beforehand, but I'd be a hypocrite if I didn't forgive you that particular flaw. Faran?"

She nodded at Jax. "If you'll forgive me for spending the past month trying to decide exactly where and when I ought to cut your throat, I'm willing to call it even."

"Then, I guess we're going to have a problem," said Jax. "Because you haven't done anything that needs forgiving, and I have."

Faran shrugged and smiled. "Fair enough. You're off the hook as far as I'm concerned."

"Thank you, both of you." Sshayar coughed pointedly, and Jax looked at her and then winced. "Oh, bugger." She turned back our way. "Triss, Ssithra, my profound apologies, both for my behavior and the oversight."

The Shades accepted more gracefully than either Faran or I had, and we settled in to discuss what Jax knew about the abbey where the captured Blades were being held. It would have been the perfect time for me to bring out my map and the signet ring if it weren't for two tiny details.

First, I still didn't trust Jax any farther than I could easily throw her. She'd lied to me too many times and too easily over the last month for me to rely on her word now. Second, I agreed with Kelos that it would distract Jax to know he was still alive. At least, I hoped it was that I agreed with him and not simply that even now I had trouble going against his word. I had good reasons for my choice not to tell her.

I just wished that doing it didn't make me feel like such a bastard.

Shan had dandruff. I found that reassuring. I *knew* that the Emperor of Heaven never manifested himself outside the mother temple at Heaven's Reach, but the dandruff made me *believe* it. It also made me wonder about the devotion of Shan's servants in Tavan.

I wasn't really lying in a bed of dandruff, just the accumulation of dust and other detritus atop the huge sculpture of the god that dominated the temple's sanctum. But the fact that neither the temple's novices nor its servants had bothered to clean the area inside the enormous iron crown for what looked like the last several years, didn't speak well of their piety.

When Jax had checked in with the Sword of Heaven in Tavan she'd received orders demanding a midnight meeting with the Signet. At that point I'd absolutely insisted that I should go in ahead and set up where I could hear the whole meeting and cover her back if she needed it. Jax had resisted, but eventually given in.

Faran had supported me in my argument with Jax, then given me a serious chewing out once she could do so beyond the range of Jax's hearing. I had to argue long and hard before she grudgingly agreed to allow me to go alone. Of course, I was pretty sure that she was lurking somewhere close at hand, in case things went wrong.

I shifted Triss away from my face now and peered down through the gaps created where Shan's irregular stone hair met the lower edge of the iron crown. Nothing below had changed from the last time I'd checked, approximately two minutes ago. Neither had the careful positioning of my blowgun with its preloaded poison dart—I didn't want to have to move much if I needed to shoot someone. Same with my other equipment.

Everything was as ready as I could make it, and fidgeting with it wasn't going to help. I took a couple of slow breaths and for about the dozenth time wished that I had a couple of efik beans I could chew to take the edge off my nerves without dulling my wits. It was an old familiar craving and one I'd managed to beat by substituting booze for beans back when I returned to Tien after the fall of the temple.

It was the worst idea I ever had, and it probably saved my life. In responsible-sized doses, efik was a much less self-destructive sort of habit than alcohol, but the chances of my handling it responsibly were pretty much zero back then. I'd rather be a drunk in the gutter any day of the week than a sleepwalker cutting gashes in my arms so I could pack them with powdered efik and smile my life away in a filthy alley.

Alcohol might be slowly killing me now, but efik would have done for me in a matter of weeks back then. The switch kept me alive then, if for no other reason than how much I initially hated the booze. It took time and real effort for me to get to the place where I *needed* alcohol. Slow suicide is still suicide, but it gives you a lot more time to change your mind along the way.

I was very aware of time at the moment. The great bells of Shan ring on the quarters of the hour. His temples are the arbiters of time in most cities of the eleven kingdoms, though they compete with the universities for that distinction in the Magelands. Here in Shan's sanctum, I could hear the faint gurgles and clunks of the huge water-clock that the timekeepers of Shan used to measure time during the hours when the sun hid its face from the world. Every five minutes it rang a gentle chime, so I knew how long I'd been waiting for the arrival of Jax and the Signet—one hour, thirty minutes, and change.

If the Signet was prompt, I'd have another twenty minutes to contemplate the god's dandruff. If not, at least I'd be able to keep an eye on Jax while the Signet kept her waiting. For perhaps the dozenth time that evening I reached for the efik in my trick bag only to stop my hand halfway there when I remembered. The only efik I carried now was mixed with opium and packed in robin's eggs to make an easily delivered and quick acting knockout drug.

Patience, Aral.

Easy for you to say. What does time mean to a shadow?

Shade, and not all that much in the divisions you normally use. Though, I must admit, your twitching makes me more aware of its passing than usual. I—hold on, the door behind the statue is opening.

I flattened myself even more tightly against the god's stony hair, though I left the hole in front of my face unshrouded. I wanted to see if I could, and I didn't think the risk too great. A moment later, the Signet entered my vision, coming around the sculpture from the right.

Now would be a good time to hold your breath, Triss sent in a mental whisper. *The Signet's Storm is directly above us, and I don't know what it can and can't sense.*

I stopped my breath and slowed my heart as much as I could, which made me miss the efik all the more. With a few beans in me I could have easily gotten my heart rate down as low as thirty beats to the minute, and held my breath for as long as six or eight minutes at the same time. Without it, I would have trouble pushing it down much below forty, and holding my breath past three or four minutes was beyond me.

And the whole effort went for nothing when I felt the statue move beneath me and my heart rate exploded while my focus on not breathing gave way to an effort directed at not screaming.

The god wasn't supposed to manifest anywhere but the mother temple!

14

------◆------

Flesh, like stone. The assassin's art calls for the mastery of stillness in the face of shock or surprise. Even in the face of the impossible. In this case, perversely, stone, like flesh. I forced myself to
stillness as the giant statue on which I lay slowly shifted its position.

Shan had been carved with multiple arms, as the gods usually
were—four in this case, though I had seen sculptures of him with
as many as ten. As the Signet passed around in front of the statue,
she touched the back of her left hand to the cross-legged god's knee.
That's when Shan's lower arms began to move, sliding forward and
down with a dull grinding sound like the world's largest knife being
sharpened. Dust fell from the ceiling here and there, bringing with
it the damp smell of rotting mortar. The whole thing made me want
to shriek like a child and bolt for the exit.

Two things kept me in place. The first was a lifetime's indoctri-
nation in the need for stealth. The second, and far more important
factor, was that the statue didn't *feel* alive. I had witnessed Namara's arrival in her stone avatar many times after I became a full
Blade. The living statue that housed her soul would rise from the
deeps of the sacred lake to give us our assignments or accept our
obeisance after a successful mission.

The bright burning core of that experience was the feeling of
vitality that radiated out from her physical form in every possible
way. When you stood before the goddess you were aware of her
presence in the same way that you were aware of the heat and light
when you stood beneath the summer sun at noon. You couldn't not
know that it was there.

The sculpture of Shan had none of that *presence* to it now. In fact, when I thought to look for it, I could see a strong glow of magic about the arm that moved. The whole statue partook of the spell-light, but everywhere but the arm, it was more like the dim glow of a ghost fungus or honey mushroom. That was deeply reassuring. Divine enchantments, like that on my old temple blades, cast no spell-light. Which meant the statue's motion was driven by mortal magic.

The mill-wheel-like grinding noise should have been another clue, since Namara's statue had always moved with silence more perfect than any living flesh. The grate of stone on stone continued as the sculpture turned its lower hands palms up, bringing six-fingered hands together into a sort of cup. Climbing the toes of Shan's left foot like a set of stairs, the Signet now ascended to the god's knee.

From there she moved to seat herself in the lowered hands, taking possession of the religious throne they had formed. That gave me a perfect shot at the back of her neck—she'd even tied her ice blond hair into a thick braid and pulled it aside. It took a real effort of will on my part not to take the shot.

Do all of Shan's idols do that? Triss asked into my mind.

Maybe. I'd never had an assignment that involved the temple of Shan, and the subject of the other gods hadn't really interested me when it came up in my education. *Jax might know, or Faran, but I've no idea.*

Siri would have. She'd always been more interested in matters theological, which is why she'd ended up with the assignment that earned her the name Mythkiller. Well, that and the fact that she was probably the best mage in the recent history of the temple, Kelos not excepted. So good that she'd been sent to study at the magical university in Uln for a few years after she became a full Blade. She could do things with shadow and spells that made my head hurt to even contemplate.

I'd once seen her step into the shadow of one tree and out of the shadow of another almost twenty yards away. When I'd asked her about it, she said it was a magical effect she'd been experimenting with. Then she went off into a rather abstract explanation that started out with a discussion of the way the fringes of the everdark interacted with normal reality and ended with something she called geometrical mathimagics. My big take-away from the conversation was that she would attempt to teach me to do it if I really wanted her to, but that she didn't think she'd try it again herself since it felt rather like being frozen into a block of burning ice.

I'd never taken her up on it, though I was thinking it would be awfully handy right now if I knew I could use the shadow of the crown as my exit strategy if I needed to. The way the Signet's Storm kept darting here and there around the upper reaches of the temple and poking its scytheblade head into various nooks and crannies left me feeling very exposed.

Jax is here, Triss said into my mind, *near the front door.*

Thanks. I couldn't see that part of the room from where I currently lay, and moving to get a better view seemed like a particularly bad idea at the moment.

She's coming closer now. The Signet either hasn't seen her yet or is ignoring her.

She walked into the narrow semicircle of space I could see clearly, coming slowly toward the seated Signet. She stopped about ten feet short of the double-hand throne and silently glared up at its occupant. If she was at all curious about where I might have set up to keep an eye on things, she didn't betray it by so much as a sidelong glance. All of her attention remained focused on the woman seated above her, even when the Storm flew down to hover behind her.

"You're early," said the Signet.

Jax nodded, but didn't say anything.

"That's good. It speaks of obedience, and you need to learn obedience. I've had time to think over our last encounter, and it wasn't at all satisfactory. Our deal was that you would cooperate with me and none of your people would get hurt. You violated that deal, and there's a price to be paid for breaking your word to Heaven."

Jax stiffened. "What have you done?"

"Nothing irreversible." The Signet reached into her robe and pulled something out, flinging it to the ground at Jax's feet. "Five right ears. If you do exactly as I say going forward, I'll have one of my best leeches regrow them. If you take one more step out of line, the next thing I throw at your feet will be the head of the youngest of the prisoners. I know how you and your lover value your students, so I'll make sure to have her killed in front of Master Loris."

Aral! Triss barked into my mind.

I froze with the blowgun I hadn't even realized I'd picked up, halfway to my lips. Below me, Jax's hands on her sword hilts were shaking. Her face looked very much as I imagined mine must, twisted into a mask by a fury that burned in the blood and bones.

"If you draw your swords, Blade, one of your students will die.

If you or your familiar attempts to harm me, all of them will die, as will you and your lover. If you kill me, the message that spares them will not be sent in the morning and they will die by torture. If you do the slightest thing to make me annoyed with you, I'll harvest you a matching packet of left ears. Do you understand me? A nod will suffice, but it had better happen damned quickly."

At a cost I could only imagine, Jax removed her hands from her swords and nodded her head once.

Are you sure I can't kill the Signet? I asked Triss.

Yesss, he hissed angrily in response—his loss of human speech patterns a clear sign of his own rage. *Too much remainsss at ssstake right now, but sssoon, I hope. Very sssoon, though I think Jax dessservesss firssst rightsss if ssshe wantsss them.*

I can't argue with that.

"Better," said the Signet. "I don't tolerate disobedience from my subordinates, and I certainly won't tolerate it from a slave like you. The only reason you or your precious charges have lived even this long is that the Son himself has ordered that the death of Aral Kingslayer takes precedence over everything else to do with your failed religion."

That left me blinking. What had I done to piss the Son of Heaven off that much recently?

"Here." The Signet pulled a packet from her robes and threw it down beside the string of ears. "Your marching orders. There's a map of the abbey with your route marked out and when you are expected. We set things up exactly as you suggested originally. Deviate one jot from the assigned path and your comrades die. You strike in two nights at moon-dark. Your Kingslayer should like that. Now, get out of my sight."

Jax turned around and walked away almost casually. I wondered how much that feigned nonchalance cost her, and admired her for her ability to pull it off. I don't know if I could have done the same in her place. Nor if I could have stopped myself killing the Signet on the spot. I'd barely been able to hold back with Triss speaking directly into my mind and infinitely less provocation. Loris was never my lover, nor the journeymen my students.

If Faran's ear had fallen on the floor at my feet, could I have walked away like that? What if Jax's had fallen with it? I had my doubts. Only the fact that my fellow Blades' lives depended on the life of the Signet prevented me from killing her even now.

The Signet rose from her throne, and walked down the toes of the great statue. This time I saw her ring of office flash as she touched it to the giant's knee. Flesh, like stone. Again I disciplined myself to stillness as stone moved unnaturally beneath me.

I didn't move until the Signet and her familiar had long since departed the sanctum. Then I rose and, slipping back out the way I had come, I went to find Jax and Faran. We had plans to make and blood to spill.

I caught up with Jax about halfway back to the snug at the inn. Or, maybe I should say, she let me catch up to her. Like all the great cities of the Magelands, Tavan was built around a university and magic was everywhere. Even most of Tavan's thieves were minor sorts of mages, so the chimney highway was rife with tangles and blinds and other sorts of charms designed to confuse the unwary and prevent pursuit.

If Jax had wanted to, she could easily have used that environment to avoid dealing with me till we got back to the snug. Instead, she chose to dawdle along the main route leading from the temple quarter—the Magelanders confined the religious orders to one small area of their city—to the neighborhood that held our temporary snug.

"Jax," I called before I dropped down onto the roof behind her—I didn't want to startle her.

She turned and waited for me to get closer. "You saw?"

I nodded.

"I'm going to make the Hand pay for that, and not just the Signet either."

"I'll help."

"Do you think we can really save them?"

Don't you think we should take this conversation somewhere a little more private? Triss asked.

"Maybe," I said to Jax, "but we shouldn't talk about it here." I looked around for someplace we could speak without being overheard. "Come on." I pointed up to a small water tank on top of a tall apartment block off to our left. "How about there? It's close and it looks as isolated as anything around here."

She raised an eyebrow. "Faran?"

"Can wait till we've had this conversation."

"All right." She frowned but led the way.

Like most such tanks, the top was slightly dished to act as a collector for rain water. Since the building was also the tallest one within a half mile or so, that put the center of the roof out of line of sight for pretty much everything but the university bell tower— over a mile distant. With Triss and Shayar standing guard up at the lip, we had as much privacy as it was possible to have without using magic.

Jax settled into a cross-legged seat. "So, I know why I wanted to have this conversation now and just between the two of us. What about you? Why did *you* want to leave Faran out of it?"

"I could go for the half truth and tell you it's because you so obviously wanted a private conversation. And that I owed it you to honor that desire, since that's true enough."

"But?"

I took a deep breath while I tried to sort out how to tell her about Kelos. "But I have things that I need to talk to you about that are going to be hard enough for both of us without trying to include the junior division."

Jax laughed a bitter little laugh. "I'm not going to like this one little bit, am I?"

"Probably not, no, though it *will* improve our chances of pulling this thing off." I paused before asking, "How could you tell?"

"Because you're wearing the exact same expression you had the day you told me you were breaking our engagement." She straightened her back and shoulders. "Might as well get the hard stuff over with. Hit me."

I reached into my trick bag and pulled out the shade stick. "Here." I handed it across to her.

She turned it in her hands. "Looks like a map, and a fairly complex one, if I'm any judge. What's it for?"

"The abbey where Loris and the others are imprisoned. They're confined in a series of crypts underneath the sanctum. The only practical way in or out goes right under the idol."

Jax held up the map. "So, this is the good news. How did you come by it?"

"That's the bad news."

"I kind of figured. And?"

"Master Kelos gave it to me."

"That's not possible," Jax said flatly. "Kelos is dead. I've seen his name on the obelisk."

"Devin's name is there, too."

"But Devin's a traitor. You told me that yourself."

"So is Kelos. In fact, Kelos is *the* traitor, the one who set us all up."

"That's not possible," she said again. "Kelos could no more betray the goddess than he could cut his own heart out."

"Actually," I said lightly, "if anyone I know could actually manage to cut his own heart out, it'd be Kelos."

Jax ignored my half-assed joke. "It can't be true, Aral. Kelos *was* the order, the bedrock on which all of the rest of us stood."

"He claimed that he was trying to salvage what he could out of an inevitable circumstance. That that's why I wasn't at the temple when it fell. He sent me away along with Siri and Kaman and some of the others, because he knew we would choose to die before we'd take the Son of Heaven's deal. He wanted to save us for later use."

Jax's face slowly twisted into the same hate-filled expression I'd seen in the temple of Shan earlier. "You're serious, aren't you?"

"I wish to everything I ever once held as holy that I weren't. . . ."

"Then it's all his fault. The death of the goddess. The fall of the temple. All the ones we've lost then and since. Kaman, Tamerlen, Viera. My torture. The wreck you've made of yourself. Even what's happening to Loris right now. It's all down to Kelos, and you're working with him now?" Jax leaped to her feet and leaned down over me.

She's going to hit you. Triss's mental voice sounded dry, almost detached.

I know.

And then she did, a full-armed backhanded slap intended to inflict maximum pain without causing real harm. I rolled with the blow, but it still stung and it would probably bruise. It was exactly the same way she'd hit me when I broke our engagement. It told me two things. First, she was really mad at me. Second, she was fundamentally still in control of herself. She knew what she wanted to do to me and how far she wanted to go, and she'd chosen the exact tool she wanted to accomplish that task.

"Feel any better?" I asked. I kept my voice calm because I knew it would irritate her.

"No! And you're an asshole, you know that, right?"

"You're certainly not the first to say so. Are you going to hit me again?"

"No. I'm sorry, that was a stupid move."

"See, I told you she could be taught," Sshayar said from her place up on the lip of the water tank.

"And fuck you, too, dear," replied Jax, this time without the heat, then she laughed.

Quick to anger. Quick to cool down. Quick to move on to the next step. That was Jax all the way, and that's why I'd pushed her. I wanted her to hit the top and bounce back so we could move on. I wasn't one jot less furious than she was, but we didn't have time to waste on theatrics.

She flopped back down on the roof and gave me a hard look. "Don't think I didn't see what you just did there. You used to do the same damn thing when we were engaged. On the upside, the make-up sex generally made up for how much that calm mask thing you do used to piss me off. Do you ever miss that? What we had together."

"No," I lied, pushing aside memories of Jax naked and wanting to make up for the bad times. It wasn't easy. "I don't."

"You're lying."

"Probably," I agreed. "But it's still true. Can we talk about how we're going to make the Hand pay for what they've done?"

"Soon. You still haven't explained why you're working with the man who destroyed us. I'm not doing anything till you answer that."

"I think the Son of Heaven and his god probably have to take some of the blame for the fall of the temple, too."

"But Kelos was complicit. Without him . . ."

"Maybe." I held out my hands like balances. "I don't honestly know what would have happened if he'd tried to stop things dead instead of cutting a deal."

"You're starting to piss me off again. Answer the fucking question, Aral."

"I'm not working with him. I'm using him. I'm taking his help to do something I was going to do anyway."

"Don't give me weasel words. That's not what I'm asking, and you know it."

"Fine. I'm doing it because I don't see that I have a lot of choice. When I drew on him, he knocked me down and disarmed me as easily as I might do the same to some back-alley pinch-purse. He's *the* master, Jax. If he wants to help us, I'm not seeing any good way to get him out of the picture. Unless *you* think you can take him?"

Jax shook her head. "Of course not."

"Well then, what do you want me to do? Throw away the map? Give up the other advantages his help can give us in getting Loris and the others free?"

"No." She looked at her feet.

"How about blowing off the mission completely and letting them all die? Would that be better? Because that's the only other fucking option we have!"

I bounced to my feet and started to pace in a tight little circle.

"Do you think I like that fact that when he called me I came to him like a dog? Do you think I like that I can't figure out how I should feel about the man who was the closest thing I had to a father? Do you think I like the fact that I don't have any clue if I'm doing this because he's our best chance, or just because it's Kelos telling me to do it? Because I sure as shit don't like any of it one tiny fucking bit!"

"Old man, you need to get a hold of yourself or you're going to wake the whole damned neighborhood." The familiar voice came up from somewhere below us.

"Little monster," I sighed. "Get your ass up here, Faran. How much have you heard?"

"Pretty much everything after the slap." She pulled herself up over the lip of the tank. "I figured that you'd both be hot enough for a bit then that you wouldn't hear my getting in close."

"Triss?"

"She's damned good. I didn't so much as catch a hint of her."

"Me either," agreed Sshayar.

"Have you told her about the finger yet?" Faran asked as she took a seat a few feet to Jax's left.

"No. Just the map. As I recall, I didn't tell you about the finger yet either."

She shook her head sadly. "That's right. I had to pick your pouch to find it, and I'm really quite hurt about that."

"I don't think I beat you enough. You are a most disobedient sort of apprentice."

"Probably because I'm only your apprentice for the assassin stuff. Where it comes to spying, I kick your ass."

I looked at Jax. "Are your students like this?"

She smiled. "Only the very best of them. Come on, Aral. Don't pull that obedience line with me. I know what kinds of crap you used to get up to. In fact, I'm pretty sure that you broke about six dozen rules by sneaking out to the sacred island and asking Namara to give you the Ashvik assignment a year before you were slated to become a full Blade. That was right before you vanished into the night without a word to anyone including the council, right?"

"I can verify that," said Triss. "Though, Master Kelos did wish us good hunting, and Devin knew about it even before we went out to the island."

"Thanks, Triss." I sighed. "Can we move on now?"

"Sure," replied Jax. "You were just going to tell me about the *finger.*"

"Oh good," said Faran. "I've been wondering about it for days now. I mean, I've seen it. And I think I can guess what it's for, but if there were instructions that came with it, somebody destroyed them before I got a chance to read them."

I told them about the ring and what it could do, and while I was at it, I told them about the moving statue, and brought Faran up to date on what had happened at the temple. When I was done, they both wanted to see the finger. So I pulled out the box and opened it up.

"Damn," said Jax. "That could come in very handy." She poked it with the tip of her own finger and shuddered.

Jax didn't like touching it any more than I did, but Faran blithely reached over and pulled it out of its box, turning it this way and that to get a better look at the glyphs. She seemed completely blasé about the idea of a living finger preserved a hundred years after the death of the hand that had once worn it.

"That's one tricky little spell," she said after a moment. "I'm sure I could replicate it easy enough, but I don't know if I'd be able to cook it up from scratch." She shrugged. "No surprise, I guess. After Master Siri, Master Kelos was always the one who taught us the most about practical magic."

"That's a hit," said Jax touching a fingertip to her chest. "Point, Faran."

"Huh?" Faran canted her head to one side quizzically. "What'd I do?"

"You just made me feel incredibly old," replied Jax. "Siri is nearly a year younger than I am. No one should ever refer to her as Master Siri with the same tone as they refer to Master Kelos when talking about their teachers. It's wrong."

"Weird." Faran looked genuinely puzzled. "I can't imagine that. You all looked pretty much the same age from where I was sitting in those days. You know . . . old."

Jax's eyes widened and she started to open her mouth. Then she paused and scowled for a moment. "You're pulling my leg aren't you?"

Faran held her wide-eyed innocent look for one more beat, then dropped it for a wicked smile.

"No wonder you call her little monster," Jax growled at me.

"Oh come on," said Faran. "It was a fair point." She jabbed the Signet's finger at Jax for emphasis. "I mean, you *are* old, right? Maybe not as old as Aral, but then, he's half as old as Kelos."

"Not yet thirty!" I said.

"Children, please." Triss plucked the finger from Faran's hand and put it back in its box. "We've got things to plan. If we're done with the show-and-tell part of the evening, maybe we could move on to the main event?"

"I don't know how much planning we have time for," I replied. "The Hand will be expecting us the night after next. If we're going to have any chance at taking them by surprise we'll have to hit them tomorrow, and without surprise the hostages are all dead."

"Point." Jax's voice was grim. "We know the where, and our window really narrows down the when. We might manage a bit of extra surprise by coming in during the day, but that would cost us too much of our Shades's strength. It's still summer, which cuts down the available hours of full dark, and it's going to take at least a couple of hours to manage the job. So, sometime between full dark and the first hour after midnight."

"Agreed." Faran nodded. "These are the people who killed Namara and the order and they've taken people we care about, so there's no question of tactics. We kill everyone we see without hesitation or mercy. What's left to discuss; which door we use?"

"That and who goes for the prisoners," I replied.

"You do," Jax and Faran said in near perfect unison.

"Why me?"

"Loris is my lover and the others are my students," said Jax. "That's going to make my thinking less clear overall, and more so as I get closer to them. I *want* to be the one to free them, and we both know that means I'll be less professional and more likely to get them or us killed."

She closed her eyes for a second and her jaw muscles tightened. "It also means that if something goes wrong and someone dies, I'm going to regret it forever. I'd take point if I had to, but I don't know if I can hold it together if everything goes to hell. Not after what I went through when the temple fell. That puts me on eliminating the reinforcements duty."

I nodded, and didn't add that if things went to shit, it'd probably be better for her to have someone else to blame. Me, for example. "Faran?"

"You're too sentimental. You don't really like killing people who aren't directly in the way. If you're going after the hostages, everyone you meet will be directly in the way, and you won't think twice. But someone's going to have to do clean up on the periphery.

That's going to involve cutting a lot of not obviously guilty throats. I won't hesitate. You might. End of story."

"I guess that means I'm going after the hostages."

"And we'll make corpses," said Jax, and there was a cold fire in her eyes. "Lots and lots of corpses."

15

---·◆·---

K illing people. It's what I do best, my art as well as my craft. It's not nice. It's not pretty. It's not romantic. Any number of times I've found myself wishing for a world where it wasn't so often necessary. But in the end, I'm an assassin, one of the best, and I love my work even when I don't like it. But these were the people who'd destroyed the temple, some of them had killed people I loved. This time I would get to do both.

We arrived outside the high stone walls of the abbey just as the trailing edge of the sun kissed the horizon good-bye. We'd spent much of the day in a coach, which had allowed Faran and Jax time to memorize the map along the way, and Ssithra and Sshayar time to make copies just in case. We'd left the coach hidden in a ruined barn a few miles back, with the coachman inside wrapped in spells of sleep.

With sunrise, the spells would fade and he would be able to depart the barn with a much heavier purse. If anyone touched him or the barn before then, the whole place and all its contents would burn away to nothing in an instant.

"Last check," said a dragon-form Triss. "Everyone know what they're doing?

"We go in through the escape tunnel that comes out in the southwest tower," I said. It was about a third of the way around the abbey from the route that had been picked out for Jax and me by the Signet. "The ring opens the doors and the wards for us. There'll almost certainly be a guard in the tunnel proper." Under normal operations, there wouldn't have been, to help preserve the route's secrecy. But with the nature of the current situation, they'd have a trusted noncom down there.

"If we're lucky," I continued, "it'll be one of the Swords of Heaven, and he'll have some sort of alarm ward on him triggered by death because he'll be out of touch with the main perimeter. If we're not lucky, we'll be facing a member of the Hand. In either case, they go down, and they die as soon as we silence any death wards. Then we split up."

Blades rarely work together in close proximity. In the vast majority of situations over the many centuries of our history one of us has usually been enough to get the job done. Beyond that, our greatest asset is stealth. Working as a team throws a significant portion of that advantage away.

When you're functionally invisible, visual signals don't do you a lot of good. Add in that people tend to notice it when the shadows start talking to each other, and any attempt at communication significantly compromises your effectiveness. Shades can communicate silently to a degree, but with the lone exception of Triss and myself, that communication doesn't extend to their bond-mates.

Also, when you can't see your compatriots, you are much more likely to accidentally hit one with something lethal. So, on those rare occasions where it becomes necessary to act together, we generally prefer to split up and spread out. It preserves our advantages and reduces the chances of killing one another.

"Once we make the split, I'll take the most direct route possible to the crypt," I continued. "Depending on who and what Triss and I run into, I hope to have the first cell open somewhere between twenty and forty minutes from now. I'll arm the prisoners and we'll start cutting our way out. Once we're clear of the main building, I'll light things up to let you know we've made it."

"I'll start by heading back to the wall and clearing out the perimeter guards on this side of the abbey." Faran smiled a nasty little smile and Ssithra flexed shadowy phoenix claws. "Call it twenty minutes if nothing goes awry. Then I'll work my way inward with a goal of leaving you a wide-open path to freedom."

Jax rolled her shoulders to loosen the thick pack hung from her sword rig, while Sshayar stalked back and forth behind her looking every inch the hunting tiger. "I'll go straight for the guesthouse and set glyphs of destruction on the main supports and bindings on the doors. That's where the Hand will be quartered. Once we've prepared the way, Sshayar and I will bring the building down and try to kill the lot of them in their sleep. I'd prefer to slit throats, but . . ."

I nodded. For every Storm that died with their bond-mate, the weather was likely to get that much worse. That was going to wake people up sooner rather than later, which is why we'd picked up the destruction wards. That was one place where having this go down in the Magelands made our lives much easier. The destruction glyphs were devilishly tricky to make, and damned expensive.

Jax's brother was going to have palpitations when he saw the bill for that, but we'd had no choice. None of us had the skills to make them in quantity, even if we'd had the leisure. Time had foreclosed the theft option as well, that kind of play took serious planning. One useful side effect of the truly horrendous weather the destruction of the Storms was going to bring down on us was that it would make for a hell of a distraction once it hit.

Triss flexed his wings and looked at us all very seriously. "And if anything goes wrong?"

Jax snorted. "If it happens before Aral's signal, I try to make sure that if I die, I do it very quietly and take the bastards with me."

"Likewise," said Faran.

"I blow the roof off and holler for help," I added.

"Then we're off." Triss nodded and then collapsed back into my shadow.

From there he climbed my body, briefly covering me in a chilly skin of shadow before blossoming outward into a full shroud of darkness. The others followed suit, and we headed for the concealed entrance to the tunnel. According to our map, it was hidden in a rough outcropping of rocks in the side of a deep-carved creek bed that ran parallel to the nearer wall of the abbey.

We probably could have gotten in over the wall undetected, though it stood a good fifteen feet, and had both spikes and obvious wards protecting it. Those defenses were the kind of things that Blades dealt with all the time, and the abbey had been built more with an eye to holding off the occasional bandit attack or rampaging manticore than a group of assassins. But the tunnel had two major advantages.

First, it would get us past the outer wall and into the very heart of the abbey in one step. Second, the over-the-wall route was the way we were supposed to come in tomorrow, which meant there might well be extra layers of defensive spells in place at the moment.

"They really did a good job on this," Jax whispered when I finally came to a stop in front of a slightly higher section of the creek bank.

Without the map and accompanying instructions we'd never have found the spot. Even with it, I couldn't be positive we'd gotten it right until I actually got the door open. I reluctantly slipped the warm finger out of the little pouch I'd hung on the straps of my sword rig at chest level—I wanted it quickly and easily accessible.

Suppressing a desire to "accidentally" lose the awful thing in the stream, I stuck the finger and my whole arm into a deep hole half-concealed by the root of an old oak. It had a shallow bend about eight inches in, that prevented anyone from seeing the spell-light from the ward that was supposed to be at the back of the hole.

"I hope we've got the right spot and nothing poisonous has moved in since the last time someone did this," I said.

"Don't be such a worrier," said Faran. "There'll be a nest-not ward to keep the creepy crawlies out." She laughed. "Well, there will if you're sticking your arm in the right hole. If not, I'm sure we've got some antivenom around here somewhere."

"*Very* reassuring," I grumbled with my cheek pressed against the stone. "Why don't you stick your advice where . . ." But then there was a faint but definite sense of magical contact as I poked around the back of the hole with the severed finger. "I think I just got it."

"Yeah, we can tell." That was Jax. "I'm impressed."

"What?" I craned my neck back to see what she was talking about but didn't pull the ring out yet. "Oh. Wow. That *is* impressive."

Without making any noise or giving any other sign, a portion of the rock face had simply vanished. That bit wasn't all that unheard of. The fact that the door lay mostly below the stream's surface on the other hand . . .

About two feet of the low stone archway stuck up above the waterline. The rest extended down to the floor of the streambed. Opening the door should have filled the tunnel with water. It probably would have, too, if we hadn't used the Signet's finger or some other authorized magical key to open it—I imagined that the abbot's ring would have worked as well.

But not only was the water not pouring in across the threshold, it was actually flowing away from the hole in a very definite pattern. One that formed a flight of liquid steps leading down to the entrance. The entire shallow stairwell shone with a deep blue spell-light.

"Do you think we can actually walk on the stairs?" Jax asked rather dubiously.

"One way to find out." Faran jumped lightly down onto the top step . . . and didn't go through. "Huh." She scampered down the five remaining liquid stairs to the entrance. "Feels a bit like walking on planks laid over mud. I'll go ahead and look for guards."

Before either of us could say a word, she was gone.

"Jax," I said.

"I know, go after her." Then she, too, jumped down to the watery stairs and vanished.

"I sure hope this thing stays open for a while after I pull the ring away from the seal," I said aloud.

It wouldn't be a very well-designed spell if it didn't, Triss replied into my mind. *This is a very pretty piece of magic, I doubt they'd flub the exit.*

You're probably right.

No, I'm always right.

Smug shadow.

Silly human.

I think Faran might be a bad influence on you, Triss.

Just do it.

All right. I pulled the finger free of the seal and jumped down to follow the others.

The stairs did indeed feel like planks over mud, and I very much wished I had time to study the spell that made it work. But I kept picturing them suddenly collapsing, or the stone wall reappearing before I'd gotten all the way through the gap, so I hurried. I needn't have worried though. There was a rather obvious seal of opening and closing a few yards into the tunnel. When I touched the ring and finger to the seal, the dim light filtering in through the doorway abruptly went away. Hell of an enchantment that.

I took control of Triss so that I could use his senses to suss out the lay of the land. The tunnel was perhaps seven feet tall by three wide, and rough finished. From the entrance it sloped down and away from me in a none-too-straight line.

Jax and Faran were nowhere in evidence, but there was only one direction they could have gone. Adjusting the slender but heavy pack I'd strapped between the sheaths of my swords—it held weapons for our imprisoned brethren—I headed down into the dark after the women. I caught up to them after perhaps a quarter mile, at a sharp bend.

"About time you got here," said Jax when I came around the corner. She was waiting with her back against the wall, swords drawn.

"Finger," said Faran. She was squatting on the floor hunched over a cocoon of shadow, just beyond Jax.

I pulled the finger out of its pouch and leaned forward to hand it to her. She glanced back and neatly snatched it. Once she had the finger in hand, she pressed it against something inside the dark cocoon Ssithra had spun for her.

"Yes! It works." She pulled the finger free and handed it back to me.

Her shoulders bunched briefly, as though she were making some physical effort. In response, the cocoon gave a single pulse before flowing back to hide Faran in a lacuna of shadow once again. It left behind the body of a young man in the uniform of Heaven's Sword. A corporal, dying now as blood poured from his freshly torn out throat. Faran touched a dull brass badge pinned to his chest.

"Death ward, and completely deactivated by the old Signet's signet. That's a hell of a toy Master Kelos loaned you. I'm glad you're willing to share it with the other children."

I blinked several times—though no one could see it through my shroud. A sudden sense of wrongness was tugging at my mind. This magical key Kelos had given me went way beyond toy. Too far. The Shade stick would have been sufficient to set us up for this mission. More than sufficient. With a full map of the abbey showing all the modifications the Hand had made to hold our fellow Blades prisoner and three of us to carry out the task, we didn't really need the finger.

Oh, it would make things a good bit easier, but the most likely ways this could go wrong had never been about getting through the locks and wards. If we failed, it would be because we ran afoul of a too-alert Hand or Sword, not because bypassing some warded door took us an extra minute to open silently without the key.

So, if we didn't absolutely need the finger to make this work, why had Kelos loaned it to me? What did he want me to do with the finger that I couldn't do without it? He had to have a damned good reason to give me such a powerful tool to use against his new masters. Unfortunately, I couldn't for the life of me figure out what he wanted or why he wanted it. At least, not now, with the fate of so many of our remaining brethren at stake and precious minutes dripping away into the dark.

"Aral?" Jax touched my shoulder through the shadows that surrounded us both. "Are you all right? Because you didn't respond the first time I spoke your name."

"Sorry. Just thinking."

"About Kelos," she stated flatly. "And what his game might be.

I've been wondering that, too, from the first moment I found out about his involvement." There was a definite reproach there. "But we can't worry about it right now."

"Can we afford to wait?" I countered. "What if he's setting us up for something right here, right now?"

"Then we're fucked," she said. "This is our one chance to get the others out alive. If we don't take it, they die. The Signet's deal has always been a lie, and tomorrow is too late."

"I know. But it just feels like we're walking into a trap."

"At least today's trap, if there is one, belongs to Kelos and not the Signet. Kelos wants something more than seeing us all dead, and that's a hell of a lot better than the Signet's vision."

She was right, and I knew it, but that didn't make my misgivings one little bit easier to bear.

"Come on, Aral, we've got to go on. Faran's already well ahead of us."

Jax didn't say anything more, and in the total darkness her shrouded presence was invisible even through Triss's borrowed senses. But I could feel her absence as she headed on down the tunnel. I followed after, wondering with every step what Kelos was up to, and coming up empty again and again, no matter how I looked at things. The passage ended at a narrow spiral stair where Faran waited for us with obvious impatience, her head unshrouded and a frown pursing her lips.

"About time," she said when I pulled my own shroud aside to let her see me.

"I'll go first," I said, holding up the finger.

Her frown deepened, but she turned sideways to let me pass, reshrouding behind me. There was another magical seal on the left hand wall at to the top of the stairs.

I turned to where I knew Faran must be standing behind me. "Did the guard have a token or a ring of some sort? I didn't see one."

"No, but I found a lunch sack, and a bottle of small beer tucked under the stairs. This clearly isn't a general use sort of escape tunnel, the Signet or the Abbot probably locked him in for the duration of his guard shift. The bottle was unopened and the sack full, so I don't think anyone's going to miss him soon."

"Good."

I released my hold on Triss and asked, *I don't see any cracks here, do you?* I was hoping that with his better command of Shade senses he'd see something I missed.

No, he replied. *No gaps at all. Same as at the other end. We're going to have to go through blind.*

"I'm going to open the door in a moment here. The map shows it opening into a meditation chamber in the library basement. Hopefully it's empty."

"If not, I've got it," said Faran, sliding up next to me.

"Then, in three, two, one . . ."

I touched the ring to the seal and the wall in front of me abruptly vanished. I felt Faran move past me into the room beyond.

"Clear," she whispered an instant later, not that I needed her reassurance.

The room was maybe seven feet across and shaped like an inverted bowl with a low domed ceiling of polished stone. The only things in it were a couple of carefully rolled prayer mats and a small hemispherical magelamp affixed to the exact center of the ceiling. The latter was currently shuttered, leaving the room in a near-total darkness. Only the dimmest thread of light showed at the base of a door a quarter of the way around the circle from where I stood.

A moment later, that line of light abruptly vanished, occluded by Faran's shroud. "I don't hear anything through the door. Shall I move forward?"

"Not yet," I replied. "I want to find the door seal on this side so we can close the tunnel."

"Gotta be in the lamp," said Jax, as she slipped past me as well. "Faran, keep the door shrouded. I'm going to open the shutters and have a look-see."

I braced myself, but even so, the bright white magelight hammered at my borrowed senses. After the near total darkness of the tunnel, the light smashed into the matrix of Triss's being in a quasi-physical way, forcing me to contract the area enveloped in the stuff of shadow. It took a good five beats of my heart for me to recover enough from the impact to really look at the magelight in any meaningful way. It was a particularly intense enchantment, blazing both with spell-light and the light of the world. Try as I might, I simply couldn't see inside the lamp.

"Damn, that's bright," said Faran.

"Too bright," replied Jax. "Though I bet several of the other meditation chambers are just as brightly lit to cover for this one. Hang on a second. . . ."

Her right arm abruptly emerged from the darkness of her shroud, and she stuck her hand in through one of the gaps in the rotating shutter of the lamp. The quality of the light changed as she covered the stone holding the enchantment with her hand, going dim and red. I stepped in close, and the comparative darkness allowed me to see another seal. This one was etched into the stone of the ceiling above the light proper. I used it to close the tunnel behind us.

Jax doused the light. "Everyone ready?"

"Of course," replied Faran.

"Yes." I drew my swords and resumed full control over Triss. This was going to be messy and bloody and the chances that there would be at least one or two fewer Blades in the world at the end of the night were very good.

"Then," said Jax, "Faran, if you'd be so kind as to get the door, we move. Aral goes first."

The door squealed as it opened, and I silently cursed as I ducked through. A monk was walking through the dimly lit hallway beyond. I took his head off before he finished turning to see who might be coming out of the meditation chamber. Without pausing, I leaped over his falling body and headed for the far stairs. Jax went for the nearer set that went past the passage that led to the abbot's house and thence to the guest complex.

Behind me, I saw the pale ball of the monk's head vanish into Faran's shroud as she picked it up and tossed it into the meditation chamber. I was just ducking through the arch that led to the stairs when Triss's senses showed me a dim flare of spell-light along the floor back by the door—Ssithra cleaning away the blood I'd spilled. Then I was fully on my own.

I went up two flights, passing another arch. Beyond it I could smell old leather and dust and all the other scents of a lot of books crammed into a confined area. I couldn't help but smile. At the next landing, I unlatched the window shutters above a reading bench and stepped through into the night. It was a short drop, no more than ten feet, and ended in grass instead of cobbles—part of my reason for choosing this route. I had to take the shock with my knees because my pack precluded rolling out of the fall.

"Who's there?" Another monk stepped out of the shadows beneath a willow, his too-wide eyes showing white in the pale mage-lanterns that stood at the corners of the small courtyard.

Dammit. I smelled the rum on his breath as I slid forward to break his neck and I paused. He didn't see me, and I twisted aside without touching him. His corpse would tell a much more believable tale than anything he might say to a guard this side of morning, so I let him live and moved on across the courtyard.

On the far side I turned into a narrow paved way that ran between the locutory and the chapterhouse. The latter abutted the temple proper and helped support the larger building, so I went up one of the buttresses between two windows as soon as I left the courtyard.

From there I catfooted my way around the edge of the domed roof to the larger building where I killed a guard by slicing his throat. As I wedged him down into the darkest corner I could find, I glanced up the side of the temple while I decided my next move. The shortest path from here to the crypts went through the clerestory windows that lighted the sanctum, two floors above me. But there was certain to be some sort of guard on watch up among the bells in the tower.

If the guard in the tower was a Sword or Swords, it made sense for me to take the extra time to kill them and disable the bells. If it was one of the Hand, I couldn't afford to kill them now, for fear the death of their Storm would give warning of our presence. I hadn't yet decided when my ears popped and I felt a sudden chill breeze come rolling down from the western hills.

In response, lightning flashed in the tower above and a cloud-winged wheel of dark fire slipped out through the windows. Hand then, and nothing I could do about it. I braced myself in the shadowy corner between a buttress and the wall and started climbing as quickly as I could. I hoped the extra darkness there would hide me from the aroused Storm above, because I didn't have the time to do this gentle and quiet anymore.

Someone had started the killing before I was in position—probably Faran and probably not willingly. I didn't think it was Jax because I hadn't heard the sounds of a building coming apart. She'd had enough time to get at least some of the destruction glyphs in place by now, and I couldn't see her going for half measures in her current state.

I was just coming up on the level of the clerestories when two things happened at once: A tremendous boom and crash sounded from the far side of the temple as the guesthouse came apart and took our plan with it. The Storm above dropped straight down toward me, the fiery wheel that formed its body spinning wildly between lightning laced wings.

16

Indecision is a luxury for the quiet times. If you let it become more than that, it will kill you.

Kelos had taught me: "Think ahead, act in the moment, dither later." In the split second I had left, I made the only choice that had any chance of keeping me alive. It might have been a stupid choice, but it was all that I had.

As the Storm dove on me from the bell tower, I discarded my shroud, collapsing the cloud of shadow-stuff down into a tight, quasi-solid ball haloing my left hand. With one foot braced on the buttress and the other wedged into the interstice between two of the huge stones that formed the temple wall, I reached my shadowed hand back to the hilt of the sword resting against my hip.

Leaning far out from the corner to give myself the room I needed, I drew the sword with a sharp snapping motion. The point dropped down in the beginning of a circle that took it past my ankle and then up and around to intersect the path of the diving Storm. I could feel myself overbalance as the sword came up past waist level—had known that was inevitable. I ignored the warnings of my stomach and my inner ear as I began to fall outward. Focusing my will on the sword and the shadow, I sent the head-sized ball of darkness up the length of my blade, which threw me even more out of balance.

Storm met shadow four feet over my head with an impact that drove me down and back into the wall. The base of my skull hit the hilts of the swords in my pack so hard that the whole world flashed bright purple for an instant. I ignored the pain and the way my right foot had started to slip, concentrating everything I had on that ball of shadow. It was pressed against the hub of the burning wheel that formed the central matrix of the Storm's physical form. With an effort that felt like it might tear a hole in my mind, I contracted the shadow sharply, folding it into a pinpoint and twisting. . . .

A giant pillar of lightning connected the sky and the earth, punching a burning hole through the dome of the chapterhouse. The noise and the light came as one, so close I could feel the heat. The thunder hit me like a giant's slap, shattering what was left of my hold on Triss. My right foot finished losing its toehold, and I pivoted into a weak jump, kicking off the buttress with my left. I caught the sill of the clerestory with my right hand as I smacked into the stones.

For a brief instant I dangled there, one-handed. Then, as I started to slip, I let my sword go and brought my other hand up and around. All the while I expected to catch a burst of lightning in the spine.

It wasn't until I was pulling myself onto the window ledge amidst the first spatters of rain that I had time to realize my gamble had worked. I would live at least a little longer. But with our presence now revealed, I had to move fast or the hostages wouldn't.

Triss? I sent, but there was no response.

That worried me more than a little, but I couldn't do anything about it. Not until I got my ass out of the gigantic storm that was about to hit and into some kind of shelter. As I started in on breaking the window, I quickly reviewed what I had just done, trying to set the memory in case I ever had to do something like it again. Shades are elemental in nature like the great dragons or salamanders. That makes them into a sort of living gateway to the everdark, the elemental plane of night.

A year ago, I had seen Triss open that gate in a fit of rage, sending men who had tortured me through it, into the dark and the cold beyond. It was probably the scariest thing I'd ever seen a Shade do, and to this day I didn't fully understand how it worked. That hadn't stopped me from trying to replicate the process.

I'm not much of a sorcerer. Oh, I can follow directions on the complex stuff and I do well enough with the basics of low magic like magefire and magelightning, but I'd known that none of that was going to hurt a Storm. Hell, most rough magic would probably just feed the thing. But I'd seen how Sshayar had taken on the Signet's Storm, and I figured that if I could pull something fancy with shadow magic, I might live to see tomorrow. And it had worked. I'd sent an eight-inch sphere of the Storm into the everdark, tearing a giant hole in its chest and killing it instantly.

The aftereffects of that death and those that had occurred when Jax took down the guesthouse had begun with the pillar of light-ning. The rain, which had opened with a pitter-patter only seconds ago, was already rising into an icy and continuous hammering like a barrage of sling stones, while the building winds tried to tear me free of the ledge.

I wasn't done with the many-paned window, but if I stayed out-side much longer I was going to take a long fall. Beyond that, I still had to get to the prisoners as quickly as I could. So I forced my head and shoulders through the jagged-edged and too-small hole, picking up a number of nasty gashes along the way.

What the hell? Triss's mental voice sounded muzzy and con-fused as I glanced around the dimly lit sanctum I was entering.

I was delighted and relieved to hear from him, but didn't have time to answer. *Later,* I sent as I pulled my feet free of the hole in the glass, pivoting into a momentary handstand on the inner ledge. *Right now, I need a skin!*

Triss didn't respond in words, just wrapped himself around me as he released his will once more. The cool shadows took the worst sting from my cuts and scrapes as they slithered over my skin. It felt wonderful, and I wished I had the leisure to enjoy the sensation, but I was already tipping forward and letting go. I somersaulted into empty space forty feet above the floor of the sanctum, spinning myself dark wings to break my fall as I went.

The window exploded above and behind me as a burst of light-ning hit it from somewhere on the far side of the huge space—another Storm somewhere within the sanctum. Expected but wholly unwel-come. I half folded my left arm in response, partially collapsing the shadow wing it scaffolded, and sending me into a sharp spiraling downward turn. The next bolt sizzled through the space I'd have occupied if I'd continued my forward glide.

I hit the floor hard as I finished something that was not quite a straight forty-foot fall but well short of the gentle glide I'd originally intended. I let myself collapse, calf-knee-hip-ribs-shoulder, since the bag of swords on my back made a forward roll impossible. It hurt, but I didn't quite break any bones, so I had to call that a win. I rolled onto my chest and got my hands under me just as something came down on the small of my back with the metallic clash of steel on steel. Most likely a sword or an axe. Judging by the impact, it would probably have sliced me in half if it hadn't hit the blades in my pack.

The angle of the blow told me where to look for my attacker, and a glance to my right confirmed the presence of a pair of darkly clad feet and legs. I released Triss then—hoping he could give me some cover—as I snapped my right arm, sending the dagger from my wrist sheath into my hand.

Before I could do anything with my dagger, Triss shrieked in pain and my opponent's blade—an axe, glowing with spell-light—smashed into the stone of the floor a few inches above my head. Triss must have deflected it just enough, but at what cost I couldn't say. Sparks flew where the steel met the flags. I could hear a woman swearing in the tongue of Heaven's Reach, as the missed strike put her momentarily off balance. Twisting as far as my pack would allow, I drove my dagger sideways into the woman's foot, hitting just below the ankle bone and sliding back to sever the big tendon above the heel.

She screamed and her leg collapsed under her, so that she fell across my shoulders and head. I heard the axe striking the flags again as she came down on my back, though this time I didn't see where it hit. Lightning shattered stone off to my left, peppering my side with shards that bit and burned, but the Storm hadn't dared to strike me directly. Not while I was so tightly intertwined with its bond-mate. Before it, or she, could move again, I half rolled onto my left shoulder and flicked my wrist to put that dagger in my hand. Stabbing up and back, I slid the blade along the inside of her leg, slicing open the big artery in her groin.

Lightning rained down all around me then, shattering stone and temporarily deafening me, but not one bolt hit me—for which I thank the Hand that shielded me from her familiar. Within seconds, the fallen woman stopped thrashing as blood loss robbed her of consciousness.

Triss, can you *see anything?*

Not right now, no. Not with all the lightning. His mental voice sounded tight and pained. *But thanks for asking. Also, ow, ow, fucking ow!*

Right. What I really wanted at that point was just to lie there for a while and rest. Then, after I'd had my break, I wanted to take my poor tattered shadow and go the hell home. Instead I kept right on moving. By the time I'd twisted myself out from under the dying Hand and dragged myself back to my feet, she was all but gone and the indoor lightning had ceased to fall. Outside, the storm intensified yet again.

I had a couple of heartbeats of breathing space to look around then. The lightning-struck bodies of three or four of the Swords of

Heaven lay close by, while another dozen or so were coming toward me from various places in the room.

With a roar like the world's biggest manticore complaining about a twist in its tail, the whole wall of clerestories above me blew inward. Shards of glass and twisted bits of lead fell like sharp-edged hail and I had to throw myself back against the base of the outside wall to avoid the worst of it. The rain followed, soaking the interior of the sanctum in instants, and I lost track of most of the soldiers of the Sword in that sudden chaos.

Time to shroud up again, I think, I sent.

Yes, and you're welcome. Shadow covered and concealed me.

Thanks, Triss! I forced myself out and away from the wall—I didn't want to move, but I needed to get clear of my last known position as a first order of business. *How badly are you hurt?*

I've had much worse, though the spell on that axe burned like a son of a bitch, he replied. *How about you?*

About the same. Nothing's broken and I'm in no danger of bleeding out, though I've a myriad of new holes in my skin. I really wish I had a couple of efik beans and that I dared to eat them. It'd sure take the edge off.

Triss snorted. *The first couple might, but we both know how that would end.*

Which is why I wouldn't dare take them. But a guy can dream, can't he?

The rain sheeting in through the ruined windows was playing merry hell with my ability to make sense of what I was getting through Triss's unvision. I knew where I wanted to go—the entrance to the crypt behind the statue of Shan—and I had long since learned to navigate blind. But it didn't normally rain inside, and the storm just kept getting worse. The roaring was so loud now I could barely think. At least it was washing some of the blood off of me. I'd gone perhaps twenty feet in what I believed was the right direction when the windows on the other side of the temple blew in as well.

I couldn't see a thing in the darkness beyond, but the only other time I'd ever heard a storm anything remotely like this bad was when a series of cyclones had ripped through the plains of northern Varya when I was a teenager. One of them had flattened a couple of the temple's outbuildings. Another had ripped a pretty big stripe out of the nearest town. Dozens were killed.

Thinking of it now made me wonder how that sort of damage had been avoided when the Son of Heaven sent his forces against the temple. Though they had won the battle that day, I knew that a lot of the Hand had died to do it, taking their familiars with them. Perhaps, given time to prepare for casualties, the other Storms could soothe the weather before it went wild.

Then I almost ran into one of the remaining Swords, literally—I didn't see him till I was practically treading on his toes. I no longer had time to think, only to react. I drove one of the knives I was still carrying into his belly, and then had to use the other on a companion drawn by the first's scream. A moment later, I left my right-hand knife behind when it wedged between the ribs of a third. I ended up throwing my left at a fourth, hitting her in the neck, but probably not fatally. After that, I had a brief clear space. It lasted all the way to the entrance of the crypt, where another pair of temple soldiers stood waiting.

I had just drawn my remaining sword, when the farther of the pair quietly fell forward and landed on his face—dead, a knife sticking out of the back of his neck. The second turned to see what had taken her companion, and went down in a spray of blood as a line of steel flashed out of nowhere and sliced her throat. Knowing the cause, I was able to infer a faint dark lacuna mostly invisible amidst the craziness of the storm pouring in through every available opening. The curtain of shadow parted just long enough to show me Faran's face, then closed again.

Trusting Faran to cover my back, I stepped up to the crypt door and pulled out the finger. "I thought you were clearing the perimeter," I said over my shoulder.

"I had to change the plan rather abruptly. I was heading for the outer wall along the top of the buttery when the big winds first hit. Blew me clean off the roof of the building, and then halfway back to the temple proper when I opened a shadow sail to keep from breaking my neck. At that point, I was in the back courtyard of the temple and it was pretty clear the original play had gone in the shit. I figured getting the prisoners loose as quick as quick could be was higher priority than forcing my way back out to the perimeter through a wall of whirlwinds."

I nodded though she couldn't see me. "Sensible." Then the door to the crypt opened and I turned to the nearer of the two fallen soldiers. "Give me a hand here."

Together we chucked the body headfirst down the long steep stairs. As it tumbled down the last few steps, I more than half expected a burst of lightning to hit it, or a sheet of magefire. But nothing happened.

"Is that good or bad?" asked Faran.

"Hopefully good." If it signaled the absence of a lurking Hand and not clever restraint on such a lurker's part. "But there's only one way to find out." I shucked out of the pack holding the swords and passed it to Faran. "Block the light from the door." I wanted it as dark as I could make it before I started down.

Faran complied, filling the space with her shroud as I stepped onto the first stair. *Fast or slow, Triss?*

Slow might be smarter, but I don't think we have the time.

I don't either. Which is why I'd removed my pack. *This is going to hurt.* I reached through our link to borrow Triss's senses, but left him in full control and sent, *You can be my eyes.* The choice would impede my ability to perform magic, but it had other compensations.

Understood.

I shifted my sword into an underhand grip—less likely to accidentally stab myself that way—and dove headfirst down the stairs. I aimed down instead of out, staying low, and mostly skidded along on my chest until I hit the soldier's corpse, which tipped me into a roll. The entire front side of my body was screaming at me as I came to my feet in a low crouch just beyond the foot of the stairs.

I had at least one possibly cracked rib, but I couldn't afford to stay still. I immediately dove into a second roll, and then a third, moving down the narrow hall toward the nearest junction.

Soldier, on your right, hiding in the arch, six feet forward.

Though we were both sharing the same unvision, I simply wasn't aware of the soldier until Triss pointed him out to me. Which was exactly why I'd chosen not to take control this time.

Triss "sees" in every direction equally and thinks that way, too. I never will, though years of training and practice have taught me how to interpret what comes in through Triss's otherworldy senses via a sort of spot-sampling technique. For me it will always be like translating from a fundamentally alien language, whereas Triss speaks it as his native tongue. He can make sense of it far better than I ever will.

As I came out of my third roll, I flipped my sword around to a front grip and straight on from there into a backhanded lunge that took the soldier through the throat.

Drop! Triss yelled into my mind. I threw myself at the floor as a burst of lightning from the side passage passed through the place I had occupied only a moment before.

Storm right, Hand left! Triss yelled into my mind.

Then my shroud was suddenly gone as he collapsed into dragon form and leaped from my back to meet the oncoming Storm. That was the last I had leisure to pay attention to him, as a spear stabbed down at me from the left. I managed to avoid a skewering by rolling toward the spearman. But I didn't have enough room to dodge the thrust completely, and I felt the edge of the blade open a shallow gash along my right hip.

I swung my sword at my attacker's ankles, but he jumped back beyond the reach of my swing, pulling his spear back as he went. *Must be my day for facing death from above,* I thought as I braced my feet on the wall and kicked myself over into a backward roll. A spray of icy rain splashed across the back of my neck from the place where shadow fought Storm behind me when I came up onto my feet.

I barely had time to register it as the spearman lunged in again, this time with a thrust at my belly. A cross body parry deflected the spear a few critical inches so that it ripped a hole in my shirt instead of my side. I turned sideways to present the spear-wielding Hand with a narrower target, extending my sword forward and down in a high guard.

He stabbed at me again, going for my eyes. This time I had the leisure to make a much more careful parry, following on with a riposte at his forward hand—the only part of him I could easily reach. But the hand is a difficult target, and he neatly avoided my slice. The narrow confines of the hall and his much longer weapon gave him a brutal advantage unless I could get inside his guard.

Triss? Though I could feel through our link that he was heavily engaged, I wanted to check how he was doing and didn't dare turn to look.

Busy! Handle it.

Right. When the spear came at me again, I jumped forward with my parry, trying to beat the point aside and get in close before he could withdraw it. But my opponent was no tyro. Now that I was on my feet he'd shifted to a more careful sort of short thrust. That allowed him to easily hop back and put his point between me and where I needed to go. I drew the dagger at my left hip to give me a second weapon both for block and attack, but the next couple of quick passes ended with much the same result as that first. If I'd had a heavier sword, I might have been able to use it to hack the spear apart, but I didn't.

As we were dancing back and forth, I got the chance to study my opponent. He was tall, almost too tall for the low passages of the crypt, but not quite. As well as slender and well muscled. His loose Hand's robes hung open, exposing partial armor—a cuirass and vambraces as well as shin plates on his boots. About the only good thing I could say about the situation was that we were both too separated from our familiars to make any use of magic. Otherwise, he'd probably have cooked me by then. I tried a couple of attacks, cuts high and low but he easily deflected them without offering me any openings.

Apparently that raised his confidence, because he laughed, "I sent my men to kill your fellows when the crypt door opened, Blade. All I need to do is keep you here for a few short minutes. You're too late already."

Fuck. If his goal was to provoke me into doing something desperate and risky, he'd just succeeded. Now we would see how that worked out for him. After I made my next parry, I raised my sword into a high guard again to give me chopping room. Then, I edged my left foot forward until it offered a more tempting target. I wanted him to come in low. He did. Rather than deliver a proper parry, I hopped aside while simultaneously bringing the edge of my blade down as close to in line with his spear shaft as I could, swinging with everything I had.

I hit the spear about six inches behind the head, edge on, with a motion that brought the sword down and back toward me. It was a very precise move and very fast, only possible because I kept my blade sharp enough for shaving, and it worked. My edge sank into the wood and stuck fast. If he'd known it was coming, he could easily have wrenched my sword out of my hand. But by the time he knew what was going on, it was already too late. I'd let go of my blade the second it stuck, and now I leaped forward.

He yanked his spear backward, trying to bring it into line to block my advance, but the trapped sword added a lot of tip weight and threw the balance off completely, twisting the shaft to the side. The effect wouldn't last long, but it didn't have to. I just needed long enough to get fully inside his guard, and it accomplished that. He was a veteran, and smart, letting the spear go the instant he realized what I'd done and reaching for his own belt knife. But by then I was on top of him.

I drove my knife deep into the flesh of his thigh, just above his knee, and left it there. As the pain momentarily doubled him up, I brought my now empty left hand up to catch his descending chin. I'd already jabbed a spearfist at his throat with my other hand, but he'd avoided the worst of it, twisting to avoid the blow. That put my right hand next to the ritual cord that bound his ponytail in place. Now I grabbed the knot and yanked at the same time that I twisted

with my other hand. His neck broke with a dull wet crack, and
thunder rattled the passage as his Storm followed him into death.

"Faran!" I yelled as I retrieved my blade. "Bring the swords!"

There was no response, and I spared a moment to worry about
that, but only a moment. If the Hand hadn't been lying to me, the
prisoners might already be dying.

I didn't see her, Triss sent as he followed the line that connected
us back to rejoin me in my mad dash down the hall.

She can take care of herself, I sent.

*Better than you can, in many ways, but that doesn't prevent me
worrying.*

Me either.

A metallic snap sounded ominously from around a corner in
the hallway ahead. It was followed by a flare of light so intense that
it burned. Wincing at the brightness I leaped around the corner to
find a pair of soldiers standing between me and an iron door pried
off its hinges. The light spilled through from whatever lay within.

The closer of the two held a broken sword, the farther a spear.
A heart thrust killed the swordsman in the same instant my thrown
knife took the spearwoman in the eye. It hadn't killed her—thrown
blades rarely do, but she screamed and dropped her weapon, reaching for the knife. A palm strike to the back of her clutching hands
drove the blade deep and finished the job, though it would take her
a little while to figure it out.

I went past her falling body and through the door into the narrow tomb beyond. The light was almost unbearably bright, despite
the soldier who had preceded me blocking the worst of it. All I
could see was the silhouette of a head and shoulders, but that was
all I needed to drive my sword into the back of his neck. He fell like
a string-cut puppet, exposing me to the direct assault of the light.

My shroud dissolved as the light forced Triss to collapse back
down into my regular shadow to protect himself, and the brilliance
of it stabbed at my dark-adjusted eyes. I staggered a half step back
at the sudden pain and had to throw up my free arm to cover my
face.

"Who's there?" the voice was weak, barely a croak and totally
unidentifiable, but it galvanized me into action and I began to grope
around for the light. "It's Aral. Who am I talking to?"

"Loris," and this time I could hear the pain as well as the weakness. "Jax?"

"Alive and well last time I saw her, but that was before this whole play blew up in our faces." My groping fingers found a metal rod hanging from the ceiling.

I slid my hand down the rod. As I reached the knob on the end the light dimmed. It was vibrating ever so slightly—in tune with the storm above—as was the floor now that I thought about it. If it got much worse it'd tear the whole abbey apart stone by stone. The cell stank of blood and piss and all the other horrible smells of torture and imprisonment.

". . . 's trap," said Loris. "She shouldn't have . . . *you* shouldn't be here."

"I know." I closed my hand around the magelight, darkening the room enough to allow me to open my eyes. My fist glowed red and I could see Loris hanging limp on a wooden framework at the back of the tomb. "She told me. I came anyway." I gave a yank on the rod, but nothing happened.

Summoning Triss to edge my sword in shadow, I snapped it around and cut the rod loose from the ceiling. Then I shoved the light under the body of the Sword at my feet. The light leaking out from underneath was still plenty to see by, but it was dim enough to allow Triss to slip back into dragon shape beside me.

Loris looked awful, naked and covered in bruises, bleeding freely from a deep wound in his side and minus his right ear. He was hanging on an elaborate wooden rack built in the shape of a glyph of binding. Heavy leather straps bound him at the wrists, elbows, throat, chest, knees, and ankles. The device was called the pillory of light. It was devised by Tangara, God of Glyphs, to hold captured Blades as a part of the war of Heaven against my goddess. I had spent some time on one a year ago, and the sight of it now set a fire in my blood.

The magelight that I'd just removed was the part that kept his Shade from acting. Now Issaru began to stir, appearing first as a tendril of shadow that reached around to cover Loris's wound and staunch the bleeding. Another severed the straps at ankles and knees. Loris hissed in pain as limbs that hadn't moved in who knew how long suddenly changed position. Remembering my own agony in a similar position I was glad that Issaru had the sense not to cut him free all at once.

"Let me help you—" I began, but Loris gave another sharp hiss.

"No. Cut the others loose. Issaru will take care of me."

"Aral?" the voice came from up the hall behind me, low but urgent. Faran.

"Here." I turned and went back through the broken door. "With

Loris." For the first time, I noticed the broken-off stem of a heavy key in the door's lock. "Thank Nam . . ." But she was gone. "There's luck."

"Too much luck, I think," said Triss. My shadow licked out and touched the lock. "This tastes of tampering and . . ."

Before he could say more, Faran appeared at the corner, having dropped the shroud across her face—how long she'd been there I couldn't say. The bag of swords hung from her left hand.

"We've got—"

Before she could finish, there came an incredibly bright flash from behind her, then a boom like a dozen thunder bursts going off all at once. The floor jumped beneath me, and a wall of pressure and dust came shooting around the corner from the direction of the flash, turning out all the lights as it knocked me flat. Dull thuds and splintering cracks told of stones falling from the ceiling around us. The temple was collapsing.

17

---◆---

Spend enough time in darkness and you will discover that it has every bit as much variation as light does. The absolute blackness that surrounded me now had a soft weight to it, like lying under a blanket with six inches of sand pressing it down.

The air felt thick and hard to breathe, almost syrupy, heavy with mold and the stink of ancient stonework. I couldn't hear a thing. Not with my ears at least, though there was a buzzing in my mind that grew into words as I focused on it.

Aral! Aral, wake up!

It was Triss, but his mental voice felt as though it was coming from a terribly long way away. It had a sort of moist echo to it, like someone yelling in the depths of a sewer.

I'm all right. I tried to get an idea of my immediate surroundings from Triss's senses, but it felt like that part of our connection had temporarily closed down. *At least, I think I am. What happened? Where are we?*

I'm not sure yet. The big flash stunned me and now I can't see. I can still feel the hammering of the storm though—it makes the whole world shake—so we can't have been out too long.

I tried to move, but felt that same heavy resistance I had before. This time, I pushed against it, trying to force myself upright—discovering only in that moment that I was lying on my stomach. For several long slow beats nothing happened. Then the silence fled before a deep ringing sound and I began to move, almost infinitesimally at first, but with a steadily increasing sureness. As I forced myself onto hands and knees, the ringing was interrupted by a couple of dull clunks, like falling stone. Then it slowly began to fade.

"Aral?" It was Faran, sounding more than half frantic.

"'M all right."

I felt hands on my shoulders in the same moment that I began to "see" things again through Triss's senses. I was lying three-quarters buried in a heap of dirt and small to midsize stones—fill the builders had packed in around the crypts and other foundations of the temple. Once I'd rubbed the worst of the dirt out of my eyes I could actually see better that way than through Triss. About half the dim magelights that had illuminated the passage before the collapse had fallen along with various sections of wall. But there was still so much dust in the air that Triss's unsight was practically blind from all the weird shadow echoes.

"How are you doing?" I asked as I finished clearing my eyes.

"Not bad considering," replied Faran. "I stayed upright and managed to avoid the worst of the collapse."

"Good plan, that." I rubbed the back of my neck where I could feel a nasty bruise rising—at a guess one of the bigger stones had clipped me. "I should probably try it next time a ceiling falls on me."

"Does it happen to you that often?" asked Faran.

Triss slid down into dragon shape and nodded sadly. "This is at least the fourth or fifth time. You'd think we'd be better at it."

I took a few steps forward. The passage that used to lead to the surface now ended in a pile of broken stone and rubble about ten feet in front of me. The blockage lay just this side of the corner where Faran had been standing. Behind me, the tunnel continued to another turn, though more wreckage half blocked the way there as well. Not that it mattered. I knew from the maps I'd memorized that there was no way out in that direction either. We were trapped, at least for the moment. Us and . . .

"Loris! You still with us?" I called.

"As much as I was before." He stuck his head into the hall, then followed it out, using the fallen soldier's sword like a cane. "What about the others? My students?"

"I don't know." I noticed he hadn't mentioned Jax, but I wasn't about to bring it up when we didn't—couldn't—know anything more about her fate. "I haven't had a chance to check on the others yet."

"Why not? And, who's this?" he asked then, looking more closely, "Faran?"

"Master Loris." She gave him a small formal bow. "I'm sorry the circumstances of our reunion aren't happier."

He gave her a warm smile and shook his head. "I presume you're part of Aral and Jax's rescue. All things considered, that ranks pretty

high on my auspicious meetings scale." Then he turned and gave
me a much more worried look. "Speaking of which, shouldn't you
be opening doors?"

I nodded. "That and trying to figure a way to get us out of here."
Though nothing came to mind. Dust was still falling from the ceiling here and there in response to the ongoing battering the structure was taking from the storm.

The tomb directly across from Loris's also had a newly fitted
iron door on it, so I moved to that one first. The frame was badly
sprung from the collapse and I had my doubts about whether we'd
be able to open it in the conventional manner. But it never hurts to
try the easy way first. While I was working on that door, Faran
handed the bag of swords to Loris and headed for the next one
down the line.

"Triss, if you would."

The shadow of a dragon climbed the door, and poked at the lock
with a foreclaw. After a moment, he let out a little hiss.

"Having trouble?"

It's not that, he replied mentally. *This lock's been tampered with.
Put a normal key in here and it's going to fuse the lock and weld itself in
place in the process. A shadow on the other hand . . .* The lock opened
with a sharp click.

Kelos? I reached for the handle and gave it a good solid yank.
The door didn't budge.

Has to be.

How recently was he here?

No more than an hour ago, probably less.

*Dammit, what's his game? And how did he get in and out of here
past the guards without leaving a shadow trail?* "The door's stuck," I
added aloud. "Triss, see what you can do."

I glanced to my right, where Faran had started working on her
door. Ssithra had slipped up to whisper something in her ear, and
now she gave me the faintest of raised eyebrows, and indicated Loris with a flick of her eyes. I made a cutting motion with my hand
out of sight of the older master. Faran shrugged and tapped the lock,
sending the phoenix back to its task.

Meanwhile, Triss had risen up to cover a substantial portion
of the door, pressing himself flat against the surface, and straining
with an effort I could feel through our bond. I knew what was coming, and that it took both time and concentration. So I waited quietly for him to do what was necessary.

Another loud click came from Faran's lock then. Her door must have fared better than mine, because it opened with a sharp pull. Painfully intense light spilled out through the opening, and Ssithra let out a little shriek of protest before diving behind Faran to hide from the brightness.

"Who's there?" The feminine voice that came through the opening sounded weak and pained, but angry.

"It's me, Loris." He started to limp toward the door. "With Aral and Faran. We'll have you out of there as soon as we can, Maryam."

I remembered a shy, quiet young woman with black hair and big eyes. Tall, sweet, and absolute murder with swords or staff. Loris had reached the doorway by then. Though I could see how badly he wanted to go to his student, Loris stopped to one side of the threshold, just beyond the edge of the light pouring across it.

"Faran, kill that for me, please," he said.

His reluctance to do it himself made me wonder how bad the wound in his side really was—if he didn't dare let the light force Issaru away from it. . . . Faran pushed forward into the cell, which darkened a moment later. At the same time, I felt the effort Triss had been making crescendo. With a sudden snap of his wings, he contracted down into a tiny spot of absolute blackness. A good-sized section of the door went with him, vanishing into the everdark and leaving a dragon shaped hole into . . .

"Dammit!" No light spilled out of that opening, nor ever would.

"Aral?" Loris turned toward me, with a sick look on his face.

"The whole chamber's collapsed. Whoever was in here never had a chance."

Loris nodded and took a deep breath, visibly putting aside his loss. I did the same. We would all mourn when we could, but for now we had to wall away our pain and our worries and keep moving.

Just then, Faran came out of her door with Maryam leaning heavily on her shoulders. The older girl looked much as I remembered, if you didn't count the huge burn scar that started just below where her right ear had been and spilled down from there across her cheek and neck. Like Loris—or me when I'd been hung on the pillory, for that matter—she'd been stripped naked and was covered in bruises. I cursed bitterly, then headed toward Faran and Maryam, and the next prisoner's door which lay beyond them.

"Master Aral." Maryam bowed as much as her position allowed. "What's the situation? Faran says we're safe for the moment, but trapped. Give me two minutes and I can fight. Have you a sword for me?"

"We have a pair, over there." Faran indicated the bag that Loris held. "But you should sit down and catch your breath first. We'll find you some clothes, too. I know a couple of guards who won't be needing theirs anymore."

A hydra slid out from Maryam's feet to touch three of its noses with the dragon at mine, while its other heads kept watch. "It's good to see you most honored, Resshath Triss, Master Aral. Maryam is right, we are ready to fight. You need only point us at the enemy."

"I think we can afford to give you a little time to recover, young Vrass," replied Triss. "Rest and be ready."

The hydra bobbed a half dozen nods, then collapsed into Maryam's shadow as Faran helped the journeyman to a seat on the floor. Her eyes met mine over Maryam's head and they held tears and a murderous rage that I shared. I paused just long enough to examine the door of Maryam's cell before moving on to try my luck with the next one.

It was the first fully intact door I'd seen. I wanted to know why no light had spilled around the seams or through the keyhole, in case it turned out to matter for any of the others. It was tightly fitted to an extra-deep set of jambs with a similar set of seals at top and bottom, and a plate had been welded across the back side of the keyhole. The whole had clearly been designed by people who'd had plenty of practice at keeping even a shadow from slipping through the cracks.

The next door frame was sprung as well, but not as badly as the first. That gave me hope for what lay on the other side. Once I'd brushed aside the pile of debris along the bottom of the door to give me a better chance at opening it, I could even see a bit of light leaking through where the twisting of the frame had broken the seal. When I tugged on the handle, the door jiggled in the frame, but I could tell it was going to take some prying to get it loose.

I was looking around for a better tool than one of my daggers as Faran passed me on her way to the last door. A question of some possible importance occurred to me, so I caught her eye.

She paused. "Yes?"

"Why did it take you so long to catch up to me in the crypt?"

"I got hung up at the top of the stairs. You'd just ducked out of sight when a Hand ran in through the same door I'd come in by. She was leaking blood from a big cut over her eye and trailing five Swords behind her. I knew you could handle whatever you ran into down here, so I figured I should get back to my original job and clear the exits. It took me a little while to manage that lot. By the time I had, another Hand had come in and got the remaining Swords in the temple organized."

"Damn. I take it you decided to cut out then?"

Faran let out an evil little chuckle. "Oh, no. I was going to take a crack at that bunch, too, but the main doors of the sanctum blew in about then and the Signet came charging through the wreckage with several more of the Hand and a whole pile of Swords at her heels. *That's* when I decided it was time to head down here so I could play rear guard. I hadn't expected her to just drop the roof on us though, or I might have made a different decision."

Which meant the Signet and some number of troops were overhead right now, doing who knows what. Not good. But there was nothing we could do about it for the moment except get the rest of our comrades free and hope that the Signet thought we'd all died in the collapse. Glancing at the roof and the light but continuing fall of dust reminded me that we still could. We needed to pick up the pace. I spared a moment to hope the Signet's presence with more of the Hand didn't mean Jax was dead, but only a moment. If Jax was gone, that would be one more thing to put aside until I had the time to mourn her properly.

The door finally yielded to my efforts, popping open all at once and falling half off its hinges in the process. Light jabbed at my eyes, coming unexpectedly from floor level and hitting Triss hard enough to make him squawk like a punted chicken before he jumped behind me. The collapse had knocked a few stones loose from the ceiling in the tomb-turned-cell, including the one that had held the magelight, which now lay half buried. The fact that the slumped figure on the glyph-form rack beyond wasn't moving, though he or she—impossible to tell through the glare—now hung mostly in shadow, was a very bad sign.

I scuffed some rubble in front of the magelight to block it further as I stepped over it on my way to the rack. I could see that the unconscious figure was male now. But whoever he was, he'd taken enough of a beating that I couldn't identify him beyond that at first glance. In addition to the missing ear, he had a split lip and flattened nose, and both his eyes had been blacked. He looked more than half-dead, an impression belied only by the faint rise and fall of his chest.

As I knelt and reached for the buckle of the strap on his right ankle, a shadowy talon came out of the darkness behind the glyph to slap feebly at my hands. I jerked back in time to avoid most of the blow, but still ended up with a pair of bleeding scratches across the back of my right hand.

"Thiess!" snapped Triss. "Stand down this instant!"

"Resshath Triss?" The voice sounded muzzy and confused. "Master Aral? Is that really you, and not more evil visions?"

"Yes," said Triss, his tone gentler now. "We're here to free you and Javan, and the others."

Javan, I remembered the name, but not much more about him than that.

"Truly?" The shadow of a huge horned owl hopped out from behind the glyph, turning his head this way and that as he looked around. "Free?" He jerked suddenly like someone waking from a nightmare. "The light's gone!"

In an instant he'd collapsed back into Javan's shadow, but only long enough to sever the straps that confined his bond-mate all in an instant. Then, before Javan could fall forward off the rack, he'd flowed back out in front of him, retaining his human's shape so that he could catch the young man and ease him to the ground. I was about to suggest we move the two of them to the passageway when I heard a crash behind me followed by a sound like someone tipping a couple hundred gallons of water onto the floor.

Before I'd half turned around Faran called out, "Master Aral, we may have a problem here."

Another, weaker voice, spoke then, "Oh, thank Namara, I thought sure I was gonna drown."

The last cell lay across the hall and a few yards down from the one where I'd found Thiess and Javan. It stood wide open now with Faran standing in front of it in an ankle-deep puddle, with more water flowing out all the time. Fortunately, the floor of the passage sloped slightly down and away toward the bend at the back. So, the water was going that way for now. As I splashed across to see what was going on, Faran pushed forward into the flowing water and went to work on the light.

By the time I stuck my head into the cell, she had it tightly fisted, reducing it to a dim red glow. Another rack stood in the cell. It held a shaggy-haired young man built like a bog troll—deep chested and ridiculously broad shouldered, with thick arms that seemed too long for his body. Journeyman Roric, Avarsi by birth, and absolutely unmistakable. Remembering that he was almost as fast as he was strong, I didn't find it at all hard to believe he'd managed to survive the fall. As I watched, his Shade sliced the bands holding him to the rack, starting at his ankles and working up.

Behind him, water was fountaining out through a wide gap where the mortar had fallen away between two stones high on the wall. From there it hit the rack and cascaded to the floor. Judging by the filthy high-water mark across his chest, Faran had gotten the door open just in time. Like the others, Roric was covered in bruises and scabs, and missing an ear. That didn't prevent him from stepping free of the rack without any help, or waving off Faran's offer of a shoulder to lean on as he staggered forward.

"Just let me get clear of this fucking ice water and aim me at the nearest Hand and I'm good," he growled, flexing thick fingers. "I've scores to settle."

The shadow that followed him out growled its agreement as it took on the form of a gigantic six-legged badger. Ssolvey, if I was remembering correctly. The Shade was another who'd never been much of a talker, which made it harder. But when I silently asked Triss, he reassured me that I'd gotten the name right.

"Give me a hand with the door," Faran said to me as she followed Roric out. "It was holding back the water as well as any dam before I opened it and I think that's going to become really important if this storm keeps up."

"Point." The ground was still gently shaking from the battering winds above.

As I moved up and put my shoulder to the door beside Faran's, Triss darted into the room and nosed around briefly before coming back to me. *Kelos touched this door last of them all. Though the water has erased any shadow trail he might have left, there's a stronger sense of his presence in that room.*

The water had gone down enough that we didn't have much difficulty forcing the door shut, though it did require Roric's help to hold it in place long enough to relock. As Ssithra saw to that, Loris joined us. He was limping badly, and looked even weaker than he had when I first found him. Fresh blood stained the lower edge of the shadows where Issaru had wrapped himself around his bond-mate's ribs.

"Roric, Maryam, Javan." He ticked them off on his fingers. "That puts Leyan and Ulriss in the caved-in cell." He closed his eyes and his jaw tightened. "She had a lovely touch with a strangling cord, and Ulriss was the sweetest Shade you've ever met. I will miss them both. But we have no time for mourning yet. What's the next step in the plan, Aral?"

"That would be for Jax to bring down the Hand's barracks as a distraction and to eliminate as many of the enemy as possible while

I lead you all out that way." I pointed to the collapsed passage. "Unfortunately, something went wrong and the distraction happened before I'd even entered the sanctum. And now, the Signet seems to have closed the only available door."

Loris frowned. "And the backup plan?"

"Still working on that one. Why don't you have a seat with the others and let Faran and I have a look down there to make sure my information about it being a dead end is correct." I waved at the other end of the passage and then started that way—we didn't have a lot of time.

Loris's expression shifted to one I'd seen a number of times when he was teaching me at the temple, the one he used whenever I'd said something particularly stupid. "I will rest when my students are safe. Not before. Is that understood, Blade Aral?"

It was a formal mode of address used only rarely by a senior master to a junior, and it carried a strong undertone of direct orders.

How bad is he, Triss? He might be my senior, but the goddess was dead and the hierarchy with her, and damned if I was going to let precedent kill an old friend. *Can you ask Issaru?*

I already did. Issaru says he's bad, but he'll live ... if nothing happens to make him much worse.

I gave Loris a faint bow. "As you wish, Master Loris."

"Then lead the way."

The whole little power-play turned out to be moot when that part of the passage ended in another cave-in maybe thirty feet beyond the bend. Our world had shrunk to less than a hundred feet of narrow tunnel and a score or so of intact tombs including the ones which had been converted to cells. Add in the Signet and her troops above and we were well and truly fucked, unless one of us could come up with a way to move through solid stone ... or shadow.

I had been idly staring at the nearest lock without actually seeing it for a good couple of minutes when the idea clicked in my head. How *had* Kelos gotten in and out of the crypt without leaving a trail or anyone seeing him? To the best of my knowledge there was no way to travel shrouded without leaving a shadow trail, and he couldn't have gotten past the guards without his shroud.

Not if he didn't want it reported, at least. Even if Kelos worked for the Son of Heaven now, I didn't think he'd want it getting out that he'd sabotaged the Hand. But what if he didn't come in through the front door? Then he wouldn't *need* the shroud. I had an idea of how he might have managed that, but it wanted a better head for magic than mine, or possibly someone who'd been a better listener back in the day. Loris answered to both descriptions.

"Master Loris." I knelt down next to where he was sitting to put us more on a level. "I once saw Siri step into one shadow and out of another without passing through the intervening space. She said it wasn't really a spell, more like a sort of side effect of the way the everdark overlaps our world or something like that. Did she ever bring it forward to the council?"

Loris's eyes went distant and then he nodded. "She did. It involved folding shadows like paper in origami. A couple of the better mages among us even tried it." He shivered. "I was one. It was very painful and extraordinarily dangerous. Master Thera walked in shadow and never returned, and none of the Shades who looked for her in the everdark could detect any hint of her presence."

"I always wondered what happened to Master Thera," I said. A service was held in her memory, but they hadn't told us how she died—unusual but not unheard of. Sometimes the council or the goddess sent a Blade out on a mission that wasn't shared with the rest of the order.

"Do you think it would help us now?" I asked.

Loris shook his head. "Even if I remembered the exact technique, I'd be extremely reluctant to attempt it. After we lost Thera, the goddess herself forbade us from trying it again."

"Why?" asked Faran. "It seems like it would be incredibly useful in certain circumstances, and everyone has to die of something. It's not like a whole lot of us ever expected old age to get us."

"It's less useful than you might think. The distance you can cover is short, no farther than a Shade can stretch and still have enough substance at both ends to form the doorway. Anywhere from five to fifty feet depending on the light, but never more that that. The pain factor is high enough that it renders the user unfit for much of anything for a good minute or two after they've passed through the everdark. But far more important is that Thera didn't just die. She was lost."

"I don't understand," said Faran.

"While she lived, Namara made sure to greet each of us on our way to the wheel of rebirth and thank us for our service to Justice. When Namara felt Thera's death through her spirit dagger, she went to the gates of judgment and waited, but Thera never arrived. Her soul was lost or destroyed."

"Do you have a better idea?" asked Faran.

"No, but neither do I really remember how to do it."

Faran nodded, but the look on her face was one I knew well, and it wasn't acceptance. I remembered then that when I'd first found Faran hiding in the sewers under Tien, she'd performed a very intricate bit of shadow origami. She'd used it produce an item she'd been hiding in a sort of shadow tuckaside in the everdark.

"You think you might be able to figure it out, don't you?" I asked her.

"I might." She nodded again, thoughtfully this time. "It can't be all that different from the trick I use to stash things in the everdark, just larger in scale. Though I can't imagine doing it with something as irregular as a tree's shadow. Siri's a far better mage than I will ever be."

"And it's far too dangerous for someone barely old enough to be a journeyman," said Loris. "I forbid it."

Faran's eyes flashed with sudden anger. "Namara's dead, old man, and the order with her. I don't answer to you. Nor even entirely to Aral, though he is *my* master as much as anyone ever will be again." She looked at me now. "Do you want me to try?"

I didn't. Not one little bit. But if we didn't find a way out of here, and quickly, every one of us would die. If it were *my* life and soul on the line, I wouldn't have hesitated to make the attempt. Now, I wished that I'd never thought of it.

Triss spoke into my mind, *She's only a little younger than you were when you killed a king. As I recall, that involved you defying the council and asking Namara to make you a full Blade ahead of your time.*

That's different!

Why, because she's more mature?

Point.

I reached out and put my hands on Faran's shoulders. "This isn't the sort of thing that you ask someone else to do. And it's certainly not the sort of thing you want to see someone you care about attempt. At the same time, I know what you can do and some of what you have survived. I care about you. I don't want to see you risk yourself this way, but after all the dangerous things I've done, I can't pretend I have any right to tell you not to do it."

Not bad, not perfect, but you're getting better at this.

"Would you do it?" she asked.

I nodded, though I really would have preferred not to.

"Thank you."

"For what?" I asked, genuinely surprised.

"Not lying to protect me this time."

I remembered my efforts to keep her from coming along on this trip and I was ashamed. "I'm sorry about trying to keep you off the boat. It was wrong. Thank you."

She quirked an eyebrow. "For what?"

"Showing me that I was wrong."

Faran hugged me. "You're still a dreadful old man, but you're my dreadful old man."

"And you'll always be my young monster."

Much better. Triss chuckled in my mind, but his mental voice was more indulgent than mocking. *Of course, if you're going to thank everyone who points out when you're wrong, you're never going to have time to say anything else. Why, the thanks you owe me alone . . .*

Faran stepped back away from me. "If there's any chance that I can get us out of here, I have to try."

"I know you do."

18

Standing by and letting someone you love risk their life requires significantly more power of will than resisting torture. I've done both, and I'd far rather take the torture. It's doubly difficult when they're risking themselves because you weren't able to get the job done.

When Faran opened the gate of shadows for the first time I wanted to forbid her to step through, or better yet, to simply go through myself if anyone had to try it. She wouldn't hear of the latter for reasons that had to do with the structure of the magic, and Loris backed her up. He'd wanted to try it first himself, but with his wounds he simply wasn't strong enough to manage such a trip more than once.

I gave her a quick hug and a kiss on the forehead. "You take care of yourself."

"I'm only going fifteen feet, and the technique isn't all that different from my little shadow tuckaside. I'll be fine. Now, I need to go."

I'd never been more frightened for her, nor more worried. Or proud for that matter. But I just nodded, smiled as best I could, and stepped out of her way, all the while wishing desperately that I had a drink to hand. The portal didn't look like much, just a sort of deepening of the shadow cast by the broken door of Loris's cell. The off-kilter rectangle was slightly darker than it ought to be and vibrating gently in time with the beat of the storm. Another thread of shadow ran from it down the hall and across to vanish into the open cell that had held Maryam.

Without another word, Faran reached out a hand to the shadow gate, touched it, and vanished. I hadn't watched nearly as closely when I'd first seen Siri try it all those years ago. Hell, I probably hadn't watched *anything* so closely in the years since I last looked on the living face of Namara and took my final assignment.

Initially, the shadow seemed to resist her, bending to the shape of her hand like she was pressing on a silken sheet. Then the surface broke with a sort of pop and, a—for lack of a better word— flash of darkness, short but intense. Sort of like reverse lightning. In that instant, Faran had turned black and appeared to become two dimensional, like a paper doll painted in midnight. Then she was gone.

I started counting. One. Two. Three. At thirty, or about three times as long as it would have taken her to slow walk the distance, the portal vanished and Faran's voice emerged from the other cell, "Shitshitshit . . . hey it worked."

I covered the distance in a dash. Faran was leaning against the wall at the back of the cell, hugging herself and looking pale and cold. I wanted to hug her, too, but I could tell she needed the breathing space right now.

"Are you all right?" I asked. "You were gone a long time."

She bit her lip but nodded. "Hurts. So cold it feels hot, and the distances aren't the same at all. You're walking, but you're falling, too, because there is no up or down. I can understand why Thera got lost." She shivered.

"You don't have to do it again," I said.

"Yes. I do." I could see how much the words cost her and I wanted to argue.

"We can find another way."

She shook her head. "Not fast enough. No, this will work and we can do it now. We don't have time to mess around anymore. Not with the Hand above. And not with the storm trying to tear the whole building apart." As if to punctuate her words, a large chunk of mortar fell out of the chink between two of the stones forming the barrel vault over the little tomb. "We have a way out, we have to take it."

"All right," I said. "Show me how to manage this little trick."

She shook her head again, even more firmly. "That's not going to work. If you don't have the basics, I'm not going to be able to get you there in any reasonable amount of time, *and* I've got a better idea. I'll create the way and hold it open, and you can all pass through on my heels. I think it will work better anyway."

A shadow phoenix appeared on the wall behind her. "Faran is

right. I didn't fully understand what was needed until we actually did it, but now I see. It's a sshssithssha way. Each soul that passes along it will make it stronger for a time. That way the strong can lead the weak and, with us to guide you, all are more likely to make the passage alive."

Triss?

Sshssithssha, that makes sense.

Can you explain it?

Not in human words no. But Ssithra is right that each passage will make it easier for the ones who follow.

"It's your play," I told Faran. "We'll follow your lead."

"Thank you. Then we only have one thing left to do, and that's to find a shadow's path out of here." She jerked a thumb toward the nearer of the two cave-ins. "That looks far too solid for even the thinnest wisp of darkness to get through, and the other was just as bad. I'm hoping you have an answer for that."

"I've got it covered, I think. I wouldn't have brought the idea up in the first place if I didn't already have an idea."

"What is it?" Loris looked over my shoulder, inserting himself in the conversation for the first time.

"Ever stand on the bank of a clear stream with the sun behind you?" I asked.

"Of course . . ."

"Then you know that shadow can pass through clear water as easily as it passes through the air." I nodded toward the closed cell where we'd rescued Roric from the flooding. "If the water can get in, we can get out."

Loris frowned. "That water was coming in awfully fast and we don't have anywhere for it to go. *And* it wasn't anything like clear. If you're wrong, we may have trouble getting the door closed again, and that could become a major problem. What makes you so sure the distance through the water is short enough?"

"I'm not." I couldn't tell him that I believed that was how Kelos had come in without revealing a whole bunch of things I didn't want to have to explain or argue about just yet. "It's a gamble, but it's the only one I can think of that might pay out."

Not bad, Triss said into my mind.

"Madness," growled Loris. "Dangerous madness, at that. The water could kill us all."

"If we don't try it we'll all die down here anyway," I replied. "Later if not sooner. I'm no happier about the idea than you are, but it's all we've got."

Faran held out a hand abruptly. "Maybe we could extend our range." She had a very thoughtful look on her face. "Two Shades together might be able to reach farther than one. You've done this before, Master Loris, if long ago. What do you think?"

Loris's eyes went far away and he blinked several times. "I . . . maybe. I don't know. Tell me what you're thinking of doing."

Faran explained in detail, talking about shadow folds, and everdark warps, and nima sharing, and other details that I'd probably have understood a whole lot better if I'd listened closer in my high magic lessons.

"That might work," Loris said when she'd finished. And then, "Where did you learn all that? You weren't old enough to have gotten that kind of instruction before the fall of the temple."

"Here, in the Magelands. I spent two of my lost years in Har. I couldn't take classes at the university without letting them know what I was. But I was able to use my powers to eavesdrop on quite a number of lessons. Mostly at night, and mostly for the advanced students because of that." She looked suddenly wistful. "It's not really an education, but I learned a lot. I'd like to come back someday."

She shook herself. "But that's a wish for another time. We've already been down here too long."

A few moments later, Triss and I were standing ready to open the door, with Roric, Maryam, and Javan lined up behind me. While I was getting the others ready, Loris and Faran did something complicated with Ssithra and Issaru. When Triss triggered the lock, the door slammed open, smashing against the stones so hard that I half expected it to pop the hinges. A wall of filthy water fell through the doorway as a couple of thousand gallons emptied into the hallway in a matter of seconds.

We were all briefly up to our knees, and Faran waded in before it had fallen to ankle height, with Loris struggling along in her wake. I followed them into the doorway and waited there as Ssithra spun herself into a cord of shadow and slithered into the gap between the stones. Loris and Issaru stood in reserve, the former looking even paler than Faran had after her trip through the everdark. If Faran could avoid drawing on them, I knew she would, and I was at least a little bit hopeful. If Kelos had come in this way, then the distance should be possible for a single Shade to bridge.

Ssithra returned after a few minutes and resumed the shape of a phoenix. "I don't think I can do it alone. It's not that far from here to the place where the water is pouring into the channel, but it's some distance from there to anyplace big enough for a person to come out that isn't underwater. Also, the water's awfully murky. That means I have to put extra substance into maintaining the link."

"But if Issaru and I help, you can get my students out of here?" asked Loris.

"And you," said Ssithra. "Yes, I think so."

"Then let's do it."

"Resshath Issaru, are you up to this?" asked Ssithra.

The shadow bound around Loris's ribs shifted to form a hawklike face. "I am. But for Loris's sake we must act quickly once I remove myself from my place here."

A shadow hydra peered around the door frame from behind me. "Resshath Issaru, if Maryam and I go last before you, I can bind Master Loris's wounds for you until it is our turn. Would that help?"

The hawk face nodded. "A great deal, young Vrass. Come here."

They did, and the hydra wrapped itself around Loris's ribs over the top of Issaru. Once she was solidly in place, the older Shade slid out from underneath and briefly formed itself into a shadow hippogriff to bow thanks to Vrass. While they were doing that, I half buried one of the bright magelights in debris on the ground beyond the room's door. From there it cast a good dark rectangle of shadow on the wall, providing a frame for the gate.

The hippogriff climbed the wall next to the rectangle, then reared back onto his hind legs in the classic heraldic pose. From there he shifted down and back, assuming the shape of his bond-mate, sans only the sword Loris had adopted as a cane. The shadow Loris knelt and produced a flat sheet like black paper from somewhere near his belt. Streamers of green spell-light like fiery thread shot from Loris to his shadow mirror, visible only in magesight. It connected them at ankle and wrist, knee and elbow, almost like a marionette's strings.

Though Loris didn't move, the shadow did as the strings grew longer and shorter. Working quickly and carefully, the shadow Loris folded the black rectangle again and again. With each fold, a line of differently colored magical light extended itself from his fingertips to lie along the crease. When he had finished, he had built a rectangular three-dimensional box covered with faint angular lines of color where the creases lay.

It was weird to see it there, a rainbow-edged bulge of pure darkness sticking out from the wall where the shadow play had happened. Leaning forward, the shadow Loris placed the box at floor level in the exact center of the door shadow and pushed it into the wall. Where it had bulged inward before, now it bowed outward, giving an impression of a small but darkened opening extending into some other space. A mouse hole to the everdark.

As shadow Loris withdrew his hand, the hole began to grow and shrink simultaneously, thinning toward two dimensionality at the same time it expanded in height and width to match the shadow of the door. When it was done, the two outlines were in near perfect alignment and it only extended a hairsbreadth into other space. The glowing thread connecting shadow Loris to actual Loris faded as the former twisted into Issaru's hippogriff form again, leaving only a single narrow strand of shadow to connect him to the door.

"This end is ready," said Loris, and I could hear a heavy weight of fatigue under his words. "But it's taking a lot out of me. We need to hurry. I wish I could have done that half so quickly as Siri did it when she first showed us the trick."

"Issaru?" asked Ssithra.

In response, the Shade collapsed down into a thin cord of darkness to match the one that Ssithra now formed. Faran closed her eyes and spun a thread of green spell-light out from the center of her forehead. Together, the two strands of darkness and the one of light slid into the hole in the wall, spiraling around each other as they went, like the strands of a rope.

Seconds took hours to pass as we waited for them to establish the gate on the other end. From what I'd seen when Faran created one earlier, work on the far end was both much less dramatic and faster. It probably took less than a minute, but it felt like days. I spent most of the time trying desperately not to think about how very much a couple of efik beans or a big glass of Kyle's would have eased my nerves.

You'd regret it, Triss sent into my mind.

I didn't say one word.

You didn't have to, not when you want it so badly. I can feel you longing after it like a canker in my soul.

Me, too, but I won't give in to the wanting. And then, because I wouldn't lie to Triss, *Not today, at least.*

That's when the gate opened. I hadn't seen it with the last one, but this time I did. The back of that hairsbreadth of depth the shadow possessed suddenly acquired a sort of reverse translucency, as though darkness was shining through from the other side.

"Follow me." Faran stepped up to the portal. As before, there was a moment of resistance, followed by a flash of darkness. Then she was gone.

I went next, putting my palm out to touch the shadow. I was expecting to feel something like the press of cold silk against skin when you touch a bolt of fabric in the market. Instead, it grabbed onto me, and I realized the resistance didn't come from the portal. It came from a soul recognizing the hungry darkness. I tried to pull back, but it pulled me in with a sharp jerk.

My perspective rotated as I passed through the membrane between the worlds. I wasn't stepping forward into the everdark. I was falling face-first into eternity. And it was cold, so very, very cold that it burned.

I had gone with my friend Devin to Aven once, the country of his birth. It was deep winter at the time and Devin had insisted on reliving one of the few experiences he remembered from his childhood, a steam bath followed by an ice water plunge. I don't know how cold it was that day. Cold enough so that in the quarter of an hour we spent in the sauna a good skin of ice formed over the hole we'd cut in the lake.

After my time in the steam bath I was so hot I felt lightheaded and I was dying for a chance to cool down. The edge of the ice lay barely two long steps from the door of the sauna, a distance crossed so quickly I barely felt the cold. I leaped out and down, breaking the skim of ice and plunging into a sort of ecstatic agony of cold. My skin felt frozen and on fire by turns. In deeper water I could easily have drowned as sensation buried thought. The passage through the gate of shadows was like that, only more so.

If not for Triss, I'd have been lost then—overwhelmed by the cold and the pain and the utter lack of light, much as Master Thera must have been. Where I couldn't make any sense of my entry into the everdark, Triss had come home. He caught my hand and tugged at me, telling me to walk. Though I was falling and there was nowhere for my feet to find purchase, I followed his command and found that it made a difference.

No up. No down. Nowhere. Nothing. No when, even. Yet, walking moved me. Maybe it was the intent to move that mattered and not the motion, but whatever the reason, I suddenly knew that I could choose my path through the eternal falling darkness. And I did, following a strand of green spell-light that I could sense but not see—walking through pain, but walking still. I felt better then, but

Thera had been companioned by a Shade, too, and she had never come back. I knew I couldn't relax until I came out the other side.

The distance felt simultaneously infinite and yet no farther than the one might casually walk between one breath and the next. I tried to count my paces, but I found that I had lost my ability to comprehend numbers. Then, just as suddenly as it had begun, I passed through the other end of the gate. My left foot trod nothing. My right came down on rough flags tilted at a bizarre angle.

Up and down reasserted themselves, and I tumbled forward onto hands and knees to empty my stomach through a stone grate in the floor. Sound came back then, as the roar of the storm hit me like a falling wall, brutal even indoors. It was so loud I could barely hear the rush of the water below the grate.

Clear the way. Triss gave me an order and I obeyed, rolling to one side when I found I hadn't the wherewithal to easily return to my feet. The action reminded me of my bruised or cracked rib— painfully.

We were in a low wide space with a steeply angled ceiling/wall combination that hosted the gate. It was too small and strangely shaped to be called a room, more like a stone lean-to. The air smelled of damp rock and old dust and the burned air that comes with lightning.

"Where the hell are we?" I asked, my voice a ragged croak.

"Underneath a flight of stairs, I think." It was Faran, speaking very quietly and sounding even worse than I felt. She was sitting on the floor to one side of the shadow gate. "That grate there opens into a drainpipe. It's where we came in. Check around the corner, but do it quietly, I think the sanctum's just beyond. I have to stay here to anchor Ssithra."

I started to slowly crawl off in the direction she was pointing just as Roric fell through behind me. He was swearing quietly, or at least he was until Faran gave him a gentle shove with her boot. But then I was at the place where our weirdly shaped little alcove met the world with a flattening out of the ceiling at about chest height. I had just enough sense left to use a cornerbright to do my looking.

It took me a moment to make sense of what I was seeing, as much because of my perspective and the horrible disorientation I'd carried forward from the everdark as anything. We were indeed under a set of stairs. The shadow gate opened from the back of the first course. The corner where I lay was underneath a landing where the stairs turned back on themselves. From there, they continued up toward the second floor gallery at the back of the sanctum behind the great sculpture of Shan.

The area under the landing and stairs acted as a storage space for religious paraphernalia which blocked much of my view. What little I could see was further occluded by the half-open door and the raised dais where Shan's sculpture sat. The floor was visibly wet inside the doorway, and the door—obviously blown inward by the storm—kept banging against a bronze chariot built in an ancient style.

I looked back over my shoulder just in time to see Maryam and Javan fall through the shadow gate in a heap. Javan was unconscious again and lying across Maryam's shoulders.

"I bumped into him," she said as Roric helped her shift Javan aside. "Tripped over him, really. Vrass saved us both then, kept me upright and pointed us in the right direction."

"Fuck!" Faran snarled. "Fuckfuckfuckdamnit!"

"What is it?" I started to crawl toward her.

"Master Loris just closed the gate."

"What? No!"

A tiny hippogriff appeared on the angled ceiling where the gate had been, all of himself that Issaru could project so far. "Loris is dying. The effort of holding the gate open was too much for him, was always going to be too much. He'd never have made it through the everdark and we both knew it going in. Get them home, Aral. He told me to tell you he was counting on you." The shadow wavered and started to fade. "Avenge us."

And then he was gone. They were both gone. One more pair of Namara's champions fallen to the Hand and the Son of Heaven. Two if you added Leyan and Ulriss buried in the cave-in below. Tears burned down my cheeks, and I promised myself that I would make my old teachers's final requests into reality whatever the cost.

19

When someone important to you dies, they take a little of you with them into the grave. Though we'd never been all that close, Loris took the last vestiges of my childhood with him. I was now the oldest living Blade. There were no more generations between me and the void.

I didn't count Kelos and Devin or the other turncoats. They'd lost any right to that name by betraying our goddess. All the priests were long dead, too. That left me the senior heir to the tattered remnants of Namara's once great legacy. The weight of it fell heavily across my shoulders and heavier still on my heart, as I tried to figure out how the hell to get Loris's students and mine free of the trap that currently held us. Perhaps fortunately, those students didn't yet seem all that interested in looking to me for answers.

Maryam worked busily at restoring Javan to coherence, while Roric leaned in close to Faran to say something. He spoke quietly, and it was impossible to hear him from even a few yards away over the roar of the winds, but the gist of his words became obvious when Faran handed across a small knife. He used it to cut shallow slices over his cheekbones.

When he was done, he caught me looking at him and gave a grim smile. "A custom from my childhood in Avars, before the priests took me. They would not approve, I think. But they're gone now, and Loris was more than my teacher. He was my clan chief."

I nodded. "Blood for mourning. Blood for vengeance." I knew the custom well.

"And blood for blood," he finished. "You don't object?"

"No. I understand and I sympathize."

Roric nodded in turn. "I see that you *do* understand. It's in your eyes." His expression went very thoughtful and he flipped the knife over so that he held it by the blade, offering me the hilt. "In your heart, too, I think."

And, because it was, I took the knife and I slashed my cheeks as well.

Faran leaned forward as I finished and extended her hand. "Mine."

I handed the knife across, and she, too, cut her cheeks. Then she offered it to Maryam. The tall lanky young woman took it and shook her head.

"Madness," she said. "Primitive, superstitious madness." Then she cut her cheeks and passed the knife to Javan, saying "Blood for blood."

She's right, Triss said into my mind. *Both her words and her actions.*

Roric's Shade, Ssolvey, shifted into his giant badgerlike form and gave us a very formal bow. "Master Aral, Resshath Triss, what are your orders?"

Javan nodded. "With Loris dead and Jax missing, we are yours to command. What's the plan?"

What I wanted to say was, "A giant fucking mess." This was the point where we were supposed to go over the wall and head for the hills. Of course, that failed to take into account the fact that anyone who stepped outside right now was going to get blown clear to Kanjuri, on top of all the other stuff that had gone wrong.

Triss?

Your call, Aral.

We hadn't properly factored the winds into our thinking. Oh, we'd known there was going to be a big storm, planned to use it to help cover our tracks even. The fight at the cemetery had served as a recent reminder of the immediate consequences of killing the Hand and their Storm bond-mates. But we simply hadn't anticipated the scale and killing ferocity of it. Until the winds calmed, we were all trapped in the temple. Faran raised her eyebrows at me then, and I realized that I'd run out of time for thinking. Besides, there was only one possible answer.

"The plan is simple, Javan. We shroud up, we go out into the sanctum, and we kill everything that moves. Hand first, Sword as it's convenient."

"Now, that is a good plan." Roric's grim smile returned. "I like it. Blood for mourning."

"Blood for vengeance," I added.

"And blood for blood," which we all spoke as a chorus. Madness. Then, one by one, we vanished into darkness.

Though I had assumed full control of Triss and his senses, I took the risk of leaving my eyes uncovered as I slipped out into the sanctum. I wanted to give myself one clear human-eyed look at the field before I surrendered my sight. The skies obliged me with a huge bolt of lightning that momentarily lit the whole place in a brilliant eerie light. I was pretty sure it was the last clear picture I was going to have of things for some time to come, so I set it in my memory.

The temple was more than half destroyed, with all the windows blown in. Portions of the vaulted stone roof had fallen, and rain was coming in every which way. One of the cave-ins had happened over the altar and the giant sculpture of Shan. Falling rubble had torn off the arms of the god on the left side, and left the ones on the right cracked and dangling. Bodies and debris lay everywhere.

No matter what happened in the next few minutes, the Son of Heaven had suffered losses here that he would be a very long time in replacing. It wasn't nearly enough for me.

Then the lightning was gone, and the battle began. Five Blades, all of them wounded, against a half score of sorcerer-priests and a hundred soldiers in the dark of a ruined temple. I lost track of the others in the first seconds, as my world narrowed to a series of fleeting impressions and momentary flashes of clarity.

The rain pounds and the wind hammers. Lightning tears giant holes in the sky and rips irregular stripes out of Triss's unvision. The shadows of the raindrops create a million false dark-echoes that drown out the real ones. Blind fighting. I am forced to push aside the shroud over my eyes, risking visibility so that I can see.

I kill the first Hand I encounter with a thrust from behind. She falls away from me, leaving her blood on my sword. A giant bolt of turquoise lightning spikes down through one of the holes in the roof, incinerating her body in an instant funeral pyre. My shroud compresses almost to nothing, and Triss shrieks agony in his dreams with the intensity of it. The heat shatters the stones beneath her, and a wave of pressure edged with bits of hot rock throws me back and away.

I roll up onto my feet, only half dodging the spear thrust of a soldier who has taken advantage of the momentary reduction of my shroud. He misses anything vital, but I come away with a long shallow slice across the front of my right hip bone. I'm hunting the

Signet and I don't have time for a Sword, so I throw a burst of mage-fire that sets his clothes afire and move on.

A half dozen more Swords die at my hand over the next couple of minutes before I spot my real target. Nea Sjensdor, Lady Signet, right hand and heir of the Son of Heaven, a potent symbol of the forces that destroyed my goddess and my life. She stands at the base of the altar. Her back is pressed tight against the stone facing, and there is a loose pile of rubble above and behind her, guarding the rear approach. I will have to take her from the front.

That's good on one level. I *want* her to know what killed her, and I want to see the look in her eyes when she dies. But it will make my task harder. Though her sword of office lies in its sheath across her back, she is armed with a pair of the short scythes called kama. Spell-light paints them a deep purple with some sort of combat enchantment, and the handles are steel instead of the more usual oak. I can see from the way that she holds them that she's an expert in their use. With the hooked blades extending her reach, she looks ever more mantislike than when I first saw her back at the Gryphon in Tien.

I can't spot her familiar—a Storm hiding in the chaos of the greater storm, but it has to be someplace close. The rain and the lightning continue to make it impossible for me to use Triss's senses, but I want to get in tight before she becomes aware of me. I look at the thirty or so feet of debris-strewn ground that lies between us, and set it in my memory. I shroud my face before releasing my hold on Triss. Magic won't win this fight for me, and having Triss awake to cover my back might.

I tell him, *I've found the Signet*, and I quickly fill in the details as I start forward.

For Loris and Issaru, he says when I am finished.

For Namara and the temple, I add.

This was not the Signet who commanded the forces of the Son of Heaven that day. That Signet died in the battle, slain by Master Illiana and Resshath Ssuma in a suicide attack, or so I had been told. But Nea was there, third in the line of command. The most senior of the sorcerer-priests to survive the battle, she was made Signet on her return to Heaven's Reach.

The changing sound of the rain as it strikes the statue of Shan and the feel of the floor under my feet tell me that I am within striking distance.

I need my eyes.

Triss parts the veil that covers them and I swing a low cut at the

Signet's ankles with my left-hand sword in the same instant that I drive my right at her throat. The blades are cloaked in shadow, and yet somehow, the Signet anticipates them. She snaps her own right-hand weapon down in a flat block, while sweeping her left around to hook my thrust aside.

I have a brief moment to remember that her Storm had shown an uncanny knack for spotting us back at the cemetery, too. Perhaps it can read the patterns of the winds in weather like this in the same way that Triss sees dark-echoes. Then, with a twist of her left kama where it engaged my sword, the Signet points the end of the rod directly at my face. Reflexes buried far below the conscious level scream at me, and I bend sharply backward without having time to think why.

A blast of pure magical force passes through the space where my face had been only an instant before. I feel my nose break in response to the pressure wave, as I realize the kama are battle wands as well as blades. Avoiding the blast has forced me to take my eyes off the second of the Signet's weapons. I hop back awkwardly, hoping to avoid the blow that I know is coming.

Pain sears along the outside of my left thigh as the hooking slice finds my leg, and Triss grunts in sympathy as the enchantments on the blade cut him, too, but I'm lucky. The combination of shroud and my jump back is enough to keep her blade from leaving me with much more than a long deep scratch. I snap my free sword down and around, batting the kama aside before she can bring it in line for a magical attack. I can feel the blood trickling down my leg, but none of the big muscles is badly damaged.

I want to move out and away from the Signet, reshroud, and then come back in, but I don't dare. Not with the battle wands extending her range to as far as she can see. I have to stay close and keep her from getting them in line again. I move into a more defensive posture, focusing my eyes on her center but tracking the flickering shifts of her kama so that I can bat at them whenever one looks as though it might point my way. It's a weak position, but all that I can think of in the moment. Before I can even begin to formulate a new strategy, I feel my shroud leave me.

Triss!

Storm above!

Tiny lightnings flash overhead and Triss's words dissolve into a series of hisses and snarls. But I don't dare take my eyes off of the Signet, not even for an instant. If there are any of the Sword close at hand, I'm going to die in the next few minutes. I cast a prayer to a dead goddess, knowing it's futile, and yet still hoping that Faran or Roric or one of the others is close enough to act as its instrument.

Over the next few seconds, the Signet and I exchange a dozen quick blows and counters, and no one runs a spear through my back. I can hear Triss fighting with the Storm as a sort of continuing angry snarl in the back of my mind, and I can only hope that he's doing better than I am. I don't dare look up to check. The Signet's damned good. Too good for me to take her quickly, or possibly at all. Not unless I get lucky, or my prayer comes through.

That's when Jax whispers in my ear. "Aral, can you hear me?"

Her voice is low and faint, full of pain and exhaustion. To me, she sounds like a goddess. I nod, hoping that she can see me from wherever she is projecting her voice, and not wanting to speak for fear of giving her away to the Signet.

"Good," she replies. "I'm hurt, badly. Very badly. Dying maybe. I can't do much, but I can probably give you one split second of distraction. Make it count."

"Wait!" I shout.

An idea has come to me, inspired by where we stand, or where I think we stand anyway. Maybe I don't have to be lucky. Maybe I just have to be smart. I glance upward to see if I'm right. Storm and shadow tumble and twist around the remaining arms of the great statue, the scytheblade head of the Storm mirroring the paired kama of its bond-mate.

"Wait for what?" It's the Signet, responding to my yell and looking at me like I'm a madman. "Is the great Aral Kingslayer going to give himself up?"

I look her square in the eyes, I want her to think that I'm talking to her, even if what I say doesn't make a lick of sense. "No, what about you? Where are you? Where do you stand?"

The Signet shakes her head, but doesn't say another word, just lashes out with her left kama, aiming for my wrist.

"Leaned against the intact side of the altar," replies Jax. "Why does it matter?"

"Because Shan himself is about to strike you down," I say to the Signet, hoping Jax will understand what I want.

"You're mad," replies the Signet.

"Oh, I think I see," says Jax. "But how—"

Before she can finish the question, I flip my left sword into an underhanded grip, an insane shortening of my reach considering the circumstances. But I can't afford to lose it, and if I don't want to cut my own nose off, it's going to be a much safer grip for what I need to do. The Signet takes advantage of the maneuver to press the attack, and I'm in serious danger of losing the fight then and there. Twisting and turning like a madman, I manage to hold off the blades and dodge the blasts long enough to get my hand in the right position.

With a sharp yank, I rip the pouch free of my chest where it hangs off the straps of my sword rig. I use the same motion to flick the pouch and its contents to the place where Jax lies in shadow. Then I go on the offensive, pressing the Signet with everything I have. She knows something's up, but good as she is, she's not good enough to pay attention to anything but staying alive for the next few seconds. It's exhausting and I can't hope to sustain the pace, but I push her back and to my left, waiting for the sound of the first crack.

When it comes, I throw myself backward, rolling desperately as I hit the floor. The Signet gets off two or three blasts, none of which connect, but I pick up a lot of bruises and a couple of burns from the near misses. Then comes the noise I've been hoping for, an enormous crash that ends in a scream. I bounce back to my feet and see that Jax has come through.

She's taken the finger I threw her and pressed it to the side of the altar, triggering the movement of the giant statue's mighty stone arms. Its *badly cracked* stone arms. With my last attack, I pushed the Signet back just far enough to put her under the hand of her own damned god.

I don't know if Namara's ghost heard my prayer. I don't know if she answered me in the voice of the woman I once loved. I don't know if this struck her as the perfect justice for one of those most responsible for the destruction of her temple and her legacy. All that I know is that the five-thousand-pound fractured stone hand of Shan has fallen from its broken wrist as I hoped it would, crushing the Signet like the mantis she so resembles.

She's been touched by the hand of her god, Triss said into my mind. *It doesn't seem to have worked out for her.*

He's got the Storm pinned now against the chest of Shan's statue. It's still struggling, so I know the Signet isn't dead yet, but it's only a matter of time. No one survives the kind of injuries she has now. The entire right side of her skull is dished in and covered in blood, that and one arm is all that's visible under the broken stone, but it's enough. The Storm jerks violently, and there's a sharp crackle like carefully sequenced miniature lightning.

I'm letting it go, says Triss a moment later. *It wants to go to her and it promises not to attack us.*

If you're sure.

He doesn't answer, just releases his grip on the thing. It flits down to hover over the great stone hand, a wild woeful keening coming from somewhere in the vicinity of its head. I dismiss it from my mind and move toward Jax as Triss reshrouds me. I can't see her, but there's a deeper patch of shadow near the front of the dais.

"Jax?" I don't like that I can't see her and her injuries. "How bad it is?"

"Later." Her voice comes out of the shadow, sounding even weaker than it had in my ear earlier. I wonder how she did that but this isn't the time to ask. "Now, you need to finish this."

"You're right." She is, but I need to tell her about Loris. Especially if she's dying.

"That may be the first time you've ever told me I was right."

I relax a little. If she's up to giving me a jab, she can't be quite at death's door.

"It may be the first time it's been true. Look, I have to go back to the fight, but . . ." There's no gentle way to say it. "Loris is dead." I hear a sharp hiss of indrawn breath, but Jax doesn't say anything, and I can't stay. "He saved us all, but he didn't make it."

Faran screams then—an agonized sound—and I turn and run back to the fight. I can't find her in the darkness, which is good. It means she's still shrouded and not dead, but it doesn't reassure. As I'm looking for her, I see a Hand swing an axe low and fast into a patch of shadow. The scream is deeper this time, Javan to judge by the foot and calf left behind when the shadow rolls aside. I split the Hand's skull down to the teeth, losing my sword when it wedges in bone. A small group of Swords rushes me then.

Killing them takes me more time than it has any right to—I'm exhausted. More keep coming, drawn by the little knot of fighting perhaps. When it stops, I realize that I can't see any movement anywhere. I turn a slow circle there in the middle of the sanctum floor and still don't see anything but the falling rain and flashing lightning.

Unshroud me, Triss. I need to find the others.

He doesn't say anything, just collapses, first to a thin skin of darkness, and then down into my normal shadow.

Are you all right? I ask.

Have to rest a bit. That's all. Wake me if you need me. I can feel him letting go then, dropping almost instantly into sleep, and wish that I could do the same.

"I've been watching your back." It's Faran, speaking through gritted teeth from somewhere close by. "They're all dead. We won."

She releases her shroud and I feel a sick weight in my stomach. The entire left side of her head is covered in blood, and she's got a strip of cloth bound across her eye.

"It's better than it looks," she says. "At least I really hope it is."

Roric appears at her shoulder, close but beyond easy stabbing range—sensible under the circumstances. "Let me see it, Faran. Master Loris was training me in healing magics."

I want to help, but I can see that Roric's got it under control, and I've just remembered Javan. "Thiess!" I yell. "Where are you? It's over."

"Here! Hurry!" The Shade's voice is shaky with fear.

As I head in that direction, Maryam steps out of shadows in front of me, coming from the other direction. Judging by the stains on the shirt Faran had brought her from the dead Sword earlier, she's got a deep gash across the ribs under her right breast. Probably some broken ribs, too, but she seems to be handling the injuries all right. In a moment she's kneeling over the suddenly visible Javan. He's pale from loss of blood and covered in sweat, but still breathing.

"Can you handle him for the moment?" I ask. "I left Jax by the altar and she's badly hurt, too."

"Go," says Maryam, and I do.

I'm halfway back across the sanctum floor when it really sinks in that we've won. My knees go soggy, and I can suddenly feel every bruise and cut. My nose feels like some demented squirrel has been using it to hide walnuts. I'm going to have to get one of the others to set it for me, but that will have to wait. Jax first.

By the time I reach her, I've started to settle back into something resembling a normal relationship with my sense of time and space. The Signet's storm is curled against the fallen stone hand. Tiny lightnings are still occasionally crackling here and there in its wings, but faintly. They're taking a long painful time dying, but it won't be long now. If I were a better person, I might feel badly about that. I'm not and I don't.

"Jax? It's over."

"My students?" She dropped her shroud.

I winced at the sight of her—she'd broken her left leg and arm at the very least, judging by the angle of the one and the sling holding the other. There was probably more I couldn't easily see, but I knew better than to ask about her injuries before answering her question.

"Roric and Maryam are mostly fine but Javan's lost his right leg below the knee. I don't know if he'll make it, but Maryam's trying."

"Leyan?"

"Dead, crushed in a cave-in engineered by the Signet."

"Bastards. Faran?"

"All right, I hope. She's bloodied up pretty badly and she's got a bandage over her left eye."

"Why are you here with me then?"

"Roric's taking care of her, and I was the only one who knew you were even present. How bad are you?"

"Leg's broken in two places, arm in one. Cracked some ribs and I was coughing up blood earlier, but that seems to have settled down, so it's probably not going to kill me right away. Worst is my left hand." She touched the sling with her other hand, and I noticed the blood soaking it for the first time. "I'll be shocked if I don't lose a couple of fingers."

"The Son of Heaven is going to pay for this!" The words come from somewhere deep down inside me, and it felt more like they were speaking themselves through my mouth than that I was saying them. "I'll *make* him pay for it."

Before I could say anything further, there was a tremendous flash from behind me and another enormous crash of thunder as the Signet and her bond-mate died. Good. It was a start. Then a thought occurred to me, but if I was going to make it a reality, I would have to move *very* quickly.

"Jax, can you hold on a few minutes more? I've business with the Signet, or what's left of her."

She gave me an odd look but nodded. "Do what you have to."

20

I stared at the mountainside and saw my soul. The snow above the old Dalridian castle burned white in the sun, hurting my eyes, but I couldn't turn away. It perfectly reflected the cold anger I felt in my bones, frozen, deadly, and utterly unmelting even here at the tail end of summer.

More than three weeks had passed since the debacle at the abbey in the Magelands. Three weeks spent mostly in traveling to this place, Jax and Loris's refuge in the mountains. We'd started out on the river coming up from below Tavan to Uln by barge and boat, the gentlest transport we could find for our wounded.

We'd had to hire porters to carry the stretchers that held Jax and Javan over the goat tracks above Uln that were the only way into Dalridia this far south. Roric and I had ended up trading off carrying Faran for a good part of that leg, too, when she went delirious on us. We'd made the final passage of the journey by royal Dalridian coach which provided some luxury, but we'd never once stopped moving.

We all would have liked to rest and recover a while in Tavan, at the healer's hall attached to the university, right at the beginning. But we didn't dare risk staying longer than it took them to treat the worst of our collective injuries. It was just too dangerous to stay anywhere there was any chance the Son of Heaven's people might find us. We had hurt him as no one had since Namara's fall.

More than three hundred followers of Shan had died at the abbey, nearly a third at our hands, the rest in the great storm and the flood that came with it. The temple proper was the only building that had even two walls standing at the end of the night. Not long after the end of the battle it had lost the rest of its roof when the main vault gave way. We'd have been crushed if we hadn't already retreated to the storage space under the stairs to get out of the worst of the wind and the rain.

Roric and Maryam and I had spent most of the next morning digging our way out of the wreckage with the help of our three Shades, where muscle simply wouldn't do the trick. The devastation we found when we finally broke through into the daylight was like nothing I'd ever seen. The abbey had been destroyed utterly and the bodies of most of its inhabitants would never be found. For that matter so had a huge swath of the surrounding countryside.

For several miles in every direction it looked like the aftermath of some mad cyclonic country dance. Great slithering tracks of destruction crisscrossed the landscape in a pattern centered on the temple's sanctum. Not a tree stood unbroken in the surrounding orchards, nor a single stalk of wheat in the fields. Death had taken everything that lived, a death that I had brought with me into this place.

The sight filled me with a sick anger that I hadn't felt in such measure since I saw my goddess lying broken and dead on the bottom of the sacred lake. If I'd had a bottle of whiskey or anything else with alcohol in it I'd have drunk it down without a thought. But I didn't, I had to face that destruction sober and without anything to blur my understanding of my part in it.

I think that's what cemented my decision to kill the Son of Heaven more than anything. Faran was right when she'd accused me of sentimentality. I didn't like killing anyone I didn't have to. For most of my career as a Blade I'd managed to avoid ghosting very many people who didn't deserve it, mostly keeping the deaths confined to my targets and the people who guarded them. Probably no more than a couple of score total, and most of those in self-defense. Till now.

I didn't regret the Hand or the Sword, the people we killed directly with steel and magic. As far as I was concerned, they had earned their deaths on the day my goddess died. But the clergy and the lay brothers and sisters who made up the bulk of the abbey's regular inhabitants had done nothing directly to me or mine. If they were not quite innocent of the blood of my brethren and my goddess, still they hadn't done anything to deserve this. That was without counting any farmers or other bystanders taken by the storms or the floods as they flowed away downstream.

Those deaths now belonged on my tally, and I would answer for them when I faced the lords of judgment. But I would not answer for them alone. Not one drop of blood would have been spilled here had not the Son and his Signet struck the first blow by taking Loris and the others prisoner. The Signet I had already taken to account— absently, I touched the pouch at my side where two beringed fingers now resided in near matching boxes. But the Son had yet to pay his share of the butcher's bill. Both for the deaths at the abbey last month, and for the deaths at Namara's temple six years ago.

It was time Shan's chief priest faced justice. And if it was a justice tainted with that ideal's darker cousin, revenge, than that, too, was something I was willing to have on my account when I faced my own judgment. The priests and Blades who raised me had taught me that revenge was not the province of Namara, that it lessened her glory when the two commingled. But Namara was dead, and her priests with her, and my frozen heart wanted hot blood spilled to warm it.

"Master Aral, are you up here again?" It was Faran's voice, still weak and weary nearly a month on, and the sound of it made the ice in my heart burn a little colder.

I turned back to the stairhead where Faran had just poked her nose out the door. She looked gaunt and pale, and the scar that ran from her forehead down under her eyepatch and out onto her cheekbone stood out red and raw. The healers had saved the eye, though they said she had at best even odds of recovering her vision or of ever seeing the end of the headaches that had started in the days after the injury. She was under strict orders to rest as much as she could, and oughtn't have been climbing the stairs to the castle's highest tower, but I had no one to blame for that but myself.

"I'm here," I said. "Just looking at the mountains again."

"Well, Jax was asking after you, and I said I'd come find you, though Roric tried to take the task for himself. Will you come down?" She sounded sad and quiet, unsure of herself in a way that was utterly out of character—more ice around my heart.

"Tell her I'll be there in a few minutes."

You should go now. Triss sounded more than a little sad and unsure himself. *Don't send Faran away alone. Not again.*

He was worried about me, and not without reason. I hadn't touched a drop of alcohol since the abbey. Not because I hadn't wanted to. Damn me, but I wanted a drink. Wanted one more than almost anything I'd ever wanted before. Wanted to surrender to the bottle and let it blur away some of the pain.

But I didn't want it more than I wanted to hand the Son of

Heaven his own heart before he died. And I was *not* going to let anything get in the way of that goal, nor let go of one shred of the pain and anger that drove me toward it. If I lived through the experience, there would be plenty of time to get drunk after the Son of Heaven was dead. Until then, nothing could get in my way.

She's still waiting, said Triss, *and you owe her more than the Son of Heaven's heart served up in a pretty package.*

He was right, of course. I shook myself free of the cold rage, or at least as much as I could.

"Come here, Faran. I've been neglecting you, and I'm sorry for that."

She crossed the short distance from stairhead to tower wall to stand beside me. "It's all right, really. I've been spending time with the other students. Altia's here and she was one of my best friends back at the temple. Jaeris, too." Her face clouded even more. "We've grown apart though, since then. Their experiences were so different. Especially Altia's. She was one of the first Loris and Jax found. . . ."

I put an arm around her shoulders and squeezed her in tight against my side, though I didn't have any comforting words.

"For her it's almost like the fall of the temple was a brief nightmare between safe havens, horrible but fleeting," continued Faran. "She doesn't understand what I went through or what I had to do to survive. I think she believes I've betrayed my training a little. It makes me feel like some sort of actual monster, where you calling me one never did."

"You aren't and never have been any kind of monster but mine. You've done nothing that you should be ashamed of, and if Altia says that you have, perhaps I should have a few words with her . . . my young monster."

She wrinkled her nose, then smiled and squeezed me back. "You really are a horrible old man, and thank you for offering, but please don't. She hasn't said a word. It's just the way she looks at me, and I think that it will pass with time. We were good friends once." Then she settled in against my side and was quiet for a little while.

I'll deal with it, Triss said angrily into my mind. *Olthiss knows better than to let her bond-mate get away with that sort of judgmental rubbish. And if she doesn't, she will when I'm done with her. Probably best if you don't tell Faran though. Some things are better handled among Shades. We don't have silly illusions about our companion's better natures.*

Thank you. We're going to have to go after the Son of Heaven soon, and I want Faran to feel at home here while we're gone.

Triss made a sort of mental tut-tutting noise. *Speaking of not having illusions, I'm a bit worried about the state of the Blade you've chosen for this mission, companion mine. While I approve of parting the Son of Heaven from this life as soon as ever it becomes possible, making it personal makes for mistakes.*

That's Kelos talking, I replied. *And right now he's only sitting a tiny jot below the death mark on my list himself. If he'd done more than just jam those locks, Loris and Issaru might still be with us along with Leyan and Ulriss. I still don't know what his game is in all this, nor his exact role in the death of Namara, but I don't trust him as far as I could toss a stone dog, and I don't like what he's become one little bit. If he gets in my way, I may have to kill him, too.*

Or die trying, Triss sighed.

Or die trying, I acknowledged.

At least he hasn't come after that finger yet. I half expected him to show up at the abbey as we were digging out and demand it back.

Me, too, which is why I made the second one from Nea's hand. I just wish I'd done half as good a job with mine as Kelos did with his. I don't know if it'll even work.

You had a few distractions to deal with, and less time to prepare.

There is that.

Faran sighed, gave me another squeeze, and then slipped out from under my arm. "We'd better go. Jax was already sounding pretty irritated when she first asked after you, and that's a while ago now."

"I don't doubt it. She doesn't like being laid up any more than you do, and she's a lot less capable of getting around right now."

Bones took forever to heal if you wanted to make sure they did so fully and properly, even with magic speeding the process. And Jax's left leg was broken in four places, not the two I'd initially thought. She was lucky she hadn't lost it at the knee the way Javan had. She couldn't use a crutch yet either, not with that arm broken and almost half her hand gone—her luck had failed her there, though she'd probably be able to hold a sword again in a few months.

One more thing to add to the bloody bill I intended to deliver to the Son of Heaven. My broken nose and couple of dozen stitches barely even figured into it compared to the others. Only Roric had come off lighter in the battle, though the torturers of the Hand had done him enough injury to balance us pretty evenly. If the temple yet stood, we would both have been cleared back to active service, with Maryam perhaps a week or two behind us while she waited for her cracked ribs to finish healing.

I helped Faran down the stairs, though she claimed repeatedly that she was fine. Judging by the sheen of sweat on her forehead when we hit bottom, I probably should have insisted on carrying her. She led me to the solar where Jax was taking her lunch, then vanished, obviously on earlier instruction. That left just the two of us and our Shades once Jax sent away the servant who'd carried her up from her rooms.

I raised an eyebrow. "You wanted to see me?"

"Obviously. Are you still planning on going after the Son of Heaven?"

"Yes." It wasn't the first time she'd asked, nor even the fifth, and I didn't much feel like talking about it anymore.

She looked at my shadow. "Triss, what do you think of this?" It was the first time she'd put him on the spot about it.

He shifted into dragon form to speak, and Ssithra matched his change out of courtesy. "I think that the Son of Heaven needs to die," he said.

Jax rolled her eyes. "So do I. So does everyone in this whole castle not excluding the grooms and potboys. What I want to know is what you think about Aral doing it, and insisting on doing it right now."

"I'm not leaving for a week, Jax. I'd put it off longer than that if I wasn't worried about an early snow closing the passes."

"Dammit Aral, what's the hurry?" asked Jax. "It's going to take you two months to get there no matter when you leave. Why can't you at least wait till next spring?"

I sighed. I didn't want to tell her the truth, but I didn't think she was going to stop arguing with me until I did. "I'm afraid I'll lose my resolve."

"That would be fabulous, as far as I'm concerned," snapped Jax. "This entire plan is crazy, and we need you here. With Loris gone, I'm alone now. You're a full Blade, and a better one in most ways than I ever was. You have so much to teach my students, why can't you stay here and do it?"

"Because I'm not going to do your students one damn bit of good as an alcohol-soaked sponge sitting in the corner and drooling! And that's what's going to happen to me if I lose my resolve. I want a drink right now, Jax. I wanted one when I got up this morning, and when I went to bed last night. I want one like I haven't in more than a year."

"You haven't had one drink since we got here," she said.

"That's because I have a goal that matters to me more than my soul right now. The only way I'm holding it together is by picturing the look on the Son of Heaven's face when I feed him his own liver. That's what the fucking fight at the abbey did to me, Jax. It pushed me right back over the edge, and now I'm clinging by my fingernails. I have to go, and I have to do it soon or I'm going to fall apart."

"But it's madness! You don't even have a real plan beyond traveling to Heaven's Reach and using the key that Kelos the traitor gave you to sneak in."

"Not yet, no. Because I have to see the lay of the land. I've never been to Heaven's Reach and I don't have the goddess to conjure me up a map anymore. Besides, you know as well as I do that all a plan does is give you a starting point. Not once in all the missions the goddess sent me on did the initial plan survive more than about halfway through to the goal. Most of the time it went to hell the minute I actually started encountering the reality on the ground. It's not having a plan that made me a good Blade, it was being able to revise the plan to suit the conditions as I found them."

"He's got a point," said Triss.

She threw up her hands. "You know, that's half of why Devin hated you. He used to say that no matter what the plan was, you always fucked it up, and *still* came out on top."

"That's because Devin, as much as I once loved him, is an idiot. Success isn't making a good plan and following it no matter what. Success is understanding that a good plan is step one on a long journey, and then moving on to step two when the time comes."

"We need you here, Aral. To take Loris's place." I raised an eyebrow and Jax blushed angrily. "I mean at the school, not in my bed."

"I know what you meant," I said, more gently this time because that's not what I'd intended to convey. "But you don't need me. Not the me you've got at the moment, at least. I have to do this, Jax. If I don't, I'm going to crawl into the bottle again. I can feel it."

She looked away. "The Son of Heaven is a harder target to crack than the King of Zhan. Four Masters have died trying to make him pay for what he did to us at the temple. Four. Not counting the turncoats, that's more than there are left of us. You're going to die if you go after him, Aral."

"I might. But if I don't at least try, you won't recognize me in six months. More importantly, I think I can do it." I pulled out the pair of little silver boxes. "This gives me an edge like nothing any other Blade has ever even dreamed about. It's not a magic panacea, but I think it'll get me in close enough."

"Maybe, but will it get you out again? That's always the harder part."

I shrugged. "I'm less concerned about that at the moment, but yes, I hope that it will."

"Don't think I've given up on this yet," said Jax. "I've still got a week. But assuming you can make this play work, will you come back here to help me with the school afterward?"

"Maybe. I'd like to, if I can beat the bottle. I don't know if killing the Son of Heaven will be enough to get me back on the right path. What I do know is that not doing it sure as hell won't."

"Again, not giving up, but if you have to go, won't you at least take Roric with you? You've got two of those fingers, and having some backup might make all the difference."

Triss's "No" beat mine. "I agree that Aral and I have to try this. But I won't let anyone else risk themselves with us."

Jax smashed her good hand down on her thigh. "That's because you don't believe you're coming back, isn't it?"

"I believe we can kill the Son of Heaven," replied Triss.

"That's not an answer," said Jax.

"It is, you know," said Sshayar. "Just not the one you want." She sat back on her haunches and gave Triss and me each a small bow. "I wish you success and good hunting. I will pray that you come back to us, but even if you don't, know that I agree that the target is worth the cost." Then she collapsed into Jax's shadow.

"Well, I damn well don't," she said.

"Neither do I," Faran added when I slipped back out into the hall. "But I've seen you drinking where Jax hasn't, and I think I understand you better than she does. If this is what you need to do, I'm not going to fight with you about it."

"But you'd follow after me if you were well enough, no matter what I said."

"Of course I would." There was no heat in her voice, but I could see it burning in her unbandaged eye, and I thought that her not being up to coming with me on this might be the sole good thing to come out of her injury. "You need someone to watch your back."

"Little monster."

"Horrible old man."

After that and my conversation with Jax there wasn't much more to say but good-bye. I left the castle on foot a few days later, though Jax offered me a horse or a coach. A man afoot is much less obtrusive than a rider, and he can go as fast or faster over longer distances if he's willing to push and keep pushing day after day. There would be horses later, and boats, but only as necessary.

I was riding when I finally arrived at the border of Heaven's Reach. The shortest route took me through the high grasslands of the northern Kvanas, and they're a horse people. Anything else would have looked suspicious. I'd joined a group of Radewalder pilgrims coming east to see the great temple of Shan and pay tribute to Heaven's Son. With my new face I blended right in, and I'd learned the accent long ago and well enough that they believed I was a countryman well met in foreign lands.

I had a few tense moments when the border guards looked through our packs. But they didn't dig deep enough to find the fingers or other bits of magical gear. I'd hidden those in a concealed bladder in a fat water skin that I'd had a Dalridian smuggler make around them. Without my old temple blades, none of my other gear was strange enough to draw any real comment. Not when I'd strapped my swords to my saddle and disassembled the rig that normally held them into its component straps and rings.

Heaven's Reach, the domain, is small, one long valley running west to east along the border between the Kvanas and Aven. It's also rich, both in terms of the land, which is very fertile, and the tributes it draws from satellite temples and pilgrims across the eleven kingdoms. Shan is the Emperor of Heaven and all the other churches pay him tribute. We were coming in on the western border, so it took us three days of gentle riding to reach Heaven's Reach the city.

We took rooms in one of the many overpriced inns the church has built to fleece the pilgrims, and I pleaded a bout of illness when the others went to visit the outer shrines the next morning. It was an obligatory tour for the truly devout, but of no interest to me. While they were gone, I reassembled my rig and trick bag then hid them in the floor of my room. I spent the next three days playing pilgrim with the others as they went through the inner shrines and lesser temples that lay within the sacred boundary of the temple precinct—an enormous and extremely well-guarded stone wall.

I feigned a return of my sickness on the final day when they went to the great temple itself. I would have loved to do a thorough scout around with my newfound friends providing moving cover, but I couldn't justify the danger it would put them in. The risk of one of my traitorous brethren stumbling on my shadow trail was just too high. I hadn't run into anyone else's shadow trail yet, but if the Son of Heaven had any of my former comrades around to help provide him with security, he'd keep them close at hand.

By begging stories of the wonders of the great temple from my "fellow" pilgrims, I was able to assemble a pretty good map of the public parts of the inner complex of buildings. They were quite happy to make corrections to my charcoal sketch, showing off their new knowledge of this holiest of Shan's temples—but sad that we would be parting ways on the morrow. They were heading back to Radewald as soon as they could, to beat the snows, and I'd long since told them I was going on to Aven for business reasons.

I spent another night and day at the inn, to give my erstwhile companions time to move on. I wanted to give them a good head start so they'd run a lower chance of getting into trouble if I was caught. I spent the bulk of that time wandering the outskirts of the temple precinct, studying my map, and putting together a plan for my initial approach. After I passed beyond the limits of the map I was going to have to improvise, but there was nothing I could do about that. Finally, I paid my bill, hid the bulk of my traveling gear on a rooftop, and strapped on my swords.

It was time for the Son of Heaven to die.

21

You can inscribe a lie in letters of gold, but that won't make it into beautiful truth. The temple complex was supposed to provide a sort of imperfect reflection of the gods' own Celestial City here in the world of man. It *was* gorgeous, even I had to admit that, but for me it was like the beauty of a will-o'-wisp—a pretty falsehood meant to lead the unwary astray.

According to holy writ, the Celestial City's streets are paved with ivory and pearl, its walls carved from jade, and its buildings roofed with purest gold. Not even the Son of Heaven could afford to counterfeit that kind of wealth, nor had he or his predecessors tried. To do so, they claimed, would have been blasphemy. No, Heaven's Reach must only reflect heaven, not strive to imitate it.

So the streets were paved with plain stone, but crushed shells had been sprinkled over them and fixed in place with magic, so that they shone silver and white under sun and moon, and blue and gold by magesight. The walls were faced with pale green marble, and the rooftops covered in terra-cotta tile that was sheathed in silver foil enchanted against tarnishing. A thousand slaves came out at night to polish every surface so that it all shone and sparkled like a ghost of the city it was supposed to reflect.

I could easily have gone in through the gates with the rest of the pilgrims during the day. I chose to go over the wall after the sun went down instead, though it required more initial effort. I had the best reason in the world.

After I'd left the inn and parked my gear I'd conducted a small experiment that I'd been itching to try for the better part of two days. I split my medallion.

Every pilgrim was given a little cast pewter medallion when they made their "voluntary" donative at the gate shrine and was told to wear it openly for their time in the city. Of course, you didn't get a medal if you didn't donate, and no one without a medal got to enter the temple precinct. Even the priests wore them, though theirs were cast in silver.

The spells that bound the medallions were very slickly done. Wrapping each one in permanent self-sustaining spells would have been prohibitively costly of magical resources. What they'd done instead was enchant the major gates at the entrance to the precinct and between neighborhoods within it. When a medallion passed through any of these gates, powerful enchantment, built into the very stones of the arch, activated and energized the medallions.

When they placed the medallion around your neck at the gate shrine it looked like nothing but a cheap bit of religious jewelry of the sort any moderately prosperous and devout peasant might be able to afford. Magesight revealed nothing more about it than the regular sort, and it remained apparently ordinary until your group knelt on the threshold of the temple precinct and recited the prayer after the priest. There, each medallion flashed bright blue for a moment, and not just to mages' eyes.

For the rest of the day, it would flash each time you passed through one of the "holy gates" that divided the sacred city into a series of individually defensible baileys or wards. In between, the medallion was infused with a very faint blue glow visible only to magesight. That remained after you left the temple precinct, but had visibly faded by the next day.

I couldn't figure it out at first, not until I'd thought to split my medallion open along the casting seam. The medallion was actually two medallions, the outer religious piece, and the inner magical tracking device and key. There were four glyphs inscribed within. Finding, binding, sympathy, and identity.

From back to front, each medallion had a unique signature, each one keyed itself to its wearer, and would sound an alarm if separated from them, each one could be tracked using a simple spell. If you had a medallion, the temple could tell who you were, where you were, and probably where you'd been. If you didn't, anyone who saw you knew you were an invader. It was a slick system.

Very slick. Roughly fifteen minutes after I broke mine open, a Hand and five Swords were sniffing around the well I'd thrown it down. A few minutes after that, the Hand had said a few words over the well and the broken medallion had flown up out of the depths to land at her feet.

I couldn't hear what she told her escort from where I was perched on a nearby rooftop and I didn't think it was worth risking a hearsay, but she didn't seem too alarmed by the find. I figured I was probably not the first irreverent pilgrim who broke his shiny little toy and then panicked afterward. Triss agreed with me. Still, I was very glad I'd given the gate shrine attendants nothing but lies about my name and my business. Likewise the Radewalders, though I hoped no one would bother to go after them for questioning.

Getting over the outer wall wasn't all that difficult. It never is. All it took was patience, climbing skills, a shroud, and the judicious application of tried and true magical techniques to the basic security wards. I was just moving from there toward the center of the precinct via one of the curtain walls that divided the baileys when a very unpleasant thought occurred to me.

A smart and paranoid magical architect might well have built the gates to do double duty: charge the medallions *and* scream bloody murder if someone without one passed through, or even over one. Since the mage who'd designed the security for Heaven's Reach was clearly both paranoid and smart, it gave me more than a moment's pause. I released Triss from his dream state and brought him up to date on my thinking.

Seems likely, given the circumstances, he sent back. *What do you want to do about it?*

We could go down and head inward at ground level, staying away from the gates, but that's going to slow us down a lot.

Not to mention the fact that there may be other places besides that gates that have the same spells on them. Probably are, actually. He made a sort of mental "hmmmming" noise then that I didn't like.

What is it, Triss?

As much as you or I may find the thought repulsive, the Son of Heaven is the representative of Shan here in the mortal realm.

And?

Do you suppose some of the gate spells are god magic?

As in, invisible to magesight? Oooh, that's not a happy thought at all. It means that if there are some of them in places other than the gates, we'll have no way of spotting them.

Exactly. Which brings me back to my original question; what do you want to do about it?

I guess now is the time to see if our secret weapon is going to work. I pulled out the finger that Kelos had given me—I still didn't trust mine, though I found the idea that I had a backup reassuring. Looking at it closely I found the glyphs of binding and sympathy inscribed on the bezel, though not the ones for finding or identity. *At least this way, we have a much better chance of running for it if it fails.*

We do if it fails in a way that's visible to us.

Have I ever told you that I find you too much the optimist?

No.

Good. A faint mental laugh tickled the edges of my mind as I resumed control over my familiar.

Moving very slowly and with the beringed finger well out in front of me I slipped forward along the top of the wall. A few yards shy of the nearer gate pier, the ring's bezel began to glow very faintly blue in magesight. Reluctantly, I extended my shroud to cover the ring, blocking my own view. It was more important that I not attract the attention of any fortuitously placed guards than that I keep an eye on it. As I got closer still it began to glow with the same sort of worldly light as the medallions had earlier.

The pressure of the light coming off the ring prickled uncomfortably against the shadows that hid it, like a light sunburn late in the day. That amped up to a real burn that had me wishing I could uncover the damn thing as I passed over the central arch—normally Blades go out of the way to avoid carrying lights of any kind inside a shroud. Fortunately, it quickly faded again on the far side.

I could only hope that the lack of a finding glyph on the ring meant that the Signet was an important enough officer of the church that the monitoring system had been designed not to track and inconvenience whoever held the post. I did have an important secondary bit of positive evidence for that idea, if you assumed that Kelos had been keeping the finger close at hand over the few years since he'd changed his allegiance. If not, well, if not, I was probably going to die without ever getting anywhere close to my target.

I tucked the finger back into the divided bag I'd made for it and its mate, and moved on. The temple precinct was shaped a bit like a nautilus shell, spiraling inward through a series of walled baileys, each with its own shrines and temples, toward the central complex. My next check came as I crossed over another curtain wall, this one part of the encircling wall dividing the first of the inner rings from the next one in.

No sooner had I stepped from the transverse wall between two baileys to the larger ring wall, then I felt an intense flare of light from the pouch holding the Signets' signets. Even through the thick fabric, the light chewed at my shroud and continued to do so as I made my way from there to the next transverse wall. It dimmed, but continued as I moved across to the next loop of the ring wall where it flared again.

At that point, I hopped down to the roof of a lesser temple and squatted in a sort of alcove made by the intersection of the two walls. Facing into the corner, I shifted the shadow away from my face and chest, moving it back and up to create a pocket of darkness before releasing Triss. When I opened the pouch, I could see the ring still glowing, but very dimly—I wouldn't have been able to see it even by moonlight. Pulling out the finger, I moved it closer to the wall.

In response, and as expected, the glow brightened dramatically. Whatever magic tied the rings and the medallions to the gates was present in all of the major walls here in the depths of the precinct.

I don't know what we'd do without this ring. I tapped the signet with my thumb. *If Kelos hadn't given it to us for the abbey attack, I don't think we could have gotten even this far.*

I don't either, and I don't like it. It makes things too easy, and it's magic that's not under our direct control. This is tied to Kelos's life force. If he died or chose to sever the connection while we're here, we'd be in the shit deep.

That's why we made one of our own. I touched my free hand to the pouch at my breast. *In fact, why don't we check it?*

I put the first Signet's finger away and pulled out the one I'd made, moving it close to the wall. It was slimmer, coming from a woman's hand, and the ring dimmer—its glow wasn't even visible initially—and almost as much green as it was blue, but it did light up. The finger felt colder, too. Warm, but not quite blood warm, which might account for the dimness and green tinge.

But then, I wasn't the mage that Kelos was, and I hadn't had a slice of unicorn horn handy when I made it, nor a silver nail. I'd had to make do with a wedge of dracodon ivory and a bent sliver of silver, both pried loose from the altar furnishings beneath the stairs at the abbey. Not to mention that I hadn't been able to harvest it until a few moments after the Signet's death.

I liked touching it even less than the other one. It was bound to *my* life force, a connection I could feel as sort of a feathery tickle at the back of my mind. Most of the time I could ignore it, but when I actually handled the finger, that feathery feeling grew stronger and extended a line to the point of contact. It felt like a ghostly string running from the finger through my hand and up my arm to the back of my neck where it spiraled around my spine and on into my skull. Very disconcerting. I put it away as quickly as I could after I'd verified that it, too, glowed.

What do you think? I asked Triss.

It's certainly connected with the magic of the precinct, but I wouldn't want to bet my life on it actually working.

Me neither. Let's hope it doesn't come to that.

For that matter, I don't much like betting my life on the other one either. It's a shitty choice, really. With yours I trust the man but not the magic. With Kelos's I have the reverse problem.

Does that mean you want to turn back?

No. I still think we stand a decent chance of killing the Son of Heaven, mostly because of the ring. That's worth the risk. Go.

I took control and shrouded up again. Between gates and guards and places where I had to double back on myself, it took me almost another two hours to get to the part of the complex that held the great temple and the Son of Heaven's apartments. It was difficult and dangerous to get that far, but I never really faced anything that shadow and the Signet's ring couldn't get me past, and that made me deadly suspicious. It couldn't possibly be this simple.

Oh, I made up reasons to explain the ease of my passage. The relative absence of the Hand was high on that list. I'd passed at least a dozen guard posts that had obviously been set up with a single watcher in mind, but which currently held three or four or even five of the Sword of Heaven's soldiers. I couldn't help but think that they would normally have been staffed by one of the Hand with a Storm hovering close by.

I would have liked to believe that, that weakness in the sorcery department was on account of the nearly three dozen members of the Hand that we had killed at the abbey. It was probably even true to some extent. No ruler, not even one as powerful as the Son of Heaven, could easily cover the loss of that many elite mages. But somehow I was certain that wasn't all there was to it. Some other need or force was pulling the Hand away from the city and the temple complex, though what, I couldn't say.

Whatever the reason, I soon found myself looking down on what had to be the several balconies that fronted the apartments of the Son of Heaven. It was the splendor that gave it away, which was one of the fundamental elements that had always made the work of the Blade easier. No matter how security conscious they were, the kinds of targets that drew the attention of my goddess and my brethren couldn't resist the temptation to make their power manifest in their surroundings. In this case, a huge garden courtyard roofed entirely in spell-hardened glass to keep out both elements and assassins.

The cost of the glass alone was staggering, without adding in construction or the magic and the staff to maintain it. The garden itself was filled with all manner of tropical rarities that had no business growing here in the north, on the cold side of the mountains.

Here, too, was that counterfeit of the Celestial City that the Son of Heaven claimed was blasphemy. The garden paths were strewn with chips of real ivory and bits of pearl, the balconies railed with jade that matched the jade tiles facing the walls. There was even a small gold-roofed pavilion beside the fishpond. The security was very tight here, with every pane of glass and tile on the roof marked by wards of alarm.

Without the Signet's ring finger I would never have been able to approach from the rooftops. With it, not only was I apparently invisible to the wards, but I had a key that allowed me to open an access panel in the garden's glass roof. From there it was no work at all for someone with my skills to make his way down onto the balcony to the left of the garden terrace—the most logical one to be attached to a bedroom or withdrawing room.

Peering through the curtains, I found that I had arrived outside the latter. The presence of a pair of the Swords of Heaven on either side of the doors to the inner chamber told me all that I needed to know about whether I'd found the right place. I paused then to set one of the few spells that I know well, a cantrip that would create a zone of silence around me for a quarter of an hour. I used that quiet to kill the Swords where they stood.

Then I was alone. Nothing but one door and at most a few short yards stood between me and the bed where the Son of Heaven lay sleeping. I was seconds from making the man responsible for the death of both my friends and my dreams pay for his crimes. I reached for the handle of the door and found that I was shaking. I backed up and took several deep breaths. I wanted to be calm for this, to completely occupy the moment so that I wouldn't miss the slightest nuance of this most deserved of deaths. As I tried to recenter myself, I forced myself to look away from the door, and really see the room, and . . .

Aral, are you all right?

What? I had no memory of releasing Triss. *I mean, of course I am. I just want to treasure this moment.*

Then why are you standing with your back against the wall as far from the Son of Heaven's door as you can get?

Am I. I blinked, forcing my eyes to focus, and realized that I was. *So I am.*

What's wrong?

I looked around and once again my eyes fell on the large wooden plaque on the wall just to the left of the balcony door. This time I made myself take in the sight and think about what it meant.

It was a display mount of a sort more typically seen in the audience hall of a castle than the bedroom of a high priest. Someone had sawn a ring out of a giant ebony, trimming the edges to make it into a perfect circle, perhaps six feet across. It was polished to a brilliant sheen that showed off rings marking hundreds of years of growth. Spaced around the edge of the ring were iron brackets each of which held the hilt of a sword of my goddess, its point directed inward, so that they formed a sort of pinwheel.

Looking at it made me want to vomit, but now that I had really seen it, I couldn't look away. Without any conscious thought, my feet took me slowly across the room toward this proud display of purest sacrilege against my goddess. As I went, I remembered the rumor that the soul daggers of the remaining living Blades, mine included, were supposed to be imbedded in the wall of the privy that lay beyond the bedroom where the Son slept now. That way, he could start each day by pissing on them.

Somewhere in the back of my head I had the sense that Triss was calling my name, but I couldn't really hear him over the buzz that filled my mind with pain. I just kept walking forward, stopping only when I physically bumped into a small table standing directly in front of the ring. I hadn't even seen it until I put my hand down to catch myself on its edge.

When I did, and looked more closely at what it held, I let out a screech of pure rage. Fortunately, my cantrip had not yet faded, and though I could feel the force of my scream tearing at my throat, no sound of it reached my ears. You see, on the table was another display, smaller, simpler, a low rack, designed to hold two swords. Loris's swords. Nothing could have hurt me more just then, and no better tool for the death of the Son of Heaven could have been delivered into my hands.

Turning, I crossed the room in a couple of quick bounds before silently kicking open the inner door. The room beyond was huge and opulent with a great canopied bed at its center. The Son of Heaven lay on his back in the middle of the bed, his arms crossed on his breast as though someone had laid him out for burial. Though

I had not seen his face in person since before the fall of my temple—
and that at a distance—I had viewed its likeness in a thousand
places. There was no mistaking the man . . . the monster.

In a moment I was standing over him, Loris's swords raised for
a double beheading stroke. Now, he would pay for all that he had
done to me and mine.

I paused then for one brief instant, to savor what I was about to
do. A mistake perhaps, for in that moment I began to do something
I had not since I first entered the Son of Heaven's suite. I began to
think instead of simply reacting. By doing so, I missed my chance to
kill the Son of Heaven from within my armor of rage, missed the
moment when his death would have been the sweetest release.

Aral?

Yes?

Kelos?

One lone word. Nothing more, and yet, once he'd uttered it, I
recognized the truth, and what had been driving me toward this
moment, or rather, who. Still, I was here, and I needed to finish my
business with the Son of Heaven before I dealt with my old master.

I did what needed doing, but I took no pleasure in it. It wasn't
my triumph at all. It belonged to Master Kelos. And when I was
done with the Son of Heaven, I left the apartments and climbed
back up the wall, passing through the glass panel to the roof. Once
it was closed, I dropped my shroud.

"I know you're here, Kelos. Come out where I can see you. We
need to talk."

Even knowing to expect him and what to look for, he surprised
me, seeming to simply fade into existence a few yards directly in
front of me.

"It's done?" he asked.

I nodded.

He cocked his head to one side. "You don't have Loris's swords.
I'm surprised. I expected you to take them back to Jax in Dalridia."

"I'll get them some other time. Them and all the others. I won't
take them to Jax, though. I will return them to the goddess as I returned mine, as they used to return themselves at the death of their
owners. It's the honorable thing to do, and I will always choose honor
over revenge. It's what I was taught by the man you once were."

He raised the eyebrow of his good eye in a gesture I suddenly
realized I had learned from him. "So it was honor that filled your
heart when you killed the Son of Heaven?"

I smiled then, and I could see from his expression that Kelos didn't like the color of my expression. Which was exactly as I wanted it.

"Oh, I didn't kill him. He deserved it all right, and you gave me more than enough reasons. But then I stopped to think, and that was your undoing."

"Aral, what are you talking about?" He spoke sharply, but his expression looked more curious than concerned.

"Everything I needed to know to figure it out, I learned in that little play you staged for me with the Signet back in Tien. I'm not sure if that was the one mistake on your part, or if she said something she wasn't supposed to, or what. In any case, you won't become the next Son of Heaven today. The throne still has its current ass to keep it warm. Actually, I don't think you'll become the next Son of Heaven at all."

"It's not like that," said Kelos. "I don't want the throne for the throne's sake. I want the power it will give me to make things right in the world, and I *will* have that power even if you're not the one who gives it to me."

"No, I don't think that you will. For a number of reasons. First, you can't harm the Son yourself, nor any other member of the church hierarchy. Not directly. You're bound by a mortal geas— harm so much as a single hair on the head of the least priest and you die. That's half of why you just wedged the locks at the abbey, because you *couldn't* act more directly. The other half, of course, was so that some of the prisoners would die, because you wanted me angry. Too angry to think or hesitate. You needed me to kill the Signet to make you the Son's heir, before I killed the Son himself."

"Very good, boy." And he smiled, like he was proud of me, and damn me to hell but it still felt good to see him do it. "Very good. But you always were the best strategic thinker among my students. So, I can't kill the Son of Heaven. Nor any of his servants. Funnily enough, that even includes my fellow apostates in Heaven's Shadow. What else have you figured out?"

"That you need *me* to kill the Son of Heaven for you."

"Why? Why can't I just set up that brilliant young apprentice of yours to do the job? She's got the hate for it, and once she recovers from that head injury—she will, you know—she'd do the job up very prettily."

"I don't know the why yet. Not that one nor some others that are important, like why the Son doesn't like to have the Hand too close to him, though I'll figure it all out, given time. No, it's me you need. Well, needed. Killing the Son won't put you on the throne anymore. Not now."

"Really? What makes you say that? What could you have possibly done to prevent me?"

"I left Loris's swords in the Son's bedroom—sunk into the head of the bed to be specific. When he wakes he's going to cut his face on them unless he gets very lucky."

"And a couple of swords are going to turn the Son against his personal Shade."

"Is that what you call yourself now? Really?"

Kelos shrugged. "I don't much like it either. The head of the Hand of Heaven is the Signet. The chief of Heaven's Shadow is the Shade. It's a little cute for me, but then I intend to change it. I intend to change everything."

"It's not going to happen."

"What makes you so sure of that, Aral?"

"Because the Swords weren't all that I left him. There's a note, too. It's short, and insulting, but I think the paperweight I used when I set it on his chest will get the point across."

"What have you done?" And, for the first time in all my years of dealing with the man, I finally saw him look alarmed. It was a tiny thing, barely a widening of his one good eye, but it was there.

"I think you know, but I'm going to tell you anyway, because I want to tell you I've beaten you, not just have you figure it out. I left the Son of Heaven a finger along with the warning, a living finger that's connected unmistakably to your life force. Even a half-witted hedge wizard would be able to tie the magic in that thing back to you."

"How did you get through the wards on your way back out?" he asked.

"You are not the only man to kill a Signet."

Kelos nodded, but didn't say anything.

"When the Son wakes," I continued, "and I expect that to happen any minute now, the first thing he's going to see are the sharp edges of a pair of swords. The second is incontrovertible proof that you've been playing him. And you can't even raise your own sword to defend yourself against his soldiers. If I were you, I'd start running right now."

Kelos nodded again, and then he did the last thing in the world that I might have expected. He threw his head back and he laughed. Not just a little laugh either, a full-throated roar that was probably loud enough to wake the Son of Heaven all by itself.

"I don't understand. . . ." I said, and I really, really didn't.

Don't you? Triss asked. *He's proud of you.*

Before I could respond, Kelos raised a hand. "Oh, very good, lad, very good indeed. I've been waiting two hundred years for someone to beat me fair and square, and you're the one who's finally done it. I can't tell you how pleased I am that it was you."

"You're mad, you know that, right? Completely mad."

"A little, certainly. But not completely. You are my child as much as any Blade I ever trained. I don't know if you can understand what that means yet, but you may someday. When you killed Ashvik you showed the whole world that you had become exactly what I wanted to make you, a perfect weapon in the hand of the goddess, and I was damned proud.

"But this, this is so much more." He smiled and shook his head, spreading his hands in a gesture that indicated all of me. "You have become the hand that wields the weapon, the mind behind the blade. That takes you beyond what I had hoped for you to someplace I can't predict. That's more reward than I expected to see this side of the grave."

Now he was crying and so was I, and I wasn't sure whether I wanted to cut his throat or hug him. Perhaps fortunately I was spared the decision when an alarm bell started ringing.

Kelos laughed again, more softly this time. "I believe that means I need to start running. You, too. Shall we run together at least as far as the edge of the temple precinct? It would be an honor."

And damn me if I didn't fall in beside him. "To the edge of the precinct, and not a step farther."

"Done."

You're as crazy as he is.

You might just be right.

Epilogue

A man walks into a bar. It's the beginning of a thousand stories and the end of a thousand more.

This time the bar was a hole in the wall in a tiny town in western Zhan and the man was me. The passes to Dalridia would long since have closed for the winter and I had business yet in Tien, so I was taking the long way back to Faran and Jax and my new responsibilities.

Three weeks had passed since I said good-bye to Master Kelos at the edge of Heaven's Reach, and he'd told me he was proud of me again. I still didn't know how I felt about that or him. He hadn't said where he was going, and I hadn't asked.

He'd given me a message for Jax, too, but I wasn't at all sure I was going to deliver it. No matter how much Kelos might have meant it, I don't think Jax was going to be ready to hear that he was sorry about Loris. Not once she heard the rest of what I had to tell her.

Aren't you going to find a seat? Triss asked.

It was only then that I realized I'd frozen just inside the door. It wasn't the first time in the last couple of weeks, and I didn't think it would be the last. With Triss's prompting I headed deeper into the bar, finding a seat beside the fire, where I could put my back to a wall and keep an eye on the door.

The talk was all about the Son of Heaven and the two parallel slices the Son now bore on his forehead and cheeks. The news of strange goings-on at Heaven's Reach was traveling faster than I was. This time the story included a new detail: that nothing anyone could do would heal the Son's wounds. That was a fresh variation on the story, and though I doubted it, I hoped it was true.

When the boy taking orders came to get mine, I asked for a plate of noodles and a pot of tea, and I could feel Triss smiling through our link. I've never liked tea and I still wanted whiskey, had even ordered it and gotten falling-down drunk a couple of times in the preceding days, but I wasn't doing it every night, nor even most of them. It was a long battle and I had no idea if I was going to win it.

But for today, and just for today, I wasn't going to drink. And when tomorrow came, well, maybe I would be able to say the same again. If I didn't, I wasn't going to beat myself up over it. I would just move on to the next day, and the next.

The tea that came with my meal was just as lacking in appeal as I'd expected it to be, but I drank it anyway.

I'm proud of you, said Triss when I paid the bill and didn't order anything more, and unlike my confusion with Kelos I knew exactly how it made me feel when Triss said it.

Proud.

Terms and Characters

Alinthide Poisonhand—A master Blade, the third to die making an attempt on Ashvik VI.

Altia—A onetime apprentice Blade.

Anyang—Zhani city on the southern coast. Home of the winter palace.

Ar—Main port of the Magelands, home to one of its five great mage universities.

Aral Kingslayer—Ex-Blade turned jack of the shadow trades.

Ashvik VI, or Ashvik Dan Pridu—Late King of Zhan, executed by Aral. Also known as the Butcher of Kadesh.

Athera Trinity—The three-faced goddess of fate.

Balor Lifending—God of the dead and the next Emperor of Heaven.

Black Jack—A professional killer or assassin.

Blade—Temple assassin of the goddess Namara.

Blinds—Charms of confusion and befuddlement, mostly used by thieves in the Magelands.

Cairmor—A Crown castle in Dalridia.

Calren the Taleteller—God of beginnings and first Emperor of Heaven.

Caras Dust—Powerful magically bred stimulant.

Caras Seed-Grinder—Producer of caras dust.

Caras Snuffler—A caras addict.

Channary Canal—Canal running from the base of the Channary Hill to the Zien River in Tien.

Channary Hill—One of the four great hills of Tien.

Chenjou Peninsula—The peninsula to the north of Tien.

Chimney Forest—The city above, rooftops, etc.

Chimney Road—A path across the rooftops of a city. "Running the chimney road."

Clanarch—Formal title for a Vesh'An clan chieftain.

Coals—Particularly hot stolen goods.

Cornerbright—Magical device for seeing around corners.

Dalridia—Kingdom in the southern Hurnic Mountains.

Deathspark—A piece of magic that turns a human being into a trap triggered by their own death.

Devin (Nightblade) Urslan—A former Blade.

Downunders—A bad neighborhood in Tien.

Dracodon—A large magical beast, renowned for the ivory in its tusks.

Dragon Crown—The royal crown of Zhan, often replicated in insignia of Zhani Crown agents.

Drum-Ringer—A bell enchanted to prevent eavesdropping.

Durkoth—Others that live under the Hurnic Mountains.

Dustmen—Dealers in caras dust.

Eavesman—A spy or eavesdropper.

Eian Elarson—King of Dalridia and brother to Jax.

Eilif Uvarkas—Lord Signet and preceptor of the Hand of Heaven in the year 3130.

Ekilikik—A clanarch of the Vesh'An.

Elite, the—Zhani mages. They fulfill the roles of secret police and spy corps among other functions.

Emberman—A professional arsonist.

Erk Endfast—Owner of the Spinnerfish, ex–black jack, ex–shadow captain.

Eva—With Eyn the dual goddess worshipped by the Dyads.

Everdark, the—The home dimension of the Shades.

Eyespy—A type of eavesdropping spell.

Eyn—With Eva the dual goddess worshipped by the Dyads.

Face, Facing—Identity. "I'd faced myself as an Aveni bravo."

Fallback—A safe house.

Familiar Gift—The ability to soul-bond with another being, providing the focus half of the power/focus dichotomy necessary to become a mage.

Faran—A onetime apprentice Blade.

Fi—A township upriver from Ar.

Fire and sun!—A Shade curse.

Fortunate Lamia, *the*—A trading vessel.

Garret—A onetime apprentice Blade.

Ghost, Ghosting—To kill.

Govana—Goddess of the herds.

Gram—The name of the world.

Gryphon's Head—A tavern in Tien, the capital city of Zhan. Informal office for Aral.

Guttersiders—Slang for the professional beggars and their allies.

Hand of Heaven—The Son of Heaven's office of the inquisition.

Harad—Head librarian at the Ismere Library.

Hearsay—A type of eavesdropping spell.

Highside—Neighborhood on the bay side.

Howler—Slang name for the Elite.

Huddle Bird—A game bird native to the Magelands and the Sylvani Empire.

Illiana—A Master Blade, killed in a suicide attack at the fall of the temple.

Ismere Club—A private club for merchants.

Ismere Library—A private lending library in Tien, founded by a wealthy merchant from Kadesh.

Jack—A slang term for an unofficial or extragovernmental problem solver, see also, shadow jack, black jack, sunside jack.

Jaeris—A onetime apprentice Blade.

Javan—A onetime apprentice Blade.

Jax Seldansbane—A former Blade and onetime fiancée of Aral's.

Jenua, Duchy of—A duchy in Zhan.

Jerik—The bartender/owner of the Gryphon's Head tavern.

Jindu—Tienese martial art heavily weighted toward punches and kicks.

Jinn's—A small cafe near the Ismere Library.

Kadeshar—Chief city of Kadesh.

Kaelin Fei, Captain—Watch officer in charge of Tien's Silent Branch. Also known as the Mufflers.

Kaman—A former Blade, crucified by the Elite, then killed by Aral at his own request.

Kanathean Hill—One of the four great hills of Tien.

Kao-Li—Fortress retreat of the Zhani royal family, upriver from Tien.

Kayarin Melkar—A master Blade who joined the Son of Heaven after the fall of the temple.

Kelos Deathwalker—A master Blade who taught Aral.

Keytrue—A charm to prevent lock picking.

Khanates, the Four—A group of interrelated kingdoms just north of Varya. Also known as the Kvanas.

Kila—The spirit dagger of the Blade, symbolizing his bond to Namara.

Kip-Claim—Pawn shop.

Knotsnake—A poisonous snake found in Zhan and Kadesh.

Kodamia—City-state to the west of Tien, controlling the only good pass through the Hurnic Mountains.

Kuan-Lun—A water elemental, one of the great dragons.

Kvanas, the Four—A group of interrelated kingdoms just north of Varya. Sometimes referred to as the Khanates.

Kyle's—An expensive Aveni whiskey.

Leyan—A onetime journeyman Blade.

Liess—A Shade, familiar of Sharl.

Little Varya—An immigrant neighborhood in Tien.

Loris—A former Blade.

Magearch—Title for the mage governor of the cities in the Mage-lands.

Mageblind—Mage term for those without magesight.

Mage Gift—The ability to perform magic, providing the power half of the power/focus dichotomy necessary to become a mage.

Magelands—A loose confederation of city-states governed by the faculty of the mage colleges that center them.

Magelights—Relatively expensive permanent light globes made with magic.

Magesight—The ability to see magic, part of the mage gift.

Mage Wastes—Huge area of magically created wasteland on the western edge of the civilized lands.

Malthiss—A Shade, familiar of Kelos Deathwalker.

Manny Three Fingers—The cook at the Spinnerfish.

Marchon—A barony in the kingdom of Zhan. The house emblem is a seated jade fox on a gold background.

Maryam—A onetime journeyman Blade.

Maylien Dan Marchon Tal Pridu—A former client of Aral's.

Meld—The overarching consciousness of a Dyad.

Mufflers—Captain Fei's organization, so known because they keep things quiet. Officially known as Silent Branch.

Namara—The now-deceased goddess of justice and the downtrod-den, patroness of the Blades. Her symbol is an unblinking eye.

Nea Sjensdor—Lady Signet, preceptor of the Hand of Heaven.

Nest-Not—A ward to prevent vermin infestations.

Nightcutter—Assassin.

Nightghast—One of the restless dead, known to eat humans.

Night Market—The black market.

Nima—Mana, the stuff of magic.

Nipperkins—Magical vermin.

Noble Dragons—Elemental beings that usually take the form of giant lizardlike creatures.

Old Mews—An upscale neighborhood in Tien that burned to the ground.

Olen—A master Blade who taught Aral.

Olthiss—A Shade, familiar of Altia.

Omira—A onetime apprentice Blade.

Orisa—God of sailors.

Oris Plant—A common weed that can be used to produce a cheap gray dye or an expensive black one.

Others—The various nonhuman races.

Palace Hill—One of the four great hills of Tien.

Patiss—A Shade, familiar of Master Urayal.

Petty Dragons—Giant acid-spitting lizards, not to be confused with noble dragons.

Poison—Gutter slang meaning toxic or too hot to deal with.

Precasts—Active spells kept precast and at the ready.

Qamasiin—A spirit of air.

Quink—Slang word meaning, roughly, freak.

Rabbit Run—An emergency escape route.

Resshath—Shade term of respect meaning, roughly, teacher or sensei.

Restless Dead—Catchall term for the undead.

Riel—Currency of Zhan, issued in both silver and gold.

Risen, the—A type of restless dead, similar to a zombie.

Roric—A onetime journeyman Blade, Avarsi by birth.

Sanjin Island—Large island in the river below the palace in Tien.

Seldan, Dukes of—Varyan nobles, two of whom were executed by Jax.

Sellcinders—A fence or dealer in hot merchandise.

Sendai, Master—The sailing master and first officer of the *Fortunate Lamia*, Kanjurese.

Serass—A Shade, familiar of Alinthide.

Shade—Familiar of the Blades, a living shadow.

Shadow Captain—A mob boss.

Shadow Jack—A jack who earns his living as a problem solver in the shadow trades.

Shadowside—The underworld or demimonde.

Shadow-Slipping—The collective name for the various stealth techniques of Namara's Blades.

Shadow Trades—The various flavors of illegal activity.

Shadow World—The demimonde or underworld.

Shan Starshoulders—The god who holds up the sky, current Emperor of Heaven, lord of stability.

Shatternot—A charm to keep windows from breaking.

Sheuth Glyph—A glyph for the binding of shadows.

Shinsan—A water elemental, one of the great dragons.

Shrouding—When a Shade encloses his Blade in shadow.

Silent Branch—The official name of the Mufflers.

Siri Mythkiller—A former Blade.

Skaate's—A premium Aveni whiskey.

Skip—A con game or other illegal job, also a "play."

Sleepwalker—An efik addict.

Slink—Magical vermin.

Smuggler's Rest—The unofficial name of the docks near the Spinnerfish.

Snicket—Alley.

Snug—A resting place or residence.

Son or Daughter of Heaven—The title of the chief priest or priestess who leads the combined religions of the eleven kingdoms.

Sovann Hill—One of the four great hills of Tien.

Spinnerfish, the—A shadowside tavern by the docks.

Sshayar—A Shade, familiar of Jax.

Sshssithssha—A Shade word denoting a sort of path through shadow.

Ssithra—A Shade, familiar of Faran.

Ssolvey—A Shade, familiar of Roric.

Ssuma—A Shade, familiar of Illiana.

Starshine—Elemental being of light.

Stingers—Slang term for Tienese city watch.

Stone Dog—A living statue, roughly the size of small horse. The familiar of the Elite.

Straight-Back Jack—A shadow jack who gets the job done and keeps his promises.

Stumbles, the—Neighborhood of Tien that houses the Gryphon's Head tavern.

Sunside—The shadowside term for more legitimate operations.

Sunside Jack—A jack who works aboveboard, similar to a modern detective.

Sylvani Empire—Sometimes called the Sylvain, a huge empire covering much of the southern half of the continent. Ruled by a nonhuman race, it is ancient, and hostile to the human lands of the north.

Tailor's Wynd—An upscale neighborhood in Tien.

Tamerlen—A Master Blade killed in the fall of the temple.

Tangara—God of glyphs and runes and other magical writing.

Tangle—Charms of confusion and befuddlement, mostly used by thieves in the Magelands.

Tavan—One of the five great university cities of the Magelands.

Tavan North—The Magelanders' quarter of Tien.

Thauvik IV, or Thauvik Tal Pridu, the Bastard King—King of Zhan and bastard half brother of the late Ashvik.

Thera—A Master Blade, killed in a magical experiment.

Thiess—A Shade, familiar of Javan.

Thieveslamp/Thieveslight—A dim red magelight in a tiny bull's-eye lantern.

Tien—A coastal city, the thousand-year-old capital of Zhan.

Timesman—The keeper of the hours at the temple of Shan, Emperor of Heaven.

Triss—Aral's familiar. A Shade that inhabits Aral's shadow.

Tuckaside—A place to stash goods, usually stolen.

Tucker—Tucker bottle, a quarter-sized liquor bottle, suitable for two or for one heavy drinker.

Twins, the—Eyn and Eva, the patron goddess or goddesses of the Dyads. Sometimes represented as one goddess with two faces, sometimes as a pair of twins, either identical or conjoined.

Ulriss—A Shade, familiar of Leyan.

Underhills—An upscale neighborhood in Tien.

Urayal—A Master Blade, killed in an attempt on Ashvik.

Vangzien—Zhani city at the confluence where the Vang River flows into the Zien River in the foothills of the Hurnic Mountains. Home of the summer palace.

Veira—A Master Blade, killed after the fall of the temple.

Vesh'An—Shapechanging Others. Originally a part of the same breed that split into the Sylvani and Durkoth, the Vesh'An have adopted a nomadic life in the sea.

Vrass—A Shade, familiar of Maryam.

Wandersea Ceremony—A ceremony propitiating the Vesh'An and asking for their protection.

Warboard—Chesslike game.

Wardblack—A custom-built magical rug that blocks the function of a specific ward.

Westbridge—A bridge over the Zien, upriver from the palace and the neighborhood around it.

Worrymoth—An herb believed to drive away moths.

Wound-Tailor—Shadowside slang for a healer for hire.
Zass—A Shade, familiar of Devin.
Zhan—One of the eleven human kingdoms of the East. Home to the
   city of Tien.

Currency

Bronze Sixth Kip (sixer)
Bronze Kip
Bronze Shen
Silver Half Riel
Silver Riel
Gold Half Riel
Gold Riel
Gold Oriel

Value in Bronze Kips

~ *0.15 = Bronze Sixth Kip*
1 = Bronze Kip
10 = Bronze Shen
60 = Silver Half Riel
120 = Silver Riel

Value in Silver Riels

0.5 = Silver Half Riel
1 = Silver Riel
5 = Gold Half Riel
10 = Gold Riel
50 = Gold Oriel

Calendar

(370 days in 11 months of 32 days each, plus two extra 9-day holiday weeks: Summer-Round in the middle of Midsummer, and Winter-Round between Darktide and Coldfast)

1 *Coldfast*
2 *Meltentide*
3 *Greening*
4 *Seedsdown*
5 *Opening*
6 *Midsummer*
7 *Sunshammer*
8 *Firstgrain*
9 *Harvestide*
10 *Talewynd*
11 *Darktide*

Days of the Week

1 *Calrensday*—In the beginning.
2 *Atherasday*—Hearth and home.
3 *Durkothsday*—Holdover from the prehuman tale of days.
4 *Shansday*—The middle time.
5 *Namarsday*—Traditional day for nobles to sit in judgment.
6 *Sylvasday*—Holdover from the prehuman tale of days.
7 *Balorsday*—Day of the dead.
8 *Madensday*—The day of madness when no work is done.

About the Author

KELLY MCCULLOUGH was raised and educated by free-range hippies. Later he received a degree in theater and worked in improv. That combination was the perfect preparation for his current career as author and cat herder. He lives and writes in the Midwest with his physics-professor wife, Laura. He enjoys hiking and biking and his role as self-heating cat furniture. He is the author of the WebMage and Fallen Blade series. More information can be found at his website *www.kellymccullough.com*.